ARCANE LEGACY  BOOK 2

STORMS
OF THE ANCIENTS

SEVER BRONNY

STORMS
OF
THE
ANCIENTS

Arcane Legacy
Book Two

SEVER BRONNY

This book is a work of fiction. Names, characters, places and incidents either are the product of the author's imagination or are used fictitiously, and any similarity to actual persons, living or deceased, establishments of any kind, events, or locales is entirely coincidental.

Bronny, Sever, 1979-, author
Storms of the Ancients / Sever Bronny.
(Storms of the Ancients ; book two)
Series: Arcane Legacy

Issued in print and electronic formats.

ISBN 978-1-990624-07-0 (paperback)
ISBN 978-1-990624-06-3 (ebook)

   I.   Title. II. Series: Bronny, Sever, 1979- . Storms of the
             Ancients ; bk. 2

AL710837091789238100   0

A310423790129866392301001
A91045720104r765165179777

Version 1.0

The writing, editing, formatting, audiobooks, and cover design of this entire work are all 100% human labor.

Visit severbronny.com to chat with fans, duel in the arena with fellow warlocks, explore world lore, see character academy class schedules, peruse photos, read frequently asked questions (FAQ), and meet the author. Spell glossary and lore can now be found at the back of this book for both paperback and ebook versions.

ALSO BY SEVER BRONNY:

THE ARINTHIAN LINE

Pursued by a murderous tyrant, fourteen-year-old warlocks Augum, Bridget and Leera train under the legendary Anna Atticus Stone — while exploring the secrets of an ancient abandoned castle.

Arcane
Riven
Valor
Clash
Legend

FURY OF A RISING DRAGON

When a kingdom threatens invasion, sixteen-year-olds Augum, Bridget and Leera attempt to resurrect an ancient and forbidden order of warlock-knights, hoping to summon dragons to their aid.

Burden's Edge
Honor's Price
Mercy's Trial
Champion's Wrath

CHRONICLES OF ANNA ATTICUS STONE

Young warlock prodigy Anna Atticus Stone is tormented by her vile sister as she tries to get into the mysterious Academy of Arcane Arts. But her sister has other plans.

Prodigy of Thunder
The Arcane Artist
Flames of Stone

 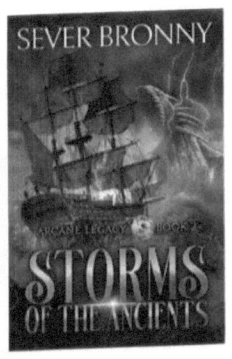

ARCANE LEGACY

Augum, Bridget and Leera face an overwhelming demonic menace from an unknown land. But who is predator and who is prey?

Whispers of Wrath
Storms of the Ancients
Future titles to be announced

All available from Amazon

Guided by The Fates go I
Alone
Lashed by the waves
Of a mighty storm

CREAKING BEAMS

BRIDGET

Somewhere on the icy and vast Eastern Salt Ocean, amidst the ceaseless clatter of men and women slaving deep in the bowels of a twelve-masted ship, Bridget Burns stabbed a coil of gargoyle manure with a shovel. As primitive oil lamps swung overhead, she heaved the sodden pile up, which mercifully stank only as bad as cow manure, tottered along the caked-over planks to a hole as wide as a well, and dropped the muck into it.

The trick was not to get too close to the hole as the floor was unforgivably slippery. She still heard the echo of a man's sudden yelp after he had accidentally slid into a hole, never to be seen again. He was quickly replaced, and things carried on, with the other slaves barely taking notice.

There came a sodden *thwack* as another coil landed behind her, followed by the usual spatter against the back of her robe. Bridget, being the only one in her vicinity with a hood, risked what few others dared to do and stole a peek upward.

High overhead, gargoyles perched on a lattice structure that went all the way up the ship, one that was strengthened by horizontal beams as massive as a grain silo. But whereas a normal ship had walled divisions, this one was mostly open, for the gargoyles needed space to fly. The gargoyles with wings flew down to the lowest lattice to drop their indignity on the tired field of slaves below. The rest climbed rope ladders.

Like insects they fly and crawl, she thought. She estimated that the ship was fifteen hundred feet in length and two hundred and fifty feet in width, but could only guess its height as she could not see the ceiling through the lattice floors.

Not wanting to risk notice from the area overseer, she turned about, dug the crude shovel under the newly formed coil, grunted as she raised it, and with burning muscles dropped it into the nearby hole.

She desperately wanted to wipe the sweat from her brow or scratch the itch on her nose that had been tormenting her like the incessantly buzzing flies, yet she dared not touch her face with her hands. It was better to endure the discomfort—or use a wooden splinter scavenged from the cleaner parts of the ship. Her formerly crimson robe was as brown as a constable's, and disease was as rampant as the rats.

She did, however, press her thumb into the iron collar around her neck and gently nudged it, providing precious relief by scratching another itch.

Her pen was a ten-by-ten-foot area cordoned off by square waist-high wooden beams as thick as a castle column, beams that also doubled as structural integrity for the ship. Sixteen hours a day, every single day, this was home.

She glanced about at the other unfortunates occupying similar pens, toiling and waiting for the gifts to drop, and wondered what they had been doing the moment the gargoyles had snatched them. Perhaps readying for bed or rocking a baby or reading a good book or, if they were aware of what was happening, quietly hunkering in their room praying the demonic invaders would pass them by.

And now you're cows in a pen, she thought. *Just like me ...*

These low-walled pens stretched along the bottom of the ship, hemmed in by lattice walls at the bow and stern, where the slaves ate and slept and the gargoyles managed and kept stores. Below this floor was a waste drainage system, hinted at by the well-sized holes and the occasional gurgling burp, as if the lowest parts of the ship were a giant stomach.

A new itch, this one on the back of her head, prompted a scratching delivered carefully with a broken nail. While sighing in relief, Bridget marveled at being enslaved inside what amounted to a floating city, for by factoring the dimensions of the ship and the pens, as well as how many slaves she had seen with her own eyes—all working in staggered sixteen-hour shifts—she had estimated the number of kidnapped souls to be a whopping *ten thousand*. And more might reside on higher tiers— one slave had supposedly glimpsed wolven cubs scrapping over a flank of raw pork in a corridor before an overseer had whisked them off.

There came a *crack* from a whip, followed by a nearby yelp, and a startled Bridget hurried to the next coil. As she carried the slop to the hole, she stole a peek at the pen the noise had come from and saw a hunched older woman haul herself back to her feet, only to slip again. It finally took her using her shovel as a support before she could stand and wheezingly totter to the next coil.

Poor thing won't survive another tenday, Bridget thought, tossing her coil into the hole. She had already witnessed one elderly woman expire due to exhaustion, her last words being, "Merciful heavens, thank you." It was times like that she wished she had become a healer instead of an earth warlock.

Bridget jabbed another coil and heaved it up, thinking, *And now you are nothing but a shoveler of poop*.

The "poop deck," as some of the slaves had taken to calling this area, was segmented into work blocks, each block composed of forty-nine pens. A platform occupied the center pen of every block, upon which a gargoyle overseer perched, protected by a small roof to prevent an accidental soiling from above. Woe be to the wretches who found themselves in the first ring of pens around that platform, for they were within easy reach of the whip, as had just happened with that poor woman.

All along the base of the ship people worked in identical slave blocks organized by the kingdom they had been captured in, with the other kingdoms bunched closer to the stern, which had its own mess hall and sleeping area. Since everyone around Bridget was Solian, she knew that her kingdom had taken the brunt of the kidnappings—unless there were other ships, of course.

Bridget had only spotted a few warlocks among the masses, recognizable as such by their robes, with the vast majority being Ordinaries. Some of her fellow slaves had recognized her at first, but their reactions of shock and hope had quickly been snuffed on the very first day of toil, when the gargoyle "mud"—thinking of gargoyle excrement as mud saved some of Bridget's precious dignity—caked everyone and their clothes and their thoughts. After that, she had kept her head down and her hood up, unsure how to behave amidst a sea of Ordinaries—and feeling like an Ordinary herself.

With the mud erasing her identity, she passed herself off as just another slathered wretch. The degradation, the despair, and the sheer randomness of it all made it pointless to get to know anyone. Besides, once herded out of the work pens, the slaves would lose sight of one another and, in their exhaustion, muster only enough strength to eat before collapsing onto the closest unoccupied plank bunk.

Bridget delivered the coil and took her time walking to the next one. This pen was not as bad as some of the others. Some had multiple holes, creating a deadly obstacle course that preyed on a single inattentive moment.

The only other areas she had been to were the mess hall and the sleeping quarters in the bow. Every day one slept in a different "bunk" — meaning a tiered system of nothing but bare planks—ate on a different spot on the floor in the mess hall, and was herded into whichever pen was going off rotation. As for privies, everyone was expected to do their duty wherever it suited them, which usually meant within their pens, a humiliating endeavor one simply got used to.

In these places Bridget had found crude string necklaces and bracelets, strips of mended cloth, and the occasional primitive shoe, all evidence of occupation prior to this voyage, indicating the gargoyles had taken slaves at some point in the past. The items she had found resembled human belongings, but all were tiny, as if made for children — or perhaps an unknown race that was smaller than humans; it was hard to tell. Whatever the case, it seemed another people had shoveled the coils on the voyage over, yet those people seemed to have mysteriously vanished.

Come to think of it, these shovels are small too, Bridget thought as she tracked down a new coil. Whilst delivering it to the hole, she searched for evidence of small footprints in the mud. Finding none, she dumped her load into the hole—and slipped. Out of sheer reflex, she lashed out an arm and telekinetically latched onto a nearby support beam, stabilizing herself and preventing the fall. Then she let go and glanced about, but no one had noticed what she had done.

In that moment, the nearby hole burped like a bar patron after downing a tankard of ale.

Not today, you bastard, Bridget thought, edging away and reminding herself to be more careful. She hoped to never discover what frightful sewage mechanism waited below.

Despite her admiration of the sheer engineering of the ship, she fantasized about turning into a dragon, roaring a mighty war cry, and tearing gargoyles into pieces, starting with the block overseer.

Except that the collar around her neck heavily suppressed arcanery. And some spells, like Teleport, Shrink, Frenzy, the Spirit of the Dragon simul, or the ability to summon the Arcaner vault, were impossible to cast at all. Still, she could perform weakened versions of other spells like Telekinesis, which she occasionally used to aid in her shovel efforts, allowing her to conserve physical energy. She had discovered this early on during her secret daily cycle of mentally running through every spell.

She just had to be careful, for she did not want to reveal the extent of her abilities.

Bridget had performed those early trials a month ago now, during the days of constant putrid nausea and wide-eyed shock at her new station in life until she gained her sea legs and learned to plug her nose with strips of cloth. The routine had since set in, each day feeling like a month. Mercifully, the collar also partly suppressed The Callousness of the Predator. Or perhaps unfairly, for she could do with a more potent dose of callousness to cope with reality.

As she worked, she wondered why the gargoyles collared Ordinaries. Did they fear that all humans could cast arcanery? Or was there more to it? And did the gargoyles use such collars on other beings back in their kingdom or had these been made just for this expedition?

Two pens away, a twelve-foot muscled beast of a gargoyle, with his shark-gray skin and leather whip and ratty wings, glanced over at her with his yellow eyes, and she hurried to another pile lest she suffered the same fate as that older woman. She had done all she could do to avoid the whip, for the overseers were liberal with their dispensations, painting strokes at a whim. If they happened to split skin, infection invariably set in—and then gangrene, followed by either a blubbering death or fodder for the arena.

The arena was the only form of entertainment the gargoyles seemed to enjoy, or at least the only one visible from the depths of the ship. It hung centrally one lattice floor above, a rectangular structure attached to the beams by thick rope. Every evening the gargoyles gathered there to drink their foul-smelling concoctions and hoot and whistle and growl at the unfortunates they had pitted against each other—or some beast. Bridget had never laid eyes on the arena, hearing second-hand whispers passed on from its survivors instead.

The creak of the rope above as gargoyles settled on their perches in the arena stands indicated the start of the nightly festivities. Sometimes a severed leg, arm, or even a torso would drop onto the poop deck, only for the gargoyles to collect it—she suspected for necromantic purposes. Bridget well remembered staring at an arm with smooth and flawless skin, wondering if it was perhaps from a young woman her age, before it was snatched away by a flying gargoyle. Meanwhile above, gargoyles would screech in celebration of witnessing a thrilling death, then drunkenly fly by and shout or claw at the shovelers.

But not all gargoyles got to participate. The wingless low-caste workers, who were shorter and scrawnier than the winged ones, did the more general labor of maintaining the ship, moving slaves about, and managing the food stores, among countless other menial duties. They were subservient to the winged ones and at times appeared terrified, keeping their heads down. Bridget wondered if they had been the ones previously assigned to coil duty on the voyage to Sithesia, and now feared getting sent back to the foul labor.

To protect her mind, Bridget took shelter in the past. In memories of womanhood ceremonies and attending class at the Academy of Arcane Arts and chatting with her friends Augum and Leera and her other fellow Arcaners and reading a good book by the fire and playing with her dog and cuddling with her man—oh how she missed Olaf and Sabby and her friends! So much so that she sometimes imagined whole conversations with people, to the point she had caught herself mumbling under her breath—anything to get her mind off the present moment, off the stench and filth and indecency and especially off the gloomy uncertainty of what awaited at the conclusion of the voyage. The future was to be avoided at all costs. Thoughts of making a family were like smoke, freedom a dream for fools.

Just as Bridget slid her shovel under yet another coil, a deep *thwoom* began outside, and the beams and planks of the great ship groaned as it abruptly tilted, forcing her to use the shovel as a crutch. A rhythmic drumming started against the curved hull that loomed fifty feet away.

"I know that there sound," a man said from a neighboring pen.

Bridget glanced over her dung-slathered beam to the top half of a reedy man with deep-set wrinkles under a layer of filth.

The man nodded to himself. "That be hail. We is about to roll into a—"

The ship lurched, and there came a chorus of alarmed shouts from the slaves, many of whom were thrown off their feet. That included a telltale yelp from the man.

Bridget dug her shovel into a coil for more stability. Whereas most quickly got back onto their feet, the old man failed to rise within his pen. Her innards went cold from the knowledge of what had happened.

The crack of whips rang out as overseers growled at the wretches, and the sounds of mud-scraping resumed. Bridget joined the throng in her toils but kept stealing glances at his pen. She hadn't even spoken a word to him. One moment a human being had been there, with his hopes and dreams and memories, and the next he was drowning in mud soup that even loosed a long sewer-like *burp*. The thought made her want to hurl, and so she forced herself not to think about it and resumed the monotonous work.

The noise of hail plonking off the hull got louder, and the listing increased. The wind began as a low scream that steadily rose in pitch. The ship started to vibrate as its bulk carved a path through waves that kept getting larger, until the ship was rocking through a high range of motion, indicating it was climbing monstrous swells before crashing toward their valleys.

This brought the queasiness back. Bridget, being an earth warlock, suffered more than most, and it was all she could do to stay focused on the task at hand. To keep the putridness from invading her thoughts — and thus her stomach — she imagined performing spell cycles with Jez — and even Mahmoute, that strange Black Eagle woman who had taken an interest in Bridget's training. Anything but the terrible reality.

A leathery flap of wings caught Bridget's attention. She positioned her shovel against a fresh coil, hoping to catch a glimpse of the man being hoisted from his pen. Instead she saw a fourteen-foot gargoyle carrying a muscled beef of a man, the beast's claws grasping his shoulders and making him wince. The gargoyle flew over Bridget, slowing just enough to drop its prisoner into the pen the old man had recently occupied. On his way down, the new man smashed into the barrier between his pen and Bridget's with an "Oof!" before rolling out of sight on the other side. After a long groan, a muddy hand slapped onto the barrier between them as the bearded man hauled himself up.

"What is you starin' at, wench?" he snapped upon catching her gaping into his red eyes. Everyone here had red eyes. Everyone sniffed and coughed and wheezed, for besides the mud, the air stank of oil and metal and tar and all sorts of strange burning salts and acids, which the gargoyles used for who knew what.

"Nothing," Bridget mouthed as she dropped her head below her hood, hardly in the mood for confrontation.

The man called her a word that, even under the circumstances, sent a shock zipping down her spine. It was a terrible word certain men called women they deemed far beneath their station, a word that made her raise her eyes once more.

"You 'eard me," the man said with a sneer. "Ain't so dainty now, is you?" he added. "See, I come from the hard iron. Meanin' prison, girl. Prison. So this ain't nothin'. And I can see through the mud, and you look fresh, yes you do. Yum-yum fresh."

Warlock Bridget would have narrowed her eyes, perhaps snapped off a caustic remark or two. Arcaner Bridget would have delivered a speech about propriety. Dragon Bridget would have licked her chops and roared. But slave Bridget dropped her eyes, cheeks prickling with shame from her meekness. It was the same meekness she had displayed in the king's presence upon being told she and Augum and Leera would be used as weapons to expand the kingdom. The same meekness she had yet to root out of her soul, earned during a childhood spent with older brothers, a little girl wanting everyone to get along.

The bearded goon smirked. "I was a warlock too, you know. Till they took it from me. That's right, de-robed. Arcastrated. Snuffed for life. Got to the 7th before I let it all get out of hand. What you think of *that*, girly-girl?"

Bridget had never met someone who had been arcastrated. She wanted to say that it must have been for a good reason, that he must have been a most vile human for the authorities to take such a drastic step. Instead she kept her head down, avoiding his gaze but keeping him in her periphery. She wondered what warlock prison was like and knew it paled in comparison to their current circumstances.

He chuckled. "Oh, you're going to be fun. Fun and *easy*."

Keep believing that, Bridget thought, though did not reply or react as she kept shoveling.

He too turned his attention to his labors, but ignoring the bearded criminal only seemed to embolden him, for he kept making remarks, sometimes snide, sometimes rude, sometimes so downright awful it would have made anyone's ears go pink.

"I bet you'd love that, wouldn't you?" he said after painting a particularly vile picture. As he snorted and bent down to work, Bridget, blood raging—mostly at herself for enabling the behavior with her cowardly silence—slid her shovel under a fresh coil. She glanced about to check that the overseers were busy before gruntingly swinging the shovel to throw the coil at the man. Weak as Bridget was from lack of nutrition, the coil shouldn't have flown far, perhaps should have hit the barrier, but she opened a hand and, using every bit of arcanery she had access to, telekinetically nudged the slop just enough so that by the time the man looked up, it sloshed into his face with a satisfying *thwack*.

While he dropped his shovel and gagged and spat and cursed and used his dingy shirt to clean himself, Bridget retreated to the opposite side of her pen, where she continued to shovel with shaky hands, keeping him well in view.

What a stupid, stupid thing to do, she thought. *What were you thinking! Should have continued to ignore him, and now you've made an enemy instead. Well done, you hasty fool!*

As the ship tilted ever more and the beams creaked and the *rat-tat-tat* of hail rose to a drumline rhythm, so too did his cursing. "You witch! You vile harlot! You rotten skunk of a wench!" The cursing continued as he shoveled a coil and heaved it at her.

Bridget merely stepped aside, allowing it to slop against the beam behind her.

Beard quivering, he went for the barrier between them, surely aiming to climb over, only for a screech to sound from the overseer platform. There came a flap of wings as the gargoyle took to the air, its long whip uncoiling.

The bearded man pointed at her with the shovel. "No! That wench there's the one who done it first! She's the one you ought to—" The whip snapped at him with a vicious *crack*, and he cried out and fell, his whine protracted and childlike and pathetic in its pleading. "Staaaawp!" he cried. "Don't! I didn't do nothin'! Pleeeeease! I didn't do nothin'!"

The gargoyle flapped overhead, casting its shadow over Bridget as he loosed a stream of incomprehensible growls at the man.

A shameful side of Bridget hoped he would get carried off, but that almost always meant the arena. Instead, when the man dared to say "I didn't do nothin'!" once again, the gargoyle arched its back, flung back the whip, and slapped the man down a second time. He cried out in a blubber and fell back to the floor, out of sight.

Meanwhile, the ship crested a monstrous wave and fell so swiftly that Bridget felt herself lighten. The gargoyle, in mid-flight, shot skyward. The ship splashed into a wave trough, throwing everyone onto the planks. The gargoyle crashed beside Bridget—and screeched the screech of someone slipping in their own manure.

For the briefest moment she met the gargoyle's yellow-eyed gaze before quickly looking away. But it was too late. Where was her meekness when she needed it? The whip whistled toward her. Bridget instinctively rolled aside, and the *crack* snapped at the plank beside her, sending manure flying.

The gargoyle growled menacingly and rose, a behemoth of a beast twice her height. Battle instincts kicking in, Bridget rolled onto her back and raised her legs, not caring in the least that doing so had exposed her undergarments to the fiend in the other pen who had popped his mangy head above the barrier to watch her get her comeuppance. This was about survival. Sure, she'd committed the sin of witnessing the gargoyle's humiliation, but she couldn't let the whip break her skin.

The gargoyle reared up with a mighty arc of a swing. Bridget watched carefully and lowered her legs toward where she thought the whip would break the air, then kicked out. The whip smacked the base of her shoes with a *crack*, sending pain shooting up her legs. It was not hard to sell that pain with a loud cry of anguish.

"Yes, yes! Get that there witch! Whip 'er raw! Whip! Her! *Raw!*"

The shouting caused the gargoyle to turn on the bearded man, and down came the whip again. Two *cracks* sounded out, each followed by a pained and rather childish yelp. Up went the ship, pressing the gargoyle close to the planks. When the ship crested, the gargoyle growled in annoyance, launched itself into the air, and flew back to its platform.

As the man whimpered in his pen, Bridget examined her shoes and found a tear in the base of the right one. *Shoot, shoot, shoot*, she thought. Noting that the man was surely writhing on the planks and thus out of view, she drew the foot into her lap, spread both hands over the shoe, and whispered, "*Apreyo.*" *See two halves become one*, she thought as she guided the fabric back together. But the oppressive collar slowed the repair, making it take so long that by the time she finished, she noticed the man watching her from the barrier. His face was streaked with angry welts and his shirt was torn and bloody.

"You're a walking dead girl," he frothed. "And your art ain't goin' to help you 'ere. I'm going to enjoy watchin' you cry and beg and scream for mercy. But mercy ain't comin' to you, wench. Only pain and then a bloody end."

Bridget let go of her foot and clambered back onto unsteady feet, the planks rising and falling most unnaturally now, for a side-to-side motion had begun as well. She made a show of glancing at his wounds. She thought the words instead of speaking them. *Not if sepsis gets you first.* They were mean words, words she was not at all accustomed to thinking without the presence of The Callousness of the Predator.

A whistle pierced the rocking motion, indicating mealtime. A small mercy, for the deposit hole was a tenacious devourer in maelstroms on account of how slippery the pens became. The question was, who could keep their food down in such queasy seas?

WHIRLPOOL

LEERA

"Oh, *yeah*? Watch this, then," Leera Jones said, steadying her feet against the rocking deck of the ship. She gazed up at the central mainmast, the highest of the three masts, and homed in on its very tip, which swayed against the sky like a plumb bob. She then touched the back of her head to make sure the leather thong that connected the arms of her spectacles was in place.

"Don't take the bait like a fool, Jones," her mentor, Jezebel Terse, said. "We don't need you showing off and accidentally—"

"*Impetus peragro!*" Leera vanished and reappeared with a *thwomp*—a full five feet away from the top of the tallest mast, for the swaying ship had hit a side wave and gone the opposite direction she had been expecting.

Leera's cat-like reflexes kicked in, and she telekinetically latched onto the mast and snapped herself to it—albeit too violently, knocking the air out of her lungs and sending the spectacles clanking into the mast, only for the thong to halt their trajectory. After replacing them on her nose and regaining her bearings, she glanced down and saw the entire group watching her. Alanna Haught—the scheming, amber-robed 8th-degree warlock who had goaded her and was openly trying to steal her man—raised a hand to shield her eyes, though the sun was hidden behind clouds.

"You all right there, sweetie?" the pasty-faced witch called from below.

"Fine," Leera wheezed, voice stolen by a stiff wind and her mast-punched lungs. How she wanted to slap that sly smile off the woman's stupid face—a thought that brought a certain viciousness to the forefront of her mind. This time, however, Leera closed her eyes and tried to take a deep breath to center herself as the training demanded—except she still couldn't quite catch her breath. She heard someone calling from below and looked down to see Jez cupping her hands around her mouth.

"I said, are you going to zip back down so we can continue, Jones, or cling on there like the monkey you are?"

Leera imagined herself turning into a beast of the sky, diving into the deck, and showering everyone with splinters. *The training. Remember the training.* She recalled sitting in a meadow with crossed legs, listening to the chirp of birds, the buzz of grasshoppers, and the gentle sway of tall grass as it brushed against her robe. *You're not the only one suffering from such fantasies,* she thought, reminding herself that Augum and Bridget struggled with the same ruminations.

"Have you gone deaf, girl?"

"I already know how to 'port on the fly," Leera wheezed back. Just because everyone else was behind in Teleport training didn't mean *she* had to suffer.

"Can't hear you, Jones. Speak up!"

"We're moving on without you!" Lady Haught eventually shouted when Leera failed to respond.

Leera flapped a hand in a *Go on then* fashion. Holding onto the mast and not yet ready to Teleport back, she took time to savor the view.

The top of the mast was a full seventy feet above the waterline and swung back and forth in a long motion. Just below, the square-rigged sails, depicting giant roses in honor of the ship's name—*Rose of the Seas*—were taut against the wind, their edges vibrating. The deck was busy with sailors and warlocks alike, who from that height appeared to mill about like lost sheep. A side chimney belted out puffs of gray smoke from the kitchens. The black-tarred ship cut a neat wedge through the waves, its metal-clad bow parting the water and leaving behind a trail of froth.

She looked back at a pair of trailing black-tarred frigates. Both were Solian navy support ships, each prepped for war with multiple arcane deck ballistae and filled with navy and army personnel, including army warlocks. Then she looked beyond.

They had been at sea for two tendays now, and the horizon was nothing but water in every direction. Somewhere beyond that horizon to the west sat the continent of Sithesia—home. Safety, security, friends. To the east, where the ship pointed, the horizon sank into a dark gloom. Not a nightly gloom, but a lightning-addled frenzy of a storm that waited for them, a predator anticipating prey.

A swath of sunlight pierced the southern sky, illuminating the waters in dancing patterns that lent Leera a sense of peace. She pointed and looked down, but the others were busy teleporting back and forth on the ship.

"You're missing the show," she told them despite knowing they wouldn't hear her even on a windless day.

The air smelled heavily of salt, the wind was as dry as her frizzy hair, her crimson robe flapped, and all of it meshed with the creaking of the ship and the rhythmic lap of the waves. Whereas others got sick at sea and hated that motion, Leera found it soothing, like being cradled in a mother's arms.

"Beautiful," she whispered to the ocean. "You. Are. *Beautiful*." *Now implement the training*, she heard the founder of the Arcaner order, Isobel Roseheart, say in an echoed voice from the past.

Leera closed her eyes, took a deep breath, and stilled her heart and soul, trying to touch eternity by listening to and feeling the moment. It had been months since she'd last trained with Isobel Roseheart, but that would change shortly—she and Augum had brought the means to continue that training on the voyage.

In the meantime, the two of them had been reviewing what they had learned so far—a tough proposition when pressed for time and worried about one's friend. The sheer number of hours required to finish the dragon courses triggered by Isobel's crest tablet always sent anxiety through Leera's soul, yet they had to be at least attempted, even though some of those classes were downright dangerous. That training was scheduled to resume later that day, specifically the meditation portion which was supposed to help ward off The Callousness of the Predator. She looked forward to it as much as she looked forward to laundering her clothes—it was a task that needed doing, nothing more.

"And that's exactly why little of it stuck over the years, you lazy turd," Leera muttered at herself.

The distant darkness in her peripheral vision lit up with a silent flash of lightning, and she looked to it. "Beautiful and dangerous," she whispered.

She had no illusions about the ocean. Knew the tales of sailors slowly drowning or getting eaten by sharks after watching the bow of their ship sink into the sea, or dying of hunger and thirst in huge patches of dead wind known as doldrums, or having a serpent smash a hole in the hull or capsize the vessel outright. There were even absurd tales of ships lost to mysterious loop traps, condemned to sail the same bit of ocean forever. Of those who attempted to breach the iron storm curtain, the vast many were never heard from again, and none had returned from overseas in living memory. The odds of survival were grim.

In the tenday prior to a hasty departure in pursuit of Bridget and fellow citizens, they had done everything they could to stock the ship with provisions. At first she and Augum had wanted to charter a private ship with its own crew, but the costs made it unfeasible—and not a soul wanted to enter the forbidden seas that prevented passage across the ocean.

They were thus forced to work with the Royal Navy, with Augum successfully convincing the king to aid them, showing his progress in courtly affairs. And Augum wasn't the only one with a silver tongue. Alanna Haught, seeing an opportunity to further her graces with Augum, had convinced the king that she too belonged aboard.

"Just 'cause you're a lightning 'lock and as comely as a doll don't make you handy," Leera hissed at the wind, her resentment of the woman only growing over the course of the voyage. She'd prefer to trade places with Bridget than be stuck in the same hull as the insipid butt-kisser. On second thought, that would mean leaving her to attempt her cheap solicitations on Augum.

"Better *you* trade places with Bridge, you pasty-faced goat," Leera muttered, taking delight in imagining Alanna begging some gargoyle not to have to work the mines on account of she'd sully her robe or, heaven forbid, chip a nail.

Even though her feet had found a perch against hemp rope slick with whale oil, her arms were growing tired of holding the mast, and so she searched what she could see of the swaying ship through the bulky sails. Spotting Alanna chatting amiably with Augum, Leera narrowed her eyes, envisioned the exact place where she would stand, and snapped off, "*Impetus peragro.*"

The *thwomp* of her arrival was accented by a satisfying shriek from Alanna, for Leera had appeared directly behind the woman. Even as the blond-haired princess wannabe swung about, Leera swooped in to grab Augum's elbow and press herself against him.

Augum pecked the top of her head with his lips. "Er, hi."

"Hi," Leera said, batting her eyelashes up at him in what she had to admit was a ridiculous display of affection even by her standards. But seeing the torment on Alanna's face was worth the price.

Alanna, a year younger at nineteen, tall and thin, with braided platinum-blond hair and wearing her best gold-threaded amber robe, crossed her arms. "We were having a perfectly civil conversation. You needn't smother the commander with jealousy."

"I'm sorry, I can't hear you, I need to make out with the commander," and Leera grabbed the back of Augum's neck and pressed his lips to hers.

Alanna smacked her gums. "I have to say, you are the most immature twenty-year-old woman I have *ever* had the displeasure of meeting." Alanna curtsied properly. "Commander, I am sorry that you have shackled yourself to a *child*," and her robe twirled as she strode off.

Augum unglued himself from Leera and chuckled. "No need for claws. She's harmless."

Leera slapped his chest as she shoved him off. "Stand up for your girl, would you? She's a lecher who's been trying to hit her mark with you for the whole voyage. Actually, even before that!"

"*Actually* we were having a discussion about the tactical advantages between short hops and long hops."

"You daft fool, that's her way of weaseling herself into your good graces!"

"Don't call me a fool," Augum whispered, eyes darting about at the gawkers, especially the nearby crew whose ears were notoriously alert for ship drama. "I'm still a commander."

"And I'm still a captain of the order *and* your betrothed. Watch yourself, mister. Bah," and she marched off, steaming at Augum for not standing up for her, at herself for allowing Alanna to one-up her once more when it came to her man, and for not being more mature about the whole thing. After all these years, after the wars and heroism and all that learning and taking flight in the skies as a dragon and seeing myriad wonders, the feisty scrapper in her who had punched a girl in the mouth at six years of age for stealing her candied apple stubbornly refused to grow up.

With the ship listing in a stiff wind, Leera, using ropes and tackles and barrels and ballistae strapped to the deck as handhold guides, marched up to Jez and grabbed her arm. "I'm done with 'porting," she hissed into the woman's ear. "I don't need more than a few reps anyway. Let's move on to something else already. Maybe new spell training or something—*anything* except for this repetitive tedium."

"*You* might be done with 'port training, kiddo, but everyone else needs to catch up," Jez replied without so much as glancing over at Leera, making a *move-it-along* motion to a nearby Jengo to continue. "If a snuff comes along, or we get surprised by a serpent, or face who knows what out there in those gods-forsaken seas, they need to be able to pop off at the drop of a—" and she snapped her fingers to make her point. "Now get your externally rebellious keister out of the way, missy. I've got lessons to impart."

Leera glanced about at the scattered troupe. Alanna Haught stood with her back turned, speaking with Bridget's apprentice, the preening Carter Southguard, and his cousin entourage of Digby Bloomington-Southguard and Teague Bloomington-Southguard.

How Leera wished her apprentice, Revel, had allowed herself to be persuaded to come on the voyage! Alas, the foolish young woman was terrified of the open ocean, something Leera found ridiculous considering she was a blasted water warlock. Come to think of it, the girl struggled with diving, having passed on the opportunity to dive into Horren's Keep when she had had the chance. Unlike herself, Revel did not like adventure or taking risks, but Leera supposed it was for the best, for Revel was young and inexperienced and did not have the temerity or skill for such a risky voyage. At least Leera wouldn't have to babysit her.

Carter, one year older than Revel at seventeen but just as inexperienced, was learning Teleport for the first time under war conditions. Being the heir to the throne meant everything took ten times longer as no one wanted the potential next king to accidentally fuse his hand to the hull—or appear deep underwater. His insufferable snot cousins, although older, provided accompaniment to his constant attempts at womanizing the few women on board—at least the ones who would put up with him, which strangely included Alanna Haught, who seemed to find his charms amusing, though he might as well have been trying to seduce a plank for all the distance it got him with her. The only chance the young man stood in life was Augum, who had taken him under his wing as his apprentice in Bridget's stead.

Regarding her betrothed, he stood gesticulating with his fellow Arcaners—healer and almoner Jengo Okeke, and standard bearer Olaf Hroljassen, who kept glancing at the horizon as he oft did, playing with Bridget's betrothal ring, which hung on a cord around his neck. Olaf had found it after she had left it behind in her temporary room in the Black Castle, and carried it in the hope that he would one day be able to slip it back onto her finger.

Even now she saw him mouth his most-asked words, "Any word from *the thing*?" meaning the Arcaner vault, which if Bridget were able, she would have left a message within.

Beyond, mingling on the top deck near the captain's quarters, stood the perpetual thorn in everyone's side, the royal butt-sniffing Lord High Commander Strout. He was speaking to the captain of the ship, an overbearing, broad-shouldered man with a hulking salt-and-pepper beard. Both kept looking to the ship's sailblower—a freakishly tall, olive-skinned woman who was holding up her arms as she manipulated the wind so that it slid over the sails at an ideal angle. She was so thin she looked like the slightest gust ought to shove her off the ship, yet she gracefully rocked along with the motions of the deck as if born to the ocean. She wore round spectacles far too large for her face, reminding Leera of her apprentice Revel.

Watching over everyone were two Black Eagles, one of whom was Samira Mahmoute, who had given Bridget some lessons—and had hinted to Leera that she was open to doling out more. And that gave Leera an idea.

"Fine, but I hope you don't mind me filling my brains elsewhere, then," Leera said to Jez, and strode past.

"Don't be spiteful. What's gotten into you, anyway? You're being unusually petty—even for you."

Leera flapped a hand over her shoulder, not caring one hoof about propriety. Her feelings were raging, and she wanted to corral them in her own way. She hopped onto the central ladder and climbed to the wheel deck, skipping every second rung, arriving with a double-footed *thud*, causing the captain, the Lord High Commander, and the two Black Eagles to look her way—and the sailblower to cease her airy manipulations.

Leera waved a hand at them. "Hi. 'Scuse me, Miss Mahmoute—er, Black Eagle Mahmoute—I was wondering if I could take you up on your offer of training. Side training. Training on the side. Whatever." *Gods, bring your tongue to heel, girl,* she thought, frustrated that her tongue had been cowed by the hard looks the captain and the Lord High Commander were giving her.

The captain opened a questioning hand at the sailblower. "Your conclusion?"

The lanky sailblower looked skyward. "Resistance optimized for current wind strength," the woman said in a surprisingly deep voice for her youth, "but that could bite us should the winds jump. When the gusts begin, we'll need to exchange the slippiness with roughness. Strong skies ahead." Her head bobbed as she nodded at the horizon, idly playing with her ponytail in thought.

Samira Mahmoute, a former Tiberran who had adopted Solia as her home kingdom after being expelled from Tiberra for blasphemy, stared at Leera with pitiless eyes. "I do not recall offering—"

"Well, whatever. Let's say I'm the hen asking for a temporary mentor as mine is busy training the chicks." She thumbed over her shoulder at the others taking lessons from Jez. "Listen, I could use a hand with Arcane Drain and Greater Repair—actually, the latter more so than the former. And I don't want to waste time on Enchant Weapon right now as I've got too far to go with it to make a dent in battle anyway — not that I'm planning to go to war alongside Ordinaries, but you get my point. Yeah, yeah, I know we're expecting to land at the Spice Islands soon before the big dip into —" Leera double-pointed at the dark horizon. " — but there's loads of time before that. It's not like the crew will attack the royals as you got this other one —" Leera thumbed to the other Black Eagle, a late-middle-aged man with a bulldog face and over-combed gray hair. She and Augum had witnessed him talking into a speaking orb to communicate with the royalty back home. "Not that that would happen as we're amongst allies. The Lord High Commander himself hand-selected the crew, after all." When they only stared at her, Leera sheepishly added, "Er, you know what I'm saying." She perked up and whapped the sleeve of the tall sailblower. "Hey — beanpole. You want in on this training or what?"

The woman, who looked to be in her mid-twenties, started at being smacked. She smoothed her sleeve and cleared her throat. She opened her mouth to reply, closed it, frowned in thought, pointed at the sails in an *Aren't they interesting?* manner, and redoubled her efforts to look perplexed by the skies.

"Fine, you'd be missing out. So, what say you, Miss — er, Black Eagle Mahmoute?" Leera made her eyebrows dance in a similar manner to Olaf whenever he tried to con Bridget into something.

The thirty-eight-year-old Lord High Commander, also known as the Sword of the Oak, turned his chiseled face to the captain. "You believe the gods awarded the power of the dragon to a dilettante?" Whenever he spoke, his overly waxed and paper-thin mustache twitched in a manner Leera loathed. She fought the urge to ask him if he had once been a rat that had been transformed into a skeevy human.

The captain did not immediately reply to the Lord High Commander. Instead he glanced Leera up and down in a manner she was most familiar with. "Were she a deckhand, I would have her whipped before the entire crew."

"Lucky I'm not one of your deckhands, then," Leera muttered under her breath.

"Beg your pardon?" the man said.

"Just saying how I admire your leadership at keeping the crew in line, sir." Not wanting to get into any more trouble, she clasped her hands behind her back in a show of pretend meekness, faced Mahmoute, and rocked back and forth on her heels. "Please?" she whispered at the old woman. "Pretty please? Begging-your-forgiveness-for-my-recalcitrance please?"

"I might be a lowly Ordinary," Strout remarked with a sly smile, "but what does Greater Repair have to do with our quest to chase down a gargoyle ship?"

Leera scratched the back of her neck. "Well ... it's, uh, a natural progression ... the next spell I need to learn ... I mean ... you never know when ... something like that will be needed ..."

All but the sailblower stared at her.

"Right. So it's a no, then. Fine, I'll go twiddle my thumbs with cycles for the umpteenth time," and Leera whirled about.

"I would think a young woman of your stature would find a more constructive use of her time," Strout said after her.

Leera halted at the top of the ladder. Her good sense screamed at her, *Don't you dare say anything. Keep your fool mouth shut!* But Mahmoute spoke before she could ignore that good sense.

"Perhaps I ought to have some time with the young dragon," the old Black Eagle said with a sigh. "Perhaps I could help tame some of her ... youthful proclivities."

"Perhaps you ought to, Black Eagle. Pray, do not go easy on the girl. She is an orphan without a proper father figure and thus needs a firm hand."

That's bait! That's bait and don't you dare act on it! Leera turned around and cleared her throat. Instead of saying how she was an accomplished 10th degree warlock Arcaner and graduate of the esteemed Academy of Arcane Arts and former pupil of none other than the legendary Anna Atticus Stone and a war hero and that she could turn into a dragon and rip that mustachioed head off and shove it up his butt, she curtsied deeply and said, "I am forever aiming to grow as a lowly woman and dutiful soldier."

Strout snorted again. "Soldier. That's rich."

Yeah, that may have been a bit much, she thought, and stepped aside to indicate the ladder invitingly. "Black Eagle Mahmoute."

Mahmoute pursed her lips, gathered her gold-fringed crimson robe to ward against the cold, and climbed down the ladder.

Now it was the sailblower who cleared her throat before blurting in rapid tones, "Having studied the winds and the skies at length, I conclude we have three hours until we ought to start reeling in the topsails. Captain. Lord High Commander. Excuse me." She bowed and followed Mahmoute, earning raised eyebrows from Leera. The gangly woman ignored her and slid down the ladder after Mahmoute.

Leera looked to the captain and the Lord High Commander and shrugged. "Thanks, I guess, uh, sirs." She clumsily curtsied, hopped onto the ladder, slid down after the women—and was surprised to find the sailblower waiting for her at the bottom alongside Mahmoute.

"We're both 10th degree, so-so-so I thought I could join in," the sailblower blabbered, red-faced and repeatedly adjusting her spectacles. "And out at sea one so rarely gets a chance to play apprentice to such a highly respected mentor—" She curtsied awkwardly at Mahmoute. "— begging that the esteemed Black Eagle will briefly accept this humble servant of the arts as a temporary apprentice despite a mismatch of elements, that is."

Mahmoute expelled a tedious breath instead of replying.

In the mean, Leera raised an index finger and wagged it uncertainly at the tall woman. "Sammy, right?"

"Tammy, actually. I know, I'm not much of a talker."

"Tammy, right. I thought you windies were all *bluster*." Leera snickered at her own pun and then thrust her hand forth. The pair shook. "There, now it's official. Never met a sailblower before. Is it sailblower or windblower, anyway?" She jestingly kept hold of the woman's hand even though it had started to squirm.

"Er, either works."

"I like sailblower. Windblower sounds so … full of hot air." Leera snorted. "Like me." She kept shaking the hand before tossing it back at her.

Startled, Tammy rubbed her hand and chortled nervously.

"You'll get to know my sense of humor in due course," Leera went on. "Everyone does. And if they don't, I toss them overboard. Anyway, I saw that blond oaf slathering his words all over you earlier. No, not that one," Leera said when Tammy glanced at Olaf. "The other one. The heir to the throne. Tell me he got nowhere. We're trying to teach that dog manners."

"Spare me your banal blathering," Mahmoute interrupted, "lest I start rolling my eyes in teenage fashion."

"Aww, Moohie, I'm just trying to get to know the resident sailblower."

Mahmoute, who had turned about to stride indoors, halted and slowly turned about to glare at Leera.

"Black Eagle Mahmoute it is," Leera squeaked. "Er … if I may, Black Eagle Mahmoute, has anyone ever told you that you remind them of Mrs. Stone? That's *the* Anna Atticus Stone, I mean. You have the same frown and deploy it in the same manner. You also have that same—" Leera flicked a hand from foot to head. "—air of disapproval." She brightened. "I think we're going to get along swell."

The old woman took a dangerous step forth. "Let me make something perfectly clear to you, young lady. I am not your friend, nor am I your mentor. I do not care for trite lollygagging nor do I care for intransigence of any sort. Your sister-in-war well understood that. I suggest you take a careful moment to comprehend it as well." She whirled about and flicked a finger. The galley door flew open, slamming against the wooden wall, and she strode inside.

"*Exactly* like Mrs. Stone," Leera mouthed at Tammy as she passed, following.

"So the rumors are true?" Tammy said as she followed Leera inside and closed the door after herself with a flick of the hand. She was so tall that she had to bend over quite far to fit into the cramped corridor. "You lot trained under *the* Anna Stone?"

"Of course they're true. But everything else you've heard is a lie. Unless it paints us in a good light, then it might be true. Or not. Let me ask *you* about a rumor. Is it true that windies in particular like huffing their own farts?"

"Excuse me?"

"Just a jest the rest of us throw about behind your backs. How'd you get into the wind-pushing grind, anyway? And don't say it's just because you're an air 'lock."

"Mama was a sailblower until the sun and salt and labor got to her bones and put her in a wheelchair. Papa also was a sailblower until the sea swallowed him up. Went missing during a late-night watch. His mates reckoned a rogue wave knocked him out against the railing before sweeping him overboard." Tammy bent a palm. "Ship near capsized. One of my older brothers is a sailblower, but he sails the Western Salt as we speak." She shrugged. "Air blows in the family bloodline, so it was expected that I became one."

"I'm sorry to hear about your parents."

Tammy wordlessly inclined her head in thanks.

"Your whole family is a testament to the inherited element theory," Leera went on.

"I suppose."

They pressed against the wooden wall as two short crew members walked past, each mumbling an "'Scuse me, miss." Most of the ship personnel were short, as if the cramped corridors and low ceilings naturally weeded out the tall.

"Does your back not hurt bent over like that?" Leera asked as they resumed walking.

"That's why I prefer to keep above deck. In the summer I sleep in a hammock tied to the first mast."

"What about your other siblings?"

"Just one other brother, who's a carpenter and an Ordinary. We're a rarity with so many 'locks in the brood."

Leera nodded along. It was a mystery how some families developed multiple warlocks while the vast majority of the population were Ordinaries. The prevailing theory argued that proximity to arcanery led to higher adaptation rates, but that ignored those who grew up with a warlock in the family and yet failed to move so much as a pebble.

They slipped into Mahmoute's cabin, a small room with a single overhead lantern, which Mahmoute did not bother lighting as plenty enough daylight filtered in through the stained-glass window, the colorful panes decorated with a rose.

"So what say you, Moohie—I mean, Black Eagle Mahmoute. Up for training us lowlies in Greater Repair?"

Mahmoute looked to the window and stared at it as if seeing the very heart of the unknown.

Leera and Tammy exchanged looks. Neither said a thing, waiting patiently for the old woman to speak.

"The odds of us making passage through the ocean storm walls are low," the Black Eagle finally said. She looked up to Tammy, down to Leera, and back up again. "Are you prepared for failure?"

Leera straightened out of her slouch. "Failure is not going to happen. We're not leaving our countrymen—and my dear friend Bridget—with those beasts. Even if Augum and I have to build a raft and paddle, we're going after them."

"At what price, young dragon? Hmm?"

"Sorry, but what do you mean what price?"

Mahmoute once more looked up to Tammy and back to Leera.

Leera glanced up at Tammy, hunched painfully under the ceiling, and watched her face darken with concern.

"Look, we all know what we signed up for," Leera said, feeling it a rather heartless thing to say, which awakened an eye that peeked in from behind the curtain of her mind. Immediately she felt herself go cold and hard, and her own eyes narrowed slightly. But with Mahmoute watching her, Leera pressed her eyes shut for the third time that afternoon and forced herself to take a calming breath.

"I was ordered on this quest," Tammy said, her deep voice slicing through Leera's thoughts. "But I've always wanted to visit the farthest outpost of the kingdoms—and see what's beyond."

Leera wanted to say that her allies in the Order of the Coastal Guard would help them, but secrecy demanded she stay quiet about their existence. She wanted to reassure them both, yet doubt had already jammed its foot in the door, and she resisted the urge to also look out the window at the dark horizon.

Instead, Leera forced herself to brighten. "So what do you think, Moohie? Greater—" Even before she finished, Mahmoute smacked her lips and strode past her. "I meant Black Eagle Mahmoute! Wait, don't go! Please, it's just a habit for me to call people nicknames. I'm awfully sorr—"

But Mahmoute had left the cabin, slamming the door behind her and leaving in her midst a beam-creaking silence.

"See, this is why people can't stand me," Leera said. "I can't help myself." She grabbed the lapel of Tammy's robe and looked up into her large, round spectacles. "I'm incapable of taking things seriously when it matters."

"I'm sure that's not true. From all accounts, you're a wonderful and funny person and—"

Leera let go, brushing the lapel. "Spare me the pompous drivel from those teenage rags they peddle at the academy. I don't need you blowing more smoke up my robe. Everyone else does enough of that." She sighed. "Shoot, I was really hoping to get some training in with that spell." She took off her spectacles, withdrew a red satin cloth from a pocket in her robe, and began rubbing off the salt-spray grime that built up all too quickly on the lenses.

"That's a smart idea," Tammy said, nodding at the thong attached to the arms of Leera's spectacles.

"Already saved me from losing them a few times," Leera replied as she carefully wiped. "Surprised you haven't thrown a cord on yours, what with all the sailing you do."

"I don't live as violent a life as you."

Leera snorted. "Fair enough. You know what? There's something *you* can maybe help me with."

"Oh?"

Leera replaced her spectacles and, seeing that Tammy's spectacles were a touch dirty as well, opened a hand. "Gimme, gimme."

Tammy's cheeks reddened. "Er …"

"Ugh, would you just—" and Leera flicked a finger and telekinetically snatched the spectacles right off the hunched woman's face, proceeding to clean them gently. "There's a book I've been pulping my brain against. I'm sure you know—everyone knows as it's the scandal of the kingdom—that I'm barren. What they don't know is that I'm not barren by choice, but by force. The product of a necromantic curse flung at me in the war. The thing is, I think I've found a possible cure." She handed the clean spectacles back to Tammy, who accepted them with a gracious nod of the head. "But it's locked behind a kargeyasnara I've been unable to solve."

"A slip-rune sequence puzzle," Tammy whispered, hooking the arms of her spectacles behind her ears.

"You know your arcaneological lore. Very good. Anyway, everyone I've shown it to hasn't been able to untwine it."

"Untwine?"

"Yeah, I'll show you what I mean. It'll be fun." Leera exuberantly threw open the door and shot forth—and slammed right into a woman. She got a full inhalation of vanilla, which she had to admit smelled divine, before realizing who it was.

"Were you *spying* on us!" Leera roared.

Alanna Haught scoffed, but the tell was that it sounded forced. "I was *passing* through, and you barreled into me like a beastly goon. We're done with 'port training, and I was heading to my cabin to have a read and a nap before—"

Leera shoved Alanna's chest so hard she slammed back against the wall. "Liar."

Alanna threw up her hands. "Fine, fine! I was curious, all right?"

Leera ballooned. "I *knew* it—"

"You should consider asking me," Alanna blurted. "One of my Arcaneology Class projects was on how kargeyasnaras went out of favor due to certain complexities—"

Leera shoved Alanna a second time. "I wouldn't give one *hoof* if you had traveled through time and founded the very *idea* of kargeyasnaras!" It felt good to shove the preening interloper.

"We don't have to be enemies."

Leera stepped toward that powdered face, hating that she had to look up at it. "I know what you're doing," she whispered. "I know, I know, I *know*, all right? I'm not new to noble games. I'm not new to your type. I'm not new to any of it. You try anything at all, and ..."

Alanna folded her arms. "And what?"

Leera wolfed her eyes.

"Would you *really* turn into a giant lizard and chomp down on my flesh over petty jealousy? Really? What if I told you I have a vested interest in being here, an interest *other* than what you think?"

Leera folded her arms as well. "Fine, I'll bite. That interest being …?" Even though her arms were folded, she opened her hands and raised her eyebrows as far as they would travel.

Alanna stared at her and smirked. "You know what? You don't deserve to know," and she whirled away.

Leera grabbed her arm and twirled her back about, only for Alanna to shove Leera this time, making her fall back on her butt in the corridor. "You forget yourself, woman," Alanna hissed. "I may look like a noble, brown-nosing tart trying to steal your precious Augum, but the truth is I'm still an 8th degree warlock on a quest to save our people—and that includes your friend Miss Burns."

She strode off, leaving Leera gaping. Tammy offered a hand, which Leera accepted, allowing the sailblower to haul her back to her feet.

"I take it that noblewoman isn't exactly a friend?" Tammy said.

"Friend? Try mortal enemy." Yet Leera was puzzled—and even curious—by what Alanna had said. "She's playing vapid games with me and Augum. There's an angle there. I just haven't figured out what it is yet. She wants my man because she thinks she's a better match for the bloodline. You can only imagine how salaciously she licked her chops upon finding out I was barren."

Tammy nodded. "You know, it's an honor to actually meet you, Dragon Jones. Both you and your betrothed. It's not every day one meets *real* heroes. Not the fictions blown up in the heralds but—"

"You sure about that?" Leera asked, glaring at Tammy with such a hard stare that the woman swallowed and looked away. *Yes, yes, push everyone away. That will show them!* the voice of reason mocked Leera. *Make an enemy of them all. Then you can take to the skies and—*

"Shut up!" Leera roared, punching the side of her own head.

Tammy, witnessing this, placed a hand over her mouth and took a step back.

Leera felt a flush of shame sweep over her. "Er … I don't suppose you could, uh, ignore what you've just seen …"

Tammy slowly lowered her hand, yet her mouth remained gaping.

"Look, it's complicated. There's a lot you—there's a lot people in general—don't know about us. We have certain … certain challenges."

"I see."

"Um. Anyway. Shall we get to this book and—"

There was an enormous *crash*, and the ship lurched sideways so violently that they were thrown into the walls with a *thud*, the pair then crumpling to the floor. A bell began to ring above decks, and voices shouted in alarm.

Tammy, holding her head where it had thumped against the wall, struggled to get back to her feet. "What the heck was *that*?"

Leera, battle instincts kicking in, was already back on her feet and helping the woman stand. "Either we hit something or something hit us. Let's find out." Once Leera managed to get the tall woman to stand awkwardly, which she did whilst holding the side of her head and wincing, Leera raced off, leaving Tammy to stumble along behind.

Leera careened through the door in time to hear a great splintering noise and see a shadow swing overhead. Her eyes widened at the realization that it was a falling mast. She shot right back inside, shoving at the air toward a wide-eyed Tammy, roaring, "*Baka!*"

As the shocked sailblower flew back, Leera raised her arm and summoned her crest shield—just as the cabin exploded. The roof slapped into her shield, which in turn slapped into her chest and slammed her against the floor, crushing her. Immense pressure from above squished the air out of her lungs. Darkness enveloped the corridor as she felt herself pressed into a lump of flesh, her shield jammed into her chest and face, legs buckled backward underneath.

Oh dear me, this is a bit of a pickle, she thought amusedly. *Imagine if I started thinking like an old lady. Oh my, gods be merciful, sweet heavens …*

"You saved me!" came Tammy's muted voice in the darkness. "Dragon Jones? Are you there? Unnameables help me, say something—anything—that you're all right!"

Just peachy, Leera thought, running out of breath. *Enough shenanigans. Get yourself gone, girl.*

She envisioned herself straddling the ornate prow of the ship and used what remained of her breath to wheeze, "*Impetus peragro.*" With a *thwomp*, she appeared straddling an iron semi-nude woman holding a thick sword forth as if calling others to battle—in nautical terms known as the bowsprit, which also doubled as a battering ram. Behind her, chaos reigned. The mainmast had collapsed onto the deck cabins, and warlocks and archers were firing spells and arrows into the water off the port side.

The ship crested a mighty swell and began a stomach-lightening fall toward the ocean. Not wanting to get soaked by freezing water yet, Leera looked to the top of the rear mast—known as the mizzenmast—and incanted, "*Impetus peragro!*" She appeared just behind it—and once more snapped herself to the tarred wood, taking care to avoid knocking the wind out of her lungs this time around.

At that height, swinging back and forth on a wild arc, she glimpsed a massive serpent, twice the length of the ship, slither its way under the hull, the water protecting it from the various missiles thrown at it from the deck of the ship.

"Gods, look at you, you monster," she whispered into the whistling wind. The route to the Spice Islands was notoriously dangerous for this main reason—another being pirates. Port authorities thus strongly advised all ships to have as many high-degree warlocks aboard as they could afford prior to undertaking the voyage.

This serpent had smashed a hole into the side of the ship. Already the lower compartments were filling with seawater and slowing the ship down, giving it a slight list. They were in serious trouble.

Being one of only two water warlocks aboard—the others had been assigned to the sister ships on account of Jez and Leera being aboard— Leera knew what she had to do, and she summoned ten watery arm rings around her forearm. Then she girded her thoughts, incanting, "*Endura o prassa ata o codola.*"

The 3rd degree off-the-books water spell Endure the Deep immediately toughened her innards, armoring her against the cold and pressure of the depths. But she still wore her robe, which would act like a sail underwater. Thinking on the fly, she flexed every muscle in her body, incanting, "*Virtus vis viray!*" and whilst her thighs clamped the mast, tore at the robe with all her might. It ripped at the seams until only scraps hung onto her flesh—she could easily arcanely repair the damage later, not to mention she had a spare robe in her cabin. Lastly, she snapped off the incantation to the 1st degree off-the-books Breathe Water, "*Bratta fil aqua.*"

Below, spells and arrows kept sending up small shoots of water from the ocean surface as the monster silently slid by underneath.

Pebbles against a storm, Leera thought. *You leave this to Jez and me, people.* She waited until the swing of the mast had reached its apex before diving off. As she plummeted, torn robe ribbons flapping madly, she focused on the 9th degree off-the-books water spell Speed of the Dolphin. She pointed at her feet with both hands, incanting, "*Kwiko au o dolfa fusio fota talla,*" whilst bringing her hands together, fusing her feet into flippers. Then she straightened and threw her hands over her head in time to slice through the surface of the water.

The force from that height was so great that it ripped away what remained of her clothes, meaning her undergarments—and even her spectacles.

Nope, can't do without those, she thought, and swam back up to snag them, slip them over her neck, and leave them hanging by the leather thong. She had perfect underwater vision and thus did not require them. *"Virtus null,"* she incanted, snuffing the now unnecessary Strength spell. Then she glanced about until she spotted the tail of the serpent whip away into the gloom, away from the racing ship.

Choosing to stay with the ship, Leera flicked her flipper and shot after it. Even though she was naked as the day she was born, she felt at home, for it allowed total sleekness. *But it's going to be a little awkward getting out later*, she thought. *Bah, I'll figure it out.* Maybe she could teleport directly into the cabin—except with the ship's erratic movements that would risk an accidental fusion.

"Focus, would you," she warbled underwater, and with her fused feet flapping up and down, she finally caught up to the rear of the hobbled ship, reached out, and telekinetically latched onto the giant rudder, which barely moved. She hauled herself forth, then lashed out at the side of the hull and swam past the rudder. She moved along the hull, sometimes using the barnacles as attachment points, until she was directly underneath its bulk. There she waited for the beast to make another run for the ship.

It was not the monster that splashed into the water, but another warlock, one with seventeen watery rings glowing around her robed forearm.

"Finally decided to join the fun, eh?" Leera shouted underwater.

Jez, who hadn't stripped down, no doubt to keep her dignity intact, gave Leera a wide-eyed double-take. Not wanting to get left behind by the still-racing ship, Jez telekinetically latched onto the hull and hauled herself alongside Leera, keeping her face averted. "Where the hell are your clothes, Jones!"

"Uh, had a slight accident hitting the water. You know how it goes. Will you stop gawking already?" Leera needled, cognizant that Jez was doing everything in her power not to so much as *accidentally* peek.

"I'm not gawking, you freak! Unnameable gods, why did I have to be saddled with such a weird apprentice?"

Leera had to snort at the remark. "You watch that side, I'll watch this side. How's the ship looking?"

"What do you think? The worm punched a hole in the hull the size of a shed."

"Can we repair it?"

"We'll see. Shoot, here it comes. Get ready to hit it."

"You got it, boss," Leera said. Noting Jez hadn't fused her feet into flippers, Leera realized she'd be quicker underwater. Hopefully that wouldn't matter and they could blow its head off now.

A hundred feet away, the serpent's massive maw opened as it snaked toward Jez. The women, each having one arm raised, telekinetically holding onto the ship's hull, waited until the beast had closed within firing range. Jez was the first to let go, shouting, "Now!" The water instantly ripped her away. "*Annihilo dio!*" she roared, shooting four jets of water.

Leera let go a moment later, shouting, "*Annihilo bato!*" shooting two jets.

The monster changed direction toward the ship, and only half of the jets drilled into its skin, albeit at an oblique angle. Flesh was torn away, leaving behind a stream of fishy debris, but they might as well have been needle marks on the side of a bull for all the damage they had done.

While Jez grabbed the hull underneath the stern with one arm and waved the other one about, surely casting another spell, Leera kicked her flipper, shooting forth and squeezing herself against the side of the ship. Hoping to blunt or redirect the monster, she reached out telekinetically, latched onto the hull, used her other hand to reach out toward the beast's massive lower jaw, and tried to use her Telekinesis to wedge the two apart. But it was like holding back a battering ram, and she felt her Telekinesis get squeezed down until it snapped, sending her tumbling from the force of the whipback—she was no Augum when it came to that spell.

There was a *crash*—but a slightly muted one, meaning she had blunted *some* of its ramming force.

With an expert kick of her flippered tail, she halted her tumble and zipped toward the massive tail and its razor fins. That tail lashed at her so quickly it took all her reflexes to dip over it, with the water curling her about as if she'd been thrust into a pinwheel.

"Whoa," she said, and reached overhead to telekinetically grab the tip of the monster's fin before it slipped away. Once latched, the beast yanked her forth so violently her stomach hit her feet. She was only glad to have avoided injury, for getting healed whilst naked would have been quite the awkward experience for all involved.

"Easy there, girl," she said as if riding a horse, "Whoa, whoa, whoa."

Almost in slow motion, she flew right by Jez, still latched to the rear of the ship, and watched her finish a spell that turned the waters by the monster into a maelstrom. Leera identified it as the 19th degree off-the-books water spell Whirlpool, which she had never seen Jez cast before — or suspected the woman even knew. The whirlpool was so massive that it sucked the side of the beast inward, folding it in half — and taking Leera right along for the ride.

"Get off, you fool!" Leera heard Jez shout underwater before vanishing around the other side of the underwater maelstrom.

Leera, seeing that the head of the beast was rapidly coming about, for it was being folded in on itself within the maelstrom, its jaw clacking, had another idea. Still holding onto the fin and with the water churning violently mere feet away, wanting to suck her in, she waited until the giant head was within Telekinesis distance, then latched onto its snout, yanked, and flippered forth. She zipped up to the clacking mouth with its rows of razor-sharp teeth and worked her tail as hard as she could, aiming to dip above the snout, toward the eyes.

"Come here, you ugly bastard," she said.

The clever beast seemed to sense her intention. It raised its snout, opened its maw — and sucked water inward. The pull was so strong it slurped Leera right inside. The jaw closed, and Leera's whole life — from her first memory as a toddler playing with a wooden stick she pretended was a sword, to running away from the Legion, to falling in love with Augum, to her celebrated graduation from the academy — flashed before her eyes. Not wanting to get ground into fish paste, she thought of the first place that came to mind — and for some stupid reason that was the rudder.

"*Impetus peragro!*" she snapped, and shot away through the ether, only to reappear in the ocean, grasping at nothing but water, no rudder in sight.

"That's because it moved, you dum-dum," she said. Things might have been different had she had eyes on the rudder in that moment, allowing for a battle teleport.

She punched her head through the surface of the water, grateful to be alive. The ship was a couple hundred feet upwind and hobbling around the whirlpool in a slow arc, its list perilous. The water to its starboard was foamy with repeated watery explosions as the serpent thrashed about, caught in the whirlpool. Warlocks and archers continued to shoot spells and arrows at whatever the beast happened to reveal above the surface, though its skin was tough to pierce. Other warlocks were frantically trying to repair the ship's fallen mast, which was laying on the damaged cabin, its ropes and sails hopelessly tangled with the other two still-standing masts.

Refocusing, Leera checked her stamina reservoir. "Still got some juice," she concluded, treading water. She next studied the splash of the serpent, trying to get a good read on the position. Then she focused on the water just above the thrashing and incanted, "*Impetus peragro!*" A naked Leera popped into existence ten feet above the head. For a moment, beast and girl were eye to eye.

Then Leera unleashed an epic wrist-smack, roaring, "*Annihilo bato!*" Two prongs shot forth. Even though she'd been aiming for a perfect skewer along both sides of the fish's snout, only one jet connected with the serpent's eye, bursting it like a fish egg. The other caromed off the slippery scales and vanished into the depths.

The beast roared, its open maw ready to chomp down on her flesh — and there was no time to Teleport away.

In Leera's peripheral vision, Jez shot out of the water nearby and shoved at the air, shouting, "*Baka!*" She felt her body get shoved a mere foot above the closing teeth. She zoomed sideways — and splashed right into the center of the giant whirlpool. Were she a mere Ordinary, her lungs would have instantly been expunged of air. Instead, she took in harmless lungfuls of water that she could use to breathe — all while she spun about like a top, getting sucked down into the whirlpool's dark heart.

A normal human, even a non-water-element warlock, would have drowned, but Leera simply got dizzy. So dizzy she almost puked.

So this is what seasickness feels like, she thought. *And what a slippery bastard!* Unable to fight against the whirlpool even with flippers, and not wanting to waste her precious stamina on yet another Teleport, she waited until she was spit out from the very bottom of the whirlpool.

Some fathoms down, she looked up to see an awesome sight lit by a piercing blade of sunshine — a massive whirlpool spinning a gigantic serpent about, its body pretzeled in on itself. Nearby was the outline of her ship, its rudder keeled over to its maximum angle, indicating the helmsman was trying to stay within range of the serpent.

Leera kicked her flipper and shot upward, keeping away from the suction of the whirlpool, inside which flesh was being thrown like debris from a tornado. They had damaged the monster. She caught a flash of speeding white to her left. Reacting on pure instinct mid-flipper kick, she turned her body, slapped her wrists, and roared, "*Annihilo!*" A jet of water smashed into a shark, exploding its head into red mist.

Leera gaped in shock, for she was staring at an enormous shark with rows of shovel-blade teeth. She watched the beast fall, pluming forth a cloud of guts and flesh. Had she not been a seasoned warrior in her own right, had she hesitated only a moment, she might have lost an arm—or worse.

This ain't no lake, girl, she thought. *This is the blasted ocean. No muckin' about here.*

Other white shapes began to appear in the deep gloom below, no doubt drawn to the serpent bits slowly falling like underwater feathers. *Gods, it's going to become a frenzy,* she realized and shot upward, leg muscles straining as she kicked the water with her flipper, aiming to hit the surface at the same moment the serpent's head was coming about. She was going at such a speed that when she broke the water's surface, she launched herself into the air like an arcane missile.

Leera immediately saw that the serpent's head was flailing out of the water, absorbing shots from the ship. Taking an eyeblink to aim, she slapped her wrists and shouted, *"Annihilo!"* The jet shot forth and smashed into the beast's other eye, splattering it.

Leera dove back into the water and, once she leveled below the surface, witnessed Jez daringly swim up to the head, take aim, and slap her wrists together, roaring, *"Annihilo dio!"* Four jets of water smashed into its open mouth. The mouth expelled a plume of flesh, and the beast went limp.

Working together, they'd vanquished it.

Jez opened her hands and arcanely manipulated the whirlpool downward, shoving it deep toward a circling swarm of sharks. There the whirlpool dissipated, leaving behind a revolving and tangled serpent pluming its guts to the assembled predators. The sharks dove in like underwater vultures to ferociously tear at the entrails.

Jez swam up beside Leera, her gaze fixed on the feeding frenzy below. "Give me thirty heartbeats to find you a blanket, then pop up on the very rear of the ship. Don't want any of those fiends catching eyefuls of you, do we?" She punched Leera's shoulder, taking care not to so much as glimpse her nakedness. "Good work, kiddo."

"You too," Leera said with a proud smile. She couldn't remember the last time her mentor had complimented her. Usually it was all snark and sarcasm—or variations thereof. "Think you can teach me that spell?" she blurted.

Jez, who had begun to incant the Teleport incantation, halted to choke on water. She thumped her chest a few times with the side of her fist. "Are you crazy? It's a massively complex 19th degree spell that would suck your stamina pool dry—that's even assuming you have the brains to learn it."

"I learned Group Teleport, didn't I?"

"Which is like the easiest high-tier spell to learn."

Leera shrugged. "I figured you'd say no. You *always* say no."

"I don't always say—ugh, you're incorrigible. You know that? Incorrigible." She sighed. "Let me think about it, but probably not. You got other spells you need to learn."

Leera tried not to wobble her head about in a self-satisfied fashion, yet it happened anyway. Luckily Jez wasn't looking. "Great," she only said.

"*Impetus peragro,*" Jez snapped after a huff, and vanished with an underwater *thwomp*. She had been close enough for Leera to feel the subtle pull of water that swooped in to fill the space Jez's body had vacated.

Leera continued to tread water as she stared at the frenzy below, which followed the slow fall of the serpent. Having plenty of flesh to satisfy their hunger, the sharks posed no immediate threat. Yet watching the primal nature of the feast woke something within her, and she wanted to turn into a dragon, dive down, and tear into them all before claiming the prize for herself.

Splashes from the area of the ship stole her attention, and she finally resolved to get back up top and lend a hand to what surely would be a difficult repair.

If repairing the ship was even possible.

HOLE IN THE HULL

AUGUM

At the bottom of the heavily listing ship, Augum Arinthian Stone shivered violently in waist-deep water. His pale and pruned hands were spread before him, teeth chattering as he shepherded splinters and planks back into place. Jengo and Olaf stood nearby, having accepted his order to follow him below to attempt a repair of the damage. The hardier of the crewmen, all Ordinaries, gawked from the steep stairs, many with hands clasped as they prayed for the gods to help with the efforts.

But there was a problem—the hole was so large that one could fit a cart through. Half of the hole was above water, the other below, and with every heartbeat, the ship's list slowly increased.

An equally shivering Olaf winced, dropped his hands, and retreated to the stairs. "I'm out!" he declared, referring to having drained his notoriously meager stamina pool.

"How come it's not working?" Jengo asked, hands wringing.

Augum saw a barrel get sucked out of the hole. "The missing planks," he blurted. "They're floating somewhere behind the ship." He needn't mention the implication that those planks had floated out of range of their Repair spell.

Seeing that the hull had ceased to respond to his attempts with Repair, Augum dropped his hands and waded back to the stairs to join the wide-eyed crew. "You there," he said to a young man. "Run up top and fetch the Black Eagles. Tell them we need an emergency Repair. Go!"

The young man nodded and sprinted up the stairs. The ship groaned as it tilted ever onward toward the ocean.

"She's gonna capsize if we don't fix 'er," the burliest of the crew said. "Can't the water 'locks do somethin'?"

Augum didn't hesitate. "They can." He pointed at the next youngest man, for he looked lithe and quick. "Hop up top and drag the water warlocks down here. Tell them we need their—" But he was cut off by Jezebel Terse practically swinging her way down the stairway, using the steep handholds as guides. Right in behind her was his betrothed, Leera—and for some reason, she was wearing a curtain.

"Shut up," she said as he opened his mouth.

"I was only going to ask what took you so long," he quipped, flashing her a wry smile. Had they been in private, he would have playfully pinched her butt, just as she did to him whenever he wore something outlandish.

Jez took one look and snapped her fingers before Leera's bespectacled face. "Evaporate. Go, go, go!"

Leera elbowed Augum aside, muttering, "Move it, mister." Then she and Jez spread their hands over the water and chorused, *"Evapa loa aqua."* With a *whoosh*, whole swaths of water began to vanish. Jez, being 17th degree, made three times as much water vanish as Leera area-wise, but Leera was faster with her castings. From what Augum recalled her telling him once, she surged the spell, meaning she paid more stamina-wise. That became evident when her spell work eventually failed.

"I'm out," Leera declared, climbing and then plopping on top of a large crate by the stairs. She crossed her legs, straightened out her slouch, and closed her eyes. "Going to meditate."

He wasn't surprised considering how busy she'd been in the water. He had glimpsed her zipping about down there—and had even caught a distant flash when she'd launched above water. Thankfully no one had said anything about her missing her clothes—at least within his earshot.

As Jez continued to evaporate the water, the ship began to list the other way, and the sailors cheered. But Augum knew it was only a temporary victory, for a full third of the hole was still below the waterline.

"Tell the captain to change tack!" he told the closest man. "Port to the wind! Go! Now! And tell him to backtrack over our course so we can fish out the rest of the hull planks!"

The man flew up the stairs—and smashed into the muscled Carter Southguard, sending them both splashing into the waist-deep water.

"Watch yourself, you clod!" the seventeen-year-old spat after picking himself up, blue robe drenched. He took a moment to fix his wavy blond hair, which he no doubt spent too much time grooming to perfection.

Augum flipped his hands at his temporary apprentice. "Help him up, would you," he said, nodding at the slow-moving crewman who was so addled from the collision that he was struggling in the water. *This kid, I swear*, he thought.

Carter yanked the sailor to his feet, hissing at him under his breath to be more careful next time.

"Yes, m'lord. Sorry, m'lord," the young man stuttered—all the sailors knew Carter was the heir apparent.

Watching this display, a shadow reared up behind Augum's mind. *How dare the boy overstep his bounds like that! And he thinks he can pass his dragoon trials? Not a chance in hell.*

"How can I help?" the hefty teenager asked after giving Leera a double-take and splashing his way over to join them.

Augum, feeling shadowy wings spreading from his back and too annoyed and tired to quell the darkness, grabbed Carter by the scruff and throttled him, roaring, "Don't you *dare* treat them below you, boy!" He shook him. "Do you understand me?"

Carter stared at Augum with glassy eyes. "Y-y-yes," he gibbered. Those eyes watered, as if he'd never been properly reprimanded before— at least by someone he respected. And the boy respected few.

"Aug!" Leera snapped.

He glanced over to see her flare meaningful eyes at him from her sitting position atop the crate, a hand flipped in a *What are you doing?* manner.

Augum let go of Carter with an annoyed grunt. There was no time to battle The Callousness of the Predator—though he ignored the protestations of his training, which told him he should *always* make time.

Carter sniffed, looked away, and wiped his face with his sleeve. "What are you looking at?" he snapped at the tiniest deckhand, who immediately dropped his eyes and mumbled, "Nothin', m'lord. Nothin' at all."

Raging but aware that there were more pressing concerns, Augum refocused on the deluge spilling in through the massive gaps where the missing planks should be.

"Your counsel," Augum spat to Jengo and Olaf, who, other than sharing a knowing look between themselves, kept mum on the subject of his temper—as they did whenever he overreacted.

Cowards, Augum thought derisively. He needed to whip them into shape. Thank the gods they had granted him the power to do that as their commander.

Olaf glanced about. "Block it with whatever we can get our hands on here. Whatever we can lift, that is."

"And we seal the cracks," Jengo suggested, one arm folded over his robe and the other propped up against it, hand rubbing an old scar on his chin. "It'll slow the intake and buy us time until we can muster a proper repair."

"We can use cloth for that," the oldest amidst the crew offered. "There's a crate of textiles about somewhere here meant for trade."

Augum nodded. "Hop to it, soldiers," and as Jez tirelessly worked on vanishing water, everyone else pointed or carried whatever they could to the hole—pallets and barrels and crates and anything with any heft. The eldest deckhand quickly found the correct crate, cracked it open with a crowbar, and began throwing colorful textiles toward Leera, who had joined in to help jam the textiles between gaps.

"Captain's goin' to be right pissed about that," the deckhand muttered upon seeing Augum drag a square rope-bound sail over by the hole, where he left it to float in the water.

"Captain ain't going to have much of a ship to be pissed about if we don't rig up a patch double quick," Augum replied, earning him a nod from the deckhand. "Let's step up the sealing efforts."

He started by organizing his thoughts in line with the expectations of the Seal spell, a staple of the 6th degree. But just as he was about to cast it, he caught his apprentice, well known for his lecherous ways with women, gaping at Leera as she bent over to stuff a sodden textile between a barrel and a crate. Charitably, Carter might be wondering why she was wearing a curtain. But Augum wasn't feeling particularly charitable and telekinetically flicked at the air toward Carter's ear.

"Get over here, Southguard," he snapped after Carter had slapped the side of his head. "I need you to hold this crate against the hole. Come on, move it, 'prentice!"

A red-faced Carter waded over, grabbed the crate, and stuck it against the edge of the hole.

"Put your full weight into it," Augum ordered.

"I *am*, Commander," came the indignant reply.

Like a scolded schoolboy, Augum thought. But he saw the teenager struggling against the water and indicated for Olaf to help. Olaf, being a big man himself, put his back against the crate and used his feet as leverage.

"*That's* how it's done," Augum said.

As the boys used their combined strength to hold the crate in place, Augum raised a finger. "*Obdura del boundera sen*," he incanted, using the finger to trace an arcane fusion between the crate and the hull. But with the hull being slightly bowed, there remained a gap between some of the sealing, allowing in water. Resolving to deal with that after, Augum continued working, with Jengo and Olaf and Leera helping with the Seal spell as needed. Luckily the captain changed tack with the wind, allowing most of the hole to rise above the water, making their job easier.

"Out of textiles," Leera reported, having jammed the last piece into place.

With the majority of the hole sealed up and the water down to their knees on account of Jez's efforts, Augum pointed at the rope-bound sail and telekinetically lifted it over their heads. "Cut the rope!" he shouted.

The eldest deckhand unsheathed a nautical knife from his belt, waded through the water, and cut the rope that held the sail in place like a giant parcel. The sail flopped forth, unfolding until it slapped into the water. "Now work together to jam it in place!" Augum ordered, and everyone used their hands to punch and jam the sail into the gaps. Augum, Jengo, Olaf and Leera then continued with Seal, until the water was down to a trickle.

"We can take care of the rest with gum plaster," the eldest deckhand said. "Good work, sir." He inclined his head at Jez, who was resting with her hands against her knees. "Miss."

A soaked Jez nodded, though she was glaring at Augum.

What the hell do you want? he thought at her, glaring right back, the callousness surging in the face of her anger.

Leera hooked an arm around his neck and patted his chest, whispering, "Remember your training, my love."

He slapped her hand aside, hissing, "Not in front of —"

"—the crew, yeah, yeah," Leera muttered, unhooking her arm from his neck and rolling her eyes.

Augum wanted to shove the curtain-wearing girl into the water slopping about at the bottom of the ship, but some dignified and quiet part of his mind croaked, *You really ought to remember the training. Maybe even continue it shortly.*

"Bah," Augum said, hating that the weak, rational part of him wanted to train up. He much preferred the anger that came with The Callousness of the Predator, which didn't give a hoof what anyone thought about him. He was a lord of the skies who could bring terror to all. Why was he even wasting his time with these useless people?

He had hoped that Leera would take more offense at his discarding of her, but all she did was start a conversation with Jez about their efforts. Leera glanced back at him and made a show of closing her eyes and pressing the air downward with flat hands, mouthing, *"Don't forget to breathe."*

She's right—you're giving the callousness too much rope of late, Augum thought. Yet he warred with himself. The last thing he wanted to do was meditate or bother with the ancient lessons, all of which he found nauseatingly boring. If anything, he wanted to find more monsters, dive at them from high up, and eviscerate them with his claws.

There came the clunk of heavy boots on the stairs, and the deckhands stiffened. Paying them no attention, Augum closed his eyes and forced himself to meditate. *It's supposed to make you stronger in the end,* he thought. *So give it a try.*

As per one of the dictums of the training, he focused on one sound — the rhythmic creak of the ship. Then he heard the waves as they whooshed by the hull and the trickle of water as it dribbled from the gaps in the repair work. He felt his heart slow and his breathing settle, and he opened his eyes.

"What say you, son?" the imposing captain said, staring at him with his hulking beard and piercing eyes. Behind him stood Lord High Commander Strout, twirling one end of his already pointy mustache as he surveyed the repair work with a grimace. Strout's beady eyes kept flicking to Leera, who brought her hands together before her impromptu curtain dress as if to shield against his gaze.

"Answer me, boy."

Augum, figuring the man had to be referring to their work, replied as he looked to the repair, "I'm not your son, I'm not your boy, and the work speaks for itself."

"You will hold that tongue, warlock!" Strout snapped. "And you will respect leadership. Why is this such a common problem for you Arcaners? Is the dragon too much to handle? Power got to your heads, did it?"

More than you know, Augum thought.

The overbearing captain considered him. Augum, still enticed by the predator, wanted to antagonize the captain into an argument, giving him an excuse to rear up with the might of the dragon.

The captain grunted, as if having experienced such stubbornness many times before. "The Black Eagles report that, on account of the wind and waves, it would be exceedingly difficult to retrace our course and pick up the smashed pieces necessary to conclude the repair." He nodded at the impromptu sealing. "Will your work hold?"

"No," Jez threw in, straightening. She rested an elbow on Leera's shoulder. "But I'll work on it with the boys—" A finger from the leaning hand danced as she indicated Olaf, Jengo, Carter, and the nearby crew. "—until we have a robust solution than can stand up to a storm. You two—" She unglued her elbow from Leera's shoulder to shove her toward Augum. "—go do your special training."

Augum caught Leera and held her for a moment before she shrugged him off. Feeling human again, he felt the sting of rejection, which prompted the callousness to again rear its ugly head, coaxing him to lash out at her. This time, he did not take the bait. But he was annoyed. After everything he'd endured, and at this stage of his life, it was frustrating to fall victim to its capricious whims. Until he could learn to control it, he would never become the commander he envisioned himself being.

Jez smirked at Leera. "And unless you want to decorate a window, missy, you might want to change out of that curtain."

"I'll think about it as there are a lot of curtainless windows around here," Leera said, nudging Augum. "Come on, butt-breath," she muttered, and led the way, only to halt before the captain and throw him an over-the-top salute complete with a heel-click. "That is, if we're excused, sir."

Augum for sure thought she had over done it, but the captain's gray eyes merely flitted between them before he waved a dismissive hand. Leera performed a lazy half curtsy in her makeshift curtain dress, and the pair walked up the steps, squeezing—and in the case of Leera, shouldering—by the Lord High Commander, who hissed, "Excuse *you*, woman."

Leera shrugged. "What? It's a tight squeeze."

All the man could do was throw her an angry lip-smack in reply.

"I like antagonizing him too," Augum said as they ascended, imagining meeting the turd of a man outside the confines of rank and bullying him mercilessly. By now, he thoroughly doubted the stories about the Lord High Commander and how he had supposedly killed seven men under an oak tree, earning him the appellation Sword of the Oak. Something told him he had made the whole story up to gain esteem.

"He *is* quite the rodent, isn't he?" Leera impersonated a squeaky sound whilst sucking repeatedly through her teeth. "By the way you won't win Carter over by being a grouch for a commander."

"I know that," he snapped. "You think I *want* to be a grouch?"

"The callous part of you does."

He sighed. "I suppose."

"Let's hit my cabin so I can change, then hop to training."

"I thought you wanted to hang yourself in front of a window," he blurted without thinking. "Wait, that came out wrong." *You don't have her wit*, he reminded himself.

She snorted and stepped aside upon reaching the ladder that led up to the cabin floor. "Girl's got to keep her dignity," she said, indicating her curtain with one hand whilst waving at him to go first with the other. Then she pressed a finger to Augum's lips, which had opened to lob a reply. "None of that gross boy stuff, mister."

"I wasn't going to be gross," he replied when she let go. "But the crew *was* gawking at you as if you were on fire," he said as he ascended the ladder. "I was steaming with jealousy."

"Big of you to admit that," she replied from below.

"It's easier to be honest when it's just me and you. Now I want to pinch your butt, Jones," he said when she hopped onto the cabin floor, joining him.

Leera swatted at his playfully pinching fingers, singing, "*Pshah.*" Then she winked, slyly adding, "We can pinch each other later."

"Oh, definitely. Any transmissions?" he whispered as they wound their way through the wreckage. The Black Eagles were working together to arcanely repair the third mast before attending to the cabin.

Leera shook her head. She'd been using her coastal defense ring to communicate with the Order of the Defense of the Coasts, which had an outpost on the Spice Islands.

"Are we going to sink, lowlander?" a growly but tired voice asked from behind.

Augum turned to find Rogor staring at him from the ruined entranceway to the cabins. Being nine feet tall, he stood awkwardly hunched over. He was the only wolven to have joined the voyage, hoping to rescue his brethren on his pack's behalf.

Augum shook his head. "We managed it."

"Honored highlanders do not belong on boats. This constant sickness is a curse."

"I can see that." At least it kept his grumpiness confined to his cabin.

Rogor's bloodshot eyes fell upon Leera. "Is that a ceremonial costume?"

Leera gaped at him. "Yes. It's for worshipping window frames," she deadpanned.

Rogor grunted. "Another inane lowlander custom. How much farther? Wolven stomachs are not made for lowlander journeys."

Augum looked to Leera, who was leaning up against the cabin wall. She shrugged, and so he half-shrugged at the wolven. Rogor grunted again, turned, and awkwardly shuffled off through the ruins of the doorway that led to the deck, growling under his breath something about being stuck on a floating lowlander coffin.

"He really thinks he can bring their cubs back all by himself, doesn't he?" Leera said as they slipped into her cabin and closed the door behind them.

"The beasts kidnapped wolven adults too. Anyway, his quest is the same as ours. Too bad there's only one of him, though."

"Because he was the only one brave enough to step aboard a lowlander ship."

"He volunteered."

"Honestly, I'm glad it's only him. They're an insufferable lot with their constant whining about us lowlanders."

Augum grunted in mimic of Rogor, and was about to sit down on her bunk when she flicked a hand at him, telekinetically yanking him forth.

"With that soggy robe? You think I like sleeping on a wet bunk? Are you jesting me, good sir? Let me dry you first."

"Yes, m'lady," Augum mumbled, suddenly tired from the ordeal.

Leera stepped up to him and opened her hands before his soppy robe. Then she grabbed his lapel and planted a wet kiss on his lips. At first he resisted, angry with her for a reason he couldn't remember, until his annoyance gave way to tenderness, and they lovingly kissed each other until the shadow within him retreated well out of sight.

"I ... I needed that," he whispered.

She smiled up at him. "So did I." She stepped back and ran a hand over his robe, incanting, "*Evapa loa aqua.*" He watched her take her time drying his robe, not bothering with the surge, likely to conserve her stamina.

"How's Ollie holding up?" Leera asked after straightening.

"Dark and brooding and full of self-blame. And constantly asking if we got word."

She nodded as she untied the curtain cord holding her makeshift robe in place. By the time she reached her miniature wardrobe to withdraw fresh clothing, the sodden curtain had fallen to the planks. "Hope you haven't been snapping at him like you have at Carter," she said as she slipped on undergarments, keeping her back to him, which was her signal that she wasn't in the mood to frolic. "Did you bring the *Codex Arcanera* book so you can continue training as a leader?" she asked as she dressed in the antiquated crimson robe she had found in Horren's Keep, with its frilly lace edging and cuffs.

"Of course not." He hadn't brought his Telekinesis training cube, Isobel's golden breastplate, any of the arcane artifacts from Castle Arinthian's vault, or any additional equipment—he hadn't even brought Burden's Edge, which he'd left in the care of the order in case something happened to him. He'd only brought what he absolutely needed—spare clothes, some basic necessities, and Isobel's tablet, which would allow them to continue Isobel's training against The Callousness of the Predator before that callousness ate them alive. At least the tablet could be hidden within the summonable Arcaner vault, although it was still a risk to use it on a ship. Augum had already suffered a nightmare about finishing training with Isobel, stepping back through the tablet-summoned portal—only to discover the cabin full of water, the ship at the bottom of the ocean.

She finished changing, but before she could turn around, he came in behind her and slipped his arms around her waist, whispering, "I love you."

"And I love *you*," she whispered, placing her hands over his and giving them a squeeze.

"Any progress?"

"With the book?" Leera shook her head before leaning it back to rest on his shoulder, allowing him to smell the ocean salt in her hair. "Got some ideas but nothing solid. Plucking away at it."

"You'll figure it out." The idea that his lineage might one day continue and they could have children together alongside Bridget's future family was more than tantalizing—it was a dream. Still, she'd warned him she only wanted to solve the root of the problem and wait to have kids for some years still. All assuming, of course, they survived the quest to save Bridget.

As the light outside the window darkened, he entwined his hand with hers and led her out of the cabin. On the way, they passed a deckhand who lowered his head, mumbling, "An honor, dragons."

They both smiled in response. Augum couldn't remember the last time he had genuinely smiled at a stranger, not only on account of the callousness, but also because of the events his kingdom had endured.

Life had been a whirlwind since the gargoyle ship had left the continent. The two gargoyle prisoners Augum had captured were put to the question, but both chose to remain mute and refused any food, resulting in them starving to death—this despite arcane efforts to keep them alive.

Meanwhile, an accounting of the kidnapped took place, with the results showing that the vast majority had come from Solia's capital. The best estimate was that the gargoyles had snatched a staggering eight thousand souls from Blackhaven alone. The one bit of fortune had been that, other than Bridget, no Arcaners or aspiring Arcaners had been taken—but plenty of the Black Castle's servants and soldiers had not been so lucky.

The calls for retribution came in swift and strong, yet with the enemy having fled, all the nobles could do was sputter and shout and point fingers. The more hawkish even dared to argue that it had been the Ohmish kingdom that had "conspired with the talking wolves in summoning the ungodly demons" and the Solian kingdom "would thence be justified in using its two remaining weapons to acquire their lands."

It had taken every bit of courtly guile Augum possessed—and then some—to convince the king not to start an unfounded war against an ally, and to instead let him and Leera pursue the gargoyle ship. Both sides had made a bevy of arguments—and subtle threats. The two arguments that eventually convinced the old boar were that Augum and Leera would not survive as dragons without Bridget, and that they promised to consider the other continent—which was surely full of countless treasures—as a potential land grab.

It had thoroughly disgusted Augum to make the second argument, which had forced him to be careful not to swear on his shield in its support lest he be held to account for such an evil idea. Nonetheless, the only thing that mattered was bringing Bridget and their kidnapped people home, and if that meant pretending to sound greedy on behalf of the kingdom, then so be it.

After the king had relented, he demanded absolute secrecy, not wanting the kingdom's enemies to know the dragons were away. As a result, few knew Augum and Leera were coming until they teleported aboard after the ships had left dock, surprising the crew.

Augum came up to his cabin door, but just as he placed his hand on the handle, he looked to Leera. "We forgot something."

"A watcher," she said, nodding along. "Shoot." She looked over his shoulder. "What about her?"

Augum glanced back to see the gangly sailblower woman exit her cabin, bow toward them, and walk away toward the galley.

Leera shrugged. "What? She's pleasant."

"You know we can't."

"I suppose you're right. No, of *course* you're right. Sometimes I don't think things through." She whapped his shoulder with the back of her hand. "Shut up."

"Didn't say anything."

Leera slipped two fingers into her mouth and whistled sharply. "Oi! Tammy! Can I trouble you for a small favor?"

The tall woman reemerged from within the galley and readjusted her spectacles. "Uh, sure, I guess?"

"Can you fetch either Olaf or Jengo? Tell whichever one you find first to come to this one's—" Leera gently elbowed Augum in the ribs. "—cabin."

"No problem." The woman sheepishly smiled as she tottered past but avoided eye contact.

"Shy thing has to hunch inside," Leera explained upon seeing Augum's quizzical expression. "To answer your unasked question, she comes from a family of sailblowers. And I bet they're all freakishly tall. Do you think they're all shy like her though? Probably not. I bet the rest of them are full of hot air. Oh, I'm on a roll with these puns today."

Augum, not particularly interested in Tammy's family background at the moment, only chuckled.

They entered his cabin, a tiny room with half the space taken up by a bunk that sat above a nest of cabinets and drawers and shelves—yet it was a grand luxury to even be assigned a cabin, as the crew slept in hammocks below. A single unlit iron lantern hung from a rusty chain, swinging with the motions of the ship.

He also had a small trunk, which he kicked open, revealing his neatly packed clothes. Out of habit, he crouched and pushed aside a layer of clothes to check that the pyramidal pentastone was still at the bottom. Upon seeing its black metal surface glinting, he replaced the clothes neatly on top. It was the only other artifact he had brought, with a second one remaining back at home for the arcaneologists to examine. This one they had studied to exhaustion, frustratingly having made little progress. Nonetheless, they hoped it would one day come in handy against the gargoyles.

Still crouching, he took hold of a fresh crimson robe but did not lift it out of the blanket box. "Should I change into my spare robe? I feel like I should change. I stink of sweat and salt."

"I happen to like that stink, mister." She drifted close to his ear to give it a playful sniff, causing him to recoil. "But only on you."

Augum smiled as he flipped the lid of his trunk shut. "You're a freak, Jones."

"You love it, you fiend."

"More than you know." He straightened, rolled out his sore shoulders, raised his left arm, summoned his shield, and incanted, "*Summano vaultus arcanus.*" With a *whoosh*, the ancient Arcaner vault, composed of three square side-by-side doors emblazoned with the full golden Arcaner crest, appeared in the cramped cabin space above the bunk. As always upon laying eyes on Bridget's still-lit crest, he expelled a sigh of relief, for it indicated she was alive.

Augum flicked open the central door. "Let's see if Bridget left a note," he muttered, inspecting the space within, jammed with countless ancient documents, as well as a stone tablet. "Nothing as usual," he reported.

"No surprise there," Leera replied. "I have this image of Olaf's ears pricking up from that subtle *whoosh*, and him sprinting through the ship to poke his head in through your door and ask for the umpteenth time today if we've heard anything." She dramatically opened her mouth wide and pointed at the door in expectation, but no knock came.

Augum chuckled at her antics as he carefully withdrew the tablet from a top shelf in the vault. It was crafted from orange clay and intricately carved with ancient runes that had required many minds to translate. Every time he laid eyes on the ancient runes, he heard the words as they had been carved eons ago.

Behold, for herein lies the soul of the founder of the Order of Arcaners, Isobel Roseheart the Noble, the Gallant, the Chivalrous, the Fair, the Brave, the Eternal. Dared she believe in the myth of the dragon. Dared she believe that she could learn from it. Dared she believe that she could become the dragon for the greater good. And thus Isobel Roseheart the Noble, the Gallant, the Chivalrous, the Fair, the Brave, the Eternal returned with sacred knowledge that set the kingdoms free from the tyranny of the mighty Rivicans. But she lived not without suffering, for she had been the first to experience the wrath of the dragon, and it was that suffering that led not only to her freedom, but the freedom of those whom she loved.

"I do that too," Leera said.

"Do what?"

"Recall the translation." She flicked her chin at him. "I saw your lips moving."

He smiled, returning his attention to the tablet, for what was hidden inside the crest mattered most—ancient arcanery that allowed Arcaner dragons direct access to lessons on meditation, flight, strategy, and warfare, each taught by only one person—none other than Isobel Roseheart.

"We have been spending too much time reviewing instead of progressing," Augum said. "The time has come for that to change."

Leera nodded in agreement.

There came a knock at the door, and Augum slid the tablet under his blanket, swiped at the air whilst muttering "*Vaultus null,*" vanishing the vault, and called, "Come in!"

Leera threw the door open for Augum, revealing the large figure of Olaf, who greeted them with a double rise of his eyebrows. "What'd I say!" Leera sang triumphantly.

"Say what?" Olaf said as he slid by the narrow frame, waving a hand in thanks to the gangly Tammy.

"You're welcome," Tammy replied, stealing a hunched peek inside whilst smiling that sheepish smile of hers. She then flapped an awkward goodbye and walked off.

Olaf thumbed over his shoulder. "She's a weird duckling. Would hardly say a word when I asked her questions."

"She's just shy," Leera said.

Olaf ran a hand through his greasy mop of blond hair and dully glanced about the room. Augum and Leera leaned in, expecting a certain question or perhaps a jest, but Olaf's face told the tale of his thoughts — it sagged, with puffy, dark circles under his eyes.

Augum clapped his beefy arm. "Just checked the vault, big guy. No word yet."

"And her door?"

"Still lit," Augum and Leera choroused together.

"We'll find her," Augum threw in. "Don't you worry, good buddy."

"Oh, I worry," Olaf replied, playing with Bridget's betrothal ring that hung from his neck. "All I *do* is worry. It's my strong suit. You know it's my fault, right? All of it. If I'd only had the patience and strength to put up with that vicious callousness —"

"Stop beating yourself up, Ollie," Leera said. "Aug and I struggle with it too."

"All the time," Augum said, nodding along.

Olaf was about to sit on the bunk when he realized his amber robe was sopping wet. He sighed and looked to Leera, flicking a hand at his sodden robe. "Do you mind?"

"Not at all." She ran a hand over his robe. "*Evapa loa aqua*," she incanted, and the cloth dried itself before their eyes.

"That is one of the most useful off-the-books spells there is," Olaf said. "Think it's teachable to a dullard like me? I mean —" He opened his palms and moved them up and down like weighing scales. "Ice and water are practically family. Shouldn't be *too* difficult, right?"

Leera folded her arms and nodded fervently. "Oh, yeah, *super* easy. Just a few thoughts and gestures and you're on your way to drying every wet rag you find."

Olaf blinked at her before leaning over to whisper to Augum, "That sarcasm was so thick we could have slathered a loaf of bread with it."

Augum smiled at him. "*There's* the Ollie we know."

"Bah. So what's happening? We having an order meeting?"

"Not quite," Augum said. "Need you to watch our backs." He slid back the blanket, revealing the crest.

Leera made a diving motion with a hand. "We're going in."

"'Bout time, ain't it?" Olaf said. He slapped his big belly. "I'll barricade that door with me fats. They'll need one of them harpoons to dislodge this here blubber."

Leera flashed Augum a grin. "Yep, there he is."

"I hide my misery behind jests."

"Well, you don't need to play sunshine bear with us, big boy," Leera said. "You can be sullen. Sometimes we might even prefer that, given all the smoke-blowing happening around here. Dragon this, hero that. Blah, blah, *blech*."

Olaf nodded at the tablet. "How long's it been, anyway?"

Augum squinted as he searched Leera's face. "Before graduation …?"

"Two months prior, I think," she said. "Maybe three."

"That hard, huh?" Olaf said.

"You have no idea," Leera muttered. She nudged him. "Want to do the honors?"

Augum summoned his lightning crest shield, with its Arcaner motto and dragon sitting atop an imposing castle, all shining in gold. "Here we go," he said, and pressed the shield to Isobel's crest tablet whilst incanting, "*Semperis vorto honos.*"

The tablet and his shield flared with light, and a ghostly woman with aquamarine eyes and wearing a silky amber robe and a floral wreath atop her head appeared in their midst. Due to the cramped space, however, she appeared within his bunk, so that half of her was standing in the cabinets below.

"*Alianos,*" the woman said in a graceful and lilting tongue.

"*Alianos,* Pelagia," Augum said, returning the greeting in the old tongue.

Pelagia glanced between the three of them. "*Mio nominos io Dragoon Pelagia. Arcan languino?*"

Augum groaned. "You know we took too long when she has to tune to us all over again." Usually she spoke to them in the common tongue.

"Cut us some slack. We've been busy with the order," Leera replied. "Not like there was a war on anyway to motivate us."

"She's so stately," Olaf said, staring at Pelagia. "She reminds of …" He pressed a fist to his mouth, choking up. "… of Bridge."

Leera patted his back. "Don't you worry. Bridget's a big girl who can take care of herself. Probably whipping those gargoyles raw as we speak."

Olaf snorted. "I doubt that, but I appreciate the sentiment. Poor thing is probably slaving in some mine or something. Gods how I wish I could have protected her. If I could have only passed the dragon trial I would have—" He ground a white-knuckled fist into a palm whilst grinding his teeth. Then he sniffed and smoothed his robe. "Sorry. Ignore me. Go on then."

"And you *will* protect her again when we find her," Augum said before turning to Pelagia, who patiently stood half inside his bunk. "*Commona languino Solianos*," he said in reply to her question.

Pelagia opened her hands and tilted her forehead toward Augum. "*Ata ueno bonda.*"

"Let us bond indeed," Leera muttered, twirling her hand in a *move it along already* motion.

Augum awkwardly pressed his forehead against Pelagia's over his bunk. She closed her eyes as light emanated from her forehead and pulsed for a while before fading. All Augum felt was a mild tingling in his brain. She then stepped back and repeated the gesture with Leera—and even offered to do it with Olaf, who merely scrubbed the air with a hand, saying, "Needn't bother with this sack of spuds. I don't even qualify to look upon your graces," which earned him a lip-smack from Leera.

Pelagia stepped back into the center of the bunk. "Dragon Stone, Dragon Jones—I now understand your language. You have opened the sacred course of the dragon, meticulously crafted over the span of one thousand years using the most advanced arcanery available to us. This is the final iteration of the course before we put it into stasis. Awakening it means that Sithesia has fallen upon calamity. We hope you will prevail. We designed the course to be taught by a single mentor—Isobel Roseheart. You must listen to her carefully and heed her warnings, for controlling the dragon will be a challenge to your dying day. Since you are secret-keepers, you may keep this tablet safe in the vault. Should the course ever return to a stasis state, please return the tablet to Isobel's tomb, located in Endraga Ra. Your arcane strength means you have fourteen lessons available to you."

Augum and Leera exchanged wild looks. The last time they summoned Pelagia, they'd only had Class One and Two available from each course!

"We graduated!" they chorused.

"Reaching the 10th degree unlocked more courses," Augum said.

Pelagia, waiting patiently for them to finish, continued. "Meditation Class One, Meditation Class Two, and Meditation Class Three. Flight Class One, Flight Class Two, and Flight Class Three. Strategy Class One, Strategy Class Two, and Strategy Class Three. Warfare Class One, Warfare Class Two, and Warfare Class Three. Dueling Class One, Dueling Class Two, and Dueling Class Three. You may take these lessons as many times as you wish and in any order, but only after passing the first will the second be open to you. Understand that some lessons may take decades to master, and some you might not ever master. I highly recommend that you begin with Meditation Class One. Please state the name of the class you wish to attend. All who qualify may enter the portal. *Semperis vorto honos.*"

"*Semperis vorto honos*," Augum and Leera mumbled out of habit, lost in thought. *Each* class was one hundred hours in length.

"She just added four hundred more hours," Leera blurted, thinking along the same lines.

"And you lot haven't even graduated to Class Two yet, have you?" Olaf asked.

Augum and Leera shook their heads.

"Wait, she reset," Augum blurted, realizing something. "Does that mean …?" He turned to the ancient ghost. "Pelagia, one hundredth hour of Flight Class One."

Pelagia did not hesitate. "You have yet to pass the seventy-fourth hour of Flight Class One, Dragon Stone."

"So she *does* have some sort of memory," Leera said, pushing her spectacles back up her nose. "Figures …"

Olaf stuck his hands into the pockets of his robe. "Might be some sort of arcane protection system to prevent people from jumping the queue." He shrugged. "You know, and wreaking havoc and stuff."

Augum rubbed his eyes. "These lessons haven't been sticking. Why is that?"

"It ain't because you lot are lazy, that's for sure," Olaf muttered. "Lost Bridge to this course countless times. She kept redoing some of the hours. I wonder if she's thinking about the course right now. Or about us …" His words trailed off as he stared through the window, once again twirling his betrothal ring.

Augum glanced through the stained-glass panels to see snowflakes silently brushing against the glass. Beyond, seen through the clearer panels, swells rolled by. The creak of the ship increased along with the wind.

A knock came at the door.

Augum raised a finger, telling them he had this, and opened the door a crack. "Yes?" He was surprised—only mildly—to see Lady Alanna Haught standing there.

"Forgive me, Commander, but they're saying we need to batten everything down as a storm's on its way."

"I see. All right. Thank you, Lady Haught."

"Er ... do you have a moment to spare for a word—"

"No!" Leera shouted behind him. "He's busy. Piss off, you powder-faced ghoul!"

Augum chuckled awkwardly.

"Ever charming, that one," Alanna muttered.

Augum flashed a tense smile. "Er, we're busy. Maybe later."

"How about never?" Leera shouted behind him. "Maybe she should find company on one of the other two ships. Plenty of hungry sailors there for a loose strumpet."

"Forgive my intrusion, Commander," Alanna murmured, curtsying properly—and a little too deeply. Her cheeks reddened as she glanced up at him before she departed, her silk robe swooshing with elegance. There was no denying she was pretty, and clearly she had an angle on him, but Augum loved Leera more than anything and was careful not to send any mixed signals. To him, Alanna was but another warlock who might be able to aid in a pinch, nothing more. No woman's charms could penetrate the castle of love he and Leera had built, no matter how attractive she was.

He closed the door and found himself in front of a glaring Leera, arms folded, one foot tapping loudly against the planks. Behind her, Pelagia stood in serene stillness, whilst Olaf pretended to be lost admiring a book about sail positions relative to wind patterns, flipping the pages and frowning at each one as if they contained the most interesting facts in the world.

Leera opened her mouth to speak—only for Augum to kiss her on the nose. Then he pressed it, holding back a smile.

"Ugh, you annoy me so much sometimes," Leera muttered, but pecked him right back.

"That's a first," Olaf muttered, shoving the book back on its shelf, probably referring to how Leera tended to go off at times like this instead of letting Augum simmer her down.

"Come again?" Leera snapped.

"Nothing. Er, Pelagia's waiting. Go and spread your wings, you two. Or whatever it is you do in there."

"We're actually going to do Meditation Class—"

"Wait," Augum blurted. "What if we *did* do a dragon class first?"

Leera searched his eyes. "You mean …?"

"Think about it. We always take time after to let the callousness run its course. We've never tried to dip into Meditation Class whilst—"

"—suffering the side effects," Leera finished for him. She slapped her forehead with a *smack*. "By gods, do you think that's what we've been missing?"

"Only one way to find out." Augum turned to Pelagia. "Pelagia, seventy-fourth hour of Flight Class One for myself and Dragon Jones, please."

"Seventy-fourth hour of Flight Class One for Dragon Stone and Dragon Jones." She turned to her right and drew an oval, creating a vivid black portal—except half was clipping through the bunk.

"Oh, go on already," Olaf said. "Just cause this here manly man—" He used his bulging stomach to bully Augum and Leera toward the portal. "—wouldn't fit through that sliver, you two reeds certainly will."

"All right already, yeesh!" Leera said, fighting him off with a snort. "Go back to being sullen, would you? Wait, I didn't mean that," she blurted, seeing his face fall. "I'm sorry."

"It's all right. I'll be here, ready for you lot to be as grumpy as ever. I'll make sure you get to Meditation Class after. That's the plan, right?"

Augum clapped his shoulders. "You're a good egg, buddy."

"Thanks, Aug." Olaf then pressed three fingers over his heart in the Arcaner salute.

After Augum and Leera returned it, Augum opened a hand in invitation. "M'lady."

"M'lord," she said with a smile as she clambered onto the bunk and crawled into the portal.

Augum took a breath, girding himself for the exhilaration of flight and the fear of what came after, exhaled, shared a nod with Olaf, and squeezed in after his girl.

SLAVE MESS HALL

BRIDGET

In the compartmentalized bow of the gargoyle slave ship, Bridget stood amidst a winding line of slaves waiting for their evening allotment of food. Every single one of them clung to what meager clothes they had, for all were sopping wet, having been splashed by a deluge of salt water to wash off the gargoyle manure. The swinging braziers cast their light from the rafters, barely keeping the damp cold at bay.

The itching from the salt had begun, particularly under the slave collar, and people were scratching themselves. Some huddled to keep warm, others rubbed their hands and danced from foot to foot despite the exhaustion from the day's work.

The ship rode the angry waves at a relatively steep tack, so that everyone stood at an awkward angle, the masses swaying back and forth as one. The hull rang like a drum from the incessant sound of hail, and the rhythms of the wind-tossed ship made many a stomach queasy.

As usual Bridget, being an earth warlock used to keeping her feet planted on firm ground, suffered more than most and was already weak from having retched once today. Shivering and fearing she would come down with a fever, which might as well be a death sentence on this blasted ship, she held herself as she had done as a sick child.

"You're her, ain't you?" an unfamiliar gruff voice said from behind Bridget. "The so-called dragon girl. One of the saviors of Solia." The cynicism was as thick as porridge.

Teeth chattering and long hair plastered to her oily face, Bridget glanced back to see a gaunt man in his fifties watching her with ice-cold eyes. He possessed a scraggly gray beard and a bald head surrounded by a tufty ring of hair. The man was among the few who weren't shivering, but held himself nonetheless. She noted his sway with the ship was more fluid, suggesting he'd been to sea before.

"They said you was here, but I didn't believe it until I saw that pert nose. Recognize a nose from anywhere, even a drawn poster. And you got a button of a nose, little lady."

The line moved, and Bridget took a step along with the others. Despite the ongoing queasiness, she was eager to put some food in her stomach.

"Reckon it must be humbling for a highborn like you to shovel dung all day," the man said. "That's quite the fall from grace, ain't it? Being the kingdom's princess and hero and bein' fed with a silver spoon only to, well …"

Bridget didn't want to waste precious energy on the man, so she pressed her eyes shut and ignored him, hoping he'd stop talking to her. She hadn't uttered a word all day and wanted to maintain that silence as some paltry means of control over her own fate. To show her soul she was still in charge of *something*.

"But you didn't really turn into a dragon, did you? I reckon the royals summoned the beasts and said you did it, didn't they? All so the kingdom could have its heroes. You're dupes, the three of you. Dupes for history. For the myths our children's children could yap about around the fire, study in the books."

The line moved once again, and Bridget did not think she could stand the cold and misery and itchiness and queasiness and hunger and this boorish man blabbering in her ear.

"You thought you was lucky, but you don't know luck. You want to know luck? They call me Mud. That's why I feel at home here. I *am* mud, you see? Now *that's* luck."

Shut your fool mouth, you fool of fools! Bridget wanted to roar at him. But she maintained her precious silence, the only thing she had left besides her sopping robe.

But that's not the only thing you have left, is it? She still had her arcanery, albeit a fraction of it. Yet in her sodden, teeth-chattering, and feverish state, what spell could she cast?

As Mud yapped on behind her about how the gods had favored him and he was destined to survive this ordeal, a scroll unfurled in her mind detailing a list of 1st to 10th degree spells. At the bottom of that imaginary scroll were two handfuls of off-the-books elemental spells and three precious Arcaner simuls. After perusing the list, she realized that none of the spells in her arsenal made sense against Mud in that moment.

Unless you want to try muting the oaf, she thought. She wondered if she should channel Augum and somehow train her arcanery to strengthen up. Except to do that she'd have to perform arcanery often, to the point of nosebleeds and headaches, which would bring perilous risks whilst trying to perform hard labor sixteen hours a day. That sort of training was thus decidedly out of the question.

The ancient Leyan 3rd degree off-the-books spell Centarro was also an option. It would help her creatively focus on her predicament, but that would mean suffering its side effects of disorientation, stupidity, and mental fog, which was also too great a risk to take.

What she ended up doing was subtly pointing at a scrap of cloth on the ground and lifting it up and down ever so slightly, remembering Augum doing the same thing but with casks of water, just to see what training would feel like.

"You can still make the magic? I suppose your lot calls it arcanery, ain't that right? Why are you bothering with that witch business for, anyhow? Just goin' to draw the attention of them foul beasties. Hey, you listening to me? Did they do something to your voice, girl?"

I have a voice and I will use it when I choose to, Bridget thought, raising and lowering the rag, which kept her mind off how cold and nauseous she was and lent her a precious splinter of hope.

She heard Mud smack his gums behind her. "I survived human prison and I will survive gargoyle prison. Look at everyone. They've already given up. And I reckon, so have you."

She wanted to whirl about and hiss into his face that she had far from given up, but she had learned a thing or two from Augum about strategy and timing—and this was hardly a time to argue, especially on account of how much energy it would take for no apparent gain other than to satiate her wounded pride. Besides, she suspected he was goading her.

And doing a good job of it, she thought. *But I will hold my ground.*

Like a spearman jabbing for openings, Mud kept chirping at her, but she continued to use silence as a shield. Meanwhile the line kept moving along, until at long last she came up to a counter, behind which stood droopy-eyed slaves serving food into wide bowls. Beyond, perched on a beam, loomed a monster of a wingless gargoyle. People called him The Brute, as he was all muscle with a uniquely stubby snout and pointed ears far too small for his oblong head. He was thirteen feet tall with a freakishly long prehensile tail he used as a whip. Bridget had heard someone say that they had seen him once slap a man down with that tail so hard he broke the man's back. Then he made the slaves carry the whimpering soul to one of the manure holes. The Brute also loved to discipline slaves for the tiniest infraction, and so not a soul ever met his gaze on purpose, and all shuffled meekly when in his presence.

About the only kindness—if one could call it that, for their motivations were suspect—was that the gargoyles allowed the slaves to make and cook fresh vegetables and meats, including the dubious mirko. The speculation was that the gargoyles had raided food stores specifically to feed their slaves, wanting to keep them as healthy as possible for the voyage over.

As such somewhere on the ship there was also a veritable barn of animals for the slaughter—their particular manure smell was the giveaway, as was the fresh meat. Yet no one had laid eyes on these animals or knew where they were, nor of the stores, which gargoyle servants carted in from somewhere above.

Being a cook was a prize divvied out at random during the initial selection process upon boarding the ship, with subsequent selections conducted based on how hard-working and well-behaved a slave was—or so the slaves desperately wanted to believe. Yet Bridget saw no evidence of the gargoyles rewarding slaves for their hard work—with the possible exception of getting to avoid the whip.

Today Bridget received a crudely carved wooden bowl from a young man of about her age, who happened to glance up at her as she stood before him. His eyes widened with recognition, and he whispered, "M'lady, had I known you were among us, I would have given *you* the banana, instead of to some boy. Bananas are a most rare treat."

Bridget tried to smile her thanks, but her mouth refused the command, and she was soon forced to move forth to collect the first slap of food—mashed potatoes sprinkled with torn green onions and leeks. Then came a whole leg of delightfully crispy fried chicken, followed by boiled and spiced carrots. The cooks even had access to spices.

"Nice talking *at* you," Mud muttered. "Not even a single polite word. What a snob of a girl …"

Bridget, relishing a small victory from not rewarding his blathering with a single word or gesture, collected a horn of water, which always had a slight taste of salt and metal. Then she wandered to find a spot somewhere on the rush floor, at last finding one where she could rest her aching back against the curved hull.

Since utensils were never provided, people ate with their hands, later washing them in large saltwater troughs. She set the bowl before her and gave it a turn to orient it—every little touch of control helped her feel like she was in charge of her fate. Then she picked up the chicken leg and bit off a crunchy morsel that yielded to a juicy interior. The sumptuousness of the salty, hot meat cut through the cold like a knife, and it was all she could do to keep herself from scarfing down the entire meal, which mercifully slammed the door on the cursed shivering.

After shoveling coil all day, these meals always felt like a well-earned luxury—one that seemed to surpass similar luxuries from home. She could not remember ever tasting such succulent meats or tang of spiced carrots or the delicate softness of a mashed potato. Every morsel was to be savored, for it was the only pleasure the gargoyles afforded them.

Across from her, a portly woman licked her lips as she stared at Bridget's bowl, clutching her own empty one like it was a baby. She had a prim haircut and wore a nightgown, as if the gargoyles had yanked her from bed. The nightgown was patterned with lilies, which for some reason made Bridget think the woman was probably a doting mother at home and had turned feral in these circumstances.

Bridget stared at her until she realized the woman had caught her eyeing her bowl. She hurriedly returned to her feast, cognizant of everyone nearby—one could not trust the starving masses. Even sharing was dangerous as it could result in a frenzy, as had already happened on several occasions, with the big-hearted victim left with nothing, not even their own bowl to lick.

"Oh, but you *will* give it to me!" hissed a garbled voice within the throng, one she recognized. "Or you is gonna have an *accident*. Those floors can be mighty slippery, boy. Mighty slippery indeed."

Bridget, having finished only half of her food, swiveled her head left and right to see through the crowd, until she spotted the familiar muscled outline of the arcastrated warlock whose welted face she had thrown a shovelful of gargoyle excrement into. He crouched in front of a thin and scared-looking boy of about eleven or twelve, hissing threats into his face in between bites of a banana he had pilfered from the boy's bowl, all the while his eyes darting about in search of threats. Even after the banana had been scarfed down, the man kept stuffing his mouth with the boy's food, his cheeks bulging like a chipmunk's.

As if all the courage had been sucked out of the room, not one other soul paid them any mind whatsoever. This enraged Bridget more than the behavior itself, and so she tilted her head, focused, and raised her hand ever so slightly, readying to cast a spell.

"Wouldn't do that if I were you," someone said in a low voice.

Bridget looked to her left and found Mud sitting behind a nearby hunched-over person. While the person was devouring their bowl like an animal, Mud was picking and choosing what he would enjoy next, his fingers shiny with grease, eyes sparkling.

"He ain't the type a girl like you ought to be playin' with," Mud went on. "They call him Porter. Do you know *why* they call him that, little laaaaadyyyy?" he asked, whimsically singing the last word. "'Cause his great joy in life was to teleport his victims into, shall we say—" His fingers danced above a crispy chicken breast as his dirty face lit up. "—rather *uncomfortable* situations."

He waved the breast about as he looked into the past. "Once 'ported a tanner into the back of a bear cave, then hopped out to hear the screams. Another time he dropped a milkmaid into a pool of acid. But he loved tormentin' plump women the most on account of having been bullied by one, a mean schoolteacher sort, when he was young. 'Ported just such a woman into a mill so her body was half fused to the grindstone. Then he calmly sat on a haybale, nibbled on a chaff of wheat, and watched the woman get all ground up. Man loved the irony of it, that he did."

Bridget wanted to break her silence to ask how he knew all this, but Mud beat her to it.

"He proudly confessed it all back in the ol' hard iron," he said. "Sort o' man to take joy from the art of the gloat. Turns out he held onto keepsakes, which is what led to his capture. Neighbor saw him carrying a missing girl's teddy bear in the dead of night, the teddy torn up as if a beast had got at it. His house was full of keepsakes. Even arcastrated and in prison, he found new ways to amuse himself."

Mud bit into his chicken breast and chewed as slowly as a cow. "He told an inmate that another inmate said something vile about his mother, told a similar thing to that other inmate, then had a jolly time watching 'em go at it. 'Nother time he rigged it so that a man would have to investigate why a large oven had failed. Soon as the sap crawled in there, Porter slammed the door closed, fired 'er up, sat back, and slurped up noodles as the man fried. Not even the guards poked about with Porter. Should have been put to death, but he told 'em some sob story about how he grew up all wretched poor with a mother who cried into a bottle and no father to put a firm hand to his antics." Mud shrugged. "And so the fools let 'im live."

Perhaps such a warning would have frightened others, and many of the nearby slaves gave Porter frightened looks and sidled further away or turned their backs to him. But Mud obviously had no idea about Bridget's sense of justice. Instead of minding her own business, Bridget heard a core edict of the Sacred Chivalric Code of the Arcaner—*Thou shalt fight for the welfare of all.*

She turned away from Mud, narrowed her eyes at the murderer he had called Porter, who was still accosting the kid, and wiggled a hand at his head, whispering, "*Flustrato.*"

"Yes, thank you for sharing your grub with—" The bearded Porter halted his loud and false words of thanks to abruptly grimace. Having once been a warlock, he glanced about, surely sensing something was amiss.

Bridget jiggled her hand three more times, murmuring, "*Flustrato, flustrato, flustrato.*" They were the first words she had uttered in what felt like days. Throughout, the man winced, pressed a heel to the side of his red-welted head, and looked about. Every time he looked in her direction she ducked behind the rows of people between them. By the fourth casting, the spells sank in and the man keeled over to hold himself and blubber, "Nothin', Mama. I wasn't doin' nothin'. I swears it …"

"You're a damn fool of a girl," Mud hissed.

Ignoring him, Bridget got up, strode over, grabbed the terrified boy by the wrist, yanked the bowl from Porter's filthy grasp, and practically dragged the kid away. When she got back, she saw that her own bowl was missing. She looked to Mud, who tipped her off by purposely looking to the middle-aged woman in the soiled nightgown. Evidently the moment Bridget had turned her back on her bowl the woman had descended like a vulture and was now rabidly feasting on it. Since they only ate twice a day and the work drew out their hunger, food was precious, and Bridget, reacting from a rage she did not know she could feel, strode over to firmly slap the woman upside the head.

"Owee!" the gowned woman cried, hands shooting to her cheek, face scrunched with the hurt look of a little girl trapped in a middle-aged body.

Bridget snatched the bowl, glaring as she loomed over her, clutching the boy by the wrist.

"I was only tasting. You didn't have to hit me," the woman protested and scooched away on her butt, sniffing loudly as if to draw sympathy that no one had the patience—let alone the energy—to spare.

"Ow," the boy squealed, and Bridget loosened her grip. She hadn't realized her nails had been digging into his skin. With a quick flick of the hand, she bid him to sit down beside her, then indicated between his bowl and her mouth.

Perhaps the callousness has not entirely left you after all, she thought, watching the larger woman crawl about in search of scraps or mercy, neither of which was provided. Ever since that first day, when everyone was hit with the brutal reality of what they would have to endure, empathy became a luxury—almost a fantasy.

The boy ripped through what remained of his food, but there hadn't been much left on account of Porter's greed, and so Bridget, hearing the code of honor echo in her mind and feeling a precious blush of empathy, slid her bowl over. He dug in, eyeing her and the other slaves like a wary animal. Bridget watched him eat, her hunger staved off by the still-blubbering threat a few rows over.

The wooden beams groaned as the ship listed so heavily that everyone had to brace against something—the wall, the floor, each other—to avoid falling over. The pounding of the hail plonking against the wood increased to a roar, creating an almost soothing cacophony.

Bridget kept glancing over at the arcastrated criminal, who had rolled into someone whilst mumbling incoherencies. The bumped person merely turned their back on him and ate faster.

The boy's eating slowed. "Are you mute?" he asked.

Bridget looked at him. He was scrawny, with sunken eyes that revealed a chronic lack of sleep. Although still dirty even after a rinsing, his hair was blond. His eyes were also hazel, the same color she and Olaf shared. Combined with the blond hair, she could imagine this boy being their son.

"M'lady?"

Bridget had to look away lest she break down thinking about the future she was losing by the league. Would her friends mount a rescue expedition? If they did, the king would hardly allow them to get far. Even if the king let them go, what chance did they have of ever finding her in this vast ocean? And oh, the irony, for like a damn fool, she'd left on a nightstand the only thing that would have given her friends a chance to find her—her betrothal ring, which was tied to Olaf's and enchanted with Object Track. She imagined him sitting silently by the nightstand, staring at it, Sabby's head in his lap, the pair pining for their Bridget.

She felt the boy's hands grab onto her arm as he frantically whispered, "That bad man's coming about."

Bridget gathered herself and looked past the throng to see the bearded man coming to his senses. *Yes, he is a bad man,* she thought.

When Porter realized the bowl and the boy were gone and that he had been tricked, he started searching about for the perpetrator, snarling at neighbors, "What'd you see? What about you, huh? Speak up. I know one of yous saw somefin'." But nobody said a thing.

The boy crawled behind her, making himself as small as possible. She straightened her back. Her meekness be damned, she would protect the boy as if he were her own. The man's eyes soon found hers. This time, Bridget did not look away. While his red eyes flared with rage at her getting another one over on him, she raised her chin.

The man stood, a lone soul standing amidst a field of hunched bodies desperate to mind their own business. Bridget, in turn, stood as well to face him, even though the boy was frantically tugging on her arm to sit back down, asking in a whisper, "Are you crazy? Please, don't make a fuss, m'lady. *Please* ..."

The Brute, noticing that they were standing amidst a sea of sitting and crouching slaves, straightened up on his perch behind the cook's counter. His long tail uncoiled and rose to wave about like a snake.

Bridget, being the only one of the pair to notice the gargoyle, for the man's back was to it, realized she best play meek once more, and so she sat back down. The bad man grinned victoriously, yet there remained a vengeful glint to his eye. As The Brute stepped off his perch, the man happened to glance back—and immediately sat back down. The muscled gargoyle grimaced as he searched for him, tail whipping about in eagerness, but he might as well have been looking for a particular chaff of wheat amidst a field of it.

Porter drew a finger across his throat at Bridget, who watched him out of the corner of her eye. *Going to have to find a secure and quiet bunk to sleep in tonight*, she realized.

"My name is Sebastian Narwal and I'm twelve and I'm from Blackhaven," the boy said, scratching at his blond scalp. "I come from a family of fishers. We live by the docks. Papa fishes them from the lake, my big sister cleans them, readies them for freezing, and an ice warlock freezes them solid for—" He winced as he looked upward into the recesses of his memory. "—I think a spine a head? Anyway, are *you* an ice warlock?"

Bridget glanced at him briefly before dragging over her bowl, but he had scraped it clean.

"I'm sorry. I thought you were done with it. Are you ... are you mute?"

"You don't have a dockside accent," Bridget remarked, her voice sounding strange to her as she hadn't used it in casual conversation since having been kidnapped.

Sebastian pressed at the bridge of his nose self-consciously.

"You're a reader," she noted.

He beamed and nodded fervently. "How'd you know?"

She mimicked him, pushing imaginary spectacles up her nose.

The boy giggled. "Gosh, you're smart. Yeah, I lost them when they snatched me coming home from school." He fiddled with his fingers. "I like reading. Papa ain't like most fishers, you know. He spends money on books and schooling and stuff. And I have a tutor who teaches me the written word. I read a lot and my teacher says I'm real smart for my age, but she also says I need to grow up some still."

Bridget wanted to smile, but her mouth had forgotten how to perform such a feat. "What about your momma?" she instead asked.

Sebastian looked down. "She's dead," he said in a dull voice. "Got robbed a few years back and put up a fuss. They didn't like that."

Bridget nodded, wanting to say something meaningful, at least give the poor boy her condolences. Instead she looked back to the bearded Porter, only to find him gone. She searched quickly and spotted him talking to a burly and bald man with a mean face and jagged tattoos all over his arms. They conversed as if they knew each other, likely from prison.

"Er … at least I *did* have a tutor," the boy continued. "Not anymore, obviously. Got nothing now. Can't even see right. Everything's a bit of a blur." He fiddled with his filthy pantleg. "My pa and my sister must be worried sick about me. I hope they're all right. I didn't see them or my teacher here, but there's a lot of people and they all look the same on account of the—" He flicked a hand at his filthy self. "—you-know-what," adding in a whisper, "the *poop*." He looked back up. "What sort of warlock *are* you, then?"

Bridget, mostly paying attention to the men, did not respond. She noticed Porter indicate the red welts on his face and then point in her direction, and the bald man looked over, nodded, and smirked. Great, she'd made two enemies now.

"I think your robe color is red," the boy continued, squinting. "So you're, like, really powerful and stuff, right? One of the rare ones. My pa is superstitious and didn't let me learn about warlocks, but they taught me about your lot a bit at school, and the rest I read in books I wasn't supposed to be reading or I heard on the street." He shrugged. "Not that I have many friends. Actually only one. She's a bookworm who thinks she's ugly but I think she's cute. Do you think we'll ever return home?"

His question cut through her focus, and she looked over at him. She allowed her silence to tell him that she did not know before returning her attention to the conspiring men. The particular way they puffed out their chests and gesticulated dismissively told her both were hardened lifelong criminals. She was in great danger and would have to figure out how to defend herself against them.

A huge fifteen-foot muscled gargoyle with folded wings and a small gold chain around its neck walked in through the large entrance way that eventually led to the manure pens. This one was emblazoned with multiple runes, which combined with the gold, told Bridget that he was of a higher rank than those assigned to oversee the slaves.

The gargoyles perceived the slaves to be such a low threat that they kept their runed brethren, who were able to use their runes to summon weapons and armor, occupied with other duties. He barked something in their growling tongue at The Brute, who'd already hopped down from his perch. The winged one indicated the slaves with a lackadaisical hand.

The Brute's tail snapped at the air in acknowledgment, making a loud *crack* sound. He raised a clawed hand several times, shouting, "*Giririg! Giririg!*" The garbled growl almost sounded as if he were trying to speak common.

"*Giririg,*" Bridget repeated under her breath to see if she could replicate the tongue, but it was like trying to repeat the growl of a dog — which made her heart pang for her husky, Sabby.

As the slaves clambered to their feet and glanced about uncertainly, the winged gargoyle went to a wall of crosshatched rope, beyond which gargoyles hauled crates about in an area that was off limits to slaves. He indicated at the wall of rope, and it telekinetically lifted aside, for it was attached to a thick timber frame in the shape of a large square, much like an unattached gate.

Bridget noted that this fifteen-footer was the only gargoyle she had seen use Telekinesis on the ship, and wondered if the ability was triggered by a rune or if it was innate or if it was something else entirely.

"*Hohol!*" The Brute roared, and his tail snapped with another loud *crack* as he waved to the now large, open doorway. "*Hohol!*"

"*Hohol,*" Bridget whispered, figuring it had to mean *go*.

As the crowd began to push toward the entrance, Sebastian grabbed hold of her hand. She looked down at him — he was a short boy for his age — and found him staring up at her, eyes wide with terror.

"Please don't leave me," he whispered, giving her hand a tight squeeze. "Please ..."

Bridget patted his hand and looked for the criminals, but couldn't spot them in the crowd. She considered moving so their backs were to the hull, but realized that would make them go last, putting them near the overseers. She thus pushed sideways through the crowd, keeping a tight hold of the boy, who did his best to fight through the throng. She glanced back and spotted Porter and the tattooed bald man emerge where she and the boy had been standing. When they glanced over, she ducked her head and kept pushing forth.

The Brute positioned himself in the rear, and his freakishly long tail snaked overhead, whistling sharply through the air as it whipped about in fearsome circles. Women whimpered while men shoved forth, and the mass of pitiful humanity scrunched in tighter and tighter, with the doorway acting as a bottleneck. The moment the first person—a young man—started to bawl, the tail came down with a ferocious *crack!* That young man howled in pain, and the masses pushed harder so that it became difficult for Bridget to breathe. She grabbed Sebastian and managed to drag him before her. Cleverly, she positioned an elbow against a large man in front of her, who was too jammed in to turn around to complain, but as uncomfortable as it surely felt for the man, that elbow was a lifesaver, giving her and the boy some breathing room.

The crowd crush made time feel like it had slowed to a crawl. While a few people collapsed from lack of air, the throng slowly but steadily pushed onward, trampling the poor souls, until at long last Bridget and Sebastian were squeezed through the doorway. Almost immediately the crowd relaxed, and she found herself able to breathe freely once more. The unfortunates who had lost consciousness were kicked until awakened. Those who failed to wake were dragged off by wingless gargoyles.

Like cattle the rest were soon herded through a rush-floored passage to what at first glance was a milking room, for it had numerous stalls, the sight of which alarmed the crowd. Bridget became worried as well, for she saw what looked like rope running from each stall to an imposing monolith located behind the stalls. It was made from black metal that reminded Bridget of the pentastones the gargoyles used, but twice the height of a person and shaped like a giant obelisk.

Someone shouted, "Gods, they're going to butcher us!"

These words caused all hell to break loose, and people started screaming and pushing back toward the entrance they had come through. The Brute was waiting for them there, and down came the whip, cracking on heads and backs alike. One of these strikes was so brutal it split a man's chest clean open, causing those who had witnessed it to shriek and run the other way once more, inciting utter pandemonium.

With both gargoyles growling at people and trying to herd them toward the stalls, Bridget kept tight hold of the boy. That was when she spotted a sudden flash of metal coming in from her left. Training and war instincts kicking in, she simultaneously shoved the boy aside with her right arm and raised her left arm in time to parry an arching stab attack from a tattooed arm—the bald criminal was using a shank made from crude iron and sharpened to a point. She then jammed a knee into the bald man's groin, spun her arm around, grabbed the man's wrist and, combining her frantic strength with every bit of meager telekinetic might she could tap into, thrust the dagger into his stomach.

The tattooed man gasped, but Bridget didn't hesitate and shoved at the air, hissing, *"Baka!"* But she might as well have thumped his chest with the heel of her palm for all the good it did, as he was so large and her collar-suppressed Push spell was so weak that he barely stumbled a step backward.

With the crowd in a wild and panicked frenzy as they struggled to get away from the whips, for the winged gargoyle had now joined in on the fun, people were too occupied to pay attention to what was happening in their midst.

Out of sheer frustration over being beaten at his own game by a mere girl, the bloodied bald man roared a spittle-flinging war cry—and charged. Bridget attempted to jump aside, but he was like a runaway cart of lumber. He smashed her into the planks and fell on top of her. The pommel of the makeshift iron knife, still embedded in his abdomen, poked her in the stomach. As if experienced at fighting warlocks, his meaty hands closed around her throat and squeezed. She batted uselessly at his giant head with her fists, feeling an immense pressure build within her skull that caused the veins on her forehead to bulge and her eyes threaten to pop out of their sockets.

Sebastian screamed a childish war cry of his own and jumped on the man's back, adding his puny fists to the battering, two mice taking on a tiger.

With black walls of unconsciousness rapidly closing in on her vision, Bridget had to think of something. She tried Telekinesis, but the bull of a man did not budge. Then she realized she could try Entangle, the 1st degree extension to Shine.

With her head about to explode, she pressed both hands to his face and wheezed, *"Shyn ... eo ... shyneo."* Had she still been an apprentice, the spell likely would not have triggered on account of the panic that came with choking—not to mention the suppressive collar. But she had *just* enough breath left in her lungs, which desperation pushed past the meaty fingers around her throat, to form the words that caused her hands to light up with weak vines. She focused on those vines and made them elongate. Like snakes they writhed onto the man's face, their tentacles probing around his eyes. But they were too ethereal, more light than density.

One of Sebastian's fists smacked the man in the cheek, making him let go of Bridget's neck with one hand to attempt to grab the boy and fling him off. Doing so allowed Bridget to inhale a sharp breath, pushing back the black walls of unconsciousness. She refocused on the Shine spell, throwing all her mental acuity into solidifying the vines.

The criminal managed to grab Sebastian by the scruff and send him tumbling away. His free hand then shot back to Bridget's throat. But by that moment the vines had turned from ethereal to opaque, and she made them rear up like miniature cobras on his face before plunging them into his eye sockets.

He jolted up with a scream, grabbing the vines and tearing them off his face, leaving behind bloody streaks that dribbled from his eyes. This gave Bridget access to the iron shank. Roaring in desperation and with her life flashing before her eyes, she withdrew it and stabbed him again and again and again, her roar lost amidst the panic of slaves still attempting to evade the whip. She kept this frantic onslaught up until he blindly tried to protect himself with fumbling arms, at which point she adjusted and viciously plunged the shank into his neck.

With blood running down his face and his chest, the man grabbed his throat, his tattoos stained with blood. It looked like he wanted to choke himself, but he was only trying to keep his life from ebbing away.

Someone gripped her under the arms and dragged her from underneath the criminal. Still in the throes of fighting for her life, Bridget kept screaming and throwing her fists and kicking at the air, but she did not feel in control of these actions. Instead, she watched as if from a distance, looking on at the hysterical wench covered in blood and sweat and filth.

She was barely cognizant of wingless gray beasts climbing down from the rafters like monkeys. Of being held by someone who struggled to lift her onto her wobbly feet. Of the wild and terrorized look in people's faces as they pressed together in a great throng. Steadily she returned to herself, or some fragment of who she was, and glanced about in a daze.

"I got you," a voice whispered in her ear. "I got you …"

"Ollie," she whispered, grabbing the hands and holding them close — only to look back and see an unfamiliar face, someone who would surely strangle her at any moment. She whirled about and shoved him away, and the man stumbled back and fell — but he was unusually small for a man.

Then she saw it was only the boy. What was his name? "Sebastian …" she mouthed, trying to understand. People trampled and tripped over something on the planks. She saw sausage legs and a bloody tattooed arm. Her eyes unfocused as she remembered a blur of thrusts.

The beasts closed in and the people screamed, but all the gargoyles did was grab them one by one and march them up to the stalls.

The boy shot to Bridget's side, blubbering, "Please don't push me away. Please don't push me away ..." He stood before her and placed her arms around his chest like a child desperate for protection.

With her heart still ramming her innards and her thoughts in disarray, she nonetheless limply allowed him to do this, her eyes flicking between the sight before her and the nearby bloody arm sticking out from underneath the crowd. An arm that did not move.

Meanwhile, the struggling human cattle were shoved into the stalls, where the gargoyles attached the rope to their slave collars. Pulses of blue energy began to emanate from the collars. Bridget followed those pulses with her eyes as they ran up the rope and vanished into the obelisk, which began to glow with the same blue light. She looked between the slaves and the obelisk, and saw that it was steadily brightening.

Then it hit her. A realization so profound it made her stagger, as if a fist had struck her brain, shaking the very foundations of everything she thought she knew about arcaneology.

Almost everyone there was an Ordinary, yet the gargoyles were harnessing arcane stamina from them. That meant even Ordinaries possessed *some* stamina! It was an idea that had long been theorized but never proven. An idea that implied Ordinaries should be able to learn the arcane arts ... at least in theory.

Bridget's mind sharpened as it worked quickly with deductions. If all Ordinaries possessed a low level of stamina, then all Ordinaries should, in theory, be able to tap into that stamina and even grow it. That meant the slow decline of the warlock could be reversed and the tide of history turned in the other direction and —

The boy, still clutching her arms over his chest, stole her attention. He was frantically shaking her arms and whimpering. Bridget followed his gaze to the tattooed arms, and saw that the bearded criminal known as Porter who had begun this whole mess had removed the iron shank from his cohort and was staring up at her with eyes devoid of soul. With black eyes of death.

For a moment they stared at each other before strong gray arms grabbed Bridget and forcefully separated her from Sebastian, who whimpered after her. She reached out to him and their hands briefly connected — only for one of the arms to lash out at the boy, smacking him aside so violently he whirled about and landed face-first onto the planks, where he writhed weakly.

"Don't you dare touch him!" Bridget shouted and vainly struggled against the grip, which felt like trying to bend iron. She watched the bearded criminal swoop in with his shank—until the winged gargoyle grabbed him by the neck, lowered that neck to waist height, and marched him forth. That same gargoyle also reached for the boy and raised him to walk in the same prostrated manner. Bridget thought they were to be excluded or taken to the arena or made an example of, but they were marched to nearby stalls along with the others.

Bridget was thrust head-first into a stall, a shoddy wooden affair that resembled a privy with a low back wall. Her captor roughly grabbed her by the hair, yanked her head up, grabbed a rope that was resting over the back wall, and attached the metal-encased end of the rope to her collar with a *click*. Where she expected to feel the cold soul-sucking feeling of a total stamina drain, she instead felt nothing—yet the pulses still emanated from her collar.

That could only mean one thing—the collars had been draining them throughout and storing that energy within. It explained her perpetually low reservoir of stamina, which seemed to run out prematurely during protracted usage of spells like Telekinesis.

Whereas other collars were sucked dry within moments, hers kept pulsing. The gargoyle, which had already reached for her rope and was standing by, growled impatiently at it. Yet her collar kept pulsing and pulsing and pulsing, until the gargoyle raised his snout to growl at the winged one. The fifteen-footer came over and leaned down to inspect her collar, gold neck chain clinking, then straightened to glance her up and down. Bridget stood with impertinently folded arms, feeling like livestock.

He reached out and almost gently made her unspool her arms, revealing the blood. Then he raised her chin to look down at her face from his great height, and those demonic yellow eyes wandered over her flesh as if judging horsemeat. He focused in on her cheek in particular, which she knew had been smeared with the bald criminal's blood in the melee. The gargoyle then leaned near, opened his snout, extended a long tongue that had her trying to squirm away, and licked her face.

A disgusted Bridget recoiled, but the winged one merely let her go with a flick of the wrist that was nevertheless violent enough to send her twirling against the stall wall. Still her collar pulsed and had now drawn multiple gargoyle eyes.

The winged fifteen-footer turned about, calmly extended a clawed hand, and beckoned at the body. It tumbled forth along the planks with awkward thuds, pulled by strong Telekinesis, then floated up to meet the fifteen-footer's snout. With the body floating in midair, the runed gargoyle's beastly tongue extended toward the neck wound, and he licked the blood.

He's comparing the taste, Bridget realized.

The winged gargoyle dropped the body with a *thud* back to the planks and looked to Bridget.

She stood gaping up at him, not knowing what to say or do. At last the collar's pulsing stopped, something the gargoyle noticed with a slight flick of his yellow eyes and a raising of his bulky brow.

Feeling vulnerable and condemned, Bridget looked to the man she had slain.

They had found her out as a strong warlock … and a killer.

DUST

LEERA

The air roared past Leera's ears as she dove toward a phalanx of archers standing amidst glittering torchlight. The night rain pelted against her dragon hide in a rapid *rat-tat-tat*, reminding her of the snares of war. All at once that torchlight shot forth in a wave of fiery arrows the rain could not snuff.

"Not one strike is permitted," she remembered Isobel Roseheart saying prior to the lesson. That was the rule—they were not allowed to sustain one strike from the enemy, whether it was a flung spell, an arrow, or a thrown rock.

With the wave of arrows taking up her entire field of view and her speed too great to dodge it even with a violent wing maneuver, Leera was forced to improvise. Choosing not to teleport as it was too dark and the terrain unknown to her, she shoved at the air, roaring, "*Baka!*" Her dragon-amplified Push spell blew through the middle of the rising wall of arrows, creating a hole. She then tucked in her wings and spun. The arrows *whooshed* by, not a single one hitting her hide.

With only fifty feet to go, she flipped the edge of her wings enough to halt her spin, then spread them a little whilst lowering her paws. Down she swept across the line, claws raking bronze-armored soldiers, throwing them skyward. Most satisfying of all was the feeling of a claw ripping through a ballista and the way the timber splintered and exploded. The soldiers did not scream as they ran to avoid her lethality. Like a school of fish, they broke as one unit, the archers failing to take so much as a potshot.

Ahead was a line of hundred-foot siege towers, half of which were already destroyed. Each had a ballista sitting atop it primed with a different elemental blast. The three within easy striking distance were loaded with bolts of vibrant green, crackling blue, and swirling black light—meaning bolts of earth, lightning, and necromancy.

To her left, and just behind, came the same crashing noise—Augum had swept in with his own raking attack.

"Tower, tower, tower, left, left, left!" she shouted over her shoulder, passing on her intentions, her powerful dragon voice easily bridging the distance to Augum.

But Augum was too busy blowing through the enemy lines, raking the soldiers and ballistae to bits.

Leera refocused on the towers, giving her mighty wings two powerful flaps to gain speed, aiming for the farthest one on the right. The three ballistae aimed at her and fired as one. She dipped, rose, and swerved. *Whoosh, whoosh, whoosh* went the elemental bolts as they zipped mere feet from her body.

Once she got to the tower, she turned on a wicked bank, tucked in her wings, dropped her head—and plowed through the structure, which exploded around her in a shower of timber. She gave one powerful flap of her wings before tucking them in again and slamming into the second tower. The explosive collision slowed her momentum too much, however, and even with a flap of the wings all she managed to do was bump the third tower. Nonetheless the structure groaned, teetered, and fell, splintering against the rocky ground like a house made from kindling.

Reorienting herself and launching off the rain-slick rock with her rear paws, she madly flapped her wings to rejoin Augum.

Suddenly a mound up ahead exploded, showering archers with mud and debris. A pair of skeletal forepaws burst from within that mound, followed by a skeletal dragon snout and unfolding wings.

Leera spread her wings to their maximum, angled skyward, flapped, and shouted down to Augum, "Necro, Aug! Necro! Phase three, phase three, phase three!"

Augum, who had just finished plowing through a line of towers, angled his snout upward to reply, only for a mound ahead of him to explode—and it wasn't the last one. Two other mounds belched forth undead dragons.

"Watch out!" she shouted.

He veered around the mound from which came a skeletal swipe. "Thanks!" he called from below, ascending on her tail. "Form up!"

She slowed her ascent. "I got left flank!"

"I got the right!" he replied. "They're regrouping! Rise above firing range!"

They joined up, wingtip to wingtip, their flapping synchronizing as they ascended together.

Leera looked down and saw that the soldiers had regrouped, and another blanket of fiery arrows was rising. "Incoming!"

"Higher, higher!" Augum called.

Leera's wing muscles burned as she struggled to climb. The arrows gained rapidly, then began to level off, a fiery wave that crested, broke, and fell back to the ground.

Leera checked for the undead dragons, spotting a cluster gaining rapid altitude. "Four at five hundred and closing fast," she reported.

"Got it. Check in. Five-sixths empty here."

Leera got in touch with her stamina pool, which was like checking in on one's arcane soul—a novice would find it a difficult and nebulous task, but for a 10th degree it was instinctual.

"Same," she replied. Gods, how were they supposed to defeat this scenario? *No wonder we failed our first try*, she thought. As had happened on their first attempt with this training hour months ago, they had expended too much arcane energy to get to this point—the necromantic dragons only appeared after a critical number of soldiers and ballistae and siege towers were destroyed.

"What do you want to do?" she asked. He was better at choosing maneuvers.

"Let's try hightail this time."

"You sure?"

He nodded.

She shrugged. "Hightail it is." *Daring and risky, but fun as heck*, she thought.

Leveling off, they slowed a touch, allowing the four pursuing undead dragons to catch up before speeding back up to match their velocity.

"My count," Augum said.

"Your count," Leera echoed.

"Three. Two. One—now!"

The pair gave a mighty flap, threw out their wings, and pitched steeply skyward, curving up and about. Leera could have reached out and snagged her tail like a cat. As expected, the undead dragons angled upward as well, each moving to smack their wrists. Augum and Leera beat them to it, however, simultaneously slapping their wrists together whilst roaring, "*Annihilo bato!*"

Leera shot two jets of water and Augum two prongs of lightning. Being so close, all four connected in some manner with two of the dragons—which was enough in this scenario for those undead dragons to burst into falling bones.

The remaining two finished slapping their wrists, roaring a garbled, *"Annihilo!"*

Augum and Leera tried to twirl aside, but they were too close—one blast of black light clipped Augum's wing, and the other smashed into Leera's belly. The strike instantly brought back a terrible memory of the same thing happening in the war against Canterra, when an ancient necromantic dragon named Tyranecron had cursed her. She remembered her innards feeling poisoned on a deep level, the delirium that came after, the soaked bed sheets, the nightmares, and the harrowing truth …

Since all the enemy needed was one strike against either of them, the rain ceased and the sodden and ruined field vanished, the sky clearing as if brushed away by a giant invisible broom. The air went silent, the space dark. In all of existence, only one light remained far below, reflected against the shiny floor.

"Damn it," Augum said as the pair descended in a slow circle toward the light.

Leera, too shaken by the memory of being cursed, said nothing, following on his tail.

The pair of dragons descended to a roaring beacon fire, before which stood the lone figure of Isobel Roseheart. They landed in front of her and sat back on their haunches, dwarfing the woman.

The founder of the Arcane order merely looked up at them. She cut a striking figure with her thick blond dreads piled high, and her sun-browned face marked by a horizontal streak of blue that crossed a pierced nose. A crimson skirt left her scarred knees visible, and her chest was cinched tight with leather and buckles.

"During the final onslaught, you chose to perform the Hightail maneuver. It was unsuccessful. You have failed to pass this hour. Explain yourselves."

"Their formation was too tight," Augum said, his deep dragon voice lost to the void.

"We, uh, we each shot a pair of prongs at them," Leera distractedly added, innards still shaken. "But they, uh, they were too close and got the jump on us with their own offensives."

Isobel rested a hand on the battered pommel of a bronze sword hanging from her hip in a plain scabbard. "That is not the reason you failed," she said, glancing between them.

Augum and Leera sighed in the same manner.

"You must be bolder and more strategic."

"Or you could simply *tell* us what we did wrong," Leera muttered.

"You must be bolder and more strategic," Isobel repeated like a mother admonishing her children.

Leera, feeling the urge to roar a profanity, flipped a dismissive paw at her. "Yeah, yeah," she said, and looked into the surrounding darkness, the memory of the war replaying through her mind on repeat. Again and again she saw herself getting struck, then lying feverishly dying in bed whilst receiving the news that she would never bear a child, that her future was no more.

"Do you wish to repeat this hour?"

Leera snorted. "Hell no."

"So be it. You may now return." Isobel gracefully indicated at the summoned portal they had entered through, and stood watching them, a light wind ruffling the wolfskin draped over her shoulders.

For a time, the two dragons sat there, each stewing in their own thoughts of failure. Augum's tail lightly whapped against the floor as he looked to the side, while Leera's tail curled about her forepaws like a cat as she vacillated between the memory of the war and how they had performed during this training hour.

As the lesson hours had progressed, Isobel became less and less helpful, much like real arcanists at the academy preparing their pupils for exams. The expectation was to apply the lessons without too much aid so that one earned the knowledge that came next.

"What hour of Meditation class did we finish on?" Leera asked.

Augum winced, exposing his long dragon teeth, as he struggled to recollect. "We last completed a non-combat challenge that had us trying to keep our heart rates down whilst sitting amidst a volcanic eruption, which was ... the thirty-ninth hour, I think? Yes, that's it, thirty-ninth."

"So we're on hour forty ..."

Augum absently nodded before giving a deep dragon sigh. "Might as well get it over with," he said. "Ready?"

She shrugged. "I guess."

"All right there, my love?"

She did not answer. The part of her that was human, that was in that moment rapidly dying and giving way to The Callousness of the Predator, wished they were in bed in Castle Arinthian, readying to cuddle. The rest of her wanted to rage at the injustice done to her and her future.

"*Xae carna null,*" Augum growled, shrinking back down to human form. He looked up at Leera with cold eyes. "Hurry up and revert already or I'm going without you."

She glanced down, conscious that his arcanery would not reignite for a while. Her dragon glare seemed to unnerve him, and he quickly dipped into the portal, leaving her alone with Isobel.

Leera looked to the ancient woman. "Why can't you be more helpful?"

As she had done many times prior when Leera said something like that, Isobel simply replied, "To progress, you must apply everything you have learned thus far. If you find yourself at an impasse, consider taking the other lessons before returning to this one. It is ill-advised to progress too far in one course without similar—"

"—progression in the others," Leera finished, chorusing along with Isobel's words. "Yeah, yeah."

Since being in dragon form perpetually siphoned stamina, she finally hit the stamina wall of an empty reservoir—there was no overdraw available in dragon form—and she reverted on the spot, shrinking down to her human form. She then placed dead eyes on Isobel, wondering what it would be like to duel her one-on-one.

"I bet you can fling some interesting ones, eh?" Leera said with a goading sneer. "Being one of the original famous wrist-slappers and all. Until people forgot you over the eons, that is …" She shrugged. "But I guess we'll all be forgotten in the end, won't we?"

Isobel said nothing, merely watching her as if she knew Leera was no more, that a predator had replaced her.

"Then again, you live on, don't you? Or part of you is still alive. What say you to that, so-called ancient one?"

Isobel stood silent, warrior face placid.

"You bore me," an annoyed Leera snapped. She stepped through the portal—and was met with the sight of a huffing Olaf wrestling with a groaning Augum. Sweat beaded Olaf's red face as he struggled to keep Augum from opening the door. The cabin rocked about as the wild ocean battered the ship. The now-dark window rattled and whistled from a fierce wind, and the lit iron lantern swung about on its chain.

Leera snorted. "Is he trying to weasel out?"

"He wants to go tell everybody off," Olaf said, keeping his back to the door.

"Move aside, fat ass," Augum hissed. "That's an order."

"You know I can't do that, Commander. Your initial order stands, which is that I am to summon Pelagia for you so that you can—"

"Cancel that order, you tub of lard."

"Nothing you say will change my mind. I am merely following your own orders."

Leera, seeing Augum struggling in the big man's grip, saw her opportunity. She opened up her hand, splayed her fingers wide—and slapped Augum's exposed cheek—*hard*. "You heard him! Ain't no goin' in to that there ship!" she drawled in a dockside accent, dancing away from his enraged swipes.

Olaf had to work extra hard to hold a frothing Augum away from Leera, not an easy thing to do in such a cramped space. "Commander, you need to let me summon Pelagia before the callousness runs out, or you will have failed your quest to learn how to control it."

Leera folded her arms and leaned forward, goading Augum by dipping her chin back and forth between his swipes. "Hear that, bonehead? We're on a quest and you're holding us up."

Augum was seething. "Come here, witch."

"I'm right here." She tapped her chin. "Come on. Hit me. Hit me, you dumb goat."

Augum tried, but each time Olaf, who was much stronger, held him back.

Leera enjoyed this very much. "Loser. Can't even fight his way free from that fatso."

"Darn it, how am I going to do this?" Olaf muttered to himself, glancing between the tablet on the bed, Augum, and Leera.

Leera, seeing he had blockaded the door, leaned back against the bedframe and rested one foot up against the cabinets that ran below the bed. "You can try using that oaf brain of yours," she replied. There was a sense of freedom that came with The Callousness of the Predator. She was not burdened by the base sufferings of her humanity—empathy and anxiety and shame and especially that most boring thing of all—prudence. Fear of the future, that sort of stuff. There was only the moment, and whatever pleasure could be derived from it.

Olaf looked at Leera.

She smirked. "What?"

He narrowed his eyes.

"Oh, look, his brain is kicking in. Are the noodles too congested with fat to function properly? What are you cooking up in that pea brain of yours?"

Just as she finished, Olaf threw Augum at her. Surprised, she barely had enough time to duck Augum's ham-fisted swing.

"*Paralizo carcusa cemente!*" Olaf shouted, and Augum froze, his other fist a mere hand's width from Leera's wincing face. Olaf then summoned his icy shield and pressed it against the tablet crest on the bed. "*Semperis vorto honos.*"

A ghostly Pelagia once more appeared. "Alianos," she said to Olaf.

"Hey," Olaf absently blurted, eyes on Leera as he stayed back from her. "You try anything and I'll hit you too." He nodded at the tablet. "You have to summon the lesson."

She considered punching Augum, but thought it'd look too weak on her part to punch a paralyzed person. "What about him?" she said instead, nodding at her so-called betrothed.

"I'll shove him in afterward."

"Why should I summon a stupid lesson?"

Olaf thought about it. "If you do, I'll shove him in such a way so you can laugh as he rolls inside."

Leera chortled at that. "Creative, but this fish ain't biting."

Olaf spun the betrothal ring on his finger as his eyes flitted back and forth in thought.

"Aww, look at the oaf trying hard to think of something. No wonder Bridget had to help you at the academy. Miracle she got you as far as she did. Guess you're hooped now that she isn't coming back, eh? No more coddling the silly dope. She's probably frolicking with another slave as we speak. A thinner one. Better looking by a league. How does *that* make you feel?"

Olaf's face went one shade redder, though she suspected from shame, not anger.

"Coward," she hissed. "You don't deserve Bridget and she's never coming home anyway!" How she wanted to anger him and rile him up and hurt him!

Olaf opened his mouth.

"Oh, here we go," Leera muttered, hoping he'd lose it. "This should be good."

"You should summon the portal to Meditation class. Otherwise you will only grow weaker as a dragon."

Leera deflated. She had to admit the goon was right. And she wanted to become stronger, to dominate the skies as the queen she was. "Fine, whatever. Pelagia, fortieth hour of Meditation Class One for myself and—" She kneed a paralyzed Augum in the stomach, toppling him toward Olaf. "—and this pathetic loser."

Olaf caught Augum's stiff body. "Easy there, Lee, easy."

"Shove that easy up your butt. You don't pull the reins back on a *Dragon*." Leera said her title with malice, enjoying the implication that she could destroy him — and this entire hunk of floating junk — with a few swipes of a claw. And she probably would have if she'd had access to her arcanery.

Olaf kept hold of Augum, refusing to meet her gaze.

"Like a lamb for the slaughter," Leera muttered, shaking her head in disgust at the sack of weakness before her.

"Fortieth hour of Meditation Class One for Dragon Jones and Dragon Stone," Pelagia said, and again drew a portal that clipped through the bedframe.

"Make sure you fling him in hard," Leera told Olaf and squeezed into the black oval.

She stepped out, surprised to find herself staring at a hellscape, for fire and distant explosions and the telltale flashes of multiple arcane attacks filled the black horizon. The air stank of flames and iron and mud. Surrounding her was a vast army of tents, and milling about those tents, mostly around cook fires, loitered men and women draped in ancient steel armor that looked vaguely familiar. Some drank out of horns, others out of waterskins. Some ate, and others played card or dice games. None paid any attention to her whatsoever.

Now and then, some of the brighter attacks lit up a great structure in the shape of an upside-down horseshoe that stood two leagues away, where the action was happening.

"Devil's Gate," Leera whispered, having seen depictions of the great structure at the academy and in books.

Someone slammed into her back and fell into the mud. Annoyed to have missed seeing him fumble out of the portal, she turned to scowl down at Augum, who dragged himself up.

Augum scowled right back at her and opened his mouth to say something stupid, no doubt, only to catch a glimpse of the army — and then the same horizon.

"Devil's Gate," he blurted.

Leera snorted. "Aren't you a quick study."

"Long after my time, prior to the Age of Reason, the Dark Age took its last breaths," the familiar voice of Isobel Roseheart said from behind them. They turned to see her standing in her usual battle regalia, her chin straight. It was not uncommon for her to take them back to a historical occurrence, even one that had occurred long after her death, for the more powerful and wise Arcaners who came after her had added to the course's teachings, with her as the teacher dispensing those lessons.

"The battle before you was one of the greatest the continent of Sithesia has ever seen. I speak of the conclusion to the War of the Scions."

Despite themselves, Augum and Leera glanced at each other. None of the prior lessons had approached this particular time in history. What was more, how was it that Arcaners kept adding to the dragon part of the lessons long after Arcaners stopped training as dragons? Had Arcaners actually traveled to Endraga Ra after Arinthian's time to update the tablet, or was there more complex arcanery involved with the order they had yet to discover? However it was done, it surely involved incredibly powerful arcanery.

Isobel looked past them, and they followed her gaze to the spot where occasional flashes lit up Devil's Gate. "Under that arch, the great necromancer Occulus awaits those bold enough to face him. Seven scion holders march toward him, unaware that six of their number will perish in the battle. But it is the army that will bear the brunt of the suffering."

Leera glanced about to see that all the soldiers kept stealing nervous glances at the arch.

"Their lives hang on the decisions their leaders make," Isobel continued, drawing their attention once more. "This scenario ordinarily demands that each of you lead them against overwhelming undead forces. You would thence use the art of meditation to come to terms with what you had witnessed. But since you suffer The Callousness of the Predator, you have triggered an alternate lesson."

Once again unable to help herself, Leera glanced over at Augum, who met her gaze with the same look of shock. Despite suffering the callousness, they recognized the implication that each Meditation class had an alternate lesson, one that only triggered if entered in a callous state. It was a novel discovery that would change their entire outlook on the lessons. In fact, she couldn't believe they had never thought about entering a lesson under its influence before.

She looked to Isobel and grinned. At long last, they could become truly powerful …

Isobel glanced between their faces. "For the duration of this lesson, The Callousness of the Predator shall not abate."

"Whoa, really?" Leera blurted, thumbs hooked into the pockets of her robe. "Awesome."

Isobel ignored her. "The question before you is a simple one. Are you the horse … or are you the rider?"

As Leera scoffed at the strange question, Isobel looked beyond, and Leera heard the stomp of boots behind them. Turning about, she saw two soldiers hurrying forth. Both wore armor emblazoned with a lion and sported identical red beards—in fact they looked like twins.

"Arinthian's forces," Augum said from beside her. "These are his troops."

"Dragon!" the male soldiers said upon arriving, one facing Leera and the other Augum, creating a chorus effect as they spoke. "Begging your pardon, Dragon, but you must follow me. Something terrible has happened."

Leera, feeling whimsically spiteful and simultaneously curious about how they would react, leaned forward and, with her thumbs still hooked into her pockets, spat a gob to the ground. "I ain't goin' nowhere," she said in a country twang.

The soldiers vanished, and the scene before them reset. The same flashes began in the distance, and the same soldiers who had paced to their tents or cook fires did so once again.

"What happened?" Augum asked Isobel.

"You have failed the lesson. You may try again or step back through the portal."

He looked to Leera. "Idiot, you made us fail."

She rolled her eyes at him. "Whatever."

Augum made an impatient *Move it along* motion with his hand. "Again, then."

"The trial has already reset, Dragon Stone."

Once more the two soldiers ran up to them, chorusing, "Dragon! Begging your pardon, Dragon, but you must follow me. Something terrible has happened."

Leera folded then unfolded her arms and sighed, wanting to show how bored she was—despite feeling otherwise. Rather, she was intrigued. She flipped a hand at the soldier before her. "Go on, then."

"Follow me, Dragon." The men led her and Augum away, but in separate directions—and to separate tents. The soldier leading Leera threw open the tent flap and stepped aside, allowing her entry.

The tent was cold and smelled sweetly of lavender and tallow, the latter coming from a lone candle that threw long shadows on the tent wall. But none of that mattered, for what Leera saw before her made no sense whatsoever.

"She asked to see you for her last words," the soldier whispered behind Leera. "I shall leave you with her, Dragon," and he left, letting the tent flap close with a soft rustle.

Leera stood staring at herself, except it wasn't her, but some soldier dressed in Arinthian armor who looked exactly like her, down to a smudge of dirt on her cheek, which Leera confirmed matched her own by wiping her cheek and looking at her fingertip.

"Unnameables heard my prayer," the fake Leera wheezed, raising a shaking hand.

The real Leera scoffed. "You want me to comfort you, an imposter?"

The tent vanished, and she found herself standing alongside Isobel and Augum. As before, soldiers moved to and fro, the distant horizon flashing in the same manner.

Augum shoved Leera so hard she fell back on her butt. "How'd you screw it up?" he barked.

Leera jumped back to her feet, wiped her bottom with her hands, and snarled, readying to pounce on Augum, only to be interrupted.

"You are not ready for this lesson on The Callousness of the Predator," Isobel said. "I suggest starting from an earlier lesson and progressing to this one."

"But you allowed this lesson to take place," Leera replied. "So it must be possible for us to pass its trial. Is that not so?"

Augum snapped his fingers at Isobel the way a foul lord would at his servant. "Besides, we don't have time to start from the beginning, woman, so repeat it for us already and get us to those doppelgangers." He wagged a finger at Leera. "Try not to mess it up this time. Unlike you, I *want* to become a more powerful dragon."

As the pair of soldiers once again ran up to them, she flashed him a wicked and sarcastic smile. The whole time, Isobel said nothing.

"Yeah, yeah, just take us there," Augum said during their spiel, and both of them once again went to their separate tents.

"Fine, I'll listen," Leera said to the fake Leera upon the latter raising a trembling hand and beckoning the real Leera to kneel beside her. Leera reluctantly did so, but did not accept her hand, which remained outstretched. "Learn from me," the girl whispered, placing that hand on Leera's knee. "For I am breathing my last …"

Leera squirmed away from it, snapping, "What have you to say already?" *You don't even talk like me,* Leera thought, wanting to voice the remark aloud.

"You are fragile. You must choose who you are at all times. I thus ask thee a sacred question … are you the rider … or the horse?"

"The rider," Leera snapped. "Who the hell else? I'm obviously the one in charge." Leera proudly slapped her own chest. "Me."

"The question shall linger until it is answered."

"So I haven't answered the question?"

Her likeness coughed weakly.

Leera glanced her doppelganger over but saw no obvious sign of injury. "Where are you wounded?" she asked, curious what sort of wound would have brought her down. She also couldn't help but wonder if it was a portent of things to come.

The other Leera weakly patted her own armored heart. "In here."

The real Leera cocked her head. "Tell me what I'm supposed to say to pass this stupid trial and I will say it and—"

The tent vanished, replaced by the camp, and she was back alongside Augum and Isobel. Seeing the slack look of surprise on his face, as if he'd been speaking, she got the jump on him and shoved him onto his butt. "*You* screwed that one up this time!" she hissed, knowing it could easily have been her again. "What'd you say, you dumb clod?"

A snarling Augum got back to his feet, but now it was he who Isobel interrupted.

"You are not ready for this lesson on The Callousness of the Predator," Isobel repeated in the same tone as before. "I suggest starting from an earlier lesson and progressing to this one."

"We heard you the first time, you nag," Leera snapped.

Augum ran his hands through his hair as he looked to the distant flashes that lit up the silhouette of Devil's Gate. Even as the pair of soldiers ran up to them, he narrowed his eyes and spat, "*Impetus peragro!*"

Nothing happened of course, except for the scene to reset.

Leera shook her head, muttering, "Moron."

Augum pressed a hand over his eyes and rubbed his temples with his index finger and thumb. "We can either give up or give this a genuine go. But I do want to beat it so what would …" He rolled his hand along. "… the proper thing or whatever to do be?"

Leera hated that he was right. She hated him and Isobel and everything about this—except for the fact that that stupid oaf of a friend Olaf had been right. Passing this type of lesson would make them stronger as dragons.

Even as she heard the bootsteps approach, she looked to Isobel. "What's that thing you said about the rider and the horse again?"

Isobel merely watched her.

"Are you the rider or the horse?" Augum replied on her behalf.

"*Obviously* I'm the rider," Leera snapped. But a seed of doubt took root, and after the soldier led her back to the tent, she found herself once more sitting beside her soldierly visage, where she went through the same back-and-forth until the other Leera weakly patted her armored heart. "In here."

"I'm the rider," Leera answered, trying to instill maximum confidence into her tone.

"Why?" the weakening Leera replied.

"Wha—what do you mean, why? That's what I said last time, so why did your answer change?"

Her armored doppelganger merely stared at her.

Leera scoffed. "Fine, um, I'm the rider because … well … because …" But a concrete answer failed to materialize.

The other Leera's eyes drooped as her breathing slowed. Were it anybody else, Leera would have told her to die already. But because it was her own self, even a fake version, she couldn't do it. Some deep sense of self-preservation overrode the callousness.

That got her thinking, which in turn resulted in her moving from a kneeling position to sitting cross-legged. Doppelganger Leera responded by opening a trembling hand at the real Leera, who scowled at it. What she wanted to say was, "Gods, that's gross." What she did instead was accept the stupid hand, if only to move the darn trial along. The hand was cold as death, but the shivering stopped upon her touch.

The lone tallow candle in the tent wavered. Since The Callousness of the Predator failed to abate, time strangely felt like it froze in place. For once, she could settle *into* the callousness instead of subconsciously fearing it would end, thus ending who she truly was.

Leera propped up her chin on her palm whilst she fiddled with her doppelganger's hand. "Am I the rider or the horse?" she whispered. "Am I the rider or the horse …" She whispered this to herself many times, which got her thinking about the art of meditation and its purpose.

To become the moment, she thought. *To self-reflect.* But all that was obvious, and it led her down the same old paths that eventually bored her, so she turned to musings. During one of these musings, she imagined herself riding a dragon that was also her, meaning she was riding herself. Invariably her focus shifted as if she were the dragon beneath the girl. That confused her, and suddenly she had a hard time picturing which one she was, and instead found herself staring down at both of them from above, as if she were a raven trailing two warriors about to fly into battle.

That very idea shifted her perspective, and she sat up, uncomfortable on a deep level. So uncomfortable, in fact, that she threw the fake Leera's hand back at herself. It flopped off her face, and only then did Leera notice that her doppelganger's skin was white as a sheet, her lips parted, eyes sightless, meaning she had died sometime during her musings.

Leera sat staring at her dead self, mouth hanging open in the same manner as the body, unnerved by the sight. She knew she ought not to care, but part of her *did* care. Or perhaps it was fear? Morbid fascination? Who knew ...

Yet the trial did not reset, meaning that idiot Augum must have reached this point as well. They were both sitting there staring at their doppelgangers, trying to fathom what it meant.

"Am I the rider or the horse?" she whispered, hearing both Isobel and the dead Leera asking the very same question. Again and again all three of them asked that question within her mind, with the real Leera repeating it in a whisper and a loud voice and even a yell. Still, the trial continued.

The hourglass of time rapidly trickled by, unnaturally so. The dead Leera's face began to go purple, then sink inward as it deteriorated. A gust of wind blew outside, rustling the tent wall, which began to wear away and tear, blowing the candle out. The blush of dawn had come by then, lighting the interior in a cool glow.

Before Leera knew it, she was staring at a pile of ashes within a husk of armor. The tent collapsed into scraps around her, and the sky brightened as the sun rose—but it rose far too quickly, already past the noon point. She stood and watched it crawl across the sky like a ball rolling across the plains, the clouds zipping like arrows. All around, soldiers zoomed about in a blur, eventually abandoning the camp.

She looked across the way and saw Augum rise from within his collapsed tent. Beyond him, a full moon replaced the sunset. That moon sped up, and the sky began to revolve between night and day, so rapidly that Leera fell to her knees, in awe at the sight.

Onward the days revolved, with everything decaying around them, leaving a muted blur of sky, an uneven landscape of dirt and snow and rock, with rusted remains scattered between, which eventually deteriorated into dust.

"Am I the rider or the horse?" Leera whispered, remembering herself riding the dragon.

But she *was* the dragon too, so ...

Someone approached. She looked up to see Augum.

"You're still young," she remarked, her voice an echo amidst the great blur of time.

"I'm still young," he said, the sky zipping overhead.

She stood. "We are beyond." It felt like the right thing to say, the smart thing. She looked skyward, finding the blurry revolutions of the sky interesting. "I saw myself riding a dragon. But I ..."

"You *are* the dragon," he finished for her.

She nodded along. "But I am the dragon."

"Am I the rider or the horse?" he asked, a phrase she echoed in a whisper.

Silence fell between them, and the blur continued. Yet it also began to fade, as if eternal darkness were on its way. Amidst that vast passage of time, Leera looked down at her hands. What good was the power to turn into a dragon if it would all end in dust? What good was rage without resolution? What good was hate without love? What good was birth if it only led to death? What good was any of it?

The sky dulled to dusk and continued fading, threatening to snuff all light. In that moment, Leera wanted herself back. To be normal again. To feel something, *anything*. The Callousness of the Predator grew boring. It had no purpose, no goal, no direction.

For the first time, she saw herself as neither the dragon nor the rider, but observing them both. Which meant only one thing …

In that last glimmer of dull light, Leera returned to Isobel at the same time as Augum. She then raised her chin and declared, "I am the watcher."

To her great astonishment, she heard her betrothed say the same thing beside her.

LEADER BY CHOICE

AUGUM

Having sent Olaf on his way with a hearty thanks and an apology for his behavior, Augum sat on his bunk holding his betrothed in his lap, his back pressed against the plank wall. The lantern swung overhead, but he had snuffed it as oscillating light, combined with the rolling of the ship in high seas, had been making him queasy.

Lightning flashes from the distant horizon occasionally lit the dark cabin through the stained-glass window. The howling of the wind, the creaking beams, and the roar of ocean waves rhythmically crashing against the hull felt rather soothing—when juxtaposed against the intense ordeal he had experienced within Isobel's alternate lesson.

He still felt the relief from hearing Isobel say they had passed the trial, but the idea that each single hour of the one hundred hours had an alternate lesson for The Callousness of the Predator overwhelmed him—and that was only for Meditation Class One! There were two other tiers, each consisting of a hundred hours, and he could deduce there was still a fourth tier, Meditation Class Four, which likely began at the 15th degree.

He wondered if the other classes—Flight Class and Dueling Class and Warfare Class and Strategy Class—had alternate lessons too. Then he realized this was unlikely the case as combining The Callousness of the Predator and Flight or Dueling class made no sense.

"I thought Isobel had been exaggerating when she told us it would take a lifetime to master the art of meditation," Augum mumbled, eyes distant. "I'd completely underestimated the sheer number of hours just to ..." He opened his hands in Leera's lap and clawed at the air in frustration. "Just to ... ugh! I mean, come on, four hundred hours of *that*? Are you jesting me?"

Leera grabbed his hands and returned them to her lap, where she caressed his callused palms. She leaned back to rest her head on his shoulder so that they were cheek to cheek, her hair tickling his neck.

"No wonder the callousness has been getting a larger toehold on our consciousness," she remarked. "We're way, *way* behind."

His chin bobbed as he nodded along. "I'm exhausted from that one lesson—and it was only one blasted hour."

"That's because the callousness drains our—" She twirled a floppy hand around her temple. "—spirit or whatever. Like running uphill for the mind. It's exhausting being that mean and vindictive."

He kissed her cheek. "It is. But you know which part I love?"

She looked up at him, and the window lit up several times with distant lightning, revealing a sly grin on her lips. She raised a sharp eyebrow. "Which part is that?"

"This part—" and he kissed those soft lips. She kissed him back, and soon they were tearing at each other's robes as they lost themselves to passion.

Sometime later, sweaty but profoundly satisfied, they lay in his bunk, Augum with his head on a folded arm as a pillow. Leera lay on her side, resting her head on his chest, a hand drawing circles on his bare shoulder.

"Want to help me with the book after supper?" she whispered.

He squeezed her midriff. "I've got lessons with Carter." That Zygothika book was a bit beyond him anyway—complex arcaneology was more Bridget's thing than his.

A knock came at the cabin door.

Leera placed a gentle hand over Augum's mouth. "Don't answer it," she whispered. "Let's lie here a while listening to the waves and the wind."

As the ship creaked around them, he gently took that hand away and, instead of replying, kissed her forehead. "Yes?" he called out, soliciting a groan from Leera.

A throat cleared. "Commander, I believe we're supposed to have our lessons together?" came the teenage voice of Carter Southguard. Another voice spoke up, whispering obnoxiously loud, "I bet she's in there with him and they're *you-know-what*."

Augum recognized it as belonging to one of the Bloomington-Southguard brothers, a pair of insufferable highborn cousins to Carter and assigned to keep watch over him. As part of the deal Augum had made with the king to let him and Leera go on this expedition, he would train them alongside Carter.

"Or he's cheating on her with that Haught woman," said yet a third voice belonging to the other brother, and they both snickered. The two of them were far older than Carter—well in their thirties— yet goaded him on as if they were teenage hoodlums.

Leera shot up in bed, roaring, "Shut your damn pie holes!"

"Told you she was in there," one of the brothers muttered.

"Quiet, you're going to get me in trouble," Carter hissed.

Leera started to pull on her clothes, muttering, "I'm going to slap them upside the—"

Augum placed a hand on her shoulder. "Let me handle this."

She thrust a stern finger before his face. "No appeasement."

"I know."

"You're their commander. *Don't* let them get away with disrespecting me and us."

He patted her shoulder, nodding. He was sick of their dumb jests and snarky comments and constant undermining of his authority, all because they were highborn snotbags who resented someone half their age teaching and ordering them about. Sure, he was more advanced than them in the arcane arts, but that only made them resent him more.

He got dressed alongside Leera, but when he playfully pinched her butt—as was their habit—she slapped his hand away and smacked her lips at him. He knew he had to deal with the problem of the men before returning to her good graces, and so he kissed the top of her head, which she allowed, and once she had stepped behind where the door would swing, for she always took longer to dress than he did, he opened that door.

"Oh, hey, Commander," Carter said, flashing a nervous smile while he brushed aside his wavy blond hair.

Augum looked between the smirking Bloomington-Southguards, both trying to steal peeks into his cabin, prompting him to step into the cramped corridor and close the door behind himself. They were clean-shaven and their faces were powdered to milkiness, as were their curly white wigs. Digby, the thirty-four-year-old 7th degree fire warlock, was as tall and beefy as Carter, but with a wolfishly mean face.

His thirty-seven-year-old brother Teague was an 8th degree lightning warlock. He was shorter and thinner than his brother, with a sniveling muskrat face and a huge brown mole on his nose.

All four men pressed a hand against a cabin wall to steady themselves against the high swaying of the ship.

Teague raised his imperial chin. "Pray, what will our illustrious hero commander train us on this fair eve?" He interlocked his fingers, reversed the hands, stretched them out, and cracked his knuckles. "Myself, I would not mind working on my offensives."

Digby flashed a crooked-toothed smile—for all their wealth, neither brother had taken very good care of their teeth. "As for me, I would not mind some work on my counter thrusts." He closed his fists before him and humped the air, grinning lasciviously as his brother laughed and Carter hid his mouth behind a hand.

Augum raised a hand and pronged two fingers between the brothers. "For disrespecting my betrothed, I'm putting you two on *proata mentora* duty." As the brothers scoffed, Augum jerked a thumb down the hall. "The privies need scrubbing. Hop to it."

Digby gave Augum the classic noble once-over. "The nerve."

"The absolute nerve," said the older brother.

"It is a breach of the covenant—"

"A betrayal of the bargain—"

"He insults our honor—"

"He certainly does—"

"A kid half our age—"

"—trying to boss his elders around."

The pair of snobs snorted in unison.

Augum folded his arms across his chest. "No part of the bargain said you could insult the honor of my betrothed without repercussions. Your lord king placed me in charge of this one—" He nodded at a red-faced Carter, who was too ashamed to look him in the eye. "Him I will train. If you want to make amends, you will scrub the privies to my satisfaction. Only after I deem your work up to my standards will I consider continuing your training." *That should keep them away from me*, he thought as the pair of brothers scoffed.

Augum looked to Carter. "A quick sup then you and I train."

As the brothers continued to play dumb, something they were all too good at despite their age, Augum looked past them at an approaching Jengo. "What's the word, Almoner Okeke?" he asked.

The gangly Jengo, holding onto the walls lest he lose his balance in the swaying ship, stopped behind Carter, who stepped aside for the tall Sierran. "Most of us finished supper. Captain said no sight of the Spice Islands yet on account of the storm. Maybe tomorrow. A few of the crew have once again begged me for my services. We've got two cases of dysentery and one mild case of scurvy, which really only needs fresh orange or lemon juice, something we should stock up extra on after landing. Anyway, with your blessing, I'd like to continue, Commander."

"You have it." Augum was grateful for the request as Jengo often used up his arcane stamina for *proata mentora*, even though he needed to keep a reserve in case of a sudden entanglement.

Jengo nodded his thanks and flicked a finger at the floor. "Ollie's in the hold barrel-freezing fish the seaman hauled in over the stern this morning, and Jez is scarfing down supper and wine while heckling that Black Eagle woman about the usual."

"Great," Augum muttered. "Anything else?"

"The hull's been repaired by the crew working with warlocks. Captain says she's slipping through the waves at top speed again and that you are to be commended."

"Mmm."

"Need anything from me, Commander?"

"You get your cycles in?"

"I did, but I was hoping you could help me with the nuance of some of the defensive spells, although something tells me you're going to be busy."

Carter whapped Jengo on the shoulder. "I already snagged him, Almoner."

"Almoner *Okeke*," Augum corrected, "or Dragoon Okeke."

"Right, sorry, Commander. Almoner Okeke."

The reedy Teague stuck two fingers into his pasty mouth and opened it wide for Jengo. "Hey, tall boy, can you eliminate this gap between my teeth? Make me a better fancy for the ladies?"

"Not if you paid me," Jengo muttered, nodding at Augum. "Commander," and he squeezed past them.

"How rude," Digby said.

"So very rude," Teague added, the pair nodding like powdered parrots.

A right pair of morons, Augum couldn't help but think, and considered it a miracle they had gotten as far as they had at the academy. *It's called the miracle of private tutoring,* he thought amusedly. Noble parents had offered him staggering sums to train their bumbling teenagers, but he had never once accepted, considering it beneath the station of the commander of the Arcaner order to perform such services. Though he did not prohibit other Arcaners from raising money for themselves in such a way, as it was outside the purview of duty. Besides, the order demanded a ten percent tithe from everyone, which meant they needed to work the odd job now and then. More if they wanted a home or fancy clothes.

The door behind him burst open. "Gods how you all yap on," Leera said and swished by, muttering something about how she had been waiting far too long to go to the privy. "Bunch of yakking goats ..." she added, a comment that earned raised eyebrows from all but Augum.

"Come eat with us after," Augum called after her, but she only flapped a hand over her shoulder, which could mean anything from her. Upon noticing how all three Southguards followed her walk with their eyes, he waited until she had turned the corner of the narrow hall before opening a hand and swinging it in such a fashion that he slapped all three of their cheeks in one go.

When the brothers reared up in affronted insult, he flared his eyes with lightning, brightening them so much they all had to look away. "You ever disrespect my betrothed again ..." He left the threat unsaid and strode off toward the galley, snuffing his eyes as he went. It was perhaps not the most commander-like thing to do, but he was sick and tired of their games, especially the way they openly ogled all the young women—even Jez, though only behind her back, for she was a 17th degree who took no guff from anyone.

And it was to Jez that Augum went, straddling the bench opposite while Carter and a grumbling Digby and Teague took up a table on the far side of the low-ceilinged room.

There were a mere six tables in the galley, which was reserved for officers and passengers, with the crew taking their meals in the general cabin belowdecks. Each table was surrounded by benches attached to the floor, forcing cramped knees. Each table had a dimly lit lantern fixed to the top of an iron bar, mimicking a torch. Sailing souvenirs decorated the walls—small anchors, paintings, old tackle, a ship's steering wheel, and various trophy weapons. One wall had a classic supper-hall style service area manned by crew cooks who cheekily loved to pepper everyone with attitude, even the captain.

"Oi! Lizard boy!" called a stubby and sweat-faced man with a soiled rag tied over his hair. "Chicken, duck, or fish? And sorry but we ain't got lamb. Dragons like lamb, don't they?" he chuckled.

"Fish," Augum replied with a grateful nod, for his stomach felt like a hollow barrel.

"Potatoes, carrots, or leeks?"

"All three."

"Can't 'ave all three, *yer majesty*," the cook said. "But I'll slop you somefin' special." He winked at Augum and got to work clattering dishes.

"… and just so you know, you won't ever win either of them over because you're a spy and you *will* always be a spy for that lot," a weaving Jez finished saying, nodding her head sideways at the newly seated Southguards. She ignored Augum as she raised a pewter goblet toward Black Eagle Mahmoute, who sat alone at a table, minding her own business as she methodically cut up what remained of her chicken and potatoes and took a small bite.

"To spies!" Jez toasted. "What would the kingdom do without them?" She took a long gulp, only to animate upon pretending to see Augum. "Oh, my," she said, delicately placing a hand against her chest. "Thou hast lent a fright to this dainty lass."

Augum propped his chin on the base of a palm and idly nibbled on the pinky nail of that hand. "Making friends, are we?"

"Always and forever. I'm nothing but sunshine and flowers."

Augum tactfully cleared his throat and tapped the corner of his mouth with his pinky whilst looking away.

Jez grimaced, brought her arm up to her face, and dragged her sleeve across her lips, wiping away the wine stain. "Where's that saucy twerp of yours, anyway?"

Augum gestured over his shoulder and indicated vaguely at the hall.

"Well, she certainly earned my attention with her spell work." Jez clumsily shoved Augum's shoulder with her free hand whilst taking a sip of her wine. "Both of you have," she said into her goblet.

Augum, hurt as usual upon seeing her in such a state, barely managed a nod.

"So how about it? Shall we get you slaving on Greater Repair and Arcane Drain? Or would you prefer trying your hand at Enchant Weapon? Or do you want to learn something off-the-books? Maybe even press ahead on a more advanced spell? That's what you wanted, isn't it? Something like that? I don't have all night, kiddo, so stop chewing on that finger like a baby and speak up."

Mahmoute must have offered to take over training again, Augum thought. He glanced over at the venerable old woman, only to receive a smack on the hand.

"Never you mind the spies in our midst," Jez hissed. She raised her index finger. " 'The sheep' —" She paused to thump a fist against her chest, muttering, "Excuse me … damn indigestion …" The index finger rose again as her glassy eyes expanded. " 'The sheep shall not stray beyond the pen, for in the forest the wolf awaits.' "

"Uh-huh."

"Don't *uh-huh* me! Don't you *uh-huh* me, mister! What, is the commander too high and mighty to listen to his mentor? Has the mentee outgrown his britches? Is the dragon ..." Jez jiggled a hand at him dismissively. "... something, something?"

Augum, unable to muster the energy to argue with a drunken Jez, nor wanting to out of sheer loyalty for the woman, sighed. "I'd love to train with you," he began carefully, knowing that training with her in this state could easily result in injury, "but I promised to train my apprentice after supper."

"Oh, I see. I see. The drawbridge is down and the pasty-faced weasels have infiltrated the keep. My apprentice has an apprentice, who is an heir, who probably has an apprentice of his own secreted somewhere under his bunk bed." She leaned forth to wheeze gaspingly into his face, dramatizing her words like a minstrel, "It's apprentices all the way down ... to the very bottom of the sea."

Augum recoiled at the noxious wine breath that still reminded him of the drunk who had enslaved him as a farm boy, a man who had painted scars on his back with a whip. He wanted to tell Jez that it was a mistake to have brought her, to have believed she could control her impulses with the goblet. She was placing herself—and everyone around her—in danger, for if something should happen, how could they rely on her in such a state? She was liable to teleport herself into the hull or, worse, far off ship, where she would drunkenly lose sight of the vessel and eventually drown or get eaten by something with countless rows of teeth.

"He's judging. Oh, he's a judging, all right." Jez drew circles with her index finger at him, circles that progressively came closer until she pressed his nose. "Look at him juuuudge," she sang. "Enjoying this, kiddo? I bet you are. Just saaaaaalivating over his drunken fool of a mentor whining—oh, that's a pun!" She raised her goblet and indicated it with a flat hand. "I done just punned me a pun!"

Augum, conscious of everyone staring at him out of the corner of their eye, was about to snap, when a dish clapped to the table before him, followed by a napkin, a polished fork, and a knife.

"Buttered redfin with a squeeze of lime, gravied potatoes, and peppered hot bread slathered with spiced blue cheese." The cook bowed. "I, my good dragon, sir, am an *artist*," he said in his best highborn accent. He straightened. "I shall take my accolades now, if you please."

The ridiculousness of the display juxtaposed with Jez's antics made Augum crack a smile. He clapped the man on the arm. "Thank you, sir. This looks absolutely divine."

"Oh, and I done almost forgot—" The cook danced to the counter and brought back a horn. "On orders of your miracle-making healer, a dose of freshly squeezed orange juice. Your own ice warlock, the chubby one, kept them frozen fresh for us."

"Olaf," Augum said, smilingly accepting it. "I do not deserve such a feast."

"Ah, but you do. My father fought in the ranks against the Canterrans. Said if it hadn't been for you slicing through the enemy like a hot iron, he wouldn't be around. So this one's from my Pa. And wait until he hears about who I got to serve!" The cook did a little dance as he traipsed back to the galley kitchen.

"As if he needs more smoke blown up his butt," one of the brothers muttered under his breath, a remark Augum chose to ignore ... for now.

Jez, however, positioned herself to opine, only for her attention to get snagged by someone behind him.

Augum, looking forward to grabbing his girl, reached back. She accepted that hand.

"How gracious of you, good sir," said a voice that made Augum jump, for it was not the voice of Leera, but of Alanna. She primly sat down beside him, smoothing her robe beneath her.

"Er, I thought you were—"

She rested a gentle hand on his shoulder and patted it, whispering, "I know." She placed those hands neatly in her lap. "I was rather hoping we could perform some cycles together after supper, Commander. A girl like me could learn a lot from a boy like you." Her immaculately sculpted eyelashes fluttered.

Augum was all too quick to point at Carter. "I'll actually be training my apprentice—"

"Perhaps later, then?"

"Er ..."

"Later he'll be busy too," Jez slurred, goblet waving about before her. "You mark my words, he'll find some excuse to stay busy. He always finds some excuse. Order this, duty that, pageant here, *proata mentora* there. And that's whenever you can unspool him from his better half. Busy, busy bee, this one here is. Too busy for his mentor, even—and look at that, still rolling his eyes like a fourteen-year-old." Jez leaned forward. "You are a twenty-year-old commander and a dragon. A *dragon*, kiddo. Maybe you should act like one? Hmm?"

"Maybe you ought to stop infantilizing him, Miss Terse," Alanna threw in so abruptly that she pressed a hand to her chest and cleared her throat. "If I may be so bold as to say."

Jez recoiled. "You may certainly *not* be so bold! You may *not*! You smarmy, trumped-up little court ghoul you, how *dare* you insinuate—"

"I was hardly insinuating—"

One of the brothers began to sing, "Oh, the hens are a—" He opened both hands at his brother, and together they chorused, "—cluckin'!"

"What'd I miss?" sang another voice Augum was all too glad to hear. He reached back with both arms, singing, "Save me, my fair princess, for a storm hath come!"

Leera swooped in, practically crawling over Augum in a ridiculous display no doubt intended for Alanna, who pointedly looked away. "Hey," she said, face appearing upside down before him. She pecked him on the lips before sliding onto the bench on his other side, making a show of draping an arm over his shoulder.

Augum, hoping they'd all behave and let him eat, picked up the knife and the triple-pronged fork and began slicing his fish. He didn't get far, for everybody stiffened as a shadow descended upon the room.

"Talking furball incoming," Teague whispered, playfully punching Carter and his brother in the arm.

Rogor, the perpetually angry and seasick wolven, strode by, head low to avoid scraping the ceiling. He stepped up to the galley, reached over the counter, grabbed a whole plucked chicken, and yanked it forth. He turned about to look at them all. No one met his gaze.

Except for Augum. "Care to join us?" he asked, and immediately felt an annoyed pinch from Leera's hand on his shoulder.

Rogor's reply was to walk over and flop the chicken down onto the table, making Augum's dish bounce. Rogor then grabbed Augum's knife, but just as the table erupted with protest, Rogor howled a belly-grabbing roar.

Augum was sure the others thought it a battle cry, judging by them shooting to their feet and raising their hands in defensive positions.

But Rogor kept howling. He jammed the knife into the table, grabbed the chicken by the neck, and swept out of there, howling his way down the hall.

"Never heard a wolven laugh before," Leera said as everyone visibly relaxed.

One of the brothers said something under his breath, and the pair of brothers chortled, looking away, while Carter kept to his own plate of potatoes and chicken and spinach. Augum stilled the waving knife before freeing it from the table, leaving behind a small gouge.

Jez whirled about. "And for another thing, Mahmoooooo, or Mahmoootie, or whatever your Tiberran name is, they don't *like* or *trust* you, so you can forget about taking my place. You hear me? You can forget it."

"She always this drunk?" Alanna asked Augum, which made Leera jolt up in her place and Jez slowly turn to Alanna as if she were possessed.

Feeling that the women were about to explode on Alanna, for both were ballooning in that particular fashion he had learned to spot a league off with Leera, and that the brothers were about to make another idiotic remark, he thought it was high time he stepped into the shoes he had crafted for himself.

"Oi, you lot!" he shouted at Carter's group without looking at them, throwing his knife onto his plate, making a clatter. "Get over here!" Having had enough, Augum dabbed at his lips with his napkin, readying to put his foot down.

"You go on ahead, dear cousin," Digby said, patting Carter's cheek, voice oozing with condescension.

"Yes, do go on, dear cousin, and play the lapdog," Teague threw in.

Augum felt the curtain behind his mind dip aside and a shadow peek into his soul. He clenched his fist, ready to smash it down on the table and roar. Instead, he took a deep breath, organized his knife and fork beside his plate, gently removed Leera's arm from his shoulder, straightened, and fixed his gaze on Carter until the seventeen-year-old cleared his throat, got up, and made his way to sit beside Jez. Mercifully, the women backed down from firing at Alanna to give him space to perform his duty.

"You want to be a dragoon," Augum said in an iron tone, forestalling Carter's reply with a raised hand. He held that hand aloft—and with it, the table's silence—before continuing. "You want to be a dragoon, but you lack the discipline and the skill to prevent an untimely death. You want to progress within the order and gain rank. You want to be a leader. I shall give you the opportunity to lead. From now on, you will be fully responsible for your cousins. Yes, they are twice your age, but you are the heir apparent to the empire, and kings rule all ages. Your cousins *will* listen to you, for they have been commanded to do so by royal decree."

The pair of cousins shifted uncomfortably at this.

"Thus," Augum continued, "for everything they do out of turn, I shall hold *you* responsible as their leader."

As Carter sat with an open mouth, that cocky grin having slipped from his face, Augum lowered his hand.

"When I was your age," Augum began, aware of how silent the room had gotten as everyone listened to him, "I had already taken command of a warlock army. We went to war together. We bled together. If you want to progress in this order, you will obey *my order*." He leaned forth. "You have a choice, Squire Carter. You can continue idling about at court, playing with fancy lordlings as they puff you up for kinghood, or you can callus your hands working for the order, in turn getting stronger as a warlock ..." Augum sat back. "... and as a *man*."

For a long moment, the only sound was the wind and the creaking and the waves, the ship rolling in rhythm to all three.

Hearing a soft padding, Augum glanced back to see that Olaf and Jengo had quietly stepped into the room. Not wanting to be interrupted just yet, he cocked his head at Carter and resumed.

"We cannot choose brethren of birth, but we *can* choose who we associate with and how we comport ourselves." He gripped his napkin, feeling quite at ease. "Tomorrow we are expected to make landfall on the farthest islands known to our kingdom. There we shall quest to discover how to make the final passage over the most dangerous seas in existence." He glanced around at them all, realizing everyone, from the cooks to Mahmoute, were watching him. "Seas that have almost always claimed ships as prey. So I suggest we start to take the matter a *little* more seriously."

He looked to Jez's goblet. "For we do not know when we will have to rely on each other." With his meal half complete, Augum stood and took one final look around at them. "Three ships, countless men and women, and you all think it's a mere sojourn. A tromp around the lake. As if safety is guaranteed. As if we will all return home."

He looked beyond them, seeing what was to come. A daring and dangerous crossing. Already he could envision the vicious storms he had read about. The ominous rising of waves taller than the ship. The howl of the wind. He, a lightning warlock, had a vague idea of what chaos truly sounded like within the fury of a maelstrom.

"Gird yourselves," he told them, neatly folding his napkin. "For we soon enter uncharted waters none alive have traversed." He placed the napkin over his utensils. "Now if you will excuse me, I could do with some fresh air," and he stepped over his bench and strode past Jengo and Olaf, both of whom gave him a solemn nod of respect.

Leaving the galley in ringing silence, Augum navigated the cramped corridors out onto the deck, where he slowly inhaled and exhaled the ocean air. He moved past the crew working the ropes and securing equipment and crates and barrels to the deck. Some nodded at him as he passed, and others kept focused on their tasks.

Augum stepped up to the wooden rail, grabbing it with one hand and a thick rope connected to the freshly repaired mast with the other. The bitterly cold winds blew his hair about, and his hood flapped behind him like a flag. The horizon was black as ink, the seas choppy with curling rolls that foamed like crazed mouths.

He envisioned rising above the ocean as a dragon and meeting a giant gargoyle. He saw himself fly just beyond the gargoyle, only to whip up over his own head. *Hightail*, he thought, identifying the maneuver. Then he saw himself performing other maneuvers he had learned during one of Isobel's Flight Class lessons. The battle was glorious to behold, the noise alone tectonic.

"I love you," blurted a soft voice.

Augum pressed his eyes shut. *Unnameables, why must the Fates torment me so?*

"I know it is impossible and I know you love *her*, but I cannot help how I feel, sir. I cannot."

Augum slowly turned around to see Alanna, cheeks stained with tears.

"It *is* impossible, and I *do* love her. More than anything. More than life itself." When she opened her mouth to reply, he raised a firm hand in the same manner he had done with Carter. "You have played the game publicly and privately. That game ends now. Where we sail, there will be no room for games. Where we sail, it will be life and death."

"Commander, I—"

Augum forestalled her by pressing his hand forth, silencing her. He held it in place. "Where we go, we will have to rely on each other like men and women of iron. Like men and women with honor. And we will have to be brave." He lowered his hand. "That is why I too have an order—no, a *request* of you."

"Anything, my lord."

"I have it on good authority you are a capable arcaneologist."

"I can hold my own. Took just about every Arcaneology class the academy offered."

"I want you to aid my beloved in deciphering a book that has been tormenting and confounding her."

Alanna opened her mouth—and kept it open, gaze searching his eyes, as if trying to comprehend his meaning. "Is … is that a jest, good sir?"

"I want you to understand her and learn to respect her. Do this so you understand what true love is. Do this not for me … but for yourself."

Alanna dropped her gaze. "How can you ask such a thing of me? To aid the woman who responds to me with vitriol, who rebuffed me when I did offer help. The woman who … gods, how I am loathe to admit it … who drives such profound jealousy within me?"

Augum watched her, this beautiful flower of a girl he had nothing in common with other than being a lightning warlock. "One day you shall find your prince. In the mean, aid those of us who could use your help. And Leera could use that help, even if she doesn't want to admit it. Please take your time considering it."

He once again forestalled whatever she was about to say by properly bowing his head at a slight incline, the classic signal between the nobility that the conversation was over—he'd learned a thing or two leading the order from the headquarters at the Black Castle. Then he turned his back on her and gripped the rail to survey the sea, eager for the journey to come.

A CURSED SCENT

BRIDGET

Bridget fought hard to keep both arms between herself and the filthy planks to prevent her face from getting torn up. She had never been dragged by a single foot before, let alone with her stomach facing the floor—and let alone by an overly muscled beast of a gargoyle the slaves called The Brute.

Feeling like a recalcitrant sheep that had tried to hop the farm fence, she vividly recalled the relief on the other slaves' faces that it wasn't them upon her first getting snagged, a relief in stark contrast to Sebastian's horrified gaping stare. She had tried to awkwardly raise a hand to tell the boy not to worry, but only ended up with her face nearly meeting the floor.

She was soon hauled into the rear of the kitchen area, which bustled with more collared slaves hurrying to and fro as they moved barrels and crates, likely food stores, as well as steaming vats of what she hoped was mere soup.

There, in an open space amidst a series of bloody butcher blocks, she was unceremoniously thrown against a wall splattered with animal guts. The intensely pungent stench, combined with her already fragile stomach, amplified her nausea to such an extent that Bridget slapped a hand over her mouth and nose and squeezed her eyes shut to stop herself from retching.

Thinking back to the meditation techniques she had learned from the founder of their order, she exhaled, inhaled deeply through her mouth to avoid the smell, held the breath for a count of eight, and slowly exhaled. In and out she breathed like this until her stomach settled. Only then did she open her eyes.

The Brute stood guard nearby, looking up through the ceiling of crisscrossing timber that allowed gargoyles to swoop down into any room.

He's waiting for someone, Bridget realized, and used the opportunity to take stock of where she was. The wall above her was filled with iron kitchen implements hanging on hooks—ladles and prongs and skewers. On a butcher block was a leather-wrapped set of what appeared to be human-sized steel tools.

Knowing she might only have a few heartbeats, Bridget raised a finger and telekinetically latched onto the handle of one of those tools. Whilst keeping one eye on the overseer, she wiggled her finger back and forth, and the steel implement began to wiggle in the same manner. She kept this up, struggling with her weak Telekinesis until the instrument pulled itself free—and fell.

She gasped and stuck out more fingers, telekinetically catching the implement a hair's breadth from the floor. She floated it over, fighting to keep hold of it, which forced all her attention into the effort. It was a small steel rod with a sharp point, perhaps a needleworker's tool—or a jabber used by those with ill intent.

The Brute idly glanced down at her, and she hid the jabber up her sleeve whilst scratching her nose with her other hand to draw his attention away. He watched her with disinterest before glancing at the hard-working slaves and then returning his gaze upward.

Bridget also looked about, but in search of a way out. If these were her final moments, she wanted to try to escape, maybe get up top and see if she could hide out long enough to spot land, then jump and make a swim for it. As improbable as such a plan was, she had to try.

Then she remembered the frightened face of Sebastian and realized she couldn't leave the boy behind.

There soon came the rustle of wings as the fifteen-footer that had licked her face descended between the rafters—and in his clawed feet he held a ghastly creature of a gargoyle, which he let go of at a surprisingly high height. The creature, a wingless and disfigured male, landed on his feet with remarkable agility, straightened, and bowed in supplication before The Brute, who took little notice of him.

But the creature took notice of Bridget, glancing at her briefly with one good eye—the other scarred over, no doubt through violent means—before looking back to the floor. He was unusually short for a gargoyle, only about seven feet in height, though mostly on account of his pronounced hunch. His arms were stubby and curled inward, and he had a nub of a tail that had, judging by the damage, been hacked off. Two more nubs protruded from his back, indicating his wings had been ripped or cut off. His snout was permanently bent as if having been violently slapped, and scars covered his body.

The winged overseer landed beside him, gold neck chain clinking. Although he wasn't as muscled as The Brute, he was taller and possessed runes and wings. The Brute deferred to him with a bow.

The overseer indicated Bridget and growled something to the hunched gargoyle, who nodded and tottered forth.

"Yer var bog varlok, yoss?" the disfigured gargoyle asked in a garbled tongue that sounded like a dog trying to make human words.

Bridget wanted to shake her head to indicate she did not understand, but realized they could interpret the movement as a *no* to whatever question he had asked. Instead she simply said, "I do not understand," and was careful to enunciate each word.

The hunched beast moved his crooked snout about as if trying to decipher her. After receiving another annoyed command from the winged overseer, he nodded placatingly and said, "You big *varlok, yoss?*"

"You speak common," Bridget blurted.

"Yes, I spaek little. You spaek tell. Spaek me say what—" He indicated his own arm. "You spaek."

"I do not understand."

The overseer looked to The Brute, who uncoiled his massive tail—and lashed it, aiming for the side of Bridget's head. Had she not raised her sleeved arm in a battle-honed reaction, he would have certainly split her face open. Instead the tail struck her forearm, which she had protected with the hidden steel implement clutched in her hand. Only a bruise would form.

Seeing her instinctive reaction, the pair of large gargoyles glanced at each other, as if confirming a suspicion.

The hunched one tapped his arm. "Spaek."

"Oh, you mean *speak,*" Bridget said, playing as if The Brute hadn't tried to snap her head off.

"Speak, *yoss.* You speak."

Bridget at last put his meaning together. "I can try," she said, and raised her left forearm and focused. Ten weak bands of floating green ivy flared to life around her arm and fizzled soon after. She tapped her forearm and then her collar. "I can't flare them because of this. If you want to see them in full, release me and I will show you." She hadn't meant for the rebellious anger to slip in like that, but suspected the wretched beast wouldn't understand anyway.

Sure enough, the hunched one growled out what she thought was a question to the winged overseer. She was careful to pay attention to their words. Although she hadn't progressed far with the 12th degree Tongues spell under Jez's sporadic tutelage, if she could string enough words together, she might be able to cast the spell in the future—if she lived that long.

The hunched one placed a hand against his chest—his claws cut short. "Me Grak."

"That's your name? Grak?

"*Yoss*, Grak. You. You who?"

Not wanting to reveal her true identity, Bridget blurted out her middle name, "Abigail. My name is Abigail."

"Abigaal …"

"No, not Abi*gaal*, Abi*gail*. Ah. Bi. Gail."

"Ah. Bee. Gail. Ah-bee-gale."

"Close enough."

Grak flashed a grin that revealed broken and stained teeth as he nodded proudly to himself, earning himself a cuff on the side of the head from The Brute, who growled a choice word at him. Grak, evidently used to such mistreatment, nodded and returned his gaze to Bridget. "Ah-bee-gale much fat."

"Fat? I don't understand." She felt she was the skinniest she had been since nearly starving to death during the war with the Legion, which she had experienced as a teenager. Although the food on the boat was delicious, there were only two meals a day, and the hard labor made short work of it.

"Er … much fat—" and Grak jabbed at the air.

"Oh, you mean *fight*? Is that what you mean?" She made a fist and punched forth. "Fight?"

"*Yoss, yoss*, fight. You much fight?"

"Do I fight a lot? Only in training."

Grak looked uncertainly between his overseers, both of whom growled impatiently.

"What do you want with me?" Bridget asked, sounding meeker than she had wanted.

"You kill. Ah-bee-gale kill. *Yoss?*"

Bridget swallowed, eyes unfocusing as she saw a past filled with regret. She was supposed to be an apprentice to an arcanist by now, perhaps in the countryside. Or maybe the apprentice to an arcaneologist. She was supposed to be surrounded by books and farm animals and a dog and a husband, her eyes fixed on a horizon of hope and family, of kids and laughter and harmony. Instead she'd been thrust into two wars, with all their anguish and terror. Most vivid of all was the fresh memory of having to frantically stab a tattooed and bald criminal that had almost choked her to death.

"Yes," she said dryly, seeing a squirt of blood shoot out from a neck. "Yes, I kill …"

The winged one snapped a growl, and The Brute's tail lashed out, curling around Bridget's neck and raising her off her feet. Thinking she was about to be strangled, she wheezingly scrabbled at the tail with her nails, feeling like a dangling mouse fighting with a python. In the struggle, the steel jabber slipped down her sleeve and pricked her armpit.

Meanwhile the overseer extended his wings and took to the air, gripping his clawed feet into Grak's shoulders to lift him away. As Bridget gasped for breath that would not come, he pointed at Bridget. The Brute's tail unwound, allowing the winged one to lift her skyward telekinetically. Up she gaspingly went, rising through the rafters, until Grak grabbed her.

"I hold Ah-bee-gale," he told her in a cooing tone, as if glad to have saved a pet. He clutched her to his chest, and she clutched herself, using both arms to press the jabber against her skin to prevent it from slipping down her body and falling out the bottom of the robe.

They flew through structures in the bow that revealed various pens, each affixed to the ship's beams by thick rope. Many held groups of animals—she saw cattle and bears and cougars and mirkos and wolves and deer and lions and monkeys and beasts she had never laid eyes upon. She'd even caught a glimpse of what she swore were wolven adults and cubs. There were open crates overfilled with wood and grain and hay and piles of silver and gold and spices and stacks of books and countless plundered riches.

She was flown sideways toward a long rectangular platform, with a thick edge and held on all sides by huge knots of rope, a platform laden with yellow sand—the arena. Already gargoyles had begun assembling along its side perches, drinking their slop and getting rowdy by shoving each other and growling in what she assumed was drunken mirth. The whole thing rested at a tilt, for the giant ship was speeding through high but steady winds.

"Please, no," she begged as they descended toward it. "Please, no …" She was not a dueler like Augum and Leera or some of the more battle-focused Arcaners in her group. As a warlock, she was an archer who shot from a distance, a person who avoided close combat whenever possible.

Grak held on tighter, cooing, "Grak hold Ah-bee-gale. Ah-bee-gale Grak hold. Pretty *hooman*, pretty girl, pretty name. Ah-bee-gale, Ah-bee-gale, Ah-bee-gale, *yoss*?"

"I'm not your pet …" she whispered. "I'm not your pet …"

Twenty feet above the sand, Bridget felt a stomach-lightening drop as the winged gargoyle let go of Grak. The disfigured hunchback deftly landed on the sand whilst holding Bridget in such a gentle manner that she briefly felt like a babe in her father's arms.

Sickened by the thought, she tore away from the disfigured beast, leaving him standing with open arms, as if hoping she would return to his embrace. The winged gargoyle flapped overhead, growled a warning at Grak, and took off to join the spectators. Bridget, holding herself, with the jabber pressed against her lower stomach inside her robe, backed away from Grak and glanced about.

They were in the very center of the spacious arena, and already a hundred gargoyles had descended to perch along its sides. New and old blood, turned brown over time, stained the sand. Her breath caught upon the sight of a freshly severed human arm, as if lying in wait for its owner to return, pick it back up, and reattach it to their body. Then a wingless gargoyle carrying a huge basket on its back sauntered by, grabbed it, threw it into the basket, and walked off in search for more.

Bridget watched the heavy sway of the basket, indicating it was already full of body parts, with a sick stomach.

"They want fight," Grak interrupted in a melancholic tone. "Ah-bee-gale show survive. Pretty Ah-bee-gale, Ah-bee-gale, Ah-bee-gale, please survive."

"Stop saying my name like that," she blubbered.

Grak watched her with pity in his lone eye.

Not wanting to keep facing the strange beast, she turned in place, whispering, "I have become the entertainment …"

Gargoyles rose from below, each clutching a slave in their paws, and dumped these poor wretches onto the sand before her. She recognized only one of them—the plump middle-aged woman in the nightgown who had stolen some of her food earlier. The woman looked at Bridget with feral eyes—and bared her teeth at her.

A cold dread swept through Bridget's soul. What would she do if they made her fight these poor souls? Would she capitulate, allowing her life to be snatched away? How could she take the lives of innocents?

In search of answers, she turned about to question Grak, but he was gone, having shuffled off to join his brethren.

More slaves kept getting dropped off, and she almost yelped when one of them turned out to be the boy, Sebastian, who landed roughly in the sand nearby. She ran over and yanked him to her chest, pressing him tightly against her whilst backing away from the throng.

"I didn't know where you got taken," the twelve-year-old gibbered, crying and whimpering, snot dribbling down his mouth and chin. "And that mean man was trying to find me and so I ran and hid behind people but he kept coming and just as he got to me the beasties came and took me ... I was so scared ..."

Bridget wound a hand around his head protectively. Then she remembered the jabber and withdrew it from within her robe. She pressed it into his shaking palm. "You take this," she whispered. "Take it."

"What ...? What is this?"

"A weapon. Use it like a knife if you have to. Until then, keep it hidden."

Sebastian whimpered as he stared down at the implement, until Bridget showed him how to hide it up his long sleeve. As the growling and hooting reached a fever pitch, she kneeled before the boy and took his face between her hands.

"Stick anyone who threatens you," she said, looking deep into his watery hazel eyes. "Do you understand? *Anyone.*"

The boy nodded quickly, eyes streaming tears that left mud lines on his cheeks. She wiped those tears and his snot with her dirty sleeve, making a mess of his face, but she kept on nonetheless, until his face was a little cleaner. Staring back at her was the face of a boy she swore looked like Olaf. It was as if The Fates were mocking her, saying, "You wanted a family? Here's a glimpse, you fool."

Tears wanted to well, yet she refused to let the boy see her terror, and so she whirled him about and kept him close.

Meanwhile the gargoyles kept dumping more slaves onto the sands, until twenty stood, all apart from each other and wary—and amongst the last were none other than two bearded men—the thin tuft-haired Mud and the muscled Porter, clothing ripped and chest slashed from having been whipped. The latter immediately spotted her and began striding in her direction with a look of pure determination.

"*Gohihol!*" an amplified gargoyle voice boomed, summoning everyone's attention and halting Porter in his tracks. "*Gohihol!*" the voice repeated, and from up high descended a large gargoyle on extended wings. He did not settle onto the arena, but rather flapped just above. "*Gohihol!*" he repeated, which Bridget assumed meant *Attention!*

The gargoyle rapidly growled a series of phrases, reminding her of the masters of ceremonies who oversaw arena duels back at home. Upon concluding one of these diatribes, the gargoyle opened its arms toward one side of the arena, and all gazes—slave and gargoyle alike—looked to a raised perch platform, atop which sat a retinue of mighty gargoyles festooned in gold chains and gold-accented bones and other stringy ornamentations. Likely the leadership of the boat, which included the face-licking fifteen-footer with the golden neck chain.

Also among them was the largest gargoyle on the entire ship, a muscled seventeen-footer whose torso was covered in runes. His snout was long and fierce and his folded wings covered in battle scars. A pronounced frowning brow lent intelligence to his iron gaze. Wingless servant gargoyles catered to his whims, bringing him platters of titan grapes and a whole roasted goat, which the gargoyle waved off with the flick of a black-clawed finger, and they were instead served to his gold-chained coterie.

The announcing gargoyle raised both arms and roared a phrase, which caused all the gargoyles to rise and cheer—or jeer; it was hard to tell with their beastly behavior. They waved their horns filled with concoctions and gesticulated wildly at the arena, devilish tails waving about like legions of snakes. The slaves moved apart, sensing a coming call to attack. Whereas Mud positioned himself far from Bridget, Porter edged closer and closer.

Sebastian began shaking uncontrollably. "I don't want to die. I don't want to die ..."

Bridget wanted to assure him that he was not going to die, that she would protect him, but the words would not breach the lump in her throat. What she wanted to say was, *You won't die alone. I'll die alongside you,* but even that was too painful to say. She kept retreating as she stared at Porter, his eyes black and flat. He advanced so close she saw bits of food peppering his filthy beard.

He only halted when a roaring wave leaped from the crowd of gargoyles, and the slaves looked up to see four winged gargoyles flying over, clutching ropes that held an iron cage full of beasts.

"Mirkos!" a slave shouted.

The slaves screamed, for the ferocious hyena-like beasts, with their sharp teeth and patient stalking behavior, were frequently depicted in children's stories. Parents warned their children never to venture alone in the wild, for a mirko could pick up their scent and begin stalking. The moment the child rested, the malignant beast would pounce with throat-ripping ferocity. Such tales, embedded in every Solian's childhood, infused a particular shrillness to their screaming.

"Give us weapons!" Mud shouted, a call the others quickly took up.

"Yes, give us weapons! For the love of the Unnameables, allow us to defend ourselves!"

Their prayers were answered when a gargoyle dropped a large wooden crate into their midst. It smashed into the sand and exploded, spilling wooden clubs.

"Clubs!" the nightgowned woman shrieked. "Are you jesting us! Those are *mirkos!*" Yet even as she protested, the slaves descended on these pathetic weapons, fighting for the largest bats in the pile.

Meanwhile the gargoyles placed the cage full of mirkos a hundred feet away. Upon spotting the slaves, the beasts began yipping and clawing and jumping at the bars in their eagerness to get at the prey.

The slaves huddled together. Porter jogged away from Bridget to swipe a club from a feeble old man—despite there being more than enough clubs in the crate. He bared his teeth at the old man until he shuffled off to find himself a new club. Then he placed himself between the smashed crate and Bridget, who kept trying to walk around the crowd to snag herself a club. But Porter eyed her the entire way, repeatedly flexing an exposed and slashed pectoral muscle as he gripped the club with both hands like a sword.

"I don't want them to rip off my face," Sebastian blubbered, holding onto her tight. "I'm awful scared …"

Bridget clutched his chest, knuckles white. A quick count of the mirkos told her there were twenty, one for each slave. Badly wanting a club to defend herself but unable to get to one, she realized she had to do something before the gargoyles opened the cage.

She stuck the boy behind her, telling him, "Stay here."

"No!" the boy shrieked. "No, no, no, no, don't you leave me!" and he threw his arms around her waist from behind with an iron grip of sheer terror, refusing to let go.

Porter grinned through his beard. "Come on, momma bear," he said, swinging the club in a beckoning motion. "Come and meet your fate …" With each swing, he took a measured step in her direction.

As was her practice, Bridget unfurled a scroll within her mind that detailed her spell knowledge. Push and Disarm and Fear and Confusion and Paralyze and Slow and Blind and Centarro and the volatile Frenzy and her elemental spells—Entangle and the First Offensive and Elemental Armor and Summon Weapon and Summon Minor Wall and Snaking Vine and Fissure. Then there were her Arcaner simuls—Birth of the Dragon that summoned a miniature earthen dragon and Bluster of the Dragon that infused her arrows with Confusion and of course the mighty Spirit of the Dragon, which turned *her* into a dragon and was unfortunately impossible to cast on account of the suppressive slave collar.

On the list, one spell stood out. A spell that would lend her an advantage—perhaps even lend an advantage to the group as a whole.

With Sebastian still clutching her waist from behind, she pivoted to allow herself to drew an invisible bowstring, incanting, "*Summano arma!*" A wispy bow blinked into life in her hands, an arrow already nocked on the string, a quiver on her back. But the bow was a shadow of its usual might. It even lacked that certain heft that instilled confidence and allowed for better aim. Still, she hoped it was an improvement on a mere club. Upon its appearance, the gargoyles howled their approval. The bow also made Porter, who at that moment stood twenty feet from her, halt his advance.

Bridget wanted to shoot, but the boy's deathly embrace made it hard to aim—not to mention Porter had placed himself on the outer ring of the throng of slaves, meaning a miss could impale an innocent. They had gathered into a single group, leaving Bridget and the boy as the lone outliers—a dangerous position against a pack of mirkos.

Gods help me, I'm going to die a screaming death, she thought, picturing a mirko grabbing her throat and rabidly rag-dolling her about and, within sight, the same horror happening to Sebastian.

Focus, damn you! her trained mind shouted at her. She looked to the cage. Of the four gargoyles that had descended with the cage, only one remained, standing atop it and holding onto the cage door. He was staring at the seventeen-foot rune-emblazoned leader—surely the captain of the ship—waiting for the command.

The captain slowly stood up to his full height and extended his wings, giving him the appearance of a giant demonic bat. He raised an arm and held it there, snout high and proud. When the crowd settled down to an anxious burble, his arm dropped and his wings abruptly folded. Up rose the cage door, and out shot the yipping mirkos, sprinting like dogs.

The slaves shrieked as one. On the other side of the group, a woman screamed, "Gods, don't! Don't you do it! Please, I didn't do nothin'—ack!"

Out of the corner of her eye, Bridget saw that Porter had dragged the nightgowned woman by the scruff away from the group and shoved her onto the sand, offering a sacrifice to the mirkos. Despite possessing a club, which she held close to her chest with both hands, she scrambled to straighten her nightgown and rejoin the group—only for a leg to shoot out and boot her in the stomach, sending her reeling backward until she tripped over her own feet and rolled.

Bridget couldn't worry about the others and, having kept her bow trained on Porter, swung it toward the mirkos. The pack split into two, with ten sprinting at the woman and the other ten after Bridget. With a child in tow, she surely looked like salacious prey.

"I don't wanna die I don't wanna die I don't wanna die—" Sebastian gibbered at a rapid clip, hold stiffening to an iron grip that was at least stable enough to allow for better aim.

Bridget barely heard him. For her, time slowed to a crawl as her Arcaner training kicked in. A brief memory flashed across her mind of practicing shooting down summoned vultures in Combat Reflex class, one of a slew of specialized courses available through the ancient Arcaner course back at the academy.

The bow swiveled only slightly now as she kept honing her aim. The noise dampened to a background roar, replaced by the high-pitched sound of blood rushing through her ears. Factoring distance, she kept the arrow tip above her target. She had plenty of room and needn't worry about missing and accidentally hitting a gargoyle. When the mirkos hit fifty feet, she fired. *Twang* went the wispy bowstring as the arrow shot forth.

The lead mirkos jumped aside. The arrow zipped past them—and struck the face of a mirko running just behind the leaders. The beast slammed into the sand, tumbling end over end before coming to a halt. The audience of gargoyles hooted in approval. It was a lucky strike, for the forehead showed a hole where the arrow had struck true before vanishing back into the ether, whence it had come.

Forty feet and closing, nine remaining in this pack, Bridget observed. She drew back and fired in rapid succession, her arms working with fluid precision. *Twang! Twang! Twang!* One arrow struck a flank, another a front paw, but the last hit the sand. The two wounded ones slowed to a limp, trailing the group. With the remaining mirkos galloping at twenty feet, she drew back to fire again, only for the bow to blink out of existence. Heavily weakened by the collar, the spell had fizzled.

Sebastian descended into a screaming puddle whilst clutching onto her. Her ears also picked up the gruesome sound of a shrieking woman getting torn up, but she kept her focus on the charging pack of seven, which had clustered together, with two injured ones loping in just behind. That cluster gave her an idea, and she pressed the backs of her hands together before pushing them apart and sweeping them forth along the ground.

"*Fiuria girata fissura!*" she roared, incanting the 7th degree off-the-books Fissure spell.

Although not as wide as usual, a fissure cracked the ground open and snaked forth in such an unpredictable way that four mirkos, which had attempted to jump over it, slammed into its sandy wall and plummeted. The two injured mirkos who loped in behind tried to avoid the randomly snaking fissure but were too slow, and they too fell in.

The echo of them all yipping told her they had fallen *through* the arena floor itself and would surely perish hitting the beams or planks below — or so she hoped, at least for the sake of the slaves working obliviously in their pens. In a matter of heartbeats, she had vanquished seven mirkos. The gargoyles again roared their approval.

Three mirkos remained in this group, all of which had jumped over the chasm, which vanished, once again demonstrating the suppression effect of the gargoyle collar. At ten feet, Bridget grew desperate and slapped her wrists together, roaring, "*Annihilo!*"

Not a wisp emanated, the collar preventing the First Offensive from even lighting.

She pivoted to jiggling a hand, hissing, "*Flustrato!*"

The lead mirko's head recoiled, indicating a true strike. The Confusion spell was *just* strong enough to cause that mirko to bite its neighbor, and the two mirkos crashed into each other — and tumbled by, descending into a biting frenzy that was so ferocious the pair mauled each other to death. The final mirko lunged at Bridget. Pressing Sebastian to her, she ducked and pointed at it, telekinetically nudging it just enough to send it whooshing overhead. It hit the ground, turned about, and lunged again.

She raised her arm to summon her shield, but nothing appeared. A glint of metal caught her eye as the boy reached up from underneath — and stabbed the mirko through the jaw, pinning the mouth closed. The mirko fell to the ground yipping and scrabbling at its mouth. Bridget gave it a mean kick in the side, sending it tumbling.

With only one mirko still alive from her original pack of ten, and with a pinned jaw at that, she grabbed the boy and hauled him toward their fellow slaves, who had devolved into a mass of panicked shrieking and clubbing, hands and faces bloody. Three mirko lay dead at the mob's feet, alongside half a dozen human bodies. Porter was not among them, so he had to be within the chaotic throng.

Bridget, half-dragging and half-carrying a whimpering Sebastian, remembered Augum leading a training raid back at the academy during their 9th degree. "Cluster, cluster, cluster!" she shouted, but she might as well have been trying to corral panicked fish for all the good her command did.

She briefly let go of a Sebastian to fluidly draw out a series of gestures—palm forward and up, establishing a mind-body connection to the arcane ether, palm down to initiate arcane draw, palm curling into a fist to grab hold of the forming tendril web, open the palm once more to slice a line across the air and throw those tendrils along an invisible line she drew well ahead of her, before curling her palm into a fist and slamming it into her other palm, forming a *T* shape and thus finishing the spell—all whilst incanting, "*Summano valla minimus girata barricada!*"

A vine wall of stubby bush appeared along the line she drew, between the people and the mirkos. It was only ten feet in length and a few feet in height, but the first mirko to jump onto that wall was immediately entangled in the vines, allowing the slaves to pulp its head in with their clubs. It was such a clumsy attempt however that a few lost their clubs to the hungry vine wall.

As Bridget closed in on the throng, a total of seven mirkos remained alive, six of which were growling and yipping at the slaves, angling for another attack. The seventh was still behind Bridget and fighting with the jabber that pinned its jaw closed.

Noticing that most of the mirkos were close together, she considered Focal Quicksand, a spell she had learned a couple years ago whilst training for her 8th degree, a dangerous spell that came with an ethics warning from the Academy of Arcane of Arts.

She flapped both hands up and down, careful to have one hand in the up position and the other in the down position, moving them back and forth in precise sequence. She thought of softness and granulation and liquidity whilst incanting, "*Arregando rapidio sedzat!*"

On account of her experience with the spell, usually the area of effect was a modest sixteen-by-sixteen-foot space. In this case, the sand beneath only three mirkos softened and barely swallowed half their bodies. But that was enough for Mud and two other men to descend upon the mirkos and club their heads. Unfortunately one man made a clumsy go of it and slipped into the sand, allowing a mirko to chomp down on his leg. He screamed and fought valiantly until the mirko got hold of his throat, silencing him forever with one ripping tear.

"Gods please help us," Sebastian whimpered. "I'm so scared …"

Bridget checked behind her and saw that the mirko that was fighting with its jaw had drifted too close to the spectating gargoyles, all of whom were wildly waving their arms at it, trying to get it to reengage in the fight. When it continued to scrabble at the jabber in its jaw, one of these gargoyles lost patience and grabbed the mirko by the hind legs, twirled it over its head, and launched the growling beast back toward Bridget.

It was such an accurate throw that her instinct was to step aside. Instead, she pushed Sebastian away and threw a vicious kick that connected with the mirko's head. There was a *crack* from its neck and the mirko slammed into the sand, tumbling a few times before going still.

The gargoyles roared their approval.

After Sebastian shot back to embrace her, she returned her attention to the throng and saw that her summoned wall had blinked out of existence, leaving behind numerous clubs and the body of a mirko.

The remaining three mirkos noticed Bridget and Sebastian, who were still ten feet from the safety of the throng. They loped away from the area of the quicksand and the clubbing humans, with one circling in from the left and two from the right.

Keeping the boy close to her back, Bridget made a run for the group—only for Porter to emerge from the crowd and deliver a kick to her chest, sending her and the boy shooting backward.

As she fell, Bridget reflexively pointed at the man and telekinetically yanked with everything she had, yet all her suppressed Telekinesis achieved was to stagger him forth a few steps. It was enough to draw the attention of the lone mirko sprinting in from the left, which jumped at him. Adept with his own reflexes, he smashed its head with his club, felling it on the spot.

Meanwhile, the pair from the right lunged at Bridget and Sebastian, who lay side by side. Sebastian, frantically kicking out, booted one in the snout. The other landed on top of Bridget. In a panic and having missed the mirko with her own clumsy kicks, she roared the only thing that came to mind—"*Shyneo!*"

Her hand burst with vines that were much thinner than usual. She nonetheless smacked that hand over the snapping snout, and the vines entwined the mirko's jaw. It began to thrash like an alligator as it fought to free itself. Despite its animalistic might, a grunting Bridget held on, knowing that if she let go, the vines would let go too. Thus, tied to the movements of the mirko, she flopped about like a fish.

The gargoyles trilled and hooted throughout, amused by the display.

As the other mirko again lunged at the boy, who lay beside her kicking at the air, she pointed with her free hand and hissed, "*Flustrato!*"

Even amidst the violent flopping, her spell miraculously smacked into the mirko's head. Against an animal with an unshielded brain, the weakened spell was strong enough to cause it to hesitate, which allowed Sebastian to give it another boot to the snout, sending it tumbling backward.

Porter kicked the mirko in the rear, punting the confused animal right back at them. The mirko finished tumbling near Bridget's leg—and chomped down on her ankle. Busy flopping about with a hand entwined to a mirko's snout, Bridget screamed in pain. But that pain also sharpened her senses and she used her free foot to kick the confused mirko in the gut, unclamping it from her ankle.

Perhaps because Bridget had vanquished so many mirkos already, her fellow slaves descended on the animal she had kicked in the gut, pulping its head in—and in their swarming, enveloped Porter.

Bridget was left nearby, gasping from the ankle pain as she was getting thrashed about by the mirko whose snout she still had a hold of, the boy feebly kicking at it. Amidst the thrashing, Bridget found herself flopping behind the beast. She seized her chance and threw her free arm around its neck, then let Shine die and drew her first arm around as well, choking it. They rolled away from the throng, Bridget screaming as she put everything she had into crushing its windpipe.

The beast's spasmic movements steadily slowed. Bridget kept a grunting hold until it went completely limp, at which point she ran out of strength anyway and flopped aside, panting deep breaths. The nearby beast lay staring at her with vacant eyes.

Body burning from exertion, she raised her head to look down at her bare toes, noting the way the sand stuck to the crevices in between. Tentatively, she pinched her lower robe and drew it up her leg, revealing a ghastly bite wound on the ankle. The series of holes barely bled, yet laying eyes on those holes made the pain acute and fiery, and she gnashed her teeth to prevent from crying out.

She let her head fall back against the sand, the fight completely drained from her. This was it. She was a goner. In the next few days, infection would take root. She would slowly descend into weakness and madness and then death. Of all the ways to die …

A life she had always longed for but was never meant to have paraded before her mind. A husband, kids, the farm, children to teach. All as ghostly as candle smoke. Like the slow pounding of a heavy funeral drum, her heart seemed to tire, for she felt and heard each thump against her chest. Perhaps Porter would swoop in and bash her skull in then and there. At least that would spare her the inevitable feverish torment.

How quickly you give up, she thought. *Do not let hope slip away.*

She wished the predator would return to her. Lend her the resolve to face death like a warrior.

Then it did. As if someone had left the door open to a blizzard, her innards cooled as she felt it peek into her mind with its icy eye.

You want to die? it asked. *Then hope must die first. Give in and you will know peace …*

Bridget considered it. Almost let out what would have been a most satisfying sigh. Even the thought dulled the burning pain. Yet a foul stubbornness remained, and she shook her head and simply mouthed, "No."

A blurry shape appeared above her. For a moment she expected a gargoyle to swiftly come down upon her vision. Instead, a boyish voice whispered, "Oh, no, you're hurt. Oh no, oh no, oh no …"

The phrase jolted Bridget from her reverie. Sebastian was shaking her, and something was happening. The others were regrouping and shouting.

"You're hurt really bad," Sebastian repeated.

Not all my wounds are visible, Bridget wanted to say, but had not the courage. Instead she groaningly sat up and, seeing that everyone was gazing toward the cage, including Porter, glanced over her shoulder. Her already shallow breath caught, for a new cage had replaced the old. Within stood a ten-foot ape-like monster with glossy black fur. It sniffed ferociously at the bars with vent-like nostrils. Its muscles were larger than the gargoyles', its arms so powerful and large they looked distinctly out of proportion with its body, as if a child had drawn a beast to life. Its enormous claws, perfect for digging, kept clamping the bars of the cage like a human.

A banyan beast.

Bridget had faced a banyan beast before, and she had read up on them at the academy. They lived underground in the deserts of Sierra and were susceptible to arcane manipulation, allowing them to be used as slaves — or sicced against one's enemies.

The mass of people screamed as shrilly as the winds that battered the hull. The ship tilted to a steep enough bank that the top layer of sand trickled toward one side. Slaves and gargoyles and the caged monster responded by leaning against the tilt.

Sebastian kept shaking Bridget, crying, "Help us! Help us help us help us!" Others too, having seen what she could do, had surrounded her, calling for her aid.

I'm too tired, I can't, she wanted to say.

But it was that gaunt-faced Mud who managed to rouse her, for he leaned down—and slapped her face hard, hissing, "Get on up, you lazy wench, and do something useful."

The shock alone was enough to snap her into action. She wanted to throttle him, but instead she pressed a hand onto Sebastian's shoulder and allowed him to haul her up, careful to keep her ankle elevated above the sand, every muscle aching. Then she hopped about to face the cage. Of the slaves, half remained, a miracle all things considering. The rest, including the nightgowned woman, lay amidst mirko bodies, each bloody and stiff with death, some in pieces.

Voices clamored around her, everyone spouting a different opinion—even the villainous Porter gesticulated wildly at the beast, going on about how if she didn't do something, they would all die, for their clubs were useless against such a beast. That explained why he hadn't finished her off—he wanted to use her to save himself.

With her leg bleeding onto the sand and her muscles burning as if she'd run a thousand leagues, Bridget ignored them all and channeled Augum's ability to focus in battle. The gargoyle above the cage was staring at the captain, whose hand would rise at any moment, loosing the beast.

Bridget looked down at her foot. Seeing her own blood dribble to the sand made her feel like a human hourglass with precious little time left. She glanced over at Sebastian and saw a boy frantic to live, to have someone like her beside him to protect him, love him, cherish him like his sister and deceased mother had.

Her gaze returned to the huffing banyan beast—and her eyes narrowed. She knew what she had to do.

As the captain's arm rose, Bridget stilled her mind. She felt the throb of her ankle, the deep ache in every part of her body, the way her other foot had sunk into the sand, and how the boy supported her arm. She heard the growling roar of the gargoyles as they anticipated a final blood match. She felt and heard everything.

She then lowered her chin, whispering, "*Centeratoraye xao xen.*"

The ancient Leyan spell of Centarro, which she had learned what felt like forever ago, was a most unique spell, as it amplified focus *and* creativity. But it was also a deadly spell, as the caster fell into a foggy stupor after its effects had faded, becoming susceptible to happenstance.

Because of her collar, she felt the spell as a bare tingle, and the heavy clouds of common thought parted only slightly, nonetheless allowing a precious ray of focused sunshine through.

As the arm fell and the cage rose and the surrounding slaves screamed and began pushing and shoving to be the furthest away from the beast, leaving her and Sebastian at the very front of the group, Bridget tilted her head and considered the possibilities. The beast was particularly susceptible to arcane manipulation. Perhaps she could attempt *Communathabanalamistro*—the ancient name for the 7th degree off-the-books elemental spell Commune With Animals. It was a long shot with the suppression collar choking her arcanery, but she had to try.

As the banyan beast sprinted toward her with sand-shaking force, she heard everyone behind her running off, and even Sebastian fell back on his butt and scrambled backward along the sand like a crab. Bridget raised a hand, flat palm facing upward. Thoughts aligned, she calmly incanted, "*Ba nalma communa.*" Although significantly reduced, she felt the cool draw of stamina upon her soul.

The beast's vicious charge halted and it skidded along the sand, coming to a stop before her. She looked up at the looming mountain of muscle, placed a gentle hand upon its enormous furry knee, and said, "Banyan, I am your friend." The beast's reply was to flare its nostrils as it sniffed her head, reminding her of her dog Sabby doing the same, but to her hand.

Ever so gently, she raised her hand and pushed it into the monster's chest, whispering, "Speak to me."

Strange imagery appeared within her mind, although it was not so much imagery as physical sensations—and she realized it was because the beast possessed no eyes.

A cascade of impressions flooded her mind—the feeling of being ripped up from the earth by a giant hand, then tight bondage within a confined space. That space rocked in tandem with the motions of a ship. Feedings of goat and boar and human. Then the memory of being starved for a day, and now a raging hunger that would be satiated one way or another.

There was no way around it. The beast would feast and feast soon. Already she felt her grip on it untwining like an overstretched vine. Only one thing would save the group.

Still with her hand upon the beast's chest, she turned her head to look back at the other slaves, which had run all the way to the stands, where they were rebuffed by the crowd of hissing gargoyles that waved at them to run toward the beast and fight it with their clubs, which might as well have been twigs. Knowing she had to communicate in a way the beast understood, she passed on the only thing that separated one from the many.

Take the one who smells like the curved fruit, she thought at the creature, the back of her slightly Centarric mind racing to come up with the right scent as she recalled a certain man feasting on a banana he had stolen from a certain boy. *It is a sweet and fruity scent. Take him. He is delectable and we will give him freely without hurting you.*

The beast made a rumbling noise that seemed to come from its very stomach. The moment she took her hand away from its chest, it barreled over her, smashing her into the sand and accidentally stomping on her bad leg, causing her to howl.

Clutching her wounded ankle whilst writhing about in the sand, she looked up to witness her fellow slaves jumping aside as the beast sniffed its way through the throng. Some took to their knees in prayer, hoping the gods would spare them. Others had discarded their clubs and curled up into tight balls to make themselves appear less threatening.

The beast sniffed them all, allowing those who it bypassed to run away to the opposite side of the arena. At last, one man remained, hiding behind someone. When Bridget saw it was Sebastian, she tried to leap to her feet, only to fall upon accidentally using her wounded ankle. She sank to the sand, then sprang forth on hands and knees like a deranged animal, complete with snarling.

The banyan monster reared over the boy, whom Porter kept thrusting forth as a sacrifice, roaring, "Take him, demon!" The boy had frozen stiff, catatonic with fear, and merely stared glassy-eyed through the beast as if hoping it was not real. "Take him!" Porter kept shouting, beard quivering, sprinkling the sand with spit. "Take him already, damn you!"

Bridget scrambled and, despite knowing she was well out of range at an incredible fifty feet away, shot a hand out to violently and repeatedly yank at the boy. The boy did not break free or show any indication that her suppressed Telekinesis had touched him.

The beast's nostrils flared, opening and shutting as it smelled the boy. With its mighty arm, it reached forth, grabbed the boy, and flung him aside. The boy tumbled a few times before coming to a halt in a catatonic state.

Porter kept backing away as he frantically pointed at Bridget, shouting, "There she is! There's the wench that bewitched you! Get her! Get *her*, you monster!"

With her thoughts fogging up, Bridget scrambled forth until she got to the boy and pressed him to her chest, hiding his horror-stricken face.

Ahead, the banyan beast reared up, snatched the top of Porter's head with its monstrous clawed hand, lifted him, and as he screamed the shrill scream of the damned, silenced him in one ripping bite. Like a contented gorilla, the beast then plopped into a sitting position and feasted on the spot, and Bridget had to look away from the grisly sight.

The gargoyles howled and hooted and stomped their feet on their perches and saluted the arena with their drinking horns. With her thoughts fuzzing rapidly, a wounded and utterly exhausted Bridget fell back against the sand. She tilted her head up to see with upside-down vision that the captain had unfurled his wings, and he and his coterie took off.

But not before sending a lackey to walk toward her. Unable to recall his name, she only watched as the disfigured gargoyle with one eye came to fetch her. The last thing she remembered thinking was that she was hurting the boy with her clenched hold.

THE SPICE ISLANDS

LEERA

Muted by the cabin door came the distant shout, "Laaaand hoooooo!" The long-anticipated call rang throughout the ship, and sailors began to thunder through the hall as they scampered deckward, echoing the call as they ran. "Laaaaand hoooooo!"

Leera, studying the Zygothika book's tendril geometries with a splayed hand for the last hour, trying to make that key breakthrough that would allow her to open the cursed book, closed it and nuzzled up to Augum. She had snuck into his cabin last evening as it was unseemly for unmarried couples to bunk together, especially a pair of Arcaners expected to set an example.

She pressed her nose, ice-cold from the frosty cabin air, into his cheek. "Land ho, my love."

A snoozing Augum groaned, turned away from her, and dragged the triple layer of blankets over his head.

Leera followed him with her cold nose, this time pressing it into his neck. "Laaaaaand hoooo," she whisper-sang, and was amused to see Augum clumsily flap a sleep-addled hand at her face. Those fingers probed about until they squeezed her nose in a judging manner.

"Yes, my snog is freezing, and you should either get up or *warm* me up."

His response was to grab her arm, drag it around him, and scooch his butt back so they spooned. He began to snore in a gentle manner that reminded her of Sir Pawsalot, who would curl up around her head and purr-snore and wheeze his way through sleep.

The cabin door rattled with a triple bang. "Get up, lazy bones!" croaked Jezebel Terse from the other side. "Land ho, fool! I'm horribly hungover and even *I'm* up! And tell that fiend of yours to stop sneaking in at night. Everyone's painfully aware of your godless ways, so maybe try acting commander and captain for a change and behave yourselves. Nasty teenagers," she muttered as she trundled off.

"We're twenty!" Leera shouted, throwing their pillow at the door, not that it did any good. "I swear she's never going to let us grow up," Leera added as Augum pawed around for the pillow. "It's on the floor. And you shouldn't have trained so late with what's-his-face—" She snapped her fingers loudly at his ears, trying to jog her Zygothika-obsessed memory. "—that blond oaf. Not that one, the other one. Carter."

"Muuuuh," Augum moaned as he sat up and blearily smacked his lips, running a hand through his unruly mop of hair.

Leera, finding him utterly adorable, pecked his cheek. "Oh my gosh you look like you've been struck by a massive bolt of lightning," she cooed, brushing her nose back and forth against his cheek.

Augum looked over at her with puffy eyes. After blinking several times uncomprehendingly, he let his forehead rest against hers and closed his eyes. She felt more and more of his weight against her until she bumped against the cabin wall, and he melted into her arms.

She pushed back on the blanket he was trying to cover them with. "No, mister, no falling asleep. Duty awaits. Your charges need direction. The sheep need their shepherd."

"You're a captain too."

"Who is subordinate to the commander."

"Then I command you to let me sleep."

"Unlawful commands shall not be obeyed."

Augum groaningly sat back up with closed eyes. "Ugh, why did the gods saddle me with inferior wit ..."

She pressed his nose, enjoying seeing it crinkle. "So that mine may shine brighter, sleepyhead. Now move aside. I'm bailing from this stink hole of a cabin. Let's go see what these so-called Spice Islands look like, then begin our quest." She shoved him over. He fell back into the mess of blankets and clumsily gathered them around himself.

Leera pointed at her antique and frilly-cuffed crimson robe, which she had thrown onto the floor the night before, and zoomed it up to the cabin ceiling. She used both hands to angle it in such a way to open the bottom before letting it slip over her head and shoulders, then wiggled into it, adjusting the robe down her body. She grabbed the yellow rope belt from the floor next, then decided to cheekily flay Augum with it, singing, "Get up, get up, geeeet uuuuup!"

From within the mess of blankets, a hand flailed about, until Augum snatched the rope, which he used to drag her over. He shot up, planted a wet kiss on her lips, and shoved her away, throwing the rope back at her face.

"Your breath stinks," she said with a coy smile, tying the rope belt around her waist. "Brush your teeth."

"Yours too."

"And wash your face and comb that mop."

"Yes, Mom."

"Ew, gross." She raised a finger. "But point taken. No more nagging my grown-up man."

He grunted in agreement, then began looking about the cabin with a single half-open eye.

Leera, having put on her spectacles, pointed at a latched drawer. The latch unclicked, she drew her hand back, and the drawer slid open. She raised her other hand, and his neatly folded robe and rope belt floated out to him.

"How far did you get with him, anyway?" she asked.

Augum accepted his robe and belt, dumped them onto his lap, and rubbed his eyes with the heel of a hand. "We did some reflex training with balls of yarn in the infirmary before going on to do …" He winced. "… I think it was four cycles in total? Crew didn't much appreciate the noise, and kept—" He flippantly signed skywards. "… making prayers and stuff in the hall. One even threw salt under the infirmary door."

"Sailors are a superstitious lot," Leera replied, smoothing the creases out of her robe. "Can barely stomach us warlocks in their midst, let alone that giant talking furball. I bet you that they think the ship's doomed on account of having triple bad luck on board."

"Wait, what's the third bad luck?" Augum stuck out one finger and then another. "Wolven, warlocks, and …?" The hand opened invitingly.

Leera did a fanciful twirl and indicated herself.

"You mean *women*?"

Leera nodded. "There's three of us on board too, and three is the witch's number, so I think there's like a multiplication component. Bad luck factor of nine or something."

Augum snorted a laugh, then his face scrunched. "But Tammy's been on board for ages …"

"And she told me it took them forever to accept her as one of them — and some *still* think she brings bad luck."

"Wait, there's *four* women on board," Augum said, adding, "besides Tammy, that is."

Leera gaped at him blankly before blurting, "Mahmoute." She shrugged. "I guess no multiplying factor then. So did you do anything with Carter after cycles?"

"I gave him some lessons on leadership so he can better control his charges."

"Those two goons will only respect him as long as he's heir. The moment he isn't—" She threw a thumb over her shoulder whilst making a quick whistle. "—they'll dump him like refuse. Oh, and speaking of women, did you talk to him about how he treats our lot?"

Augum fiddled with the folded robe still in his lap. "A little. Told him he needed to respect you all if he ever wants to find a girl who respects him back. That is, if he ever wants to find true love."

"That's all?"

"Er ... I guess I'll keep working on it."

"Hope so. He's a total boor, and if you don't rein him in, you mark my words he's going to make every woman in his circle miserable, especially as king. By the way, did you check the you-know-what?" Multiple times a day they took turns checking the summonable Arcaner vault in case Bridget left a note. The only safe place to summon it was in their cabins.

"Before bed. Nothing."

"I checked it first thing this morn. Same result. Anyway, the island is supposedly civilized so you won't mind if I hop on ahead, right? I don't want to turn into an old lady waiting for you to get dressed and then comb your hair and brush your teeth and hit the privy and probably munch on breakfast like a sloth." She shook her head and *tut-tutted*. "Look at you moving as slow as a snail. Mister Molasses. And here I thought it's us women who took forever getting ready ..."

Augum blinked, unimpressed. "Thought you said no more nagging your man."

Leera opened her palms in surrender. "You got me." She gently slapped each cheek. "Bad Leera! Bad!"

He smiled and shooed both hands at the door. "Go on and abandon me then, why don't you."

"Thanks." She pecked his lips before throwing open the cabin door and zooming out, eager to lay eyes on these fabled and remote islands, the last bastion of their kingdom before the mysterious and open ocean.

Their quest was clear—learn how to traverse the ocean, but especially the part in the middle that was supposedly uncrossable. She wanted to aid that quest by meeting up with a fellow flipper—one of the playful terms the Order of the Coastal Guard used.

After washing up, Leera hurried to the deck to gaze out at the horizon. Sure enough, a low-lying group of islands waited dead ahead, their yellow beaches bright against the stormy darkness that loomed beyond. While the backdrop constantly lit up with tiny flashes of lightning, high above was the bright blush of dawn. In every other direction, the sky was a cloud-saturated gray.

The deck was a hive of activity, with sailors scampering about securing lines, heeding commands to ready cargo for trade, sweeping and washing the deck for inspection, and steadily taking curiously named sails down—fore royal, main moonsail, mizzen skysail, spanker, and countless others. She looked back to see that their sister ships were also taking down sails in preparation for docking. Much money was to be made selling precious cargo, with the raised money promised to be used to outfit the coming expedition.

Amongst the crew, the lanky sailblower, Tammy, caught Leera's eye. She was standing on the windward side of the ship, both arms raised as she manipulated the tempestuous winds. Leera went up to lean against the rail behind her and watch her work. That was when she caught Alanna Haught staring at her from across the deck. The vile temptress pretended to delve right back into conversation with her lecherous and snobby friends, the Bloomington-Southguards.

" 'Shades of manure,' " Leera muttered, echoing a sailor proverb she'd heard, staring at Alanna with narrowed eyes, daring her to look at her again. "I know what you're doing," she said under her breath. "You think I don't know? I *know*. Look at me again. I dare you. That's what I thought, you cowardly snot rag."

The presence of a shadow loomed behind the curtain of her mind. It wanted to throw that curtain open and roar itself forth. "Stop being the horse," she whispered, knowing she had to learn to neither be the horse nor the rider, but the watcher. Based on that lone lesson with Isobel, it seemed to be the only path forward. But then they still had hundreds of hours of learning ahead. The problem was time.

A voice cut through her thoughts. "Morning, Dragon Jones."

Leera, still glaring at Alanna, unspooled her folded arms—which she hadn't realized she had been holding so tightly—and turned her attention to the sailblower. "Morning, Tammy. I was just wondering if there's something I can help with. Whip the rudder about. Take in sail. Hoist a sail back up as a prank. Maybe splash a recalcitrant deckhand or two. That sort of thing."

Tammy chortled. "Er, I believe the captain has things well in hand."

Leera shrugged. "Just thought I'd make myself useful."

A sharp whistle sounded.

"Oi! Gather up!" called the bosun, a swarthy fellow with a perpetually tilted cap. "Captain's got a few words for y'all." He stepped aside to allow the captain to lumber forth, staring people down with his imposing gaze, a man used to being obeyed. He began a long speech about keeping in tight groups, watching each other's backs, and, above all, maintaining "operational security," which had something to do with people not speaking about having *the* dragons aboard. But he lost Leera the moment he began lecturing them on propriety, pointing out that their behavior reflected on the Solian Navy and thus the kingdom, and so on and so forth.

With her breath steaming in the frigid air, Leera stuffed her hands deep into the pockets of her robe and swung impatiently on her heels. She considered checking in with her coastal order contact, but thought she'd surprise him instead. Besides, talking over the ring to a stranger just felt weird.

As the captain droned on, she kept her gaze on the approaching main island, the largest of a chain known as the Spice Islands. The port bustled with activity, for a line of square-riggers and cutters and whalers sat broadside to the docks, some accepting cargo, some offloading, others undergoing repair or maintenance. Gawkers were already assembling, probably local denizens curious about the approaching trio of ships.

Beyond the docks stood a small trading town, its buildings painted cheerful colors like emerald green and glacial turquoise and cherry red and sunset orange and banana yellow. The land itself was composed of wind-scarred rock and dotted with hardy shrubs and trees that from a distance looked suspiciously like palms.

What she looked forward to the most was not so much the exploration, but the anonymity. Back home, everyone seemed to know who she was, for her face was painted on posters and scrolls and flags and walls and in the heralds, and these days, even woodblock-printed on napkins. The saviors of the kingdom and all that.

As some sailors hopped up onto the guardrails, ropes in hand for the dock workers to catch them, Leera became cognizant that the voice of the weaselly Lord High Commander had taken over the lecture.

"For security reasons, the following names are expressly *forbidden* to depart the vessel." And then the bastard went on to list every single Arcaner.

Leera was not at all surprised. This time, however, she only nodded to herself and, after taking one last but careful look at the coastline, slipped down below—rudely before the meeting's end. The moment she stepped into her cabin, she visualized the exact formation of rocks south of the docks and incanted, "*Impetus peragro.*"

With a deep *thwomp*, she appeared on the rocky coastline, where she looked to the ships—and flipped them a rude gesture. Scoffing disdainfully at the so-called Lord High Commander—an Ordinary, no less, who had no right restricting their movements—she tossed up her hood to ward off the stiff wind, only to realize it would look suspicious upon stepping foot into town, and so left it down.

The ground was rocky, with patches of dry yellow grass. Boulders and dried-out thorn bushes littered the land alongside palms with needle leaves.

Leera took a step but, used to the rhythms of the ship, promptly tripped over her own feet. "Whoa, whoa, whoa, girl, take your time. Balance is off after being at sea so long." She wiggled her shoulders and hips and did a little dance to shake off the vertigo. "That's a little better."

She started to hum happily and was about to continue to the town when a pair of *thwomps* sounded behind her. She whirled about to see Olaf and Jengo, only the latter of whom was grinning, for little cheered poor Olaf up these days—and understandably so.

"Aug told us to keep you company while he argued his way out of the restriction," Jengo said as the pair walked over.

"You mean watch over me."

Jengo shrugged. "He's looking out for you."

"He was expecting it," Olaf added, looking to the ships. "Mentioned it last night that they might restrict us to the ships. Even said you'd 'port off anyway and that if you did, to follow you."

"Bah, I'm a—"

"—woman grown, we know, we know."

"I also happen to be an—"

"—Arcaner Dragon, yes, yes," Jengo threw in, wincing as if worrying he had overstepped.

Leera wagged a finger between the two of them, aiming to say something caustic, then dropped it. "Fine, you can be my goons, but try to keep up. I'm not dallying about."

They set off toward the town, with both Olaf and Jengo commenting how their bodies felt weird on stable ground and Leera telling them they still had their sea legs on. They then bantered how it was good to be off ship for a change before taking notice of the town. The folk here seemed to come from all over—there was the loose garb of the Tiberrans and Sierrans, the curved blades on hips that denoted Nodians, the colorful flower-embroidered robes of the Ohmish, the stiff upper jaw and high chin known to the Canterrans, the zanka-chewing habit of the Abrandians, and so on. All races and creeds appeared to mingle, but there were almost no warlocks among them. The lone visible one who wore a blue robe staggered about as if drunk, and his long beard was so thoroughly tangled that Leera wondered if the man was a common sailor who had stolen the robe.

Being that the three newcomers wore warlock robes themselves, the townsfolk noticed their approach. As they walked past a decrepit building used for fish storage, with men and women hauling in that morning's catch on their shoulders, eyes turned to them. Children swarmed in, trailing them as they walked.

"Begth uth a coin?" one boy asked, which Leera translated as "Begs us a coin?" The boy was missing his front row of teeth, making him speak with a lisp.

"Wanna buy a turnip? Only one castle!" said another. "How about a rock nut? Sweet nut? Coconut?"

"Sorry, little ones, but we don't have any money," Olaf replied.

"Then make the magic!"

The loudest child, a sun-bronzed little girl with raven hair, shouted, "Yes! Make us the magic! Magic, magic, magic!" She tugged at Leera's robe—and at her heartstrings.

"Want to see some arcanery, do you?" Leera sang.

"What's *arkwanewy*?" the girl mumbled.

"Another word for sorcery."

"What's *sowsewy*?"

"The word for *real* magic. Not cuppers—" Leera raised her hands and moved them over each other. "But the real thing, which we call arcanery."

"Oooooohhhhh."

"Is one of you a healer?" squeaked a little girl with brown skin, one eye puffy and red. "Can you fix me?" Her cuff rose, and from it poked the stub of what had once been a hand.

Jengo halted in his tracks, which in turn made Olaf and Leera do the same. Jengo knelt before the girl. "I'm sorry, my dear, but no healer can regrow a hand." As the girl wilted, Jengo lifted her chin with two fingers. "But I *can* heal that eye." He glanced up at Leera and Olaf. "Likely an infection of the cornea and the aqueous humor of the anterior chamber. Can you spare a few heartbeats?"

"Of course we can," Olaf blurted before Leera could speak.

"What do you take me for?" Leera snapped at him. "You think I'm in *that* much of a hurry? By gods, heal the poor girl!" She whapped Olaf's meaty shoulder with the back of a hand. "Can't wait to find Bridget again so I can complain about you to her," she muttered.

"You find her and you have my leave to complain all you want," Olaf replied. "As long as you find her."

Jengo bid the girl to sit before him. "I have to examine your eye a moment, little one, so just sit tight." He opened his hands before her face, a gesture that made some children jump away and others step near. "*Examino potente morbus aurus persona.* Yes, I was correct, a corruption of the cornea, the aqueous humor of the anterior chamber, with an additional minor inflammation of the iris."

In the mean, Leera smacked a small hand away that had wandered into one of her pockets. "Told you I got nothing," she hissed at a teenage girl, who scuttled off as if bitten.

"Now on to the good stuff," Jengo went on. "Hold still, please. *Remedia rexo excella vindiv infecta poisa venoma extracta.*"

Leera half paid attention to eye healing and half to the ever-growing throng, some of whom acted too suspiciously for her liking, oft looking away when she glanced at them or changing direction or turning their back, hoping not to be noticed.

"There, all better," Jengo declared, standing. When the other children leaned in, they shouted out from joy and surprise and wonder, and some sprinted off to scream, "He healed her! He healed her and it's a miracle and healers are as real as real is!"

This had a reaction Leera did not expect—adults dropped their baskets and fish and whatever they were carrying to sprint to them. Leera quickly found all manner of folk—young and old and stubby and tall and disfigured and perfectly healthy looking—pawing at her.

"I'm not a healer!" she protested, thankful she had nothing in her pockets, which were being rifled through as if they held luxuries beyond imagining.

Olaf was under the same onslaught, until the children pointed at Jengo, causing people to push Leera and Olaf out of the throng. Jengo, for his part, took it all in stride, holding up a single palm as if waiting for everyone to calm down. When they did not cease their bleating for his attention, he waved that hand back and forth, slicing at the air with the side of his palm.

"Form a line that way!" he shouted. "I will see to you all and do what I can!" He looked to Leera, his head floating above the crowd. "You two go on ahead without me. I've got a lot of *proata mentora* to catch up on, anyway. Go on. I'll be all right. You'd be surprised how often this happens in the city too."

"Braver than I am," Leera muttered, elbowing Olaf. "Let's leave the poor sap to it."

They walked off, each glancing back to see what looked like half the town had swarmed in on poor Jengo. Yet Jengo was smiling, treating every person with compassion, particularly the children, to whom he gave priority.

"He's a good soul," Olaf said.

"And has way more patience than I do," Leera replied, throwing in, "I'd have made a terrible healer." She snorted. "Actually, I'd have hit my ceiling at the 1st degree." She knocked on the side of her head, adopting a dockside accent. "Don't have them smarts for all the memorizin' that element needs."

"You and me both," Olaf muttered, adding, "barely got enough to survive class as is."

The town had a single uneven cobbled road running through its heart, which hosted its major markets and attractions. The colorful homes pitched up three stories and overhung the street, and every single one had a shop at its base. Beyond stood smaller homes and shacks amidst tight alleys and winding backstreets.

Leera and Olaf stepped to the center of this bustling street, whereupon Leera glanced toward the docks to see that the *Rose of the Sea*'s gangplanks had been deployed, and the crew was offloading cargo. There was no sign yet that anyone had departed the ship.

"Looks like we can take our time window gazing."

"Crowd should keep us hidden," Olaf added.

It was surprisingly busy for such a small town, likely because the majority filling the streets were sailors with bunks on their ships. Despite a salty wind that made signs creak and rustled hair and clothing, the air smelled heavily of tar and rope and stone and fresh fish and roasted fish and all sorts of oils, mostly fish or whale.

Most shops had something to do with the shipping trade, and many stuck to the traditions of alliteration—The Bearded Bait & Tackle, Eckhart's Engraving, Aaron's Apothecary, Nella's Pilots & Navigators, Father & Sons Rope Weavers, Mother & Daughters Chandlers, and so on. Other shops were simply named—Shipwright, Pickler, Cobbler, Cooper, Blacksmith, Leatherworker, Tinkerer, Carpenter, Craftswoman, Sailmaker, Wheeler, Scribe, and countless others. Some shops exclusively sold fish or crabs or lobsters or other specific sea creatures.

There was also an overabundance of seedy-looking taverns already filled with raucous sailors. The Jaded Harpoon, The Rusty Anchor, The Pelican and the Whale, The Tilting Deck, and so on. One tavern, The

Singing Sailor, was living up to its name, for a dozen sailors were belting out, "*An' it reared up into the sky rumblin' like thunder, ready to fall and smash the ship asunder,*" a line from the ironically titled sea shanty *Leviathan's Lullaby*, which Leera had heard so many times on the voyage over that she absently hummed along.

Singing minstrels and fruit sellers and trinket hawkers and concoction dabblers and pie makers and countless other food vendors accosted them. Street criers shouted out the best deals, old news from the mainland, and fresh news from the seas. Throughout, people gawked at them from all sides, for other than sailblowers and fish freezers and fire makers, who were often of low degree, warlocks were a relatively rare sight on the known edge of the kingdoms.

The most colorful shop was The Spice Emporium, which was twice as wide as other shops, with four bleacher-style shelves that held containers brimming with spices: saffron and sage and cinnamon and thyme and ginger and nutmeg and pepper and salt in all colors of the rainbow, each neatly stoppered with a cork and sealed with fancy wax. It was one of the busier places, and so Leera and Olaf allowed themselves to drift along with the river of the crowd.

As a gigantic hanging flank of fish steak caught Olaf's attention, Leera's was caught by a dignified older woman carefully weaving fine lace undergarments. She sat in a rocking chair behind a raised window for all to see, and was working on a frilly shirt with lacing that glittered in the street torchlight. Passing sailors whistled appreciatively at the straw mannequins behind her that showcased her work, which looked frightfully expensive.

Like a moth drawn to flame, Leera gently pushed her way to the window and imagined wearing that shirt and matching undergarments and sashaying into Augum's room with a devilish grin. She absently patted her pockets and rope belt, searching for her coin purse, only to remember she'd left it back in her cabin as she'd heard there were plenty of pickpockets in town.

"Should have thought things through before jumping ship so quickly," she muttered, forcing herself to turn away just as the old lady looked up to smile. If anything, she could have hidden the purse in her undergarments. It's just that she'd been expecting the usual hodgepodge of stinky ship-oriented businesses and not such a delightfully interesting town.

"Hear ye, hear ye!" a nearby teenage crier called out, waving a fistful of rolled-up heralds. "The mysterious winged beasts known as gorgles have fled over the ocean! Will anyone pursue? Will they return? In

further news, King Darby Sepherin of Canterra agrees with our Solian King Rupert Southguard to a knowledge trade of spells once thought lost to the kingdoms! Only three castles for the scroll!"

"It's *gargoyles* not *gorgles*," Leera corrected after approaching the scrawny teenage crier, cutting him off midway through repeating the headline.

"Huh?" he held a tied bundle of scrolls under his arm that constantly threatened to tip him over.

"*Gargoyles* not *gorgles*. Never mind," she muttered when he gaped at her blankly. "Which spells did the kings trade, anyway?"

The crier proudly raised his chin. "That information will cost ya three castles, miss."

Leera turned her pockets inside out. "Please?"

"Gots to make me livin', sorry. But you're a pretty lass if you don't mind me saying so. In a wild sort of way." He looked to her ring finger. "Your husband is a lucky man."

"Husband-to-be," Leera replied.

"Oh." As the boy's caterpillar eyebrows worked this way and that on how to continue the conversation, Leera spied a tear along the side his trousers, held together with strands of frayed rope tied around his leg. "How's about a barter?" she said, and nodded at the pants. "I repair that tear for one scroll."

The boy's eyes enlarged before narrowing. "That's too good a bargain. What foul witch thing do you also want in turn? Ain't one of them brewing types of witches who wants ter make a potion out of me, is you?"

"I don't want a thing, and no I don't want to …" Leera flipped a hand at him, trying to keep a straight face. "… brew you into a potion or whatever."

"Not one of those soul-suckin' types then?"

Leera sighed. "Just the scroll in barter, please and thanks. News is hard to come by on the water." She thumbed toward the docks. "Left my purse on the ship and don't want to be bothered to fetch it."

The boy glanced over her shoulder. "All right, but you swear on your life and soul no shenanigans or jinxes with that there magic of yours? No blood or brain or soul stealin'? No turnin' me into the undead to haunt my family forever and ever?"

Leera pressed her tongue against a cheek. "Well, I *was* secretly thinking of slipping your juicy brain into a delicious witchy concoction, but now that you said you don't want that, I *guess* I could restrain myself."

But she'd said it jestingly, and he relaxed. Still, Leera muttered, "You'd think someone who sells news about warlocks would know a *little* more about us. Now hold still." She spread her hands over the tear, focused, and incanted, "*Apreyo.*" Thread by thread, the tear closed and sealed with a white light.

As a few people who noticed what she'd done gave her dirty looks and signed skyward, Leera dusted her hands. "There you go."

The boy glanced down. "Gods, that's absolutely brilliant!" He promptly handed her a herald scroll. "Thank you so very much, miss. So *very* much indeed as I reckon I've never had anyone—" He halted abruptly, and those caterpillar eyebrows scrunched together as he got to studying her face. "Say ..."

Here it comes, Leera thought.

"... have I seen you somewhere? You look *awful* familiar ..."

"Meh, I get that a lot." *Probably from the very heralds you're hawking*, Leera thought, and flipped him a whimsical two-fingered thanks before walking over to Olaf, who was drooling as he watched a pastry maker sprinkle powdered sugar over dough.

"Huh, look at this, Ollie," she said, reading through the unfurled scroll as people bustled by. "The king made a deal with the Canterrans to trade Shrink for Decoy."

The 12th degree Shrink was a standard spell the trio had unearthed in the war. Their adversaries, on the other hand, had learned the 12th degree Decoy. The core rudiments that made both spells workable solutions in the field, rudiments once presumed lost to time, had been rediscovered. Now that the former enemy kingdoms were on trade terms, it seemed progress was being made. Despite the trio's—and their former mentor Anna Atticus Stone's—wish otherwise, Shrink had been declared a state secret, one only to be shared with close allies. To keep the peace with royalty—and other senior warlocks at the academy who agreed with the king on the subject of restriction—the trio went along with the statecraft, for they wanted to establish the budding Arcaner order on stable political ground.

"Maybe we could learn Decoy when we get back," she threw in, imagining making a second copy of herself in dragon form. "The chaos that could cause ... hey, you listening, Ollie?"

Olaf's response was to pinch her robe and drag her over to him. "Look at this," he whispered, licking his lips, eyes entranced.

Leera looked over. The vendor wrapped slices of candied salmon in pastry, dipped the wrap into oil, where it sizzled and let off a mouth-watering scent, then dipped the wrap into powdered sugar before

placing it onto a square of rice paper. The vendor, who had bulging red cheeks, had a steady stream of eyes gawking at the fare, and there was no shortage of hands offering five copper castles for the treat.

"I need to get my money pouch right now or I am going to die," Olaf declared.

"You go back and they won't let you off again," a refined voice interrupted.

Upon hearing it, Leera's blood flashed-boiled, and she whirled to face the woman who was constantly trying to steal Augum's attention. Alanna Haught stood with highborn poise, fingers pressed together in a professorial *A*. Her platinum-blond hair elegantly framed her swan face, which naturally drew the male gaze.

"Surprised you're not running off to tattletale on us, you brat," Leera snapped.

Alanna withdrew a ruby-and-pearl-encrusted coin purse from within her robe. "I owe you an apology. Sir, how much for three of those?" she daintily asked the vendor, who cut someone off to reply, "Fifteen castles, fair miss."

"I don't want your stinking charity," Leera snapped, and she was about to slap the coin purse to the ground when Olaf shoved her aside, wheezing, "Don't listen to her we definitely *do* accept charity let's just call it *proata mentora* or something oh my gosh this is such crazy luck that you arrived in the nick of time you're amazing as my stomach is a squealing beast that would kill me if I passed on this golden opportunity." His hands opened and closed toward the pastries as he cooed, "Gimme, gimme, gimme …"

With the crowd thick, Leera was forced to watch as Alanna paid for three pastries, handing Olaf one.

"Oh, sweet merciful gods, this looks absolutely sumptuous …" He took one nibble, and his eyes rolled into the back of his head as he crooned, "Mmm, mmm, *mmm!*"

Leera couldn't help but salivate. Her taste buds pleaded for her to relent to the sugary crisp she could hear with every small bite, the morsels delectable to the eye and tongue and stomach and —

"Oh for the love of gods give me that," she snapped, telekinetically snatching the pastry from Alanna's offered hand. "Gods I hate your guts and I wish you'd have stayed behind in the city where you belong with your powder-faced ghoul friends kissing your—Unnameables help me why is this so good?" The very first bite almost made her go weak at the knees, and she even glanced about for a place to sit down and fully enjoy such a treat.

Alanna, who had yet to take a bite of her own pastry, held it before her as if thinking it would be a sin to so much as taste its sugary goodness. "As I was saying earlier, I owe you an apology for my behavior with your betrothed. I will never have him, and I will cease trying." She bowed her head. "Forgive me."

Leera, who'd already finished stuffing her pastry into her mouth, crumbs tumbling all down her robe, wanted to smack the bowed blonde before her. Instead she snatched Alanna's pastry and eyed her distrustfully as she took small nibbles to savor this one.

Alanna straightened, hands returning together in an elegant manner that annoyed Leera. That annoyance only rose when Alanna's ridiculously blue eyes did not covet the sweetness of the pastry. She wanted to roar into her face that she ought to be normal and succumb to the pleasure of the pastry as she could well afford another treat what with being so damn thin and all so why in hell *wouldn't* she try one? Was it to show how strong her will was beyond Leera's? Gods how the dilettante infuriated her so much that she wanted to clench her fists and roar in childish frustration—

Leera cleared her throat and forced herself to behave. It would not do to debase herself into a *total* barbarian. She waved the pastry about as she ate with bulging cheeks, not bothering to place a hand before her mouth as was expected of a civilized woman. Suspecting what had happened, her head bounced up and down along with the pastry. "He rejected you, didn't he?"

Alanna straightened and smoothed her finely embroidered amber robe. "I ... I overstepped and deserve your hand to my cheek. Thus I offer it." She indeed offered her cheek, but closed her eyes and winced in anticipation of a decking.

Leera halted her chewing as she became more than tempted, her hand even balling into a mean fist. She allowed herself to imagine the doll-like hair whipping about as the girl gasped from the indignity of a right proper *smack*.

Instead she sighed and turned to the vendor. "Another, please, sir."

"Right away, young miss."

As Alanna gaped with a look of confused revulsion, surely thinking Leera was about to scarf down a third pastry, a look Leera found most amusing, Leera snatched Alanna's coin purse. She dug out five copper castles, mildly relieved they were the old coins with the sovereign's head on the face instead of the dragon, and threw the purse back at Alanna, who flinched upon catching it.

"Stupid lordlings and their stupid lordling games …" Leera kept muttering under her breath as she accepted the pastry and offered it to Alanna. "Oh, for the love of gods, here," Leera had to say, grabbing Alanna's hand and jamming the pastry into it, squishing its soft exterior into a mush.

Leera felt Olaf's face loom over her shoulder. "Say, uh, is there any more of that charity for those of us of a more … rotund nature?"

Normally Leera would have said something snarky, but instead she looked to Alanna and raised an expectant eyebrow. *Want to make amends?* she thought. *Start with my friends.*

Alanna animated to life. "Oh, uh … of course, uh … how many were you—"

"Four," Olaf blurted. "Four would suffice nicely for this here belly. Er, three maybe? All right I'll settle for two. Yes, two would sure go a long way into making good graces. Erm … please and thank you, Miss Alanna, er, Miss Haught … whatever."

Alanna looked to the puffy-cheeked vendor, who was keeping a sharp eye on her. "Three more, please, sir."

The vendor grinned knowingly and began on her order.

"I saw you staring at those nice garments," Alanna said as they waited.

Leera felt her face go beet-red. "Shut up I don't know what you're talking about I wasn't staring I was merely passing by and glancing over like a normal person would as the woman works behind glass on a rocking chair weaving stuff which you have to admit is a bit unusual and even interesting—" Leera barely took a breath. "—why, are you thinking of buying that for me too because I might just consider it wait no forget it I don't know what I'm saying here gods how you *infuriate* me will you just go away or something why are you even here?"

Alanna pressed a hand over her mouth to cover the snicker that had escaped. She slipped her pastry under that hand and took a dainty nibble.

That dainty nibble made Leera want to drag the stupid predator by the ear from behind her mental curtain and toss it at the cursed woman. And yet Alanna's seeming earnestness wilted Leera's anger, and so she refrained, knowing it would be unwise to rouse its passions anyhow. Yet even thinking about it made a shadow pass over her soul, mimicking the cloud shadow that in that moment passed over the city, bringing with it a cold and stiff wind that made all bundle up that much more.

"Would you just eat the damn thing already!" Leera snapped. "No one cares about your fancy dignity here."

To her surprise, Alanna lowered her hand and seemed to delight in daring to take a slightly larger bite.

The vendor handed over the pastries to a salivating Olaf, who crammed the first pastry into his mouth as the women watched. Munching with bulging cheeks as large as the vendor's, Olaf waved one of the pastries before Leera's face.

Leera scrubbed the air with a hand. "I really shouldn't as I've already had two and they're really quite sugary and—" but Leera somehow found herself not only clutching the offered pastry but chewing on it as she spoke. "—and surely it can't be good to have this much sweetness I don't want to get sick later—*merciful gods,* these are ridiculously good, one might even go so far as to say *unfairly* good, right? Why can't they make stuff like this in Blackhaven, anyway?"

"With all due respect, miss," the vendor threw in, "'cause no city dweller ever has time to learn the full art of the sweet tongue. Too busy being busy, I reckon."

"Do you take apprentices?" Olaf blurted. "I jest, I jest," he told Leera when she whapped his shoulder with the back of a hand. "Or do I ...?" He nodded firmly at himself. "Yes, of *course* I jest."

As they ate in silence, Leera felt a tap on her shoulder and a meek voice say, "'Scuse me." She turned to see a young woman with scraggly blond hair, rough homespun woolens—and a pregnant belly. The young woman kept her eyes on the ground as her hands fiddled below her protuberant belly. "Begging your pardon, m'ladies and good sir, but would you have some spare coin for a woman whose rotten man had abandoned her for the greener pastures of a younger lass?"

Leera gaped at the belly, acutely feeling her failure to crack the ancient *kargeyasnara* puzzle locking the Zygothika book's potential womb-healing knowledge.

"I have coin for thee," Alanna said gracefully. The moment she pressed a spine into the girl's eager hand, a rush of new hands appeared, and in heartbeats people were clamoring for her charity. Alanna yelped and retreated, clutching her purse high and close, but the swarm followed.

Leera, watching all this unfold, cupped a hand around her mouth after taking another bite and, with mouth full, shouted after her, "Guess we'll see you on the ship! And don't mention that you saw us! What a tart," she said to Olaf, who shrugged before realizing Leera was staring at him and promptly correcting himself with, "Yes, an absolute tart who can't keep from playing stupid games and who ... ugh, gods, can we go back to the ship to fetch our pouches? I think I need another one. I mean I don't *need* need another one, but I suppose I could use one. Okay, fine, I *want* one, all right? Happy now?"

Leera's reply was to snort. Her eyes followed Alanna's hasty retreat. She had to—albeit very grudgingly—admit that the woman had done right. She had taken her shot at her man, realized how futile it was, and tried to make amends. That was far more than most women would have done.

But she didn't want to let Alanna occupy too much of her thoughts, for she was still right jealous of how damn pretty and perfect in every way the girl was, and she still hated her for trying to steal her man in the first place.

Having finished pressing the tail end of her third pastry onto her tongue, Leera whirled about and whapped Olaf once more. "Onward with the quest, dragoon." They had a coastal guardian to see.

"Onward with the quest," a still-chewing Olaf echoed. "Gods how I can't wait to introduce these to Bridget. She's going to squeal with delight …"

DARING WORDS

AUGUM

"You will obey this edict of ship confinement as you would obey the king himself, for I stand in his stead," Lord High Commander Strout explained whilst picking at a nail, not deigning to so much as glance at Augum.

The pair stood in his office, located by the captain's quarters at the rear of the ship, a finely carved campaign desk between them.

"You may be a kingdom hero, but on this ship, you are a passenger like anyone else. Remember that you are only twenty years old and barely in charge of a lowly order of younglings playing as warlock knights. I may be a mere Ordinary, but were it not for the fact that you can summon the dragon, you would hardly have convinced the king to approve this foolhardy venture."

The man deigned to look up, sticking one hand in a pocket of an ostentatious gold-buttoned uniform pinned with an overabundance of medals and honors that looked like they'd been purchased from a fair. "Our kidnapped people are likely long deceased. The sooner you accept that fact, Stone, the sooner we can return home."

Augum's lip curled. Of all the insults, hearing this mustachioed turkey call him by his surname rankled him the most. Still, Augum represented an honorable order and had to comport himself accordingly. "Sir, if I may—"

"You may *not*, young man, for I am not finished." He went to stand before a gilded oval mirror to fiddle with the already perfect part in his brown hair, pale gaze regularly flicking to Augum through the reflection. "You've pulled the wool over my predecessor's eyes and blown smoke up everyone's robes, but you will never fool me. I know you long for the skies and you wish to wreak havoc on everyone who has crossed you. It's in your eyes, young man, and I can read eyes better than most. I am the Lord High Commander and you will do as I say, for *I* am in charge of this here fleet. Not the captain, not the other captains, but me." He turned to glare at Augum with an overly fierce expression, as if trying too hard. "*Me*."

Augum stared at him, his anger catching the attention of a certain shadow that salivated at the idea of goading the man on. *Do not be the horse*, he thought, knowing the shadow wanted to take him for a ride to serve its own ends. Until he learned how to suppress—perhaps even vanquish—The Callousness of the Predator, he needed to refuse its constant incitement.

"I see you have tamed your ..." The Lord High Commander strolled over to press the fingers of one hand into the campaign desk as he awkwardly tried to present a fearless countenance, only to change his mind and instead fold his arms. "... inner child. That's a start, I suppose. Now you leave the island quest to me." He had to unfold his arms on account of all the silly awards on his chest, which clinked and bent and got in the way. "If there is a solution forward through the storm wall, my men will find it, that I assure you of. Dismissed, soldier."

Augum eyed the ribbons and medals and pins, finding them suspicious. How many of them were fake? How much of what the man had claimed about his so-called past was a fabrication? What else was he hiding?

The man seemingly did not appreciate Augum gazing at his accolades and so pulled the bottom of his uniform and gave it a double tug, raising a weak chin that hardly suited his chiseled face. "I said dis*missed*, soldier." He jiggled a hand at the door. "That means get out."

Augum pressed three fingers over his heart in the Arcaner salute, a salute that was lamely—and rather sarcastically—returned by the Lord High Commander, who added an effete mock to it with a wiggle of his thin mustache.

Augum turned about and strode out of the cabin. The moment the door closed behind him, he gently knocked on the cabin opposite. When no one answered, he quietly opened the door and slipped inside, glad to find it empty. There he waited until he heard the distinct squeal of the Lord High Commander's door as he exited. After waiting a little longer for the sound of his boots to fade and checking that the coast was clear, he slipped back out and into the commander's cabin. From there he went right to his desk and began searching through the parchments, but there were so many that the task quickly became overwhelming—and who knew when the man would return.

"I know you're hiding something," Augum muttered. He splayed a hand and, focusing on what was hidden nearby, incanted, "*Un vun deo.*" The 1st degree Unconceal, a favorite of adventurers and the incurably curious, allowed him to look for and trace the intent to conceal, imprinted in the arcane ether.

Sure enough, a slew of tendril tugs pulled at his soul, but only three were pronounced and fresh and close by. It was those three that he followed. The first led him to a hidden half-finished bottle of Nodian fire whisky tucked in behind a trunk, which he left as found. The second was a book of accounts hidden under a drawer in the desk. The list of expenses included all sorts of fine liquors, visits to bawdy houses, gambling losses, and various other shady expenses—it seemed the man felt a need to catalogue every spine and castle. But it was one expense in particular that made Augum snort a laugh that he promptly suppressed.

"I'll be damned, you really *did* buy those cheap awards at a fair ..." he whispered with a scandalized grin, carefully sliding the book of accounts back under the drawer. He suspected that if push came to shove, he could always dig the account book up and see if there was anything actually illegal in there. But that was an option of last resort that would hopefully be unnecessary as there was too much at stake.

He had to relight the spell in order to trace the last tendril trail, which led him to a bookcase. His hand trawled over the books until it centered over a compendium series titled *A Detailed Accounting of Ledgers of the Ancient Imperial Solian Fleet.*

"The most boring title in all of existence for a reason," Augum muttered, and was about to reach for the books when he realized they could be alarmed. He thus switched focus, incanting, "*Un vun asperio aurum enchantus.*" Reveal made visible a panoply of Object Alarm tendrils stuck to the spines of the books. The tendrils were tightly woven, indicating an expert casting, likely by either Mahmoute or that other Black Eagle.

Too curious to leave them be, Augum changed focus to whisper, "*Exotus mia enchantus duo dai ideum exat,*" the incantation to Disenchant which allowed one to grab hold of tendrils. He caught the end tendril bit and plucked it with his fingernails, but because the casting was advanced, he had to hook it under and through several tendril loops before it began to unwind. The effort took an anxious amount of time, and more than once he worried that he might have accidentally triggered the spell.

At one point he stiffened as he heard boots in the corridor and readied Teleport on his lips. But the boots passed by the door, and Augum proceeded to fully undo the enchantment until it fell apart, vanishing back into the ether from whence it had been wound. He then took a deep breath, pinched the end of the line of books where there was a smudged area from overuse, and pulled. The spines all swung out as one panel, revealing a hidden compartment—and a strongbox requiring a key.

"Shoot," he muttered. Defeated by a simple locking mechanism. There was only one place the key would be found—on the Lord High Commander's person. Augum closed the panel and withdrew from the room, quietly closing the door behind him—and just about ran into Rogor. The towering wolven, whose head and back were bent low and yet still pressed against the ceiling, grimaced.

"Your commander thinks I would cause a mass panic among the islanders. I have a good mind to jump off the ship and roar, as my feet— and my stomach—long for stable ground."

Augum refrained from patting the fierce wolven on the shoulder as he would Olaf. "You and me both, friend. But we have been confined to the ship, and so within the ship we shall remain."

"Until we are useful. But you would be a fool to think they wish to cross the oceans in search of a few thousand souls. Your silver tongue may have convinced your king to allow this quest, but these so-called captains fear the crossing more than they fear you. This I can see in their weasel lowlander eyes. Now my ill stomach demands rest. Curse this ship and you lowlander fools," and Rogor pushed past Augum to find his cabin, which Augum heard had been extended into the neighboring cabin to accommodate his great size.

Knowing the two Black Eagles were keeping watch on deck, Augum went in search of the Lord High Commander, and heard him in the first place he went to—the captain's quarters, within which a quiet discussion was taking place. The only challenge remaining was how to get inside …

Ah, but the captain has a steward, Augum realized, and thus a plan formed. He would wait for that steward to come, then slip through under the guise of a certain spell. He ran a hand over his body, whispering, "*Armari obscura chameleano traversa*," the incantation to the 8th degree Chameleon spell, with the added travel extension he'd learned some years back that allowed for movement without snuffing the spell—as long as that movement wasn't too sudden.

Luck was on his side, for there came a distinctive bell sound from within, indicating the captain had tugged a bellpull to summon his servant. The young buttoned-up steward soon arrived carrying an empty silver platter. Augum, pressed up against the opposite wall, stiffened upon the steward knocking on the door.

"Come in," the captain barked, and the steward opened the door. Careful to be slow but efficient, Augum slipped in right behind—and had to put a hand to the door, closing it a bit slower than usual. This the steward noted with a casual glance backward, but the captain quickly snatched his attention.

"Fresh bottle of wine, son."

"Of course, Captain."

"Er, I prefer whisky, Captain."

"And a bottle of whisky for the Lord High Commander. Bring that Canterran swill."

"Right away, Captain." The steward excused himself with a curt bow and departed, leaving Augum to lower himself to all fours and prowl forth like a cat stalking up to its prey. Except this prey was unaware of his presence and continued casually conversing.

"As I was saying, Captain, the little witch hopped off the ship before I even finished speaking. The young fools are quite predictable."

"Then she'll deserve banishment to the brig, won't she?"

"She's been a thorn in my side since the beginning. The mouthing off, the snide remarks, that cursed slouch—she has no respect for authority, and that includes your authority, Captain. If she were my daughter, she'd feel the back of my hand upon her cheek on the daily."

"I was never one for malcontents myself, Lord High Commander."

As they yapped on about Leera's unruliness, Augum ever so slowly reached into the Lord High Commander's left pocket. Finding it empty, he went around to the right, and his hand closed over a single key—just as there came another knock on the door.

"Bring it on in already, boy!" the captain shouted.

The steward opened the door and carried in a bottle of wine, a bottle of Canterran whisky, and two crystal-cut tumblers. As the servant poured the drinks and a chameleonic Augum slithered through the door, he heard the Lord High Commander raise a toast.

"To the riches of the Spice Islands."

"May our trade bring us great fortune," the captain replied.

Augum suspected he knew what he would find. Even so, he returned to the Lord High Commander's office and reopened the hidden panel of book spines. The key turned with a soft *click*. Inside the strongbox, a single document made itself available to his nimble fingers.

"Cursed bastards," Augum said as he read the contents of the page, sealed with a giant royal wax stamp. The ships were ordered—by none other than the king—to make a show of looking for the gargoyle ship, but not to progress farther than the Spice Islands. The section that truly made Augum's blood boil stated that "the two remaining weapons were to be returned in good stead to protect the kingdom from further incursions," and were to be "mollified with platitudes and reassurances that all was being done to make the passage possible," while simultaneously doing little other than making good trade.

"And that's why you confined us to the ship, you back-stabbing weasels," Augum said, shooting the document back inside the strongbox and slamming it shut—harder than he had intended. Then he rested his forehead against a nearby wall and closed his eyes, disappointed in the king. After all the support they'd thrown his way …

The door ripped open behind him.

"Well, well, well," crooned the Lord High Commander with a devilish smirk, slapping one hand with a pair of leather gloves, the crook of his mouth upturned enough to skew his thin mustache. Behind him stood both Black Eagles and the captain. "What do we have here? Only some light *treason*, I see. What, did you think none of us would notice your pathetic little attempt at Chameleon? You think one such as *I*—" He slapped his own chest with the gloves. "—even as an Ordinary, would attain the rank of Lord High Commander without knowing the trickery you witches get up to? That some of our best would not train me—" He flapped the gloves at the surrounding Black Eagles. "—to spot those very signs?"

Augum stood his ground. "You have betrayed the bargain."

Strout scoffed. "What bargain? The one with the king?" He flopped the gloves toward the shelf holding the strongbox, his medals clinking cheaply. "The king signed that order himself. I'm just a soldier doing his duty. And you will do yours and be confined to your cabin—or, if you wish, the brig. Unless, of course, you desire for your precious *order* to be dismantled. What good would you two dragons be as outcasts then? Hmm?" He took a step forth. "Let me speak plainly, Stone. You are hereby confined to your quarters, and there you shall remain until our return to home port."

"Now let *me* be plain, Strout," Augum replied, taking a step toward the man so they were nose to nose. He took a moment to savor the pleasure of using the man's surname in the same manner, but loathed the sharp stink of rose oil that invaded his nostrils. "The lot of us are going after our brethren whether you like it or not. If that means departing your ship to find another means of transport, so be it. But we will press on— with or without you. You are free to return to the king empty-handed—

well, not exactly *empty*-handed," he added with a sly wink, referring to the trade cargo being dragged off the ship using its gangplanks, the sound screeching through the windows.

"Our quest continues," Augum went on. "A great ocean awaits, as does a mythic storm. The question is, which of you will be brave enough to join us?" He nodded at Mahmoute and the other Black Eagle. "Of course, I expect you to order our distinguished Black Eagles to keep us Arcaners confined, but if you are at all aware of our history, you will know that we have gotten mighty crafty at breaking free of all sorts of chains. Even *if* you succeed in holding us until we reach home, you cannot chain us forever. At some point, we would begin the quest anew, but *without* your aid. I gave you the benefit of the doubt. I shall extend it one last time."

"You two weapons must come to terms with the fact that the third weapon amongst you is lost *forever*." The Lord High Commander flashed a smarmy smile. "Surely you realize the kingdom still needs protecting. The gargoyles, after all, could return at any time. The order from the king is plain. You are to return to Blackhaven, and that is that."

Augum patted Strout's shoulder in the most condescending fashion he could. "Ah, but it doesn't say *when* to bring us back, does it now? And I believe this is yours?" He raised the key and dropped it into the Lord High Commander's waiting hand, then took a long moment to stare at the man's fake accolades, making him squirm, before shooting an expectant look at the captain and the Black Eagles, particularly Mahmoute.

Conscious of the gamble he was taking, Augum slowly raised a finger and tapped his temple, gaze wandering between the captain and the two Black Eagles—but pointedly ignoring the Lord High Commander. "I can still hear them," he said, voice as cold as winter iron. "Those who screamed …"

He let the purposely unfinished thought settle before continuing. "Our brethren have been taken overseas. If we do not uncover their fate, do you really think, in time, there will be a kingdom to return to? If your loyalty truly lies with the kingdom, your only choice is to press on into the great unknown with us. We rescue our brethren and see with our own eyes the lands of the enemy. Take into consideration their size and strength, then report back." Augum shrugged. "Or destroy them."

He used that moment to let the callous shadow slip into his soul, and the Lord High Commander and the captain recoiled at what they saw— the eyes of the dragon, blinking at them.

You know nothing of the destruction I have already wrought, Augum thought acidly, taking predatorial delight seeing even the Black Eagles stir in discomfort. But he had a clear quest and so he briefly closed his eyes and thought of a tent rapidly decaying to dust under a zooming sun and moon, until nothing but darkness remained. *I am the watcher, noticing the passage of time*, he thought, opening his eyes after winning back control.

"Now if you will excuse me, I must query these islanders to find a way across what awaits—" He nodded toward the window, the horizon filled with a perpetually brooding storm. "—out there."

He remained relaxed as he squeezed past the Black Eagles, expecting the Lord High Commander to order them to seize him, but that order did not come—the Lord High Commander's courage had failed him, just as Augum had hoped. Yet silence wasn't the only thing that followed him, and as he stepped up to Jez's cabin, he became conscious of a figure in tow.

"I am glad they sent you, Black Eagle Mahmoute," he said without looking over, for her stealthy movements made her robe swish in a manner distinctive to her—that and she smelled faintly of cloves, the scent carried by the drafts slithering through the ship. "But do they send you to persuade?"

"You need not bother with her as she is still recovering, Commander."

Augum, well aware that Jez was perpetually hungover these days, hovered a knuckle before the door. "Except she was up earlier and eager to hop off the ship and—"

"You go on ahead. I'll be out in a bit!" Jez's hoarse voice interrupted from within before he could knock. There came a rustling and banging noise as if she were pawing around for something, followed by the sound of a tin scraping against wood, which Augum suspected was a bowl, followed in turn by the revolting sound of retching. He took an involuntary step back from the door and winced.

"Ignore that!" a panting Jez wheezed from the other side of the door.

Augum sighed and dropped his hand. "That does not answer my question, Black Eagle."

"They have sent me as a chaperone. They are convinced you will fail to find a means across the ocean of your own accord and will return to the ship with your tail tucked between your legs. Despite my expectations otherwise, it seems that your commander tongue has won you a chance to prove your quest possible."

"Should I be concerned that you would attempt to bind me in some manner, Black Eagle?"

"What do you think, Commander?"

He glanced over at the former Tiberran. The old woman stood with hands clasped before her, relaxed as ever, her long and gray hair flowing down her gold-fringed crimson robe, with its famous crest depicting a black eagle, its wings spread, claws ready to tear the enemy apart. Although her hard eyes showed no pity, her actions thus far had shown that she possessed the all too precious virtue of empathy. She shared that particular trait with his famous great-grandmother Anna Atticus Stone, endearing her to him more than he wanted or dared admit.

He nodded his acquiescence—and knocked loudly without breaking her gaze. "My mentor is hurting from having lost her beloved in the war," he explained. "She was there for us when no one else was. She will thus *always* deserve a chance."

"Even though she is failing you in almost every way? You lot ought to be training for the 11th degree. From what I understand, you can barely squeeze a lesson in with ..." Those hard eyes flicked to the door. "... Ms. Terse."

Hearing a belabored moan from within, Augum knocked louder. "Get on out, lazy bones!" he shouted in a passing imitation of Jez. "You wanted to come see the town, didn't you?"

From within came a weak, "Ugh ... need to puke again ..."

"Then puke, gather yourself up, and hop on out. I'm not going anywhere until you crawl through that door, whether you be green as snot or covered in your own filth."

"Is it wise to bring someone in that state along on such an important quest, Commander?"

"Why do you hate her?"

"I do not hate Ms. Terse, but her incompetence is inexcusable. She is failing you and thus failing the kingdom."

"And I suppose you think you can do a better job."

"You know I can."

"You want to take over our training because the king ordered you to spy on us."

"I have indeed been ordered to spy on you, but that is not the reason I wish to take over your training. You know the reason."

He nodded. He *did* know the reason. Mahmoute wanted to strengthen the kingdom. Having been condemned to death in her home kingdom for blasphemy and then accepted in Solia wholeheartedly, she was a loyalist through and through.

"The gargoyles will spare no mercy," Mahmoute said.

"So you believe it is possible to follow them across the seas?"

"I know not of such things as ocean crossings, but you have proven to be able to move mountains … so to speak. I would like to see that mountain-moving in person."

As the clamor from Jez's room increased, indicating she was probably getting dressed, Augum couldn't help but smile. "You have said more in the last few moments than I have ever heard you say."

" 'The path of persuasion is walked not in silence, but with a lively tongue.' "

A wise proverb spoken by a wise woman, he thought. He had been lucky to know many wise women in his life, and he longed for more of that wisdom. Hearing her speak in such a way made him miss the company of his beloved great-grandmother—and, of course, his sister-in-war, Bridget. Every time he thought of the latter his heart constricted with worry and sorrow.

The door at last creaked open. Out stumbled a peaked Jez, hair in tangles, turquoise robe spotted with wine and food stains. She pressed the base of her palm against her forehead and squeezed her eyes shut. "Ugh, I've got to stop drinking."

"You say that every morning."

"Yet by evening I partake. I know, I know. I am—what the hell is *she* doing here? You surround yourself with obvious spies now?"

"She is my chaperone—"

"*I* am your chaperone!" Jez smacked her chest. "*Me!*"

"*You* are my *mentor*."

"I—" Jez cleared her throat as she smoothed her robe. "That I am indeed. As your mentor, I—" She abruptly pressed the side of a fist against her mouth. "Excuse me," she mumbled and rushed back into her cabin, from whence came a second round of retching.

Augum did not glance over at Mahmoute as he did not want to see the subtle look of condescension on her face.

Jez soon reappeared, gripping the door frame. "As I was saying, as your mentor …" She winced and squeezed her forehead. "Wait, what was I saying again?"

"Let's get some bread in your stomach, fill you with some tea—"

"Coffee," she blurted. "The galley makes strong Nodian."

"Coffee it is." He stepped aside and let her trundle by, trying not to wince at receiving a pungent waft of vomit.

She flashed Mahmoute an irritated scowl, but Mahmoute only watched her as she passed, allowing Augum to go next before taking up the rear.

As Jez grabbed coffee and bread from the galley, Augum quietly filled her in on what he had learned about the Lord High Commander's—and the king's—betrayal of their quest. Predictably, she exploded, and it took some time for Augum to calm her down with the reassurance that he would not be arrested, at least for the moment. He told her that the Lord High Commander believed any attempt to cross the ocean was doomed to fail, and that they needed to accept that Bridget was forever lost to them. Upon hearing this, Jez was more resolute than ever.

"Then let's prove to the bastards that it *can* be done and Bridget *can* be saved, eh, kiddo?" she said, striding out of the galley with a chunk of bread in her mouth.

Carter stepped into the hallway from his cabin. "Can we come?" he asked. Two more heads popped out from behind like parakeets—the Bloomington-Southguards. Augum, wondering if the pair of court snobs knew that the ship had been commanded to return rather than attempt the ocean crossing, shrugged. "Sure, why not?"

Jez flashed him an *Are you serious?* look, which he pointedly ignored as he wondered if including the two snobs would help Carter bring them to heel. *Since the squire worships me so much, let him watch and take notes*, his thinking went. Having won a small victory against the smarmy Lord High Commander, he felt more confident in his leadership—and wanted to keep building it.

They left the ship along one of its gangplanks, taking care to step around the cargo cluttering the dock, and walked on into town. Being that they were a party of no less than six warlocks, one of whom was a Black Eagle and another a turquoise-robed grandmage, people gave them an unusually wide berth and watched them with wary eyes.

At least having this many warlocks will help with negotiating chartering a new ship, Augum thought.

"Yes, we could smoke you lot in one go," Teague said to a pair of sun-bronzed fishermen, and his brother Digby cackled a laugh.

Digby then whistled appreciatively at the sight of a passing young woman wearing a pink dress decorated with hearts. "Did you see *that*?" he whispered to Carter and Teague, digging an elbow into each of their ribs.

Augum placed an expectant gaze on Carter, who blurted, "Let's keep focused here, boys."

"Right you are, sir," Teague muttered, and the brothers snorted to each other.

Carter pressed his lips flat and nervously looked away from Augum, who refrained from saying anything, for the lessons of leadership were teaching themselves at this point.

Augum naturally headed up the group and went to the first place he saw where he could begin his queries—Nella's Pilots & Navigators, a dingy office under an overhanging wooden building. The interior stank of tar and seaweed and was festooned with harpoons and anchors and fishing nets and ship wheels. A wide counter lined the front, behind which stood two thin old men in fishing slacks and a blue and red coat respectively. They gazed at a wall of charts, a pipe in their mouths, taking turns muttering as they stroked their gray beards.

Augum and his lot strode up to the counter with Mahmoute posting herself by the entrance.

One of the fishermen glanced back and did a double-take. He punched the other one on the arm and they both gawked at the throng with open mouths that barely clutched onto their pipes.

Augum cut right to the chase. "We need to get across the ocean," he said.

The two men glanced at each other—and burst with wheezing, beard-shaking laughter.

Augum, having expected this, raised a finger to argue, when Carter slammed an open palm against the counter, startling the pair of men and knocking over a luckily stoppered ink bottle.

"Hey!" Carter snapped. "Do you know who you're talking to here? You're looking at *the* Augum Arinthian Stone. The Arcaner. The *dragon*." He raised his hand and swooped it past the counter. "You know, the fella who cranked through a whole column of Canterrans back in the war …"

The one in the blue coat removed the pipe from his mouth. "Uh-huh. And I'm Anna Atticus Stone and this here—" He indicated his red-coated cohort with the pipe. "—is the Lord of the Legion himself."

"In the flesh," threw in redcoat.

Carter puffed out his chest and began, "Look here—" only to be stayed by a calming hand on his shoulder from Augum.

"All we want to know is, how can it be done?" Augum pressed, giving Carter a double pat before withdrawing his hand.

"Done? It can't be done," redcoat said.

"Never *been* done," bluecoat added.

"Not in millennia."

"Maybe even only in myth."

"The gargoyles did it," Jez interrupted.

Redcoat gummed his pipe. "What, them beasts you all summoned?"

Bluecoat waved his pipe about. "Or made up to scare the wee ones?"

Augum, sensing where this was going, chimed in before the others could. "What's the farthest our people have sailed? Lately, that is?"

"The whalers," both men chorused before taking turns speaking in their thick dockside accents.

"They hit the outer banks," redcoat said.

"Skirt the storms," bluecoat threw in.

"They might know a thing or two about traveling that far."

"But ain't no one dares to cross the storms."

"Wouldn't survive it."

"Sinks even the biggest whaler."

"And if the storms don't do it—"

"—the serpents will," they chorused, clasping their pipes in their teeth and nodding in tandem.

"Right," Augum muttered. "And the whalers are ...?"

The men waved their pipes toward the street.

"Down yonder," redcoat said.

"Check The Singin' Sailor—"

"'Cause they're a singin' bunch."

"Right. Right ... uh, thanks." Augum thumped the counter and they moved on out.

The men made awkward mock curtsies as they chortlingly sang, "M'liege."

"You can't let them sully the Arcaner pride like that, Commander," Carter said once they had reentered the bustling throng outside, which parted like a school of fish making way for sharks.

"What pride?" Digby muttered, snickering alongside his brother Teague.

"If the order's pride is so easily harmed, we have much greater concerns," Augum replied, keeping his eyes steeled ahead. "Learn to spot harmless words, Squire, and do not allow them to breach the castle of your mind." It was something his great-grandmother would have said, a thought that lent him confidence.

"Now *that's* what an Arinthian sounds like," Jez, walking beside him, whispered, giving him a friendly nudge—and a proud wink, which he appreciated. "The lion we know and love. Wait, not lion, dragon. Yes, dragon."

Augum wanted to remind her that Arinthian's sigil was a lion, but he also did not want to spoil the moment.

With his thoughts turning to the negotiation he knew would have to take place, he stopped to untie the leather pouch of coins at his belt, one he had brought from his castle reserves. He weighed it in his hand, conscious that others in the crowd had spotted this, some with a nefarious glint to their eye. *Try it if you dare,* he thought, feeling safe amongst his learned colleagues.

"This isn't enough," he said after considering the pouch. Nonetheless, he handed it over to Carter. "I want you to step forth with it on my signal."

"Er, sorry, Commander, but what are you talking about?"

"You'll see."

Jez grinned as they resumed walking. "*I* know what he's talking about," she crooned.

They heard the singing well before laying eyes on The Singing Sailor, which had already devolved into raucous mayhem.

"Sun's barely hit noon and they're drunk as skunks," Jez said. "Rather impressive, actually."

Augum saw her fidgeting and knew she craved a tankard. When she noticed him looking at her hands, she promptly smoothed her robe and straightened, snapping, "Get on with it, monkey."

It hurt his heart to see her pining for a drink like that. Yet any time he so much as hinted that she had a problem, she dove head-first into that problem.

The sailors, most of whom were bearded and wore fishing trousers and jackets and who were singing a sea shanty about bringing a woman on board the ship and how it would thence doom the voyage, slowly took notice of the newcomers. Augum and his retinue waited for the song to end, which it eventually did with a hearty toast and a final hymnal note that went on for so long that some of the more red-faced among them had to take a second breath.

After the cheering died down, one of the stouter young men of about Carter's age got up, adjusted his slacks, nodded, and asked the warlocks, "You lot lost?"

"I'll get right to it," Augum said, not wanting to waste time. "We're here with the navy and we need an expert to help us pass the storm wall and then cross the ocean." Even as his audience chortled and wheezed with laughter, Augum raised his voice to add, "A daring pilot willing to risk it all to save thousands of souls."

"Do none of you recognize him?" Carter shouted. "Not a one?"

"Makes no difference who ye are 'ere," said a burly man with a tilted cap and a proud walrus mustache that would put the Lord High

Commander's frilly fluff to shame. "You pick up that there 'arpoon—" He nodded at what Augum had thought was a metal support beam but was in fact a gigantic and long sea spear. "—haul us some blubber, and we might 'ave us somefin' to ta' about. Till then, go on back to them wizard towers and keep slurpin' up them cauldrons of blood."

"'Sides," threw in another fisherman, "ain't nothin' but the edge of the world beyon' that storm. It's uncrossable 'cause it ain't *supposed* to be crossed."

As the men clinked their tankards in a toast to these sentiments and returned to conversing amongst each other, Augum stepped forth. "We can pay. At least for a genuinely sincere plan on how to penetrate the wall of storms that awaits the voyage ahead." He looked back at Carter, who took his cue and stepped forth, proudly holding up and dangling Augum's pouch of coins.

This sent the men grumbling, with many scratching their beards or drumming their tankards as they mumbled about the offer to their neighbors. Yet not one word that Augum picked up was in support of the effort, but rather how to con them out of the money.

"That ain't enough for a fully stocked ship," a gravelly voice cut through.

Heads turned to a gnarled old man with a long gray beard and a low winter cap who had been surveying them from his stool. He wore a knitted brown sweater over faded green trousers and possessed a face so wrinkled by the sun that it was tough to see where the crease of his mouth began. The others quieted down, showing that the man held their respect.

"You're with the fleet," the man noted, idly gumming a pipe longer than his arm. "Aye, I recognize you. The sort that believe Mclidian the Mariner's tales weren't tales at all. Some of us reckon they weren't tales either, though. Even so, that storm wall is full of furies that ain't like the little squalls that bully your dinghies about the harbor, son. Them storms …" He tapped the side of the pipe with a tobacco-stained finger. "… them storms stack waves taller than fifty men."

"A hundred," someone threw in, earning a nod from the old man.

"Waves that toss ships like driftwood. And the serpents out there …" He swiveled the mouthpiece of his pipe to point at a dark window, through which the distant sky flashed repeatedly. "… they ain't like the serpents from your little ponds. Can drag down a ship with the snap of a tentacle. There's some strange goings-on out there too. Unexplainable things. Dark things. And you got to remember that the storms just *begin* there. They go on and on and on—"

"Some say forever," another man chimed in.

"Not forever," Jez corrected. "For our enemies sailed through it, stole our people—your people—and sailed through it again."

"Landlubbers all," the youngest fisherman of them said, searching about for support, which he received with nods and chortles of agreement that reddened his cheeks.

"How long until they come for you?" Augum asked, letting a bit of his farm boy youth slip into his speech, twisting his tone with the slightest of country twangs. "They got a taste of us, saw our weaknesses. It's a shorter path to you than it is to us, after all. Who's to say they won't return looking for more slaves? Or maybe next time they take a liking to killin' instead of slavin', eh?" He shrugged. "Who's to say they don't wipe this island off the map entirely? Then what?" He thumbed between himself and his group. "How much regret would you have over passing on this here opportunity to help a bunch of landlubbers out, landlubbers trying to save everyone's hides?"

Augum nodded at the pouch of coins Carter continued to hold up. "No, it ain't enough. We know that. But you ought to be doing it for nothing. All of you ought to be thinking up every which way how to punch through that storm wall and get across that there sea." He cringed internally that he'd let too much of their jargon slip into his speech, as if he was trying too hard. It was that bullied farm boy side of him that wanted to fit in, but there was no going back, and so he plowed forth. "Ships we have, but we need—"

"Those ships ain't nothing against what's out there," the gnarled man with the long pipe interrupted. "I know those ships 'cause I sailed those ships since I was a wee lad. I know those ships 'cause I *commanded* them." He let this warning drift amidst them like the pipe smoke choking the room. "Those ships would get torn apart like a seal in the jaws of a white-and-black."

"How many of those ships sailed with a whole squad of high-powered 'locks?" Augum countered. *Let alone two warlocks able to summon the power of the dragon,* he wanted to add, but didn't want to overdo it.

The old man's gaze flitted across the group, but all he did was grunt and take a puff of his arm-long pipe.

"What sort of ship would we need?" Augum pressed.

"A blubbin' ship," the man with the tilted cap and walrus mustache said. "A proper, cut-to-the-sea, harpoonin' whaler. Or at least one converted from one."

"And a right wide ship," the old man added. "So she sits low in the waves. Then you got to outfit 'er with a nasty prow. Even if you get all that, you still have to man 'er. The sturdiest of our lot and the craftiest of yours. Out there ..." He looked to the window again. "... you'd be facing the elements, so yous got to *bring* the elements."

Augum, thinking he understood the man's meaning, glanced about him. Even here among them, Jez was a water warlock, Mahmoute earth. He was lightning. There was a wind warlock already on the ship. Olaf was ice, Jengo healing, Leera water.

He looked past the Bloomington-Southguards to Mahmoute. "Your Black Eagle cohort. Would he happen to be fire?"

"Ice. Though he would not come on such a voyage."

"But you would."

Mahmoute's gaze flicked to the Bloomington-Southguards, telling Augum she was not at liberty to reveal her true feelings on the matter.

Thirty-four-year-old Digby Bloomington-Southguard swung his shoulders as he stepped forth and thumbed his chest. "I'm a fire warlock, good sirs!" he announced theatrically, causing a ripple of laughter through the saltblood audience.

"A mere 7th who hit his ceiling?" the old man replied with a scowl.

"How did you—"

The old man indicated with his pipe. "I can read a robe, son. An' I can smell the stink of uselessness from ye even from 'ere. Ever set light to a rammer? Jabbed a headhorn? Had a plate-sized sucker latch on to yer powdered face? I reckon not. Them beasts don't mess around, boy. Your fellow 'locks would be needin' someone a lot more darin' than a court jester who maybe once speared a pond fish from the side of a dock."

The crowd laughed as a suddenly red-faced Digby slithered back to stand beside his brother.

"There's also a low-degree fire warlock on the ship," Carter said when they calmed down. "The meat scorcher. But I think he's only like a 1st degree or something."

The old man chortled. "No scorcher's gonna square up against the swashbucklers—let alone a kraken, son. No, you need a ringer." He indicated his own arm, which did not flare. "10th an' up at the least. Only sort who could burn a ship and maybe take on an ice beast."

Pirates we could handle, Augum thought. *But ice beasts are another matter.* He raised his chin at the gathering and boldly challenged, "Is there no one on this island who is a 10th degree fire warlock or higher that would step forth?"

"Aye, there's a man," one of the other fishermen said. "But he's a black flagger prowlin' the islands searchin' for bounty, an' he ain't right in the 'ead no-how," which caused another burble of laughter.

Augum, suspecting *black flagger* was another term for *pirate*, looked to the old man. "Can we get by without a fire warlock?"

"You can't get by even if you find one. And that's cause you don't have the salt in your blood, young man. Aye, you is a warrior, that much is plain. Maybe could even summon a dragon to your aid, as they say," a sentiment that caused skeptical chortles to ring out. "But monstrous beasts lurk out there amidst those waves, monsters so big they would see your ship as nothin' but a tadpole snack. And what good would a summoned dragon do, anyhow? The thing would only flap about the waves while the ship be sucked down into the dark and cold and deep abyss …" He drew out the *s* in the word *abyss*, until the word died out, leaving behind a silence broken by the bustle of the street and a cool wind that rattled the storm shutter chains.

Augum saw something in the way the man was looking at him, or rather *through* him, as if seeing a great adventure from his younger days. "Old man," he began, choosing his words carefully—but speaking them boldly, "if I got you a ship, would you be interested in piloting it into the heart of an unpassable storm … past unknown serpents … into uncharted waters … to an unknown land … filled with beasts of legend?"

Not a man spoke as they looked to the old captain, who chewed on his pipe as he stared Augum in the eye. After drawing the moment out, the old man stood with a groan, tapped his pipe against the counter, and looked to the barkeep. "Better whip us up a bowl of chowder, laddie, as I got a voyage to plan."

MONSTERS

BRIDGET

As Bridget felt prodding and dabbing against her ankle, she numbly sat with her back against a wall, hands limp in her lap, eyes boring through the wooden hull that separated her from the mighty ocean. She didn't bother scratching the itch underneath her slave collar, for the annoying pain had settled into a constant tingle that kept her awake. Yet how she longed for a long and cozy and perhaps eternal sleep! But not yet. Not yet …

The air was thick with a drowsy incense, a type of myrrh that smelled like Northern Monk sandalwood, but spicier and sweeter. It mingled with a smoky meat that suggested the gargoyles were feasting on roasted boar.

The room was small and dark, its floor littered with hay and rush. The gargoyles had taken her here after the battle, separating her from the others. The fog of Centarro, as weak as it had been, had been strong enough to prevent her from memorizing her location.

Low torch lamplight spilled in from the corridor. It was relatively warm here, suggesting nearby heating, but whether that heating came from a furnace or some other means, she did not know.

As the ship listed to its greatest degree, threatening to toss her against the hull, she looked in the direction of what she imagined was home and wondered what the others were up to. Were they grieving her loss, or had they mounted an expedition to find her and their fellow citizens? Even if they had, what hope had they of tracking down a ship in an uncharted ocean full of storms and monsters?

Ah, but your crest is still lit on the door of the Arcaner vault and so they know you're alive! she realized, a thought that gave her comfort. Unless she was too far from the mainland … *Wait, that makes no sense. The door would be lit regardless of where you are. Stop fearing the unlikely.*

She could hear rain lash parts of the ship exposed to the fearsome weather. Being an earth warlock with no interest in the sea, she knew little of sailing, but she did know the tack had changed. Sometimes she could hear the water trickle by on the other side of the hull—or perhaps multiple hulls, it was hard to say. The integrity of the ship was strong yet nimble, and far more advanced than the knowledge accumulated over the millennia by Solian shipwrights.

A stabbing pain in her ankle made her jolt, and she looked over at the seven-foot-tall gargoyle called Grak. He was now pressing white paste into the mirko bite wounds. The demon sat on his stubby knees, using the nub of his tail as a stool, the stumps of his wings protruding from his back like tiny mountains. His one good eye studied the wounds while his broken-clawed fingers worked on her ankle in a surprisingly delicate fashion.

Bereft of hope, she almost wanted to tell him not to bother, that an infection would set in eventually and she was a goner. Instead, she asked, "Where is my son?" She did not know why she had called Sebastian Narwal, a twelve-year-old boy with family back home, her son, but it made her feel needed. Like her existence had purpose—at least for the time being.

Grak looked up from his work. "Sss … son?"

"Yes. Progeny. Offspring. Child. Boy." She raised a flat hand and pushed it down, indicating a small human. Then she pressed that hand against her belly. "Son." *You cursed liar,* her thoughts spat at her. But she shoved them aside, not wanting to hear the pathetic bleating of her so-called conscience in that moment.

"Where is he? The boy I was protecting. His name is Sebastian."

Grak pointed at her belly. "But you … young, no?"

Ah, see! He is not as stupid as he looks! Yet the thought pricked her conscience, for all this wretched beast had done was show her that most precious gift not even her fellow slaves had shown—empathy. Compassion. Kindness.

Tears rolled down her cheeks as she shook her head and mouthed, "I'm sorry. I'm so sorry …"

Upon seeing those tears, Grak tilted his mangled head. He reached out a claw, only to rescind it, as if not knowing what to say or do. And so he returned to pressing in the white paste, scraped from a tin container, paste that had begun to sting like fire.

"It's starting to hurt," she said, not bothering to wipe her tears.

"*Ga*," he said with a nod.

"*Ga* and *yoss* mean yes in gargoyle, don't they?"

Another nod. "*Yoss*."

"And no? What is *no* in gargoyle?"

"*Gen.*"

"Both with a hard *G*," she whispered, the interest keeping her mind off the burning ankle. "Why do you help me, Grak? Hmm? Why do you help this wretched slave who will die soon anyway?"

Grak replied with a fluid sentence in the gargoyle tongue. Even as he spoke, Bridget shook her head. "Your language is too difficult to understand. Why do you help me?"

"You … honor." He pointed to the doorway. "*Bog karr.*"

"*Bog karr* …" she whispered. One of the words jogged her memory, a memory trained on countless hours spent memorizing spell texts and history and obscure arcaneological phraseologies. A memory born of a valedictorian capable of the studious power of *context* which now pieced together words she had heard the gargoyles say.

"*Yer var bog varlock, yoss?*" she said, startling Grak. "You are big warlock, yes? Not you, obviously, but the words mean that, right?"

Grak gaped at her with a slightly open mouth that revealed his broken teeth.

"So *bog* means big, and you have more than one word for *yes*, which is similar to our tongue. And you sometimes bend your tongue to fit ours, which tells me that you are either a quick study, or that you learned our words a while ago. The latter implies that you already have human slaves. If so, where are they?"

Grak winced with his one eye and shook his head—not in a manner that said he disagreed, but that he did not understand.

"I know, I threw a lot at you," Bridget went on. "Let's start simply. What does *karr* mean? You pointed at the doorway, suggesting big …" She grimaced. "Big what? Boss? Is that right? Boss? Perhaps captain?"

An out-of-sight gargoyle barked a command from the hallway, and Grak shot to his feet and scurried out, leaving his tin behind. Bridget picked it up and sniffed the paste. It smelled of a mix of mint and various medical-smelling substances, though which ones she did not know, for she was hardly an apothecarist.

Putting it back on the floor, she checked on her stinging ankle, noting that it had swelled up rather grotesquely. She'd never been bitten by a mirko before, but she had heard tales of untreated bites festering into harrowing conditions. The future looked bleak indeed, for what would gargoyles know about healing humans from mirko bites? And even *if* they were somehow familiar with mirko bites, did they care enough about her life to heal her? No, she was certainly done for …

Hearing nothing but the distant din and clatter of feasting gargoyles, Bridget's curiosity got the better of her, and she stood up — only to slap a hand over her mouth to suppress a yelp upon putting the slightest weight on her ankle. She thus hopped forth but, finding it too tedious, dropped to all fours and crawled to the doorway.

The bare wood hallway branched off, with the left leading to a kitchen manned by wingless gargoyles. To the right, the direction Grak had gone, the hallway once more branched off. Checking that the kitchen gargoyles were busy, she hurriedly crawled toward the right. Upon reaching the juncture, she peeked around the corner. To the left was a dark room with hanging metal implements that looked like rusted iron. To the right, a light with moving shadows — and the sound of low gargoyle voices, one of which she thought she recognized as Grak's, but it was hard to tell with their growling tongue.

She crawled to the left, stifling a whimper when her ankle bumped into the wall, and soon reached the solace of the dark room. There she crawled out of sight of the light and hallway, and took a closer look at the implements. Most of them were giant cleavers, the handles worn from use, but the blades kept sharp. There were giant forks and spoons and iron pans and griddles and ladles and countless other oversized cooking implements, either spares for the kitchens — or butchering tools.

Since there was no door, she dared not attempt to light her palm — not that her collar-suppressed light would be bright enough anyway. Yet even in the dim light that filtered in through that doorway she was able to make out a large slab in the center of the room with smooth sides. She crawled to it and caught a glint of shiny metal, telling her the top surface was steel, the sides wood.

The height of the table was made for gargoyles, meaning she would have to stand to look upon its surface. Yet the length was far shorter. Curious, she pressed her hands against the side — and snatched them back upon touching something sticky. The scent alone told her what it was and awakened something within, the flicker of a monster that had been hiding behind a curtain. But the callousness vanished as quickly as it had appeared, leaving her to gape at the vague outline of her sticky hands.

Breathing rapidly, she scraped her palms against the plank floor, hoping it was only animal blood. Yet her fearful mind could not know for certain.

A gargled shout came from down the hall, startling her. She scrambled around the butchering table and peeked out from its corner. Grak's disfigured shadow emerged from the adjoining hallway she had crawled from, soon joined by a much larger winged shadow with a long tail. That tail rose before lashing down repeatedly, and Grak tried to protect himself with his arms, but the powerful tail blasted through his paltry defenses, and he was soon a blubbering heap on the planks.

The winged gargoyle then berated Grak in a rapid stream of growls and gesticulations, and Grak only nodded from the planks, until he was bid to rise with an annoyed flick of the claw. The mismatched pair soon strode out and around the corner, and Bridget ducked back behind the table. Following a pregnant pause, she heard their footsteps echo toward her, footsteps that halted within the entranceway to the room.

"*Giri fi,*" snapped a deeper growl.

As rapid footsteps shot forth, Bridget, heart thundering and mind focused on the need to get away, remembered seeing mirkos fall through the arena floor. She hurriedly pressed the backs of her hands together and spread them apart below her, hissing, "*Fiuria girata fissura.*" A relatively small crack formed in the floor, and her knee fell through—but she had hastened the spell. Combined with the suppression of the collar, she found herself jammed halfway down to another room below. It was then that a harrowing thought occurred to her—the weakened fissure casting could close at any moment, slicing her in two.

The footsteps thundered over, and Bridget shrank herself as much as she could behind the table, covering her head out of instinct—and praying her fissure spell did not fail.

A clawed hand roughly punched through her arms, grabbed her by the hair, and yanked her up and out of the fissure. She dared to open her eyes to see that Grak was holding her forth, presenting her to the mammoth gargoyle like a captured chicken.

The monster before her was festooned with golden chains and an intelligent yellow-eyed gaze she recognized from the arena—this was likely the captain of the ship. He was immensely muscled, his torso crammed with various runes, and he possessed the longest and fiercest snout of all the gargoyles, giving him a naturally mean appearance.

The captain flicked a claw for Grak, who was less than half his height, to raise her still higher. Grak adjusted his grip to grab Bridget by the waist and hauled her up until his arms were fully outstretched. The captain smacked his toothy gums, apparently still unsatisfied, and he reached out, grabbed her by the neck with his cold claws, and raised her to his full seventeen-foot height. Grak let go, and she hung there gasping for breath, hands scrabbling at the claws and feet kicking at the air.

In the glint of hallway torchlight that reflected off his yellow eyes, she could see her own frantic face. As he studied her much like a human would study an insect they were about to dissect, his claws almost whimsically squeezed harder, and she thought for sure her head was about to pop off her body like a cork. Just as the black walls of unconsciousness closed in on her vision and her struggles slowed, the leader let go, and she plummeted to the planks, collapsing in a heap she barely felt.

Coughing and gasping whilst holding her sore neck, she struggled to come to her senses. "What … what do you want?" she wheezed.

The leader flicked a claw onward, lazily commanding, "*Te fi*, Grak."

Grak roughly grabbed her by the hair for a second time and yanked her to her feet. She hopped on one foot, for the pain of the wounded ankle was too much to bear. Satisfied to see her standing, the captain turned his immense back on them, allowing her to see that his giant wings were neatly folded—and covered with battle scars. More scars appeared when they stepped forth into the light of the hallway, where Grak transitioned to holding her gently but firmly by the elbow.

"I'm sorry I got you into trouble," she whispered to him, hoping it was possible to make an ally of him, at least on some level.

He made no reply, though the lower lip of his stubby snout gave what appeared to be a sad grimace, as if he were either accepting her apology—or apologetic himself. It was hard to tell.

As Grak dragged Bridget along the hallway, forcing her to hop but allowing her to leverage him for balance, she noticed that her hands and her robe were covered in blood from the butcher table. *Or dissection table*, a morbid part of her mind thought.

Here, the ship was more refined and carefully finished. The wood displayed simple carving work, with grooving and curving and even inlay on a finer table within a room they passed. Yet it was hard to envision a huge gargoyle hunched and laboring over such delicate work. She had no idea where within the vessel she was, but it had to be higher up, perhaps in the bow or stern.

They soon stepped into a spacious room with a monstrous redwood desk, behind which sat a felled redwood log stripped of its bark. Judging by the clawed indentations covering this log, Bridget suspected the captain used it as a perch.

The giant gargoyle confirmed that suspicion by leaping over the desk, giving one flap of his wings, and settling on the log. He rocked from side to side like a giant owl as he slowly turned about, drawing his knees up and making a comfortable perch for himself. His wings untucked from behind and settled around him like a cape.

A hopping Bridget was left to stand on her own, for Grak took up position behind her and to the left of the doorway. This allowed her to inspect the room. Various skulls hung on the walls, few of which she recognized—but then, she wasn't an expert in such things. Among those she found familiar were the skulls of a mirko, a deer, a bear, and a human, each emblazoned with a golden runic description underneath the mounting. Below the skulls hung weapons of different makes. Among many Solian pieces she recognized a Nodian curved pirate-style blade and an Ohmish sickle sword. She even spotted a blade she was sure once belonged to the vanquished Legion.

The captain growled a short phrase, capturing her attention.

"*Yer var … soil, yoss?*" Grak said to Bridget.

"I don't understand. Am I soil? What does that mean?"

The captain poked a hand out from within his winged enclosure, and from the claws of that hand extended leaves on a long vine. The five finger-vines coiled on the floor like snakes, before the captain flicked his claw and the vines shot upward, falling about his massive countenance like thick strands of hair. They brushed against his wings, catching along the sharper edges, and hung there for a time before dissolving.

"You're an earth gargoyle," Bridget whispered. "Not soil, *earth*," she told Grak, and raised her right arm to make a demonstration, only to hesitate. She ought not to reveal she was a 10th degree warlock—and had been suppressing her rings for that reason. Instead she attempted to light her shield, but it was a wispy ghost of a thing that promptly flickered out. She flared the fingers of her hand instead, incanting, "*Shyneo.*" Vines sprang from her palm, throbbing with a weak earthen light.

"Earth," she said, indicating between herself and the captain. Was *that* why he had overlooked her insolence in trying to make an escape?

"*Grak, grak fi!*" the captain roared, and Grak raised a palm and slapped Bridget so hard she hit the floor, where she gasped from the shock of it.

"*Yoss gen krekri karr,*" the captain hissed.

Grak pressed his hands together like a sage, voice soft. "*Gyot* … must … not like captain."

"Fine, I won't compare myself to him again," Bridget replied, wondering why the captain had used Grak's name twice in his command. Such an oddity in the language. Wondering if his name had a double meaning, she hauled herself back to her feet and smoothed her bloody robe to regain some dignity. With one foot raised slightly to keep the pressure off, she boldly raised her chin in defiance to stare at the captain, knowing it was impertinent—but wanting to see what he would do and whether or not—

She felt the slap before she saw it, and was once more thrown to the ground. It had been so hard and so quick that a shower of sparks had exploded in her vision, blinding her.

"Must ... never ... not ... equal. *Yoss?*"

Bridget pressed a hand to her stinging cheek, tasting blood in her mouth. She had never been slapped so hard before. Yet Grak stood above her with watery eyes, as if about to cry. It made no sense.

"You want me to submit fully," she mumbled, once again hauling herself to her feet, where she wavered on one leg. "Yet I am a dead woman standing." She raised her wounded ankle and waved it forth, channeling the strength of her beloved sister-in-war, Leera. Oh, how she missed her best friend so dearly! Even thinking of her lent her the courage to spit a gob of blood at the planks. "Dead, you understand?" This time she jumped aside and the slap *whooshed* by her ear.

Having swiped and missed, to her surprise, Grak stood in place instead of advancing. Bridget, shoulders heaving as she breathed rapidly, waited along with him for the command to come.

"Finish it," she whispered, her ankle stinging as if someone had poured lemon and salt on the wounds. "Finish it, damn you ..."

The captain sat unmoved. If anything, he showed interest by revealing both hands and interlacing the long-clawed fingers. He growled out a phrase to Grak, who continued to stare at Bridget with a terrible pity that confused her more than anything else.

"You show *varlock*," Grak said.

"You want me to demonstrate my arcane arts?"

"Arkan arrrts," Grak mimicked in an undertone, rolling the *r*, as if wanting to learn her tongue as much as he his.

"Arcane arts," she repeated, patiently enunciating each syllable as she had done to many a budding Arcaner. Even while suffering a mortal wound, she could not hold back the part of her that wanted to become a teacher. "Yes, I am a warlock and I am human and I have dignity and I have so much to teach," she said, not knowing why she was explaining herself.

The captain barked an impatient command, and Grak repeated himself.

"All right, all right," Bridget said, raising open palms. She was weakening and did not know if she even had the energy to haul herself up from the planks if he slapped her down as violently as the last time.

She thus went through the most basic cycle she could think of—wispy castings of Shine, a blurry casting of Shield, various impractical vine spells, another weak Fissure casting, summoned her half-ethereal bow, which she kept aimed at the floor—and which resulted in Grak jumping between her and the captain, who only growled a chuckle when she merely moved on to the next spell. Throughout, she kept back the true extent of her knowledge, keeping each casting exceptionally weak. Even so, she attempted to cast Summon Minor Elemental just to see if she could, but by then she was so weak from the wound and her arcanery so suppressed and her stamina pool so low that only a flash of an outline appeared before the spell fizzled. It left her wavering in place, a hand still raised from the spell attempt, until that hand slowly fell along with her head. Somehow, she felt like a failure.

After a thoughtful silence, the captain declared, "*Deh fi fi gu gur gop gyot,*" pronouncing every *G* as a hard *G*.

"What did he say?" Bridget asked, looking to the disfigured gargoyle staring at her with that same pitying expression.

Grak struggled to form the common tongue. "Tell it … it is … my … slave."

Bridget murmured the words back to herself, transcribing their tongue. *Now you are a fi,* she thought, using the gargoyle word for *it.*

Grak raised his snout as if proud of himself. "Tell it that it is my slave." He nodded at the captain. "You slave to Captain Gravak."

"That is his name? Captain Gravak?"

"Captain Gravak."

"And I am his … *gyot*?"

"*Gyot, yoss. Yoss gyot.*"

"What a foul word," Bridget muttered. She was a *fi* and a *gyot*. The latter reminded her of the low and unspeakable word *gutterborn*. And it made her feel that way too. "I am a *gyot*," she said. "I *am* a *gyot*, which sort of rhymes with idiot." She wanted to laugh, but the very idea of mirth felt foreign, as if it belonged to a different Bridget still stuck in a different time, a Bridget who had not acclimatized to her new station in life.

Gravak the captain made an *off-with-it* motion with a claw, and Grak roughly took Bridget by the elbow and dragged her out, with her wincingly hopping on one foot. The moment they were out of view of the captain in the corridor, the hold loosened and his gait slowed. As he led her onward, the ship began to tilt and vibrate with a deep *thwoom*, injecting hesitation into Grak's steps. He watched the walls as if worried they would implode.

It would be a drowning death, Bridget thought. *Perhaps a mercy in the end ...*

A deep rumble ripped through the ship, making its timbers squeak and squeal as if whipped.

"Thunder," Bridget whispered. The thunder must have been particularly loud for it to penetrate the ship so thoroughly. Again it sounded, louder, and then louder once more, the rumbling so intense a crack spidered through a nearby beam.

Suddenly the ship listed to such a fearsome degree that Bridget and Grak were pressed against the wall, with Bridget thinking it would surely capsize. Then the ship swung violently the other way, and the floor came up to her chest, then steadily fell away, meaning they had crested a massive wave, one that gave her the feeling of riding a great wooden dragon.

As she and Grak struggled to maintain their footing, with him keeping hold of her arm, a screeching of gargoyles sounding the alarm seemed to come from all parts of the ship. As they screamed, a command came from behind, and Grak whirled about with Bridget. The gargoyle captain had emerged from his office and was sprinting toward them at a frightful pace, for with each stride he gave a quick flap of his wings, lending him leaping momentum.

For a frightful moment Bridget thought the captain blamed her for whatever was happening, and was about to flatten her into mush. But the formidable gargoyle merely barked a command as he swished by, gave a powerful flap of his wings, and shot up through a gaping hole in the ceiling and floor ahead. In a mine, such a hole would have been a shaft for a rope-and-crank elevator.

Grak followed with Bridget in tow, and the pair leaned over the shaft, which went all the way from the bottom of the ship to the top deck, a remarkably long way up. Above, winged gargoyles streamed into the shaft from all sides, eager to get to the source of the trouble. Another thunderous smashing sound came from up high, and in between flitting gargoyles, she glimpsed something thick whipping by the shaft whilst pulsing with blistering lightning.

"Gods ..." she whispered, goosebumps rising on her skin. She had seen depictions of such monsters in books of mythology, but never with her own eyes.

"We're about to be destroyed," she said to Grak, whose eyes were also glued upward. Sure enough, a gigantic tentacle with numerous suckers stuck itself to the inside of the shaft. It pulsed with frantic lightning that quickly charred the wood, until the timbers lit with a *whoosh* of flame. But then a gargoyle swooped from a nearby floor and shot a jet of water at the flames, extinguishing them—only for the lightning to leap along the jet of water and envelop the gargoyle. The winged demon sizzled and fell, and they watched it, blackened and smoking, plummet past them until it smashed into a floor below.

The ship strained and tilted once more, and the tentacle began to rip into the timber as it used its suction cups for leverage. But at least it halted its lightning attack, as if it wanted to conserve its energies.

"It's climbing onto the ship," she said, the shock robbing her voice of emotion and making her sound as if she were stating a common fact in class.

More winged gargoyles swooped in to attack the tentacle, chopping and hacking at it with summoned elemental weapons. Some clawed and others bit. But the tentacle was so large and the skin so thick that they barely penetrated.

The ship lurched violently, throwing them forward. While Bridget instinctively lashed out with her weak Telekinesis and grabbed onto the wall, Grak fell into the shaft—and let go of Bridget at the last moment, as if not wanting her to suffer the same fate. Their gazes met as he fell, and she caught a profound glimpse of pity in his lone eye. A heartbeat later, he smashed into the planks two floors down, and his body rolled out of sight from the momentum.

She held her breath and waited to see if he would reemerge, wanting him to live. When he failed to appear, she turned about and bolted—and promptly slipped and fell, having forgotten in her panic about her wounded ankle, only to then use the rolling motion of the ship to haul herself right back up and continue hopping onward.

Desperate to find Sebastian, she ignored the hoarse screaming in her head that told her he was not her son and she was a fool to risk herself for him and ought to go topside instead of to the death trap that was the bowels of the ship.

Terrified of drowning and uncertain of where she was, she hopped about through the labyrinth of passages searching for a safe way down. As the ship rumbled with echoes of violence, she soon found herself staring at the dead end of a wooden wall. But instead of turning around, she pressed the backs of her hands together toward the floor and ripped them apart, roaring, *"Fiuria girata fissura!"*

The floor parted with a fissure wide enough for her to hop through. Below was a dark room, and not wanting to impale herself on something, she put her arm through the crack and incanted, "*Shyneo.*" Her palm lit with ivy, and the light was *just* strong enough to reveal a floor twenty feet down. Lashed to the sides of the room were towering stacks of crates, but none were close enough to jump to.

With the fissure weakening and readying to close, Bridget spotted a chain hanging from the ceiling, swinging wildly with the motions of the ship. She pointed and, after a few tries, telekinetically snagged it. But she had to be careful, for attached to the end of the chain was an iron hook that could easily skewer her.

As the fissure began to close, Bridget aligned the chain to hover below her, then hopped off her one good foot through the chasm, with the fissure slamming closed a heartbeat after her head passed through. She grabbed the cold chain and swung, the hook whipping about below like the stinger of a scorpion.

She swung about, getting her bearings, palm still lit. One of the leather lashings that kept a stack of crates in place was coming undone due to the ship's motions. Yet as much as she tried to telekinetically snag the leather, her attempts failed, probably on account of the cursed slave collar—that and she was not as accomplished with precise Telekinesis as Augum.

"You're going to have to take a leap of faith, Bridget," she said, swallowing.

Like a kid on a swing, she used her body to gain momentum. At the apex of the swinging arc, she let go, launching herself toward the closest stack of crates. Then she lashed out telekinetically and grabbed a strong enough hold to swing herself toward the crates on an invisible tendril line that loosened by the moment. She crashed into the crates near the bottom at such a speed that her body smashed through the wood. As she cried out in pain from her ankle, the crate regurgitated a river of dry red beans. The damage caused the crate to collapse, and the lashings from above loosened enough for the remaining crates to tumble.

Bridget instinctively raised her arm to summon her shield. The crest blinked into existence before fizzling out. Instead she grabbed a chunk of the crate and threw it over her head just in time for one of the crates to smash into it—and slam her back against the floor. Weight upon weight pressed on top, and it was only the violent motions of the ship that prevented her from being buried alive, for the crates, instead of tumbling on top of her, mostly tumbled off to the side.

Buried under a mound of beans and splintered wood, Bridget could barely move—or breathe. Once again, the motions of the ship saved her, for the beans and damaged crates steadily sloughed off, until she was able to free a hand, then an arm, and finally slap enough beans aside from her face to suck in a breath.

After spitting out a gob of beans, she lay gasping in the darkness, almost marveling at the bizarre turn her life had taken. There she was, a collared slave, mired in red beans deep in the bowels of a gargoyle ship under attack by a tentacled monster somewhere in the middle of the ocean. Were the situation not so urgent, the ridiculousness of her circumstance would have made her snort, maybe jab a fictitious Leera with an elbow and say, "You believe this lunacy?"

But the sound of rushing water jarred her to her senses. Water was cold death, and now there was no mistaking the urgency. The ship was going down. She had to find Sebastian and get the heck off.

But to where? her mind asked as she struggled to free herself from the grip of the beans. *Don't think about the reality. Just focus on what's in front of you.*

Having finally freed herself, she hopped out of the room. After taking a few turns in the corridors, she found another shaft. This one was thinner and mostly empty of gargoyles, though she could see a few flying up high toward the deck.

The sloshing sound of water came from below, but the water was not yet visible, which she supposed was a good sign. She swung her body over the edge of the floor, lowered herself so her hands clamped the planks, waited for the swing of the ship to align with her target destination, and let go. She fell to the lower floor with a *crash*, and even though she had done everything she could to avoid putting weight on her ankle, it still screamed with pain.

Yet the maneuver had to be repeated, and so she continued falling and crashing down three more floors, until she was a gasping heap of a woman.

"One more to go," she said through gritted teeth, the pain from her ankle white-hot now. "Only one more to—" The words caught in her mouth as she found herself staring at none other than The Brute, the thickly muscled gargoyle overseer from below. Spotting her, he uncoiled his massive tail, which rose up like a cleaver ready to split her head open.

Out would come the beans, Bridget thought. Maybe gallows humor was the closest she would come to actually having a sense of humor. The idea made her want to laugh and say, "Go ahead and split me open, you bastard."

Instead the instinct to survive kicked in, and she rolled aside as his tail smashed into the floor, flipping planks up like playing cards. Seeing that The Brute was on the edge of the shaft, she shoved at the air, roaring, "*Baka!*" But she might as well have thrown a bean at him for all the good it did.

Forced to roll aside a second time to avoid another smash of the tail, she lashed out at his gargoyle feet, incanting, "*Summano midus vinat!*" *Middling Vine, 6th degree, off-the-books, elemental*, her trained mind thought. One could use the spell without the incantation if a vine was already present. In this case, she fashioned one from the arcane ether, latching it between the gargoyle's feet. It was a paltry thing that tore the moment The Brute moved—yet *just* strong enough to cause him to trip. He swung his arms about in wild arcs as his tail shot about in search of leverage.

"Got you, you bastard," Bridget hissed, and shoved at the air once more, roaring, "*Baka!*" This time her little nudge was enough to send him windmilling backward into the shaft. She glanced over the edge and watched him plummet toward the arena floor, where he smashed into a central log support that the arena ropes were tied to. He hit it at an angle, and his body spun in a blur as it fell all the way down to the poop deck, where it crashed into an overseer platform with such force he punched through the floor, vanishing into the darkness below.

"Good riddance," she snapped, and searched about for any sign of the slaves. What she spotted instead was water cascading in from the port side, toward which the ship listed. Already a quarter of the poop deck was flooded, and the water was rising fast.

A flash of light from the bow partition caught her attention. Her gut told her that was where her fellow slaves were being kept, and so she hopped around the shaft, careful to hold onto the wooden plank walls, before continuing toward the bow.

Halfway there, hopping like a madwoman whilst glancing over her shoulder, she slammed chest-first into something hard that had careened around a corner. After bouncing off and landing on her butt, she looked up to see a wingless ten-foot gargoyle gaping at her in surprise. Before he could fathom what a slave was doing there, she jiggled a hand at his head, repeatedly incanting, "*Flustrato, flustrato, flustrato!*"

The gargoyle's head nudged back with each strike. By the third one, his eyes unfocused, and when he awkwardly swatted about for her, she crawled through his legs. Clear of him, she thought to try a spell she hadn't attempted on the ship yet—the 5th degree Darkness.

She made a circling motion with an arm, incanting, *"Voidus vis!"* A pale and wispy cloud the color of pipe smoke appeared. Yet combined with the gargoyle's confused vision, it was enough to allow her to hop onward. Glancing back, she took a small measure of satisfaction upon seeing the beast prodding at the wall with one hand and rubbing his eyes with the other.

Eventually she reached another shaft, this one built with rope rungs tied between four log supports. The only problem was that each rung was meant for wingless gargoyles—and they were thus a whopping six feet apart. The shaft shot past the arena floor all the way down to the poop deck.

With the ship listing at a critical forty-five degrees now and trembling as if repeatedly stung, and with ungodly noises screeching from above, Bridget saw little choice but to turn about and jump, stretching her arms out in time to hook one of the rungs. She swung wildly, stabilized, then dropped to the next rung, repeating this maneuver until she found herself swinging above one of two massive central support beams that doubled as perches—meaning they were round.

Luckily there were enough gouges in these supports to allow her a handhold. After a swing back and forth, she timed her jump—and landed on the edge of the beam, which she promptly flattened against. Once balanced, she got up and crawled onward, trying not to look down, sweat dripping from her brow. Below, her peripheral vision caught sight of brilliantly blue but deadly cold water that was starting to fill the angled bottom of the ship. Streaming in the opposite direction like rats, countless terrified slaves desperately vaulted or climbed pen walls, their gargoyle overseers having deserted them to attend to the battle above.

After a perilous crawl, Bridget reached the entrance to the bow section where the mess hall was, and promptly took shelter behind its wall, where she leaned back and caught her breath. This was all too much. She shouldn't even be here. Had she been more aware back home, had her head been on a swivel, had she not been so gullible and trusting and brave ...

As she used her wrist to brush aside a sweaty lock of hair from her cheek, a distant chorus of screams reached her ears. Jolted, she jumped to her good foot and hopped forward, bracing against the port wall. She took numerous twists and turns in corridors that looked increasingly familiar, until she found herself peeking around a corner into a room of stalls with a massive black metal obelisk. A single disfigured gargoyle, whom she instantly recognized as Grak, albeit with a hobble of his own as if he'd wounded a knee in his fall, was having a hard time organizing a group of about a hundred slaves, all of whom were cowering in a corner. One of those slaves was none other than Sebastian.

Another was Mud, the man who'd warned her about Porter. Mud was holding a woman before him, using her as a shield.

Something else caught Bridget's attention. The obelisk behind the stalls, which had previously been full of blue light, was now half empty — and draining fast. That could only mean the gargoyles were using the energy for something, likely to cast a spell.

Meanwhile, Grak was frantically grabbing whatever slaves he could by the neck and shoving them into the stalls to keep feeding the obelisk with slave stamina, all while hissing and gesticulating in a threatening manner at the group of slaves.

"No run!" he kept shouting. "Must live!" Bridget had never seen such panic in a gargoyle.

Nearby was a long cattle hook with a sharp point. Bridget envisioned picking it up, swinging it about behind Grak, and skewering his temple with the hook. Here at last she had a chance to make a difference and possibly allow for their escape.

But the rational part of Bridget, the part that could analyze arcaneological differences in complex tendril patterns, the part that could reason through arguments with apprentices and mentors alike, had an epiphany. Time slowed as she processed the idea. A crazy idea. Yet it was the only chance they had.

Girding her courage, she placed a hand to her throat, incanting, "*Amplifico*." Feeling her vocal cords strengthen a little, she hopped out of her hiding spot, hands raised with open palms visible. "Stop!" she shouted, voice amplified just enough to cut through the anarchy of screams.

Grak whirled about—and his eyes enlarged. Before he could do anything, she pointed at the stalls, shouting, "We must feed it! Help them or we sink! Trust me with your lives and do it now!" Just as Grak shot toward her, Bridget slipped into the nearest stall, grabbed a cord, and hooked it into her collar.

Grak ran up to her, slowing his last few paces, until he stood before her, mouth agape as he tried to comprehend what she had done. "Help them or we drown!" Bridget shouted as the cord began to siphon blue energy from her collar.

"Help them or we drown!" Sebastian shouted and ran to a stall. Mud followed, which turned the tide. Everyone ran into a stall, intuitively understanding what Bridget was getting at.

Sure enough, the obelisk's pace of energy depletion slowed significantly. Everyone, Grak included, watched with bated breath as the level continued to fall. Then, just before it hit the bottom, the level froze. A bright flash of light came from somewhere far above, filtering down through the many shafts and deck perforations peppered throughout the ship.

As Bridget and Grak stared into each other's eyes, there came a great gargoyle roar from high above that shook the very floorboards.

The gargoyles had summoned a protector.

The ship now stood a chance.

MOLLUSK AND LIMPET

LEERA

On the eastern edge of the island, with the town still in sight behind them, Leera and Olaf stood on dry grass at the precipice of a cliff, staring at a distant ruin sticking out of the ocean like a bent thorn. Far below the overhang, violent surf battered rock walls. Like a dreary curtain backdrop, the horizon, filled with angry black clouds, silently and repeatedly lit up with flashes of lightning.

"Is that really where we're going?" Olaf asked, chewing on a long yellow straw of grass.

Leera shrugged. "That's what my contact said."

"What even … is that? Some sort of … flooded, decrepit lighthouse?"

"Looks more like a ruined castle battlement to me."

"Am I supposed to come with you? And how are we to get to it, anyway? I'm not swimming in that—no matter *what* you enchant me with. I'm an ice warlock, not a swimmer. I don't even like getting wet, which annoys Bridget to no end because she tells me I need to take daily baths. Who takes daily baths? A man ought to stink a *little* bit. Don't look at me like I'm feral. Just ask him, would you already?"

"Fine, and you *are* feral," Leera grumbled, raising the wave-engraved ring to her lips. "Contact Mr. Mollusk."

"*Mr. Mollusk?*" Olaf mouthed, cracking a grin.

Leera held up a finger, indicating for him to wait, and stepped away. "Hello, Mr. Mollusk. Uh, Leera here again. So, uh—"

"Hi," came the curt reply, spoken directly into her mind in a bored drawl.

"Yes, hi, right, uh, so, I'm here—well, that's the thing, *we* are here—"

"We?"

"Yes, we. I know, I know, I know. The order's super secret and all that, but can I, uh, can I ..." She winced, anticipating a lambasting. "... bring a trusted friend?" She pressed a hand against the air as if seeing the man before her. "He's a fellow Arcaner and very, *very* trustworthy."

There was a pregnant pause, then a simple, "Fine."

Her eyebrows rose. "Wow, really? That's ... that's great! Very kind of you, Mr. Mollusk. We'll be right over. Oh, one last thing. He's not exactly a water person—actually, I don't think he's ever bathed before in his life—yes, that was a jest," she was quick to blurt, forcing a stilted chuckle while Olaf glared at her. "My point is he's not much of a swimmer, so how, uh, how do I get him to the—"

"The rowboat."

She quickly nodded. "Right, right. Makes sense. Thank you and see you soon, Mr. Mollusk. Cease contact."

Olaf flipped a questioning hand at Leera, who stepped right up to the cliff. "Whoa, whoa, whoa, there, missy. We're *not* jumping! It's, like, a hundred feet straight down into rocky surf!"

"Riiiiight ..." Leera raised the same finger, then used that finger to wiggle at the air along the boulder-strewn shoreline below, until she stabbed the air. "... there!"

Olaf tepidly prodded a foot forth and leaned his head forward enough to catch a glimpse before jumping back. "That ain't no dinghy, it's a death trap! If we don't drown after it inevitably tips over, a monster with a big enough jaw will eat us in one bite!"

Leera snorted. "Don't be so dramatic."

"Well excuse *me* for not wanting to die." Olaf clamped both sides of his waist with his hands. "You know what? I think we should forget the dinghy and just 'port on over."

"Can't 'port. Mr. Mollusk told me you'll need a rowboat to get into the tunnel. Or you can suck it up and swim."

"I'm *not* swimming in that maelstrom of an ocean. Those currents look downright dangerous."

"Well then, see you when I get back."

"Wait, but—"

"*Impetus peragro!*" Leera snapped, and with a *thwomp*, she appeared on a slimy boulder recessed into an alcove. Nearby, an upside-down and distressed rowboat rested on a higher rock. A frayed hemp rope attached the bow to a rusted iron stake. Careful not to slip on the slimy rock, Leera took her time scaling the boulder, then got to untying the rowboat.

There came a second *thwomp* below, followed by the sound of slippage—like a cat scrambling with its claws. "Ye, gods!" Olaf exclaimed. "A hand, please?"

Leera, standing ten feet above and beside the rowboat, glanced over the edge of the boulder to see Olaf clamped to the side of another boulder, face white as a ghost as he barely hung on. She reached out a hand, latched on telekinetically, braced her feet, and helped haul him up.

"I am *so* not built for this bunk," Olaf grumbled, wiping the slime from the front of his robe. "This guy better be worth it. Does he sound crazy?"

"Not really. Just a bit, uh, quirky."

"Quirky. Great. Just great. He's a jerk, isn't he? Don't even say it. I can read faces."

"Here, catch," and Leera telekinetically raised the rowboat and lowered it to him. With one hand propped against a boulder, he raised the other one to take over, but with Olaf not as competent in the art of Telekinesis, the boat dipped and bumped its way along the rocks as he awkwardly guided it into the sloshing water below.

Leera, wincing at every scrape, asked, "Does ... does it float?"

"Barely," Olaf replied, walking toward the bobbing rowboat as if on eggshells. "Unnameables, I'm definitely going to drown. You'll be sure to notify my next of kin, right?"

"Just hop in, will you? And if you fall, I'll save you like a damsel in distress."

Olaf kept grumbling as he delicately padded his way toward the rowboat. "So dumb ... thing is a deathtrap ... probably full of holes ... sink halfway there ... I'm not as buoyant as I look ..."

Finally he got in, and the boat veered away. Leera, being the spritely hellraiser she was, jumped off the boulder, causing Olaf to shriek like a little girl. When she landed dead center in the rowboat, using her sea legs to stabilize it, Olaf whapped her thigh with the back of his hand.

"Gods, you're *such* a brat!" he said with a mock whine. "Can't be*lieve* you did that!"

Leera kept standing, legs straddling the width of the rowboat. "Are you rowing or am I?"

Olaf pressed a hand to his chest. "I'll be doing the rowing, thank you very much. Need *some* control over my fate," he added in a mutter. He withdrew two small oars wedged under the seats, hooked them into the oarlocks, and began rowing. "What do you expect him to do for us, anyway?" he asked, cheeks already red from the exertion.

Leera plopped down on the rear bench and shrugged. "Honestly? Not very much. I'm going to pick his brain though, see if something nudges free." She pushed her spectacles up her nose, then adjusted the frilly cuffs of her antiquated robe. "A man who sits on the farthest watch has to know *something*."

"He *better* know something," a huffing Olaf grumbled.

Leera, sitting facing him as he rowed with his back turned to the way ahead, wished Bridget were there so she could needle her about the whole bathing thing.

"Why are you looking at me like that?" Olaf asked as they bobbed about.

"Like what?"

"With narrowed eyes. Like you're suspicious. Spit it out already. Everyone knows it causes you tremendous suffering to hold anything in."

Leera wobbled her head about in a *That's certainly true* fashion. She drummed her chin with her fingers before flicking them forward. "You don't reaaaaally hate baths, do you?"

"Of *course* not! Well, not really. I just … have a thing about enclosed spaces like tubs and stuff."

"Go on …"

"Come on, you don't want to hear this."

"Maybe I don't, but *someone* has to fill in Bridget's shoes. Then I can tattle on you when we rescue her."

That elicited a snort from Olaf. "All right, when I was a young and recalcitrant boy, which mind you was a lot, Papa used to teach me a lesson by pretending to drown me in the tub. Exceeeeept sometimes there was a *wee* bit more spite to his pretending. But the lessons certainly stuck … and then some."

Leera, having been expecting something a little more adventurous, deflated. "Oh. Sorry."

Olaf waved the sentiment off with an oar. "Bah, ages ago, anyway."

"Still, you ought to, you know, scrub between the toes and stuff." Leera grimaced at the thought of Olaf sticking his tongue out one side of his mouth as he lathered his crusty feet. "Bridget might be an earth warlock, but, yeesh, Ollie, no girl likes a man who, uh, who reeks." The grimace turned into a recoil as she regretted pressing the point.

"Maybe you should shut up," Olaf said with a smile.

Leera flicked both index fingers his way. "Yeah, maybe I should."

They soon floated up to the ruins of the tower, which did indeed appear to be the top portion of a castle, for the kelp-encrusted crenellations were still visible below the water. After rowing around it, they found a cave entrance with a ceiling so low they had to duck.

"High tide," Leera explained, reading Olaf's quizzical face.

"Figures," he said.

The tunnel meandered snakelike, which Leera suspected was by design to minimize the waves. Sure enough, by the time they floated into the inner sanctum—its walls a series of arching, calcified bricks the color of ripe mango—the water had gone nearly pond-still.

But they were not alone, for the scrawny figure of a pale-faced boy with the reddest hair Leera had ever seen awaited them. He looked to be about twelve and wore a dated burgundy apprentice robe with a faded golden band embroidered into the upper sleeve of the arm. Chewing on a finger, he watched them with curious round eyes.

"Reel us in, would ya," Leera said, and threw him the rope, only for a loop of the rope to catch on an oar.

Before the rope could splash into the water, the kid pointed, telekinetically caught the rope, and guided it to his hand. After grabbing hold of it, he crouched to slip the end through an iron shackle before tying a bowline knot.

"Hey-oh, someone's got salt in 'is blood," Leera said in a dockside accent, playfully swinging her elbows back and forth as she ignored Olaf's offered hand and hopped right onto the dock.

"You're a girl," the boy blurted, returning to chewing the already mangled finger.

Leera patted herself down and made a shocked face. "Holy gods, is *that* what I am?" She turned to look at Olaf, who had just clambered rather unsteadily onto the landing. "Ollie, you'll never believe this—"

"Whoa, you're a *whale*," the kid interrupted upon getting a good look at Olaf.

"I don't accept judgments from toddlers playing dress-up," Olaf countered.

"I am *not* a toddler! I'm fourteen and a 2nd degree, thank you very much!" He flared two bright watery rings around his forearm. "I blossomed at thirteen. What do you think of *that*?"

"That's great, kid," Leera said, pushing her spectacles up her nose with one hand and patting him on the shoulder with the other, feeling as awkward as Jez. "Now where's your dad at?"

"He's not my dad. He's my mentor, and you're an idiot."

"You little snot—"

But the boy whirled away and thumped off.

"At least I don't still chew my finger!" Leera called after him. "We've just been greeted by a talking baby playing dress-up," she said over her shoulder to Olaf.

"Uh-oh, someone's met her match," Olaf muttered.

"What's that?"

"Nothing," he squeaked.

"Thought so."

Annoyed, Leera smoothed her robe, tried to straighten her slouch, and walked after the kid into an arched brick hallway that opened into a voluminous tower. Its construction reminded her of the inner sanctuary at the top of the Library of Antioc, for bookshelves lined the round walls at the bottom. Countless rotting pennants and flags hung from the walls above the shelves, most of which looked nautical in theme, though some were royal as she recognized a fresh crest on a flag that denoted the Southguard throne. A thin and crumbling staircase that lacked a banister snaked along the wall all the way to the top.

"That looks safe," Olaf quipped.

Despite the exterior looking like a ruin, the walls were well kept, and the floor was black basalt, polished to a mirror-like luster that reflected the light from the torch sconces, reminding Leera of the Academy of Arcane Arts. In the center of that floor was a descending spiral staircase, which the kid had taken, not bothering to wait for them.

"He's a rude little turd, eh?" Leera said, and they followed along down the staircase, which was lit by tiny iron lamps that looked like miniature prison cells.

"What's with ancient castles and these sorts of lamps?" Olaf asked. "It's like the lords of old loved to remind people they could be put to the question at any time." To demonstrate the point, he poked and prodded Leera in the back, causing her to shrug him off and smack her gums at him in annoyance.

"What, you think annoyance only goes one way?" Olaf said, prodding her so hard she stumbled a step and whirled about.

"Damn it, Ollie!"

He expelled a dramatized sigh. "Fine, I'll go back to being depressed."

Her shoulders wilted. "Damn it, Ollie," she repeated, this time in resignation, and continued descending.

The spiral staircase opened into a free-standing structure that descended into the center of an expansive room. They both stopped and gasped, for there, well below the waterline, was the giant living room of a fully furnished castle. Except unlike a real castle, this castle's windows looked like aquariums, for they showed the splendor of the ocean beyond.

"Well slap me fats and prance me a pony," Olaf mumbled. "Wish Bridget was here to see this ..."

Between the windows hung gigantic gilt-framed oil paintings depicting brooding figures of old. The floor, also made of the same highly polished basalt, was spattered with sprawling Tiberran carpets. Numerous long puffy red couches sat in random locations, each with a different table—a table made of barnacles here, a driftwood table there, a fallen marble column table over there. Large bronze statues of various mythological beasts stood about the room, gazing inward like sentinels protecting their master, a man who stood in the center with one hand tapping his vibrantly turquoise robe and the other massaging an aquiline nose.

"Behold, Apprentice, for adventurers cometh to our humble abode to sweep thy soul away," he said in a clear voice that rang throughout the hall. The man had a thin face, owl-like eyes, and a crop of dark hair. He bowed his head then angled it to the side to gaze at them studiously. "An honor it is for one of the dragon rank to enter my sanctuary—and an honor for the order that she has chosen us as her compatriots."

"Er ... hello," Leera said as she continued down the staircase, trying to square this animated version of the man who was quite curt to her whilst speaking through the ring. "This is my Arcaner friend, Dragoon Olaf Hroljassen—"

"But I had it on good authority—" Mr. Mollusk chuckled as he approached, robe swishing silkily. "—if the heralds could *be* considered an authority—that you were betrothed to another."

"Oh, yes, he's back on the ship playing leader—*being* leader, I mean. Because he is a leader. Of men. And women!" she blurted, raising a finger. "Lots of women. He's a commander." *Gods would you shut your fool mouth, woman*, Leera thought, forcing herself to straighten as she cleared her throat and smoothed the ruffles of her robe, trying to regain her poise.

Olaf flopped a hand in greeting as he glanced about. "Hi. Nice place you have here, uh, Mr. Mollusk."

"Built by a husband-and-wife team of warlocks generations ago and arcanely reinforced since." Mr. Mollusk, possessing wolfishly hairy ears that did not suit his smooth features at all, stepped up to stand ten feet away, where he bowed more formally. "Baron Von Mollusk, of the Kenton line, at your service," he said, pressing the tips of his fingers together and using them to indicate the boy. "And this is my stalwart apprentice, Limpet."

Olaf snorted a laugh, only to descend into a coughing fit after Leera elbowed him in the ribs.

"Jeremy Jenkins," the flame-haired kid said a little too loudly, making Mr. Mollusk wince.

Leera, not wanting to insult the man any further with their crude manners, gave a small curtsy. "Dragon Leera Matilda Jones, of the Artemesia line." As proper as she had tried to sound, she couldn't help but feel like an ale maiden trying to play at court.

The kid continued to chew on his mangled finger. "She doesn't look like a dragon."

"That is because the young lady can turn *into* one, my incurious little—" Mr. Mollusk said through clenched teeth, then pressed his lips together, withholding what he had been about to say. "You must forgive the boy. He suffered the grievous injury of orphanhood when his father was eaten by a black whale and his mother by a spear squid. As a derelict orphan, he has had the pleasant adventure of being passed around within the order. Having inherited his parents' aquatic element, he now gallantly awaits his own *nemana*. Do you remember what that word means, boy?"

Limpet rolled his eyes as he replied in a bored tone, "It's Henawa for a spiritual quest that turns a boy into a man."

"Yes, indeed. The order takes care of its own, but at some point, a bird must take flight from the nest. Is that not so, Limpet?" The man made a *pop* sound with his mouth when pronouncing the boy's name.

"Yes, sir," the boy mumbled, shoulders sagging.

Leera found herself drifting toward a towering bronze sculpture of a man with ten tentacles as arms and a squid's beak for a nose. "What about the academy?" she absently asked, raising a finger toward one of the tentacles.

"Don't touch that!" the kid shouted, making her hand recoil. "It's not yours."

"Nor is it yours, my boy," Mr. Mollusk said. Then he smiled politely and wandered to a tall window, behind which swam a large jellyfish, its globular body rhythmically puffing and collapsing. "Nor is it mine, for that matter. We are all mere guardians of our possessions, which we take on loan paid for with time. A loan that comes due upon the moment of death, whereupon all our—*things*—" He said the word as if it disgusted him. "—are forfeit, to be drooled over by another, until they in turn have to relinquish those very things when the particles of sand in their own hourglass trickle to expiration. Hence the common and rather hopeless pursuit in search of ..." He turned about, fingertips still pressed together. "... the eternal."

Leera, finding the point a wise one, turned to acknowledge the man with a nod of the head. It was her not-so-subtle way of trying to intimate that, despite her uncouthness, she was not entirely an idiot.

Olaf scratched the back of his neck rather loudly. "You, uh, certainly have a way with words, sir."

"I don't want to go to the academy," Limpet blurted. "I hate that place. People there are stupid."

"Young Limpet here is home-trained," Mr. Mollusk said. "We ... tried to enter him into the academy, but the boy is rather spirited and refused to even take the entrance exams."

"And the teachers are dopes," Limpet added. "And the classes are boring. I like reading and studying on my own. I'm smarter because of it."

Arrogant little fart, Leera thought. "Er, about my visit, Mr. Mollusk."

"Yes, about your visit. You have sailed in on an armada that will, upon having enriched itself from the island's spices, turn one hundred and eighty degrees about and sail right on home, its proverbial tail tucked between its proverbial legs, yet its snout proud with victory, its coffers rich with spoils."

"I ... don't know why you would think that, sir. The king gave us his blessing to sail beyond the—"

"Oh, my dear girl, if you knew the admiralty like I do, you would know they would never throw their balsa ships into the maelstroms ahead. Those storm curtains wait like hungry wolves licking their chops as they prowl beyond the farmer's torchlight. Solian navy ships are sheep hardly built for such wolfish winds."

Leera didn't hesitate. "Then we'll charter a ship that can punch through."

"With what money? Do you truly think the powers that be would ever allow their remaining two dragons to stray beyond the light of the torch?" The fingertips of his hands drummed together as he raised an eyebrow. "Hmm?"

Leera bit her lip, not wanting to say something she would regret.

"Forgive me, my dear, but you are frightfully naive to the machinations of your own kingdom. They paid you lip service, you bought the rhetoric, and now you prance on in here thinking it is possible to pierce the molten storm curtains that have kept the continents apart for countless generations—" He stabbed the air. "—for good reason, mind you. Terrors await deep in the storm wall, my dear," he whispered, voice lowering as he spoke until he mouthed, "Terrors await ..."

Leera walked up to a statue of a woman who had flippers for hands, gills for ears, and a long serpentine tail instead of legs. The end of the tail wound around her torso like a vine. "We are resolved to boldly plow through the storm curtain before us, sir," she said loudly, hoping to sound half as smart as him. "We will not let our brethren become slaves to those beasts."

She glanced back to throw him a determined stare that made a shadow within her rise, before walking to one of the tall windows. *Do not become the horse,* she thought, closing the curtain on the shadow. *Stay as the watcher.* That last lesson with Isobel had been pivotal, and she couldn't wait to see what else awaited them. Already she felt more confident in dealing with The Callousness of the Predator, yet she also well recognized it had yet to be truly dealt with—and would take a lifetime to master.

A large barnacle had suckled itself onto the glass, and a seahorse floated near it as if on patrol. "We're going to attempt the crossing with or without the help of the royals—" She turned about and pressed her own fingertips together. "—or the order. And if I may say so, if the Order of the Coastal Guard fails to aid us on this sacred quest, a quest that could benefit us all, I see no reason ..." She made a show of playing with the coastal ring. "... to continue being a member." Not that she was a full member anyway, more like an ally, but the point stood.

"Yeah, she doesn't need you lot," Olaf clumsily threw in, folding his beefy arms across his chest. "She's a *dragon.* And she already has an order. And friends. Loads of them. And a great man at her side who happens to be my best friend. So ..." He gave a proud nod. "... yeah."

Leera smiled her thanks at him.

Mr. Mollusk sighed deeply as he rubbed his chin in a motion that made him look like he was smearing it with cream. "I rather think that would be hasty, and a loss for all."

Leera, feeling like she was getting somewhere, thought the man needed a push, and so she walked up to the bronze statue of a huge squid with tentacles so long that they trailed on the floor. "I've seen some large ones," she said, stepping over one of the bronze tentacles. "Deep in the dark and cold. But I know there are larger ones out there ..."

"Oh, indeed there are, my dear. *Monstrosi del o duva, monstrosi infenatti. Defenda, defenda, defenda.*"

"Monsters in the deep, monsters beyond. Defend, defend, defend," Leera said, translating the coastal guard's motto. She turned to face him and raised her chin, silently telling him she would not be dissuaded and that the decision to aid in their quest was his.

Mr. Mollusk smiled curtly—and knowingly. "Seeing as I cannot deter you from your quest, I suppose it would serve everyone's interest that we equip you for the attempt."

"You'll help us?"

"I've discussed this with Mr. and Mrs. Seahorse, and some of the others, and I've been granted permission to make an exception to an old rule. Although you have not technically earned the privilege, I would consider teaching you a certain power the ring possesses ... for a price."

"What?" Limpet shouted. "That is *not* fair! You won't even teach that power to *me*!"

"You are hardly ready for such power, my boy," Mr. Mollusk snapped back.

"Yes, I am! I'm smart and strong and I can whip anyone in a duel!"

"You're a mere burgundy who has hardly dueled a soul. Now be *silent*!" Mr. Mollusk roared, then quickly cleared his throat. "Forgive me, but the boy is most inclined to try one's patience."

Leera twirled the ring around her finger as she idly paced from statue to statue. "What's the price, because—" and for the second time that day, Leera stuck her hands in her pockets and turned them inside out. Then she flicked her hands open in a *Ta-da!* motion.

"Call it a condition. Non-negotiable, of course."

Leera tucked her pockets back into her robe, folded her arms, and strolled by a tall lizard man, from where she raised an eyebrow at Mr. Mollusk. "That condition being ...?"

"You take the boy with you as your apprentice."

Leera choked on her own surprise. Anytime she tried to speak, the choking would restart, and she had to raise a finger as she calmed her body down. "Absolutely not," she wheezed. The last thing she wanted was to attach herself to some brat. And then there was the unspoken expectation of having to be his big sister or mother or whatever. Ew ...

"Oh, I'm definitely coming," the boy sang.

Leera shook her head furiously. "No way—"

"It's going to be *so* much fun!"

"I already have an apprentice and I didn't bring her because she's far too inexperienced—and she was a 5th degree Arcaner squire, mind you! The kid's a mere 2nd degree finger-chewer!"

"You're going to be a terrible mentor but I don't care I just want to go on an adventure!"

"He's going to get himself killed!"

"This is his *nemana*," Mr. Mollusk said. "As you can plainly see, he has been sheltered to his own detriment and will become an expense to society if he does not learn the ways of the world. Besides, with the boy in tow, you will have added motivation to succeed — and survive."

"I don't need motivation to survive! I have plenty enough as is!" *Except you are barren with a dead bloodline ahead of you*, her mind hissed at her, but she kicked that part of her in the shin and folded her arms. "No way am I taking on a spoiled, rotten little brat who still plays with toys."

"Do this for the order, Dragon Jones, and the order will give you a *chance* by granting you the power I can teach you."

Leera's hands remained firmly pressed to her chest. "What sort of power is it, anyway?"

"Only one that allows us to battle the serpents and keep them from our shores."

"It's called The Final Flush!" Limpet shouted with a giggle.

Olaf snorted a laugh, but quickly composed himself upon earning a look from Mr. Mollusk.

Leera shared her friend's skepticism. "What's it do, squirt turds at serpents?"

The boy belted out an obnoxious laugh.

Mr. Mollusk seemed unperturbed. "Its ancient name is *Slaiyusserpenteros* —"

"Serpent Slayer!" the boy shouted. "And you're going to suck at using it because you're a dumb girl, so you better teach it to me so I can slay those serpents for you!"

Mr. Mollusk pressed his eyes shut so tightly that the gesture reminded Leera of whenever her old mentor, Anna Atticus Stone, lost patience with the trio.

"It is an ordained power, *Limpet*," Mr. Mollusk said through gritted teeth. He opened his eyes to look at Leera and raised a finger. "But it does require some careful training."

"What are the mechanics?" Leera pressed.

"Surely you are aware of the principle of surging …"

"I've put it into practice myself, actually." Using only the 4th degree off-the-books water element spell Evaporate to dry her wet clothes and hair quickly, but the man needn't know that.

"The Serpent Slayer power takes the principle to its logical conclusion. It greatly amplifies The First Offensive — or Second or Third, so on — at the expense of surging your stamina."

"So it amplifies like a scion."

"Precisely. There are two catches, however. The first is that it can *only* be cast underwater."

"And the second?"

"The second is more of a challenge. One must be extremely careful to time the surge so that one leaves enough stamina to be able to teleport home. Or back to the ship, in your case."

"So take the kid on as an apprentice and learn a dangerous new power in return." Leera ran her hands through her raven hair. "I need to think about it," she muttered and paced to the window. Countless arguments against the idea erupted in her mind, all of them involving the finger-chewer torturing her with inanities. Yet the lone argument for it was a mere image—that of a wretched Bridget in chains.

Mr. Mollusk stepped in beside her to admire the ocean beyond the glass, hands behind his back. " 'Guided by The Fates go I, alone, lashed by the waves of a mighty storm' ..." He whispered. "Mclidian the Mariner was the boldest of our lot, and now you attempt to follow in his footsteps. It is fitting that you learn the same power he once possessed. Yes, he was a coastal guardian."

An impressed Leera nodded. As a water warlock, she'd learned plenty about Mclidian's legendary voyages. "I'm surprised you haven't asked to come along."

Mr. Mollusk chuckled. "I experience more than my share of adventure simply guarding the coasts. Besides, I've been spoiled by this outpost. A ship's confines would be ..." He shuddered at the thought, only to reanimate. "So what say you to my bargain?"

Leera, having already concluded what she was going to do, turned on her heel to face him and thrust out a hand. "Deal."

As Mr. Mollusk accepted the handshake, Limpet did a taunting jiggy dance, singing, "I'm a gonna get me some f-u-n, yes I am!"

Leera narrowed her eyes at him, thinking, *I'm going to leave you crying on the dock, you little turd.*

"And in case you were thinking of pawning him off to someone else or stranding him on shore," Mr. Mollusk said as if reading her thoughts, "remember that young Limpet over there is a full-fledged member of the Coastal Order."

The boy grinned as he showed off his own ring.

Leera almost groaned. *Damn it.*

"Further, you will swear on your Arcaner shield that you will take him with you. Limpet will also provide regular reports at my command. Won't you, Limpet?"

Limpet shrugged. "Sure, whatever."

Mr. Mollusk leaned closer to Leera, voice quiet so only she could hear. "He will be your apprentice, yes, but I implore you to treat him like your son."

Leera couldn't stop her face from twisting with revulsion.

"He needs a mother and a father, and if even a quarter of what the heralds wrote about you two is true, I can think of no better pair than you and Dragon Stone."

Leera's nostrils flared. "You read that foul piece and think that because I am barren I am therefore desperate to adopt whatever kid comes bouncing my way? Well, guess what—I'm going to overcome that curse and have kids of my own. You mark my words, *sir*."

"Then be a good mentor to the boy. That is all he requires."

"I'll take him along, but I'm not promising anything beyond that."

Mr. Mollusk considered her a moment before surrendering a nod. "I suppose I can live with that, for the gods know how difficult he can be. Luckily, the misfortunes that have befallen him have also taught him an independent spirit, allowing him to learn of his own accord. Do what you can. The gods will be grateful."

"Yeah, I am sure they will be," Leera muttered, looking past the man to see the boy picking his nose and eating the booger. "And he's how old? Fourteen? Looks twelve. Acts ten."

"Stunted by neglect. Including my own, I admit."

Leera sighed the longest sigh of her life. "Fine. *Fine.* Let's get to this Serpent Flusher power or whatever." She shook her head, watching the boy gleefully offer a booger to a disgusted Olaf. "Gods, I'm so going to regret this …"

SALTFANG

AUGUM

With his entourage in tow and the old man gumming his arm-long pipe beside him, Augum stood staring at *Saltfang*, the toughest-looking ship he had ever seen. She was anchored at the end of the dock, a low-profile double-master with tightly furled square sails, hull wide and stubby and mean.

The old captain nodded, pipe waving about as he spoke. "She's been converted into a merchant ship for long-haul sailing into southern hurricane seas. Don't let the conversion fool ye, though, son. They might have added fancy cabins and dropped her blubbin' gear, but she's still got the iron heart of a whaler."

The sweater-wearing salt flicked his pipe. "She's double-hulled yet nimbler than your heavy cutters on account of her smaller size, and wide and low enough to right 'erself from her mast kissing the waves. Just no further as she'd flounder. She's got a heavy lead keel as sharp as a surgeon's blade and her bottom's lined with long carving strips that will rip up a curious beasty. Front's been fitted with a serpent cutter. You get 'er lined up just right, and she can carve most of 'em in two. She's a pricey commission, and o' course you'll need supplies. If you can secure the funds, we can have 'er fitted and ready to go in short order."

"How much for everything?" Augum asked.

"A hunny, I reckon. Give or take."

This made his entourage chortle. Even Jez snorted, while the Bloomington-Southguards each had a choice thing to say about not having a chance in hell the admiralty, let alone the Lord High Commander, would ever spend royal funds on a suicide quest.

If Lord High Commander Strout doesn't arrest me first, Augum thought as he paced up to a massive iron dock cleat, wrapped with hemp rope thicker than his leg, which led up to *Saltfang*. He rubbed his forehead, knowing there was only one path forward. The challenge was to sound convincing.

He turned around to look at his entourage, all of whom awaited his decision. As he searched their gazes, his mind raced with possible solutions. He drummed his lips with his fingers as he considered them all. One in particular stood out. Lord High Commander Strout was an arrogant Ordinary. If he could be convinced of a power beyond his understanding …

"Jez," he said, stepping forth. "Care for a short sojourn?"

His mentor sneered victoriously at Mahmoute before raising an eyebrow. "What've you got in mind, monkey?"

"Let's have a stroll and talk about it." Augum looked to the old man. "Can you start organizing?"

"Aye. But you'll need to have the funds ready within a couple hours, son. Can't load unpaid-for supplies."

"Understood." He turned to his entourage. "Aid the captain as best you can. I will send word when you can transfer ships and load your things."

"You're dreaming," Teague said, shaking his head alongside his brother Digby. "The Lord High Commander's never going to allow it, let alone lend you the money."

Carter grimaced. "It *is* rather quite unlikely, Commander," he sheepishly muttered. "At least knowing how stubborn the Lord High Commander is."

"Leave that to me." Augum returned his gaze to Jez and opened an inviting hand toward their ship, which sat moored a ways down the dock. "Shall we?"

She skipped over and hooked elbows with him. "You bet, monkey. Let's walk so you can fill me in on your fiendish little plan."

* * *

After having a hearty laugh alongside the Solian navy captain, Lord High Commander Strout swished a hand across his desk, practically singing through his tears of mirth, "You are completely out of your mind, my boy. What makes you think that I am going to contravene a direct royal order, sign a royal promissory note for one hundred *thousand* crowns, and hand over our supplies?"

Augum, standing beside Jez, placed his hands behind his back and waited for the man to finish getting his kicks in.

After lobbing mirthless jests at the silent captain whilst playing with his thin mustache, the Lord High Commander looked at Augum. "Enough. We are about finished loading the new provisions. You lot are returning with us and there is nothing left to discuss."

"You have a speaking orb," Augum said, "which your bulldog Black Eagle has been using to communicate with the fleet, and with home."

"So?"

"Please query the king directly. Tell him I am willing to offer my castle as collateral for the loan. If he refuses the request, tell him my mentor—" He flicked his head sideways at Jez, who stood with arms folded across her chest. "—has the power to teleport-hop me home, at which point I will secure a loan from the Black Bank myself and have it here by nightfall."

Augum took a step forth. "This quest will move forth with or without the admiralty. You can either help us get fitted properly or see us depart with half the chance to survive had you given us your aid. You have one hour to convince the king before we make our own arrangements. We'll be on deck waiting for your response." He gave a proper bow of the head. "Lord High Commander. Captain." He and Jez then turned on their heels and went to the door, where Augum paused to add, "Oh, and tell the king I am disappointed in him."

He left the Lord High Commander gaping alongside the captain, who Augum noted had a slight smirk, almost as if he respected Augum's daring.

"You're getting good at their games," Jez noted once they had stepped onto the deck, where the wind had picked up, ruffling the many flags that hung on all the ships. "But the king might call your bluff that I can hop that far."

"Either way it's a gamble," Augum said. "And I can't think of any other way to raise a hundred thousand crowns."

Jez nodded at the town. "I can sell myself for a couple days."

Augum recoiled. "Eww, Jez."

She shoved his shoulder with a hand. "I didn't mean *that*. I meant sell my *skills* with the arts. Gods, kiddo, really? *Really?*"

"Oh. Of course. Sorry."

"Apology accepted." She sighed, a hand idly slapping her thigh as she glanced about the deck. "The crew is spying. We should show them we are unperturbed. I think it's high time for a lesson, Augie boy."

"What? Here? Now?"

"Damn straight."

"Fine, but just don't call me Augie. I hate it."

"Sure thing, butt-for-brains. Arcane Drain or Greater Repair?"

Now it was Augum who sighed, as pushing Jez just made her dig in further. "You know I need more help with the latter."

"Right on, kiddo. Quick recap. We can only repair arcane objects that have been damaged, meaning—"

"—parts of the original incantation must remain," Augum said, making a twirling *move it along* motion with his hand.

"Don't imitate that fiendish rascal girl of yours."

"Sorry."

"And stop apologizing so much. It's unbecoming of a commander."

"You're starting to annoy me now."

"Good, as it means you're paying attention. We just have to find something to fix." She snapped her fingers at someone behind Augum. "Hey! Stick-legs!" Then she snapped her fingers repeatedly at Augum, whispering, "The heck's that sailblower's name again?"

"Tammy, Ms. Terse," Tammy said, walking up to them whilst adjusting her large and round spectacles.

"Tammy, right." Jez flicked a fingertip at her. "10th?"

Tammy nodded. "10th."

Jez condescendingly patted Augum on the shoulder. "Look, I'm about to impart a critical lesson on Greater Repair to my prodigal apprentice here, also known as the lord of the skies and dragon of the kingdom. Well, one of *three* dragons anyway—"

"How may I be of assistance, Ms. Terse?"

"We need something to repair. Anything arcane on the ship that's broken? The older the better. Preferably something that's sunk to permanence, as I want to ramp up the challenge here for my green-eared apprentice—and by that I mean green-eared with the spell, of course. He's *mostly* capable in the stuff he ought to know by now."

Tammy nodded toward the bow. "Well, we *do* have a wyrmspike that's been out of commission for as long as I've been a member of this crew."

Jez thumbed between herself and Augum. "Do we look like sailors to you? What's a wyrmspike? I'm assuming it's not a literal thorn sticking out of a literal wyrm, is it?"

Tammy chuckled. "It's an arcane device that launches spears and harpoons."

Augum felt like being cheeky, and sang, "Sooooo ... liiiiike ... a ballista?"

"No. Yes. Sort of. But yes." Tammy shrugged. "I guess we saltbloods like to be different."

Jez windmilled both arms theatrically before pointing them at the bow, singing, "Weeeeeelll theeeeeen let's go!"

Just as the three of them started walking, a *thwomp* sounded from behind. Augum turned, and his heart did its usual leap of joy upon seeing his girl. Olaf was with her too, and so was someone else—a red-haired kid dressed in a burgundy apprentice robe and holding a canvas bag almost twice his size.

Leera jogged up to Augum, grinningly slapped her hands on his shoulders, whirled him about, and leapt upon his back, singing, "Hiiiiii, sweetums!" whilst planting kisses all over his head.

Forgetting himself, Augum twirled her about, then pointed her in the direction of the kid, who was glancing about the deck with a look of disgust. He used his whole body to lean forth, making a body-length nod at the boy. "Uh ... who's that?"

"Oh. *Him.* Yeah, uh, long story short, that's my snot-eating new apprentice, Limpet."

As the kid dumped his bag onto the deck, gesticulating at a sailor to carry it to his stately cabin, a command the sailor snorted at, Augum let Leera down to gape at her.

"You're jesting, right?" Jez said. "You took on a little baby playing dress-up? Kid looks ten."

"'Fraid not," Leera said, and after explaining that she'd had no choice and that the kid had come with the exchange of a power that would aid them in their crossing, and that his former mentor had made her swear on her shield to take him along, she grinningly patted Augum on the shoulder like Jez had.

"I think I need a drink," Jez muttered.

The women in my life ... Augum thought with a sigh.

"So, maybe he might look at you like his dad now," Leera threw in. Had it not been for the playful twinkle in her eye, he might have reacted by throwing up.

"Hey, what're you lot doing?" Olaf asked upon approaching. "Whoa, look at your faces. She told you about the kid, didn't she? Yep, there he is, pickin' his nose as we speak. Oh, and eating it too. Lovely."

"I'm going to pretend none of this is happening and continue my lesson," Jez said. "Greater Repair. If there's any room left in those marshmallow brains, you two are welcome to come and learn a thing or two."

"Don't mind if I do," Leera said, and once again hopped onto Augum's back. "Hey! Shrimpy Limpy! Get busy scrubbing the deck or something!"

"Piss yourself!" the kid replied.

"Isn't he just a peach?" she said, pecking Augum on the cheek. "Missed you, lovebug."

Jez grinned. "I cannot *wait* for you two to experience what it's like managing brats."

"Oh, it'll be a hoot," Leera muttered. Then she gave Augum a gentle jerk. "What's the news?"

Augum quietly filled her and Olaf in on his plans.

"So it's a bluff," Leera whispered.

"Sort of. We'll obviously move forward with or without them, but it would be easier with them on board."

"Not literally, though, right? They can follow us in their trio of driftwood dumpsters."

"Ooh, good one," Olaf crooned.

She acknowledged him with a cheeky finger point.

"I don't know," Augum said, rubbing his scruffy neck. "I guess we'll see."

"Think they'll really go for it?" a skeptical Olaf whispered.

Not wanting to show the crew, who were indeed watching them out of the corner of their eyes, how uncertain he was, Augum stopped himself from shrugging. "We'll see," he whispered. "We'll see ..."

Jez pushed Tammy. "Go on already as the wind's starting to gust."

"I can temper it, if you like," Tammy said, leading the way to the bow.

"Finally someone with some brains. Please do, Twigs. Mind if I call you Twigs? Those legs are long enough to make secondary masts."

"Er ... sure, I guess."

"That's her way of saying she likes you," Leera threw in.

"Oh." Tammy smiled uncertainly. "How nice."

Once at the bow, Tammy showed off the old mechanism, which was built into the bowsprit. The damaged portion was a log-sized rod with an open end, where the harpoon or spear would be loaded. Then she stepped back and swept her arms about in an orchestrated manner whilst incanting, "*Ipulato aero marjorus.*" Augum recognized the spell as the 9th degree off-the-books Major Shape Air, which allowed her to calm the surrounding wind, enabling full concentration. As she kept an eye on the winds, she politely asked permission to stick around for the lesson.

"Knock yourself out, Twigs," Jez said. "Let's go, kiddos. Flare 'em."

Augum, Leera and Tammy each opened a hand and incanted, "*Un vun asperio aurum enchantus,*" while Olaf's face fell.

Jez flipped a questioning hand at him. "Well?"

"I, uh, I'm only 7th, so, uh, I—"

"—have yet to learn the 11th degree Reveal. I get it, big boy."

"I'll rectify that," Augum blurted. It was legal in times of war for warlocks to learn more than two degrees ahead.

"No, I will," Jez interrupted. "Let me do my job, monkey," she told Augum. "And you, blond loaf-for-brains. Lessons every morning before lunch."

"That'd be great," Olaf said. "Er ... will that be, uh, a little too early for you, or ...?"

"What are you implying, meathead?"

"Nothing," Olaf squeaked. "Nothing at all."

"Good. Now shut up, hang about, and listen."

"I wanna learn too," a voice chirped nearby.

They turned to see the kid—*Was his name actually Limpet?* Augum thought—staring at them, his bag lying abandoned on the deck where Leera had teleported in with him.

Jez raised an expectant eyebrow at Leera.

Leera didn't miss a beat. "Then flare your hand with Reveal and get to learning."

"Fine. Teach me Reveal."

"Maybe after you grow out of that squeaking voice and learn to respect people a little," Leera snapped.

The boy stood there gaping before he mumbled in a small voice, "I'm going to tell on you."

"And say what? 'Dragon Jones was being mean to me by not teaching me a spell I'm far too young and inexperienced to learn?' That the way of it? Look, your old mentor dumped you for being a brat. I suggest you start behaving because no one around here is going to coddle you." She indicated between herself and Augum and Jez and Olaf. "The four of us? We went to war. Bled together. Almost died countless times. We don't have the patience for brats. To be honest, the best thing for you is to keep whining until you give up and go back home. Everybody would understand. What we're about to do is dangerous beyond measure, and there's no place for a kid on deck."

"No place," Augum echoed, nodding sagely.

Olaf and Jez—and even Tammy—joined in with their own nods.

"She's right, kid," Olaf added. "We're going directly into a wall of storms. You're a leaf that'll get blown overboard with the first big gale."

"I'm not a *leaf*!" the boy shouted, fists balled. "I'm a 2nd degree warlock who's going to be the greatest water warlock *ever*! You'll see!"

"Uh-huh, sure," Leera said, nodding patronizingly. "Anyway, uh, please seriously think about quitting. Maybe take a job on the dock hitching bowlines or whatever."

"I'm coming along whether you like it or not!" Limpet shrieked, and he whirled about and stomped back to his bag, where he slumped against it with folded arms, pouting.

"A little tyrant in the making," Olaf noted with a shake of the head.

"Take it easy on him, kiddos," Jez said. "Mentoring is harder than you think. Now clam up and focus. Where'd we leave off with our last lesson together, anyway?" she asked Augum and Leera.

"Tendril interlacing, tendril completion probabilities, and tendril cut-offs," Augum replied, well remembering the lesson.

"That was a tenday ago too," Leera added.

Jez's brow rose. "A tenday? Has it really been that long?"

"Yes," Augum and Leera chorused.

"Shoot, guess I got a little side-tracked. Anyhoo, have a study here."

Augum, Leera and Tammy leaned in over the mechanism, with Olaf craning his neck over their shoulders.

"Note where the tendril enchantment weavings end and *how* they end. These ends here are decayed, whereas these here have been sliced clean off. That means multiple and various direct hits, with follow-up decomposition when no one repaired the enchantment. This ship saw some battle, all right—and its crew failed on the upkeep side of things."

"Black flaggers have their warlocks too," Tammy said, then checked over her shoulder to make sure the other crew members were far enough away before adding in a whisper, "And I'm the highest degree warlock they've had on the crew in like a decade. The army tends to steal the best of us, dumping the leftovers for the navy."

"Well, they certainly had some competent people in the past," Jez continued, face scrunched with concentration as she pointed out tendril orientations of note. "The original enchantment never sank to permanence because it wasn't a strong enough casting—typical of most castings, of course, seeing as how rare a perfect casting is. Instead, they kept repairing the accumulating damage as they went, reinvigorating the core enchantment, which, judging by the oldest tendril line here, I'd say is about two hundred years old."

"That's far older than the ship," Olaf said. "How can that be?"

"Think about it," Jez replied.

"They must have moved the mechanism from another ship," Tammy concluded before Augum could say the same thing.

"Exactly. You can see the old repair work here, between the decomposing tendrils. See how the repaired ones show up brighter, with cleaner edges, while the old ones are fraying and cracking?"

"Ooh," the group sang in unison.

"Ugh, I really regret not pushing myself when Bridget offered to teach me Reveal," Olaf muttered from behind Augum.

"We're lucky here as the enchantment wasn't completely destroyed, nor did it slough off and fall back into the ether. That tells us ..." Jez opened her hands. "... what?"

Leera winced. "The enchantment was cast with some competence?"

"Not in this case. It means all the repair work over the years calcified the enchantment a little, making it grab onto its structure that much more. You can see the evidence of that if we lower ourselves and look at the tendril geometries from a shallow angle."

As the sky darkened and the winds strengthened without affecting them, and the ship creaked and groaned and the flags snapped, Augum crouched along with the women. Sure enough, he saw that portions of the tendril work clung to the metal like crabs, while others barely floated above the rod.

"The work that's fighting to hold on there was done sloppily and quickly," Jez went on, a finger dancing over the tendril patterns. "But that's not always the warlock's fault—"

"As sometimes they're in the middle of a battle," Augum was quick to throw in before Tammy could.

"Exactly, monkey. Exactly. That's something you'll have to learn—how to perform the most optimally effective advanced repair whilst embroiled in chaos. Perfection has no place in battle when good enough is all you need to survive."

"This is the smartest I've heard you sound in ages," Leera muttered.

Jez playfully smacked her head. "Shut up. And it ain't even mine—"

"It's an old military proverb," Augum threw in. "I recognize it from Military Strategy class."

"That's right. Now consider how *you* would repair this. One at a time, starting with you, monkey." She looked expectantly to Augum. "How would you fix 'er up?"

"Er ... I would start by focusing on the weakest substrates and rebuild them one at a time from there."

Jez's gaze swiveled to Leera. "Monkey number two?"

"I'd start from one end and work my way to the other."

Jez raised her brow at Tammy, who sheepishly said, "I'd bridge the missing gaps with a basic web before strengthening and tweaking that web to completion."

"None of you are right. The very *first* thing you have to do is study the complete tendril landscape before you."

"Riiiight," the group chorused.

"Bit of a trick question," Olaf muttered.

"Nobody asked you, fart-for-brains. So let's study this enchantment. We know it's two hundred years old. What else do we know?"

"It's mostly crimson, indicating an explosive," Augum replied.

"And the blue variegations point to a Push enchantment," Leera said.

"You all are moving so fast," Tammy said, shaking her head. "Much faster than I'm used to, even when I was at the academy."

"These two grew up training on the fields of war," Jez said, "so they had to connect concepts right quick. And if they got it wrong—" She sliced a finger across her throat, making a "*Kchhh*," noise with her mouth. "Nodian smile. Not to mention they had the privilege of studying under none other than *the* Anna Atticus Stone."

"I've heard plenty of stories, but what was the esteemed archmage really like?" Tammy asked.

"She was a no-nonsense grump who could put you in your place with a mere look," Jez replied.

"But she also had a massive heart," Leera added. "Er, still does, that is. She's, uh—" She pointed upward. "—she's still alive, but in Ley."

"Let's keep on topic here," Jez continued, cutting Tammy off before she could press further. "What else can we learn by studying the tendril landscape? Anyone? No? Look closely." She leaned in, a fingernail hovering over a particularly complex area of weaving. "See this tendril pattern here? How it seamlessly fuses the explosive and the supportive together? That's the trigger, codified into solidity by the complex thought patterns involved in the crux of the spell. And I say *crux* because the trigger is the most important mechanism of this enchantment."

She adjusted her crouch. "So what does that all mean? Stop drooling and focus. It means the enchantment is salvageable. Otherwise what? Wow, slow day, huh? Brains took a few too many knocks sleeping in the cabin bunks? It means that otherwise we'd get nowhere, and it would behoove us to wipe the added enchantments off with a Disenchant and simply start the repair from scratch. And that of course would be difficult to do as the arcaneological mechanics—that includes the later additions and repairs—were cast by experts with a narrow focus on crafting such mechanisms. And we don't exactly have many of those experts around anymore, do we?"

"That explains why they haven't repaired it," Tammy mumbled, pushing her spectacles back up her nose, which prompted Leera to do the same.

"Let us now spend time studying every facet of this tendril web, from one broken end to the other, including the patches of repair work." Jez snapped her fingers. "Let's go. Hop to it, kiddos."

They did just that, studying the enchantment with their splayed hands, barely listening to the wind as it whistled through the rigging or to the bark of the bosun commanding the crew to secure the decks.

"All right, now let us begin the actual repair process," Jez said once they completed the study phase. "The golden rule, in times of calm, is to start with the simplest repair possible and work your way up. In battle it's occasionally the reverse—you repair the most complex damage first and hope it gets the spell working enough to fend off whatever's about to hit you."

She jiggled her open palms. "But I digress. This part here. The outflow of tendril geometries that secures the outer edging to the framework of the rod. This is what we will repair first, and the reason being …?"

"It's the simplest," Leera answered.

"Someone's paying attention. Because the exam—" Her eyes flicked to the gathering storm. "—might one day be in the real world. Anyway, I'll start. I want you to take turns attempting to continue what I begin. Watch carefully. Hey, are we watching?"

"Like hawks," Augum replied.

"Good. Here we go. Having done the Reveal analysis, we switch to Greater Repair, where things really get interesting. Of course, we'll keep things simple to start. The key here is to reconstruct the original intent and function, which means we don't have to perfectly recreate what had been there originally. Get me?"

They nodded uncertainly.

Jez blinked at them before waving idly. "You'll figure it out." She then refocused on the enchantment and, after a surprisingly long think, incanted, "*Apreyo enchantus delicato obiectum roa,*" and began to carefully weave a web that dovetailed nicely with the current tendril construction. But it was such a complex weaving and took so long that by the time she was finished, everybody watching gaped open-mouthed.

"There, I fixed it," Jez said with a nod, dusting her hands. "Perfectly functional now." Then she noticed them. "Why do you all look like deer staring at a crossbow?"

"Because ..." Leera stuttered, hand flipping at the enchantment. "I mean ..."

"That was *way* over our heads," Augum said on her behalf, with Tammy nodding along beside them.

"One small hoof step at a time, my antlered apprentices. It *is* a spell that takes years to get a grip on, and decades to master. And I haven't even delved into complicators yet, which are their own barrel of pickles, let me tell you! Wait, you didn't really think you'd get a shot at casting the spell right away, did you? Don't answer that. All you needed to do was pay careful attention because the first lessons are always about watching a repair and making distinctions. You *were* making distinctions ... right?"

"Oh, *yeah*," Leera said, nodding emphatically. "Plenty of distinctions."

"Loads," Augum threw in.

Jez looked between them and muttered what distinctly sounded like, "Morons ..."

"You are an excellent mentor," Tammy blurted. "I-I-I am sure I cannot afford your rates, but would you consider—"

"Of course I'll consider it, Twigs," Jez replied. "But that means that—"

"It means *exactly* that," Tammy interrupted in a whisper, eyes darting about in search of the lurking crew.

Augum nodded approvingly at the tall woman, glad to welcome a competent air warlock among them—if the old sea captain let her aboard, that was, and, of course, if he secured the funds.

"Also, these two mischief-makers—" Jez pronged two fingers between Augum and Leera. "—along with that blond loaf there, get my attention first. And I'm a busy woman—ignore their rolling eyes," she added, precluding Augum from sharing a skeptical look with Leera and Olaf, for half of Jez's time was spent with a drink in hand taunting whoever crossed her path.

"Of course, Ms. Terse. Any time you can spare beyond training these three fine heroes I would be grateful to receive."

"Speaking of moving ship," Leera muttered, looking past Augum.

Augum turned to see the captain come up on deck. He spoke a quick word to his bosun, who blew a whistle. "Meeting on deck!" the bosun shouted in turn. "Move it, move it, move it, saltbloods!"

"Let's leave it there and see what the decision is," Jez said, and they snuffed Reveal and moved on to stand behind the gathered throng of sailors.

But it was not what the bosun declared nor the inscrutable face of the captain that revealed the answer to Augum, but rather the face of Lord High Commander Strout, who had at last emerged from below.

And that face was glum with defeat.

MUD AND ICE

BRIDGET

Bridget picked up a large basket of stale hard bread and carried it toward the kitchen area, bare feet thumping on the planks. To the contrary of her expectations, Grak's salve had miraculously staved off infection and her wound had indeed healed. For the time being the burden of a slave life would continue. But for how long?

She stopped at a glassless window that overlooked the poop floor. Even a tenday after the gargoyles had defeated the sea monster that attacked the ship, a few scattered pools of seawater remained, trapped in sections between beams that did not have adequate drainage. Only a handful of gargoyles labored over that water, methodically using their beastly arcanery to evaporate the liquid from the vessel.

"Just like a water warlock would," she whispered. But their castings were not as efficient or practiced, telling her humans were more adept at some spells than gargoyles, a point of interest she hoped to one day pass on to her friends and fellow warlocks. "If I ever see them again, that is," she muttered, trying not to think about the many smiling faces she longed to lay eyes on once more.

Her gaze swept to the slaves shoveling coils, and she located the cubicle in which Sebastian struggled with a shovel. Weak and scared and exhausted, he had been reduced to either staring at nothing or gibbering to himself, reliving past memories. Stabbing a mirko's mouth shut and seeing arena atrocities first-hand had traumatized the poor boy, and it was all Bridget could do to soothe his poor nerves.

At least the boy didn't have to worry about their former section overseer, The Brute, who was the worst of the lot. No one had seen him since the day she shoved him to a deathly fall. No one knew it was she who had vanquished that monster, not even Sebastian.

She had been keeping an iron eye on the boy ever since the summoned gargoyle vanquished whatever monster had tried to capsize the vessel. That massive gargoyle remained clinging to the deck, on watch, fending off multiple sea monsters since.

Sebastian would slice under a coil, totter over to a hole, toss the coil in, pause to use a sleeve to wipe the sweat from his brow, then repeat the cursed maneuver, his lips moving soundlessly throughout as he kept up a running narrative.

My poor son, she thought. *Your false child*, the shadow behind her mind countered. The Callousness of the Predator had been showing up more of late. Perhaps it was gaining strength because she hadn't had the energy or time to use Isobel's meditation techniques against it.

From above came the raucous sounds of an arena duel. Another group of pitiful slaves was facing who knew what, steadily eroding slave numbers, which made little sense to Bridget—unless the gargoyles thought they would return to enslave the entire continent of Sithesia and thus have no shortage of slaves to inflict their amusements upon.

You should have let them all drown, the second part of her mind thought. *That would have been the merciful thing to do.* Instead, she had saved them, gargoyles and slaves alike. Grak, in his broken Solian, later told her that the serpent had been about to capsize the ship, and if she had not won the crowd over and told them to aid the effort of filling the obelisk with their precious stamina, the ship would have surely sunk. As a result of that aid, Captain Gravak promoted her to the top position of the slaves—overseer of the kitchen.

She managed the stores and dispensed food justly and fairly, making sure all were fed, quietly saving the very best for Sebastian. In between, she served as the gargoyle captain's personal slave. Luckily he rarely called on her, and when he did, it was usually to scrub his crusty gargoyle feet or offer him food from a telekinetically raised platter or simply sit leashed like a dog by his side at the arena to watch slaves get torn apart, their severed limbs carted off in baskets, her presence further enhancing his prestige amongst his beastly peers.

She had used what meager power she possessed to prevent Sebastian from getting thrown back into that arena—and she only succeeded by convincing them he was her son. Her tearful pleading had won Grak over, but the captain and others remained irresolute. She had yet to witness any sympathy from any gargoyle other than Grak. To them, only strength and dominance mattered, much like The Callousness of the

Predator. She wondered how the lowliest among them, a pitiful creature with one eye plucked out and both wings torn off, had the greatest empathy.

Seeing that Sebastian was all right, Bridget continued carrying the basket toward the kitchen. The plank floor was angled at about thirty degrees, causing everyone to walk at a tilt. The storms raged on. Today it was wind and rain; yesterday, wind and hail. But the ship was built for the weather, though it creaked and groaned as it flexed mightily upon its long log supports.

It was the month's long storm that convinced her the others would never be able to save her. No Solian ship could puncture that ferocious wall of maelstroms, let alone the massive serpents that awaited. No ship was large or strong enough.

Odds were she was never going home. Her former life was over, replaced by a shell of herself that scooped gargoyle dung and served her masters and acted as a stamina vessel to be regularly siphoned. She would never see the clear outline of her crest again or turn into a dragon. Bridget Abigail Burns was no more, replaced by Ah-bee-gale, as Grak called her. But even that was a veneer, for she was a *gyot*, the gargoyle word for slave, rhyming with *idiot*. She was also a *fi*—an *it*, as Captain Gravak and his gargoyle brethren sometimes referred to her.

As she mutely withdrew loaves of bread from the oven and stacked them on a counter for another slave to cut for supper, she thought of Olaf smiling. The way his pudgy hands fidgeted whenever he wanted to say something to her, invariably something kind. The way those hands patted Sabby or stroked her long cinnamon hair, back when it was shiny. He was a distant memory now, yet one she cherished nonetheless, holding him close to her heart. She also remembered being mean and vindictive, injuring him with her callousness, and thus injuring their future.

What future? she thought, wanting to scoff. If only scoffing would come as easily as it had before. Despite these thoughts, her face remained plain, beaten to placidity by so much callousness—from the gargoyles, from her fellow slaves, and from the cold creature that perpetually lurked behind the curtain of her mind, longing to be set free. Interestingly, the more she drew on that callous creature's strength, the easier it came to the fore. Her training told her to suppress it, but her predicament begged otherwise.

A grumpy-looking old lady air-sliced at the bread with the side of her hand. "Ye want 'em cut on the quarter or torn apart, miss?"

Bridget's response was to chop at the air twice with her own hand. She did not smile or speak, which was common for her now. The less she got to know her fellow slaves, the more insulated she felt from them—insulated from caring, for she had seen too many of them ripped apart on bloody sand, reduced to mere musings for gargoyle entertainment.

She glanced over at a wingless gargoyle minder the slaves had nicknamed Cracks. He sat on a perch, picking at the claws of a foot like one of those bored exotic beasts Bridget had seen caged in a traveling caravan. Except in this case, it was she who was caged and he the slaver. His immense muscles would allow him to snap a human in two—as she had witnessed when a slave had a mental breakdown. The poor man had come raving at the gargoyle, saying it ought to stop the prank and turn back into a human. Cracks had simply grabbed the man by the leg with one arm and the neck with the other and bent him backward until there came a series of sharp *cracks*, earning himself the appellation.

Cracks was mean and unempathetic, even to the gargoyles he deemed beneath him—yet he dared not step one claw out of line when facing a superior. To those he sucked up like a teacher's pet, hopping to their commands and only showing extra aggression toward the slaves.

Few spoke within earshot of him, for he was the suspicious sort that always thought a plot was afoot. Within his vicinity, the kitchen noise was at a bare minimum, for even a dropped pitcher could attract his attention—and no slave wanted his gaze upon them.

It annoyed Bridget that she had vanquished one mean gargoyle only for him to be replaced by another, but then she supposed they were all like that. Still, it made it feel futile to fight them, which was probably the point.

She received a basket full of yams from a curly-haired and brown-skinned nineteen-year-old girl, a new addition to the kitchen team after Cracks had skewered the last girl with his tail for the offense of accidentally stepping on his foot.

"Chef," the girl said.

Bridget acknowledged the handoff with a nod, placed the basket on the wooden counter, and withdrew the first yam, which she was planning on adding to the soup that was boiling away in a huge iron pot nearby. Right away she noticed that the yam was unusually cold in her palm.

Bridget took up a dull knife and pressed it against the skin. Sure enough, the yam refused the slice, indicating it was still frozen. Bridget rapped the counter with a knuckle and the girl, who had turned away toward her station where she was responsible for cutting carrots for the soup, turned about. Bridget raised the yam and tapped it on the counter with a double *thunk*.

"Oh," the collared girl said, eyes darting to the gargoyle. "I'm so sorry, Chef."

Bridget nodded at a steaming pot.

"Yes, Chef, I'll thaw them right away, Chef," the girl said, and took the basket from Bridget, poured more hot water into the steaming pot, and then emptied the basket of yams into it. The girl had long curly hair woven into crude braids and was dressed in rags, her clothing having long rotted away, a common problem due to the salt and mildew and toil, forcing slaves to craft clothing from rags.

Bridget had not asked for her name, nor was she planning on it. It was the same with the others, for she could not risk sparing what little caring she had left on anyone but Sebastian.

The girl suffered from the attention of men on account of her beauty—a fair and oval face and large green eyes that shone like forest stars. Among those men was Mud, who currently also worked in the kitchen, having been arbitrarily assigned by Cracks. Mud had stayed away from Bridget after her arena victory and ascension to chef, yet now and then she felt his eyes on the back of her head. He was a strange and shady fellow, suddenly appearing in places, observing with his beady eyes before walking off. She always got the impression he was scheming, but having no one to scheme with, he schemed all on his own in silence.

The girl edged closer to Bridget. "Chef, there's a rumor that you're *the*—"

Bridget interrupted her by sharply tapping the counter with a knife, loud enough for Cracks to look up—something she had not intended. The girl yelped, jumped away, and pretended to be very busy poking and prodding at the yams.

Bridget almost reached out to apologize, but her arm remained by her side. She moved on instead to cutting potatoes, which would also go in the soup.

"These are ready, Chef," the girl mumbled when Bridget finished cutting the potatoes, and carried the pot of yams over to her on the counter. "I'll fetch the turnips from the freezer," she added and walked off.

Hearing hurt in her voice, Bridget watched her go. She absently fished out a yam from the still-warm water and squished it in her palm. It was indeed ready for cutting. Just as she was about to direct her attention to the task, she spotted Mud walking after the girl. Checking that Cracks was busy picking his claws, a suspicious Bridget put the yam down and walked after them.

The freezer was located at the very end of a meandering hall of stores and was frozen daily by an ice gargoyle. Bridget kept well back, only turning corners after Mud had already gone. After a series of turns, there came a yelp from down the hall, and Bridget shot forth.

There in the dark, amidst a room pluming with ice, she found Mud holding the girl tight against the wall, a hand clamped over her mouth. Acting on pure instinct—and a rage she had not felt in some time— Bridget picked up an ice shovel and swung it at the man's head. He looked over in time to feel the *smack* of the cold metal against his nose. Blood exploded across his face as he fell like a limp noodle, curling backward, head thumping against a snowy buildup.

Breath pluming in the frosty air, Bridget let the shovel slip from her hands to the icy plank floor, where it *thunked* to stillness.

The girl shot to Bridget and enveloped her in a crying hug. Bridget did not pat her back, but stood staring down at the moaning form of Mud. Yet it was not his face that caught her attention, but what had spilled from his pocket.

Bridget opened her right hand, incanting, "*Shyneo.*" It lit up with weak vines, revealing a square of torn and bloody cloth. Curious, she gently pushed the girl behind her, leaned down, and lifted the cloth, finding the lily pattern familiar. After a think, she recognized it—it was the identical pattern of that old lady who had stolen her bowl early on. She remembered Mud telling her about Porter and how he liked to keep souvenirs. She remembered a leg shooting out from the crowd, kicking that desperate woman toward the mirko.

The man, who had been squeezing his eyes shut and blubbering from the pain, abruptly shot forth with surprising quickness, first grabbing her lit palm with one hand then snatching her throat with the other, precluding her from spell casting. They shared gazes, and she saw that his eyes were those of a shark, devoid of anything, before he opened his mouth and growlingly tried to bite her nose off like a rabid dog.

Bridget tried to jerk away but he was far stronger and easily wrestled her to the planks, keeping himself on top. Then he proceeded to growl and snap his teeth at her nose, each time making a *clack* when she spun her head away, all whilst dribbling blood all over her face. Feeling the veins of her forehead bulge, she searched for the girl—only to discover that she had run off, leaving her to her fate.

Curse you, coward, Bridget thought.

As the blasted black walls of unconsciousness closed in from the choking, Bridget feebly punched at the side of his head with her free hand, but the man simply tilted his head so that she punched the top of his thick scalp, doing no harm. Getting nowhere, she turned her attention to her still-lit hand and used all her remaining focus to urge the vines to move. The green fronds crawled up the man's arm, onto his cheek, and reared up—before plunging into his eyes like ice picks. He screamed and shot away, scrabbling at his face whilst rolling about as if he were on fire.

A gasping Bridget wanted to run, but she knew what could happen if she did. To the girl. To herself. Then Sebastian would be alone. So she shut the thick ice door behind her, plunging them into near darkness. All that remained was her palm, pulsing in time to her beating heart. Thump-*thump*. Thump-*thump*. Thump-*thump*.

The blinded man stood, blood streaming down his face whilst he again growled like a rabid animal.

Bridget picked up the shovel. Thump-*thump*.

Mud stretched his arms out, roaring, "I'm going to tear you up, witch!"

Bridget raised the shovel. Thump-*thump*.

Mud blindly shot forth, arms swinging. Bridget aimed and swung. The shovel connected with the side of his head, emitting a grotesque *crack*, and the man fell at her feet. Thump-*thump* went her heart. Thump-*thump* went the light. Blood oozed onto the planks, approaching her naked frozen toes and soon enveloping them, the warmth almost reassuring. The shovel fell beside the pool of blood with a *clang*.

Bridget stood staring. Thump-*thump*. Thump-*thump*. Thump-*thump*, until her light died, plunging her into pitch darkness, for the collar was too strong, her arcanery unable to penetrate its suppression for long periods of time.

She stood listening for his breath, almost hoping he was still alive, that she had not taken yet another life. But no sound came besides the cursed thump of her heart slamming into her chest. Even as a chef, death followed her like a shadow. She could not escape it. She breathed it. What *was* she?

You're a chained queen of the skies is what you are, a cold voice said in the back of her mind, one she welcomed in that moment, for it was the only blanket offered to her conscience. *You are a ferocious predator all should fear. This? This is nothing. It is but a paltry burden which you can shrug off, as you have shrugged off so many others.*

The door opened with a squeal. Bridget did not want to turn around.

"Chef?" came a trembling voice.

It was the girl. And that girl yelped upon spotting the body. After muffling a cry, the girl abruptly grabbed Bridget, removed her from the room, and closed the door behind her. She kept hold of Bridget, who stood staring at the door, numb. There death lay, once again a familiar friend … and nemesis. There death lay in wait for her, as vengeance for all her sins. All she needed to do was report it, and it would be over. She would not battle in any arena. She would let them kill her—

No! roared a thought. *Do not give up!*

"I'll take care of it," the girl blurted, patting Bridget's shoulders reassuringly between giving her spontaneous hugs Bridget did not return. "You saved me. I ran like a coward. Now I will save you, Dragon." She looked into Bridget's eyes, whispering, "I know who you are. I *know*. And you're our only hope. So go. Wait—wait." She withdrew a kitchen cloth from a pocket and gently wiped Bridget's bloody face, using nearby slushy ice to aid with the cleaning. Then she made Bridget raise each foot and wiped them thoroughly.

"I'll clean everything," the girl said upon finishing, using the bloody rag to indicate the door. "And I'll take care of the body. Go. Please, Dragon. Go …"

Bridget turned to walk away, but before she vanished around the corner, she stopped and turned around. For a moment, the two young women stared at each other, both party to a crime.

"What is your name?" Bridget finally asked.

"Naomi," the girl replied. "My name is Naomi."

Bridget nodded and walked off. She numbly resumed her duties in the kitchen, breathing a small sigh of relief that Cracks hadn't noticed her absence. As she moved on to cutting carrots, the girl returned, face pale.

"It is done," Naomi whispered as she placed a bowl of celery on the counter beside Bridget. "I used the scrap chute."

Bridget's response was to push a bowl of chopped carrots at the girl, who took it with trembling hands. For a fleeting moment they shared eyes. Whereas Naomi gave her a fearful look, for there was no doubt in Bridget's mind that she had never done such a beastly thing as dispose of a body, Bridget kept her face placid, as she did not feel fear. She felt ice cold. If she feared something, it was acting on her true feelings, which were that she was a desperate *gyot* willing to do almost *anything* to survive for Sebastian's sake.

The women turned away from each other, with Naomi delivering the carrots to the steaming pot and Bridget withdrawing the celery and chopping it up into chunks. As she worked, her conscience searched the

Sacred Chivalric Code of the Arcaner, yet found no discrepancies. She had defended herself and come to the aid of someone in need.

That frail conscience nonetheless warred with itself. Other than Sebastian, Mud was the only person who had tried to get to know her, but he had also turned out to be a predator. A keeper of keepsakes. A former prisoner who had brought to slavery his prison mentality and former criminality. An inmate she had dispatched without too much of a fuss — albeit in self-defense. Still, what was she becoming? She had taken three lives on this ship alone — that bald and tattooed man, The Brute, and now Mud. Not to mention she had played a part in Porter's demise at the hands of the banyan beast. Her face felt as cold as the ice she had left the body lying in.

You're getting comfortable with killing. That's what's happening, a voice inside hissed at her. As usual, she imagined it coming from behind a certain curtain. *What happened to Augum is now happening to you.* Except her brother-in-war had suffered mightily in the wars, and he had come out all right, had he not?

Thinking of Augum made her think of Leera and then Jez and Haylee and Jengo and Alyssa and everyone else, including Olaf, and her shivering heart warmed ever so slightly.

No, that's not it, the voice argued inside her head. *It is the last gasp of a weakness you have known all your life. Let it die so that you can finally become the queen of the skies you have always been destined to be.*

"No!" she roared, slamming the knife down through the last of the celery so hard a piece flew away. It hit the ground and tumbled toward Cracks, who looked up to scowl.

Bridget looked at him with a fearsome and challenging gaze, a wolfish gaze she had seen Augum deploy. *Kill me,* she wanted to say. *Get it over with before I do any more harm.*

Cracks jumped off his perch and rounded out his shoulders.

Bridget felt a calming hand on her arm. "Chef," Naomi whispered, gently enveloping her knife hand. "Chef, the soup. If you please."

Bridget looked down and saw that her knuckles had whitened around the handle of the knife. She remembered the man who had demanded that Cracks cease the elaborate prank and turn back into a human. She let Naomi take the knife from her hand and guide her to the soup. There Bridget climbed a stepladder, picked up a huge wooden ladle from a nearby wooden pocket, stuck the ladle into the broth, and began stirring. She anticipated a lash of Cracks's tail and imagined herself falling forward into the soup.

"Ah-bee-gale," came a voice.

Bridget looked to the doorway to see Grak standing there, staring at her with his one good eye. He nudged his head sideways, his way of summoning her. She glanced over her shoulder the other way—and saw Cracks standing directly behind her, tail raised. Indeed he had been about to lash her.

Fool, you almost died because you let your emotions govern your actions, she scolded herself.

She calmly placed the ladle into its pocket, stepped down the ladder, and strode to Grak. Once they were clear of the kitchen and walking in a dark hallway, Bridget's steps faltered, and she ended up leaning against a plank wall, clasping both hands over her mouth as she desperately muffled a cry of anguish. Like the suppressive collar, she too had been suppressing things.

Grak stepped near, hands wringing as if he were debating how to comfort her. "Ah-bee-gale pain, *yoss?*"

Bridget dropped her hands. "Yes, I am in pain," she mumbled, tears rolling over her lips. "I am in pain in here." She patted her heart. *For I am a killer,* she wanted to add. *A slave and a killer.*

Grak placed a hand over his own heart. "Grak pain. Grak pain know …"

Bridget sniffed, comporting herself. "Are you a slave?" she asked. "Amongst your own kind?"

Grak thought a moment. "Grak *gerger.*"

"*Gerger*? What does that mean?"

Grak circled a palm over his chest. "*Gerger* … ah … *gerger?*" He seemed to struggle with how to translate it.

"You must teach me your language," she said. "So that we can understand each other. If you tell me more words in your tongue, I can attempt to—" She placed her wrist to her chin and opened her hand before her mouth like a flower. "—speak it using a spell I was learning. Tongues. Do you understand? It's a spell I might be able to cast despite the collar."

Grak hesitantly glanced between her and the direction they had been walking in. "We go," he said, and they took to walking again, giving her the sense he would get in trouble if they lingered too long.

Bridget's heart fell when Grak took a certain turn along the hallway, for ahead was the open doorway leading onto the log support that bridged the bow of the boat with the arena. She vividly recalled The Brute smashing into that support on his way down, his body spinning until it crashed through an overseer platform.

"Ah-bee-gale *hohol,*" Grak urged from behind her.

Bridget stepped onto the wide beam support and, as always, had to drop onto all fours to prevent herself from slipping off. Grak walked patiently behind her, the claws on his feet digging into the wood, stabilizing him. She crawled onward, seeing that a crowd of gargoyles had already assembled along the perimeter of the arena, anticipating another gruesome match.

She got as far as a blood stain and a divot in the wood, where she stopped to stare at it, guilt gnawing at her innards like a piranha. The guilt was not so much for killing The Brute as it was for having taken life, which was antithetical to her very nature.

Then you do not understand yourself yet, hissed that all-too familiar voice from behind the curtain of her mind.

"Ah-bee-gale," Grak said in gentle tones, nudging her butt with his foot. "Ah-bee-gale *hohol.*"

"Yes, I go, I go," she said, and she gritted her teeth as she mutely continued on. *Armor your mind,* she told herself, and entered the sanctum of her mental castle. There she turned about and raised the drawbridge. *Armor your mind ...*

She watched herself walk along the arena floor, her bare feet enjoying the granulated feeling of the sand between her toes. Grak remained just behind, patient with her slow movements in relation to his usual walking speed. She was led to the captain, who was waiting beside his commanders, a legion of powerful winged gargoyles who took drinks from trays offered by wingless gargoyles. For these massive beasts, humans were too short to wield trays even when the beasts were perched, for they perched on engraved beams that gave them stature. That was partly why Captain Gravak enjoyed Bridget as his personal slave, for she was the only slave strong enough in the arts to telekinetically heave aloft one of those trays, impressing the other gargoyles.

Captain Gravak flicked a claw at Bridget, and Grak dutifully clipped a thin chain to her collar, one that was twenty feet in length, as required to reach the captain's hand. He then gently led her to sit before the captain's perch, hands in her lap, and reached up on his clawed tippy-toes to give the captain the leash. Bridget mutely obeyed, face as impassive as it had been in the kitchen. She was safe inside her castle, where she bid the scared little girl of her youth to sit before a roaring hearth, pick up a thick book, and read. Meanwhile Bridget moved to another room within the castle in her mind to perform spell cycles.

As a small group of helpless and muddy slaves was herded onto the sand, clinging to one another like children, Bridget uttered the incantation to Shine within that imaginary castle and saw her hand flare brightly. Then she summoned her shield, lit with the golden glow of the entire Arcaner crest—a golden dragon perched atop a golden castle, above the golden words *Semperis vorto honos*—Courage, fortitude, honor.

Fortitude. Yes. That was the key. She would not only survive, but grow stronger within. Her sanctum would flourish.

She took charge by uttering the incantations that saw the castle's heat turn up and its curtains open, allowing in bright sunshine. Through its stained-glass windows she heard the echoed laughter of children playing in the bailey. Out there she imagined her husband playing with the kids while she worked at home.

I will build this sort of life, she thought. *One day, somehow, I will have my husband and my kids and my future.*

A cage was lowered, this one filled with wolves, and the slaves started screaming. Bridget looked through a window in the castle, stealing a peek beyond the walls. Sebastian was not among the slaves. Neither was Naomi, meaning she wouldn't have to once again grovel before the captain. She did not know these wretches. These poor people she could not help.

After waving at her imaginary children and her husband, throwing them kisses like a loving mother, she closed the curtain and withdrew into the dark interior of the castle, where she resumed casting spell after spell, each imagined with full potency and lethality. Practice targets were hit and enemies spawned and destroyed. And as wolfish howls rose from beyond the walls, which prompted terrified screams from the damned, the enemies Bridget had summoned turned into gargoyles, and she began trying variations on them, seeing what worked and what failed. She saw them touch runes and used Telekinesis to yank their hands away. She attacked their minds and saw them wilt to their knees, whereupon her arrows would meet their foreheads with sickly *thunks*.

The very last incantation was performed deep within the castle, in a subterranean cavern. There, with a mammoth gargoyle enemy before her, she raised her arms and legs and spoke the sacred incantation that sprouted wings from her back, her vision rising until she became a queen of the skies.

As the wolves tore apart the slaves in the real world, she tore apart the giant gargoyle in the imaginary one. Throughout, her real face was placid as it gazed at the arena, for she did not see with her eyes that which the others saw.

She had been so focused on her inner training that by the time the drawbridge came down and she allowed herself to venture beyond the safe confines of her mighty keep, she realized she was no longer in the arena, but sitting, once again like a dutiful dog, on her knees in the captain's office. Waking up as if from a trance, she looked about—and found that she was alone.

Seize your moment, she thought, and jumped to her feet—only to get yanked back hard to the planks, for the chain was still secured to her collar. Frustrated, she angrily wrestled with the blasted collar like a feral dog, until noticing that the other end of the twenty-foot chain had been placed on a hook seventeen feet up or so—easily within the captain's reach, but far too high for a human.

A fixated Bridget hauled herself up off the floor and padded to stand below the hook, examining it. She had not trained her Telekinesis up like Augum, so it would be a challenge. Nonetheless, she raised a hand and threw all her focus into snatching the hook. The ring at the end of the chain clanked about as if prodded by a ghost, but failed to rise above the tip of the hook. Her hand began trembling from the effort.

You're trying too hard, she thought, gasping and dropping her hand. For some reason, she pondered how Sabby would do it—and promptly smacked her forehead, snapping, "You dolt!" She reached up to her collar with both hands and fiddled with the mechanism, unclipping herself. She'd done the classic over-focusing on an idea instead of stepping back to analyze what was happening.

She gently rested the chain against the wall to avoid making it clink, then paced over to the desk. Although oversized, the build was very human-like, for its base was partitioned with multiple drawers. She reached up for the top central drawer—only to shoot her hand back.

"Be wary, for they have the power to alarm," she whispered. In an attempt to further understand the ship and its protections, she'd surreptitiously cast the occasional collar-suppressed Reveal, which had shown her that certain doorways and crates were enchanted with alarms.

After taking a calming breath, she splayed her hands, wanting to use both in the hope of strengthening and stabilizing the casting, and incanted, "*Un vun asperio aurum enchantus.*"

Unusually crude blue tendril geometries revealed themselves on each drawer. They were widely spaced apart and very fresh, as if cast by an apprentice performing their first alarm casting. Already barely visible due to the collar suppression, they promptly flickered out, but their afterglow remained. Like a late-year arcaneology student whose entire future rested on the exam, Bridget studied that afterglow from memory. She even practiced pinching the tendrils and unwinding them a certain way that should lead to dissolution.

"You can do this. Just got to concentrate," she whispered, girding her soul for the next crucial casting. "*Exotus mia enchantus duo dai ideum exat,*" she whispered, the incantation to Disenchant. The webbing flickered back to life, weaker than before. She identified the lead tendril on the top drawer and pinched at it, but her fingers went through the noodle and she winced, scared she'd triggered the alarm. Yet the webbing remained, as bright blue as ice in the sunlight.

She tried again, slowing the pinch and focusing on the arcaneological principles of rigidity and permanence. She barely felt it, but her fingers caught onto the tendril vine. Just as gently, she pulled on the vine. Then it flickered out. Had it come undone? Running out of time, she decided she couldn't wait, and so she wincingly hooked her fingers under a lip where claws usually ventured and gently pulled.

Nothing seemed to happen, and the drawer opened to reveal a series of neatly wrapped scrolls, each inked with a crimson gargoyle rune — except for one, the central scroll which was inked in blue. Tilting her head, she withdrew this scroll and splayed it open on the desk.

What she saw took her breath away, for it was a detailed illustration of the ship revealing multiple views — top-down, cross-section, and length-wise, all drawn as if by a human craftsman. Yet upon closer inspection, it was evident that there were complexities involved that no human could know. Glyphs and cartouches and runes she had never laid eyes on before, not even at the academy. The closest historical example was ancient Rivican runic workmanship, but even that felt like a stretch.

The illustration, inked in rich black with tones of gray for the inner workings and supports and walls, showed the arcaneological workings of the ship — and there were many such frameworks, from how the bow was arcanely aided to cut through the waves, to how the keel could electrify with lightning, to how the hull could be iced up. But that was just a guess, for although some symbols appeared familiar — fire was a wavy flame within a cartouche, ice an icicle, lightning a lightning bolt — others were obscure and inscrutable squiggles and complexities.

Bringing her face near, she looked closely at various sections of the ship. One, shaped like a pyramid, stood out.

"A pentastone," she whispered.

The hairs on the back of her neck stood on end, for upon referencing its location between the cross section and the top-down view, she realized where the pentastone had to be.

Bridget turned about, allowing the scroll to furl up with a *shloop*, and looked up. Twenty feet above, within high reach of the captain, was a golden panel engraved with an intricate rune. The implication nearly knocked her over. Her intuition told her the pentastone had something to do with either protecting the ship … or aiding it in its transoceanic crossing.

"Ah-bee-gale?"

Bridget yelped and whirled about to find Grak watching her from the doorway with a puzzled expression. When he noticed the plan on the desk, his lone eye bulged as if about to pop out of its socket.

Bridget, a hand pressed to her chest from the fright of being discovered, slowly lowered that hand. While maintaining eye contact with Grak, who stood almost as horrified as her, she picked up the plan, placed it back in the drawer, and slid it closed. She paced over to the wall with the chain, picked it up, clipped it back on, and took a kneeling position once more, facing forward like before.

"Ah-bee-gale bad," Grak whispered, pacing back and forth. "Ah-bee-gale bad, bad, bad …"

"Don't tell him," Bridget whispered, staring straight ahead before looking up at him with pleading eyes. "Don't tell him or he'll kill me. Please keep me alive. *Please* …" Then she returned her gaze forward upon hearing the soft swish of Captain Gravak's wings in the hall. As Grak stiffened, she shut her eyes and meditated, trying not to think about the risk she had taken. She calmed her heart and walked over the drawbridge of her castle, but did not raise it, waiting in anticipation by the mechanism instead.

The captain barked some questioning growls at Grak, who replied a little too quickly for Bridget's liking. The chain clinked, and she was roughly bid to stand, as if Grak was angry with her. Bridget opened her eyes to see the captain jump up on his perch, holding a gigantic furled scroll. His long claws handled it with delicate ease, pinching it gently, much like she had the alarm tendril only moments before.

The captain absentmindedly growled a phrase and Grak hauled Bridget to a huge barrel with a tap, where she picked up a wooden bowl and filled it with water. Relieved not to have been caught, she performed the duty expected of her, which was to kneel before the captain and wash his grimy toe claws.

As she did so, lathering up a rag with a pungent and oily soap unfamiliar to her, the captain unfurled the scroll and read it above her. This particular scroll was dense with cartouches, confirming that the gargoyles were literate. Or at least this one was.

After that, she was careful to keep her eyes down while she slowly washed her master's claws. Yet a tiny smile crept into the corners of her mouth, for Bridget had retreated to her castle, where a fond memory awaited—that of her brother-in-war Augum washing her tired feet in the sacred plane of Ley whilst performing an ancient ritual of restitution. She remembered their banter and how he had spoken of his beloved Leera, and how Bridget had spoken of her love, Ollie.

A memory that felt like it belonged to a life she no longer had.

THE FIRST STRATEGY

LEERA

As the wind whistled through the rigging and whipped her hood about her head, Leera watched her former ship, the *Rose of the Seas*, carve waves a quarter league behind *Saltfang*, their new ship. The other two ships of the fleet trailed in a line behind it. Augum had negotiated that the three cutters would accompany *Saltfang* as far as they could before the storms inevitably forced them to turn back.

Leera could almost see the look of pure resentment on the Lord High Commander's face from here. He, most of his men, and the bulldog-like Black Eagle had remained on the *Rose of the Seas*. Interestingly the king's nephew and heir to the throne, Carter Southguard, had disobeyed a direct order to stay aboard, forcing the Lord High Commander to order Black Eagle Mahmoute, the scheming Alanna Haught, and the immature Bloomington-Southguards to come aboard *Saltfang* and watch over him.

"And for all your bluster, you were too cowardly to come along yourself," Leera said into the wind, glad the Lord High Commander had not done so. He was an awful man with poor leadership skills, and the ship and its crew were all the better for his absence, for some men weren't cut out for voyages that required camaraderie and trust. He was so awful that she envisioned pinching at his foot with her claws, tossing him skyward, and enjoying his screams before he fell down her gullet.

Rogor the wolven had also come aboard, complaining about lowlander ships looking like deathtraps. Perpetually seasick, he continued to mostly remain below, sometimes pawing at a human book, sometimes a scroll, all in an effort to "better understand your lowlander barbarisms," as he had said.

Behind her, the old captain snapped confident but quiet commands to his bosun, a burly man with a gigantic walrus mustache and tilted cap, who in turn shouted the commands to the crew in a thick dockside accent. Sailors, young and old alike and each hand-selected by the captain, clung to the swaying masts above, adjusting sails as needed. Ropes were constantly pulled or loosened, and something was always being scrubbed or cleaned or oiled or repaired or tarred, yet the men seemed happy and convivial, oft singing sea shanties or telling tall tales or cracking jests that would turn any landlubber's ears pink.

Swells as large as a house rolled by underneath the ship, creating a steady rhythmic motion Leera rather enjoyed, just as she enjoyed her alone time. It had been a long series of days getting the ship prepared. When not transferring supplies, she had been training alongside Augum and Jez. She and Augum had also been training with Isobel, which had taken a toll on them mentally, for the shadow once again slunk about, eager to make itself known. But at least they'd made some headway in keeping it behind the curtain.

In her spare time, she'd been thumping her brains against the Zygothika book, desperate to unlock its secrets, as well as despondently checking the Arcaner vault. She'd also been putting up with Limpet, who was about as interested in being an apprentice as she was in being a mentor. The kid mostly strolled about the decks, sometimes humming to himself, sometimes staring at people as they worked, sometimes pawing through a book he had brought along or borrowed from the bookshelf in his cabin. He never helped, and if he said something, it was usually a criticism or an insult. He had yet to make a single friend, which seemed to suit him just fine.

Having gorged herself on a hearty lunch of hot and spicy chili and buttered and peppered bread, Leera yawned and stretched her arms, ready for a nap. As she turned about to walk to the cabin and flop onto her bunk—on this boat she shared a cabin with Augum, for propriety can stuff itself—she bumped into Alanna.

"Hey," the woman blurted, red-cheeked.

Leera walked around her without a word.

"So, uh, whatcha workin' on?" Alanna asked in a sing-song voice that made it all too obvious that she was playing cute.

Leera's reply was to halt her steps and sigh loudly.

"It's just that I saw you poking at a book in your cabin."

"Maybe *you* shouldn't be pokin' about where *your* beak don't belong," Leera mocked in the same cute-style voice. *Rise up. Let her feel the cold of your shadow*, The Callousness of the Predator hissed into her ear.

"Must be a challenging book if you're constantly trying to decipher it. Maybe I could help."

"Or maybe you could mind your own business," Leera snapped, continuing on.

"We don't have to be enemies, you know!" Alanna shouted after her.

"Don't have to be friends either," Leera sang back, not bothering to flap a hand over her shoulder. Why waste the effort on a tart who was no doubt angling for something else? "Did she think I was going to forget how she tried to steal my man?" Leera said to herself.

"Why would she do that?" squeaked the kid.

Leera, who'd entered the hold, happened to have walked past Limpet's cabin. She backtracked to see him sitting on his bunk, legs swinging underneath, hands gripping a thick book.

"Is it because you're so ugly and she's so pretty?" The red-haired little monster grinned evilly.

"Stop pretending you can read and go back to what you do best— eating your own boogers." *Now this one ought to see you bare your teeth. Imagine him pissing himself and*—Leera pressed her eyes shut as she shoved the voice away. Too many castings in too short a time meant a bleed-over effect. She needed to work on controlling it.

"I don't eat boogers, you do!"

"Sure thing, booger-eater. Is that a book on booger-eating?"

"No!" Limpet adjusted the wrinkled lapel of his burgundy robe as he raised his nose.

"Surprised you can even read," she threw in.

"It's actually a *very* complicated book on navigation using astrological signs."

Leera thought she glimpsed a look of hurt flash across his face. *Hmm, maybe he's got a heart somewhere under all that arrogance after all*, she thought.

But then he threw in, "It's for smart people like me, not dumb people like you. I'm going to help the captain when you stupid lot eventually get lost."

"The captain is far too skilled to get lost," she muttered and walked on.

"Why don't you stop being lazy and train me in something awesome!" he shouted after her.

Leera backtracked again to lean against the doorway, where she folded her arms. "Great, let's do that. You're a, what, aspirant?"

"I'm a 2nd degree and you know it! Stop playing dumb."

"Oh, wow, a whole 2nd degree? My gosh, almost a master."

"Your jests are *so* dumb."

Leera shrugged. "Well, *I* like them."

"*I* don't."

"My heart is broken."

"I hate you."

"Oh no, whatever will I do?" Leera asked in a tone as flat as a countertop. "You sure you don't want one of us to 'port you back home? Ain't no turning back once we slice into those storms."

"Told you a thousand times no. I'm coming along. And you should train me on something awesome. Right now."

"Well as a mighty 2nd degree, I suppose we should get you working on the 3rd degree spells you'll need to learn in order—"

"I don't *want* to learn those stupid spells! I want to learn awesome stuff like Teleport and Strength and Bewitch."

"You want to learn an 8th, a 9th, and a practically illegal 14th degree spell."

"That's what I just said, you oaf!"

"But the 3rd degree *is* awesome." She held up a fist and raised fingers as she listed off spells. "Mind Armor. Object Alarm. Object Track. The First Offensive. Don't you want to learn The First Offensive? You'd be a natural at terrorizing people." Then she added in a mutter, "Which will send you straight to the brig once you inevitably abuse it."

"I already know it, dum-dum. And my mind is as strong as iron."

"Yeah? So if I cast a spell against you, you won't wilt like a flower?"

"Of course not."

Leera considered testing the kid, but suspected doing so would only humiliate him. Besides, it was almost more fun seeing his arrogance play out naturally. She would just have to keep him from getting into a real battle lest he get blown to bits.

"I guess Object Track could be fun," Limpet said. "But sticking something in your pocket and following a dullard like you about a tiny ship would get boring quick."

"Uh-huh. Look, it really isn't too late to change your mind, Limpy." She thumbed toward the stern. "I can drop you off at the other ship and that bulldog-looking Black Eagle can probably hop you back to the island by nightfall. Or maybe Jez could do it if she gets in the mood." *And if she's sober*, Leera thought.

"You hate me and just want to dump me. I'm telling on you."

Leera shrugged. "Fine, whine like a baby. Go on." She affected a bratty voice as she pretended to talk into her nautical ring. " 'Hi, Mr. Mollusk? Yeah, hi. I wanted to report that they're being *so* mean to me because they're all so dumb and all they have to do here is stupid chores and I didn't even bring any of my toys' ..." She ignored what the callousness wanted to add, which were horrible things not even this kid deserved.

"I don't sound like that and I wouldn't say that!"

"You sure?"

Limpet raised his ring to his lips, threatening to reach out to his former mentor. When Leera only raised her eyebrows and drummed her thigh in anticipation, he dropped his hand and pressed his lips together in a firm pout.

"Seriously, kid, reconsider all this. Once we hit those storms, there's no crying to daddy. We might get thrashed and sink right to the bottom. Then what? Nobody's going to save a brat."

"He wasn't my *dad*, idiot."

"Is it because I'm a girl? You'd rather talk to a man, that it?"

"No, you're *all* morons. Insipid morons."

"Whoa, big word. *Insipid*. Did you learn that one today?"

"And obtuse. Insipid and obtuse."

"Obtuse. Good one. What's a fancy word for booger-eater?"

"Shut up."

"Right. Enjoy the reading and eating," and she strode off, disappointed with herself for stooping to a dumb kid's level. "That's why you'd make a terrible mother," she muttered as she stepped into her shared cabin, slamming the door behind herself. *You think you will be a mother? The only thing you will birth are eggs in a jungle filled with prey—*

"Shut up!" she hissed, punching the wall. "That was stupid," she wheezed, wincing and shaking the pain off.

Amidst the timber creaking and whistling of the wind and the rattling chain of a tiny unlit lantern, she flopped onto the bed, kicked off her shoes, and rubbed her eyes. She had to work harder at solving the shadow problem. Having an earful of terrible thoughts at every turn was no way to live, and she was sick and tired of second-guessing herself and especially of the sheer vindictiveness of the blasted voice.

A knock came at the door.

"What!"

The door creaked open, and Olaf's head peeked through. "Hey."

"Hey," she replied glumly.

"Any word yet?"

"I literally checked an hour ago."

"So ... nothing?"

"Ollie, the moment Bridge sends word, I'll be hollering your name all over the ship and pounding on your cabin door until you choke on your snoring and spring up."

"Right. Great. Uh ... you all right?"

"Fine. Why?"

"You look a little down."

"Peachy."

"Okaaaaaay. See you later, I guess. And thanks."

Leera flicked a couple of fingers goodbye and returned to rubbing her eyes with them, one arm under her head. Then she realized what she wanted to do and bolted upright. "Wait, Ollie! Ollie!"

The door flew open. "What, you heard from her is she all right is—"

"No, no, nothing like that. Uh ... are you busy by chance?"

He thumbed over his shoulder. "Just finished freezing fresh stores in the hold and was going to do my dailies."

"Instead of cycles, want to do me the *wee* favor of watching my back? I was thinking of hopping in again." She flicked her head at the empty space above her and clicked her tongue, adding, "I can also check if there's been word from Bridgey-poo."

Olaf beamed as he stepped inside and went to close the door behind him, only to catch it with his foot before it clicked shut. "Want me to fetch Aug?"

Leera stood to wave a hand aside. "Nah, leave him be. He's training what's-his-face, Carter. I won't be long."

"Are you going to cast ... *the spell*?"

"Yes, but this time, I'm going to stay inside with Isobel."

Olaf breathed a sigh of relief, probably because it was a particular sort of hell for him to have to goad them into stepping back into the portal to continue the lessons while under the influence of The Callousness of the Predator.

Leera summoned her shield and incanted, "*Summano vaultus arcanus.*" The vault *whooshed* into existence, making the already small cabin feel that much more cramped. As was her habit, she immediately checked that Bridget's far-right door was still lit, indicating she was alive, before opening her left-most door and letting her shield vanish. Then she reached into the vault to grab hold of Isobel's tablet crest, which had been stuffed into the vault in such a way that it straddled both her side and Augum's. It was jammed in there so tightly though that she had to prop her foot up against the edge of the vault to yank it free—and was sent flying against the back of the cabin when it popped loose.

"Thought you once said that the vault only accepted paper," Olaf said, swooping in to poke and prod about Leera's side, hoping to spot a note from Bridget. "No luck," he muttered.

Augum and Leera had mutually decided that they implicitly trusted Olaf with the vault. After all, if he couldn't be trusted, what hope was there for anyone?

"The creators made a few exceptions," Leera replied, dumping the crest onto the bunk and slapping her vault door shut. Then she swiped at the air. "*Vaultus null*," and the vault vanished with another *whoosh*.

Olaf sighed as he stared at the empty space the vault had occupied. "You think she's thinking about me?" he whispered in a distant voice.

"More than you think, big guy." After seeing his face light up with a pained smile, Leera resummoned her shield and pressed into the clay tablet resting on the bed. "*Semperis vorto honos*." Pelagia appeared, legs vanishing into the bunk. Leera launched right into it. "First hour of Meditation Class One, please, Pelagia."

"First hour of Meditation Class One for Dragon Jones," Pelagia replied, and drew a black oval that clipped through the bunk.

"Shoot, I should have positioned the crest better," Leera muttered. Pelagia always appeared at a certain position relative to the crest, and there was a trick to doing it so that the portal was not impeded or cut off by objects.

"Wait, are you starting at the very beginning?" Olaf asked.

"Just following a hunch. I want to see if Isobel says anything different. Should have done it from the get-go," she added and crawled onto the bed. "See you soon."

"Good luck, and don't take too long. You don't want to crawl out into the bottom of the ocean," and he chuckled nervously.

She breathed a half-hearted laugh, yet he had a point. Each time she or Augum went through the portal, they risked something happening back at the ship—and there was no way to reach them once inside, and that included setting alarms. For some reason, they failed to penetrate whatever world Isobel conjured for them.

Leera crawled into the portal and appeared on a grassy hill facing vast rolling plains, the hazy outline of snow-capped mountains rising in the distance. Nearby stood a rough-stone hut with a grass roof, silently puffing out a column of smoke. Today the sky was gray, with low cloud cover, markedly different from the first time she took this lesson with Augum and Bridget, when it had been partially sunny.

"Greetings, Dragon," said the primitive voice of Isobel Roseheart from behind Leera.

Leera's reply was to raise both arms and one leg in the praying mantis pose and, after a few heartbeats of concentration, incant, "*Xae carna draca arcan doma legenda rava.*" Her body bulked up into the greatest predator of them all. After settling into her form, she looked down at Isobel, with her warrior face and thick dreads and wolfskin. Despite being awash with Leera's natural Fear aura that splashed ahead of all dragons, the ancient founder of the Arcaner order merely gazed up at her with serene calm.

"I will return," Leera said and leaped skyward, where she gave mighty flaps of her wings, cutting into the air and climbing higher and higher.

Rain pelted her skin, yet she did not feel wetness like a human would. Her dragon form distanced her from small sensations like that. Because of the thick hide, she could bathe in mud and feel perfectly comfortable, for example.

She ascended to three thousand feet and skimmed along the bottom of the clouds, enjoying the sight of the green hillsides rolling by like ocean waves. To speed things along, she thought she ought to perform cycles, and so she began by slapping her wrists together and roaring, "*Annihilo bato!*" Two massive jets of water shot toward an approaching mountain. They slammed into a rocky outcrop, exploding its base and sending the entire shelf tumbling down the mountain in a roaring plume.

Leera angled into a dive, chasing after the rockfall, practicing her aim by shooting First and Second Offensives at various tumbling boulders, tail and wings moving this way and that as she dipped and rose around obstacles. When the debris smashed into a field of pines, cracking and splintering their trunks with a most satisfactory *crunch*, she flew above the trees, allowing her wings to skim their canopies like a child walking through tall grass with outstretched arms. She felt her natural Fear aura splash ahead of her, and pictured enemies screaming as they dove for cover.

Except one of those trees was a large and gnarled oak, and thus particularly tough—and it caught one of Leera's wings and sent her spiraling about. She went with the momentum and rolled amidst the leafy forest, then sprang onto her hind legs and drew the outline of the offending tree, incanting, "*Paralizo carcusa cemente!*" The tree, being immune to Paralyze, stood as before, but that didn't stop Leera from treating it like an adversary.

She twirled aside, imagining a giant spear shooting by, and shoved at the air, roaring, "*Baka!*" The tree swayed back before straightening. She sprang forth to dip her snout below the encroaching trunk and slammed the base of her palm into one of its thicker branches, as she would have under the chin of an enemy. She next whipped her tail about and slapped the tree's trunk, imagining her opponent doubling over in agony. Then she whirled about and whapped the tree with the back of an arm before jiggling a hand up at an imaginary head, hissing, "*Flustrato!*"

She followed up with a flurry of spells—Fear and Deafness and Paralyze and Mute and Slow and Blind and Sleep, among others.

The more she cast, the stronger the whispers sounded at the back of her mind, goading her into ever more violent acts and inflating her confidence. Here she was, the queen of the skies, able to cause terror with a mere look or flyby. Here she was, the queen of the jungles and forests and mountains, practicing for the wars ahead—for her own ascent into the dominion of rule by claw and spell, by might makes right.

Her stamina steadily drained as she continued the fearsome barrage. When it neared emptiness, she ended by casting Strength on herself, at which point she grabbed the oak by the base and near the top and, muscles screaming, bent its thickest branch off until it splintered—and finally cracked right off. Acorns fell by the hundreds, and she took a step back to raise the stricken branch above her head, imagining holding the bloody appendage of a vanquished gargoyle.

"You shall know dominance soon enough!" she roared into the quiet forest, the rain pelting her with large droplets. "I am coming for you ..." she whispered, lowering her arm. She was a dragon. Leera? Who was Leera? Some useless girl left behind.

Then you admit to turning into the horse and leaving behind the rider, she thought. *What then of the watcher who watches?*

She looked down at the branch, noting its fragility before letting it go. It dropped to the ground, a broken symbol of ... something. Maybe her heart. Or her humanity. Or her future. She did not know.

"It's just a mirage," she said to the wounded tree, the human part of her feeling sorry for it. "An arcane figment. I cannot hurt what is not real."

She raised her snout and closed her eyes, listening to the quiet pitter-patter of the rain, feeling her dragon breath steaming into the cool mountain air.

"Bah," she said, and she stretched out her wings and took to the air, returning all the way to the hillside with its cozy cabin, where she landed before Isobel in time for a forced reversion to take place.

As the rain petered out into a mist, a cold-eyed Leera raised her chin at Isobel.

Isobel paced around her as she had that first time around the trio. "Welcome, Dragon," she began. "Thus you come with a splintered soul, suffering the agonies of The Callousness of the Predator. I too have suffered this callousness, as did those who came after me. Those who aid in the efforts of this training. Now *you* shall reap the lessons of old, quietly passed down from generation to generation, across eons of time."

"I wish to be the watcher," Leera declared. "Neither the rider nor the horse, yet in full command of my future."

Isobel continued to pace around a callous Leera. "In my era, we tried everything known to us at the time. Incense and prayer and sacrifices and oaths of blood. But in the eras that followed, the progeny of the idea of the dragon learned the simplicities of the masters of the mountains. Those with shaved pates and quiet demeanors."

"The Northern Monks," Leera whispered, taking cool pleasure in hearing herself bring solemnity to the moment. Existence revolved around her, and despite being cut off from her mighty arcanery, she felt like a goddess.

"We came to understand that the callousness has an opposite—the human, for to be human is to know empathy. Then came the question of whether empathy could be taught to a beast, for in its primal form, the callousness is but a beast." Isobel ceased her circling to stand before Leera. "The more you give in to the demands of the beast, the closer to the beast you grow, until you *become* the beast."

"So I *can* turn into a dragon forever ..." Leera whispered, hopes soaring that she could become the queen she was destined to be.

"On the contrary. Those who indulge in the callousness for too long or allow its claws to sink into the flesh of their soul shall suffer it in their day-to-day lives. Should this indulgence continue unaddressed, the callousness itself, after each casting, shall become longer and longer, until the human is replaced in totality."

"Which means I'd probably transgress the honor of the shield, causing a dim, which would in turn lose me the power to turn into a dragon."

"That is correct. In the eras that followed mine, this happened to those who could not keep The Callousness of the Predator at bay. Those souls were condemned to lose the powers of the dragon ... and in some situations access to the very powers that defined them as a warlock."

"The arcane arts ..." Leera whispered, eyes unfocusing as she imagined turning into an Ordinary. Even suffering callousness, the very thought made her shiver. "So what you're telling me is that this path is a dead end. That the callousness will not allow me the power of the dragon, but will take it away—and maybe even kill the warlock within me."

"That is correct, Dragon Jones. And so you must convince the callousness that it is not in its own interests to take over. I can aid you in this regard by teaching you fundamental techniques in meditation. These techniques vary depending on the situation." She stepped back. "You are ready for the first lesson."

Leera folded her arms and tapped her foot. "What *is* the first lesson?"

"To focus on the physical. By drawing attention away from the thoughts of predation, we can quicken the side effect, thus shortening it. Sit with me, like so," and Isobel took a seat before Leera, carefully crossing her legs, placing her hands gently upon her knees, and straightening her back.

Leera mimicked her but kept her back bent out of familiarity—and laziness. "Now what?" she snapped.

"Now we pay attention to our bodies. We start with the toes. Do you feel your largest toe?"

Leera rolled her eyes. "Obviously."

"Concentrate, Dragon Jones. Close thine eyes and empty thy mind. Think only of your biggest toe."

Leera expelled an annoyed breath but did as she was told, for there was one thing she feared as a predator—losing all her power, especially the one that allowed her to become a dragon. If it took quelling the blasted callousness that made her feel so powerful, so be it. It had to be done.

"I can feel my big toe," Leera said in the most bored tone she could muster. She still wanted to annoy her teacher, for she despised the idea of positioning herself as lesser than another, as having less knowledge.

"You can also feel the callousness attempting to take control with insidious thoughts. Pay it no heed. Instead, one at a time, become conscious of your other toes. Breathe slowly." Isobel's cadence slowed, voice softening. "Now feel your foot. Now your ankle. Now your thigh. Now your leg in whole. Now your thumb. And your other fingers. Your palm. Your hand. Your elbow. Your shoulder …"

On the lesson went. Leera followed it with skepticism, yet an amazing thing happened. By the time the exercise led her through to the head, she felt the blush of emotion return—much sooner than expected. Like a spark in a dark cavern, the light of empathy flared. With each new focus point, that spark grew into a flame and then a raging fire, until Leera burst with a cry.

She knew intrinsically that *this* was indeed the right path, as she had suffered The Callousness of the Predator for the shortest amount of time since having learned the Spirit of the Dragon simul years ago.

That cry strengthened until she was holding her face and full-on sobbing. When she finished, she looked up to find Isobel standing before her.

"You have learned the first strategy. There are others. Return and learn as needed, moving through the lesson hours. You need not attend them all, but variety will aid in your efforts to curtail the callousness. In time, with persistence and training, you will find the sacred balance."

Leera stood to brush the wet grass off her behind. "To become the watcher."

Isobel smiled.

Leera refrained from punching Isobel's arm. "I suppose I should step through that there portal so I can eat. I'm starved."

Isobel merely stood there.

"Not one for banter, I guess," Leera muttered. She nonetheless smiled at Isobel, who at least smiled back, before she stepped through—only to double over, having forgotten that the portal cut through the bunk bed, causing her legs to flip back and her body to roll forward.

When she untangled her limbs, she realized the cabin was on a steep angle, Olaf was no longer present, and what sounded like the whole ship was shouting all at once.

They were under attack.

BLACK FLAG

AUGUM

"Gods, would you look at the cut of it," a pale-faced Jengo said amidst the ringing of a bell and a call to man the decks. "Like an obsidian blade carving through sunset."

Augum, standing with him midship and under the forward mast, grabbed hold of a rope and hopped up onto a barrel to get a better view, shielding his eyes from the fiery sunset squished between the ocean and the clouds above.

"Easy there, Commander," Carter said. "Don't want you falling, sir."

The Bloomington-Southguard brothers exchanged a sneering look, as if they were tired of his sucking up. Augum paid them no heed, his attention focused on the sleek black-flagged three-masted ship that had appeared from around an island and was now slicing through the waves at a steep angle, on course to intercept *Saltfang*.

"Almost as long as a serpent," Jengo added, swallowing.

Augum looked to the old captain, who was casually barking out orders in between gumming his long pipe, his wrinkled face creased with excitement.

"She's a quick hit-'n'-dasher!" the captain shouted to his men, which Augum took to mean that she would hit them, rob them, then be off sailing before the other ships caught up.

There came a huffing sound. "Aug! Aug, Aug, Aug!"

Augum glanced down in time to feel Olaf jerk his arm, wrenching him off the barrel. Carter and Jengo immediately jumped in to prevent him from falling overboard.

"I'm fine, boys," Augum said, easily landing on the planks. *Worry not for the dragon, but for yourselves*, he thought, irritated. He was due for another lesson with Isobel, and would have been doing just that were it not for taking time to train Carter.

Olaf pressed his mouth close to Augum's ear. "Leera's inside the *you-know-what*."

Augum bolted before Olaf even finished, feet sliding on the slippery planks. He flicked a hand at the main cabin door, which telekinetically opened in time for him to plow through—and slam right into his girl, sending them both spinning to the floor.

"You all right?" Augum asked as he rushed to grab her arm and check her face.

"Of course I'm all right!"

"Are you callous?"

"Quite the opposite. I actually learned a good counter strategy you need to learn too. But I'll fill you in later. What's happening?"

"Black flagger on our rear, cutting a steep angle. She's a hit-'n'-dasher sort of ship."

"What does that mean? Never mind, I figured it out." She planted a kiss on his nose. "Let's move it, my love," and she hopped to her feet alongside him and ran outside. By then, everyone from down below had assembled on deck.

"Oh, she's fast," Jez said, taking a sip of wine.

Augum gave her a once-over and noticed her swaying more than be accounted for by the ship's motions. He made meaningful eye contact with Leera, indicating they would have to watch her. A drunk Jez was a foolhardy Jez. Then he remembered something. "Did you secure *the thing*?" he whispered to Leera.

Her subtle nod indicated she had jammed Isobel's tablet back into the vault.

"You're all going to diiiiie," Limpet sang.

"Who asked you, pipsqueak?" Digby growled, rearing his hand back as if about to whap him on the side of the head.

The kid recoiled, whining, "Shut up," and slunk to the back of the group.

Augum noticed Leera slip away from him and edge closer to the boy. By the way she was glancing between the boy and the black flagger, he knew she would do everything in her power to protect him, just as Augum would do for her.

He returned his gaze to the drama unfolding at sea, calculating the speed of the black flagger relative to the storm. "They're going to intercept us before we hit the storm wall," he whispered in conclusion and pronged fingers between Carter and the Bloomington-Southguards. "You lot keep together and keep shields."

Carter pressed three fingers against his heart in the Arcaner salute. "Yes, Commander."

"What does 'keep shields' mean?" Digby asked. "Is it some sort of secret Arcaner command?"

"Just means we're defending," Carter replied.

Augum next pronged fingers between Olaf and Jengo. "Ollie, you'll be a shield. Jengo, you're on support."

The pair nodded whilst pressing three fingers against their hearts, with Ollie adding, "Aye, aye, boss. Er, Commander."

Augum raised his chin at the others, shouting, "Prepare for an onslaught!"

Alanna Haught came to his side. "How can I help?" she asked, voice trembling.

Augum didn't miss a beat. "Watch over Leera, Jez, and the boy."

Alanna opened her mouth to argue, then swallowed her pride, nodded, and peeled away to stand behind Jez and Leera's group, something he was glad Leera failed to notice in her concern for the boy. In a quiet way, he was proud of Alanna for overcoming her covetousness and jealousy. Despite being a court flunky, a good woman existed within her, and he could see her one day applying to become an Arcaner. But his attention soon drifted to his girl.

"Cap!" he called to her. "Captain Jones!"

"What!" she snapped back.

"On shields."

"Obviously," she replied.

After smacking his lips in annoyance—Augum felt she needed to do a better job of respecting his command outside of their relationship—he approached Mahmoute, who stood beside the towering wolven in the rear.

"Any volunteers for the tip of the spear?" he asked.

Rogor bared his teeth. "A wolven does not need permission from a lowlander to extend his claws."

"Just don't kill any young ones," Augum replied. "The cubs."

Rogor's reply was to snarl and stride past to stand threateningly by the railing. The enemy vessel, which was making a beeline for them at a rapid clip and was now less than a thousand feet away, cheered with bloodlust upon seeing the wolven.

Augum looked to Mahmoute. "Captain says they usually have a couple warlocks on board and will be expecting our tricks."

"And we ought to be mindful of theirs," she replied. Her steely-eyed gaze was only for the oncoming ship, and he knew he could count on her. *These invaders have no idea what's about to hit them*, he thought as he went to the stern, where the captain was dictating short and quick commands to his crew.

"Port three."

"Port three degrees," the walrus-mustachioed bosun growled to a young helmsman, who turned the wheel ever so slightly to port.

"Star two."

"Starboard, two degrees," the bosun echoed.

"Port one."

"Port one degree."

"Steady as she goes."

"Steady as she goes, lad," the bosun said to the helmsman.

Tammy the sailblower stood nearby, arms extended as she manipulated the winds with a focused expression.

The old captain tapped her shoulder with the end of his pipe. "Squeeze 'er."

"We're at optimal slip in terms of sail to draft to beam ratio, sir. She's as sleek as she's going to get."

The captain sucked in air and gave a small shake of his head, telling Augum his calculations were correct—the black flagger would catch up before they could vanish into the storm ahead.

The ship was less than five hundred feet behind them and closing fast. Her bow was armed with long spears, possibly arcane harpoons.

The captain nodded ahead. "Well, boy, if ye truly *can* turn into a dragon, I reckon now would be the time to show 'em what you can do."

Augum stepped to the rail and considered it, but bulking up into a dragon here would certainly damage the rigging. He would have to do it from midship. Even so, something told him that if he did turn into that form, he would destroy the black flagger into splinters, sending every man to the bottom. Was slaughter what the ship deserved?

Then he saw the crew on the black flagger—and a full third looked to be only boys, some maybe as young as thirteen.

"Your hesitation tells me all I need to know, son," the captain said. "I guess those stories were just that—stories."

"Some of them are only kids," Augum replied.

The captain spoke with his pipe still in his mouth. "Kids or no, they want bounty, and that might mean the neck of your girl. Ready on my mark," he said to his bosun.

"Ready to tack," the bosun echoed.

"Prep for boarding."

"Prepare for boarding!" the bosun shouted to the entire crew, who echoed the cry up and down the ship—"Prepare for boarding! Prepare for boarding!"

There was the sound of swords and knives being unsheathed, as well as the *thunk* of shoes and boots landing on deck from crew manning yardarms. The swords the crew wore on their hips were curved slightly in the Nodian style and kept sharp, as they were sometimes needed to cut lines in an emergency.

"Why are they throwing their shoes off?" Augum asked, watching boots get dumped onto the deck by the dozen as the bosun gruffly tasked young sailors to "Hurry 'n' gather them up in baskets, lads."

"To gain better footing," the captain replied.

Augum considered him, getting the sense he had much experience with black flaggers. "What sort of 'locks should we expect?" he asked the man.

The captain looked at him like a grandfather at his daft grandchild. "The sort with salt for blood."

"How many and what degree?" *No time to play games, old man*, Augum thought. *Just tell me what I need to know.*

"Two at the least. Reckon half a sleeve apiece. Maybe stronger." He raised his pipe and pointed it, squinting with one eye. "See them kids hunkered about the ship? I wouldn't go 'portin' in there like a fool. You'll get yer throat slit before you get a word out."

Augum saw that there indeed were pirates hiding throughout the ship. He checked to confirm that the Solian ships had no hope of catching up anytime soon, nodded his thanks to the captain, and jogged back to his group, using the rails and lines for support.

"Expect at least two warlocks, 10th degree or higher," he reported. "As for the crew, they know our tricks, so no blind 'porting. Oh, and a third of them are kids."

Leera threw her arms up, muttering, "Great."

"Which means Paralyze, Slow, Sleep, and the like. We'll be aiming to take captors and offload them to our sister ships, so spread the word. Ollie—see if you can gather some rope to tie them up with."

"I'm on it," Olaf said, and went scavenging.

"Jengo, prep for—" and Augum tapped his own shoulder, chest, and temple with two fingers.

"I'll start the focus process now," Jengo said, and he shut his eyes, taking concentrative breaths as he murmured instructions to himself.

"Watch who you strike and *how* you strike," Augum said, aiming his words toward Carter's lot, as he did not trust the likes of Digby and Teague to be responsible. He nodded at Carter, reminding him that he was accountable for his cousins, a nod that was mirrored, telling him Carter understood the assignment.

Augum then flipped off his shoes. "They do it to get a better foothold," he said, forestalling the question.

The others followed his lead and threw their shoes and boots into a basket held by a passing crew member.

"Jez," Augum said to his mentor, who was holding onto the cabin for support with one hand, goblet in the other. "Jez!"

"What!"

Just like Leera, Augum thought, stopping himself from shaking his head. "Would you mind helping us with shields?" He had to be careful with his wording as she was prone to obstinacy.

"Yeah, yeah," and she took a final swig of her goblet before chucking it into an open barrel, where it smashed at the bottom. "What? I'll repair it later," she snapped upon spotting him staring.

Jengo wordlessly stepped before Augum, who gave him the go-ahead nod. Jengo pressed a hand to Augum's heart while nine rings of white light appeared around his forearm. "*Summano semperis vorto honos,*" he incanted, and his hand lit up with a gentle and warm glow.

Augum felt a surge of power through his soul, gaining an arcane potency that would bolster his spells by approximately two whole degrees. "Ally of the Dragon!" Augum called on Jengo's behalf so the healer could maintain his concentration.

Jengo turned about and raised his lit hand invitingly, and Leera jumped before him to receive that hand to her heart. She was followed quickly by Olaf and finally a staggering Jez.

"What's he doing?" Teague asked.

"Casting support simuls," Carter said and left his cousins to receive the ancient Arcaner blessing.

Notably, neither Teague nor Digby stepped forth, choosing instead to trade skeptical looks. Nor did Mahmoute, who had drifted away from the group as if preparing for Teleport.

"What is that gobbledygook?" Limpet asked. "I want to try it."

"Get away from there, kid," Jez said, yanking him back by the hood. "He can't spare his energy on you."

"Why?"

"Because he needs it for healing in case the pirates chop off your arm. Now go hide."

Limpet's face paled. He swallowed and backed away, looking for a place to hunker down.

Jengo next incanted, "*Summano stamina au draca persona*," and touched Augum's shoulder, fattening up his stamina by about sixty percent.

"Stamina of the Dragon!" Augum called on Jengo's behalf, and the line reformed, including Leera.

"*Summano minad au draca persona*," Jengo next incanted.

"Mind of the Dragon!" Augum called out, and the process was repeated one last time, with this simul strengthening their Mind Armor.

"Here they come!" a crew member shouted from above, and everyone's attention turned to the oncoming ship. With muscles as taut as lanyard lines, they watched as the black flagger cut a mean path directly toward them. For a time there was only the sound of the ship cutting through waves, the shrieking wind, and sails and flags and robes flapping madly.

"Don't forget, avoid lethals," Augum reminded his lot. "Subdue, subdue, subdue."

"Do they not realize we have warlocks on board?" Digby said.

"They do and don't care one hoof," Jez replied. "Pirates are crazy."

"Either way, they're about to get one rude wake-up call," Teague muttered.

At a hundred feet, the shouted taunts from the other ship reached them. It teemed with pirates wearing black bandanas and armbands whilst waving long curved blades and round bucklers. Like in the stories, most were tattooed, even those who looked to have barely entered their teenage years. And they were a scrappy bunch, for some had missing teeth, one lacked an arm, another had a peg for a leg. Despite the cold, many proudly bore naked chests raked with scars.

"Hit their sails!" Augum shouted, and slapped his wrists together, roaring, "*Annihilo bato!*" sending two bolts of lightning toward the largest sail—only to witness the bolts shoot away as if diverted.

Other attacks met similar fates—even Mahmoute's quadruple vine punch veered away on either side of the masts.

"They've got 'emselves an angler!" the bosun shouted.

"The hell's an angler?" Leera asked.

Augum had an idea of what the term meant and looked carefully at the throng ahead. Sure enough, someone near the front but hidden in the crowd had both arms up and was pointing at incoming spells and bending them away. It told Augum that the person possessed high expertise in Telekinesis, serving as a warning that the enemy should not be underestimated.

Suddenly there came a loud *twang!* from the front of the black flagger as a long metal harpoon shot forth, trailing a tow chain. By the time Augum thought to try to bend its arc into the ocean, it smashed into *Saltfang's* side, and a tremor ripped through the deck, making everyone stumble.

"Shields keep midship, shields midship!" Augum shouted as he ran toward the spot, accompanied by Rogor and Mahmoute. He slammed into the railing and looked down to see that the harpoon was firmly lodged in the deck below. On the black flagger, men worked as a team to wind a gigantic reel mechanism.

"Fifty feet and reelin' us in on their windlass!" a crew member shouted from the halyard.

Augum summoned his lightning shield and enlarged it to as big as it would grow, which was almost the size of his body. He angled it this way and that, showing off the full Arcaner crest to let the enemy know who they were dealing with. But the taunting shouts only grew louder as they neared, telling Augum the pirates were just like everyone else on the ocean—they did not believe in the power of the dragon, likely thinking it was a ruse or a tall tale.

"Thirty feet and closing!" came the call from above, which was echoed down the length of the ship. "Thirty feet! Thirty, thirty, thirty!"

"Incoming! Cover, cover, cover!" someone shouted from above as arrows and first and second offensives began to zip in from the black flagger. There was the clunking sound of people raising wooden shields, which joined those who had already summoned their elemental shields.

Augum kept his shield forward and felt three *thunks* against it. Every time he dipped out to fire a tempered First Offensive, another arrow zipped in, with one nearly skewering his face—a strike that would have instantly ended his life then and there. The barrage indicated that these pirates were trained to deal with warlocks and weren't playing around.

"Twenty, twenty, twenty!" came the call from above, echoed up and down the ship.

Augum felt a *whoosh* as something shot by him. He peeked out from behind his shield to see that Rogor had used the railing as a leap point to launch himself onto the other ship, his body armored with an airy crust, a summoned airy blade in one hand and an airy shield in the other. He was so strong that he easily cleared the gap and barreled into the enemy like a giant ball thrown by a catapult. Pirates went tumbling and flying, with more than one kid hooking onto the guideline ropes lest they splash into the frigid ocean water below.

Missiles shot back and forth between the two ships. Many from the black flagger were elemental—one of which was a large fireball that exploded into a lower sail, bursting it into flames and engulfing a young crew member who had been working on tightening a line. The crew member screamed as he fell and slammed to the deck—right in front of Jengo, who didn't miss a beat, immediately going to work on him whilst telling people to make room.

"Cover the wounded!" Augum shouted, waving an arm at Olaf, who happened to be standing nearby. Olaf nodded and kneeled behind Jengo, keeping his relatively small ice shield up as a ward against the arrows.

"Ten, ten, ten!" a crew member shouted at the same time as the bosun roared, "Watershapers snuff out the fire! Talkin' to you, ladies! Splash, splash, splash!"

Augum witnessed Jez and Leera aim and spray swaths of water at the sail, snuffing the flames with a satisfying *hiss*.

Another fireball went up, but this time it was met with a fierce gust of wind that pushed it just enough for it to *hiss* by one of the largest sails before falling harmlessly into the ocean beyond.

"Way to go, Tammy," Augum found himself saying under his breath, using his shield to cover a crew member who was readying a small bow and quiver of blunt arrows.

"Aim only at the adults," Augum instructed, shield consistently sustaining *thunks*.

"Yes, sir," the bare-footed young man squeaked in a trembling voice. "Never been in no scrap before, sir."

"Just do your best."

"Yes, sir. I will, sir." But every time he dared to swivel around Augum's shield and wincingly take a shot, the attempt was so wild that it either sailed well past the ship or ripped through a sail or simply thunked into the hull, reminding Augum that the majority of people were not cut out for battle.

When Augum stole another peek, waiting for the right moment to strike—ship on ship combat was wholly new to him, after all—a massive vine web shot forth from *Saltfang*. Certainly a product of Mahmoute's spell casting, it quickly expanded before enveloping the black flagger's sails, corralling and entwining them—and reducing their effect with the wind. As pirates above hacked away at the vines, someone from *Saltfang* screamed, "They're going to ram us!"

Augum felt his eyes bulge, for despite the entanglement, the black flagger plowed forth like a gigantic spear, its pronged metal bow, built for ramming, gleaming. And just behind that bow, men worked alongside a warlock to rapidly spin the windlass along.

"Tack port! Port, port, port!" came a call from the captain, and the ship veered toward the wind, which opened it up to what would surely be a lethal broadside ram. Just as Augum thought the grizzled captain had made a fatal error in judgment, the man shouted to tack the other way, and the ship veered off, throwing up a wall of wake—a clever maneuver meant to minimize the damage.

"Brace for impact!" came a chorus of shouts. "Brace, brace, brace—!"

Augum grabbed hold of the railing and the ship jolted with a loud splintering as the black flagger slid alongside, the two hulls screeching as they rubbed. Despite it being a glancing blow, it was violent enough to send the young man with the bow tumbling over the rail. Luckily for the sailor, Augum's Arcaner-trained reflexes kicked in and he telekinetically snatched him by the pants and hauled him back over the railing—absent his bow and quiver, which had tumbled to the ocean.

Before the sailor even had a chance to thank Augum, all hell broke loose as pirates spilled on board, hacking and slashing with crazed abandon. To Augum's surprise, the crew of *Saltfang* launched themselves at the enemy even before he could mount a concerted assault, as if they'd done this many times before.

A *thwomp* sounded from Mahmoute's direction, and Augum saw her appear at the very back of the enemy ship, where an earth warlock stood throwing vine punches and more web-like spells. The pair descended into a blurred volley of offensives, two earth warlocks going toe to toe.

Augum focused on the only other enemy warlock he could spy—a man who now proudly stood tall above his crew members, one foot on the rail, arms working this way and that as he either threw mind spells, the occasional fireball, or angled offensives away from his ship and crew.

The angler, Augum realized.

The man's scalp was disfigured; he wore a giant hoop earring, a nose ring, and multiple lip rings; and his face and neck were cleanly shaven and heavily tattooed. He wore a high-collared black robe, traditionally the symbol of necromancy, but in this case it seemed to be a symbol of loyalty to his pirate brethren, for his arm burned with around fifteen fiery rings—it was hard to make a snap count at that distance.

Seeing that one of the yardarms was somewhat overhead of the man and free from vine entanglements, Augum imagined seeing his feet balancing on it, with his toes gripping the wood and his back to the puffed-out sail. He let his shield vanish and snapped, "*Impetus peragro!*" He shot forth through the ether and appeared an eyeblink later on that very yardarm, where he used precious time to reach behind him and grab the edge of the triangular sail lest he fall off.

Fifteen feet below, the bald enemy warlock was surrounded by strapped-down barrels and six guard crew members, three of whom had bows and the other three curved blades. Obviously trained to listen for *thwomps*, all seven pirates looked up.

Even as Augum thought, *Uh-oh*, the bald pirate, who was quicker than the archers, swiveled his arms upward and slapped his wrists together, roaring, "*Annihilo ito!*" Three fireballs *whooshed* up at Augum. But fifteen feet of distance was plenty enough time for Augum to summon his mighty crest shield. The fireballs smashed into it with such strength that the shield smacked his jaw and his body pressed against the sail.

Realizing his position was too precarious and his back too much up against a wall—or in this case a sail, the canvas of which was far more rigid than he'd expected—he envisioned a spot ten feet behind the barrels, where there was no crew, and once more incanted, "*Impetus peragro!*"

He appeared in the empty space—and barely dodged a sword swipe, for a crew member, evidently hiding behind a barrel and waiting for just such an opportunity, had lunged for his neck. Augum kept stepping back to fluidly dip away from a ferocious series of hissing slices, keeping his shield at his side to draw wilder and wilder swings, until he earned an opening which he seized upon by violently yanking at the man. He ducked a final clumsy swing as the pirate stumbled past, then shoved at his back, roaring, "*Baka!*" sending him flying overboard, where he splashed into the icy ocean below.

He had only a moment for a pang of regret to cross his mind before *twang!* went an arrow shot, which *thunked* into a barrel directly behind him. Two more twangs followed, which *thunked* into Augum's shield, for he had swiveled it about by then.

"*Disablo!*" shouted the bald warlock, ripping the shield from Augum's arm, making it vanish.

Augum's reply was to yank with both hands at the archers, roaring, "*Disablo!*"

Both of their bows twirled skyward, while the third archer frantically reloaded. Augum made his job that much harder by flicking a hand, telekinetically tipping the bow into his groin, and causing his arrow to shoot harmlessly into the planks between his feet.

As the archer gulped from the close call, the bald fire warlock shoved at the air, shouting, "*Baka!*" forcing Augum to whirl aside to avoid getting blown overboard. '

In the mean, two of the three sword-wielders guarding the warlock closed in, with the third remaining behind to guard his boss. Augum opened his hands at the men and slapped them together, and his mighty Telekinesis, strengthened by the Ally of the Dragon blessing, warped the space around him—and sent the men crashing into each other. There was a sickening *crack* as their heads smashed together. The pair tumbled onto the planks, unconscious.

There was not a moment to take a breath, for a double *twang* sounded from the pair of archers who had tracked down their bows. Augum countered by expertly resummoning his shield and slicing it across his body in time to catch both arrows, which would have surely punctured a couple holes in his unprotected chest.

The archers were so impressed by this feat that they exchanged looks, while the third one with the arrow between his feet said, "Impossible ..."

Ignoring them for the time being, Augum, curious how the warlock would react, jiggled his wrist at his head, hissing, "*Flustrato!*" but the man ducked with ease, and the spell instead smacked into his sword guard, whose head snapped back. The guard began to stumble about as if unsure of where and who he was.

The fire warlock blocked the aim of the archers as he pressed forth, launching a combination of spells, arms and hands a blur. "*Dreadus terrablus! Flustrato! Effectus Xadius! Voidus aurus!*"

Augum ducked the Fear casting, spun away from the Confusion spell, ducked again to avoid Slow, and then let the Deafness casting hit his strengthened Mind Armor. The spell, cast at a potent 15th degree, smashed full-force into the castle of his mind, denting the walls.

"My turn," Augum hissed, and slapped his wrists together, roaring, "*Annihilo bato!*" Two lethal bolts of lightning *sizzled* at the bald warlock, who responded by flicking a finger from each hand. The bolts, which would have blown both of his arms off had he not reacted, changed trajectories to angle past his body on either side.

One smashed into a gaping archer, who took it square in the chest. He had enough time to look down at the smoking hole before falling onto his face, dead. The bumbling guard wasn't much luckier, for the second blast blew his sword arm clean off at the shoulder, spraying a fountain of blood right into another archer's face. He screamed and, perhaps in some delusion that he was on fire, jumped overboard, as if wanting to dunk his arm into water to snuff it.

Seeing the wounds and the spray of blood sent a wild predatory thrill through Augum's soul, and the shadow of the dragon reared up behind his mind, eager to be summoned to the fore.

The bloodied archer, having witnessed his mates perish in such a gruesome manner, whimpered—and threw his bow at Augum. While Augum stepped aside to let the bow whistle by, that archer bolted in a zig-zag pattern to avoid getting hit in the back.

The final archer dropped his bow, grabbed one of the swordsman's bucklers, and kept it before him as he retreated, whimpering in the same terrified manner.

The fire warlock saw all this and did something Augum had hardly expected—he laughed. It was not a malicious laugh, but rather the sort of jovial laugh a drunken fool would blurt to his friends upon seeing something utterly ridiculous.

"Ye got some whip to ye, boy," the man growled in a well-practiced sea twang. He wiped his mouth with the back of a black sleeve as they circled each other, hands ready in attack formation, the battle between the two ships raging behind them.

Augum finally had a good look at the man's face tattoo, which depicted leopard spots that went down his neck and on to the exposed part of the chest.

"Let's see how you dance to this," the bald warlock sang, and slapped his wrists together, shouting, "*Annihilo!*" A monstrous fireball whooshed forth.

Augum's thoughts aligned with the principle of perpendicularity as he summoned his shield, angling it just so as he roared, "*Mimicus!*"

The fireball whooshed off the shield—and rebounded right back at the bald warlock, who surprisingly had the wherewithal to point at his own fireball and send it caroming off into the ocean, where it missed a flailing sailor's head by mere feet and splashed into the water beyond with a harmless *hiss*.

"Fancy trick, boy," the bald man said, giving his chin a playful stroke. "Have ter admit I'm a wee bit impressed. And now that I see it clear, that's a fine painting on yer shield, if I do say so myself." He smiled a gold-toothed smile. "How's about I buy you a drink and you teach me how to toss a spell back and paint my shield up like that?"

Augum, seeing that the chaos on the boat needed his attention, decided his reply would be a classic combination. He shoved at the air, roaring, "*Baka!*" The man summoned a fiery shield and leaned into the expected attack—except it had been a feint, and as he leaned forward, Augum yanked on the man's feet. The warlock fell back, smacking his head against a barrel on the way down so hard that his body went rigid, with his arms extending and hands curling inward. He rolled about on the deck, possessed by a violent seizure.

Augum knew the man would be incapacitated for a while. He'd personally seen the effect in training when a warlock hit his head too hard, with Jengo informing him that such occurrences were a particular kind of concussion that usually required urgent healing. Either way, with a long tail of recovery, the 15th degree warlock pirate was most certainly out of the fight for now.

The predator within him licked its chops, urging him to summon his shield and cut off the man's head—or anything equally grotesque, to shed more blood, more mayhem.

Do not become the horse, he thought, disallowing the indulgence that invariably led down a certain path. Or was it the rider in that scenario? He wasn't experienced enough with the principle to know.

Having slammed the door shut on the bloodlust, Augum checked to see that Mahmoute was holding her own dueling the earth warlock pirate in the stern. Beyond, he noticed the tip of a mast bobbing between long swells. When it revealed a sail emblazoned with a rose, he knew that the *Rose of the Seas* had gained on them, with her sister ships surely not far behind. Augum wasn't at all surprised that the sniveling Lord High Commander, no doubt in fear for his own safety, had forbidden the bulldog Black Eagle from teleporting over to lend a hand in the fight.

Coward, Augum thought as he shot by the now foaming pirate warlock, for he was eager to help his friends. He went after the easiest targets first—those in the back, waiting to have their turn up front, confident that the bald pirate had handled things behind them. He strode up to a bound set of crates, using them as cover, and began with the youngest attackers.

"*Paralizo carcusa cemente*," he incanted whilst drawing the outline of what appeared to be a thirteen-year-old boy. The boy, holding a sickle, froze in place. His colleague, another thirteen-year-old, barely had time to glance questioningly at him before Augum paralyzed him too.

As Augum kept this up, he noted that his side was doing a good job of minimizing the onslaught. Already a dozen attackers stood paralyzed on *Saltfang's* deck, or had been put to sleep, or stumbled about utterly confused or temporarily blind, swinging at the air like fools. The worst seemed to be screaming not from pain, but from the Fear spell.

That was where the minimizing ended, for the *Saltfang* crew was hacking at the pirates with abandon, most of their sword play held on precarious ledges and railings and even on the sails themselves, usually on the lower yardarms, but a few were chopping at each other on the foremast and one pair was going at it on the topgallant, the highest sail. Most of the swipes were meant to keep the opponent at bay, with few taking any risks, as one mistimed strike could lead to a mortal wound or fall into the ocean.

Rogor was not holding back either. The wolven had skewered two men with a summoned blade made of dense air, both of whom lay dead at his feet, and was now dancing with three others, the lot jabbing and parrying and shield-blocking each other's thrusts. He was the aggressor, and they the defenders. His strange countenance — who knew how many wolven the pirates had seen in their lives — also drew many anxious eyes from the enemy, making them easy marks from the rear.

Augum jiggled a hand at the head of a bearish man with a hairy chest, incanting, "*Flustrato.*" The man's head snapped forth, and he began swinging his curved blade so wildly that he almost chopped off the head of a fellow pirate, who shouted, "Ye gods, watch it with that thing, ya daft sack of blubber!"

Augum, seeing the danger, yanked at the sword, hissing, "*Disablo!*" It spun out of the bearish man's hands and fell into the ocean. In his confusion, the man grasped at it so wildly that he tipped over the railing and vanished overboard.

Another death, Augum's mind chronicled. The predator within him roared with salacious delight — and to thwart that roar, Augum ran to the edge and kicked a loose crate over the railing. He peeked overboard to see that the frigid water had brought the man somewhat to his senses, and he swam for the crate.

Maybe you can save some for a change instead of turning into an animal, he thought.

"'Lock behind us!" someone shouted.

Augum whirled about to face five early-twenties pirates rushing him with curved blades. All premeditatively ducked and bobbed and weaved about, anticipating his spellcraft. They looked so ridiculous performing these kooky maneuvers, with their bouncing locks and clinking clothing, that Augum had to suppress a smile. They were fools in it for the adventure and the robbing more than the killing. Or so he hoped.

"Enough games," he said, and used a finger to draw the shape of a dragon, incanting, "*Summano elementus minimus draco!*" A pony-sized dragon made of pure lightning sizzled into life between them.

"Gods, what the hell is that?" one of them asked as all five skidded to a halt.

Augum touched his throat. "*Amplifico.* "Drop your weapons or I will command it to tear you apart," he boomed. And because it was the very *last* thing he wanted to do, he roared, "Do it!" His amplified voice was so mighty that it cut through the noise ahead, turning heads.

"You're surrounded!" another voice boomed behind him, and he stole a glance back to see Mahmoute striding victoriously forth. Behind her, the deck was painted with blood, with no sign of the earth warlock pirate.

Something else loomed beyond, making Augum's eyes widen—and others scream out in warning. "Braaaaaaace!" he roared, and grabbed the closest thing he could—a rope that bound a stack of crates.

The *Rose of the Seas* had finally caught up, its visage obscured by the sails and swells and chaos. For whatever reason, the swarthy captain of the *Rose of the Seas*, Lord High Commander by his side, had decided that the best course of action was to ram the pirate ship from the rear. Just as the black flagger lurched forth with a cacophonous splintering, the *Rose of the Seas* loosed a great *twang*. Its newly repaired weapon—the wyrmspike—shot a massive harpoon straight down the center of the ship.

Mahmoute, who'd jumped aside from a falling barrel, barely had a moment to turn before it sliced through her side. The violence of the strike spun her body in place before she fell to the planks with a *thud*. Augum dipped away and felt the harpoon miss him by a hair's breadth. It crashed through the crates he'd been holding, sending him staggering against the railing, and went on to plow a gruesome line through the pirates—and some of the deck crew—before finally lodging into *Saltfang's* cabins, leaving behind a trail of destruction. A thick rope attached the harpoon to the *Rose of the Seas*.

As pirates and crew and warlocks screamed, forgetting their fight, and both ships shook and tilted, the black flagger's stern dropped to the ocean. The *Rose of the Seas* kept coming, climbing the stern like a gigantic shark. Crates and barrels and swords and shoes and people began sliding toward the mouth of the vast ocean and the bone-crunching bow of the Solian navy ship.

Augum, incensed at the utter idiocy and senseless destruction of the maneuver, snatched the railing with one hand and telekinetically grabbed hold of a young pirate as he slid by. That kid grabbed for another kid but missed, and all the pair could do was helplessly watch that kid scream as he slipped into the ocean underneath the bow of the *Rose of the Seas*.

I'm going to throttle that captain until he chokes on his beard, Augum thought as he drew the boy, who had descended into a shrieking cry, up toward him. He stole a moment to note that the kid's face was tattooed with a swordfish, the blade of its snout inked to appear to be slicing through one of the boy's eyes. After grabbing him by his frayed hemp-rope belt, which held up a pair of scraggly shorts, Augum looked for Mahmoute—and saw her body curled around the last mast. Was he imagining it, or did her head move? *Save a life*, he thought over the callousness. *Be the watcher.* Wait, was it being the rider if he was saving lives? *No time to ponder inanities right now—just act!*

"Grab hold of something," Augum commanded and boosted the kid to the railing, which the pirate frantically grabbed hold of like a scared squirrel, repeatedly mumbling, "Okay, okay, okay ..." His tough countenance, accented by a half-shaven head and a classic loose-linen pirate shirt, had quickly broken under the reality of battle and the prospect of losing his ship to the ocean.

As the steepness of the deck continued to increase, Augum reached out his now free arm and focused on Mahmoute, who was fifty feet away, past the limit of his Telekinesis. But thanks to Jengo's Ally of the Dragon casting, the spell was two degrees stronger, and after repeatedly flicking his fingers as if fishing, her arm twitched. He finally latched on and dragged her limp body up the pitched deck, leaving behind a trail of blood. The moment he grabbed her hand, he curled his other arm around the boy, envisioned a certain open portion of *Saltfang's* deck, and incanted, "*Impetus peragro grapa lestato exa exaei!*" He vanished and reappeared with a *thwomp* on the deck of the whaler, where he shoved the boy at a tied-down barrel.

"Hold on," he said and crouched before Mahmoute.

"Okay," the boy squeaked and grabbed the barrel with shaking hands.

Augum, seeing he was no threat and only a scared boy, focused on Mahmoute. Her wrinkled face was pale and she did not move or seem to breathe, yet her eyes were open, though he couldn't tell if they saw anything. He dared to open her torn robe—and flinched at the sight, for the harpoon had cut a chunk of her side clean out. He promptly stuffed the torn robe into the spot, grabbed the boy's hand, and pressed it firmly against the wound.

"Hold here," he commanded.

"Okay," the whimpering boy gibbered and wincingly pressed the cloth against the wound with both hands.

Augum jumped to his unsteady feet, for the ship bobbed this way and that, violently shoved about between the increasingly high waves, the fearsome wind, and the pirate ship, the harpoon of which was still firmly lodged in *Saltfang's* hull. With the *Rose of the Seas* still mounted atop the rear of the enemy ship, its own harpoon rope running over the pirate ship before disappearing into one of *Saltfang's* wrecked cabins, the entire scene looked like a haphazard ocean crash connected with rope and chain and splinters.

"Healer!" Augum shouted, cupping his hands around his mouth, but he'd lost focus on Amplify during the ramming, and the spell had fizzled. The splintering and cracking and screaming, the latter mostly coming from the pirate ship, many of them too young to be experiencing such devastation, drowned out his voice.

Then he spotted Jengo amidst the panicking throng, which had long stopped fighting. The healer had just finished carrying a crewman away from the splintered cabin when he realized the man was missing both of his legs. After gaping at the grim sight, Jengo gently lowered the body to the planks and solemnly pressed a hand to the man's forehead. Then he looked about to see where he could help—and noticed Augum waving him over. Jengo immediately began running toward him.

"Healer's on the way," Augum reported to the boy and turned his back on him and Mahmoute in readiness to hop back. That's when he heard a sickly sound behind him. He whipped about in time to witness Digby, the thirty-four-year-old younger Bloomington-Southguard brother, run his summoned fiery blade through the back of the boy who'd been pressing down on Mahmoute's wound.

"Gotcha, little worm!" the powder-faced Digby sang as the boy gasped and fell on top of Mahmoute.

Augum's blood flash-boiled. He took a single step toward Digby, who sneeringly opened his mouth to trumpet, "Skewered myself a rat—" and viciously punched him in the jaw. Digby did a full twirl, his summoned blade vanishing midway, before he thumped face-first to the planks, landing unconscious beside Mahmoute and the now writhing boy.

Augum crouched by the boy and shouted at Jengo, "Hurry!"

Amidst the chaos of scrambling people, he saw the rest of his lot helping who they could, with Teague and Alanna and Olaf working together to drag people out from under wreckage. Rogor had jumped clear by then and was clinging to a mast like a dog trying to avoid getting wet. Somewhere at the back, near the cabin, he spotted Leera—and she was holding a shrieking Limpet by the collar with one hand while her other arm was curled around a stricken pirate boy. Both boys' eyes were wild and roving about, telling Augum they'd likely been hit with Confusion castings.

Just as Jengo slid to a halt beside him, grabbing hold of the lip of a barrel to steady himself, the boy at Augum's feet stiffened and loosed a shuddering gasp, then breathed no more.

Jengo went to check both bodies, while Augum took a precious moment to close the boy's eyes, whispering, "May your soul rest in peace, young brave warrior." Then he threw the still-unconscious Digby a furious look, knowing he'd have to deal with the coward later. A *murderous* coward, for that had been the cold-blooded murder of a kid who had essentially bent the knee.

"You got this?" Augum asked, still glaring at Digby.

"I got this," Jengo replied. "You go."

Augum shot up, focused on the tilted deck of the black flagger, and envisioned himself standing before its mast, which was now leaning backward at an astounding forty-five degrees.

"*Impetus peragro!*" he snapped and shot forth, appearing exactly where he'd wanted—facing the pitched mast, which he promptly clamped onto. People were screaming and sliding and falling down the deck, and many were already in the icy water, water that would shortly kill them, trying to grab hold of something. He spotted one of his own among those wretches—a drunken Jez, who herded people as if they were a school of fish, doing all she could to stop them from drowning her in their panic. Having grabbed two of them by the scruff with a single hand and another by the flailing arm, she blinked out of existence. He glanced back to see her waveringly dump them aboard the whaler.

Refocusing, he lashed out in time to telekinetically snag another pirate, this one about his age, and haul him to where he stood. The young man had a face tattoo depicting a tiger curving from one side of his forehead down to his chin. Then he did the same for a *Saltfang* crew member hiding behind a stack of crates, the roped lashings of which were coming undone. The pair of opposing crewmen nodded at each other as if they were old friends, then clung onto the mast without Augum telling them to do so.

Augum snagged another pirate—a teenager of about sixteen—who was climbing the deck with his saber. "Let it go so I can drag you up!" Augum shouted. The boy promptly let his blade tumble down the steeply pitched deck, and Augum dutifully dragged him up to cling onto his pirate crewmate.

"Thanks, eh," the teen said, surprising Augum.

Feeling he could take one more, Augum spotted the bald fire warlock tattooed with leopard spots. He was still in a daze and lying on his side twenty-five feet away, body pinned between two barrels.

Save a life for a change, he thought again and reached out. After a few attempts to telekinetically fish the man out of the swaying boat, his invisible hook finally caught, and he began dragging the man up the now sixty-degree deck.

"She's going down," one of the pirates he had saved said casually, as if talking about the weather. "Think he can 'port us, mate?" he asked the whaler crew member, for Augum was busy hauling.

Surprisingly polite, Augum thought.

"I don't know nothin' 'bout their magic," the crew member replied with a shrug.

Augum finally got the fire warlock within reach and snagged him by the arm. "Grab onto me," he told the others as the black flagger began sliding into the water.

"Didn't think she'd end like this," one of the pirates said just before Augum snapped off the Group Teleport incantation, appearing on *Saltfang* with the fire warlock, the whaler crew member — and only one of the pirates in tow.

"The fool let go," the pirate he had saved blurted.

Augum looked to the black flagger and saw the other pirate still clinging to the mast. The ship angled so steeply that the pirate signed skyward and jumped clear, vanishing into the icy water below.

"There she goes," said the pirate he had rescued. "A dark beauty to the very last ..."

The group paid the ship the respect of a brief watchful silence.

"Over here!" Olaf shouted.

Augum looked down the deck and saw that Olaf and Alanna and Leera had worked together to corral prisoners and the wounded, with most of the former either tied or stiff with paralysis, while the wounded lay writhing in a separate area. Jengo was there with Mahmoute, having evidently brought her over, and was still working on her side. Behind them, the ashen-faced Limpet peeked out from the main cabin door, his bravery abandoning him as much as it had with that kid pirate.

"Let's go," Augum said and dragged the fire warlock to them. He was surprised he didn't have to order the pirate he'd saved to come along, for the young man did so willingly, even sitting amongst his brethren and throwing one of them a friendly elbow, as if to say, *You got out too, eh?*

Pirates are an odd lot, Augum thought as he dumped the fire warlock before Olaf. "Gag and confound him," he ordered, glancing to make sure the others were all right.

"On it," Olaf replied.

Suddenly *Saltfang* lurched and began tipping sideways, and a hair-raising realization hit Augum as he grasped the issue. The harpoon the black flagger had launched was still lodged in *Saltfang's* hull. The pirate ship had also snagged the rope that ran from the bow of the *Rose of the Seas* to the harpoon stuck in one of *Saltfang's* cabins. If something wasn't done—and quickly—the black flagger would drag both ships to the bottom of the ocean.

"Get clear!" Augum roared, sprinting forth, raising and flexing his right arm as he sought to deal with the first harpoon. He launched himself over a writhing body toward the taut rope, which had cut through the railing like a hot knife and was now sawing its way through the deck. "*Summano arma!*" he shouted mid-leap, and upon feeling a lightning longsword appear within his grasp, he swung it at a portion of the thick rope still visible above *Saltfang's* deck.

There was a fearsome *snap* as the rope, so taut it had stretched and thinned, whipped by at blinding speed, leaving behind a trail of dust. For a moment *Saltfang* swung the other way as it righted, before continuing to tip.

"One down," Augum said. He shot to the railing, leaned over, and saw that the puncture hole from the black flagger's chain harpoon was now under the waterline. *That's a problem*, he thought, hearing the bubbling suction of water streaming in through the hole.

There came a *whoosh* as a crimson blur launched over the side. "Lee!" he shouted even as she splashed into the water in a perfect dive. She popped her head up—and latched onto the chain, perhaps in an attempt to cut it somehow. He wasn't sure what her plan was.

"Let go of it!" he shouted, waving her off.

Somehow amidst the din she heard him and let go. With no time to worry about a water warlock literally in her element, Augum shot off the other way, careening through the wreckage of the cabin and vaulting down multiple ladders to the lower decks. He shoved past more wreckage below, until he came face to face with the metal harpoon, which had penetrated a massive beam. The chain was pinging and groaning as it pulled on the beam, which had started to bend and crack, all while water gushed in through the hole. The ship squealed as if about to snap in half from the strain.

He raised his lightning longsword and swung it at the chain. *Brrrrrring!* the chain sang upon the blade making contact, sparks flying. Again he swung, and then again and again and again, the chain singing a spark-flying symphony as it began to glow red-hot.

Just as the ship was about to capsize and Augum was about to drop from exhaustion, there came a vicious *chwang!* as the chain split at the smash point. The metal rings ripped through the hole, spraying splinters, and the remainder snapped back at Augum, who felt a nasty hotness across his chest as he was thrown backward. He slammed into the beam and cartwheeled over it, then fell into the frigid water with a *splash*. The ship turned back to even keel and bobbed, water sloshing about him.

Groaning from the pain and muscles screaming, he heard splashing footsteps.

"Aug? Aug!" Olaf shouted, coming to him, with others close behind. "You're hurt!"

"I'm fine," Augum wheezed, gesturing at the hole. "Repair it. Quickly now."

As Olaf rushed to the hole to begin the arcane repairing process, Augum pressed a hand to his own chest. He looked down and was unsurprised to find blood. He'd felt his ribs crack, and the skin was surely split, but he'd worry about all that later—Jengo would heal him. Right now, he needed to make sure Leera was all right.

"You got this?" Augum asked.

"I got this. You go on."

Augum nodded, grabbed hold of the wrecked timber, hauled himself to his feet, and stumbled toward the ladder, only to realize he was in too much pain to climb. Instead he took a breath, pushed the pain to the back of his mind, cleared the rest of his thoughts, and focused on standing on the deck by the railing.

"*Impetus peragro,*" he incanted, and with a *thwomp* appeared where he'd intended. Holding himself with one arm, he propped the other against the railing to look overboard. He felt all the color drain from his face as he spotted Leera floating face-down in a storm-tossed pool of blood. He tried to leap over the railing, but his legs gave out as black walls of unconsciousness closed in. Obscured by the exhilarating rush of battle, the wound was more severe than he had estimated.

He groaned at the closest person he could, which happened to be, of all people, Alanna Haught, who was caring for a stricken sailor. Unable to get her attention, he lashed out telekinetically instead, whipping her about to face him.

"Help Leera," he managed to wheeze, gesturing weakly at the railing even as he fell back, barely seeing anything. Alanna rushed over so quickly she slammed into the railing. She took one look at the water, one pale look at Augum, back at the water, swallowed—and launched herself overboard.

Her robe flapping as she vanished was the last thing Augum saw before black walls choked off consciousness.

LIGHT

BRIDGET

A crowd of stinking wretches stood in a chokingly humid room, listening to the creaking of ceiling planks. Slices of light, streaming in through the cracks above, lit up swirling dust and grimy faces. Despite her weary bones and wearier soul, Bridget stood among these wretches with a straight back, eyes dead ahead, her arms draped over Sebastian's shoulders and loose before his chest.

Either the ship had traversed southward at some point or spring had begun, for the voyage had steadily heated up, and work had become sweatier and sweatier, so much so that many of the men had taken to working bare-chested. Bridget had done her quiet best to alleviate the suffering, petitioning Grak for dunks in the cold water tanks, more fresh water from their reserves, and less toil. The gargoyle captain accepted all but the last request, rejecting it outright.

The mammoth ship's motions had stilled to near imperceptibility, indicating it had docked. But docked where? An island, or the gargoyle homeland? Or somewhere else?

Any time Sebastian looked up at her, as if pining for her attention, she kept her chin level, jaw firm. They all looked to her. The young chef. The one who had guided them through the ocean passage, suffering her indignities with determination and fortitude. The personal slave to the captain. The one who had captured the ear of a disfigured gargoyle. The supposed hero of the wars—and maybe a dragon, though no one dared mention the latter. To every man, woman and child, whether they had been criminals in their past lives or jewelers or teachers, all longed for freedom—and all hoped she would rescue them. In the sweltering heat,

Bridget was acutely conscious of that hope, but the itching under the blasted collar reminded her that she was still a mere *gyot*.

Someone pushed through the crowd to join her. "What do you think is happening?" Naomi whispered.

Bridget gave the slightest shake of her head. She had learned many things from being a slave, including that people respected her more when she said less. The more time she took to think, the more weight her replies received, with silence oft yielding the most potent effect. She had also learned that when the only possession was dignity, respect was as precious as gold. She had watched the way those who had been kidnapped from prison traded respect, bartered with it, cherished and nurtured it. She had watched and learned and applied.

Throughout, she trained, for although the beasts had taken almost everything, they had failed to take her spirit. Whenever she had the opportunity, whether she was cooking or washing gargoyle feet or shoveling gargoyle coils—for the captain regularly liked to remind her of her lowly status by sending her to the pits—she entered the castle of her mind, which over time had morphed into Castle Arinthian.

There she trained with a resident talking suit of armor named Fentwick and shot spells beside her brother-in-war, Augum, and bantered with Leera and cuddled with Olaf and threw sticks for Sabby and mentored under Jez and received guests from afar. Sometimes she even took lessons with Isobel Roseheart, or with Atrius Arinthian, or with Rebecca Von Edgeworth, or other arcanists she'd had over the years.

"They're going to slaughter us," someone whispered.

"No, they're going to *eat* us," another countered.

"Shut up," someone else hissed. "They didn't float us to the other side of the ocean just to jam us onto a spit. We're more valuable than that."

"Then why'd they decimate us in the arena and dump hundreds more down into sewage holes? Huh?"

"Shut up, both of you," a third person hissed. "Or you'll get us all whipped." This last utterance brought many murmurs of support, silencing the pair of arguers.

Sometimes Bridget retreated into humor. It was never her own humor she heard in her mind, but the humor of those who could so effortlessly deploy it even in the most difficult of circumstances. In this case, she heard Olaf say into her mind, *The dirties are getting restless*, and saw him chuckle.

"Don't think I've ever seen you smile before," Naomi whispered.

Bridget felt a hot slice of sunlight shining on her face and moved her chin slightly to hide the smile, however small it was, in the darkness. Yet she kept the rest of the blade of light on her face, enjoying its sweet hopefulness, reminding her that there was a world out there still, with fresh air waiting to be breathed in and enjoyed. Trees to be smelled and climbed and read under. How long had it been since she had felt sunlight splash upon her entire body? Seen the vivid green of grass? Seen a tree?

"Must have been a pleasant thought," Naomi whispered.

Even though Naomi had helped with Mud, she kept the girl at arm's length. She was sweet and kind, but Bridget dared not let anyone into her heart, even Sebastian, telling him little about herself and asking little of him.

Yet the bond between her and the boy had strengthened even in silence, for she nurtured him in secret ways he did not know about. Assigning him the lightest duties, passing him the choicest cuts of meat, keeping him away from tussles and arguments, and generally watching over him like a hawk over its chick. Everyone sensed it too, for after the mysterious disappearance of Mud and The Brute and Bridget's rise to power, not a soul, not even the hardest of the remaining criminals amongst the slaves, dared to so much as breathe an ill word toward the boy—or her. She had proven herself in the arena, in the kitchen as a chef, and as their leader in the way she handled the gargoyles and lobbied on behalf of the wretches.

Sometimes she stood in the shadows watching those criminals, feeling the whisper of the predator as it looked through her eyes. Although it was a shadow of its former strength, suppressed by the collar that had worn a perpetual dirt line into her neck, it still pined for her attention nearly as much as Sebastian.

"What's happening?" Sebastian whispered, looking up at her.

Bridget removed a hand from Sebastian's chest to angle his head forward.

"I'm scared."

She slid her arm down his chest again to join her other arm and gave his chest a double pat with both hands, silently telling him to stay calm whilst keeping him close. Cherishing him. Yet one of the reasons she had not bared her soul to him, or the others, was the dark truth of history, which told of what happened to slaves. Unless they were kept for general labor, they were always broken apart and sold. Then broken again, sometimes in the most harrowing of ways.

She tried not to dwell on such things, but there was always a worrier within her, just as when she had been younger and studying for the academy entrance exams, reading and rereading every page and scroll, reviewing every concept and methodology, terrified of failure and desperately wanting to succeed as a warlock.

The planks above shook from a rhythmic thumping that sounded like hundreds of heavyset people dancing. Except they weren't people at all, but towering gray beasts with wings. Then came a strange and low hooting that throbbed in time with the thumping.

"They're celebrating," Naomi said. "The bastards are celebrating victory."

The hooting and thumping grew in strength, and people had to drop their heads to shield their eyes from the falling dust. A deep drum that reminded Bridget of the Black arena in the capital joined the thumping. She almost expected snares to chime in, but instead a high-pitched horn slipped into the armada of sound, until it became an animalistic orchestra so loud that many covered their ears.

Bridget covered Sebastian's ears for him. In turn, he reached up and covered hers, which melted her heart. She rested her chin on his dusty head and closed her eyes, absorbing the wall of noise, letting it thunder through her bones and soul. She tried not to think about a huge gargoyle dragging Sebastian away by the hair or a collar chain, watching him forever fade from her life …

All at once the deafening noise halted, leaving behind a ringing silence. Then, as if expelling a communal breath, all the gargoyles boomed, *Whoooooooooooooooooo* …

But it was not the hoot of an owl, and neither was it a question, but rather the satisfied war cry of a beastly race announcing its prize.

Now it's time to show that prize off, Bridget thought as the gargoyle roar died, leaving behind a restless silence. It was soon followed by a regimented scuffling noise and then by the creaking of a door opening ahead. Light streamed onto a staircase, outlining two wingless gargoyles who barked at the wretches to move. The sounds of whips cracking upon backs in the rear had the masses shuffling forward.

A shaking Sebastian clung tightly to Bridget's arms, which remained draped around his chest. Others, even some of the burlier men, nudged their way closer to her. Naomi was pushed out, until Bridget reached across a large man's chest, grabbed her arm, and dragged her over.

"Unnameables bless you," Naomi whispered, for it was the most affection Bridget had shown anyone other than Sebastian.

Onward the masses shuffled until light splashed onto their faces, which caused most to hold up a hand to shield their eyes against the brightest light they had seen in some time. They dropped their heads as they streamed past the guards and trounced up the steps, leaving behind a cloud trail of dust. They poured out of the entranceway onto the bright deck of the ship, and all along that ship more groups of slaves exited onto the deck, each surrounded by their own gargoyle minders. Some were grouped by individual kingdoms they had been captured from—the Nodians, the Sierrans, the Abrandians, the Tiberrans, and so on. Another group was composed solely of wolven and their cubs.

Squinting against the sun, Bridget peeked through scissored fingers to see a series of masts. She remembered seeing them from afar what felt like a lifetime ago and that she had counted a dozen. They were thick and tall, and the boat was wide and so long it seemed to stretch into infinity. On every protrusion—the yardarms and the railings and crates, whatever was a high point—a gargoyle sat atop, basking.

But it was not the sun they were basking in, nor was it the boat that held her attention. Her gasp was lost amidst many other gasps, for a sight she had never seen awaited, one that made her crane her neck. Far beyond the starboard side of the vessel, amidst undulating fields of vivid green grass she had dreamed about, rose countless poles that shot into the heavens. These poles, dotted with cave-like holes and parrot-like perches, were so staggeringly tall that some pierced the occasional cloud. Winged beasts flew between these poles, some ducking inside, others crouching on the perches.

Many slaves gawked with open mouths, others whispered things like, "Gods help us," and "Unnameables look at that," and "Unholy heavens." Others whimpered or cried. One woman fainted, slumping to the planks in a heap, and no one came to her aid, for after a grueling voyage of bare survival, fainting was of little consequence.

Bridget was part of the silent group, yet her mind marveled at what she saw. Atop some of these poles, or spars, or whatever they were, sat what appeared to be flat areas with structures too distant to make out. And down below, amidst the grass, there stood strange mound-like buildings that looked like ant nests. Except it was gargoyles that used them, dipping or flying into holes, with the wingless ones using ground entrances. Beyond the hills, barely visible through a distant blue haze, rose other structures, tall and oblong like termite nests …

"A city," Naomi whispered. "That's a gargoyle city …"

Captain Gravak, who had been standing on a platform erected on the deck, stepped forth and raised his arms above his seventeen-foot height. All the gargoyles on the ship stood tall and began beating their chests like gorillas. Those watching from the countless poles and perches and mounds, with more gargoyles sitting on the hills, joined in. There were so many that they resembled a swarm of bees that now droned as one massive hive.

This awesome display of a foreign and beastly kingdom, revealing perhaps only a hint of its vastness, hit some of the slaves hard. Several more fainted, several keeled over to vomit, others burst with fearful cries.

Sebastian was among those who broke down crying, turning about to bury his face into Bridget's filthy robe. She held him close, her gaze returning to level. She felt a twitch in her mouth, but controlled her face, for others kept flicking their gazes to her. She could not reveal to them the true extent of her fears, for upon seeing those vast rolling hills and towering poles and distant blue-hazed city and not knowing how many demons lurked beyond, she knew she would never be found again. Not by her kingdom, nor by Augum and Leera. Two dragons against such an empire was a mere pair of wasps against a hive. They were nothing. *She* was nothing. A mere *gyot* amidst a huddled and terrified mass of *gyots*.

Due to a combination of factors—the bright sun, the stifling heat, the overwhelming noise, and the sheer shock of the sight before her—the moments that came after were a blur to Bridget. Wanting only to keep Sebastian close and preserve what mental fortitude she possessed, Bridget found herself drifting down a long wooden plank without guardrails, one of many extending down the length of the ship for the other groups of slaves. Since there were no guardrails, a precipitous drop yawned on both sides, a stone wharf waiting far below.

A woman who dazedly walked ahead glanced back. In the light of day her eyes were profoundly sunken, her hair was utterly disheveled, and her ragged gown was a filthy mess. Those sunken eyes looked the column of wretches over and lingered on Bridget but a moment before she took a purposeful step off the plank.

The wretches yelped and screamed and some reached for her, but she was gone, the last of her existence a subtle *whoosh*. Like a dam bursting, others leapt after her, causing the screams to intensify.

All up and down the dock, a similar display took place, with people choosing to end it all rather than go on. The gargoyles, for their part, seemingly found this display amusing, for they howled and whistled and shrieked in that particular beastly way of theirs that showed animalistic delight.

Bridget did not look down after her or the others, nor did she much hear the gruesome *thuds* from below everyone else winced at. Rather, she raised her chin in conviction and was the first to continue walking, Sebastian pressed to her like jelly and a whimpering Naomi pinching the rear of her robe, urging Bridget not to leave her behind. The others saw her determination, her sheer will to live, and continued down the plank.

For her part, Bridget could not understand surviving such a harrowing voyage only to choose that sort of end. *What a waste*, she thought, then immediately chastised herself for her callousness. *Feel for these poor creatures, for they deserve your pity and compassion. Do not turn into a beast. Do not lose your humanity.*

"We walk to our doom," someone said.

Bridget looked at him. He was a parchment of a fifty-year-old man, a waif of bones and whiskers and tufts of hair. He opened his mouth to add further words to his despair, but upon seeing her eyes, he promptly closed his mouth and looked down at his feet in shame.

Let your silence do the talking, Bridget thought, eyes returning to the horizon. *Let it do the leading.* It was such a profoundly simple idea too.

Crowds of gargoyles, winged and wingless, had gathered at the bottom of each gangway plank, with a tall platform waiting nearby. Some gargoyles were adorned with golden chains, others with silken ribbons, others with bones. A wingless gargoyle dressed in the closest thing to a human robe—albeit one made from seashells—waved a chained burner of incense about, the copper pot gleaming in the sun.

The slaves were bid to assemble before this crowd, and Bridget took a deep breath. She smelled tar and sea salt and grass and masonry and the incense, which vaguely smelled like cloves. There were countless other scents mixed in—earth and sod and ginger and fragrant oils and fish. Underlying them all was the ever-present and intimately familiar soft coil stench of gargoyle droppings.

Speeches of greeting began in earnest. The lead gargoyle dignitary presented the captain with a massive skull that looked like it belonged to a giant. The gift, or perhaps trophy, was studded with glinting gems—ruby and emerald and topaz and amethyst and diamond, each cut in a spiral pattern that reminded Bridget of digging a shovel underneath steaming coils. After the handover, gargoyles cheered in their hooting manner and thumped their chests and flapped their wings like humans clapped.

Dizzy from the heat and the sun and the drastic change of environment, Bridget paid no attention to the speeches, their meaning plain despite the unfamiliar language, as it seemed all beasts enjoyed the victory of plunder.

Then came the moment she had been dreading for some time, for the first of the slaves in their group, a sorry mule of a man, was grabbed by the arm and tossed onto a tall wooden platform that had been dragged forth for the occasion. A wingless gargoyle with a tapered stick hopped up onto the platform, grabbed the man's arm, and raised him so that his feet dangled above the planks. The gargoyle shook him, turned him about, shook him some more as if hoping he'd drop treasure, then began growling in rapid tones, the stick sweeping the crowd, searching for bidders.

Hands flipped upward, wings folded forth, and claws were extended, and the auctioneer acknowledged these with a quick point of his stick.

How human, Bridget thought.

The slaves began to panic. Some tried to push beyond the gargoyle sentinels, who raised their whips and brought them down with vicious *cracks*. And so the masses huddled tighter together, with Bridget at the very center, her chin held level. Sebastian whimpered in her arms, and Naomi clung to her robe, her head buried in Bridget's shoulder. Others took hold of her, closed their eyes, and raised their heads to the heavens as their lips moved in quiet prayer.

Lean against me for I am strong, Bridget thought, clenching her jaw. *I am the reed that bends in the wind. The oak that creaks in the gale. The mountain in the winter night. Lean against me for I am strong …*

Then she saw herself standing outside a moat, and beyond the moat towered mighty Castle Arinthian, and on its terrace stood Augum. He raised a fist to her and shouted, *"Adversi alua probata!* Do you hear me, Bridget? *Adversi alua probata!"*

"Against all odds," Bridget translated in a whisper, her voice lost to the crowd and to the auction, her soul strengthened by her brother-in-war's presence.

Leera appeared beside Augum, and she too raised a fist, shouting, *"Semperis vorto honos*, Bridget! *Semperis vorto honos!"*

"Courage, fortitude, honor," Bridget whispered, nodding, seeing what no one else could see.

Then Olaf appeared and Jez and Jengo and so many others, all shouting their encouragement. She looked to them, nodding to each, until there was a scream beside her and a sharp tug on her arm. Bridget crashed back to reality—and to Naomi getting pulled away. She was shouting for help and pleading with her overseer, who happened to be the malicious gargoyle the slaves called Cracks.

"For the love of the Unnameables please just leave me alone!" she shrieked as Cracks dragged her along by her curly hair. "I don't want to be sold! I don't want to go! No, no, no!" The gargoyle of course paid her no heed, and simply kept dragging her until he threw her up to the platform like a sack of rocks, where she was caught by a wingless helper.

Bridget, clutching Sebastian tightly, pushed through the terrified throng to the front, where she looked up at Naomi, who stood shaking like a leaf on the platform, one arm clutching herself, the other raised and gripped by the auctioneering gargoyle. She locked eyes with Bridget, and they shared a moment. Naomi opened her mouth, but her lip quivered along with her chin, and no words came, only tears that dribbled down her cheeks, leaving a muddy trail.

Bridget raised a calming hand, placed it under her own chin, and raised it ever so slightly, then gave a hard-eyed nod. *Show them no fear*, she was telling her. *Show them no fear.*

Seeing this, Naomi nodded in turn, leveled her chin, and looked straight—before the gargoyle yanked her off her feet by the arm and turned her about in midair, displaying her to the bidding fiends. Although Naomi shook, she did not break again and let herself hang limply, with eyes defiantly steeled ahead.

You can survive this, Bridget thought. *Be and stay strong.*

Bridget did not see who won Naomi. What she did see was the auctioneer accepting a chain and hooking it onto Naomi's collar before unceremoniously shoving her off the platform toward her new master or mistress. The last thing she saw of Naomi were her glassy and uncomprehending eyes before she vanished into the throng.

Fare thee well, Naomi, Bridget thought, wondering if she would ever see the woman again.

One by one they were torn from around her, and she clutched Sebastian so firmly that he squeaked, and she had to un-whiten her knuckles lest she hurt him.

When there were about a hundred slaves left in their group, the auctioneering beast pointed directly at Bridget, who felt a terrible chill run down her spine. Cracks shoved slaves aside, absently plucked Bridget by the torso with a single huge hand, and effortlessly raised her skyward as he growled at another slave to step away from the platform. Bridget resisted the overwhelming urge to fight the tight grip around her waist, focusing instead on holding onto Sebastian, who kicked feebly at the air while he screamed, "No! No! No!"

Cracks noticed this and his other hand reared back, ready to slap Sebastian from Bridget's grip. But then the auctioneer accepted the handover with a fiendish chortle. When he tried to separate them atop the platform, she summoned her inner tiger, incanted, "*Shyneo*," and entwined the glowing ivy around Sebastian, tying him to her. It took tremendous mental effort to get the spell to hold, for the suppressive collar was powerful and persistent and weighed down her arcane strength like an anchor.

"No!" she spat firmly, glaring at the auctioneer, who was holding her up by her left arm as he puzzled out how to untangle them. All the while the crowd of gargoyles chortled and clucked their beastly tongues and growled their approval, as if seeing the strength of the horse they were about to bid on.

"No," Bridget repeated, dangling with an entwined Sebastian. Then she remembered the gargoyle word that Grak had taught her. "*Gen!*" she shouted. "*Gen girku!*" which crudely translated to, *No! No offspring!* To drive home her meaning, she nodded down at Sebastian, repeating, "*Gen girku!* You will not separate us! He is my son! Do you understand, you rotten beasts? He is my *son!*" She practically frothed as she shouted, "*Girku! Girku, girku, girku!*"

The auctioneer raised his free arm to slap her head off, and she winced in anticipation, when there came a sharp growl. She opened one eye and saw that Captain Gravak, who'd been lingering in the rear, chatting to high-ranking winged gargoyles, had pushed his way to the front. His disfigured servant Grak was by his side, whispering something up into his ear whilst wringing his mangled hands.

The captain sliced a hand across the air, growling something unintelligible, and the auctioneer immediately dropped Bridget and Sebastian to the planks. They landed with a *thud*, and Bridget quickly shot back to her feet, Sebastian still tied to her by her steadily weakening vines.

As the auctioneer bowed to the captain, the latter stared at her with his yellow eyes before flicking a claw back and forth, which Bridget instinctively knew was his command to separate them. Knowing the moment she had been preparing for had at last come, Bridget threw out an elbow but folded the arm back toward her head, pressing the rigid fingers of her hand against the base of her chin like a reverse salute. To lend strength to the threat, she angled her chin and moved her fingertips so that they pressed hard against the apple of her throat, then made her vine glow brighter.

"*Seppek!*" she roared at the captain, using the ancient Dreadnought word for suicide. *Come on, you bastards, be students of ancient history!* It was a vain hope, but the only hope she had. "He stays with me or I will commit the final thought of *seppek!*" she shouted, unable to hold back the tears from flowing down her cheeks. "I will end myself! Do you understand! You tell him, Grak! You tell him that I mean it and he will have *nothing*!"

The gargoyles had broken out into mutters, with many gesticulating at her and nodding, as if in respect of her gumption — or perhaps her arts, or her knowledge of history. Who knew?

"*Seppek*," she mouthed at the captain, glaring at him, putting everything she had into the bluff. "*Seppek* ..."

At long last, Captain Gravak flicked an approving claw and said, "*Gazmat*," which Bridget knew from Grak meant *all right*.

As Bridget dared to expel a sigh of relief and drop her arm, the weakened vine at last vanished, but she held onto Sebastian. The bidding began, and to her surprise, the captain was among the bidders. All he did was raise a single claw while others fought for the auctioneer's attention by flapping wings and throwing up arms or hooting in that gargoyle manner. But the captain's claw was steady, and soon he was one of only two bidding on her and Sebastian.

When she laid eyes on his opponent, her stomach fell, for he was an equally tall and muscled gargoyle, with nearly as many runes peeking out from a body adorned with bones. These, however, were not animal bones, but human bones. Multiple femurs and tibias and vertebrae, a couple pelvises, a partial ribcage, even a skull, which was the prominent feature of a pendant necklace.

"I'm scared ..."

"Shh."

"But —"

"Shh, my boy," she whispered, pressing Sebastian's face into her chest. "Shh ..."

Suddenly the boned one roared, startling Bridget and the already whimpering Sebastian. The huge gargoyle flapped a hand at her, and the auctioneer shoved her — not toward him, but rather toward the captain. Yet it was Grak who caught her, gently stabilizing her and Sebastian. That was when she knew it was Grak she had to thank.

OVER DARK INK

<hr>

LEERA

Leera's hands attacked each other as she stood in the dimly lit and tilted hallway of the freshly repaired cabins of *Saltfang*. She chewed on her lip as she stared at a door, contemplating how to do it—if she was going to do it at all.

"Nah, this is stupid," she muttered, and turned on her heel and strode off, then faltered after a few steps. She turned around in readiness to walk back to the door when it opened—and she promptly whirled about once more.

"Dragon Jones?" Alanna asked.

Leera did not turn to face her, instead blurting, "What, what do you want I was just passing through can a girl not simply pass through a hallway without getting accosted?"

Alanna sighed. "I thought I heard someone, that's all."

"Well it's a creaky ship with all sorts of noises so you're always going to hear stuff and that includes people casually walking by in the hallways." She cringed at her own idiocy.

"Right. Er … good day, then."

"Yeah good day it's a great day it's good to be alive isn't it? So good." *Gods would you shut your fool mouth*, Leera thought, thinking she ought to shrink herself to oblivion. When she heard no reply, she stole a peek over her shoulder and saw that Alanna had retreated back into her cabin—but had left her door open.

Hands attacking each other more violently, Leera slid a single foot along the planks toward Alanna's room, which caused her to start doing the splits. She forced her other foot to turn about and also slide toward Alanna's room—and that was how she shuffled her way to Alanna's doorway. She found the amber-robed Alanna sitting on her bed, back turned to the door, a book open on her lap.

Leera leaned against the doorway and, not knowing what to do with her stupid hands, grabbed her elbows instead. When that felt too defensive and unnatural, she jammed her hands into her pockets. Alanna surely had to know she was there, but she made no attempt at conversation, so Leera thought to start first.

"Sooooooo ..." She kicked at Alanna's nearby trunk, which made such a loud *clunk* she realized she was being unforgivably rude, so she instead kicked her other foot. "... a while back ..." She threw a thumb over her shoulder. "... you said that you, uh, that you ..." Her voice trailed off for some stupid reason.

Alanna turned her head just enough for Leera to catch the hint of a smile, which annoyed Leera to no end—and that flare of annoyance also made her cheeks prickle with shame.

"You said you've studied stuff!" Leera blurted a little too loudly, and a hand shot out of a pocket, wanting to cover her dumb mouth, but she jammed it back in. "I mean about kargeyasnaras ... and stuff."

Alanna did not raise her head, the blond hair of which was ridiculously and unfairly shiny. "Oh, are you referring to my class project on kargeyasnaras? Yes, amongst other studies on arcaneology. Why?"

"I'm only asking because I've been bashing my head against a bit of a riddle but it probably wouldn't interest you because it's sort of dark arcanery and stuff and it's kind of impossible because it's ancient and done in the old way and you know what that means all sorts of ridiculous complications and anyway, uh, yeah, it ..."

Alanna turned a page in her book. "It what?"

"It has to do with me," Leera said, hands jammed so far down that her arms were rigid straight, threatening to tear the seams of her pockets.

"Is that what you came to talk to me about?" Alanna asked in a surprisingly gentle and neutral tone.

"Well, yes. Er ... maybe." Leera swallowed, eyes darting to the sanctuary of the hallway. One foot began sliding out the doorway.

"You're welcome," Alanna said rather jovially, head bobbing.

Leera would have normally interpreted that head bob as a smug gesture, but in this moment, she saw that Alanna was proud of herself for having done something truly special and rare—she had performed a profound kindness.

"I, uh ... I didn't know ... I mean ... I didn't realize you had it in you." Leera winced, thinking, *You oaf, that was such a rude thing to say!* "Gods that was a rude thing to say, wasn't it?" Leera mumbled, sucking air through her teeth while she pressed the side of a fist against her mouth.

Alanna's response was to turn her head ever so slightly once more, revealing a hint of a smile.

Oh, you're loving this, aren't you? the malicious part of Leera hissed into her mind. *Preening powder-faced snotbag of a noble. Now you can lord it over me every chance you get, and every time my man looks at you you're going to have that stupid smirk and glint in your eye and satisfied head bob and I bet he finds you better looking than me with your stupid blond hair and pristine face and perfect skin and—*

"I am sure you would have done the same for me," Alanna said, turning another page.

Leera imagined glancing over the ship's railing, just as Jez said Alanna had, then seeing Alanna floating face-down in the water. "Yes, I would have," she said in a small voice, knowing she would have put aside their squabbles to save the woman's life, for it would have been the right—and honorable—thing to do. Any hesitation would have been brief. She would have absolutely dove in.

"You didn't have to do it," Leera added, straightening and girding herself. "Yet you did. And for that …" She rolled a hand forward, urging the words to come out of her mouth. *Come on, say it, damn you …*

Alanna froze, as if waiting to see if Leera would follow through with it.

"… I'm thankful," Leera finally said. "Grateful, actually. And, um, surprised." She nodded emphatically. "Very pleasantly surprised. It's not often that people you consider vile down to their very bones surprise you, you know. People you thought were out to get your man or slag you in the heralds—which you *did* do, mind you. Er … so I'm also a little confused … and stuff."

Alanna's shoulders dropped. "But you're also right. I *did* slag you in the heralds. I had a lot of pressure on me that you don't know about. Family, hereditary pressure. To advance the lineage with a great match. They … I … allowed them to get into my ear. I foolishly thought I could, you know …"

"Win him over?"

Alanna nodded. "I was wrong. Terribly, unconscionably wrong. Further, I apologize from the bottom of my soul for even *thinking* it. You two are a …" She flipped a hand at the cabin wall. "… a divinely made match. Your man practically snorted in my face when I approached him with my …" Alanna swallowed. "… my true feelings …" Now it was Alanna who pressed the side of a fist against her mouth.

Leera felt her eyebrows crawl up her forehead. "He … he did?"

"Yes. He was clear. Slammed the door in my face—*hard*. There was never any hope of a snobby fool like me ever stealing him away from you." Alanna turned her face fully sideways and forced a smile, and Leera almost looked away upon seeing Alanna's tear-streaked cheeks— tears she did not hide.

"I just … I guess I wanted to steal for myself that which you two have … something one cannot steal. Ever. I'm deeply ashamed of my behavior. Deeply. And sorry. To you and to Augum." She returned to perusing her book, casually flipping the pages—which she obviously wasn't reading—with one hand and at last wiping the tears from her cheeks with the other. "I've been watching how you two interact. The stolen hugs. The quick pecks. Your casual hand-holding. The way you two look at each other." Her voice dropped. "All your disgusting cuddles …"

Leera snorted a short laugh, which she promptly suppressed.

"You've taught me that love has to be *earned* and I was a fool to think something like that can just be … taken. I know you will probably never forgive me for that, and that's fair, but I want you to know that I came from a bad and malicious place where things like that are expected and regularly tried. Love-trapping, dowries, noble matches paid for by the highest bidder, lineage hunting, all of those courtly games that don't translate into real life. They're stupid tactics, and they'll *never* get me what I want, which is …"

"True love," Leera whispered on her behalf.

Alanna nodded. "True love. I want my own Augum, but obviously not Augum," she was quick to add.

"You need a snobby version of an Augum," Leera quipped. "Someone with a powdered face but an adventurous streak. Someone festooned with jewels who can get away with wearing a rucksack. Maybe has a mule in the shed or something—wait, no, it'd be a fine stallion of a horse, not a mule. And he'd probably have his own barn and stuff."

Alanna did something Leera had never heard her do, at least genuinely—and that was laugh. She laughed so hard, and so truly, that she keeled over to grab her stomach and bury her mouth into her sleeve to stifle that silly but genuine laugh.

Leera almost wanted to comfort her—almost. Instead she raised a finger. "You know what? Be right back," and she strode off, humming some sea shanty medley she'd heard the crew sing the other day. She went into her and Augum's cabin, snagged what she wanted, and returned. Upon arriving, she found Alanna sitting with her hands together in her lap, face relaxed and smiling in a manner Leera had never seen from the woman.

"What's that?" Alanna asked.

"The wall I've been bashing my head against." Leera tossed the book onto the bunk beside Alanna, where it bounced before settling.

" 'Zygothika,' " Alanna read. "Calligraphy carved in crimson, or I guess carved through the binding, revealing red underneath. What's the word mean?"

Leera grimaced as she recalled the exact phrasing. " '*Zygothika—Ei Rivika necromantos kusu tos murtos o utera*' —a Rivican necromantic curse that kills the, uh, the ..." Leera gestured vaguely downward.

"Kills the womb," Alanna finished for her in a whisper, not looking at Leera but at the book.

"Found it in Horren's Keep," Leera threw in.

"I thought that was just a rumor. Are you saying you actually found its vault?"

"If by vault you mean its library full of treasures, then yes. I reported the find to the authorities. Arcaneologists are probably cataloging the works as we speak," then she added in a mutter, "Assuming they found a way in there."

"Must have been quite the challenge to get in."

Leera snorted in a *Little do you know* manner and plopped down onto the cot beside Alanna, only to feel so wretchedly uncomfortable from being so close to the woman who had tried to steal her man that she shot right back up, choosing instead to hover nearby with her hands once more stretching out the pockets of her robe.

Leera cleared her throat as she swung side to side, robe twirling about her. "Er ... don't bother trying to open it as it's locked."

Alanna spread the fingers of a hand over the cover, and her arm lit up with eight lightning rings. "*Un vun asperio aurum enchantus*," she incanted.

"You learned Reveal," Leera blurted, trying to suppress the jealous tingle upon seeing the lightning rings, for the woman she considered more beautiful than herself also shared Augum's element. "Did you do it legally?"

"Money has its privileges," Alanna replied whilst studying the cover. "My family provided a generous endowment to the academy, which in turn granted me a dispensation to study Reveal before I had earned the proper degree so that I may better understand the arcaneological frameworks I would be working with."

Her fingers danced delicately over the cover as she spoke to herself distractedly. "Long sunk to permanence … the workmanship is unfamiliar … definitely a kargeyasnara … they certainly do not make slip-rune sequence puzzles like this anymore … or any, for that matter. And what's with the binding of the book? It almost looks …" Alanna recoiled. "It really *is* necromantic," she whispered, looking up. "Isn't it?"

"It's the spell that was inflicted upon me, which I'm hoping to reverse. And the only way to reverse it is to—"

"—study it and see if there's a reversal incantation or ritual," Alanna finished for her. She looked to Leera's belly, and Leera unconsciously removed her hands from her pockets and placed her arms before her, as if to block the sight. If asked, she would struggle to articulate the full extent of her discomfort in sharing such an intimate part of her soul with this attractive former rival.

Leera twiddled her fingers. "Er, I'm hoping there's a, uh, a way to undo it in the back or something."

"It's possible. Some necromantic curses can indeed be reversed."

"You think so? That's great. Apparently the mechanism—the kargeyasnara—might need malice. True malice. Or so Mrs. Stone said."

"Mrs. Stone …?"

"Anna Atticus Stone."

"Oh. *The* Anna Atticus Stone."

"She wrote about breaking a similar kargeyasnara some years back. Jez found that bit in the records, but it's only a small clue."

"I wish I'd had the privilege of being her apprentice."

"I wish I could continue being her apprentice, but she's in Ley."

"Is that part true? That she lives in Ley? That you lot visited that plane? That it even exists?"

Leera summoned the courage to sit down on the bed, with the book between them. "Yes."

Alanna stared into Leera's eyes. "Huh," she said, and returned her gaze to the book.

Leera flicked the cover. "I've been trying to solve this kargeyasnara since I got the book. Every day I've been pulping my brain against it, but I've made little progress."

Alanna brushed her hands over her hair, smoothing it down as she expelled a long breath through puffed cheeks. Then she scratched her pert nose before giving it a quick drumming with her fingers as she considered the book. "Do you know anything about its author?"

"Not a thing. Could be the devil for all we know."

"Then all we can know of the author is what he made visible to us—the decisions he made with the binding and presentation, as well as of course the tendril enchantments he left behind in the form of a kargeyasnara."

"Who's saying it was a he?" Leera threw in cheekily.

"Fair point. But how many women do you know would bind books in … whatever skin this is? Doesn't look like animal skin, I'll say that."

"And a fair point to you," Leera replied, disbelieving she was actually agreeing with something the noble scheming witch had said.

"Come to think of it …" Alanna held up the book and turned it this way and that as she grimaced at the cover. She put it down, raised the sleeve of her robe, exposing smooth and alabaster skin, and placed the arm up against the cover. "You don't think …?"

"You have disgustingly fair skin," Leera muttered, but leaned in to compare.

"It's human skin, isn't it?" Alanna whispered, ignoring the prior remark.

"What are you two idiots doing?" a childish voice asked from the hallway, startling the women, with Leera shooting away from Alanna and Alanna dropping the book, which tumbled toward the door. Limpet, who'd been standing in the hallway chewing on the edge of his thumb, as Leera hadn't closed the door behind herself, picked it up. "Looks necromantic," he said.

"Give me that," Leera snapped and swatted at the air, telekinetically yanking the book from his grasp.

Limpet returned to chewing on the edge of his thumb. "Were you about to cast a curse on me?"

"We will if you continue to bother us," Alanna replied.

"I thought you two hated each other because you—" Limpet nodded at Leera. "—think she—" He nodded at Alanna. "—is like a thousand times prettier, and you—" He nodded at Alanna again. "—are like suuuuper jealous of her—" He nodded at Leera a second time. "—for having that Arcaner commander."

Leera made a sweeping motion with her free hand. "You mean little goblin, why don't you do us a kindness and go eat your boogers somewhere else."

"I'm not a goblin, you are. I'm bored and I want you to teach me Teleport."

"Why, so you can fuse yourself with the hull? How about no."

"How about you get up off your lazy butt and teach me Teleport."

"How about—" and Leera flicked a hand at the door and it slammed shut in his face. After a moment of ringing silence during which both women tried not to snicker, there came a *bang* of the door, as if he'd punched it. Then an, "Ow, ow, ow," from the other side, and a shuffling sound as Limpet trundled off.

"You should dump him on the *Rose of the Seas*," Alanna said. "There's still time until we dive into the storm."

Leera thought of the *Rose of the Seas* and the two sister ships trailing them as they traveled southward along the storm line, looking for an advantageous spot to enter the maelstrom. "I'd love to, but I was made to swear on my shield that I'd take him and now we all have to suffer." She raised the sleeve of her robe to compare her own skin to Alanna's, but only got halfway, for after seeing all the freckles and imperfections and how dry her skin was, she promptly dragged her sleeve back down and dumped the book between them.

"Anyway," Leera sang, splaying a hand over the book.

"Anyway," Alanna echoed, doing the same, and the two women chorused, "*Un vun asperio aurum enchantus.*"

"These leading tendril edges are interesting," Alanna said, pointing out a particularly dense grouping of black tendrils with a perfectly manicured finger. "Look at the formations here and how they intertwine with these blue geometries."

Leera studied the noted portion. "Uh-huh …?"

"This is the keylock insertion point."

"The spot where the uttered phrase or word or spell meets the locking mechanism, I know, I got that far too," Leera replied, genuinely impressed with Alanna's knowledge on the subject.

"What have you tried?"

"All the usual suspects. Fear, Blind, Mute, Darkness, Paralyze, and a host of others—I even blasted it with a super-tempered First Offensive."

"And did at any time a portion of the kargeyasnara move?"

"Not a single tendril so much as vibrated."

"Then you're digging in the wrong spot."

"What do you mean?"

"You mentioned malice being one of the requirements. None of those spells have malice as a core tenet of execution."

Leera sighed. "You're suggesting I need to learn a necromantic spell with malice as a core tenet."

"Maybe."

"Maybe?"

"Maybe." Alanna bit her lip as she studied the complex tendril webs. "What if ..."

"What if ... what?" Leera wanted to playfully shove Alanna's shoulder to spur her along, but caught herself. The scheming witch had a long way to go to earn *that* sort of camaraderie ...

"There *is* a spell in our arsenal that has room for malicious insertion—"

"—Fear," Leera chorused along with Alanna. "But I tried it."

"In what manner?"

"The usuals. Injecting a fear of spiders and swords and sharks and serpents and all sorts of nightmares."

"I see." Alanna considered the matter. "Although those were subjective ideas on what a human target might consider fearful, they weren't injecting true *malice* into the tendril weavings, were they?"

"Well, I mean, er ... I guess not." Leera wanted to hate Alanna for being right about such an obvious point that made her feel stupid.

But Alanna did not appear to revel in her insights. Instead, her splayed fingers danced over the weaving as she delicately chewed on her lower lip. "What if ..." Her face slowly twisted with loathing. Then she made a claw of her hand as she swiped toward the book, hissing, "*Dreadus terrablus!*"

Leera started and practically shouted as she frantically gestured at the cover, "They-they-they rang! The tendrils vibrated! You ... you got something! What'd you do?"

"I envisioned plunging a knife into a woman's belly and hearing her scream in pain. In effect I injected the idea of creating harm—malice, if you will."

Leera blinked as her hands crawled to her belly. "Was it any particular woman or ...?"

"It was a faceless blob of a woman. You know, the *idea* of a woman. Nothing specific. You try it."

"Why belly though?" Leera muttered as she readied a clawed hand over the cover and Alanna took a turn watching how the tendrils reacted. "Malice, malice, malice," Leera said in an undertone, trying to come up with a variant of the spell that would trigger the tendril mechanism to unlock. She wanted to use Alanna as an example, but couldn't muster up the hatred required, and so she too imagined a faceless blob—albeit one with blond hair and alabaster skin. Then she envisioned stabbing the woman in the throat and clawed at the book whilst hissing, "*Dreadus terrablus!*"

"They moved, all right, but barely," Alanna reported.

"I couldn't muster up the requisite malice, evidently," Leera muttered, knowing her heart hadn't been in it.

"Hmm, I guess it has to be a more genuine loathing, then," Alanna said, brushing a finger across her lips. "I might have it. Let me try again." She took a series of deep breaths, during which her face steadily changed. Her eyes narrowed, she bared her teeth, and her lips curled in a loathsome scowl. Her fingers danced above the cover in a taunting fashion as she whispered, "*Dreadus terrablus …*"

Leera's eyes magnified as she witnessed the black tendrils vibrate in a symphony that interacted with the blue tendril mechanism portion. Then it happened. The mechanism unwound — and unlocked with a *click*.

"You did it!" Leera shouted and reached out to hug Alanna, only to recoil and instead pat her lamely on the shoulder. "Er … good work. Yeah. Well done. What'd you use to unlock it?"

Alanna shrugged. "Had a snob of a bully as a kid who stole my boyfriend. Just pictured the book being that bully and punching her face and breaking her pretty nose, causing her malicious harm."

Leera clucked her tongue. "That'd do it." She licked the tip of a finger, pressed it under the cover, made her eyebrows dance at Alanna, then lifted the cover … revealing a cover page with the word *Zygothika*, written in ink so dark red it was almost brown. Leera flipped another page and read out the inscription. " 'Let the soil dry, may the seed die.' "

The women shared an ominous look.

"Spooky as all heck," Alanna whispered.

Leera began flipping pages alongside Alanna, their lips moving silently as they skimmed the text together. It was a relatively thin book, but the calligraphy was dense and precise, outlining the composition of a complex curse that, once mastered, could be cast in the heat of battle.

"And I'm living proof that *that* is attainable," Leera murmured to herself, flipping the page. On she read, eyes zipping across the pages and over the gruesome diagrams, written in a fluid hand and nightsoil-colored ink, until she came to a pertinent chapter titled "Remedy & Reversion," at which point she pressed a hand to her chest to calm her breathing.

Alanna watched her, perfectly groomed blond eyebrows pitched with empathy. Then she jolted as if zapped by a realization and got up. "My word, I should leave you be as this is going to be a very private process." She flicked a hand at the book. "It should remain unlocked from now on. Anyway, glad I was able to help and that, uh, we're no longer enemies. I'll go," and she whirled to walk off, only to stop at the door. "Wait, this is my cabin."

Leera couldn't help smiling as she closed the cover, keeping a finger on the chapter, and rose to her feet. She passed Alanna, opened the cabin door, but hesitated. "You know, you're not as revoltingly terrible and vicious as I first thought," she said, fingers tapping the door frame.

"And you're not as insipidly stupid as *I* first thought."

"I hate how pretty you are."

"I hate how pretty *you* are."

"I hate—" Leera did a double-take. "Wait … what?"

"In a feral way," Alanna added with a cheeky smile. "No, but seriously, you are *wildly* pretty. And honestly, combined with who you are as a person, way prettier than a powdered court flower like me. It is plainly obvious that he is smitten with you on multiple levels, which is something to behold. I'm …" She swallowed. "… genuinely in awe of you two."

"Well don't be in *too* much awe now. Don't need any more smoke blowin' up our robes."

They grinned at each other. Leera then lifted the book to nod her thanks and departed—and saw the flick of a burgundy-colored robe vanish around the corner. "Stop spying on people, you little snot!" Leera shouted after Limpet. Sighing, she went to her cabin, where she found Augum lying on their bunk, an arm behind his head, a book open before him, which he lowered to his chest.

"Hey," he said with a smile.

She slithered onto him, purring, "Hey," and pecked his lips. "How's that grouchy Black Eagle doing?" she asked, sliding in beside him and resting her head on his chest.

"She's undergoing multiple arcane surgeries. Jengo has asked the captain to wait to enter the storm until he completes his work. Said he needs the day, and then Mahmoute will have to recuperate."

"And then we enter the storm?"

He idly played with her hair. "And then we enter the storm."

"And Digby's trial?"

"That's happening later on."

"Ah. Whatcha readin'?"

He flipped the book up and turned the cover over.

" '*Voyages of the Dawnchaser, a Fateful Expedition into the Storm Curtain*,' "] she read.

He cradled her close. "Make any progress on yours?"

She made a show of lifting the *Zygothika* book and letting go of the spot where she'd inserted her finger, allowing the book to flop open onto Augum's chest.

He jolted. "No …"

"Yes."

"No *way*."

"*Yes* way."

"But … how?" He nudged her. "Huh, Miss Smileypants? What'd you do?"

"I … got a little help from a rather unexpected source."

"Jez?"

"Nope."

"Olaf?"

She snorted.

Augum grimaced. "What? He's not dumb."

"Never said he was. It's just not his thing." Now it was she who nudged him. "Keep guessing."

"If I have to. The little turdling."

Her face curdled. "*Limpet?* Ew, no."

"Carter …?"

"Come on, you're not even trying." Her eyes narrowed. "Wait, you already know, don't you?"

"No idea what you're talking about."

She whapped his chest with the back of her hand. "You fiend, you put her up to it, didn't you!"

He looked away guiltily.

She shoved him off and sat up. "You conspired with my enemy to—"

"It wasn't like that," he interrupted, looking at her and raising a hand to cup her cheek, but she slapped it away, not too hard but not too soft either. Augum sighed. "I told her I'm totally committed to you."

She did a little head wag. "I know you did."

"Yeah and—wait, what?"

"We had a talk." She narrowed her eyes. "But is that all?"

"Basically, yes."

"Didn't swear to marry her behind my back?"

Augum snorted. "Come here," and threw his arms around her and made her flop back onto him, where he showered her with kisses. She let him, enjoying his scent and touch and his adoring attention, knowing he loved her and she'd long won his heart and Alanna was nothing. Things got heated, and she had to lock the cabin door for a while as they shoveled the books off the bunk.

Later, sweaty and having exhausted themselves, they unspooled.

"So?" he asked, drawing the blanket over his chest.

"So what?" she said, idly kicking her naked back with her feet while lounging beside him.

"What's the fix?"

"I was just getting to that part." She made a hand yap at him in a *Gimme gimme gimme* motion, and he reached down beside the bunk and grabbed the book for her. "Thanks, and I'm sure it's not that simple," she added, taking it from him.

Augum grabbed his own book. "Well, let me know if there's anything I can do."

"Mmm."

They settled into reading beside each other, with Leera delving into the promising chapter titled "Remedy & Reversion," whilst lying on her front and continuing to kick her own back with her heels. That kicking soon slowed to a halt, and she sat up, the fingers of one hand stabbing the page before her and the fingers of the other pawing at Augum.

"What is it, lovebug?" he asked, an eyebrow rising above his book.

She squeaked and repeatedly clapped her palms together like a seal — she only felt comfortable acting in this silly manner with her betrothed, of course. Everyone else got the obnoxious-brassy-girl veneer.

"Look at this," she cooed, fingers tapping along a certain line. " 'The necromancer may at some point feel it in his or her best interest to reverse the curse inflicted upon the victim. Perhaps the victim has fallen into line, or perhaps the terms of a ransom are paid in full, or some other change of fortune has occurred. Regardless of the reason, any healer of the 18th degree or above can perform the highly complex reversal process' —" Leera raised a finger here. " —'as long as they know the healing ritual *Apreyancrosolautera* —' " Leera snapped her fingers as she translated the components of the name. "Repair ... sacred ... soul ... womb." She punched Augum's shoulder. "Eh? Am I good or am I good? That spell should exist in the archives somewhere. Some dusty scroll sitting on a shelf no doubt."

"Is that all there is to it? Seems kind of simple."

"Let me finish, mister. 'They must also have at their disposal *three* rare ingredients for the aforementioned ritual, all of which must be ground to a fine powder and mixed with the victim's blood. The ingredients are —' " Her voice steadily weakened as she read them out. " —'the tooth of a giant, the claw of a wyvern, and the ... and the horn of an adult ...' "

"An adult *what*?" Augum pressed.

"An adult minotaur.' " Her shoulders slumped. "It wants beasts from myth."

"They obviously can't be myths if they're listed as ingredients. They have to be real *some*where. Maybe in the lands beyond." He rubbed the scruff on his neck. "Or maybe …"

"Maybe what?" She shook his shoulder. "Maybe what!"

"Maybe what the author *thought* was a minotaur is something more mundane, like an ox. And a giant was just an oversized human. You know, like Jengo, but freakishly taller. People like that are super rare but a handful are scattered throughout the seven kingdoms. And a wyvern … maybe that's just a big lizard. And if it *is* the real thing, well, we've seen *summoned* wyverns during the war with Canterra, so maybe the real thing exists out there too. Oh, and not to mention we've seen some weird beasts in Endraga Ra …"

Leera gaped at him before planting a big wet kiss on his forehead. "You're brilliant and I love you."

He wobbled his head about in imitation of her and smiled to himself.

"I should be able to figure out which beasts were mistaken for creatures of myth back in the day and work backward from there …" She straddled the book with her elbows and propped her chin on her hands as she read on, soon reading another part aloud. " 'The challenge will be to coax the curse back from the ether, where it sits lodged within the arcaneological context of the soul and its membrane parts.' " Leera scowled. "The heck does that even *mean*?"

Augum shrugged beside her.

" 'Once the curse is coaxed to the fore, it can be disenchanted, and the womb thence healed.' " She let her head slip through her hands and flop onto the book. "This might take years."

"Well, it's not like we're in a rush. Besides, years is better than never."

She moaned pitifully into the book, which prompted him to drape his leg over her back and nuzzle up to her. He ran a hand through her hair and whispered, "I'm proud of you and I love you and healing the curse would be an unexpected gift, so don't stress about it," which made her feel better.

"Thank you, that means a lot," she whispered. "And I love you too." *More than you know*, she wanted to add.

As he continued idly tracing a hand over her head and back, she shoved the book aside, closed her eyes, and sighed with some contentment, for there was hope on the horizon after all …

THE FRANTIC RING OF A BELL

AUGUM

"On the contrary, I charge him with cold-blooded *murder*," Augum corrected, pacing up to a glaring Digby, voice carrying in the stifling room. "The boy was only thirteen years old, trembling like a leaf, had been whisked to an enemy ship—and yet he had been eager to help me try to save Black Eagle Mahmoute's life."

Augum slowly ground a fist into an open palm as he held a steely-eyed gaze on Digby, whose scowl reminded Augum of the classic bully. "The kid was holding a cloth to the Black Eagle's wound, his back turned, and—" Augum punched his palm with a *smack*. "—*that's* when Digby stabbed him. Right. In. The. *Back*."

Augum left his fist in his palm, trying not to snarl, before placing his hands behind him and turning to a crowd of tense crew members and passengers. "It wasn't just a dishonorable act that Digby Bloomington-Southguard pretends to regret." Augum shook a finger. "Digby here was gleeful—" He thrust the finger behind him into Digby's face. "—*gleeful* about it, shouting, 'Gotcha, little worm!' " Augum's hand dropped. "Gotcha. Little. Worm. It was a cowardly act performed by a *coward*."

The younger Bloomington-Southguard sat white-knuckling a spindled armchair, powdered face curdled with loathing. In the back of the room, in a small throne-like chair, the captain sat gumming his arm-length pipe, having taken on the role of magistrate. The ship creaked as it tilted another degree whilst slowly cresting a rolling wave. Outside, the wind whistled against the hull, and there could be heard the distant sound of rigging clanking about.

Augum continued to address the audience. "Digby deserves a prison sentence commensurate with the crime." His eyes ran across the older Bloomington-Southguard, Teague, who wore his white wig in solidarity with his younger brother. His equally powdered face was hard as he raised his chin imperiously at Augum, his protuberant mole colored in the beauty mark manner of the royal court. Behind him, like a servant torn between two masters, sat Carter Southguard, nervously fidgeting in his chair.

Alanna, Leera, Jez, Olaf, Jengo, Limpet—and even Rogor—sat or stood along the back, with senior crew in the front. All watched with interest, especially Rogor, whose head was tilted as he examined the crowd as much as the accused.

"His act was a direct betrayal of the law of honorable battle," Augum continued, pacing to his chair before turning about to look at the captain. "An act that cannot go unpunished, for it would diminish us all as honorable people." He nodded at Teague, who the captain had appointed to represent Digby. "Council," then took his seat.

Teague jumped from his chair, launching right into it. "A mere oversight committed in the heat of battle!" he shouted to the rapt audience in an oily tone, arms outstretched. "You were all there—it was chaos! Absolute. Chaos! We took prisoners, for heaven's sake! Our brig is full, and the rest have been offloaded onto the *Rose of the Seas*. So for the commander of the Arcaner order—which my brother does *not* belong to, mind you—to come along and moralize in the heat of battle is unfair and preposterous. *Preposterous!* For Unnameables' sake, the ship was sinking!"

He paced up to the audience to repeat, *"Sinking!"* He let that thought settle. "My brother was merely defending the ship, as any honorable sailor would do. We only have the word of the commander of the Arcaner order—and yes, he demonstrated his superiority over us mere mortals by swearing on his holy shield that what he was saying is the truth. But—*but*—!"

Teague strolled up to a sitting Augum, holding his hands behind his back in a blatant copy of Augum's style, stopping to stare down at him. "It is well known that Augum Stone thinks *little* of my *little* brother. The two have been at odds every league of this voyage. Every. League."

Teague raised a finger, which he wagged about as he turned in place to make his point. "*I* suggest that the commander was inflamed by his passions and thus viewed the moment through the *biased* eyes of someone who not only *despises* my little brother, but rigidly follows a code of honor that my brother does *not* subscribe to. What Augum Stone saw was true to *him* and *his* code of honor. My poor younger brother—" Teague threw both arms at Digby, whose lip protruded in a simpering pout. "—should therefore not be held to the same standard of that code of honor, but to the reasonable demands of a terrible battle that almost finished us all. How was he supposed to know the man whose back was turned to him was a kid? He was trying to save the ship! That's all there was to it!"

Teague looked to the captain. "There is one last point of contention. My brother is a subject of the royal court and should be judged in that court by a royal committee of his peers, not by ..." He turned to throw a disgusted glance at Augum. "... a twenty-year-old soldier who thinks himself above his station."

This earned him some hisses from the audience, which prompted the captain to tap his pipe against the armrest. "Settle it down, people," he said, restraining his usual dockside twang. "Settle it down. Continue, please, Mr. Bloomington-Southguard."

"Yes, sir. Thank you, sir. For my final statement, I ask the captain this. Would you truly send to the brig a young man who made a simple mistake in the heat of battle, that mistake being his failure to identify one of our attackers as a mere boy?" He raised his hands aloft as if holding the question, then bowed with a graceful—and in Augum's eyes, ridiculous—twirl of those hands. "The defense has presented its case to you in full, honorable captain, and my brother's life is in your hands."

Augum glanced back at Leera, who expressed his thoughts by rolling her eyes and shaking her head. "Ridiculous," she mouthed, a sentiment that had him subtly nodding in agreement.

"Hmm," the captain toned, puffing on his pipe. He expelled a series of blue puffs of smoke before nodding. "Hmm." He flipped the pipe upside down, tapped it against the arm of the chair to free the ashes, and glanced about. The walrus-mustachioed bosun, who was standing by, fished out a silver box from a pocket and opened it before the captain, who picked out a clump of tobacco with stained fingers, pressed it into the pipe, and allowed the bosun to repeatedly strike steel on flint until the pipe lit.

"Hmm," the captain toned, nodding as he puff-puff-puffed on the pipe. "Mr. Digby Bloomington-Southguard, would you stand, please, young man."

The thirty-four-year-old Digby shot to his feet even quicker than his brother. He wrung his hands before him as he shifted his beefy body from foot to foot.

"Solian maritime law allows me full discretion on the matter. The charge is serious and warrants this court proceeding on this boat. In the eyes of this court, it has indeed been proven that a young lad was slain."

Many in the audience nodded at this point, with the white-wigged Bloomington-Southguards trading worried looks.

"However," the captain went on, nodding as he took a moment to steal a puff from his pipe. "However, the opposing counsel has not proven beyond doubt that Mr. Bloomington-Southguard intended to slay a boy. On the contrary, it appears to this court that Mr. Bloomington-Southguard was merely doing his duty, albeit clumsily. For that clumsiness, his honor has already been tarnished, and he has already spent days in the brig. This court believes that the younger Mr. Bloomington-Southguard will not make such a mistake again, that he will be more cautious in any future frays. This court therefore finds that Mr. Bloomington-Southguard is free of the charge of murder, free of the charge of accidental murder, and is free to continue his duties in guarding the heir apparent to the kingdom, the young Arcaner Carter Southguard."

Augum felt himself wilt a little in his chair. To him, it had been cut and dry. So either the captain genuinely didn't think the crime warranted a conviction, or he was loyal to the crown, or he feared what was to come and simply wanted every warlock on deck instead of any rotting in the brig.

The captain tapped his pipe against the arm of the chair. "Court adjourned."

Digby flashed Augum a triumphant grin as he embraced his brother.

Olaf patted Augum on the shoulder when he joined their group in the back. "You gave it your all."

"That was a travesty is what it was," Leera muttered, and hugged Augum. "You got robbed of justice."

"It wasn't me who got robbed of justice," Augum said, thinking of the pirate boy.

As people turned to their neighbor to mutter about the outcome, the captain stood, adding, "Crew, prepare to transfer the last of the prisoners. Ms. Terse, I reckon you're still up for it?"

"Not too sloshed yet," Jez replied with a nod, flashing Augum a look he interpreted as, *Dare you to say something.*

Augum was hardly in the mood to chastise his mentor and, seeing the captain was on his way out of the room, excused himself from his group to catch up to him. "Sir, regarding our earlier discussion on the subject of the *Rose of the Seas* and its captain's reckless piloting into the back of the pirate ship—"

"I've thought it over, son," the captain interrupted, "and I shan't be bringing a case about it should we arrive back in one piece. In fact, I reckon there's even less merit in that there charge than the one ye argued." He patted Augum's shoulder. "Learn to pick your battles, laddie. Besides, me thinks we both know there's bigger whales to blubber." He nodded at a window with an ominous darkness on the horizon, hinting at the challenges ahead.

Despite wanting to argue on, Augum knew it was useless, and so relented with a sigh. "Sir, one other thing, if I may. There is one among the pirates. I'd like to see if he'd take a commission to work for us."

"Something tells me I know the one you are referring to. You have my leave, son. But convincing *him* is another matter altogether." He nodded and moved past Augum.

Augum followed the captain a ways before sliding down a ladder, then wound his way through the cramped corridors of the decks below. As he walked, he began hearing a surprisingly soft male voice singing a melancholy tune about a girl lost at sea and being found by her lover, only for the pair to perish in each other's arms amidst tall waves. It was such a beautiful song that Augum found himself slow-walking the last hallway. By the time he stepped into the brig, a room filled with cages and guarded by several bored crew members, the song had winded down to a sweet hum.

One of the guards was Tammy, the sailblower. She stood leaning against a wooden wall with a book open in her hands, one eye peeled on the prisoners, who sat in cages barely larger than crates, a hand idly swaying about in rhythm to the humming.

Upon Augum's entrance, she straightened and smiled, mouthing, "Commander."

Augum smiled a hello and gestured to one of the cells, mouthing, "May I?"

Tammy indicated with her open book. "Please."

Augum approached the cage where the humming was coming from—and which held the bald man tattooed with leopard spots. He sat with eyes closed, legs crossed on the floor, hands shackled before him with the only pair of arcane manacles the crew had in their possession, which the captain had wisely commissioned from the island nautical rental supplies prior to departure for a premium—and with costly insurance to boot in case of their failed return.

Augum waited until the sweet melody died out on the man's lips, then said, "Fire warlock."

"Arcaner," the man replied, not opening his eyes, large hoop earrings dangling along with his nose and lip rings. "I'd stand to receive ye, boy, but I'm a little tied up at the moment." He rattled his manacles.

His fellow pirates, mostly young boys, sat up a little straighter in their cages. All had been told they would be turned over to the constabulary on the Spice Islands, then likely set free—unless any were wanted by said authorities.

From the angle at which he looked down upon the man, Augum saw that the scarring on his head had a particular pattern.

"I was young and stupid and robbed a Henawa," the warlock said, opening his eyes to look up at Augum. "That was back before I took to the saltbloods."

"You have a sense about you," Augum replied, impressed he had read his thoughts.

"I'm no telepath, boy. Just aware. Take, for example, your position. You stand peekin' down at me scalp in all its glory. 'Course you'd take note. Wouldn't ye, boy? Don't take no smarts to figure that out."

Augum ceded the point with a nod.

The man leaned against the back of his cage. "I never got to thank the tall one who healed me noggin'. Took a right knock, didn't I?"

"You'll get your chance, I'm sure."

The fire warlock considered him. "We had a right proper scrap."

"That we did."

"And now, having appraised this 'ere pirate, you want me to join yer voyage."

Augum kept his face placid, no longer surprised that the man had guessed his intentions. He was the street-smart sort, but also played that up, for there had to be an intelligence there as well, capable of climbing the degrees all the way up to the 15th.

"What's the pay?"

"No pay."

The fire warlock snorted as he looked to his caged crew members, who took their cue and chuckled, albeit mutely, as if afraid to bring too much attention to themselves.

"But I can offer something better, pirate. Glory."

"Glory?"

"Glory ... and adventure."

"Glory and adventure." The man smiled, and the torchlight glinted off his golden tooth. "But you reckon you'd talk to me first. See what sort I am." He nodded to Augum's shield arm. "I ain't that sort, that's fer sure."

"No code of honor?"

He nodded to his fellow pirates. "Me and mine. That's my code of honor."

"And if your mine were to include us?"

The fire warlock raised his manacled hands to scratch his chin. "Then I'd fight by yer side, wouldn't I?"

"How'd you learn it?" Augum asked, sticking his index fingers out and making them point inward then outward in dual harmony.

"Angling? Like anything else with the ol' arts."

The corner of Augum's mouth curved with knowing. "Practice," he said.

The fire warlock confirmed that with a slight incline of his tattooed head.

"What about you and that spell mirroring? Never seen that before. Or the ability to decorate one's shield. Fancy, fancy, fancy, laddie."

"I'm afraid such things are only for us Arcaners."

"Ah. Shame."

Augum crouched, resting his arms on his robed knees, hands together. He considered those hands, how they were cracked and dry and the fingernails a little dirty. How he needed a long and hot bath, ideally with Leera. "Look," he began. "The one promise I can give is adventure. I can't even truly promise glory. There will likely be no riches either, for we aim to penetrate the storm curtain. We have all the elements—"

"—except fire," the warlock cut in. "So it ain't my dazzling personality you want."

"Or your pretty voice," Augum added with a wry grin. "Although that'd raise spirits, yes it would. No, this journey isn't for us. It's for others. People you haven't even met." Augum stood, nodding to himself. "For people you might *never* meet." Then he turned and walked off, just as others, including Jez, filed in.

"That's it?" the fire warlock called after him. "That all you got?"

Augum turned at the doorway. "That's it."

"Cut and dry?"

"Cut and dry."

"Adventure?"

"Adventure."

"No glory?"

"That part's up to you."

"You haven't even asked me my name."

"Does it matter?"

Jez, who'd stepped in beside Augum, folded her arms and nudged him with her shoulder. "Making friends?"

"Don't know yet," he replied.

The pirate smiled toothily. "Leo. Leo the Leopard. And Leo the Leopard is intrigued enough to join y'all on this foolhardy errand because Leo the Leopard is curious as to what's on the other side. And Leo the Leopard might die, but then it's better than getting bored to death in the brig." His eyes went to Jez and he warbled a seductive whistle. "Why *hello*, there, pretty miss."

Jez snorted, but her cheeks colored a little.

Augum acknowledged Leo with a nod and was about to leave, only for the man's voice to halt him once again.

"I heard your name is a name mentioned often in them heralds! A historic name with a right historic story. That true, boy? Did I face a hero of the war? One of the so-called *dragons*? That why you were all quick with them reflexes?"

"It's true," Jez replied on Augum's behalf. "Cap says you might stay. We could use a scheming pirate. Got some lick to you?"

The pirate warlock looked Jez up and down. "Not as much as you, I think, my feisty mermaid of the seas."

Jez smiled cheekily before nodding down at his wrists. "Guess I'd better get those off you. Think you can handle a woman after being around boys all this time, *Leo the Leopard*?"

Leo chortled. "The gods have blessed me—and they've blessed us. Oh, how we're going to have us some fun. Do you dance?"

"Like a bird and drink like a fish."

"Gods, marry me already, my salacious queen of the ocean."

"Ugh," Augum said.

"Shut up," Jez hissed at him, albeit with a grin.

Augum only rolled his eyes at her.

Limpet shoved past Augum and Jez, pointing at one of the cages with a boy his age inside. "His name's Dirt and you have to keep him too."

"Nuh-uh, kiddo," Jez replied. "He's too young, and so are you. Dropping you both off today."

"That's not the deal!"

"It's not safe for kids where we're going."

"I might *look* young but I'm still a 2nd degree! Mostly self-taught! I can handle myself. Besides, *she* promised." Limpet flicked his chin at Augum. "His stupid harlot."

Jez slapped the boy—hard. "Watch your damn mouth, boy. This isn't a game. You're off, and that's it. Captain's orders."

Limpet's eyes flared at her as they watered. "You *dare*—"

The ship abruptly tilted, cutting the argument off. Wood creaked and the sound of a fearsome wind shrieked past the structure. Someone up top began furiously ringing a handbell.

Augum and Jez shared a knowing look.

"It's way too soon," Jez said.

"Something's wrong," Augum replied and raced off. He careened through the corridors, shot up the ladders, flew through the main cabin door—and found himself standing on a chaotic deck of crew scrambling to man the rigging. The bosun was ringing a bell, shouting, "Batten them hatches and trim them sails, lads! Skip to it now!"

What lay beyond was what caught his attention, for an enormous black cloud bank had descended onto the ocean—and was about to engulf the entire ship. It repeatedly flashed with lightning, sending forth rolling rumbles of thunder that ripped over the ship like invisible waves, shaking his innards like a drum.

Augum turned to look rearward, but a haze had formed all about, and he couldn't spy the *Rose of the Seas* anywhere. Attempting to teleport to the other ships, moving targets that could not be seen, would certainly result in the warlock finding himself lost amidst a storm-tossed ocean. In short, it would be suicide.

Just like that, they were cut off, dashing any hope of dumping the kid and the prisoners, as well as any chance of Augum being able to tell off the captain and the Lord High Commander for their reckless maneuver earlier.

"Hit us like an avalanche," the bosun said, tugging his tilted cap further down his head so it wouldn't blow away, walrus mustache whipping about. "Best get below. It ain't going to be pretty out here."

The captain echoed the sentiment and looked to Augum from near the wheel and threw down an arm, silently telling him to get below.

"With respect, son, you 'locks would only get in our way," the bosun added.

Augum returned his attention to the onrushing cloud, which reared up like a mountain. Except the lightning flashes reminded him of home—specifically, the hallway that led to the lightning elements room in the

Academy of Arcane Arts. He had no fear of lightning—he was even immune to it.

"With respect, no," Augum said, retying the golden rope belt of his robe so that it was nice and tight. "I'm staying," and he strode forth.

"Aug!" came Leera's voice from behind. "What's happ—holy mother of the gods ..." she muttered, voice trailing as she glanced around, hair flailing in the wind so much that she pressed an arm to her forehead to shield her eyes from it.

Others soon joined her—Olaf and Jengo and Jez and Digby and Teague and Carter and Alanna and the newly freed Leo—and all their faces went white upon seeing what was about to descend on them. Already the surrounding waves began to froth and crest and tumble, and the wind threw spray sideways at a velocity that stung the skin.

"Water, wind, and lightning to the fore!" Augum shouted. "The rest get below. Ollie—snag Tammy, would you?"

Almost all turned on their heels and scrambled out of there, with Olaf throwing in, "You got it, Aug."

Alanna, a lightning warlock, stayed for a bit, but her nerves failed, and she skittered back inside, which caused Leera to snort knowingly. Leo stayed, yet his grim face made Augum wonder if he regretted his choice to stay aboard—not that he had much of a choice anyhow, considering the storm had cut them off.

"I suggest ye better lash in, then, lad," the bosun said, tossing Augum a coil of rope.

Augum handed it to Leera, then fetched some more, and a crewman helped them all tie in to either an overhead line, a mast, or a cleat near a mast.

"Hear that?" Leera shouted over the wind. "Like living thunder! Bet you're loving it, aren't you, lightning boy!"

Augum, who had one leg raised on a crate and a hand on the rigging, flashed her a grin. He *was* enjoying it—to a point. He'd never been in such a violent ocean storm before, and it was only ramping up. Yet the lightning and thunder were like calls to war for him. He did not fear these things directly, but rather what they could do to the ship and to his colleagues. It was time to put his arts to the test—he needed to curtail the storm's awesome power.

As the crew ran about in a desperate attempt to trim the sails to a minimum and batten down and triple-lash everything to the deck, Augum scrolled through his spells, homing in on the lightning tiers, wondering which one would be the most effective. Although limited by his 10th degree, his theoretical and academy-taught knowledge of the element was strong enough to give him options, and that was why he craned his neck toward the top of the main mast, for lightning would seek the highest point of the ship. If it was powerful enough, it could blow the mast apart ... or worse.

He began to untie the rope from around his waist that kept him lashed to the ship.

Leera grabbed his wrist. "Don't even think about it!" she shouted over the wind.

He used his free hand to gently take hold of her wrist. "Trust me," he said and removed her hand.

She swallowed. "Damn it, Aug!"

His response was to kiss her and press her to him. She threw her arms around his shoulders, and they embraced for a long moment.

"The time has come to do my elemental duty," he said into her ear. "Please keep everyone clear of the mast."

"'Port back down the moment it gets to be too much," she replied into his. "But don't you dare 'port your way up there. Climb it, you hear?"

He drew back, nodded, smiled, and went to the taller of the two masts. He grabbed a piece of spare rope between his teeth and began the precarious climb. The mast's swaying increased by the foot, until he found his stomach being thrown about. But Augum did not fear heights, for they brought him closer to the sky. The higher he climbed and the more violent the swing, the more he felt like he was climbing closer to home, for he had flown through violent storms before. But the quest here was different as he would be hunting lightning itself. His prey was his own element.

"Excuse me," he said through the rope in his teeth as he passed sailor after sailor, all of whom gaped at him with raised eyebrows.

Down below Tammy had her hands raised skyward as she worked the winds to minimize their impact on the sails, and Jez had lashed herself to the bow of the ship, where she pointed at the occasional massive wave, tempering its strength. Leera, who had positioned herself aft of the main mast and just below the wheel deck, stood watching him more than the ocean. Wisely, she was saving her strength for the battle to come.

"Worry not, my love," he said into the wind and rain as he climbed past the last topgallant. After ascending to the pinnacle, and with his legs clasped around the mast and feet wedged into a pair of rope hooks, he took the rope from his mouth, threw it around the mast and around his waist, and used one hand to tie a bowline knot, which a sailor had taught him earlier in the voyage.

But he hadn't prepared for the icy rain, and already his hands began to freeze and his teeth chattered—and they hadn't even entered the storm cloud rising like a black mountain directly ahead, flickering angrily with internal lightning. The mast swung in such wide arcs that Augum felt like he was in a giant slingshot priming to release him into the maelstrom.

Lightning stabbed at the waters ahead. He girded his soul, for soon they would stab the ship.

Think not of the cold, he thought, war training kicking in. *Nor of the wind. Steel your soul and think of the warmth within.* Gradually his teeth stopped chattering as he took control of his inner strength. He was the commander of an ancient order. A war hero and a dragon. Weather would not defeat him. He would show that he was its master.

No, too arrogant, he thought and corrected himself. "I am the watcher," he declared. "And the watcher survives the onslaught by rising above it."

But a frightful thought remained. How long could he keep it up? What if the storm persisted and worsened? How far did they have to go to break through the storm?

Suddenly it felt like the storm wall was barreling down on them, and a handbell began to ring again below in warning, but what the sailor was yelling did not penetrate the shriek of the wind. Augum's eyes widened, for this was unlike any storm he had ever faced in his life. It felt amplified by an unseen and malignant force …

"Unnameables help us all," he whispered out of habit, almost seeing Mrs. Stone's lips form the same words as she stared at a mighty challenge. Thinking of his great-grandmother strengthened his resolve, and he tensed his muscles and tightened his hold.

The storm wall roared in like an avalanche, plunging the ship into darkness and violently putting it on its beam, nearly capsizing it, before it slowly keeled back like the reincarnated dead. The lamps below clanged as they swung in the gale—and promptly snuffed, for the wind was too great even for their reinforced cages. One by one, the warlocks on the ship lit their palms, providing the only source of light—along with the near constant flashes of lightning.

"*Shyneo!*" Augum shouted into the wind, flaring his hand with lightning. Yet all that he illuminated was a relatively small area around him that showed nothing but sheets of sideways rain. Occasionally the imposing walls of rolling water, reflecting the light from his palm, could be seen quickly approaching the mast before retreating as the ship swung the other way.

Then he felt a certain *crackle* in the air. His clothes felt clingy, and his hair stood on end. Knowing what was about to happen, he raised his lit palm skyward—and a lance of light split his skull. He felt his body stiffen and heat up, his innards vibrating with a simultaneous *crack* of thunder so loud he felt the mast shake. The air ripped around him, as did his clothes, which seemed to have been blown apart from within—yet other than the occasional char mark, his skin remained unharmed.

Robe shredded, a smoking Augum looked down to see Leera waving and shouting something. Unable to reach him, her palm light, barely visible through the sideways rain, went to her throat, and she roared in an amplified voice, "Are you all right, my love!"

He flashed a thumbs-up, which seemed utterly ridiculous, but it was the most concise way to pass the message along. In fact, he was more than all right. Every fiber of his being felt alive and hot and limber. The lightning had injected energy into him, warming his soul and body and even his reflexes. The ancestral echo, passed down from Atrius Arinthian himself, who he shared a birthday with, had saved him from incurring the wrath of the lightning. It had also saved the mast, which could have been blown apart.

The only problem was that his clothes were hanging in strips, from his robe to his very undergarments. Quickly he ran a hand over the strips of his undergarments, incanting, *"Apreyo,"* and stitched them back together as best he could—some were hidden to him on account of his awkward position on the mast and would have to be repaired later. The robe was a little easier as it was on the outside of his body, though a few random strips remained missing, for they had either been blown out of range or burnt up by the lightning bolt, meaning he'd have to switch to his only spare robe later and patch this one. The Repair spell, after all, could not mend that which had been burnt.

He quickly threw these musings aside when he felt the tug of the sky a second time. His hair straightened and his robe crackled and he felt a wicked and crisp dryness even in the rain.

Crack! went a second bolt of lightning and thunder, blistering his soul and body and whitening his vision, leaving behind a throbbing afterglow.

He flashed the thumbs-up even before Leera could shout the question again, then checked himself over. The lightning had blown off even more strips, for the first strike had weakened his robe and undergarments, yet he had once again saved the mast.

"Can't keep this up though, can I?" he asked the storm.

He felt the ship crest a gigantic wave and saw Jez's and Leera's arms waving about down below. The ship's movement softened temporarily, but soon there was another mammoth wave, and then another, and before Augum knew it, the mast had swung down to such a steep degree that he felt like all he had to do was reach out to touch the black wave that *whooshed* by like a giant rolling pin.

Gods, this is scary, he thought, envisioning one of the taller waves swatting him off his perch like a bug. And then there were the lightning blasts. If he didn't find a new tactic, the lightning would quickly fry his clothes and he'd find himself naked, a completely unsustainable scenario in such frigid cold. Further, even protected by the ancestral echo, how many blasts could he endure before one knocked him out or blew him clean off the mast?

As the water receded when the mast rose to swing the other way, an idea struck him. He wove the fingers of his free hand in the air. "*Ipulato laitna marjorus*," he said, the incantation to the 9th degree off-the-books *Ipulaitnamarjahanilus*—the ancient name for Major Shape Lightning. A web of lightning danced forth from his outstretched fingers, probing and prodding at the air.

Tilting his head, Augum focused on it, expanding it to a large branch of crackling snakes. He made this branch sag downward toward the water, pushing his knowledge with the spell, working its core arcaneological muscle. In a way, it felt similar to when he raised objects with his Telekinesis, exercising that arcane muscle to strengthen his ability.

The end of the lightning branch got so low it touched the water. He soon felt the dry and energetic stiffening come on again and braced. *Crack!* went the lightning and thunder, but this time the branch channeled the lightning to the water, where it lit up a long wave. A few fish bobbed to the surface, fried from within, but the swinging ship quickly passed them.

"Yahoo!" Leera shouted from below, a call echoed by Jez and the sailors who had witnessed the feat.

Augum, realizing his clothing had been spared this time, raised his fist in triumph. He kept the branch lit in this manner, absorbing and channeling blasts of lightning as they came—and they came often. His robe took a steady beating, but interestingly, with each blast, he felt an enormous surge of energy pass through him—and he wondered if he could somehow capture a *fraction* of that energy in his pool of stamina, which was steadily draining from holding up Major Shape Lightning.

The idea lit up his mind like one of the myriad flashes that blinked in the storm.

As the lightning continued to blast through him and strike the ocean, he tried applying arcaneological principles such as tongue-to-tendril ratios, fractaline geometries, diminishing returns, inversion techniques, tendril decomposition, geometric arcane lensing, and others—but all failed to replenish even the tiniest amount of stamina.

After hours of this destructive and wind-lashing and mast-swinging repetition, soaked and frozen to the bone, he was ready to give up on the ludicrous idea.

"But there's one principle you haven't tried," he said, the wind snatching his tired words like an angry thief. With his wet hair plastered to his face and his robe in streaming tatters, and with his bones weary and his stomach pleading for sustenance, Augum decided to draw one last bolt of lightning.

Although the storm had hardly abated, the bolts of lightning had petered out to the occasional distant flash, yet he still sensed those bolts tugging at him now and then as the boat crested certain high waves. He felt like the angry sky wanted to test him one last time, to knock him off the pedestal and win the crown of who was lord of these skies.

"It's going to be me, damn you," Augum hissed into the storm, shaking his fading branch of lightning about. Already its tip hardly touched the water, as its length had shortened due to him dredging the bottom of his stamina reservoir. "It's going to be me ..."

This time, he would apply the principle of arcane perpendicularity, a principle that governed the simul Mirror of the Dragon, which turned his shield into a spell-reflecting mirror. And he would pair it with the principle of arcane lensing, but would choose to use his branch as a focal offshoot, and the principle of arcane transmutation, which he had learned in his 10th degree final year at the academy. He structured the core of his mind to think in *perpendicular*, meaning a portion of the lightning would bounce off that perpendicularity—the mirror effect— and, ideally through the application of the arcane transmutation principle, land in his reservoir. The mental aim of it was the challenge.

The ship crested another mammoth wave, and with the winds wailing in agony, flapping his robe strips this way and that like miniature tattered flags, he once more felt the crackling dryness and the hair rise on his head. As before, the lightning struck suddenly and powerfully with a mighty *crack!* of thunder and lightning. Augum applied the arcaneological thought structure, allowing for the vast majority of that raw power to surge through his soul, out of his long lightning-branch arm, and harmlessly smash into the ocean. Yet, guided by the prepared principles, a small portion of that lightning bounced off his mirrored mind and zipped down an arcaneologically constructed cavity, landing in his pool of stamina. That pool sloshed upward an astounding *halfway*.

"Oh. My. Gods," Augum said into the wind, face splitting with an enormous grin. "Unnameables did you see that!" he shouted skyward. "Gods, did you see that! Mrs. Stone! Atrius! Ancestors of old! Did you witness that miracle!" He whipped his arm about, using the branch of lightning like a gigantic lasso as he shouted, "Yahooooooooooooooo! Yeaaaaaaaaaaah! Yeah, yeah, yeah!"

He'd performed something he'd only seen in an ancient artifact called a moon orb—and that power, which completely replenished one's stamina, was tuned to the moon, meaning it could only be used once a moon cycle. But this? This he could use when struck by lightning. Sure, that was a rare event in itself, yet who knew when it could be useful? He further suspected it was only possible because of the ancestral echo—the immunity to lightning itself, an exquisitely rare gift.

As if the gods were acknowledging his victory, perhaps a feat some might consider a feat of legend, the rain halted, replaced by the steady shriek of the wind. "Yahooooooo!" he shouted again, whipping that lightning around and jostling in his seat and shaking the mast with glee. "Yahoooo …!"

Sensing the lightning storm was over, he let the branch die, leaned his head back, closed his eyes, and allowed himself to experience the chaotic sway of the ship as it rose and fell over monstrous rolling waves. While *Saltfang* continued to sail into unknown seas, Augum savored a small but potent victory.

A NEW LIFE

BRIDGET

It was quite something for Bridget to witness the ground falling away from her. Usually she experienced such a stomach-plunging sight in dragon form. Far below, evening shadows had already descended upon the gargoyle kingdom, which blinked with tar-like fires she could still smell at that height. Yet sunset remained waiting in the sky above, painting puffy clouds with a fiery glow, taunting Bridget with a childlike hope she remembered from a youth now long extinguished.

After Captain Gravak had won her at a gargoyle auction, he had picked Bridget up and was now flying her to what she presumed was her new home. Whilst gripping a sack that contained his giant bejeweled skull trophy, his powerful wings beating at the air, the long claws of a single foot clutched her torso like a hawk clutching a fish, with she in turn clutching Sebastian tight in her arms. Having never been higher than the top of a hillside, the boy whimpered and cried and kept his eyes shut, for that had been her instruction—don't look, my child, lest you get the fear in you. He was terrified anyway.

Even though Bridget wore the suppressive collar, rising in such a manner—akin to flight—prompted the queen of the skies to stir within her soul, and she imagined herself gliding in above the captain, snatching him in her claws, and tearing off his head with one blood-spurting bite. In that fantasy, Sebastian would be on her back like a horseman riding his mount.

Meanwhile, Grak, whom the captain clutched in his other clawed foot, bobbed about to the rhythm of the climb like someone long used to such a thing. He gazed at the heavens with his lone good eye in a rather wistful manner, as if remembering what it had been like to fly before they tore his wings off.

Bridget wanted to ask him what he had done to deserve such a fate—to deserve losing an eye, to deserve the countless scars that had been inflicted upon him—but she did not want to insult him, as Grak was her only gargoyle ally, and her best chance of keeping the boy safe. She would continue to foster his friendship and learn from him, and when the right time came, she would press him for what she needed to know—how to gain her freedom, then how to find a way home. Who knew, maybe he'd come with her and teach humans about gargoyle kind, for there was one thing Grak possessed that the other gargoyles seemingly did not—empathy.

Sensing her watching him, he glanced over with his big, sad eye, as if intimating that they were both mere slaves, prisoners to happenstance. But she disagreed. And although he had witnessed her daring and initiative, she wondered if he could sense her hidden might. Yet he had shown no interest in her as anything beyond a slave. She felt more like a pet to him, one he pitied. Maybe one day she would tell him her real name, even if it would mean little to him.

At last they flew into the orange sunlight layer, where the piercing sun made Bridget look away, turning her attention to the vast expanse of towering pole homes. They stood like giant flower stalks amidst rolling grassland, winged demons flitting between like hummingbirds. Strange creations in a strange land.

The captain flew closer and closer to one of these sky stalks, until she could make out the texture. The poles were three times as thick as a grain silo and made from enormous stone blocks cut and stacked into place much like a spine. Intermittently, branch-like perches as thick as a log protruded from holes. Sometimes these holes were flanked by many little ones—perhaps windows, albeit without glass.

They passed a winged gargoyle settled on one of these perches, a droopy beast with sagging ears drinking from an enormous curved horn cup. The hole behind him was warmly lit with fire that outlined the shadowy silhouettes of other gargoyles, albeit smaller ones. Bridget heard the sound of a high-pitched growling snicker. It was the first hint of offspring—gargoyle children.

Onward they ascended, ever higher into the brilliant and warm light. As they rose, so too did the wind, drying out the sweat from Bridget's robe and skin and hair.

"What's happening? I'm not looking still. I don't want to look."

"We're going to our new home, Sebby," Bridget replied into his ear, squeezing his torso. *Sebby* sounded like what she'd call him if he were her son. So that would be his new nickname to her. So close to Sabby, too, which was a bittersweet reminder. *But he is not your pet*, she reminded herself. *He is a scared slave boy, and you are all he has left of the old world.*

"Just as he is all that is left of the old world for me," she murmured, allowing the wind to steal her words lest the boy hear them.

"Should I open my eyes? What will I see? I'm awful scared."

"You don't have to open your eyes. I can describe it if you like, though."

"Okay. Okay ..."

"We're flying high above a strange land. There's a city in the distance. A strange city. All around us, like cattails dotting hills of grass, slender stone towers poke high into the sky, so tall they reach into the heavens. On top of them sit mysterious platforms in the shape of earthly plateaus, but we haven't gotten high enough to see what's on them yet. And far in the horizon, which you feel on your face, is a beautiful orange sun lighting up an orange sky."

Sebastian gasped at her description. "I'm going to look, then! I'm going to look!"

"Only if you feel yourself brave enough, but don't feel like you need to."

"I'm going to look now. Here I go!" Clasping him tightly in her arms, she felt him take a girding breath, and then he yelped and began struggling.

"Shh, it's all right. I've got you. Don't worry. I've got you in my arms and I won't let go. Just relax and see if you can enjoy the view."

"My stomach wants to jump out of my mouth."

"I know, I know, that's normal. Just relax and take it all in, and feel free to close your eyes again."

"I'm dizzy. I'm so dizzy ..."

"That's normal too. Just breathe."

There was a pause as Sebastian took a series of deep breaths. "I see it. I see it all. It's ... it's *beautiful* ..."

"It is, isn't it?"

"It's the most beautiful thing I have ever seen. So this is what it's like to be a bird. I will dream of this forever."

"Forever ..." Bridget whispered as her robe flapped in a sudden gust, and she did not know why she was repeating the word. Perhaps because on some level she wished the moment would never end. Here she was bathed in sunlight, holding her adopted child, flying amidst a kingdom she felt at home in — meaning the sky, where she truly belonged.

"How do you know this feeling is normal?"

Bridget hesitated. The boy did not know what she could become and that she had already experienced the miracle of flight upon her own wings. "Because I read it," she blurted.

"In a book?"

"In many books. One can experience many incredible things in books."

"Then I want to read even more books."

She patted his chest with her fingertips. "You will. You will …" She ignored the part of her that doubted they'd ever see a human book again.

Thousands of feet above the ground, the captain kept rising between the poles, until they had ascended high enough to see what was atop the closest plateaus. Homes, of a type. Strange ruins and manors and castles that looked much older than everything else she'd seen from the gargoyles.

The captain headed toward one of these plateaus, a flat piece of irregularly shaped land sitting atop its pole like a pie balanced on a jester's stick. The bean-shaped plateau was the size of a small city park, with vibrant patches of grass amidst gnarled pink-leafed trees that reminded Bridget of oaks from home.

A path of flat stones wove its way by these trees, passing a fountain before culminating at a rocky outcrop. Atop that outcrop sat an imposing but plain manor made of smooth black stone. Up close it was a ruin, albeit one that had obviously been repaired. The archway entrance was open, revealing torchlight within, and the windows were tall and rectangular and fitted with colored glass.

The captain dumped her and Sebastian and Grak onto the grass, barked a command to Grak, and flew ahead toward the manor, leaving them to collect themselves.

Bridget helped Sebastian to his feet and took a deep breath of the kind of fresh air only such a height provided. She smelled the grass, the trees, the tiny yellow flowers. She caught the scent of earth and stone and wildflowers, along with strange scents she could not place. The high breeze rustled the pink leaves, and she heard the quiet but incessant croak of numerous frogs amidst the occasional gentle tweet of an evening bird, reassuring sounds that once again made her think of home.

"Are we in heaven?"

"No, Sebby. We are not in heaven."

"Are you sure?"

Instead of replying, Bridget drew Sebastian to her and kissed the top of his oily hair.

"Can ... can I ask a question?" Sebastian said. "You told the gargoyles I'm your son. Did ... did you mean that?"

"Of course I did, Sebby. Of course I did."

"Oh. Okay, then ... then can I call you my momma?"

Bridget felt her chest tighten. "I would like that very much."

"Okay, Momma."

They squeezed each other.

Grak walked forth, turning about. "*Hehi, Ah-bee-gale,*" he said, beckoning. "*Hehi.*"

"Yes, we're coming. We're coming," Bridget said, taking Sebastian by the hand and leading him on behind Grak, heart wanting to burst.

Together they walked the path of flagstones, set far apart for the gargoyle gait. Sebastian kept glancing about at the wonders before them. The oak-like trees were taller and thicker, the leaves scalloped and colored an unusually bright pink. The flowers poking above the grass were thin and tall and bright yellow. The grass itself felt coarser to the touch and was unusually vivid.

Amidst the trees, Bridget glimpsed a pond with swirling flies that caught the sunlight. From the corner of the pond, overseen by a particularly gnarled tree, rose a clump of blue weed-like marsh flowers.

On they walked, until the manor came into clear view, and Bridget gasped, for she recognized the core architecture from academy classes. "Rivican ..." she whispered, mouth agape as she held Sebastian's hand tighter. The realization of what she was looking at—an ancient Rivican ruin brought back to life through repairs and additions—raised countless questions. Where had the gargoyles found these ruins? Why did they treasure them? How had they brought them up this high? Did they use Teleportation or physical winged labor?

The captain had landed ahead and strode in through the doorway of the ancient manor house, and from within came the sounds of grunting and cooing and short whining growls that almost sounded like happy puppies.

The path up to the entrance of the manor was made of gravel and surrounded by a surprisingly well-manicured garden of large and colorful exotic flowers, not one of which Bridget recognized, but they smelled divine—and filled her nostrils so thoroughly that she abruptly sneezed. The sound elicited questioning growls from within.

"*Gehyoma,*" Grak whispered, holding up a hand and pointing at the ground, indicating for her to stay here a moment. She nodded, and he stepped up to the massive arched doorway, bowed deeply—and remained bowed. With a flick of the claw, he beckoned for her to approach.

Bridget once again placed Sebastian before her and slowly walked them up to the entrance. The moment she spied the captain standing amidst his brood, she pushed Sebastian forward into a bow and bowed beside him, making sure to keep a hand on his back lest he rise too quickly.

A series of interested—perhaps even delighted—growls sounded from the gargoyles, a bunch of whom came up to inspect their new prizes. Bridget was grabbed by the arm and yanked to stand upright. For the first time she saw a family of gargoyles up close—which included female gargoyles, who were more slender, their hips pear-shaped, their breasts small, their snouts shorter, and their faces starkly curvier—feminine as opposed to the typical angularity of the males.

There was the mother, perhaps a wife depending on whether gargoyles believed in such a custom, as well as four offspring—two males and two females. One of the males was older, likely a teenager, as was one of the females. The remaining pair was quite young—perhaps the equivalent of human ten-year-olds, even though they were both taller than Bridget. All wore colored but simple cloth to cover their modesty. Most interestingly, the two older siblings already had a few runes emblazoned on their torsos.

All four offspring poked and prodded at Bridget and a whimpering Sebastian, touching their hair and pinching their cheeks and ears and clothing. The youngest male almost stuck a claw in Bridget's eye accidentally, making her recoil. The motion made the younger male jump, causing the others to cackle and opine in quick growls, the first real sign of gargoyle humor. Now and then, Bridget caught words she had learned from Grak, the most oft-used being *gyot*—the word for slave.

The female gargoyles I shall call girgoyles, Bridget thought, putting up with the prodding by staring straight ahead, chin level, pose firm and unrelenting. She would not allow herself to be a pushover.

The towering captain loosed a series of explanatory growls, gesturing between Bridget and Sebastian. Everyone, including the wife, listened intently. As he growled on, Bridget stole a glance around the manor. The living room ceiling was over forty feet high, the walls smooth black stone and decorated with the heads of animals, while the windows were made of uneven glass and depicted mighty winged gargoyles locked in combat with various beasts—tigers and lions and lizards and minotaurs and serpents and strangely shaped elementals, among others.

There were no stairs, but rather an open second-floor mezzanine and hallway overlooking the sprawling living room. There were scant furnishings—ornately carved logs on stands for perching, towering cubby shelves brimming with parchment scrolls and tablets, a large round supper table, and imposingly sharp iron floor candelabras lit with candles. It was interesting that the idea of the candle existed overseas as well, just not the idea of books—at least thus far. Who knew what secrets the gargoyles kept.

One of these sweeps had her looking behind her. The entranceway had a pair of ancient dark wood doors that opened fully against the walls, and high above the entranceway were more heads—but these caused her stomach to drop, for they were the dried-out and slightly shriveled heads of fellow humans. There were around thirty in total, some dating back generations, judging by their darkened and dusty appearance. Perhaps it was something about the crest-shaped plaques or the way the poor wretches stared with heads bowed in subservience that told her these souls had been prior slaves of the family.

A cackling drew Bridget's attention, and she looked over to see the youngest male pointing at her with his stubby claw, laughing at her reaction to seeing her future. After his older sister questioned him, he explained, and then the others all started trilling with laughter as well, with the youngest girgoyle flicking a claw at Sebastian, trying to convince him to look up. Bridget held his head down, however, until the youngest male slapped her hand away, grabbed Sebastian's jaw with both his clawed hands, and forced him to look up.

"It's all right," Bridget whispered reassuringly to the boy. But upon laying eyes on the heads, he too seemed to grasp the future that awaited them, for his face curdled with a cry that quickly turned into a full-blown wail, causing the youngest male to shove the boy's jaw away with a malicious flick. Seeing that the wail irritated the gargoyles, Bridget gently buried his face in her chest, whispering, "Shh, Sebby, shh, shh …" He wrapped his arms around her and squeezed her so tightly she felt the blood rise to her head, yet she continued to stroke his greasy hair whilst humming, "Shh, Sebby, shh. It's all right. Shh …"

The only one not laughing at this display was Grak, who looked on with that somber eye, the lone fool to suffer the blight of empathy—until the captain barked a word at him, snagging his attention. The towering seventeen-footer proceeded to snap off a series of commands, with Grak stiffly nodding along to each one. As he did so, the younger son, who possessed unusually large ears, drifted close to Sebastian and flicked his tiny ear, causing the boy to yelp and once more bury his head in Bridget's chest.

Cackling to himself, the gargoyle reached out to do it again. This time, Bridget was ready. She had learned on the ship to stand up for herself and those around her by hitting the bully quick and hard. Hoping that concept worked against gargoyles, who only seemed to respect strength, she snatched the gargoyle kid's claw and whipped it back into his face with a *smack*.

This act made the youngest girgoyle roar with laughter, cutting the captain off. The gargoyle boy's snout lips curled with rage, and he shot a claw out at Sebastian—not at Bridget, interestingly. Bridget's war-trained reflexes reacted swiftly. She pointed, telekinetically caught the claw, and bent its arc so that the boy swiped at his own chest. He'd done it so viciously too that he drew blood on himself, and promptly yelped and sprang back, pressing a hand to the tiny wound as he gaped disbelievingly at Bridget.

"*Shyneo,*" Bridget hissed, lighting up her hand with glowing ivy. She raised that hand and angled it up and down like a cobra ready to strike the boy, twisting her face into a pitiless warlike expression, consciously drawing upon The Callousness of the Predator.

"I see you," she hissed at him, extending the *s* in *see* to sound like a python, all while making the vines on her hand wave about like miniature snakes. It took tremendous concentration to keep the spell active and prevent it from blinking out, which it was inclined to do on account of the collar. But she persevered. It was imperative that they never feel entirely safe with her, even with the collar in place.

Except for the captain and Grak, the rest of the family took a step back. The wife immediately began questioning the husband and the children discussed Bridget amongst themselves, until the captain cut them off with a quick slice of a claw and went on to explain in punchy growls. Picking up on certain words and the quick gestures with his claws, Bridget suspected he was talking about her arena victory—and that she was a prize he had won, a prize that was to be respected—or so she hoped.

As they discussed their newest acquisitions, the light in the room went burnt orange from the sun kissing the horizon. Bridget turned her head to look at it through a window, a part of her soul marveling at the sheer distance she had traveled. How many other humans had come this far over the eons? What were the other slaves like, the ones who had lived here all their lives? Would they speak common too?

"*Gyot!*" the youngest girgoyle snapped. "*Hohol, gyot!*"

Bridget looked back to find the girgoyle waving a dismissive claw at her. Grak flicked his head sideways, silently beckoning her to follow him. Bridget lowered her head in obedience and, with Sebastian clutched before her, followed Grak toward a doorway. Before she left the room, she glanced over her shoulder to see the captain reveal to his family the trophy awarded to him, and his family burbled growling coos and awes which continued as the captain raised the giant bejeweled skull to a position near the shrunken human head trophies.

"*Hehi, Ah-bee-gale,*" Grak said patiently. "*Hehi.*"

Bridget nodded and stepped through the doorway, which opened into a kitchen with a twenty-foot-high ceiling. But instead of drawers and cabinets and shelving, there were raw wood cubby holes, like for scrolls. Except these were filled with kitchen implements and food stores, mostly dried meats, with the occasional bundle of vegetables—yams and potatoes and pumpkin and squash and carrots, or cousins thereof, for each was slightly too large and oddly shaped. In the center stood a heavily worn harvest table. At the far end was an open cleaning area with enormous iron-strapped wooden tubs and copper taps, with a crude door leading outside. Visible through a glass window that hung beside a ratty door stood a rickety wooden ladder, and beyond, a drying line swung in the wind. Yet the room was empty of slaves, making her wonder where they were.

"Boy clean." Grak pointed to a twig broom standing in a corner beside a crude wooden bucket and a pile of old rags, then indicated the floor and then the living room. "Boy clean here, boy clean there." The dirty floor was composed of the same black stone as the living area and walls—basalt, most likely, which Bridget believed Rivican structures were historically made of.

"Ah-bee-gale chef," Grak went on. "*Karr Gravak* want Ah-bee-gale cook here. *Nadeha?*" Grak pressed, using a gargoyle word Bridget recognized from their prior interactions.

She nodded. "Yes, *nadeha*—we understand." So the captain had chosen her partly because she had been head chef for the slaves, which made sense.

"I'll be a good cleaner," Sebastian squeaked. "I'll do a very, *very* good job, sir, I promise."

"I'm sure you will," Bridget whispered, patting the top of Sebastian's head reassuringly.

Grak looked at the boy with pity, forced a pained smile upon his scarred snout, and walked on through a smaller doorway and down a short hallway, waving at them to follow. On the left was a small dark room with a central privy hole sized for a human and no door for privacy. Bridget put one bare foot into the room before hopping out, for it stank most foul and the floor was sticky. She hoped a good wash could remedy both problems.

To the right of that room was another, empty but for one thing—a tall metal obelisk that was dark, with multiple cords hanging on the walls.

Bridget gaped at it, imagining a gargoyle shoving her in and sticking a cord into her collar and siphoning the stamina the collar had collected.

"Hehi, Ah-bee-gale. Hehi."

"Yes, sorry," Bridget mumbled, and continued ambling along. On the other side in the hallway was a cool and dark storeroom of cubbies filled with stores.

Grak moved on to a musty and rectangular room with the same ceiling height as the kitchen. Embedded into the far wall was a blackstone hearth so massive that one could walk into it, yet it lacked logs. At the near end stood a plain bed made from thick planks of wood, one that appeared to be missing a mattress, and was instead piled with linens and blankets, all of which were frayed and soiled and coarse to the touch. A single crudely hewn trunk sat at the foot of the bed, engraved with what looked like graffiti at first glance. Cut neatly out of the far wall were three thin but towering windows, the glass within the wooden casements filmed with dirt, the cream-colored curtains unkempt and torn.

Seeing the filth of the room made Bridget realize there probably hadn't been slaves here in some time. She couldn't help but think of those shriveled heads above the entrance. Had any been her most recent predecessors?

There was also a shelf of small human-sized scrolls, which drew Bridget's interest, and she silently walked over and drew out a scroll. The yellowed parchment crackled upon opening, with dust streaming from the interior like sand. The writing was woefully crude and looked like common, but it was indecipherable, as if a drunk had written it or perhaps a child. Interestingly, the words were all short, as if they held only one syllable. She let it furl with a crackling *shloop*, returned it, and drew another one. It too had similar writing.

"Are they all like that?" she asked.

Grak did not reply but stared at her with a gaze that told her he saw history repeating itself. Perhaps the prior wretches he had gotten to know had asked the same question. Perhaps, like Bridget, he too had learned the lesson of not getting too close to those like herself lest he develop too much compassion.

"These are Rivican ruins, aren't they?" Bridget pressed, curious if she could rouse his interest. "Were they once buried, dug up, then brought up here? And these scrolls ..." She held up the one she had been examining, feeling the gentle tickle of dust cascade down her hand. "The other slaves were literate, but I don't recognize the language. Yet the scrolls are old and barely used, so only a precious few could read and write, isn't that so?"

Grak's reply was to walk to the enormous hearth. He tapped the wall with a claw, making a *tick, tick, tick* sound. "Come, Ah-bee-gale. I teach."

Bridget put the scroll back and shuffled over with Sebastian, noting that Grak was tapping a rune on the wall, one she did not recognize. It reminded her of the cartouches she had seen in history books used by ancient races such as the Rivicans—or so it was theorized.

Grak then tapped his temple. "Ah-bee-gale see here fire." He pressed his palm against the rune, loudly enunciating, "*Fra ga la.*" The hearth burst with flames, startling Sebastian so much that he jumped away. Grak kept his palm there. "*Fra ga na,*" and the hearth snuffed with a whoosh. "*Nadeha?*"

"*Nadeha,*" Bridget replied, finding it interesting that the concept of runes on objects had found its way over the ocean. *But what if it's the reverse?* she thought. *What if we took the idea of the rune from them?* She couldn't fathom such a profound idea, which would turn ancient history on its head, and settled on the premise that the gargoyles had likely learned it from the Rivicans eons ago.

Grak nodded at her to try.

Bridget stepped up to the rune, imagined the hearth roaring to life, pressed a palm against the cool stone, and said, "*Fra ga la.*" Fire burst within the hearth.

Grak opened his hands and his eyes widened, as if he did not quite believe she had done it on the first try, which told Bridget about his experiences with former slaves. "*Fra ga na,*" she said, and the flames snuffed.

Grak pointed at Sebastian. "Boy try."

"I don't know magic," Sebastian squeaked.

"Arcanery, Sebby," Bridget corrected, unable to help herself. "We call it arcanery."

"Arcanery."

"And go on and try it. *Fra ga la* to ignite, *fra ga na* to snuff."

The boy hesitated, swallowed, but stepped up to the hearth and placed a grubby hand against the rune. "*Frageela,*" he blurted. Nothing of course happened. Bridget prompted him with the correct phrase, but even after trying various pronunciations he made no progress.

"I will teach him," Bridget told Grak. "I will try."

"Ah-bee-gale teach, *yoss*."

"What were the others like?" she asked, nodding at the bed, wanting to distract Grak from any ideas that Sebastian might be a worthless slave. "The other *gyots*?"

Grak looked to one of the windows, the walls of which were thick and angled inward as if they'd served as archer slots in some long-forgotten age, well before the glass casements had been added. His eye then went to the graffiti-covered trunk, no doubt seeing into the past.

Bridget walked to the trunk and kneeled before it. The graffiti was not so much graffiti as it was two short words, sometimes three, written in that same garbled tongue, but each written by a different hand, with few words repeating.

"They're names," she blurted, looking over her shoulder. "Aren't they?"

Grak inclined his head once before moving to the doorway. There he turned. "*Hehi*, Grak teach water." She followed with Sebastian, and Grak taught her how to turn on the taps over the tubs, where more food stores and cleaning supplies were located, how the privy worked, and other such things.

Later that evening, she stepped into the bedroom with Sebastian, having been left alone for their first evening as slaves beholden to a master and his family. Bridget tested the bed, but the rough linens and woolen blankets were so filthy and frayed that she resolved to do something about them right away.

"Help me wash these, Sebby, and then I will arcanely repair them."

"But what will we sleep in? It's getting cold."

"We'll dry them by the hearth."

"Yes, Momma."

Bridget's heart swelled upon hearing him call her that. Upon seeing him staring at the bed with fear, she abruptly drew him to her once again, stroking his hair and whispering, "Don't worry. We're safe now, Sebby. Everything's all right."

"I'm scared. I'm scared of tomorrow. I'm scared I'll die here ..."

"Shh, it's all right. That's not going to happen. I'm going to protect you."

Sebastian looked past her, and she knew what he was imagining.

"You're not going to end up on that wall," she whispered. "You keep your mind off such things, you hear? Look at me."

"Okay."

"You just worry about staying clean and behaving yourself and doing as you are told. What's the word for *understand* in gargoyle? Do you remember?"

"*Na … nadeha.*"

"Good boy. Tomorrow we will clean and organize and start our new lives."

"Okay."

Bridget kept a gentle hold of him, but although she had said that, she knew her quest was different. She would watch and learn and search for ways to get home. There had to be a way back. There had to be …

They took all the bedding to the washing station, where Bridget dragged up a footstool for Sebastian to stand on and stir. Having filled the wooden tub with hot water, also triggered by a rune Grak had taught her how to pronounce, she had Sebastian pour in powdered soap that smelled sweetly of lemon. She went back to the bedroom and flipped open the trunk.

Inside was clothing, including cream-colored linen nightgowns and rough-cotton servant gowns in as plain a style as she had ever seen, almost as if they had been made for farming servants. These too were soiled and musty, and so she piled them on her arms and was about to walk off when she spied something at the bottom of the trunk. Arms full, she stuck out a finger and, straining to punch through the suppressive collar, used Telekinesis to lift the object.

A carved wooden bull rose before her vision, but this bull stood on hind legs, its horns and muscles large and surprisingly well carved. "A minotaur," she whispered. Did the other slaves share a common mythology? Or did such beasts exist on this continent?

The toy had seen a lot of play, for it was heavily scratched and dented. She put it down on the bed for Sebastian and went to drop off the gowns into the tubs, where Sebastian was already stirring. After giving him a supportive pat on the shoulder, she returned to the bedroom and proceeded to repair the curtains arcanely. It was a tedious task as she had to constantly fight through the collar, but she got most of the lower strips done. The higher ones closer to the ceiling would require a ladder, which she remembered seeing outside.

"*Gyot,*" hissed a voice, and Bridget, who had just finished a repair that sealed up with white light, whirled toward the voice. The youngest gargoyle, who stood over six feet in height, body already sculpted with powerful muscles and wings folded neatly behind his back, walked in from the doorway to inspect what she was doing.

A tense Bridget did not back away, refusing to show fear.

The gargoyle grabbed the curtain with his claws, head tilting this way and that as he examined her work. He snorted and let go, directing his attention to her. Suddenly he bared his teeth and raised his claws and his wings burst open and trembled like a rattlesnake tail as he hissed at her.

Bridget sprang back with a yelp, fearing he was about to attack—or even eat—her. Hands in attack position, she was ready for a fight.

But the gargoyle cackled a fiendish laugh, shoulders bouncing as his wings folded. That laugh halted as he looked her up and down, snout twisting with revulsion. "*Sudu, gyot. Sudu.*"

Bridget wanted to hiss at him that she was *not* stupid. That she was learning their language little by little, and even if it took years, she would eventually understand their tongue—and use it against them. Yet she remained silent, for she did not want to reveal her plans to this insipid brat. In fact, that would be his name to her—The Brat.

"*Kupa,*" he spat, hawking a gob of gargoyle spit on her bare foot.

"I don't know what that means," she said, lying. She knew what it meant—had heard the other gargoyles use it and had at one point asked Grak about the word. It was an evil word, one that meant the lowest of the low—the gargoyle version of the vile human word *gutterborn*. But she did not want this young fool to know that she knew its meaning.

His snout curled with a malignant smile and he walked off, tail idly slapping the ground behind him. Bridget raised her foot and wiped off the spit with her sleeve, knowing she would wash her filthy robe tonight anyway. She padded after him, wanting him to know that she was not like prior slaves, wanting to stalk him. Sensing her, he turned in the doorway to the kitchen, and she let him see half of her, the other half hidden behind the wall to her bedroom, her face in darkness, her visible fist balled and ready.

See me watching you, gargoyle, she thought, drawing upon the predator always hiding within her. *Know that I too can stalk. That I too can kill.* Her mind returned to the ship. She saw The Brute fall, slam into a timber support, and spin in a blur until he slammed into an overseer platform with such velocity that he punched through the poop floor, never to be seen again. *Such a fate could await you if you press me,* Bridget silently intimated with slitted eyes.

This display seemed to unnerve the gargoyle, for he walked off rather quickly, a most satisfying sight to The Callousness of the Predator that had poked its nose through the curtain of her mind.

That might have been foolish, she chastised herself. Yet it was imperative that the beasts give her the maximum respect possible under the circumstances; otherwise, she would find herself abused who knew how. Above all, that respect would protect Sebastian, for if she showed them she was a vicious mother hen, they might think twice before doing something evil to him.

After checking on and reassuring Sebastian, who told her he'd been terrified by the gargoyle's entrance, she returned to the room, where she thought to try a spell she'd been thinking about since arriving — Unconceal. She thus splayed her hand and, after focusing on things hidden on purpose, incanted, "*Un vun deo.*"

She felt some tugs, which led outside of the room — but one led to the bed. She dropped to her knees, reached underneath, and probed about the crude support planks until her hand closed on a spindle of cold metal. Checking that no one was spying on her from the doorway, she quietly unwedged it from under a plank and withdrew the object, which turned out to be an enormous and strange-looking bronze spindle with a hoop at the end. The spindle portion was molded with indentations and lines, and the hoop formed a miniature maze. There was a buildup of rust and verdigris on the bronze, as if it had been underwater.

It occurred to Bridget what it was. "A key ..." she whispered. The spindle's point was sharp enough to be used as a weapon.

Holding the key with her left hand, she splayed her right hand over it, whispering, "*Un vun asperio aurum enchantus.*" Something flickered, but her spell failed as she hadn't concentrated hard enough to push through the collar's suppression, forcing her to recast the spell. A tight tendril web revealed itself and blinked out shortly thereafter.

Too exhausted and hungry to concentrate, she put the key back and went to fetch the broom. After thoroughly sweeping the bedroom of all the dust and dirt, she turned on the hearth, washed the floor, and used a crude crank mechanism to open the windows and air out the place. The heat of the hearth would dry things quickly.

For food, she cut up a squash and boiled some potatoes in a crude pot above the kitchen hearth, spicing them with salt and pepper retrieved from the storeroom. They ate together in the bedroom, with the blankets and clothing hanging before the roaring hearth on poles and sticks Bridget had cobbled together from items in the washing room.

"Do you think we'll ever get home?" Sebastian asked, staring into the flames while he held a large half-eaten chunk of roasted squash.

"I don't know, Sebby," Bridget replied, biting into her own squash and staring into the same flames. "I don't know."

"Will you tell me a story?"

"I would love to tell you a story. What sort would you like to hear?"

"I'd like to hear a story about the Academy of Arcane Arts."

Bridget smiled. "I can tell you plenty of stories about that enchanting place," and she told him about the time she first learned how to make her palm shine with light, and how she'd found it such a delight to be able to read a book well into the evening hours without the use of an expensive candle. She went on to blissfully tell him how much fun she had had at the academy making friends and all the trouble her best friend had gotten up to and their shenanigans with immature boys, but she left out the part about it all coming to a sudden halt when the Legion took over, forcing her and her family and friends to go on the run to start a new life in the forest.

But she did tell him about the time she and her friends had apprenticed under the greatest warlock to have ever lived, a hundred-and-one-year-old woman named Anna Atticus Stone, and how they had explored an abandoned castle and how Mrs. Stone had taught them the Unconceal spell and how she and her friends had used it to discover all sorts of hidden trinkets and secrets. She also told him how Mrs. Stone had taught her the Repair spell, and even demonstrated the lessons by repairing the freshly washed servant gowns and some of the linens and blankets, until the collar and exhaustion once again prevailed.

As she continued to regale him with samples of her adventures— without letting on who she was in case he recognized her, for she did not want the gargoyles to glean that information from him—Sebastian sat with wide eyes that sometimes closed as he imagined the scenarios. Bridget only concluded the storytelling when they finished their food, at which point Sebastian asked, "Do you think I can become a warlock?"

"I don't know."

"I'm too young, aren't I?"

"For now."

"Will you teach me?"

"I can certainly try. But we have a ways to go for that."

"Oh. Okay. Promise you'll tell me more stories about the academy, Momma."

Bridget swallowed the lump in her throat. "Of course I will, Sebby. Of course I will. Now let's wash up and go to bed."

They washed up and Bridget had Sebastian dress in a freshly washed servant gown, which was too small for him, then tucked him into bed with the cleaned linens, with extras folded underneath to make a mattress. He conked out right away. Next she took her turn, stripping herself naked and, feeling the late hour, slipped into one of the tubs in the dark kitchen, where she proceeded to wash herself with a pad of soap, savoring the warm water.

Having stolen what felt like a luxurious bath, she dried herself with an oversized cotton towel, left it wrapped around herself as she fetched a nightgown, and changed before the fire, taking comfort from hearing Sebastian's gentle snoozing and from the fire-warmed linen nightgown that barely slipped over her head and down her malnourished body, telling her that the slaves that had lived there had been on the small side. With a bitter and cold wind whistling in through the windows, she closed them to a finger's width and left the hearth roaring, for her robe had yet to dry. Then she curled up beside Sebastian, who already clutched the minotaur in a hand. She lay there in the dark and wondered what the new day would bring.

Yet as she fell asleep in her new home for the first time, her thoughts drifted to her beloved Olaf, and to her sister- and brother-in-war Leera and Augum, and to all her friends, and a poignant pain stabbed at her heart. A pain of longing ... and sorrow.

INTO THE STORMY VOID

LEERA

As black clouds swirled overhead, and as the rigging clanked and whistled in a vicious wind, Leera rather lamely slapped her wrists together.

"*Annihilo,*" she incanted, sending a jet of tempered water forth.

Jez, standing twenty feet away on *Saltfang's* steeply pitched deck, lazily stepped aside even as Leera slapped her wrists, and the harmless water jet splashed into a crate.

"So, what, are you two besties now?" Jez snapped before drawing Leera's outline with a finger and incanting, "*Paralizo carcusa cemente.*"

Leera, who hadn't bothered trying to duck the spell on the slanted deck, felt her limbs stiffening and whirled about in place, breaking through the invisible tendril grips trying to cement her in place. "Hardly!" she countered with a forced laugh. "I'm just trying not to be such a vindictive prat all the time." She hooked two fingers at the air and yanked them back. "*Voidus occa.*"

Jez made her own fancy twirl, ducking the Blind spell, and stuck her index fingers out and pointed them at each other as if plugging invisible ears, incanting, "*Voidus aurus.*" Then she raked at the air with a clawed hand, adding, "*Dreadus terrablus.*"

Leera bent over backward to avoid the Deafness and Fear castings, the maneuver forcing her to slap a hand against the ground, roll sideways, and jump to her feet. "Ugh, don't make me work so hard."

"So you're bosom buddies. Got it."

"Gods no, we're hardly friends! We're mere acquaintances stuck on the same ship."

"Who giggle like a pair of schoolchildren—*effectus xadius*—and share looks and barbs and jests—*flustrato*—and who have been spending so much time together that a certain unruly monkey has been neglecting her studies—*annihilo!*"

Leera, having danced her way around the first two castings of Slow and Confusion, found herself cornered against a stack of lashed barrels and was forced to summon her shield to prevent the jet of water from smacking her in the chest.

"Hey, easy now!" she replied. "And sharing *one* look during supper and laughing at *one* jest and spending a mere hour discussing the implications of the find hardly makes us bosom buddies!" She petted the air as she would Sir Pawsalot, incanting, "*Senna dormo coma torpos!*"

Jez scoffed as she sidestepped the Sleep spell. "You could have come to me. I could have solved it with you. Moving on to Drain. Open up. Let's go, missy. I don't have all day."

Leera sighed. She didn't want to say that Jez was too drunk—even mentioning the over-drinking always resulted in Jez putting up her guard, and then she got angry, which was not a fun combination during training. So her reply was to open her arms as directed and allow Jez to throw the hooking tendril, incanting, "*Arcan rosso!*" The invisible tendril line of the 11th degree Arcane Drain smacked into Leera's soul, and Jez worked to pull in the invisible rope hand over hand, quickly siphoning stamina from Leera's reservoir.

"Enough!" Leera called. "Can I hit back finally?"

Jez did three more hand-over-hand motions before flicking a hand in an annoyed *Bah!* manner. She took her place where she had started and flipped open that same hand. "Well?"

Leera gathered her thoughts, recalling her training. Then she made her own throwing motion and incanted, "*Arcan rosso.*" She felt the tendril line catch, but the moment Jez folded her arms across her chest, the suction ceased.

"Lazy bum, you weren't even trying," Jez hissed.

"I was *so!*" Leera lied. The truth was she was tired of training for the day.

"The incantation lacked intensity, the motions were weak and imprecise, and you mistimed the fluidity. I could have batted it aside with a limp wrist. Lazy. *Bum*. That's what you are."

"I'm not a bum, and I'm not lazy. And what do *you* care if I have some extra laughs with someone new?"

"I care because I care about *you*. You can't trust pasty-faced fiends who prancy about court sucking up to each other for a living. Now should I show you how to do it or are you going to give it a real attempt?"

A hoarse shout from above interrupted them. "Rogue waaaaaave! Rogue waaaave from starboaaaaard!"

Leera and Jez ran up the steep incline, grabbed hold of the railing, and beheld a monstrous wall of water advancing toward them amidst a choppy ocean.

"Everybody hold on!" Leera roared.

"Smooth it, smooth it, smooth it!" Jez shouted in reply.

Whereas the 2nd degree off-the-books spell Minor Shape Water only required one arm, the 9th degree version Major Shape Water required both—and a lot more stamina. Both women thus hooked their elbows under the railing to anchor their bodies to it, folded their arms forward, and made dual smoothing motions at the water whilst chorusing, "*Marjorus ipulato aqua!*"

Leera felt she had hold of the water and worked hard to tame its height. Together with her mentor, they managed to reduce the monstrous wave's size, at least in the vicinity that counted, to a mere hill, which the ship rolled over like a giant bob.

"That's the third one in just as many days," Leera muttered, unhooking from the railing and turning about to watch the giant rolling pin push onward, a central portion now indented, having been weakened by the women.

"That's why we trade off at night," Jez said, leaning back against the railing. "You need to stay sharp."

Leera had had enough. "I'm not the one who's drunk on my ass half the time or suffering hangovers or—" Her cheek exploded with a stinging *smack!* "Did you just *slap* me?" Leera asked, face turned away in shock.

"Don't you dare disrespect me. I'm your mentor. Your *mentor*."

Leera turned to glare at her with narrowed eyes. "Maybe you shouldn't be, then," she blurted without meaning it.

Jez's lower lip trembled. She reached out a hand as if to apologize, only to withdraw it. "I need a drink," she muttered and glided down the deck before quickly trundling inside.

"You just got slapped," Limpet sang, laughing alongside his goonish pirate friend.

Leera looked to the open cabin door and the two boys peeking out from within.

"She just got slapped," the friend, who was apparently named Dirt, crooned, and the pair continued the chant, "You just got slapped! You just got slapped!"

"How long have you two been standing there?" Leera asked.

"Not long," Limpet said whilst his friend kept singing the refrain. "Does it hurt?"

Leera reached out in preparation to telekinetically slam the door closed in their faces. In an instant, the boys' eyes widened in horror—a rather disproportionate reaction to what she was about to do. She hesitated, wanting to crack a jest at them for being so afraid, when she saw their eyes rise above her. Sensing something was off, she whirled about. A massive tentacle riddled with suction cups had reared up above her—and slammed downward. Battle instincts kicking in, she lashed out at the railing and yanked herself toward it.

The tentacle smashed into the deck, crumpling wood and sending splinters flying. The plate-sized suction points grabbed hold, the tentacle tightened against the hull, and the wind-tilted ship lurched violently to an even keel.

Leera barely heard the screams of alarm from the sailors in the rigging, nor did she much see the tentacle before her, for a slew of other tentacles rose from beyond the railing of the ship at all points of the hull. They too slapped onto the deck and suctioned themselves to the wood. Tales of horror from the deep ocean flashed before her mind, and she thought she was in a nightmare and should probably wake up now.

But reality sharpened when all the tentacles color-changed at once to match the woody grain of the ship—octopi had the natural power of Chameleon.

Except this was no ordinary octopus. It was a monster straight out of mythology—a kraken.

From below, as if a mountain were slowly moving, came a deep rumble that reverberated through every plank in the ship. The forward momentum of the creaking boat halted, and the ship began to sink.

"She's a gonna drag us to the bottom!" a teenage sailor cried out so shrilly that his voice cracked.

Knowing she had mere moments, Leera vaulted over the railing and splashed into the frothy water. A bolt of icy shock shot through her system. *You fool, you forgot to protect yourself!* Better late than never, she mentally hardened her mind and her innards whilst incanting, "*Endura o prassa ata o codola.*" Having completed the 3rd degree off-the-books Endure the Deep spell, which quelled the cold somewhat, she quickly transitioned to the 1st degree off-the-books Breathe Water by incanting, "*Bratta fil aqua!*"

The beast's body was so immense that all she saw was a wall of flesh. Its bulky movements, combined with the already choppy sea, churned the waters, making it difficult for Leera to keep her body steady.

Time to give this Final Flush business a go—and it better work or we're about to die, she thought, readying her mind for the onslaught. *Great, and I'm halfway bled too*, she mused blackly, referring to her stamina reservoir having been drained from training and then taming the rogue wave. Leera didn't want to admit she felt it was irresponsible of Jez to have drained—perhaps a little vindictively—so much of her stamina, when she could have instead drawn only a little bit to demonstrate her point.

The serpent slayer power of the nautical ring, which surged an offensive spell, was usually a one-off as it left the caster bereft of stamina. That meant she had to be precise. The problem was, she did not feel confident in the spell causing a fatal blow were she to cast it broadside against the wall of flesh before her. She thus swam downward, but became frustrated by her robe, which acted like an underwater sail that slowed her swimming to a crawl.

She thus zipped through the mental preparations for the basic 2nd degree off-the-books spell Fast Swim and incanted, "*Akseler aqua loa!*" Quickened, she kicked her feet and swam down around a monstrous sack that kept puffing and expelling water. The beast turned, and one of these massive vents opened, sucking water in—and Leera right along with it. It was far too powerful a jet stream for Leera's relatively wimpy spell of Fast Swim to combat. As the light snuffed and she was sucked into the interior of the beast, she had but a moment to decide on whether to teleport back to the deck of the ship—or fire the lone arrow in her quiver.

Realizing that teleporting would cost precious time the ship didn't have, it wasn't much of a choice. Leera therefore placed the ring to her lips and incanted, "*Arcanarma!*" which armed the power inherent to the ring. Whilst tumbling end over end amidst a whirlpool that would surely end with her in the kraken's stomach, she slapped her wrists together, roaring, "*Annihilo bato!*" She instantly knew the serpent slayer power had triggered, for she felt a monstrous flush of stamina suctioned from her reservoir as two massive jets of water blasted forth. She was so unprepared for how quick it was that she cut the drain off too late, leaving precious little stamina in her reservoir.

The two jets exploded into the belly of the beast, and light burst into the interior, exposing a cloud of countless fleshy bits. The rumbling ceased, and the beast went still. From above came a wooden groan.

Leera kicked out, swimming through the slippery detritus of flesh. She dove around and wiggled her way past giant tentacles that had let go of the ship. They slithered by, limp and harmless. As the beast fell away, she glimpsed an enormous beak—and two wagon-sized eyes, now sightless. To see this giant kraken of an octopus roll away into the gloom, with its slimy limbs flopping about, was one of the more unnerving sights of her life.

Leera's head popped above the water. Checking in on her nearly empty stamina, she knew her reservoir was a ways off in replenishing so she could cast Teleport. The ship, the deck of which had dunked below the waterline, popped up like a giant cork, spewing off water. With the railing too high to grab and the ship already catching the wind and moving forth, Leera tried to think of a way to get on board before she froze to death—and luckily spotted a stray rope slipping away in the water.

"Come here, you," she snapped, lashing out an arm and telekinetically snatching the end. After a sudden yank, her body began to carve a frothy wave as the telekinetic hold dragged her through the water. She hauled herself along that invisible tendril line, ripping through the dregs of her stamina pool, until she managed to flailingly grab hold of the rope with barely enough stamina remaining to keep her protective water spells active.

"Cutting it a little close here, Jones," Leera muttered, grimacing at the sloshing water that was threatening to tear her robe off, for the ship was rapidly regaining its former speed.

Here comes the hard part, she thought and, putting one hand over the other, laboriously pulled herself in until she was alongside the hull. But by then, the cold she hadn't initially warded against set in, her teeth began to chatter, and her hands went numb. Besides, her sodden robe was far too heavy for her to haul herself up the rope and over the railing.

"Ack," she said. "Can anyone lend a hand!" she shouted up at the railing, wincing under the barrage of splashing water. "Hello! Jones here with a nearly empty pool of stamina and trying not to drown! Hellloooooooo!"

Alanna's head popped over the railing, her face deathly pale, surely from the terror of the ordeal.

"Hey, no rush. I'm only freezing half to death down here. And I think something just brushed up against my leg. Mind hauling me up?"

"Right. Sorry. Of course." Alanna grabbed hold of the rope and strained, but the rope did not so much as rise a hand's width.

"Try Telekin—" but Alanna disappeared. "Or not," Leera muttered, seriously considering casting Teleport, even though that would delve into overdraw and possibly cause arcane sickness—a debilitating illness that could send her into a coma.

Others soon showed—Olaf and Jengo and Jez, all of whom worked together to telekinetically and physically haul the rope up, until a soggy Leera flopped onto the deck. She made a show of it by sticking out her tongue to the side, closing her eyes, and playing dead.

"Like a speared whale," Olaf quipped.

Leera felt her cheeks get slapped lightly.

"Hey, you all right, kiddo?" Jez asked. "I'm sorry about earlier I *completely* overreacted and I feel terrible for doing it and holy Unnameables are you a damned hero, Jones. You hear me, Jones? Jones!"

Just basking in my moment, Leera thought, and she smiled, which was the signal for her friends to haul her to her feet. "And *I'm* sorry for calling you out like that," she said. Then she abruptly threw her arms around Jez, whispering into her ear, "You know I love you, right? Even though I hate you, I love you."

Jez awkwardly patted her back. "I know, monkey. I know."

"Uh, excuse me," squeaked a voice. "Excuse me."

Leera let go and saw Dirt, the young pirate friend of Limpet, standing there, wringing his hands.

"What is it?" Jez snapped.

"My friend's gone."

"Well, where the heck did he go?"

The boy pointed at the swirling ocean and every head turned. Leera felt her chest tighten and her face drain, for she realized what the boy meant—Limpet had washed overboard.

"He's not going to survive a hundred heartbeats in that," Jez said, and she began the incantations that would ward off the cold and allow her to breathe underwater.

Leera, who had yet to dispel those spells and had been holding onto them out of habit, was already armored for the ocean. Without uttering a single word, she shot to the railing and once again vaulted over it, diving head-first into the water, not giving one thought as to how she would get back.

As she swam underwater, Limpet's terrified voice barged into her mind. "Hey ... it's me ..." he blubbered, teeth chattering in between crying sobs. "I'm in big trouble! I can see the ship ... and I'm waving ...

but they're floating away and they can't see me cause of the waves. I know I said some mean things … but please, *please* help me! I'm too cold to swim and … and I don't want to die …"

Leera swam back to the surface and, whilst looking around for a waving arm, pressed the ring to her lips. "Contact … gods, what the heck was the little turd's real name again?" *It was Jeremy something,* she thought. *Jeremy, Jeremy, Jeremy* … "Jeremy Jenkins!" she blurted, recalling the moment of introduction. "Contact Jeremy Jenkins — hold on, kiddo. I'll use the tracking power of the ring to find you, starting with guiding you to me. Cease contact." She rebuilt her thoughts around the concept of Object Track, careful to inverse its core rudiments, then incanted into the ring, "*Guidosio Jeremy Jenkins tei mei.*"

Now that the ring was set to guide him to her, she reconfigured her thoughts to the standard Object Track enchantment and incanted into the ring, "*Locata Jeremy Jenkins.*"

She felt a tug along the line the ship had sailed, but couldn't spot a hand waving amidst rolling waves as large as hills. Knowing she'd now be scraping the very bottom of her stamina reservoir, she nonetheless dipped her head below the water, pointed at her feet, and brought her hands together whilst incanting, "*Kwiko au o dolfa fusio fota talla!*" Thankfully her legs fused and her feet developed a large dolphin's fin.

Cutting it close again, Jones, she thought as she kicked out, zooming underwater along the invisible tug line.

"P-p-p-p-please … hurr … rrrryyyyy …" came Limpet's teeth-chattering voice.

Swimming as fast as I can, she thought, not wanting to bring the ring to her lips, needing her arms to navigate the waters efficiently. She zipped just feet underwater, using the back of rolling waves to gather momentum. At one point she even exploded out of a wave that had crested and splashed into an opposing wave. She kicked so furiously that her legs began to burn, and she breathed rapidly, clearing so much water through her gilled lungs that they felt like they were on fire.

There was another problem too — her stamina reservoir had drained completely just by maintaining the water spells, forcing her to dip into precarious overdraw, which also meant the spells could fail at any moment. Still she swam on, desperately conscious of every heartbeat that passed, fearing the worst.

At last she shot through another cresting wave and spotted mid-flight a body floating upside-down amidst the trough of a nearby wave. She crashed back into the ocean — and felt her legs unstick. The Speed of the Dolphin spell had failed. Suddenly kicking at the water felt useless, but she furiously swam on, arms splashing at the surface, robe dragging like a sea anchor. Her breath caught water—and she choked on it, meaning Breathe Water had also failed. Then the cold washed over her like ice.

And there goes Endure the Deep, she thought. *Now you're in serious trouble.* Her hands and feet and body went completely numb. Spitting and gasping, she battled the churning waters, until she finally managed to grab hold of Limpet and turn him over. The sight of his pale face, blue lips, and sightless eyes sent a chill through her soul. He was her responsibility. Hers and hers alone.

Between waves, she might as well have been in the middle of nowhere. It was only when she crested with a wave that she spotted the ship. By then it looked like it was leagues off—and about to vanish into a rain squall, which meant she had almost no hope of nailing a teleport.

With her reservoir depleted and well into overdraw, she knew she would have to perform something she'd never truly done—dip *much* further into overdraw, which risked sickness at the very least—and death at the worst. Already her soul could sense its distant cliff, a cool void that silently beckoned her to experience the eternity of the Great Beyond.

Yet what choice was there? Jez would never find her as Leera hadn't made Jez cast Object Track on a piece of her clothing, and the ship was about to vanish anyway.

"Gods, and Group Teleport's a 17th degree spell too," she muttered. Such a high-degree spell would consume a huge amount of stamina from someone of her relatively low 10th degree.

Clutching tightly onto Limpet, Leera girded her terrified soul as she waited for her wave to reach its apex. "Gods, this better work," she said. "If not, I'm sorry, Augum, and I love you."

As she rose with the swell, she thought of the ancient mariner poem Mr. Mollusk had recited, which almost sounded like a prayer, one she now said to the wind. " 'Guided by The Fates go I, alone, lashed by the waves of a mighty storm' …"

The tip of the last mast emerged. "Get ready now …" She imagined her feet firmly planted on deck between the two masts, and whispered, "I love you, Augum, I love you, I love you, I love you …" When the wave at last reached its apex and she took sight of the deck that was already vanishing into the squall, she shouted, "*Impetus peragro grapa lestato exa exaei!*"

She yanked on herself and Limpet and catapulted them through the ether. But unlike a normal teleport, this one overdrew her stamina reservoir so severely she felt like she'd violently shoved her soul into a bath of icy darkness. She overshot the cliff of overdraw and fell right into its void, headlong, limbs flailing.

With a *thwomp*, she smashed into a stack of crates, losing her grip on Limpet along the way, and cartwheeled onward, until she slid and rolled across the deck, finally slamming into and bending around the second mast.

She emitted a wheezing groan as an acute headache, brought on by overdraw, cleaved her brain open. Combined with the pain of the crash, it was all she could do not to scream.

As people rushed in on her, she flapped a hand at Limpet's nearby body, which had come to a halt at the foot of a stack of barrels. "Help *him*!" she croaked. "Help him, you fools ..." But what came out was, "*Yelp ih! Yelp ih, ye foos ...*" Utter gibberish.

As horrified faces looked at her, she felt blood spill out of her mouth and saw it pool on the pitched deck, where it rolled away like a tiny river. *Where do you think you're going?* she thought. *How dare you try to escape. Come back in here,* and she fumbled to scoop her blood back, but her arms weren't working quite right. Then weakness overcame her and she flopped back onto the deck—or someone had shoved her, she couldn't tell.

The face of an ebony-skinned young man hovered into view, a gangly fellow she knew she ought to recognize but couldn't. He examined her face with a serious expression.

"Multiple lacerations to the mouth, nosebleed, dilated pupils, pale skin, blood from the ears ..." He glanced about at serious-faced others, one of whom was a young man she cared deeply about, but her jumbled mind couldn't for its life remember his name. "Overdraw," the ebony-skinned man concluded. "We need to warm her up and get her below. The lacerations are easy, it's just the overdraw that's a concern."

"The kid," Leera said as they hauled her up, yet all that came out was a teeth-chattering moan. She struggled against their iron grips, but it was like fighting an army of walruses. And that was what they looked like, too—big and hairy and toothy and blubbery. She recoiled from the nightmarish sight, wondering what was happening.

"She's descending," a voice echoed, her vision retreating. "It was a serious overdraw—she blew right past the shakes into the delusion stage. We've got to work fast. Get the boy!"

"Yes, the boy, the boy," Leera blathered, forgetting his name but knowing he was important. Her words were now just a pitiful squeal, barely discernible even to her. *You sound like a baby walrus,* she thought amusedly, not that she knew what a baby walrus sounded like.

As they carried her body off, her mind descended into the whirlpool of overdraw. It swirled around the drain of consciousness, until it got sucked into a deep and dense and cold void, where her thoughts evaporated into mist.

* * *

Time. Time passed as slowly as a bead of sap along the bark of a maple tree. In time, a small prick of light penetrated the saturated void. The observing girl blearily focused in on it, curious about its meaning. She felt nothing, for there was nothing *to* feel—no body, no breath, barely a mind. Just a thought observing an anomaly.

In the drip of time, that thought bisected into two. There was light, yes, but perhaps there was something more than the light and darkness. Further bifurcations begat a series. Being a girl meant there was a boy. Being two meant there were more.

Over an eon the light steadily brightened into a beacon fire of hope. And as it did so, complications arose within the structure of thought. She was a girl with a name. Leera. Yes, that was her name. Leera Matilda Jones. She was twenty years—years, not eons!—old. Born the daughter of a saddler and an ale taster, she had gone on to attend the Academy of Arcane Arts as a water warlock. She had trained partly under the legendary Anna Atticus Stone, fallen in love with a boy named Augum, become an Arcaner and a dragon, helped win two wars, graduated. And now ...

"And now what?" she whispered into the void. She wanted to remember, but like a thought on the tip of the tongue, that final leap of memory remained just out of reach. "Now what ...?" she repeated, interested by the sound of her own voice amidst the great emptiness. She could look away from the light, but there was no physical body to look at—until there was. Her hands, bare outlines against the inky darkness. Her naked chest, her curving hips, her legs.

It was like when she floated in water, blissfully alone, undulating gently with the waves, feeling the sunshine on her face. She even felt that particular sense of depth beneath her just as she felt it swimming in the ocean. Whereas others became uncomfortable with that idea of infinite depth—were even terrified by it—she welcomed it, for to her, it was like looking at the infinite sky, but in oceanic reverse.

The ocean ...

"I remember the ocean," she said into the void, and the light got brighter still. "I remember a ship. I remember a voyage and a trial and my friends and my mentor and my beloved Augum and a boy named Limpet—" She gasped, for amidst the inky darkness she saw a body floating upside down within tumbling waves, the sky stormy, looming ...

She heard the wind and felt her body rise and tumble with crashing waves and she saw lightning strike the water and the sky flicker with anger. Then a deep shiver set in, and she realized she had neglected to protect herself from the ocean, which was most unlike her.

"Most unlike me," she whispered, trying to fathom the meaning behind it all. She heard a boy's teeth begin to chatter, a chatter her own teeth caught, and her body took on a vicious tremble as the cold deepened. Voices echoed from beyond the light.

"Violent tremor ... we're losing her ..."

"Come on, come on, come on ..." someone else said. "My love ... can you hear me?"

"I'm here, Aug. I'm here!" she shouted.

"She's moving," Jengo said. "Keep talking to her."

"I love you, Lee. Do you hear me? I love you *so* much. You fight like the warrior girl you are. You fight and come back to me. You hear me? You come back to me. Please. *Please* ..."

Leera tried swimming, but her arms were stiff as planks, and the storm was only strengthening, the waves rising to building-sized proportions. She rose along the cliff wall of one such wave, until she was vertical, and then she curled along its monstrous overhang and fell along with the spray, crashing into the water, her body tumbling in the maelstrom.

Down, down, down the water pushed her, and she tumbled along in its violence, too weak to swim.

But you must swim! her mind shrieked, panicked that the light had dimmed in the sinking depths to near pitch darkness. *Swim, woman, swim, damn you!* She heard other echoey voices cajole her on. She envisioned Jez rearing back and slapping her in the face before taking her by the lapel and giving her a good shake whilst roar-spitting into her face, "Swim, monkey, swim!"

Feebly her limbs moved in a vapid manner, halting her descent. Her breath was almost gone. She had been holding it, but it was expiring, and the walls of consciousness — life itself — were fading by the heartbeat.

Death. Death beckoned with its warm blanket, offering solace from the cold and dark. Offering that final peace only gifted to those who stepped into the Great Beyond.

It spurred her on, and she fought to stroke her numb arms forth and kick her numb legs up and down and hold that last breath in as she began to rise.

High above the waters she saw a vision—the blurry form of a young man, and he was smiling.

I'm coming, Aug. I'm coming …

Because she dared to want to live, because she held that breath for far longer than any mortal normally would have, because she had a beloved who waited for her, because she had a boy she needed to save, her head exploded above the waters, and she inhaled a lungful of cold air.

The winds died, the clouds evaporated, the waters calmed, and the light brightened to a morning dawn. The placid ocean lit up in a vivid aqua, a single line bisecting all of existence. Above was light, and below was light, and in between floated a naked Leera, alone but at peace.

"She's through the worst of it," Jengo's voice echoed. "Thank the merciful Unnameables, she's through the worst of it," he repeated. "Now she needs rest. As do you, Aug."

"No, I'm staying with her."

"I miss you, my love," Leera mouthed, far too exhausted to speak. She let her body float, closed her eyes, and basked in the light, absorbing its precious warmth.

Time. Time passed. Day slowly fell victim to the night, which thence succumbed to a new dawn, and still she floated, nurturing her soul with warmth, trying not to think, enjoying hearing the occasional echo of the voice of her beloved Augum. Nights and days revolved in that state, and still she floated, biding her time, waiting for the strength to swim toward the light.

DARK STONE

AUGUM

Augum held Leera's cold hands in his own. People drifted in and out of the room, yet he numbly kept holding them, squeezing tighter and tighter, urging her to wake. Their echoey voices kept asking him to let go, but all he could focus on were her blue lips, hoping they'd move.

Then her body sank away through the bed, and he could barely hold on. He felt a shadow over his soul and saw the dragon reap its vengeance upon great cities. He screamed the scream of loss ... and of the damned.

Augum awoke with a start, practically falling from his chair. Forehead beaded with sweat, his eyes raced to Leera's form, lit by the glow of dim oil lamps swinging on squeaky chains. Her lips were full and pink, and her chest subtly rose and fell.

He leaned forth, clasped her hands again, and expelled a massive sigh of relief upon feeling their warmth.

"Dreamed I lost you," he whispered, delivering a gentle kiss upon those lips.

But his beloved failed to rouse, sleeping in a healing slumber Jengo had put her under three days ago. She was one of two people in the small ward, which had six bunks. Whaling crews were so prone to accidents that the ship had its own infirmary, albeit a crude one.

Augum glanced over at Mahmoute. The old woman, also in a healing coma, was taking an unusually long time to rouse, likely on account of her advanced age.

The wooden beams creaked as the ship rocked in a gale. Waves routinely splashed the dark porthole windows. Even down here Augum could hear the distant shrill whistle of the wind. Sometimes a gust was so strong that *Saltfang* lurched and screamed in the language of clanks and creaks and groans, as if the seas were wounding it. Somehow, she persevered through it all and sailed onward into the black unknown.

Augum used the heel of a hand to rub first one eye then the other. He looked to a dark window and wondered if it was morning or night. With the perpetual storm, it was hard to tell. He'd hardly left Leera's bedside but to eat, hit the privy, and battle one lightning storm, during which he again practiced harnessing the power of lightning to renew his stamina. Yet his thoughts had been with her throughout, and in better dreams, the pair of them fogged up the windows of their cabin from all the naked frolicking.

He'd also spent more time studying the gargoyle pentastone, which he'd brought along for the journey in the hopes of utilizing its powers against the gargoyles. He'd whispered out his theories with a snoozing Leera, but had made no progress.

On Jez's insistence, he'd tried training, but his mind was too preoccupied with his betrothed. He had kept fumbling the spells, and so she had kicked him back down here, where he could watch over Leera like a hawk. Overdraw sickness, also known as arcane fever, had its perils. Many a tale was told of sick warlocks slipping away suddenly in their sleep. It was dangerous to overdraw, yet he knew she had had no choice, for Leera never would have plunged so deep into it unless things had been truly desperate.

"Must have been one heck of a battle to find the kid," Augum whispered to her sleeping form, caressing her hands. "I'm glad you made it back to me, my love. Don't think I'd have the strength to go on without you."

The ship loosed a long series of creaks as it rose over a particularly steep wave. Augum's keen battle instincts picked up a slightly different sound amidst that creaking, that of a squeaking plank in the hallway, and he turned his head in time to see a shadow flick away.

"Boy!" he called. "Come here, boy."

The reason for Leera's closeness to death wandered into the light of a lantern, head and eyes low, hands fidgeting with his pockets. He schlepped to Mahmoute's bed first, as if pretending she was the reason he was there.

"She's old," he said.

Augum watched him, curious about this red-haired boy and why Leera had taken charge of him. Something told him it had not been so much to learn a new power as to train in the vain hope that she would someday become a mother. He entertained her quest with as much gusto as he could muster, but his soul was skeptical of its potential success.

Perhaps it was a form of self-protection, for he did not want to once again extinguish the flame of hope that he might one day continue his ancient lineage with the love of his life.

"She's going to die soon," the boy added.

Augum wanted to tell him he was stupid and didn't have the faintest idea of what he was talking about. Instead he continued to watch him, which seemed to make the boy nervous, as he quickly moved on to peruse the room, pretending it was of interest to him before meandering his way to stand by Leera's cot, albeit on the opposite side from Augum. He looked her over quickly and threw a sidelong glance at Augum, as if wondering what he saw in her, before his hand drifted to her bedside, where he twirled the woolen blanket with an idle finger.

"So what's this stupid Arcaner business all about, anyway?" he asked.

Augum let the silence linger. "Limpet, isn't it? Why do you come down and watch us, Limpet?"

"I don't."

"And why do lies come so easily to you?"

The boy swallowed. "I don't lie."

Augum leaned back in his rickety chair, its bent wood squealing in protest. "Why wonder about something you can never become?"

"I can be anything I want to be."

"Is that so?"

"It is."

"You're arrogant for an apprentice."

"Because I'm the best in my degree."

"Is that so?"

"Stop playing teacher. You're not my father. And of course it is."

"And what have you done to prove it?"

"I'm smarter than everyone here."

"That's hardly what I asked, is it?"

The boy's lip curled, but he failed to reply.

Augum folded his arms across his chest, stretched out his legs under Leera's cot, and crossed his ankles. "The Arcaner order is everything opposite of how you conduct yourself. An Arcaner follows a strict code of honor. That means he does not lie. An Arcaner does not take advantage just because advantage is available for the taking. An Arcaner seeks knowledge that contributes to the arcane craft. An Arcaner roots out corruption. An Arcaner serves others. Stands up for the weak. For justice. For goodness. I could go on, but there's no point, seeing as you're incapable of following such a path."

"I could be a better Arcaner than all of you put together."

"You would die a quick death attempting the very first Arcaner trial."

"I would *not!*" the kid hissed, fists balling, nostrils flaring.

Augum snorted, the snort breaking into a genuine head-shaking snicker. He looked to a porthole, seeing the past in the sloshing waters. "There was this one kid a couple years back," he began, scratching his nose to vanquish an itch. "Not too much older than you. Handled his challenges with grace and maturity. Rose in the ranks, paid attention in class, understood the principles. Did everything right. Convinced everyone he was ready." Augum looked back at Limpet, who was listening intently. "The trial chewed him up. There was not even a shred of a robe left to place into the sacred blue fires. I still recall the faces of his parents after placing a blade before their feet, asking for their forgiveness …"

"I'm an orphan. I don't care about parents."

"Seems to me you don't care about much at all."

"I care about myself."

"Do you, though?"

"'Course I do, idiot."

Augum leaned forth to rest his arms on his knees and interlace his fingers, feeling his wise old great-grandmother and mentor, Mrs. Stone, step into his soul. "Is it caring for yourself when you water the weeds in your garden instead of the flowers?"

The boy's face curdled, and his eyes moved about as he tried to fathom Augum's meaning. "That's dumb. Stop talking in riddles."

"Is it caring for yourself when you make no effort to understand virtue?"

"Nobody cares about that stuff. You're all *pretending* to care. But you don't."

Augum leaned back, nodding to himself. "That is why you would fail an Arcaner trial—" He raised a finger. "—not that we would even consider training you in the first place."

"Why? 'Cause I'm too smart for you dumb lot?"

"Because you're unapologetically arrogant and unable to examine yourself, and that combination kills."

The boy's mouth opened, eyes flitting about as he searched for a venomous reply. "Yeah, well, *you* can't even turn into a dragon! So *you're* a liar!"

Augum gave a kind smile. "I think I understand why Leera took you on. Even one such as you deserves succor."

"What does that stupid word mean?"

"To give aid. To help."

"I don't need your help."

"You shouldn't have come on this voyage."

"I *chose* to come."

"This is not a game. You almost died out there. You're too young, too brash, too *arrogant*. And if you keep on like this, you're probably going to die a screaming death."

"You're dumb and I *hate* you!" the boy shouted before storming off.

Augum watched him go, wondering if the message would sink in. He hoped it would, for if the boy did not start looking out for interests outside himself, he would be lost in short order.

He leaned over Leera, taking one of her hands between his own. "You sure chose a spritely one," he whispered, patting her hand. "I just hope, if your quest to reverse the curse is successful, that one of our kids doesn't turn into *that*."

Another creak came from the hallway. Augum, ready to ask the boy what he was still doing there, turned his head to see Alanna appear in the doorway.

"My lord Augum," she said with a delicate curtsy.

Augum stood and inclined his head. "Lady Haught."

"How does she fare?" Alanna asked, gliding into the room, wearing her gold-fringed amber robe and a sparkling jeweled necklace, which she idly played with.

Augum looked to his sleeping beloved. "Recuperating still."

"I am sure she will wake soon."

"Yes ..." He felt her eyes appraise him.

"When have you eaten last, Commander?"

"Er ..." He pinched his forehead and rubbed it. "What time of day is it?"

"The seventh hour of the morn."

"That early, huh? Would have preferred seventh hour of the evening."

"Allow me to quote one of my favorite plays, *Fanny's Follies*, and say, 'That nary answers the query, doth it?' " she smilingly countered in a stage accent.

Augum grimaced as his addled brain struggled with the math. "Then I ate about sixteen hours ago, I think. Maybe longer. I don't know anymore. Don't exactly feel hungry either," he added despite his stomach pleading for him to entertain it with even a tiny morsel.

Alanna scoffed. "My lord is fooling no one, for I can hear your stomach complaining. How can you expect to care for your lady if you are bereft of sustenance? Please go eat something. I will watch over her. I insist."

"Er ..." Augum's stomach grumbled for him to go, but then he recalled all the things Alanna had done to Leera, and no matter how much change he saw in the woman, years of mistrust around strangers made him take a seat beside Leera. "I'm not that hungry yet," he mumbled.

"Sir. My lord. Commander. Truly?"

"Truly."

"Shall I make you swear on your shield that thou art not hungry?"

"You sound like a friend of mine, Laudine. She loves the stage and flays people with quotes so often they have battle scars."

"A first-rate courtly deflection." Alanna brushed her necklace against her lips and sighed. "Perhaps I have overcooked the theatrical stew, then. But I understand. I do. I have not earned your trust, and who knows what sorts of antics your enemies have gotten up to over the years. Forgive me for imposing, good sir." She bowed her head.

Augum turned his back on her to look upon his beloved's sleeping countenance, not wanting his face to reveal to Alanna that she was exactly right.

"At least allow me to have the galley fix you up a meal to break your long fast."

Augum turned his head to the side and gave the slightest nod.

"Very sensible, my lord." There was the swish of her robe as she curtsied. "Commander Stone."

"Lady Haught."

She left him be, and he felt a pang of guilt for distrusting her, but it was a tiny price to pay for the safety of the love of his life. Alanna had been a scheming noble of the court intent on breaking them up, and it was only after seeing them together in confined quarters that she realized the utter futility of that quest. She had thus not yet earned their trust, and a few good deeds were a far cry from what was required. He and Leera and Bridget had spent their teenage years embroiled in violence, with enemies at every turn. Alanna could hardly expect him to let down his guard after a few paltry shows of loyalty.

Except she dove into frigid waters to save Leera's life, he realized. The thought caused a creep of shame, for had she wanted Leera's expiration, she would have chosen to stay on the boat then and there.

Unless it was a performance, the skeptical side of Augum retorted. *And she did it knowing someone else would have dove in.*

He pressed both hands to his face, gave it a good rub, and sighed. "You are getting cynical, sir," he muttered through his hands.

He gave Leera's hands a squeeze and a double pat, stretched out his arms and legs, and rolled his shoulders and torso. Feeling like he had worked out some of the kinks that had accumulated from long bouts of sitting, he went to the door, quietly closed it, and placed his back against it. Checking that Mahmoute was still sleeping, he took the time to summon the vault and perform his routine check for a note from Bridget. Seeing no such note, his eyes settled on the edge of Isobel's sacred crest, which sat jammed in on the very top shelf. He looked forward to resuming the lessons with Leera in due course. Until then, it would have to sit in place and wait.

He swiped at the air, whispering, "*Vaultus null,*" banishing the vault back into the ether, and returned to Leera's bedside. As he had done many times whilst waiting for her to wake up, he reached out to an empty cot and lifted it telekinetically into the air, then held it there, keeping his Telekinesis muscle toned, until there came a knock at the door.

"Come in," Augum said, lowering the cot.

The door creaked open, revealing Alanna holding a wooden tray filled with steaming food. But she wasn't alone. Smiling faces beamed from behind her—Olaf and Jengo and Carter and, of course, Jezebel Terse. The bunch of them piled into the room like kids attending a birthday party.

"We heard you could use some company, Commander," Carter whispered, biting down on an island apple and taking a seat on an empty cot. "Don't mind, do you?" he asked, sweeping his already swept blond hair aside with the back of the hand that held the apple.

"That's right, monkey. Let us take a turn watching over your fiendish girl for a change," Jez threw in, shoving Augum, forcing him to stand to view the tray. Before him sat a plate holding a large bread bowl filled with roasted chicken and potatoes, both of which were slathered with gravy and sprinkled with cut chives, salt, and pepper. Beside it was a cup of steaming coffee, an entire pot of freshly brewed coffee, a tankard of water, and a bevy of empty cups to share.

"My lord," Alanna said, smilingly extending the tray to him.

"Thank you, this looks utterly divine," a salivating Augum said, accepting the tray and taking it to an empty cot, from whence he poured the coffee into a cup.

"I told them you had missed supper, so they made you one to make up for it."

Augum offered her a cup of coffee whilst inclining his head in thanks. Alanna accepted it with a nodding *You're welcome*. He then proceeded to fill the remaining cups, passing them out to Olaf, Jengo, Carter, and Jez, all of whom thanked him by using his title, with Jez only grunting her thanks and muttering something about how the one thing that was missing was a dollop of Canterran brandy in hers.

"Nice to see *you* up so early," Augum said and immediately regretted it.

"What's *that* supposed to mean?" Jez snapped.

"Nothing. Was just thinking it's nice to see you suffer the indignities of dawn with the rest of us goons."

"Dawn? What dawn? Have you actually *looked* at the portholes, or have you been drooling over that rapscallion of yours the entire time? It's storm-dark out there." She glanced about at the others. "Is there a better word for that sort of darkness? Anyone? Look at you lot gaping like fools. Y'all need more of that there edu-ma-cation," she said in a country twang.

"She has followed up with slowly training me in Reveal and even delved into a bit of nuance with Teleport," Olaf threw in, taking a slurping sip of his coffee and wincing from its heat. "Seeing as it's a bit dangerous out there—" He nodded at the window, the glass of which received the slosh of a wave. "—we're mostly covering the basics to conserve arcane stamina and avoid any, uh, accidents."

"I got up fresh as a drunken daisy," Jez sang and plopped down by Leera to take her hand. While her face softened upon looking at Leera's snoozing face, Jengo checked on Mahmoute. Olaf, meanwhile, joined Carter on the cot opposite Augum, with Olaf throwing Carter some friendly elbow jabs.

"How's the greenhorn been acting, Three Toes?" Olaf jested, jostling a smiling Carter, who pretended to fend off his blows, the pair of them protecting their coffees. "Huh? He behaving?"

Augum stabbed a chunk of chicken from the bread bowl now sitting on his lap, warming his thighs through the plate. "He is living up to his duties … so far."

Olaf opened his hands. "Whoa, whoa, whoa, 'living up to'? Thems high words of praise from that there commander, young buck. What say you? Think you deserve his tutelage?"

"The commander has been an excellent tutor and mentor, especially regarding the expectations of the order. I only wish we had more time together, but I know his duties far outweigh my own needs. He has shown me that I ..." Carter revolved his coffee in his hands. "That I am not ready for the next trial."

"That's right," Jengo said. Having finished looking over Leera, he took a seat on the other side of Carter and took a sip of his coffee. "There's no rush, Squire Southguard."

"And too many rush into it," Jez quietly threw in from Leera's cot.

"So *here's* where they are!" Digby loudly belted out in song, dancing his way through the doorway.

"Shut up!" Jengo hissed, standing. "Can't you see people are convalescing?"

Digby threw up his meaty hands in false apology. "Well excuuuuuse me for trying to lighten the mood." He sniffed at the air like a rat. "Is that ... is that *coffee* I smell?"

Augum didn't so much as glance at him. "Get out," he said flatly.

Digby primped his white wig. "He says it so casually," the thirty-four-year-old replied in a singsong voice Augum found repulsive. "But you are not *my* commander, *sir*."

"But *I* am," Carter said, standing. "Get out."

"Stop playing, Cousin. You are too young for babyish—"

Carter did something Augum had least expected. Having calmly put his coffee cup down on the floor, he chucked his apple at Digby's surprised face, and it connected with a most satisfying *splat!* Digby whirled about, smacked his face into the doorframe, and groaned. As everyone, Alanna included, snickered, albeit with Alanna hiding her snicker behind a hand, Digby stood dumbfounded, hands shaking as he peeled apple bits from his red face and now skewed wig.

"How *dare* you," he hissed, readjusting his wig. "I am twice your age and charged with watching over your good health, sir. How *dare* you betray me ..."

Carter picked up his coffee cup from the floor. "Never disrespect the commander. *Ever.* You and I shall have a word later. Now for the last time—" He pointed the cup at the doorway. "Get. Out."

Digby glanced around the room with an indignance that reminded Augum of Limpet. "You'll pay for this," he hissed. "All of you." He strode out, violently shoving the door, which slammed against the frame with a *crash*.

Augum looked to Leera and Mahmoute, but the noise had failed to wake them.

"Waste of a perfectly good apple," Olaf muttered.

Carter sat back down, looking to Augum with a proud grin—and for reassurance.

Augum only sighed as he returned to enjoying the delicious chicken and potatoes. "Your heart was in the right place, Squire, but you have much to learn about leadership."

"He's only seventeen," Jez said. "I seem to recall you having your own little tantrums and the like at that age. Don't worry, young buck. You'll get there, especially if you keep listening to that one—" She indicated Augum with her cup before taking a slurping sip from it.

The grin nonetheless slipped from Carter's face. He looked down at his hands and surrendered a nod. "My apologies, Commander. I forget that I must represent the order at all times in good faith. I shall reinforce my understanding of our code of honor today with study."

Augum reached out and clapped Carter on the upper arm. "There's a good lad," he said, mimicking the sailor twang.

He resumed eating, and the others kept him company, engaging in idle banter and reflecting on the old days. Jez jested about Leera, saying she would soon shoot up in bed and demand her cuddles, drawing a round of laughter. This spurred most everyone to opine on how Leera would wake, with Jengo betting she would immediately demand a sweetcake, Olaf that she'd whine about her pillow being too stiff, Jez that she'd drag Augum out to jump his bones back at their cabin, which simultaneously drew some jeers and laughs, with Alanna pointedly going red, and Carter that she'd kick them all out to spend some quiet time with Augum, which made everyone coo and *aww* and needle Augum over how disgustingly cute they were together.

Alanna mostly kept out of it, standing by the doorway and holding her cup in both hands to draw upon its warmth. She observed them with a smile, as if hoping she could be part of this cabal one day, a thought that amused Augum. He had seen people change before—why not her?

"Does the order interest you, my lady?" he asked her in the midst of a burbling but quiet conversation among the others.

Startled, she pressed dainty fingers against her chest. "My lord, such a thing has never occurred to me."

"She doesn't have the honor required," Jez threw in, swirling her coffee. "Nor the ambition."

Alanna smoothed her fine amber robe with one hand whilst holding her cup away with the other lest she accidentally spill it upon her fine garment. "Forgive me, Miss Terse, but you know nothing of what I am and am not capable of. You know me not."

"If you say so, but your past actions speak to your fundamental character, do they not? Court women are all the same. If you ask me, I still think you're playing games."

"But I did *not* ask you, Miss Terse. Besides, what games are there to play in the middle of the ocean? I have left the court and its games behind, and truth be told, if I survive this journey, I may never return to those games. That life no longer ..." She stared into the middle distance. "... stirs the passions, if I may say so."

"Hmm," Jez only said, and took a long sip of coffee before needling Jengo to make sure Leera was arcanely fed through the 10th degree Reinvigorate spell while in the coma, and they all bantered on.

A silence fell when Olaf spoke about how Bridget loved walking Sabby and how the poor dog surely missed them both, despite Laudine taking care of her. He then sighed heavily and raised a questioning eyebrow at Augum.

"I checked," Augum mouthed at him.

"Nothing?" Olaf mouthed back.

Augum gave a slight shake of the head.

"What are you two talking about?" Carter whispered.

"Senior order business, Squire," Olaf snapped. "Never you mind."

"I understand, Standard Bearer Hroljassen," Carter replied, and went to converse with Alanna, while Jez discussed with Jengo about ways they could make Leera's convalescence more comfortable.

"I love it when people refer to me by my proper title," Olaf said, floating the coffee pot over to refill his cup. "Young man's got a bright future if he keeps learning the ropes." He snickered to himself.

Augum pronged a potato and a morsel of chicken onto his fork, dragged them through a pool of gravy, and placed them on his tongue. As he savored the succulence, he considered Olaf, who absently tapped his cup with his betrothal ring, a distant look in his eyes.

"You know she wants, like, *six*, right?" Augum quietly said as the others chatted away.

Olaf reanimated. "Who? Six what?"

Augum smiled cheekily.

Olaf's eyes widened. "Six *kids*?"

"Three boys, three girls."

"Ye, *gods*." Olaf took an unusually long sip from his coffee as he thought about it. "Guess it's going to have to be a big farmstead," he concluded, and the two friends jostled each other with their elbows as they chortled.

"She really say six?"

Augum nodded as he raised his coffee to his lips.

"Not, uh, not six *dogs*, by chance?"

Augum snorted on his coffee.

Jez, noticing them, swirled her own coffee. "Before you know it, you'll all be thirty, have beards, the order will be entrenched, and I will be an old woman of no use to you …"

After a stunned silence, Augum ripped a small chunk of his bread bowl and pelted her with it, singing, "Oh, shut up," a remark that, combined with the action, caused everyone to snort with laughter. Jez, for her part, instead of descending into a temper, rubbed her cheek, nodded, and said, "Is that the way of it now?"

"It is," Augum replied. "Your value will only grow, Jez. We love you. You know that, right? How much we love you?"

"Stop it. You're embarrassing me." Jez looked away, sniffed, and wiped a tear whilst muttering, "Bunch of stupid monkeys."

Augum shared a smile with Olaf and Jengo, both of whom knew that of everyone there, he had the most sway with her. Leera notwithstanding, of course.

"You have worthy friendships, my lord," Alanna said, drifting nearby whilst the others bantered on.

"You ought to consider it," he said. "You can always try out as an aspirant, and if you—or we—even remotely think you're not ready for the first trial, you simply don't take it. At least you would make some genuine friends who don't play courtly mind games or constantly use their station against you and each other."

Alanna idly played with her sparkling necklace as she studied his eyes. "My lord sells quite the picture. But the women of your order would never accept me as one of their own. I am too much of a threat to their men. And that of course is entirely my fault. I lilted to the expectations of my noble upbringing and have only known noble games. Being amongst you now, I find my behavior inexcusable and, to be perfectly honest with you, terribly embarrassing. As your lady would say, 'I cringe when thinking about my past behavior.' " She shrugged. "At least that's something I imagine she would say."

"That is why there is hope for you yet," he said, "for you are capable of self-reflection. And it is no mere picture I paint, but a whole new life. As to the women of the order, I would ask you to consider dropping all courtly airs in exchange for their friendship, for the friendships within the order are the deepest I have ever known."

"Darn right," Olaf said, raising his cup of coffee, having caught the tail end of their conversation.

"Here, here," Jez said, raising her cup, with Jengo raising his and echoing the sentiment.

Augum raised his coffee. "To friendship."

"To friendship," the others chorused.

On they bantered, with Alanna playing with the necklace as she pondered the matter. The very fact she considered it told Augum she was capable of giving it a serious go if she put her mind to it—heck, she'd even struck up a fragile friendship with Leera, of all people, one of the hardest to befriend once crossed!

Augum had gotten halfway through his meal when the ship's tilt and rocking abruptly eased, causing everyone to opine about how they might have passed through the storm wall—until someone began ringing a handbell above decks.

"Now what?" Jengo said with a sigh.

"Knew it was too good to be true," Olaf added, setting his cup down.

Augum put his nearly finished plate down and shot to his feet. "Stay with them, Almoner," he commanded.

Jengo nodded. "Commander."

"Let's investigate," Augum said to everyone else, and he hurried out, with all but Jengo following.

They rushed to the top deck, at which point Augum's steps faltered to a halt, for by then the ship was level with the water—and completely surrounded by a dense fog, with only the gentlest breeze to push them along. Yet the waters still lapped, and there was a distant and constant low rumble, as if they had passed through a wind wall.

Upon their arrival, the bell ringer halted and cried out, "'Locks on deck, sir!"

Augum looked to the helm wheel and saw that the captain, his bosun, and some of the crew were standing around the imperial lodestone, the compass used to navigate open waters. After exchanging a perplexed look with his group, he went forth.

"Captain," Augum greeted upon joining the group, his own crowding around just behind him.

"This I've never seen before," the captain muttered, gumming his long pipe.

Augum looked to the lodestone—an ornately carved stone needle that swung on a pivot, which in turn pointed to the degrees of a compass. The devices were so expensive that they were bolted to the deck and guarded with arcane alarms. In this case, the needle wobbled about, sometimes even turning back on itself.

"We done reached the edge of the world," a middle-aged crewmate muttered. He nodded at the fog. "Ahead looms an abyss that will see us falling until the very end of time."

"Or The Fates blew us into cursed waters," another muttered, "on account of ..." His eyes flicked between the women among them, not bold enough to finish what he wanted to say. In response many sailors signed skyward, while others picked salt from small waist pouches and tossed it over their shoulders, an old superstition to garner luck and ward off evil. Some muttered about this being a bad omen and they ought to turn about and head home.

"Maybe we reached the land of the jinxed," yet another sailor whispered in spooky tones, as if they had all gathered around a midnight fire. "Where the people talk backward and walk backward and think backward and lack eyeballs and—"

"Stow that peasant talk," the walrus-mustachioed bosun snapped, silencing the chatter, though he too stared ahead at the fog.

The captain looked to the most senior warlock among them, Jez. "Ever seen anything like this?"

Jez gripped her hips and shook her head. "No. Never. But I'm not a saltblood."

The captain glanced about at his crew. To a man, all shook their heads, mumbling things like, "Nay, sir," and "No, Cap."

"Oi!" shouted the top lookout. "Somefin' dead ahead, Cap!"

All eyes went to the bow, and the boat fell pin-drop silent. At first Augum couldn't see anything, and then a nebulous darkness began to appear within the fog. Some sailors took a step back while others signed skyward. Meanwhile, the darkness steadily formed into a tall shape.

The captain took a few hesitant steps forth. He lowered his pipe and shouted, "Reel 'em in. Prepare to anchor!"

"Reel 'em in! Prep for anchor!" the bosun echoed, and the crew shouted this command a third time whilst scurrying about the ship and climbing the masts and yardarms. Sailors promptly loosened lines and furled sails, all whilst stealing nervous peeks at the mysterious shape ahead.

As the shape continued to clarify within the fog, Augum and his group hurried to the bow, where other passengers, including Rogor the wolven and Digby and his brother Teague, had already gathered. Others piled in from behind, all gawking with open mouths.

At last the shape broke through the fog, revealing itself to be a tall mountainous pillar of black rock sitting on a small island of the same color of stone. The pillar was as thick as half a city block and rose so high that its top vanished into the fog. Most interestingly, something appeared to glow with an eerie light from on up high, as if a ghostly beacon fire sat atop it.

"What in the name of the gods is that?" Olaf whispered.

"The devil's horn," a pale crewman whispered, flinging salt over his shoulder with one hand and signing skyward with the other. "Unnameables protect us from evil, and rouse not the devil to punish us for our mortal sins ..."

"Not so sure about that," Jez said, stroking her jaw in thought. "If I was to guess, I'd think it's some sort of lighthouse. Likely enchanted."

Augum acted on her opinion by flaring the fingers of his right hand, incanting, "*Un vun asperio aurum enchantus.*" He gasped, for the entire structure, including the small island it sat upon, lit up with blue tendril webs so faded they were almost white. But what made the goosebumps rise on his arms was the fact that the tendrils seemed to distort more and more as they climbed the tower, as if stretched into curvature by an unseen force.

Others who knew Reveal took his cue and opened their own palms, until all were mumbling their disbelief at what they were seeing.

"What do the lowlanders see?" Rogor growled.

"It's ancient, whatever it is," Jez said.

"Spooky as all heck too," Alanna muttered.

"Anchor's away!" came the call from up the ship, and two anchors were dropped—one from the stern and one from the bow.

"Look up," Augum said, noticing something. "The fog is slowly swirling around the pillar."

"Maybe it's an ancient shelter from the storm," Alanna said.

Digby rubbed his hands. "Maybe there's treasure in there."

His brother Teague threw him an elbow. "We're goin' to be rich."

"You're already rich," Olaf muttered, giving them a disgusted look.

Both brothers shrugged.

The captain approached the bow holding a spyglass, which he looked through upon arrival. "I want two of you 'locks to investigate and report back," he commanded without putting it down. "The rest stay until we know what we're dealing with."

Jez smirked at Augum. "Time to practice those leadership skills, monkey—er, commander. Who do you want to take with you?"

Augum stepped past them to stand beside the bowsprit to get a better look at the island. It appeared menacing to him, a massive and ancient structure, perhaps cursed, that imposed its will over the vicious turbulence that surrounded it like a protective cocoon.

He turned about and looked to Jez. "Me and you," he said, noting that almost everyone else breathed a sigh of relief that he hadn't chosen them. "But first let's place some alarms in case there's an attack on the boat," and he and Jez each set an Object Alarm enchantment on a cleat for the crew to tap in case they were needed back at the ship.

"I'll hop first and wave when it's clear," Jez said. She took a step forth to stab at the air with a finger. "That rock right there."

Augum followed her point to the closest rock, a huge boulder that protruded toward them.

"Looks like the toe of a giant," Olaf said, a thought that made the others exchange dark looks.

"Don't wake nothing up," Digby threw in. "Don't be stupid."

"Thanks for that," Carter mumbled, shaking his head whilst looking to Augum with that perpetual want for approval, which Augum pointedly ignored. Carter was like a puppy — the more attention Augum gave him, the more he sought.

"Off I go," Jez said, and after a concentrative pause, snapped off, "*Impetus peragro.*" She vanished with a *thwomp* and appeared a heartbeat later atop that very boulder. After taking a good look around with a splayed hand, she raised an arm, and everyone expelled a breath.

Augum, who'd girded his soul to cast the Spirit of the Dragon simul, nodded at the others before concentrating on the feel of that black stone beneath his feet, the smell of the salty ocean, and how Jez would be to his left. He incanted, "*Impetus peragro,*" yanked himself through the ether, and appeared exactly beside her. He was immediately hit with the pungent smell of wet stone and moss and seaweed and salty ocean and rotten fish.

Focusing on the quest, he kneeled to allow for better study, splayed his hand, and recast Reveal. The tendrils of the rocky shore were ancient, all right, and they were also strange. The geometries were simultaneously crude and complex, but in the sense of looking at a wholly unfamiliar language. For all he knew, the language could be simple, only appearing complex to someone learning it for the first time.

"I don't recognize it," he concluded.

"It's possibly Rivican," Jez replied, her own hand splayed. "Or Sipithean, Minothean, Kargonyan — could even be Dreadnought for all we know as so little survived from back then."

"Wish Bridget was here," Augum muttered.

"This is beyond her academy learnings. We'd need someone who's spent a lifetime studying ancient tendrils, someone like a senior arcaneologist." She glanced around at the fog. "Something tells me this place would be hard to find again — and that includes teleporting to it." She nodded at him. "Keep that hand up and let's keep moving."

They walked onward, ascending the relatively gentle incline, jumping from boulder to boulder, climbing some and descending others, until they stood at the foot of the massive pillar. It imposed itself upon the sky, puncturing the fog like a giant fist, and now that they stood at its base, the light at the top of the tower appeared like a ghostly orb, illuminating the fog with an eerie glow.

"An ancient halo of light," Jez whispered.

"Really does look like a lighthouse from down here, doesn't it?" Augum said. "But then why the calm water amidst a storm? And why do I get the impression the fog is the perpetual sort that doesn't go away?"

Jez grunted in agreement.

Augum stepped closer to the tower. The tendril geometries here were loosely spread apart and nearly bone-white, as if having been sun-bleached over eons. Since there were no indications of triggers or mechanisms of that sort, Augum raised his left hand. After sharing a look with Jez regarding his intention and hearing no protest, he slowly pressed his hand against the rock. Thinking to play a prank on Jez, he violently shook as if shocked by lightning.

"Gods—!" Jez shrieked and ripped him away, only to find him snorting with laughter. "Ugh, you fiend!" she hissed, giving him a proper shove.

"Come on, when's the last time I made a prank?"

"Yeah, yeah, nice to see you relax a little, I guess. I should have known too considering that ancestral gift of lightning immunity and all." She pressed a hand to her chest in an effort to calm her breathing. "But holy Unnameables did you ever give this gal a good scare. I think I pooped myself a little."

He felt his face curdle. Somehow, she always managed to go slightly too far.

As Jez patted her chest with one hand and flapped at her face with the other, Augum, wanting to reconnect with the rock to get a sense of it, once again stepped forward to place his hand against the stone. Then he closed his eyes and took a deep breath, feeling a profound sense of history, of time, of a people and a past unknown to the temporary wanderers now facing that history.

"We are but visitors," Augum whispered. "Let us glimpse your ancient secrets, old tower." He opened his eyes to study the rock. It was akin to basalt, but richer, darker, and with fewer imperfections, like gray beach stones made black by ocean water.

He let go and stepped back to look up. The rocky edifice did not taper as it rose into the fog, making him curious about what lay in wait high above. Was it a roof with a ghostly beacon fire atop it, or something else? Was there perhaps an interior?

"Let's see if there's an entrance," he said, and they began wandering around the pillar. Before stepping out of sight of the ship, Augum raised a hand and saw hands rise in acknowledgment. The captain would be watching them through his spyglass, no doubt. As best he could, Augum signaled their intentions of walking around the tower. They then proceeded to circle the massive structure, looking for anything out of place—and found a cave-like entrance directly on the other side.

Augum took a knee to study the ground enchantments. "Tendril geometries haven't changed." He stood. "If we've been safe walking thus far, we should be safe walking in."

Jez shoved him into the cave, and he yelped. "Just checking to see if something happened," she said with a wry smile.

"But something *could* have happened!"

"Yeah, but nothing *did*, did it? Besides, it was a *prank*," she mimicked.

"I ... I can't *believe* you did that."

She gently whapped him upside the head as she passed. "Believe it, kiddo. And don't dish it out if you can't take it. And don't you dare give me that respect-the-commander speech I can see forming on your impish tongue. No one's watching, so you're still one of my rascal kids—and you always will be." She turned to smile lovingly at him.

"Ugh, you make it so hard to be mad at you," he grumbled as he entered farther with her.

"You told me you loved me. This is what you get. Affection. Isn't it terrible? Doesn't it make you feel all queasy inside?" She playfully pinched his ribs. "Huh? Huh? Awkward, isn't it?"

He whapped her hand away. "You're just getting gross now."

"How do you think I feel every time you and her—" She made her hands attack each other.

"Gods, Jez, please stop."

"I mean, at least keep it down. I can't even knock and enter anymore lest I want to bleach my eyeballs."

Augum turned around and feigned walking out. "I'm 'porting back to the ship."

"Where are you going?" She telekinetically snagged his robe and yanked. "Get back here, you little weasel."

"As long as you stop talking about ... you know. Ugh."

"You're just like your filth-minded girl," she muttered, looking up. "But fine, I'll stop."

Their echoey voices died to silence, and they allowed themselves a moment to absorb the interior, which was a tall space that shot into darkness.

"It's hollow," Augum noted.

"I can see why she fell for you. Must be difficult hauling such a gigantic brain about."

Augum had to snort at that. "Good one."

Jez winked at him then cupped her mouth and, before Augum could stop her, shouted, "Hello!"

Hello …! Hello …! Hello … the echo returned, bouncing about up and back down like in an inverse well. They waited in silence, with Augum expecting something beastly to wake with a roar, perhaps even the entire island to rise out of the water and reveal itself to be a monstrous demon with a tower horn. But nothing happened.

"Let's check the walls," Augum said, and they lit their palms, went to the entrance, and started walking leftward along the wall. "No change in tendril geometries, other than the color, that is," he reported. The tendril color was a smidge bluer inside.

Once they got to the opposite side of the entrance, a jagged and crude form appeared along the wall.

"Holy gods, those are stairs," Jez said. "Barely wide enough for a person to walk on and as steep as a pitched roof. No railing either."

"They must go to the top," Augum said, eyes following the stairs as they snaked their way up into the darkness, following the wall in a perpetually rising line.

Jez gave him that *hauling-around-your-big-brain* look that made him snort. "No, by all means, continue stating the obvious. I love it."

"Now I know where Leera gets her sarcasm from," he muttered.

"She's my apprentice on multiple fronts." Jez placed her hands on her hips and expelled a breath through flapping lips, blowing off a strand of black hair that had strayed into her line of sight. "Well, we can't climb up without saying anything—they'll think we're missing. I'll hop to the ship and tell them what we're up to."

"You go on ahead. I'll keep exploring."

Jez nodded, then pointed at the entrance. "Just in case, I'll 'port from outside. Don't trust zipping through this weird rock."

"Prudent," Augum said.

"There's a word I rarely hear you say."

Augum, a little tired of the banter and itching to explore, only nodded, and she walked off to the entrance, from whence she snapped off the Teleport incantation, vanishing with a *thwomp* that echoed into and up the tower.

Augum allowed that echo to die, appreciating the ancient stillness of the tower's interior, before walking toward the distant entrance so he could take a look at the center of the floor. Thus far, it was all composed of the same rock as outside. He brightened his palm light, turning himself into a lightning-lit beacon fire that shone in a wide circle. Strange shadows soon appeared from jagged objects, and when he approached, he realized what they were.

"Bones," he whispered, kneeling.

The bones were encased in a rusted crust, all that remained of ancient armor. Nearby was the pommel and half of the hilt of a sword, the blade long gone. Out of curiosity, he splayed his hands over the sword, imagining it whole again, and incanted, "*Apreyo*." A few rice-sized pieces of metal that hadn't fully rusted tumbled back to the pommel, but that was all. Rust was a form of damage like fire and could not be repaired arcanely. The idea nonetheless made him wonder if a stronger form of the Repair spell existed, perhaps locked deep in the archives in Ley or someplace else.

He searched the area and found more bones, some with similar equipment, others with altogether different styles, as if from different eras. One of these pieces of armor hadn't fully deteriorated and showed a huge dent, as if bashed by a huge club. Inspecting the crushed bones beneath told him these warriors had died either from battle or, more likely …

He looked up into the darkness and whispered, "From falling …"

Suddenly the idea of climbing those stairs didn't seem so tantalizing.

There came a *thwomp* as Jez reappeared—except she'd appeared ten feet above the ground and so close to the entrance wall that she yelped from fright—and took a hard tumble upon crashing to the rocky floor.

"Definitely not safe to 'port into here," she said, allowing Augum to help her up. "The enchantments here must be interfering somehow. I dare not imagine what would have happened had the teleportation distance been any greater."

"Then let's avoid 'porting. Anyway, I found something. Take a look." He led her to the bones and showed her all the rusted detritus. "Either they got clubbed to death—"

"—or they fell," she said, looking upward. "Anything salvageable?"

"Not a single thing. The salt ate it all away. I tried Repair too."

Again the *hauling-around-your-big-brain* look. "On *rust*?"

He shrugged. "Worth a shot."

She poked the remains with her foot, then crouched over a particular hunk of rust. "This rivet-work here … it's Canterran in origin—not that I'm an expert on ancient armor smithing." She moved on, examining each piece. "This one's Nodian, and this one's definitely Solian. In fact, I believe they *all* originated from our continent. Everything here can likely be attributed to a Sithesian kingdom."

"Explorers from ages past?"

"Who knows. But again, I'm no expert, and we don't have one aboard either. Should have taken a historian with us."

"And a senior arcaneologist."

She grunted, dusted her hands, and again looked up. "You got a fear of heights? 'Course you don't, what with flying about all the time. Want to wait down here or come along?"

"Don't ask stupid questions."

She looked at him. "Is that a genuine smile?"

"What, I can smile." He walked toward the staircase.

"Don't make it look so forced, then. You need to learn how to unwind."

"Oh, I *know* how to unwind."

"Eww."

"Grow up."

"Never."

They reached the staircase, and Augum went first.

"Ladies first, you rude little jerk!"

"I'm spritelier," he declared and shot off ahead, knowing the staircase was far too narrow for Jez to pass him.

"Fine, you can be the one testing the stairs. Just be ready to yank yourself in case of a sudden collapse."

He flashed her a thumbs-up and nimbly rose the first few flights as they snaked along the wall, his light guiding the way. The stairs themselves were overly tall, as if meant for a taller people, which also made them a tripping hazard, forcing care.

Upward they climbed, until their lights neither reached the ground nor the ceiling. That slowed their ascent, for they tended to press against the wall, worried about falling.

"Dusty up here," Jez noted behind him.

"No footsteps in the dust either," Augum replied. He did feel the occasional gust of wind, however, which meant that any footsteps would inevitably get erased over time.

At one point, he happened to glance up to see how high the stairs rose and noticed that the ring of stairs above, barely visible at the edge of his light, was missing an entire portion.

"We'll worry about it when we get there," Jez said when he pointed it out, prodding his back for him to continue.

They continued ascending, making a full circumnavigation of the interior of the tower before arriving at a stair that opened to a wide gulf before the next stair resumed.

"Twenty-five feet," Augum calculated, wiggling a hand back and forth. "Give or take."

"No teleporting unless we want to get half fused," Jez reminded him. "Which means we got to do it the old-fashioned way."

Augum nodded—and leaped, causing Jez to yelp. He telekinetically lashed out—and his heart jammed into his throat when his usually long Telekinesis tendril hook missed. As he fell, he snatched the wall instead and stuck to it like a frog.

"That's what you get for rushing it, monkey!" Jez said from above.

"That's not what happened," Augum replied. "There's no way that should have missed."

"You got careless and are too proud to admit it."

"Maybe." Holding onto the wall with his right hand, he lashed out with his left. Unusually, he had to try several times before hooking on, then used all his telekinetic might to drag himself up, an endeavor that warped the space around him from the strain. "Did you see that?" he asked upon clambering to his feet on the other side of the broken staircase.

"Your Telekinesis has long stopped impressing me, kiddo," Jez replied from across the gulf between them, "and you don't need more smoke blown—"

"No, not that. Did you see how many tries it took me? Hold on a moment," and he spread the fingers of his right hand, incanting, "*Un vun asperio aurum enchantus.*" The tower lit up with those ancient and nearly bone-white tendrils, all of which were distorted in a similar way.

"They're bending," Augum reported. "Some sort of perpetual field warp on the ethereal plane itself—if that's how it works. Anyway, try to latch on, but don't jump yet. I want to see how your tendril geometries behave."

"Whatever you say, kiddo." Jez casually made a lobbing motion.

Augum watched her tendril line shoot out from her hand—and veer away, as if blown by an invisible wind.

"Gods," he said.

"What?"

"It ... I mean ... the tendril line sort of—" He made his hand snake away.

"What? That makes no sense."

"See for yourself. Splay your hand and watch mine."

They switched so that he was the one tossing a tendril line down to her, and even from that distance he watched as her eyebrows rose so high they dragged her mouth open.

"That's ..."

"It's not impossible because we're seeing it with our own eyes," he said. "Maybe it's also causing the lodestone to swing wildly like it is."

"Maybe," she said, rhythmically slapping her thigh as she thought about the problem. "All right, keep watch and let me know when my line hooks on."

He nodded and monitored her repeated attempts at telekinetically hooking her tendril rope. Only when he told her to adjust her aim to the right did it finally catch, at which point he signaled the go-ahead and she swung off. When she reached the apex of her swing, he telekinetically caught her, which also took two tries, and helped haul her over the edge.

"This place is creepy as all heck," she muttered after he had helped her stand, with the pair of them pressing against the wall to catch their breath and take stock of the climb ahead. Finding no more breaks in the staircase, they soon continued ascending.

"Ever seen that sort of effect on arcanery before?" Augum asked, huffing with each step now as they'd been climbing for some time.

"Not like that, no."

"But something like it?"

"Here and there. Your field warping, for example, but that doesn't affect other tendril geometries. And I've certainly never seen an effect this strong. I'm curious what we're going to find."

After about an hour of climbing, with multiple circumnavigations of the interior of the tower, Augum's light finally reached the ceiling, with the stairs continuing on through an opening at the very top. By then he began to hear a rumbling, which he suspected was the wind, meaning the stairs likely opened to the outside.

They exchanged a look of interest and continued on, each step measured and careful, with their bodies as close to the cold stone wall as possible. At last, they reached the opening, which led to an enclosed series of steps that wound in the same circular ascending fashion. Seeing that the tendrils had not changed—other than bending at a steeper fishbowl-like angle—Augum continued forth, noting that the rumbling was now unusually loud.

The staircase soon opened to the fog, and he poked his head out—and froze, barely conscious that his Reveal spell had instantly been snuffed. The top of the tower was composed of the same roughly hewn rock as the structure, creating a round roof plateau half the size of a city block. But it was what floated at the plateau's heart that caught his breath—a massive sphere of energy, shining like a beacon fire made of brackish light. Even laying eyes on it felt brutal, and his teeth buzzed and his bones vibrated. It felt wrong to look at, dangerous even.

"What in the dark hells is that?" Jez whispered.

Augum barely shook his head, for he had never seen anything like it.

"Whatever it is snuffed me," Jez said.

"Me too."

Both of them tried to reignite Reveal, but Augum was only able to catch a fleeting glimpse of tendrils swirling violently around the sphere of light before his spell was once again stripped away.

"I don't think it's safe here for us," he said.

She agreed, and they quickly retreated to the safety of the open stairwell, where the buzzing of teeth and bones halted.

"Felt like it was eating my soul," a breathless Jez said, a hand to her chest.

Augum gently knocked his head against the wall he had pressed his back to, mind ablaze with theories. Only one made sense.

Jez beat him in verbalizing the conclusion. "A people built it long ago to slow or even halt overseas travel," she said. "There must be … who knows how many of these things out there, straddling the center of the ocean."

"Why?" he asked, searching her eyes. When neither of them verbalized an answer, he looked away, moving his jaw left and right in thought. "Whatever people built it wanted to keep the continents apart for a reason."

"And now the gargoyles have broken that boundary," Jez said.

Augum nodded. "With us following suit."

They considered the matter further, but with the rumbling so close, neither felt comfortable standing there, so they mutually decided to return to the ship. With nothing else to uncover on the island, it was best that they move along for now.

WHITE MARBLE

BRIDGET

Bridget paced the path stones alone, appreciating the bright morning sunlight as it filtered in through the pink-leafed oaks that dotted the sky plateau. Wearing a freshly washed plain cotton slave garment in an attempt to adapt to her new home, she breathed in the cool air and smelled the exotic scents of a mysterious foreign land.

With Sebastian busy washing the kitchen floor, she had stolen a moment to explore the garden, hand subtly splayed before her, tracking a tendril tug that should lead to something hidden. Interestingly, the gargoyles did not seem to have the power of Unconceal, or they had yet to discover the spell, for the key she had found under the bed had been there for some time, and the tugs all about the place were relatively old.

A quiet rustling noise followed her as she walked. Hoping to catch the offender, she abruptly turned about and witnessed one of the bushes stop shaking. Something else lived here, something small. Perhaps a cat?

The change of focus snuffed Unconceal once more, and so she refocused and whispered, "*Un vu deo*," and continued forth, following the gentle tendril tug leading toward the pond. Leaving the bushes behind, she heard the rustling transition to grass—and whirled about a second time. Twenty feet behind her stood a creature as long as a cat, but armed with a turtle-like carapace. It had a head that resembled a mouse, with big ears and small black eyes and a snuffling snout. The animal had frozen still upon Bridget catching it out, as if pretending to be a rock.

"Hello there," Bridget said, crouching as her mind worked through mythology class, for the creature looked familiar. But mythology class was not where she'd seen it depicted, and she mentally flipped pages of books she'd read, until she came across a Sierran depiction of an armored little creature that looked very similar.

"You're an armadillo, aren't you?" she asked, recalling that they were friendly creatures and sometimes taken as pets in certain Sierran circles. It wouldn't surprise her if the gargoyles kept it as a pet too, considering it would have had to be carried up here in the first place.

The creature sniffed at the air, placed a tentative paw forth and then another, until it was waddling over to her. She extended a hand, which it sniffed. To her delight, it rubbed up on her hand much like a cat or a dog and waddled around her, rubbing its armored carapace against her butt and legs and wagging its tail.

"Oh my gosh, you are just so adorable, even though you're odd-looking. What's your name? Huh? What should I call you?" She drummed her knee with her fingers. "How about ..."

It looked up at her between its quiet snuffling.

"How about Snuffles? Hmm? Do you like that name?"

The creature waddled underneath her and settled in like a loafing cat, as if taking shelter from the sun.

Bridget allowed herself a smile as she petted its thick carapace. Remembering Sabby, she almost wanted to find a stick to throw and play fetch. But having assigned herself a quest, she stood up, turned about, and splayed her hand. Since the Unconceal spell had failed upon her attention getting stolen, she once more incanted, "*Un vun deo,*" paused to sense the various tugs, and quickly reacquired the one that led to the pond.

"Are you coming?" she asked over her shoulder as she walked, and was delighted to see the little thing waddle after her.

She walked slowly, allowing Snuffles to keep pace, until she found herself standing before the small pond with its overhanging pink-leaf oak and blue reed-like marsh flowers and sun-kissed swarms of tiny flies. Here and there a frog's head poked out from between pink pond leaves. Beneath the water, small fish lazily swam about.

Bridget felt Snuffles poking her feet. She separated them, allowing him to waddle in between, and there he loafed once more, taking shelter from who knew what, drawing comfort from her mere presence.

"You are melting my brittle heart, little one," she whispered while keeping hold of the tendril tug. Curiously, that tug went directly into the center of the pond. There was no way she was going in there right now, not with the day starting. For all she knew it could be a mere coin or a shoe. She did not want to risk angering her new masters on a gamble.

"Ah-bee-gale!" came a distant shout.

She shot up to see Grak waving at her from the entrance of the manor.

"Yes, coming!" she shouted and took off running, leaving a confused Snuffles behind. Running like that brought back an old memory of being a little girl and running to her father's call. Here she was many years later starting all over again with a new life, albeit as a slave in a strange land of ruthless demons, and yet with all her memories intact.

"Ah-bee-gale what you do?" Grak said upon her arrival.

She thumbed over her shoulder. "I-I-I was exploring. Enjoying the scenery and the pond and the view, that's all."

"We go."

"Where are we going?"

Grak flicked a few clawed fingers downward, indicating for her to be quiet, and he stepped back and bowed his head. Bridget had the good sense to do the same—and good thing too, for the entire gargoyle family spilled through the open doors of the manor.

The four young ones—two brothers and two sisters—growlingly bantered with each other, while the mother organized a handful of scrolls. The captain father, meanwhile, looked to Bridget and asked a flippant-sounding question with the word *gyot* in it, to which Grak promptly replied and walked off, no doubt to fetch Sebastian.

Bridget stood with her head bowed, ignored by them all. She felt awkward, as if she was in the way, and hoped they would keep ignoring her. She wondered if that was how servants felt around the trio back at home. She wondered just how much was invisible to her higher station. She wondered if this was the gods teaching her a lesson in humility.

Grak came out holding Sebastian by the upper arm. The moment he let it go, Sebastian shot to Bridget, throwing his arms around her and burying his face into her chest. The captain growled a sharp rebuke, and Grak grabbed Sebastian and tore him away from Bridget, who felt a stab of pain in her heart. Grak then made Sebastian stand beside Bridget and pushed his head down.

"We must act like servants and all will be well," Bridget whispered to Sebastian from the side of her mouth.

"Yes, Momma."

"*Kyesos*," the captain growled, and the entire family hooked elbows with each other.

Grak stooped to hook an elbow with Sebastian, Sebastian with Bridget, and Bridget with the reluctant brat, who hissed down at her. She paid him no mind, ignoring the overly tight grip of his callused elbow that was cutting off the circulation to her hand.

The captain touched a rune on his body and the group shot off with a *thwomp*. The hurtle through the arcane ether was identical to a standard Group Teleport, and they were soon spat out onto a white marble floor.

Sebastian keeled over to vomit, for he was an Ordinary boy not used to teleportation. This caused The Brat to raise a fist. But just as he was going to slam it down on the back of Sebastian's head, Bridget threw herself over the boy, protecting his body, and she felt several hammer thumps upon her back. All she surrendered to the evil brat were a series of grunts, until the teenage male gargoyle yanked The Brat off her, snapping an angry word at him.

A wheezing Bridget helped Sebastian stand and wiped his face with the back of her sleeve.

"Are you okay?" Sebastian whispered, eyes watery with fear for her.

"Of course I am," she replied, throwing him a wink. Her back hurt like heck, and there would certainly be a big bruise there, but it was nothing compared to what she had experienced in war. And she certainly wasn't going to let some bratty gargoyle draw satisfaction from seeing her whine or cry, even though part of her girlish instincts, perhaps awakened by the memory of her late father, wanted to do just that.

The family strode away and Bridget and Sebastian had to practically jog to keep up with the long gargoyle gait. She positioned herself and the boy in front of Grak, but behind the rest of the family. Only then did she steal a glance around, and her breath caught, for they walked along a vast white-marble floor surrounded by marble pillars as thick as a grain silo and as high as a ten-story building. Atop every pillar stood a statue of a winged gargoyle, each in a different pose and with a slightly different expression. The faces were all fierce or proud or imperial or determined, with varying styles of dress—some wore robes, some sashes, some chains, others nothing at all. Bridget suspected they were leaders from ages past, or perhaps mythical figures, or even gods for all she knew.

Beyond this marble plateau sprawled an entire city, the rounded buildings of which were made of varyingly colored stonework and dotted with gargoyle holes. Gigantic sky pillars rose between these structures and even from the top of them, all similar to the one she now called home. Most buildings were between five and ten stories on average, and smaller ones could be seen in the distance—the marble area here had to be in the dense city center. The structures also lacked straight edges, meaning every surface was curved, making the city appear like a gigantic termite nest.

Other gargoyles walked to and fro on the marble floor. These gargoyles looked stately, some with chains much like the captain's, others with various strange accouterments like sashes and leather thongs ornamented with strings of bones, or ropes fitted with colorful gems, or plates of thick armor that clanked as the gargoyle walked, giving them the appearance of gigantic, misshapen and beastly knights.

Of particular interest was that almost all had a human slave in tow—except these slaves looked wretched compared to Bridget. They were short and thin and as gnarled as the oaks back on the plateau. Some were leashed by a chain or a leather strap or rope, others walked freely, but all wore slave collars.

The family and their slave entourage strode toward a marble staircase as wide as the entire plaza. Those stairs led up a long way to a raised area well out of view. As they walked, some gargoyles came up to greet the towering captain with a growled "*Karr Gravak*" and a nod, to which the captain merely inclined his head. Some, obviously lower in rank, even bowed deeply. The rest of his family was plainly ignored, with hardly a glance paid toward the slaves.

But it was the slaves that these gargoyles brought near that stole Bridget's attention. They were lowly creatures whose heads were perpetually bowed. Their clothes were often mere rags and they stank something foul. The split between male and female was equal, and the ages averaged between fifteen and thirty years of age, but hardly any were older. All were disfigured in some manner—one was missing a hand, another an arm, another an eye. They were scarred and emaciated, with blotchy, sunken skin and sallow countenances. None uttered so much as a grunt, offering only subtle movements of the body or the eyes, and they kept stealing glances at Bridget and Sebastian, with many sniffing at the air like animals.

Bridget held Sebastian's hand as she hurried along, keeping a close eye on him and helping him whenever he stumbled trying to keep up. His head was on a constant swivel as he gaped wide-eyed, mouth hanging open and occasionally emitting a pitiful whimper, for he was a tiny creature amongst giants. Every time it looked like he wanted to ask a question, Bridget squeezed his hand tightly, wordlessly telling him to remain silent. She knew he was scared, but he needed to learn to keep attention away from himself.

They began ascending the stairs, which were built for gargoyle legs, meaning Bridget had to raise each foot almost up to her waist. Sebastian had such a hard time that Grak picked him up and carried him under his arm like a pet. Bridget's pride refused such an indignity, and so she struggled up the steps as best she could. She was completely out of breath by the time they reached the pinnacle—a flat and square marble space that seemed to float amidst the highest points of the city buildings, at least the ones that weren't pillars.

Seeing more gargoyles emerge from the four other sides told Bridget they were standing atop a gigantic marble pyramid, and at the center of that pyramid stood a congregation of gargoyles and their human slaves.

The congregation noticed the captain's approach and greeted him with raised arms and nods and growls of victory. The captain raised his arm in turn, and he trilled at the air like a bird, which they returned with more trills, until all the senior gargoyles—they were all male, Bridget noticed—trilled in unison.

After coming to stand before this congregation, the captain stepped aside and thrust his arms toward a panting Bridget and a meek Sebastian, who Grak had by then put down to stand beside Bridget. The gathering of high-ranking gargoyles, all winged, all wrinkled with age, and all covered in scars and runes, gathered close, their meek human slaves in tow. They prodded Bridget and Sebastian and bent down to sniff her hair and skin, while they themselves smelled of luxurious exotic oils. She tried not to squirm or show fear, keeping her mind well away from their encroachments, some of which were most unseemly. She wanted to slap their claws away but knew such a reaction risked serious harm or even death, for these were possibly the highest echelon of leaders the gargoyle kingdom had.

She assumed as much until every single gargoyle standing atop the pyramid dropped to their knees and prostrated themselves, placing both arms above their heads as they bowed flat along the floor, with their wings angled forward, doing the same.

Simultaneously, Grak pushed Bridget and Sebastian to the floor, forcing them into the same position. Bridget dared to sneak a peek in the direction everyone was bowing and saw a massive golden gargoyle, one of the largest she had seen at a staggering twenty feet. He was festooned with golden armor and trinkets and hoops and necklaces and chains, all of which clanked and clanged as he strode toward them at a leisurely pace, grunting at the occasional underling.

A retinue of gargoyle servants followed him, some holding gold trays of food and drink, others working together to haul wooden carts full of tall shelves bolted to the frames, creating miniature libraries of scrolls and tablets and trinkets and trophies. One group worked together to haul a wide cart filled with bejeweled chests, the rickety wheels squealing awkwardly from the weight. Another group carried a gigantic throne studded with glittering jewels. Though he wore no crown, Bridget concluded this was the gargoyle's king.

Having glimpsed him and his entourage, Bridget pressed her forehead against the cold marble floor, her face obscured by her long hair, arms outstretched. The position was strangely comfortable, allowing her to catch her breath from the climb and stretch her sore limbs, so she hardly minded when the king took his sweet time sauntering over.

His clinking and clanging and rattling of chains and armor and accouterments halted directly before her. The giant claws of one of his feet did a *tappety-tap-tap* right by her outstretched hands. A noxious concoction of scented oils wafted over her like a waterfall, and she had to press her nose tight against the marble, trying not to imagine getting whipped to a pulp for the sin of sneezing.

What a way to die, she thought, unable to help the cynical amusement from slipping in.

The king loomed, the entire courtyard in silence. At last he spoke, his voice so deep and guttural that it sounded like a boulder was speaking. The voice had a slovenly cadence, as if he had all the time in the world to express himself. He ended his growl with a rise in pitch, indicating a question, but Bridget could not understand one word due to his boulder-like voice.

Out of the corner of her eye, she saw the captain rise to his feet and reply in a respectful growl. She recognized a few words, telling her he was saying something about slaves in distant lands. His clawed foot prodded her as he said, "*Gin gyot gurgur.*"

This slave … something, Bridget translated in her mind, not knowing what the word *gurgur* meant. She wished she had worked harder to understand their language, especially to attempt the 12th degree Tongues spell. But then ship life had been so difficult that it was hard to blame herself for the shortcoming.

The king pivoted his stance slightly and growled a single word, "*Girku?*"

Bridget understood this word, which meant *offspring*.

"*Yoss,*" the captain replied, which Bridget knew was the formal word for *yes*, with *ga* being the informal variant. Despite everything, she found it an interesting language.

Captain Gravak spoke on with many words she did not know. She dared tilt her head enough to steal a peek at him, and saw him open his wings wide along with his arms, and the entire retinue, servants included, gasped.

"*Gef?*" the king growled incredulously. "*Draga?*"

The captain's response was to raise a single claw and say, "*Gat draga. Gat.*"

He's talking about having faced Augum as a dragon, Bridget realized, suspecting the word *draga* meant dragon and *gat* meant one. Little did they know a dragon secretly lay amongst them, albeit as a slave.

"*Gat draga? Gat?*" The king repeated in that incredulous tone. He glanced about, accouterments clinking, before booming a guttural laugh, a laugh that all present joined in—except the slaves, of course. This laugh went on for some time and was followed by a seemingly spontaneous shout of victory. After silencing his exuberant subjects, the king commanded the captain to continue, and this time the captain spoke at length, concluding by opening a hand at Bridget, who immediately returned to pressing her nose to the marble floor.

The king mulled this additional information over, then barked out another single word, "*Gerhat,*" which sent a cold chill up Bridget's spine, for Grak had taught her this word, and it meant *demonstrate.*

There came a bustling sound as everyone rose to their feet. Grak roughly hauled Bridget up by the arm, yet when their gazes met, she saw apology in his lone eye and understood he was only doing what was expected of him. She got the impression that he had to show his masters that he was being rough with the slaves so they knew their place, yet he also despised doing so.

Or maybe you're deluding yourself, she thought as Grak shoved her away from the group so roughly she stumbled and fell, rolling a few times before nimbly vaulting back to her feet. The warlike way she'd done it, which accidentally revealed her training, caused the committee of gargoyles to grumble amongst each other, with the captain opining in such a manner that told her he was saying, "You have not seen anything yet."

She looked back and was relieved to see Grak holding Sebastian by the arm. Whatever display was about to take place would not involve the boy—a small relief. Meanwhile the king's servants placed his massive throne down, allowing him to lazily take his seat. They also hauled the various carts so that he could have them within view, the wheels squealing so absurdly that were Leera there Bridget imagined her bursting with laughter—and then promptly getting flayed for it.

One of those gargoyles, a wingless and mutilated beast much like Grak, with a missing eye and stubs where the wings had once been, dropped to all fours to act as a footstool for the king, who dumped both legs on his back. The beastly servant groaned from the strain but held the armored legs up.

As the king reached for a golden chalice, a gargoyle servant raised an ornate bronze horn—how interesting that some customs barely changed even across the oceans—and loosed a series of short blasts.

Several gargoyles, each leading a collar-chained human slave, emerged from another stairway hole in a different part of the courtyard. Bridget gasped, for one of these was the boned one, the gargoyle bidder who had tried to win her at the auction. Today he wore intricately engraved armor made solely of human bones. His helm, which he carried under an arm, was composed entirely of jeweled skulls. He was among the few who had more than one slave—three, in fact.

One of these slaves was none other than Naomi—and the girl's eyes widened upon seeing Bridget before they dropped out of fear. The second slave was a squat, balding old man with a salt-and-pepper beard and portly belly. He tottered beside Naomi, now and then flashing her a domineering scowl and hissing at her to move slower or faster or who knew what. The third was an also hunched but muscled and, interestingly, armed creature of a human whose teeth were so crooked that they stuck out of his curled lips. He was missing an ear and covered in scars, and for some reason he was allowed to carry a sword and a shield, the former hanging from a leather sheath, the latter from his back.

An arena dueler, Bridget realized, swallowing. *And likely a high-ranking one*. Some of the other gargoyle slavers also had arena slaves, for they were armed, but none were as ferocious looking as the one that belonged to Bones.

The new gargoyle arrivals lined up in a wide semi-circle before the king. They bowed in unison, each extending the chain leash that led to their slaves.

Gods, please not Naomi, Bridget thought. *Please, please, please …*

The king barked a word so guttural that Bridget could not make it out, yet she felt another chill when Bones inclined his head and stepped forth. The king mulled over his three slaves—the trembling Naomi, the scowling old man, and the grinning arena warrior. He raised a single claw and indicated the warrior, and Bridget expelled a sigh of relief.

The new arrivals disassembled to stand behind the king, while Grak stepped up beside Bridget.

"I know," she said, already tying her long cinnamon hair into a makeshift ponytail. "I must fight."

"*Yoss*," he replied, lingering as if he wanted to say something more. When she looked up, she saw that his lone eye was watery with regret. He gave the slightest hint of a smile before stepping away.

"Momma?"

"Shh, Sebby. Everything's going to be all right," she whispered, patting a hand at the air whilst staring at her opponent, assessing him. He was stubby with a short reach, something she could potentially use to her advantage. Probably slow too, but she ought not to rely on that. One thing she had learned was never to underestimate a foe.

The captain glared at Bones as the latter smugly unclipped his arena dueler and shoved him toward Bridget. While the hunched slave unsheathed a clunky iron sword and grabbed his shield from his back, Bridget raised her hands into attack position. She was conscious that the king would be assessing her skills and using that knowledge to determine what to do with her lot next—maybe what to do with her entire kingdom.

Realizing that her actions and decisions would thus carry great importance, she wondered what the best strategy was here. Would it serve her people's interests if she showed little skill or revealed her training? If the latter, how much should she show?

As the pair circled each other, Bridget, who did not possess Augum's sense or training in military strategy, chose the limited version of the latter only because the gargoyles would tell the king anyhow of her might, but she would still keep certain cards close to her chest.

The arena warrior growled and lashed out first, swinging his clubbish sword in a figure-eight as he pressed forth. Bridget stepped back with each swing, keeping her distance, assessing his style whilst trying to remember basic sword and buckler training. Her breath came in quick, for a fight was still a fight, and she feared getting cut and dying as much as anyone. Between Augum, Leera, and herself, she was by far the weakest when it came to close combat, much preferring to fire spells and arrows from a distance.

All other movement stilled as the entire courtyard watched the melee. Whereas gargoyles had been loud and obnoxious and drunk on the ship, here they were silent and reserved, respectful of their king.

Meanwhile the idea of dueling atop a marble pyramid, mixed with the exotic aromas, the cool air and bright sun and strange slaves and towering visuals of an exotic land felt utterly surreal to Bridget.

She kept stepping back as the warrior kept swinging. He raised his shield—nothing but a coconut-style husk of some sort—after every swing, telling her he was expecting counter-thrusts. The sword swings were also short and kept close to the body, as if he was used to close combat.

The warrior belted a full-throated war cry and shot forth, sword raised high overhead in readiness to cleave her in two. Bridget made a twirling yanking motion on his sword hand, incanting, "*Disablo!*" Even suppressed by the collar, the spell was strong enough to send the sword spinning through the air. She glimpsed a look of surprise cross his brutish face before he transitioned to trying to club her with a fist, which she dipped while simultaneously shoving at his torso and shouting, "*Baka!*"

He was sent tumbling only a short distance and promptly jumped back to his feet. He ran for the sword, but upon reaching for it, found it gliding away. He reached for it again, but a pointing Bridget kept a telekinetic hold of it and slid it toward her.

While some gargoyles growlingly chortled at this display, others exchanged looks—and grumbles, telling Bridget she might already have overplayed her hand. Did she really want to reveal how skillful her people were, at least to those who had not already seen her people in action back in Sithesia? One side of her said yes, she ought to show them her strength, even if suppressed, for it might prevent them from returning to her continent.

It was that part that won out, and she pushed her arcane muscle to float the sword to her waiting hand, upon which she swung it about rather clumsily, for she was not at all a swordswoman like Leera. She did this whilst stepping back, forcing the warrior to think about what to do next, which he did while cowering behind his shield, afraid of what she might do.

If you want them to fear your people, she heard Mahmoute say to her, *show them what fear looks like.* She did not know why it was Mahmoute who appeared in her mind, but she followed the directive nonetheless and lobbed the sword into the air toward the warrior. Whilst he reached for it, distracted, she made a claw of her hand and, with the utmost focus, swiped at the air whilst hissing, "*Dreadus terrablus!*" infusing into the spell the image of Bones ripping the warrior in half.

The warrior's head snapped back. He missed grabbing the blade, which clanged loudly against the marble floor, dropped to his knees, and loosed a high-pitched scream of terror that startled some of the gargoyles and slaves.

Bridget could have picked up the sword and sliced the warrior's head clean off, but she only stood there, arms by her sides, chin level, intimating that the duel had ended.

But they did not respect this signal, for the king glanced about at his audience, silencing them with a single look, and they proceeded to wait.

Bridget hesitated. It went against the code of honor to take the life of a weaponless Ordinary, so instead she drew his outline, incanting,

"*Paralizo carcusa cemente.*" Despite feeling the casting had been weak, the arena slave nonetheless froze in place, mouth agape in a silent scream.

Not wanting to waste any more stamina than she had to, Bridget stepped up to the sword, picked it up, and placed the edge against the warrior's neck. She looked to the king—and realized she had made a grave error, for the king snarled and his retinue roared in disapproval. Everyone, including the captain and Bones—even Grak—shouted for her to avert her eyes.

She of course dropped her eyes, yet the damage was done, and with a single flick of the claw, Grak was sent running forth toward her. She let the blade fall from her grasp and allowed him to yank her up painfully by the ponytail.

"Momma!" Sebastian shouted, but The Brat grabbed him, lest he foolishly run to her.

Not wanting to show them how terrified she was, Bridget let the pain of being held up by the hair wash over her, a pain that resulted in involuntary tears trickling down her cheeks. To keep the focus off that scalp-burning pain, she flexed all her puny but lithe muscles, body trembling as she focused on simply hanging there like a captured doll, teary eyes low.

Grak carried Bridget in this manner, swinging like a fish on a line, until she found herself dangling before the king, her scalp burning raw and feeling like all her hair was about to be torn out of her head.

Even sitting, the king towered over her, the jewels of his throne blinding her with reflected sunlight. He let her dangle as he considered the matter before uttering a low series of growls. Grak released her hair, and she fell to the ground in a gasping heap. She delicately touched her tender scalp. Feeling no blood, she hauled herself to her feet and remained standing with a bowed head, wanting to show that their callous treatment had not destroyed her.

The king growled a series of instructions, and Grak roughly snatched her by the arm and dragged her back to stand beside Sebastian, who tried to grab hold of her hand, only for the older gargoyle sister to smack it away, causing him to yelp in pain. When the boy looked longingly to Bridget, she allayed his fears by using a hand to pat at the air, telling him to settle down and that everything was all right. She also edged closer to him until the side of her arm touched his shoulder, sending him silent reassurance.

She looked to the warrior she had faced and saw he had overcome the Fear and Paralyze spells. Bones had re-clipped the leash to his collar and was dragging him back to stand beside a terrified Naomi, who surely feared she was next.

Bridget expected that same horror, but something else happened instead—a slew of wingless, runeless gargoyles emerged from a stairway carrying a series of marble tables. They dutifully laid these tables out end to end where Bridget had fought, rolled out a golden silk runner along the center of the table, and proceeded to run back and forth between the stairway and the table, bringing in marble trays of food. Some of these trays held entire animals—a type of boar, a type of pig, a peacock-like creature with teal feathers, and many that Bridget did not recognize.

But that wasn't all they brought, and she and Sebastian gasped upon seeing a human, bound up like a pig with a pink fruit in its mouth, brought out on one of these trays. He was a young man of about Bridget's age who was missing an ear. Just as she wondered how the poor wretch had died, his eyes glanced over at her and she had to restrain herself from yelping. The poor thing was *alive!*

Despite the shock of seeing such a terrible thing, the tray that followed was even more mysterious to her, for it held a small gargoyle, bound up in the same manner—and also alive. Despite the implications, Bridget suspected they were mere decorations, for she doubted the gargoyles would eat their slaves or cannibalize their own.

With the food arranged down the center of the long table, the king stood and extended an arm toward one of the marble staircases. All heads turned to witness a gold-glittering gargoyle emerge, surrounded by a large retinue of girgoyle servants, some of whom carried a golden throne chair similar to the king's, others a cart of bejeweled chests which they placed on the marble floor and then rolled. There was no doubt in Bridget's mind that this was the queen, for she wore a surprisingly feminine dress made of nothing but fine golden chains that tinkled gently with each step. Her snout and ears were festooned with golden rings that sparkled in the sunlight, and there was a grace to her walk Bridget had not seen in any gargoyle.

Upon her gliding approach, all gargoyles but the king bowed their heads, which prompted the slaves to do the same. The chair was placed beside the king's, and the royal couple sat, which was the signal for all to begin taking their places. Bones was invited to sit on the queen's right and the captain and his family on the king's left. Naomi and the old man were made to sit with a separate group of slaves, frustrating Bridget as she desperately wanted to talk to her. Bridget and Sebastian, meanwhile, were made to sit in a circle of unfamiliar slaves that included the arena warrior.

As the king gave leave to start the feast, all the gargoyles kept stealing glances her way. Not at Sebastian, but at her specifically. It became plain to her that she was the subject of multiple conversations, with Bones and the captain taking the liberty of filling the queen in on the grand prize of the occasion—a suddenly pink-cheeked Bridget.

She was trying to pay attention to their subtle gestures and whatever gargoyle words she could pick up when a bowl of slop was dumped before her. She looked up to see two wingless girgoyle servants, one of whom hissed at her like a cat.

Not wanting to antagonize her, Bridget looked to her slop and realized no spoon had been provided. The other slaves, all of whom kept shooting wary glances at her, dug in with their hands. Grimacing, Bridget reluctantly did the same and found the slop to be mashed potatoes mixed with bits of what she hoped was fried bacon. Being too salty, she only got so far before her attention returned to the table.

"*Ho di yi du da wi te ra ma?*" asked one of the slaves, a bedraggled woman with frizzy and limp hair, stained and missing teeth, and a crooked nose. "*Ho di yi du da wi te ra ma?*" she repeated, this time accenting the question with a grunt at the end.

The language felt vaguely familiar, but Bridget couldn't place how, and she shook her head. "I do not understand you."

Her reply caused all the slaves to reel back as if struck. They exchanged mystified looks.

The warrior leaned forth to ask Sebastian, "*Ah yi al a ra ma?*" He too accented his question with a grunt.

"I'm sorry, sir, but I do not understand your language," Sebastian mumbled.

His reply had an even greater impact on the slaves. Some wrung their hands and rocked back and forth, while others muttered to each other and made bizarre swirling gestures skyward. Bridget listened keenly and noticed that all their words were monosyllabic. Their tongue sounded simple, and she wondered if that explained the scrolls she had seen back at the house. She also wondered if one or more of these slaves were literate, but had no idea how to ask that.

The scarred warrior she had fought tapped at his chest and grunted at Bridget.

"I do not understand," she said.

He pulled down the front of his coarse linen shirt and grunted questioningly.

"Oh, I think I see what you want. No, I do not have runes on my body," she said, making a show of shaking her head. This did not appease the warrior, who kept tugging his shirt down, a gesture the other slaves soon parroted.

Sighing, Bridget used both hands to pull down the neck of her cotton slave dress just enough for them to see her bare chest bone. "See? Nothing."

The slaves exchanged looks and a slew of monosyllables. The youngest slave, a darkly sun-tanned girl of no more than fourteen and wearing a ratty linen dress, pawed at the air toward Bridget's bowl.

"Would you like some more?" Bridget asked Sebastian, wanting to make sure he ate first.

"No, thank you," he whispered.

Bridget, who had been trying to pay attention to the conversation at the table, idly flicked her hand, and the bowl moved toward the girl. She immediately regretted this decision, for every single slave shrieked and leaped up and jumped about whilst twirl-signing skyward and muttering the words, *"Ga he me!"* over and over.

Gargoyle servants descended upon them with a vengeance. Out of nowhere, whips were uncoiled and cracked, and the poor wretches screamed in agony as they were slapped back to the floor. *"Ga he me!"* they kept shouting, throwing hand spirals even as they rolled about in pain.

"I'm sorry," Bridget said, sitting absolutely still, feeling a deep compassion for these poor souls. "I'm so sorry ..." She sat listening and wincing with each *crack* of the whip, feeling a deep remorse for her casual carelessness, until the slaves had been reduced to whimpering and moaning, yet all continued to twirl hands at the sky whilst mumbling, *"Ga he me."*

It was then that something clicked in her mind. *"Gods help me ... that's* what you're saying, isn't it?" she whispered to herself after the gargoyles had retreated, leaving behind a writhing pile of moaning slaves. "Except you're saying *god*, not *gods*, meaning you worship a single deity." She raised a single finger, asking, "God help me?" Then she twirled that finger about in an echo of their dramatic gestures. *"Ga he me?"* But doing so only confused the poor slaves, who backed away from her uncertainly whilst exchanging whispered monosyllables, some now using both hands to twirl skyward.

"What's wrong with them?" Sebastian whispered.

"They grew up as slaves under a very different people and culture."

"So they're not cavemen?"

"No, they're not cavemen. Just people suffering under wretched circumstances."

Sebastian looked to the bound young man on the table, whose eyes were full of glassy terror as he watched gargoyles idly reach for foods nearby whilst conversing with neighbors. "Are they going to eat him?"

"Of course not. They did that to show their power. It's just a display. Finish your bowl."

"Okay."

After taking time to recover from their beatings, the slaves took to licking their slop. In the hubbub, some of that slop had spilled onto the floor, yet the wretches had no compunction in either scooping it up with a hand or licking it directly off the marble. They did this whilst eyeing her like animals fearful of further violence. Not one dared to touch her half-empty bowl, which sat in the same place Bridget had telekinetically moved it to.

Bridget's attention drifted back to the table, where the gargoyles appeared to still be discussing her. Watching them, she noticed a pattern. One of them would point to her or flick a claw her way, then point or flick a claw toward the distant ocean. It gave her a bad feeling.

Bridget looked at Grak, who stood nearby, at the ready to serve his master and mistress. He sensed her gaze and with his lone eye gave her a solemn look. As subtly as she could, she raised a single finger and made it arch from herself to beyond, all whilst raising a questioning eyebrow at him. But he only looked away, and her question of whether the gargoyles were planning a greater invasion went unanswered.

With her heart fluttering from nerves, Bridget thought to attempt a spell she had been longing to try, a spell she had had no success in thus far—Tongues. *But maybe I now understand enough*, she thought. Even if she got the gist of what they were saying, that would help her immensely with how to deal with the situation …

She thus lined up all the pieces to the puzzle she could about gargoyles—how they spoke, how they intimated, their gesticulations and accents and grunts and assorted verbalizations. Then she pretended to scratch her head, subtly transitioning to pressing three fingers to her temple. At the same time she pretended to wipe her mouth by rubbing it with the back of her sleeve and surreptitiously touched her throat, all whilst quietly incanting into the fabric, "*Translateo commona linguino Gargoyle.*"

She felt the spell trigger at an echo of its usual strength, yet it was enough for her to make out the occasional word, all words she had either learned on her own or Grak had told her. Tongues allowed the mind to make new connections between words that were intuitive. But the horizon of one's learning also limited the spell, and it was that horizon which frustrated Bridget, for out of every ten growled words, she maybe understood one, and it was always out of context. She closed her eyes to further her concentration, lips subtly moving along as she caught certain words.

"Slave ... get ... this ... special ... demonstration ... slaves ... more ..."

"Momma?"

"Compare ... it ... go ... tell ... my ... bring ... them ... far ... go ..."

Shoot, I haven't learned enough, she realized.

"Momma ..."

Bridget felt Sebastian tug on her dress but, desperate to understand, ignored him. Then a few key words struck her like a bell. "Bring ... slaves ... ships ..." Her eyes flew open in time to see a whip slap into her face, sending her rolling backward as pain exploded across her forehead.

She rolled with a wincing grimace, one hand pressed to her forehead and the other raised and flailing about to protect herself against the whippings that rained down upon her. She glimpsed a disfigured gargoyle servant not unlike Grak administering her punishment.

Then the captain shot to his feet and barked at the servant, who halted the beating. He bowed to the captain, stepped back, and growled an explanation, but Bridget's Tongues spell had failed by then so she understood little of it, not that she needed to—she had been caught casting a spell, no doubt because the gargoyle servant had seen her lips moving.

Sebastian went to Bridget, crying, "Are you okay? Momma, say something."

"Shh, it's nothing," she told him, bracing him by the arm and keeping him away from her. "Everything's fine, Sebby. Everything's fine. I'm fine."

"You're bleeding."

"It's just a scratch. I'm a warrior. You understand? Momma's a warrior." Yet she kept her hand pressed firmly against her forehead, knowing it was more than a scratch—it was an open wound in a foreign land.

"Please don't do anything else. *Please* ..."

"I'm not going to do anything. Don't worry."

"No, I mean, please don't do anything to make them do that to you again. Promise me ..."

Bridget sighed, but upon seeing the terror in his eyes, she gave him a pained smile and whispered, "I'll try. I'll try ..."

Meanwhile, Grak endured a barrage of growling questions. He responded simply and factually, indicating Bridget only once.

Bridget didn't care. She now knew what the gargoyles were planning, and it was nothing short of a total invasion of her continent. Yet with that realization came a most profound damnation of herself, for she was partly responsible for that future invasion. The plain truth of it was that the gargoyle race would not have made such plans had she let the damn ship sink.

FATHOMS BEYOND

❧━━━━━━━━━━━━━━━━━━❧

LEERA

Leera stretched, yawned, and raised her arms to capture Sir Pawsalot, who was warming her head, as he so oft did. As the tabby purred at her embrace, she raised a leg and slid it over her beloved, enjoying his quiet snoozing and his nakedness by her side.

The fire in her castle room crackled low, making the far end of the room glow with coziness. A fearsome wind whistled outside the windows, and the red velvet curtains swayed in the drafts. She caught a glimpse of starlight and the edge of a knife moon, which cast shadows across the old floor.

What a cozy night, she thought.

The wind outside increased in strength, and for some reason its sound penetrated the castle and made it sway about.

"Not this again," she muttered, trying to keep hold of Sir Pawsalot, but the cat hissed at the windows and jumped off the bed. Her feet felt Augum slipping away, and she reached over to grab him, but she was too late. He slid off the bed without even making a *thump*.

"Aug?" she said, frightened by the motions, which became ever more violent. Paintings and books began to fall from the walls and shelves, and the hearth snuffed, plunging her into moonlit darkness.

"Augum …?" she asked, but her voice was lost to the roar of the wind. She looked to the vibrating windows and saw that the curtains had been torn away. Her eyes widened, for water sloshed beyond the glass. Suddenly the windows imploded and in roared the ocean, overturning the bed—and sending her flying.

Leera thumped against the floorboards and woke with a start. She shot up and found herself in a small room with six cots. She blinked repeatedly, which helped her remember where she was.

"*Saltfang*," she croaked, watching as water sloshed up against the porthole windows so violently she feared it might punch through like it had back in the castle of her dream. "I'm in the infirmary on *Saltfang* ..."

This dream had been particularly vivid, more so than other nights woken like this. Too many bad dreams, and far too much sweat. She smelled disgusting after having convalesced for so long. All she wanted was to get clean and then be up and about again and useful and chirpy and training and cuddling with Augum. But Jengo had ordered that she continue to rest—and a healer's order was law.

"Except there ain't no law in the middle of the ocean," Leera said in a seaside twang.

With one hand propped against the swaying floor, she used the heel of the other to rub the heavy sleep from each eye, then blearily glanced about.

There was one other person in the ward—a sleeping Mahmoute, who remained on her creaking cot because her blankets were tucked tightly underneath her, cocooning her in place. Only one iron-caged oil lamp, swinging wildly alongside others, remained lit. A few parchments and books slid off a side table, dumping onto the floor. Her spectacles, having sat on a nightstand, now lay on the floor as well.

Leera reached out, telekinetically grabbed hold of the leather thong attached to them, and floated them to her face. Once they were on her nose and the temples curled around her ears and the thong behind her head, she pressed a hand to her chest to feel her heart thundering along. She was chilled from the sweat and a headache pulsed against her skull. A high whistle of wind, one that brought her back to the dream, sang shrilly in the night. The boat rocked about, sometimes pressing her against the floor and then releasing her as it crested a monstrous wave.

"Another storm," she muttered, wondering where her man was. There was a triple flash of light from the portholes, followed by a loud triple *crack* of thunder that shook the ship. "He's on deck, exactly where you should be," she said, hands dancing, urging her body to rise. "Let's go. Move it, girl." Using the cot as leverage, she clambered to her feet, only to be overcome by a dizzy spell so strong she had to sit back down lest she vomit.

"Ye gods," she wheezed, rolling onto the cot to catch her breath. Her mind was ready to move on. Now she just needed her body to catch up. "Where's that gangly beanpole when you need him?" she muttered to herself, wishing Jengo would appear and cast one of his rejuvenation spells to get her moving. "A bath. Start with a bath. You reek, girl."

The ship had one bath, usually reserved for the captain, but he was a fair man and let anyone use it with permission. None of the crew ever dared to ask, but the warlocks were keen on keeping themselves a bit cleaner.

She raised a finger. "To the bath!" Wanting to move, she only grunted. Again the finger rose. "I said, to the bath!" Emitting a troll-like groan, she slithered off the bed and transitioned to crawling along the planks. She got as far as the doorway before splatting to the ground, tongue lolling out, sweat dribbling off her forehead.

"Move it, move it, move it, you bum," she wheezed, trying to motivate herself by channeling her mentor, Jez. Yet she continued to lie there, feeling the swaying motions of the ship, hearing the creaking of planks and distant clanking of tackle, all amidst the whistle of a violently gusting wind.

"Maybe forget the bath," she muttered and dared to haul herself to a standing position. With wobbly knees and using the walls for support, she proceeded to walk unsteadily toward the top deck. The ladders were the hardest and used up so much energy that she flopped onto the floor after each ascent, her body feeling like it had run a league.

There came the creak of a door opening, and a large shadow, backlit by a swinging lantern, filled the passageway.

"What are you doing, lowlander?"

"Nothing special, just resting. You?"

"That is not a place to rest."

"As good as any. Am I in your way?"

"You are a dog with no shame."

"I've been called worse."

The wolven grunted and disappeared back into his cabin.

"Nice chat!" she called after him, adding in a mutter, "Annoying mutt." It was a wonder the crew hadn't thrown him overboard on account of their superstitious natures.

After catching her breath, Leera continued crawling until she found herself feet away from the door that led to the exterior. Its outline lit up with lightning, and it was constantly shuddering, either from the wind or the thunder that rolled through the ship in angry waves.

Not wanting to expend the energy to rise and grab the handle, Leera pointed at it instead and moved her hand downward. The handle turned—and the door blew open, allowing the wind and rain and sea spray to pummel the passage. Leera battled through it, crawling outside and telekinetically closing the door behind herself. The effort had once more exhausted her, and she found herself lying on the deck, staring at a black sky—and a lone lightning-lit palm at the top of the main mast. Other than the warm glow of a single cabin light, everything else was pitch dark.

"I've come to say hello and lend a hand," she wheezed, knowing how ridiculous that sounded on account of her condition. Not to mention she might as well have been whispering into a maelstrom, for the wind stole her words and tossed them into the hungry night.

"You look so alone and so far away, my love," she whispered, watching his hand wave about. His entire body lit up as a thick bolt of lightning connected him to the sky. That bolt bent from his body—and smashed into a nearby wave. The *crack* of thunder was so loud that Leera slapped her hands over her ears and recoiled. Even with closed eyes she saw the lightning in vivid afterglow.

She looked back up to the top of the mast—and found it dark. Heart jamming into her throat, she sat up, ready to call to her betrothed, only for the palm to flutter back to life.

"Gods, how does he do it?" she asked the wind, slumping back down to the deck, wincing against the sea spray and rain.

She stayed there watching her beloved ride the mast as if attempting to tame a wild horse. Luckily the rain soon stopped, and the sky began to lighten in readiness for the coming dawn. The clouds hung low and heavy and turbulent, but Augum clung on. Only when the lightning had ceased for half an hour did he start to clamber back down. Wanting to surprise him, Leera crawled to hide behind a stack of crates.

When he had descended to five feet above the deck, he jumped clear of the mast—and landed beside the crate, back turned to her. Leera rose up, grabbed his waist, and shouted, "Gotcha!"

Augum yelped, spun about—and zapped her with a lit palm, causing her to yelp as well. Unaccustomed to such a strong shock and having exhausted herself by simply standing, she turned into a noodle and flopped back onto the planks.

"Lee—!" he shouted, dropping to his knees and taking hold of her. "Can't *believe* you did that! Scared the poop out of me!"

"Surpriiiise," she sang, flashing him a tired but cheeky smile.

"Gods, I could have seriously hurt you! What are you *doing* out here, anyway? Do you realize how easily you could have been washed overboard? And then what? Huh?" He gave her an annoyed shake.

She shrugged, wheezing, "Er … I didn't think that far."

"Jengo gave strict instructions. You should be resting, my love."

"Bah, I'll only wither if you force me to keep to that cursed cot." Her weak hands caressed the torn strips of his robe. "Besides, I wanted to see my man, maybe help out. And oof, you look like you've been squeezed through a cheese grater. *Apreyo*," she added, mending some of the unburnt strips before he gently batted her hands away, snuffing the repair work.

"Unbelievable. You're as weak as a kitten and you thought coming out here was a good idea?"

"Wanted to get a sea bath. I, uh, I kind of stink."

"Quest accomplished. You're soaked."

"Better to stink of salt than convalescence."

"I don't care how you smell. You know that."

"Aww …" She pawed at him as she cooed, "You love me."

"Of *course* I love you, but I'm so mad at you right now."

"Then why are you smiling?"

"Because my fool mouth can't help but smile at your antics. You're such a … ugh! Come here. I'm taking you back down."

"My knight savior," she sang as he scooped one arm underneath her knees and the other around her shoulders, lifting her up. "But I really am feeling better, so you needn't jail me," she added, which only elicited a scoff from her beloved.

Fog rolled over the deck as *Saltfang* passed through a particularly low-hanging cloud.

"There she is again!" a lookout called from the bow. "Dead ahead! Someone fetch the cap and the spyglass!"

"Shoot, hold on," Augum said, and put her back down on the deck before running inside.

Leera, curious about what they were referring to, crawled to the high edge of the ship's tilt, where she dragged herself up the railing. About a league ahead, amidst swirling clouds so low they played with the tops of waves, she spotted a ship.

"Way out here?" she asked the wind. "Maybe they're lost …"

Augum soon returned with the captain, bosun, and a slew of puffy-eyed crew, including Tammy the sailblower. But instead of following them all to the bow, Augum came to Leera. "Come on. Let's get you back to bed."

"Not a chance, mister. I'm sick of being an invalid. This girl longs for fresh air and adventure. Take me to the bow. I want to see what all the fuss is about."

Augum sighed but relented in helping her move. "We first spotted her late last night before the storm took us," he explained, holding onto her as she used the railing for support. "She was behind us by a league or so. Now it seems she's ahead by that much."

"See any more of those towers you told me about?" Leera pressed, annoyed she'd missed out on such a glorious find.

"Nothing."

"No other islands either?"

He shook his head. "Not even a bird to give us a hint."

They got to the bow, where the captain was peering through a spyglass. "Me eyes ain't as sharp as they used to be," he said, handing his spyglass to his bosun. "But she's a whaler, all right."

"Same class as ours," the bosun said, walrus mustache twitching.

By the time Augum got his turn at the spyglass, the ship had vanished into the cloud curtain, and he returned the spyglass to the captain. "Strange spot on the ocean," he said as an aside to Leera.

"What do you mean?"

"Last night we sailed through this same sort of pocket of emptiness between low-hanging clouds."

Leera looked to the horizon. Sure enough, swirling clouds encircled their patch of ocean.

The captain lit his pipe as he searched the distant cloud bank. "Prep for comms if we see her again."

"I'll have the flags ready, sir," the bosun replied and went to give a deckhand instructions. That deckhand raced to a barrel, opened its lid, picked out a bundle of wrapped flags, closed the lid, and raced up the forward mast. He secured the flags to the top lookout and waited.

"Shall I take my lady below?" Augum asked as the crew dispersed. "Or perhaps fetch us breakfast?"

"M'lord is welcome to do the latter. M'lord can then keep his lady company on deck, as the fresh air pleases her."

Augum gave a courtly bow. "As m'lady wishes."

Leera snorted. "Eww, next thing we know we're powdering our faces and putting on airs."

"I shall start practicing holding a porcelain teacup with a raised pinky."

"Double eww."

They horsed around with jests before Augum went to fetch them a breakfast of bacon, eggs, roasted peppers, and bread slathered with strawberry jam. They settled onto a seat by the forward mast, where they ate to their heart's content whilst conversing idly. Leera then watched Augum perform a morning cycle, protecting their now empty plates in her lap. And she wasn't the only one—the crew watched him like curious children, with the more superstitious signing skyward after every casting and muttering a prayer of protection. Within the hour, others began emerging from below, including Jengo, who went straight to Leera to deliver her a version of the same lecture Augum had.

Leera rolled her eyes. "Spare me, Almoner Okeke—*Healer* Okeke, in this context. Fresh air never killed a girl before."

"No, but arrogance has," Jengo muttered, leaving her to sit with his back against a stack of crates, where he could keep one eye on a thick healing book and the other on her.

Feeling bad for not following his advice, she nodded at the book. "Which one today?"

"Regeneration, which has been causing me trouble."

"Is it higher in degree or something?"

"It's only 9th, but it's got lots of hidden arcaneological complexities."

"More than the 10th degree Reinvigorate?"

"In many respects, yes, but—" He narrowed his eyes at her. "Just ask."

"Just ask what?"

Jengo snapped his book shut and folded his arms expectantly. "Don't play dumb."

"Damn it, you're too smart for my clumsy charms." Leera sighed heavily. "May I receive a casting of Reinvigorate?"

An unimpressed Jengo kept his arms folded.

"Fine. *Fine!* Brilliant Healer Okeke, can I please utilize that massive brain of yours—so massive it can barely fit through the cabin doorways—and benefit from the unfathomably complex Reinvigorate spell which you went out of your way to learn in your spare time, especially seeing as it's 10th degree and—"

"Oh, shut up already," Jengo said and dragged himself close.

She did a little victory dance with her shoulders.

"Stop dancing. Be mindful of your energy."

"Yes, Dad."

"On second thought, I changed my mind—"

"No, wait! I'm sorry, I'll stop, I promise. Please, I'm tired of reeking and I'm especially tired of *being* tired. Just one top-up is all I need so I can do something normal for a change." She nudged the plates in her lap. "I already stuffed my gullet too." She put her hands together, whining, "Pleeeeease, Jengoooooooo ... heeeeeelp meeeeeeee ..."

Jengo looked to Augum, who had just finished casting the entire 7th degree. The latter smiled with a shake of the head before continuing on to the 8th.

"Fine, but you're aware that the spell—"

"—has diminishing returns, yes, yes. I just don't want to feel like jelly anymore. I'll be good after this, promise. I feel strong now." She flexed her right arm and flashed a pandering grin, then said in caveman voice, "Me strong. Strong girl. Woof. Wait, not woof. Roar. Yeah, roar."

Jengo's lips thinned at her display.

"Gods don't make me keep begging because I will if I have to …"

"Fine, but only because I'm sick of your bleating."

Leera threw her arms up and wiggled her fingers, singing, "Yaaaaaay!"

"Unnameables, will you stop already. And lie down."

"Yes, sir, sorry, sir, of course, sir." She saluted in the military fashion, jammed the plates between two crates, and lay down, smiling toothily.

Jengo sighed, but he went ahead and pressed his thumb and index and middle fingers together and rolled the hand along as he worked through the complex thought process that came with the 10th degree spell.

"Lie still," he finally commanded before incanting, "*Rinvara rexo inductio boda balan sustana*," all while making a series of motions, some of which seemed to draw energy from her body, while others seemed to push that energy back in, with the latter motions outweighing the former. He finished by pressing both hands gently against her tummy.

Leera, her soul and stomach and physical energies replenished, sighed happily.

Jengo gave her shoulder a shove. "You stink and need a bath."

"That bad, huh? I don't suppose you have a miracle bathing spell, then. Ideally one that makes the hair all shiny and smell nice too. Maybe even combs it."

"Don't make me roll my eyes at you," Jengo replied, moving back to his spot and opening his healing book.

Leera, feeling totally reinvigorated, jumped to her feet. When the dizziness failed to knock her back down, she threw her arms up, shouting, "Yessssssssss!" only to promptly smooth her robe when the crew gave her strange looks. "Er, thank you very much, Healer Okeke. If it wasn't for your giant brain, dullards like me would wither and die screeching, pathetic deaths of utter despair and—"

Jengo cut her off by making a brushing motion with a hand. "Just go and … do whatever it is you need to do already and stop pestering me with inanities."

"Sir, yes, sir. Thank you, sir." She pressed three fingers over her heart, giving the Arcaner salute, and threw in a bow, whispering, "Seriously, thank you, Healer Okeke." Then she twirled about and opened both arms at Augum, singing, "Ta-da!"

"Yes, very nice," Augum said with a shake of the head and a smile.

The arms fell to her side. "Does no one appreciate that my obnoxiousness stems from being cooped up in bed for a lifetime?"

Augum grabbed her lapel, yanked her close, smacked her lips with a sloppy kiss, and shoved her back. "I'm starting the 9th. Going to join or keep dancing about like a jester?"

"Don't patronize me," she muttered, fixing her lapel. "And I'll start at the beginning, thank you very much." Annoyed that her antics hadn't drawn witty repartee desperately needed after such a long convalescence, she schlepped off to the stern, where she had more space to think. Then she began a spell cycle by splaying a hand and incanting, "*Shyneo*," lighting up her hand with water. Next she flicked at a mop that a deckhand had been using to wash the deck, floated it from its bucket, grabbed it, and snapped the handle in half over her knee.

"Oi!" shouted that very deckhand, having returned from below eating an apple. "What are you doing, lass?"

"Practicing." Leera dumped the two ends of the mop onto the planks, splayed her hands over them, and incanted, "*Apreyo*." When the handle was made whole again with a sealing light, the deckhand signed skyward, muttering, "Gods protect me from these witches."

Leera tossed the mop back at him. He caught it and promptly shoved it back into the bucket before vigorously wiping his hand on his trousers.

"It's not hexed," she said.

"How do I know?" he muttered, sticking the apple in his mouth and holding it there while he walked off to coil a loose line, keeping a wary eye on her throughout.

Leera wanted to mock signing skyward, but didn't want to tempt the gods, let alone get condemned as a real witch by such a superstitious lot.

She moved on to Unconceal but didn't bother tracking down its various tugs as she was in no mood to find hidden empty whisky bottles or lewd scrolls or other such rubbish. Instead she transitioned to summoning her shield and shoving at an imaginary opponent before disarming said opponent, then making a violent throwing-at-the-planks motion whilst roaring, "*Grau!*" taking satisfaction from hearing the crew yelp from the roar of falling water, with the same deckhand shouting, "Rogue wave!" only to redden with embarrassment when she explained the Slam spell to him.

Onward she cycled, degree after degree. Mercifully the weather died down, allowing for better concentration. Whilst the ship entered the cloud bank and Leera was preparing to cast the 5th degree Darkness, which would summon a black cloud behind the ship, she spotted something in the distance, emerging from another ocean-hanging cloud bank.

"Ship off the stern!" she shouted over her shoulder, a call that was promptly echoed up and down the ship, causing crew and warlocks alike to hurry toward the stern.

Leera, meanwhile, noticed that the sister ship was the same one she had spotted earlier that morn, albeit this time it was behind them. "No way could we have gotten ahead of it in such a short time," she muttered.

The others exchanged the same speculations as before, adding that there might be a fleet of whalers from a rival kingdom about. To Leera, something felt off, and as their ship entered the cloud, she raced to the front of the ship. The bow broke through the cloud wall, and sure enough, there in the distance, she saw the back of that same whaler.

"Ship out front!" she shouted over her shoulder. Instead of waiting to tell them, she thought to test her theory and vividly imagined standing on the planks at the rear of that very ship. Then she snapped off, "*Impetus peragro.*" She vanished and reappeared with a *thwomp* on its stern — and saw deck crew and her friends rushing toward the bow.

"Gods," she said to herself, slapping her forehead. "It's us!" she shouted after them, trying to suppress the laughter from the comical circumstance they found themselves in. "The ship is *us*!"

A few people glanced back at her uncertainly, and judging by everyone else's serious expression, she suspected it hadn't quite sunk in.

"We're the ship we're looking at," she said upon everyone joining her in the stern. "Look, it even has the same signal flags."

"That's because it's trying to communicate with us, you dolt," Digby said. The commotion had drawn people from below, including the Bloomington-Southguards and the two boys, Limpet and Dirt, as well as Leo the Leopard, who strolled about jesting with the crew as if they'd been shipmates for years.

"It's the healing coma," his brother Teague said. "Made spaghetti of her noodle, if you know what I mean."

"You best hope she's wrong, lad," Leo said, hands deep in his pockets as he sniffed a guide rope. "Right proper amount of oil on this one, but a couple o' the others could do with a rub."

"Look, I can easily prove it," Leera said, even though the ship had already vanished behind their cloud curtain wall. "Next time we approach the cloud bank, I'll stand here at the stern and wave at the other ship. Anyone on the bow will be able to see me waving."

"What are you suggesting? That we're stuck in a loop?" Jez asked, searching her eyes with a serious gaze.

Leera's reply was to open her hands and throw them a *Well, what else could it be?* look. "We all heard the sea stories of strange anomalies," she went on. "It's the only thing that makes sense. Look at the clouds, the way they form a rough circle around us. It just happens to be a league wide, making it hard to discern from sea level. We're stuck in a trap or loop or whatever. Maybe it has something to do with that mysterious tower I missed adventuring out on."

Augum idly scratched his stubble. "Could be the energy vortex at the top of that tower …"

"You're not seriously taking an invalid's word on this, are you?" Digby snapped. "She's delusional and you're supporting her delusions because she's your woman."

"We can prove it in an hour," Leera snapped back, stalling Augum from blowing up. "And I'll have you know I am fully—"

"We can prove it now," the captain interrupted, turning to the bosun. "One-eighty on the needle."

The bosun flicked at his tilted cap and turned to the helmsman. "Hard to port, about face one-eighty-degree turn on the lodestone."

"One-eighty on the lodestone, aye, aye, sir," the helmsman replied and rolled the large ship's wheel all the way to port, one eye on the low-hanging cloud wall they had passed through, the other on the enclosed lodestone. *Saltfang* groaned as she slowly pivoted.

"Now some of us will stay here and wave, and the rest of you go to the bow and watch us wave at you through the spyglass." She shooed them off with her hands. "Go, go, go, hurry or you'll miss it!"

Slightly more than half raced off, with Augum leading the charge. Among those who lingered were the two kids, both of whom gawked at her.

"What?" Leera snapped at Limpet.

"Have you been drinking?"

She gaped at him.

"'Cause you're weaving and stuff," Limpet said. "Anyway I wanted to tell on you that you haven't been training me awesome spells I want to learn but I haven't been able to reach my old mentor since that stupid tower."

"Aww, did your little plan to tattle-tale and whine fail to work out? Too bad so sad," Leera sang, not surprised in the least that the ring hadn't been able to breach the arcane interference of that mysterious tower.

"She stinks like butt," Dirt said, and the pair cackled.

Leera reached out to them with both arms, singing, "Overboard you go—"

The kids yelped and shot off, which gave her a small chuckle. Then she sighed, turned about, and started waving. Sure enough, the moment the bow of the ship penetrated the cloud wall, a ship's bow appeared a league away.

"What are you lowlanders doing?" Rogor asked, being the latest arrival on the deck.

"Waving to ourselves, what's it look like?" Leera replied, swinging both arms over her head.

Rogor looked so flummoxed by her response that he said nothing, which made her turn away from him lest he see her suppressed smile. There was something ridiculous about all this, and her way of dealing with that ridiculousness was through humor. But that smile was yanked from her face by a single remark from none other than Alanna, who had remained in the stern.

"We might be trapped here forever," she noted.

"Not forever," Leo corrected, sidling up to Jez and playfully pushing her sideways with his shoulder, causing her to give him a look that was a mix of disbelief and amusement. "Only until we run out of freshies and the scurvy takes root. About a couple o' months, I reckon. Maybe three if we get creative. But probably two." He nodded a gold-toothed smile before shuffling off to inspect the lashing of a stack of barrels, leaving Jez mystified.

Leera dropped her arms. This time, no witty remark came, and she instead looked back to the ship, but by then they had passed through the cloud wall once more.

"The question is ... why?" Alanna pressed. "Why craft something of this magnitude and complexity? And who had the knowledge to do so?"

"Someone who wanted to prevent the continents from communicating," Leera replied, adding, "Or from being invaded ..."

The women exchanged dark looks. A people in the ancient past might have crafted these enchantments after experiencing something terrible. Either that, or it was a form of control. The more Leera thought about it, the more questions she had.

People soon trickled in from the bow, including Augum and Jengo.

"We indeed saw you waving," Augum said, returning the spyglass to the captain.

"You were right," Jengo threw in.

"Whoa, whoa, whoa, hold on, let me just hear that again." Leera cupped her ear with a hand and leaned awfully close to Jengo, only to receive a friendly shove in the shoulder.

"Don't push it, missy," Jengo said.

"Maybe something is activating it," Alanna offered, shielding her eyes from the sun that had peeked through a break in the clouds.

Everyone did the same, searching the ocean, but other than the surrounding cloud wall and the rolling waves, the intemperate ocean was featureless, with no hint of land.

The sun vanished behind the clouds, casting a pall over the area. As the others mingled in small groups to discuss the problem, and the possibility that they might be trapped forever, Leera's gaze went to the ocean. She splayed a hand and incanted, "*Un vun asperio aurum enchantus.*"

Sure enough, a massive tendril web appeared. It was so old that only a hint of its blueness remained. It covered the entire area, its tendrils floating just above the ocean. But unlike the ocean, these tendrils did not move with the waves, and instead sat like a floating circular blanket, albeit one with wide tendril symmetries. Those symmetries also pointed in one direction—down.

"It's underwater."

"What is?" Alanna asked, noticing what Leera was doing. "Did you cast Reveal?"

Leera turned and shouted, "It's underwater!"

Everyone looked to her.

"Those who can cast Reveal can see for themselves," she said.

Warlocks hurried to the railing and cast Reveal.

Jez was the first to look back at Leera. "We're going to have to dive," she said.

Leera nodded. "Yes, we are."

"Absolutely not," Augum said, slicing both hands horizontally. "She just convalesced and will be too weak."

"I'm fine. I ate, I'll eat some more, and this one topped me up." She thumbed at Jengo.

"She would have to be careful," Jengo said after a think.

"See? I'll be careful, now stop worrying," and Leera planted a quick kiss on Augum's lips and before he could keep arguing the point hurried away to a different spot by the railing.

Alanna and Jez joined her, as did Tammy the sailblower, and the four women looked out on the vast expanse. A whole league of water to cover was no jest.

Tammy leaned over to stare into the depths. "Merciful heavens, I'm glad I'm not a water warlock."

"Same here," Alanna threw in, holding herself. "I don't envy you two."

"Might take days," Leera muttered.

Jez scoffed. "Try a month."

Leo, who had splayed his hand over the railing to examine the tendrils, drifted near. But instead of weighing in, he scratched a tattooed portion of his bald scalp, glanced over at Jez, grimaced, and walked off.

"Odd duckling, that one," Jez said, watching him go.

"I think that was his way of worrying about us," Leera added.

The captain joined the four women. "Any suggestions where to start, lasses?" he asked, gumming his pipe.

"The most obvious spot first," Jez said, nodding into the interior of the wide circle. "The center of the entire clearing."

The captain looked to the bosun, who was always within hearing range, and said, "Get 'er ready."

The bosun clicked his heels and turned to the helmsman. "Due east, steady as she goes." He then cupped a hand around his mouth and shouted to the crew, "Top down, take in all but the forecourse, mainsail, and the spanker, lads!"

Olaf lumbered onto deck from the cabins. "What's going on?" he croaked, rubbing an eye with a fist, hair disheveled as if he'd just woken up.

"Not much," Leera replied, "except we might have sailed into a trap and could be stuck here forever."

Olaf snorted. "Very funny." He flicked his chin at Jez. "Are you training me today or the sailblower or the dragons or all of us at once?"

Jengo, who happened to have caught their conversation, draped an arm around Olaf's shoulders. "I think we better let the women strategize."

"What's going on? Why's everyone on deck, anyway?"

"I'll explain everything ..." Jengo replied, walking Olaf away until Olaf cried out, "Gods, I *knew* something like this would happen! I'm never going to see Bridget again, am I?"

As Jengo consoled him and the ship sailed onward and the speed slowed with each newly furled sail, Jez nudged Leera with an elbow. "You sure you're feeling up to this, monkey?"

"I'd rather drown than get back on that filthy cot. Need the salt bath too."

"We ought to dive together, watch each other's backs. Who knows what's down there. But let's grab some grub first. Don't want to dive on an empty stomach. They'll need time to stabilize the ship anyway in these winds. Let me just have a word with the captain first."

Jez went on to instruct the captain to measure the depth with a line, mark out the depths in five-hundred-foot increments, and throw the line back down. Leera and Jez then went below deck, where they fetched themselves a hot meal at the galley and strategized on how to make the dive. By the time they returned to the deck, the ship's sails had been furled and the sea anchor, composed of giant buckets made of fabric that dragged underwater, deployed.

The captain greeted them by removing his pipe from his mouth. "She's ready for you, lasses. Depth line maxed out, so we tied a second line, painted with increments, as you requested." The captain hesitated.

Jez flipped a hand. "So what's the count already?"

"Five hundred and thirty fathoms deep."

"What's that in feet?"

"Around three thousand two hundred."

Jez and Leera looked at each other.

"Ever swim that deep?" Leera asked.

Jez shook her head. "Bottomed out at three thousand. That was when I was a young and spritely monkey like you and could sustain the pressure."

"And since?"

"About two thousand prior to the war. Got to work that muscle to dive that deep."

"What do you mean?" Limpet asked loudly.

Leera was about to snap at him not to be rude when Jez answered, "It means if either of us for whatever reason loses our concentration at that depth and our Endure the Deep spell fails ..." She smacked her hands together. "... we're fish paste."

"Implosion," Leera clarified for the wide-eyed among them. "The body collapses in on itself on account of the pressure."

"I don't understand," Dirt said.

As Jez continued to explain the complex dynamics of arcane deep-sea diving to the enraptured throng, Augum gently took Leera aside by the elbow.

"My love—"

"I already know what you're going to say," she interrupted. "I'll be *extremely* careful."

"I'd rather you not go at all," he whispered.

"What, and leave Jez to perform the quest solo?"

"I realize I'm being selfish, but you're still weak from your ordeal with overdraw and I'm just …"

"I know." She squeezed his hand. "I know you're scared for me, but I feel good, all things considered. I had loads to eat and strategized with Jez. Don't worry, I'll be *extremely* careful."

"Promise?"

"Promise."

"It's going to be dark down there."

"Dark I can handle. Pressure, though …"

Her betrothed gulped before whispering, "What's the deepest you've dived?"

"Not *that* deep." Not even close, but he needn't know that. No sense worrying him more than his face already showed. She smiled, patted him on the chest, and pecked him on the lips. "Now you know how I felt whenever you used to go on your solo jaunts."

He gave a tepid smile and drew her to him, whispering, "I love you."

"And I love *you*," she whispered back, squeezing his waist.

"Stop snogging and hold this," Jez said, thrusting a hefty lead fishing weight the size of a small boulder between the pair of them.

"What the heck's this?" Leera asked, letting go of Augum to grab it — only to have to stop herself from falling over by leaning back with the weight.

"Our ticket to the bottom. Now listen. This part's important. What are you gawking at? Stop listening in. This ain't for your ears." She pressed a hand to Augum's chest and shoved him off.

Leera implored him to be patient by flaring her eyes and smiling, but Augum lingered nearby like a nervous husband about to watch his wife go into surgery.

Satisfied no one else could hear them, Jez leaned in to whisper, "If at any time you think that your protective spells will fail, don't waffle on it, just 'port on back to the ship."

"Of course," Leera replied.

Jez stabbed Leera's shoulder with a finger. "Hey, this ain't a jest, kiddo. This ain't even a training run. This is the real deal. The pressure down there will test your limits. Maybe surpass them. If it does, you'll have less than a heartbeat—no, less than an eyeblink—before implosion. So you need to sense it coming *before* it happens. Do you get me?"

Leera nodded quickly. "I get you."

"It'll be a long plummet, so we'll need to conserve energy. I'll keep my light on as my stamina reservoir is larger than yours. Keep the line between us at all times." Jez turned to look at the crowd, most of whom were speaking in low voices, while the remainder watched them with worried eyes. "Hey, you people there—clear a space between the masts for us in case we need to 'port back in a hurry." When they did as commanded, she turned her attention back to Leera. "Once we hit the bottom—*if* we get that far, that is—I'll keep my hand lit, we'll assess, maybe cast Speed of the Dolphin if we need to explore. Got all that?"

"Got it."

"You sure? Wouldn't rather go below to keep snogging?"

Leera, feeling her cheeks prickle with redness, adjusted her grip on the lead weight. "I'm sure."

"Don't need more rest?"

"Jengo topped me up and my belly's full. I'm good to go."

"All right. Let's prep."

As the roiling clouds lingered dark and heavy, threatening rain, and wind whistled through the lines and made the ship creak as it bobbed over long rolling waves, the two women began their dive preparations, which notably did not include stripping down to their undergarments, as both wanted to preserve their dignity before the gawking crew—that and Jez said the clothing would slow their rate of descent.

The crew and passengers looked on with unease, including the two boys, Limpet and Dirt. Even the towering Rogor, who preferred to spend his time below deck, was present and watching from the rear, where people gave him plenty of space. Nobody said a word as the women cast Breathe Water and Endure the Deep, but many waved to them and wished them good luck as they stepped up onto the railing, holding their fishing weights.

Leera, having slipped her spectacles into an inner pocket of her robe, looked back at a blurry Augum—and forced a smile. He blew her a kiss, mouthed, "*Good luck,*" and pressed a hand to his heart.

Unable to do the same, she mouthed, "I love you," and after exchanging a nodding look with Jez, stepped off the railing. The pair plunged into the cold water on either side of the depth line and began to plummet. The speed surprised Leera, a speed that steadily increased, until she and Jez reached what was in water warlock arithmetic known as the drag coefficient—wherein the clothing they were wearing reached a balance between the pull of gravity and the drag of the water. Because her arms were busy gripping the weight, she had to use her legs to keep near the line, a surprisingly difficult challenge as the speed of the fall demanded precise movements.

She looked up to see the outline of the ship rapidly shrinking and wondered if she'd ever see it again, for as brave a face as she had put on, she knew this was the riskiest thing she had ever attempted in the water.

They sank facing each other about five feet apart, with the line in between, each looking over the other's shoulder, sometimes meeting gazes, sharing silent resolve as they held tightly onto their weights. The darkness steadily deepened, yet the diffused light from above was still visible. Jez waited for that final light to die out before flaring her hand, surrounding them in a pale blue halo of light.

They soon passed the first marker, painted as a white band on the rope.

"*Five hundred,*" Jez mouthed. Even at that relatively shallow depth, only a faint blush of light remained.

Leera felt the usual tension of the depths pressing inward, but she was still quite comfortable. They passed neither fish nor critter, not even silt. On the way to a thousand feet, they slipped into darkness and saw their first jellyfish, an amorphous blob that pulsed with weak light, its edges frilly. Both watched it approach from below and silently swish by as if they were riding a mining elevator into the abyss, a tiny star in the night, vanishing above soon after. The next stop was the thousand-foot marker, which they acknowledged by nodding at each other that they were present and understood the implications.

"All okay?" Jez mouthed.

Leera, wanting to preserve as much energy as she could, merely gave a nod whilst gripping the weight. The cold steadily increased, and although it did not affect her, she used it as a secondary measure of descent—and a way to stay alert. The pressure built with each fathom, until she felt like someone was pushing against her from all sides.

With neither woman saying a word, Leera felt encased in her own thoughts. She felt so far away from the ship and from their kingdom and the academy and the order and especially Castle Arinthian. She wondered how the others were faring back home. Her friends, her apprentice, Revel, her new servant, Gertrude, and Sir Pawsalot. She hoped all were getting along and in good health, and sent them a wish of wellness from the unfathomable depths, one that made her wonder if they had abruptly perked up and thought of her in that very moment.

I'm thinking of you, she thought, smiling a small and bittersweet smile. *And I miss you all …*

As they passed fifteen hundred feet, the black depths deepened to a void that reminded her of her recent overdraw sickness, and she had to keep that feeling of unwellness from penetrating her soul. Perhaps drawn by that inky void, a certain predator peeked out from behind the curtain of her mind, but she remembered Isobel and took hold of that curtain and gently drew it over the dark eyes of the thing that wanted only advantage and suffering. Her idle mind sought comfort in distraction by thinking of better times, or walking the sacred halls of the academy, or simply lounging by the fire reading an absorbing book, but she corralled that too, knowing she needed to focus and pay attention to her limits.

At two thousand feet the pressure became so great that Leera had to work hard just to breathe in the water, and she distracted herself by constantly readjusting the weight. Jez too looked like she was struggling, her face tense and a shade darker. When her eyes began to bulge, Leera felt a fear she had never quite experienced before—the fear of seeing someone she loved pushing herself past the point of danger. She felt her own eyes bulging as well, but Jez was handling it differently.

Then it occurred to Leera what the problem was. Jez was a heavy drinker, and learned arcaneologists who were also water warlocks theorized that drinking did something to the body that changed how it handled the depths, at least when it came to Endure the Deep. Yet she knew Jez's pride wouldn't let her go, not without permission. That was why Leera forced a smile, gave a nod, and mouthed, "It's okay. Go. I'll be all right."

Jez jerked her head, indicating she would not leave, yet her face was starting to expand, which told Leera her Endure the Deep spell would fail at any moment. How Leera reacted in the next few heartbeats would mean the difference between life and death for Jez, and so she firmed her lips, raised her chin, and gave a single nod whilst firmly mouthing, "Go. I got this," then repeated, "I *got this.*"

Jez swallowed, her eyebrows pitching up with sorrow, before she surrendered a nod. She looked up into the darkness and incanted, "*Impetus peragro!*" vanishing with an implosive *thwomp* that sent Leera tumbling away, her last glimpse being of Jez's fishing weight as it plummeted.

"*Shyneo!*" she incanted after barely keeping hold of her lead weight and righting herself from the tumble, but the circle of light around her showed no rope. She searched about, frantic, yet couldn't for the life of her find the rope, not even after brightening her palm—the teleport implosion, and its subsequent shockwave, had been that powerful at this depth.

Leera looked down into the darkness and fought the panic—and, for the first time ever underwater, a sense of vertigo. The dizziness was so strong it threatened to overcome her confidence, which would in turn lead to a loss of concentration—and spell failure.

"No," she said into the void, using up precious energy. "I shall not relent. I shall not falter. I. Shall. Not. Fail." Having given her feeble mind its marching orders, she resolutely shut down any stray thought. She slammed the door shut on the girl who liked to jest and play and roughhouse. The girl who liked to idle and kick her feet up and frolic. The girl who liked to reminisce. Remaining was a coldly rational woman aware of the danger she had willingly put herself into. Subsequently the vertigo retreated like a vanquished enemy.

Twenty-five hundred, Leera estimated, feeling a pressure on her body she had never before experienced. It was so great that breathing the icy water felt like pushing iron in and out. Yet her strong lungs held on, and she continued to plummet deep into the abyss.

Time passed as it had when she was sick. And like when she was sick, she paid it no heed, minding only that which needed minding—her arcane soul. In some ways, she felt like she was undertaking a *nemana*, the Henawa word for a spiritual quest, usually signifying one's ascent to adulthood.

The voice of a kid broke into her mind. "Your weird mentor told me to tell you she's all right, and that you are doing well." Leera smiled as she heard a panting Jez urging the kid to say more in the background. "She also said not to talk unless you absolutely have to. Anyway, uh, good luck, I guess. What? I told her already! Oh, right, cease contact."

Despite it coming from the annoying kid, hearing Limpet's voice in the depths bolstered Leera's spirits. That warmth, brought on by such simple words, kept her sane until, just like that, a sandy bottom appeared. Vast and yellow and smooth, it loomed below like the floor of the entire world.

She let go of the weight just before reaching that bottom. The lead smacked into the sand, sending a cloudy plume in all directions. Among that plume, Leera's bare feet pressed gently into the sand.

She raised the water ring to her lips and said, "Contact Jeremy Jenkins. I'm on the bottom." Limpet promptly shouted her words to others, and upon hearing a round of background cheers, she added, "Now off to explore. Cease contact."

First she checked in on her stamina pool. *Half down. Not too bad, all things considered*, she thought. She'd done a good job conserving. Now it was time to utilize some of it in a meaningful manner, however, and so she steadily brightened her palm to its maximum, a bright lamp amidst an infinite void. It lit up the surrounding sand in all directions for a staggering hundred feet, for the water down here was crystal clear. Tiny paths revealed themselves, likely belonging to crustaceans. Littered sparsely about were small mounds of coral, interspersed with the occasional clump of seaweed. Fifty feet away, a school of colorful fish turned away from her light and slowly swam off.

At the very edge of that light, a fishing weight sat twenty feet away from a coil of rope, the end of which was tied around an identical lead fishing weight. That rope bounced up and down in long wavelike rhythms whilst leaving behind a steady drag line in the sand.

Leera looked up, picturing the ship bobbing three thousand two hundred feet above on the surface, its sea anchors keeping it to an idle drift. Then she glanced about, reminding herself to stay alert, but no monster showed its face.

Hopefully the light won't attract one, she thought, splaying her hand open. After a concentrative pause, she incanted, "*Un vun asperio aurum enchantus.*" Sure enough, the same tendril web as above appeared below, this time resting gently on the sand. It was flat, ignoring the coral outcrops, and the tendrils were spread well apart and thick enough that their complex layering reached the top of her ankle.

Leera, taking advantage of the steadiness of being on solid ground, crouched to inspect the pale tendril weaving—and was surprised to discover tiny knots in between the occasional junction, a most peculiar thing to find on a tendril tapestry.

Almost like a fisherman's net, she thought.

It was so far beyond her experience that it felt like staring at an entirely different language of the arcane arts. The closest style she'd seen was ancient enchantments on constructs attributed to the Rivicans—but those enchantments were never fully confirmed as belonging to the Rivicans as the race was driven to extinction around 3700 Pre Founding—over seven thousand years ago.

Maybe a different ancient people crafted these, she thought, rising to her feet to look about and see the tendril web as a whole. It was almost unfathomable to picture such a web stretching for an entire league, telling her a team of water warlocks working together in harmony must have crafted it. Except the workmanship looked too uniform, too identical. Was it the work of a higher being, perhaps?

"A god? Is that what you're saying, Leera?" she muttered aloud, chortling at her own musings.

Then she froze, for a shadow rose from behind her thoughts, wanting to open the curtain to her mind. The question begged itself—what if a dragon-like being had cast this web? The tendrils, after all, were as thick as dragon-cast tendrils, like those she had seen in the plane of Endraga Ra, the home of dragons and where she and Augum and Bridget had learned to cast the mythic Spirit of the Dragon simul.

That question begged another—had such beings existed in an unknown era, prior to the written word? Was history far older than people presumed, spanning beyond The Age of Primitives and The Age of Beasts?

Something fishy here, that's for sure, she thought, choosing to avoid speaking the words aloud as it was hard enough to breathe the heavy water as it was.

A little spooked by the echo of primordial history, she glanced around again—and almost jumped out of her skin, for a shark was floating a mere ten feet behind, studying her.

"Shouldn't sneak up on a girl like that," she wheezed, pressing a hand to her chest.

The shark, having been noticed, swam to the side as slowly as a snail, keeping one eye on her as it circled, as if curious what sort of being she was. The species was of a type she had never seen before. Its skin had a red tint, or so she thought in her cool watery light, and looked primitive in its contouring—but then she was hardly an expert on the subject of sharks.

"Maybe you can be my guide," she said to it and cocked her head, wondering if a shark counted as a fish for the 4th degree off-the-books Commune with Fish spell. *Only one way to find out,* she thought, and gingerly swam up to it. To her frustration, the shark swam away just fast enough to keep her from touching it.

A smile rose from the corner of her mouth. "Want to play hard to get, do ya? Fine." She reached out and telekinetically snagged the tail as gently as she could. The shark reacted by swimming a little faster, and her feet rose off the ground as it pulled her along. Yet it did not try to shake her off. Instead, it swam in a snake-like pattern, slowly to the left and then slowly to the right, as if wanting to fathom with each eye what she was doing following it.

Since the shark was dragging her along at a relatively rapid clip and she didn't have to expend additional stamina—other than for Telekinesis—she chose to avoid casting spells like Speed of the Dolphin and Commune with Fish—for now.

It wasn't long until something new entered her hundred-foot circle of light.

"A shipwreck," she said, heart pumping faster. Shipwrecks were her favorite things to explore.

The shark swam near enough to it that she could let go and her feet once again touched down on the sand, this time in between two old wooden beams encrusted with barnacles. The shark swam on, then turned to swim sideways once more, turning itself into a nosy lollygagger.

"You just keep a nice and safe distance with them teeth, ya hear?" Leera told it.

Mindful to keep sight of it at all times—not to mention watching over her shoulder lest more sharks show up—she next took stock of the ship. It was half the size of the whaler and had come to rest on the bottom upside-down. Its leaf-shaped hull, punctured in many places by erosion, would have sat low in the water. Leera swam up to one of these holes, raised her lit hand over it, and peeked inside.

Amidst the detritus, a glint of reflected light caught her eye, and after checking that the shark was keeping its distance, she used her other hand to snag the object telekinetically. She caught on to it, but moving it resulted in a plume of silt. Still, she kept hold and slowly maneuvered it out from underneath the debris—until a round plate-like object emerged, too big to jam through the hole. It was likely made of steel and thick enough to have survived the years largely intact.

Checking that her back was clear, she used her lit hand to brush some of the buildup away, but most of it was rust that was stuck too strongly to the metal. Still, she could make out the beginning of a word—*Trazin*, with the rest cut off. She used the word to jog her memory, repeating, "Trazin, Trazin, Trazin … It must be one of the expeditions of Codus Trazinius!" she blurted, whirling about to yell at the shark whilst holding onto the shield with her left hand. "This might be his boat!"

The shark's reply was to continue slowly circling her at a distance of twenty feet, a comfortable margin.

She hesitated, drumming her cheek with her fingers. "Or it could be one of his commissions. Famous explorers sometimes lent their names to such endeavors. But didn't he die at sea? I can't recall." She considered asking Limpet to pass the question along, but too curious by the find to waste time on communication, she turned back to the hole. Unfortunately the swirling silt obscured the interior, and unless she wanted to expend precious energy making a larger hole, there was no point loitering about.

With great reluctance, she let the shield go and watched it vanish back into its tomb. Sighing underwater, she turned to the shark. "Mind if I catch a ride again? Come on, you must be bored as all heck. Come here and let's make this interesting for both of us." She beckoned. To her amusement and surprise, the shark cagily swam forth to her. As before, she snagged its tail, and it once more swam off.

This time, however, Leera slowly reeled her telekinetic line in and enclosed her finger over its fin, feeling its sandpaper skin. She braced for a violent reaction, but the shark didn't seem to mind at all.

"I think it's time our relationship progressed to the next level, don't you?" she asked it, not worrying about expending a little energy on speaking aloud just to hear herself make the jest. "Now don't be afraid. This won't hurt a bit." She transitioned her thoughts to the Commune with Fish spell and incanted, "*Fisha thiyola communa.* Shark, I am your friend. Please show me what you saw today."

Her vision morphed to that of the shark's, and she saw herself gliding along the bottom earlier that day. Whereas the waters were dark, the shark's black-and-white vision was strong enough for her to barely make out the bottom. The shark happened to be chasing another fish and was thus swimming at a rapid clip. The first thing she noticed was the countless shipwrecks—they were everywhere, dotting the bottom at roughly hundred-foot intervals, about the diameter of her pool of light.

This ancient trap must have snagged quite a few over the centuries, she thought. There were all sorts of ships, few of which she recognized, for they were either too rotten or too ancient in design. Some had been reduced to mere skeletons, others a leaf-shaped mound of sand. A few were so large that the shark's limited field of vision could not see them completely. These larger ones were also the most rotten, interestingly, with some easily passing for natural ocean habitats, and the only thing giving them away was the occasional protrusion of a particularly hardy old beam. One of these behemoths had a long line of masts, reminding her of the gargoyle ship. Those masts, splintered and rotten, poked out like the bones of a leviathan's spine.

Onward she swam through the shark's memory, her vision clear but dim—and almost yelped aloud upon seeing the face of a monstrous serpent in the distance. It appeared to be asleep and coiled on the ocean floor, surrounding something big—it was hard to tell in the dimness. She quickly lost sight of it anyhow, for the fish the shark was chasing swam toward that serpent as if seeking shelter, while the shark veered away, no doubt fearing a predator—as it should, for the serpent's body was thicker than a grain silo.

Leera withdrew from the shark's memory and realized she was swimming in pitch darkness, meaning she'd lost focus on her Shine spell. She blurted, "*Shyneo!*" relighting her palm—and brightening it to its prior strength. Upon seeing no predators—and no serpent—Leera expelled a sigh of relief. "Don't get sloppy," she uttered.

They had swum into a new area, this one with no less than three shipwrecks relatively close together. Checking in on her stamina told her she was down two-thirds and didn't have long left down here. Still holding onto the shark, she knew there was only one place to go, and so she recast the Commune with Fish spell, then said, "Shark, I am your friend. Please take me to the area of the serpent."

The shark jerked at this and changed direction. It swam for a little while before darting away so violently that Leera lost her grip on its tail. By the time her feet touched sand, the shark was gone. She looked at her hand—and saw blood, for the jerking motion of that sandpaper fin had cut the tip of her index finger, and a small dribble of blood plumed in the water.

"Thaaaaat's not good," Leera sang and promptly squeezed her thumb against the cut. Blood in water was dangerous as it drew predators. She thus resolved to keep her head on a constant swivel. She needed to find whatever structure the serpent was coiled around doubly quick now.

Using the rough direction the shark had been swimming in as a guide, Leera incanted, "*Akseler aqua loa*," opting to cast the 2nd degree off-the-books spell Fast Swim rather than the 9th degree Speed of the Dolphin, which ate far more stamina.

She jumped up and kicked her feet and smoothly swung her arms about in a forward swim-crawl that, with the aid of the spell, had her arcanely zooming along at a respectable speed. All the while she kept glancing over her shoulder and was careful to keep her thumb firmly pressed against the cut index finger.

Onward she swam in the deep silence, over corals and clumps of seaweed and slow-crawling giant crab and passing schools of strange fish and various shipwrecks or shipwreck mounds until, at long last, her light caught the distant glint of scales. She slowed and drifted close to the sandy bottom, and soon found herself floating fifty feet away from the very serpent she had seen through the shark's eyes.

It was a true monster. Its teeth were so big they protruded from its mouth like the jaws of a giant furnace. Even bathed in the periphery of her cool light, she could see it had crimson scales. A long series of iridescent fishlike fins protruded from its thick body, each one twice her size.

But it was the object it was coiled around that made her glad she had risked coming here, for it was a structure all right—a building with a spire that rose above the serpent like those chapels the Canterran Path disciples worshipped in.

There was no chance of taking the beast on directly, for she did not have enough stamina to make serious use of the ring's serpent slayer power—the spell simply wouldn't have the punch to kill the monster. Instead, she would have to use guile.

After checking that nothing was creeping up on her, she pondered the challenge—and thought to try a trick Augum had taught her a while back. If she could correctly apply geometric arcane lensing with the principle of focal plane relativity, she might be able to offset the 2nd degree elemental spell Slam behind the serpent.

First, she needed to conceal herself, and so she ran a hand over her body, incanting, "*Armari obscura chameleano traversa,*" being sure to add on the travel extension, which cost more stamina but was necessary. Her body melded with the sand, making her vanish like an octopus. She was now a mound of sand—albeit one that emitted light from a camouflaged hand.

Limpet's voice broke into her mind. "Hey, everyone wants to know if you're all right, so, uh, are you still alive?"

Can't answer right now, she thought. Steeling her soul and readying to Teleport should the serpent come for her, she transitioned to the complicated spell maneuver she was about to attempt. Once she thought she had the focal plane lensing principle rightly aligned, she made a throwing-at-the-ground motion, roaring, "*Grau!*"

The roar of crashing water reverberated on the serpent's left—a deep rumble that made little sense here. The serpent jerked awake and looked to it. In that moment, Leera saw her hand appear—the violent gesture from the spell had broken the Chameleon casting, and she now stood out like a beacon fire.

Instead of recasting Chameleon, she froze in place, for the serpent's head swiveled back to look directly at her—and its eyes narrowed into thin slits. Whereas normally those slits would be a sign of danger, in this case, they gave Leera hope, for they told her that the serpent, which was used to deep darkness, did not like the bright light. She thus slowly brightened her palm to its maximum possible brightness—and tried not to worry about the steady bleed of stamina that was happening from the combination of Breathe Water, Endure the Deep, and now a powerful Shine spell.

The serpent uncoiled from around the structure—and swam away. Amazingly, her bright light had run it off, probably the easiest victory of her life against any monster.

"Hey, if you're still alive, you should say something because they're all freaking out up here, especially your boyfriend or whatever."

Leera raised the ring to her lips and absently whispered, "Contact Jeremy Jenkins. I'm fine. Found something down here. Talk later." Limpet passed her message on, but she cut off the distant sound of cheers with the words, "Cease contact," so that she could watch the monster's massive body snake away, its tail vanishing into the darkness beyond her protective light.

After taking a moment to collect herself—and give herself a pat on the back for having gotten this far, all things considered—she dimmed her light to reduce the stamina bleed, checked to make sure nothing was stalking her from behind, and walk-swam up to the structure.

"Now this is something to behold," she muttered, for the structure stood three stories high and was covered in barnacles and small crustaceans and seaweed and seagrass. Combined with what appeared to be the tip of a tail, the shape reminded her of a proud sitting lion, much like those stone guardians found outside royal buildings—particularly with the crusty buildup, which gave it a proud mane.

Except ...

"Wait a moment ..." The tail did not look like a lion's tail at all. On a hunch, Leera swam up to the seaweed and seagrass and aimed her lit palm, incanting, "*Aquatos*." A jet of continuous water shot from her hand, which she used to clean away the buildup, until a fearsome and scaled face revealed itself to her. It was not the face of a lion.

But of a *dragon*.

"By gods ..." she whispered, floating back to look at the statue anew. It faced a certain direction, which she suspected was east, meaning toward the distant lands. "The trap wasn't meant for us," she said. "It was meant for *them*."

With her stamina rapidly nearing the return point—the moment she needed to use the rest of it to teleport back to the ship—she figured she still had enough for one or two selective castings. She thus splayed her fingers and incanted, "*Un vun asperio aurum enchantus*."

The dragon lit up with the same tendril arcanery as the ocean bottom and surface—with one exception. Every single tendril drove *out* from the dragon, meaning it was the source of the loop trap. She swam about the statue, noticing that the tendrils didn't flow into the statue, but around it. She traced them—and saw that they emanated from the dragon's chest, which happened to be encrusted with a layer of barnacles.

"Gotcha," she whispered and let Reveal die in favor of another casting of the 3rd degree Splash, once again incanting, "*Aquatos*." She took satisfaction in watching the barnacles fly off from the pressure of her water jet. An outline slowly emerged, then the top of a shape. A head, wings, a castle, and by the time her work revealed three sacred words, she was grinning ear to ear.

For she now knew who had created the loop trap and, more importantly, how to turn it off.

SEAWEED

AUGUM

"Let me get this straight," Leo the Leopard said, dancing an arcanely flame-lit finger back and forth before his eyes, his booted feet kicked up on a galley stool. "The entire reason the ocean is impassable ... all those lives lost over the centuries to storms and monsters and traps ... is because your Arcaner lot wanted to stop them beasties coming from overseas?"

Augum let the question linger in the smoky galley, for every soul not on deck had crammed in there, paying rapt attention to what was unfolding before them—to hear about what had *already* unfolded. He sat surrounded by friends at the very back of the galley, Leera snoozing peacefully in his lap.

Upon her return from the depths, she had loudly blurted something about a giant Arcaner dragon statue being the culprit behind the loop trap and that she had turned it off and that the ship could now sail on. Then she had promptly stolen Augum so she could have a bath. While washing up, she had bubbled with giddiness, explaining everything, diving into detail only Augum would ever hear.

He had listened intently, enjoying watching her nakedness and her smile and wit and her inspiration as she blathered a league a heartbeat about the historic significance. All that was fascinating and fantastic even, but he was just so happy to have her back that at one point he placed a finger to her lips and kissed her, and she kissed him until they passionately lost themselves in each other.

Then she changed, and after Jez and Olaf goaded her to repeat the tale to everyone else, she instead crashed in Augum's lap, leaving him to explain things to the dumbfounded but fascinated throng while eating supper. Even as he spoke, his mind feverishly worked on the implications.

"Well, we're not sure about the pillars, but that trap was an ancient Arcaner construct," he replied, nodding his thanks at a sailor after the young man had taken away his finished plate of ribs, potatoes, and asparagus. "How did she turn it off?" he said, repeating the question one of the rapt listeners had thrown at him during his thinking. "Leera summoned her shield, pressed it to the crest, and apparently had the option to turn it off for one day or permanently — that is, until someone turns it back on."

"And she chose what?" Alanna asked.

"For one day, which is why we were able to sail out of the loop." Even as he spoke, the ship's degree of list increased, as did the howl of the wind that whistled through the creaking planks. They were entering another storm. If he saw lightning, he would hit the deck and climb the mast.

"And only someone of dragon rank could have turned it off?" Jengo, sitting to Augum's left, asked.

"She believes so, yes. The crest had the full shield, and she studied the tendrils, which pointed to the requirement." Annoyed that they kept interrupting his thoughts, Augum chose to express them aloud, albeit quietly so as not to wake Leera — although she slept like a rock anyway. That way he could work through the problem — and maybe then they would understand why he was so distracted.

"But it's the historic significance that's interesting here," he went on. "At some point in the distant past, Arcaners of old feared another continent — maybe *multiple* continents — and went to the measure of protecting *our* continent from all the others. So they built this trap, and possibly more, to prevent passage." With the haze of pipe smoke and the staring — even the galley crew were watching him — he felt a bit like a grizzled mariner recounting an ancient tale around a campfire.

"That means we've likely been invaded before," Jez said, swirling a goblet of wine.

Augum idly stroked Leera's shoulder, watching her sleep in his lap as he mulled this over. He took so long that Olaf, sitting next to him, quipped, "He's a cookin' something up in that there noggin', ain't he?" eliciting chortles.

Augum looked up, awed by a realization. "Sure, maybe we were attacked," he said quietly, "and maybe those attacks have been buried under the sheer weight of history. Or …"

Everyone leaned forth, with many chorusing a whispered, "Or …?"

Augum swept the crowd with his gaze. "Or maybe those able to turn into dragons flew overseas, saw something, and knew they needed to place a wall between us ... and *them*."

This resulted in a tense silence during which people exchanged ominous looks.

"Now we're heading straight to this ... *them*," Digby said, chewing on a leg of lamb. "Meaning the gargoyles."

Augum shrugged. "Maybe."

"Too many maybes," Digby added. "I don't like so many maybes."

Augum wanted to spit that he didn't care one hoof what Digby liked or didn't like, but he needed to keep the atmosphere respectful. What he wished he could do, he realized as the others broke out into quiet conversations, was search the depths of the summonable Arcaner vault. There had to be something in there, an instruction or warning, about the protective wall. Maybe even how to navigate through it safely. The only problem was he would never risk emptying the vault on the ship, for if something happened, all of its contents would be lost to the sea—not to mention nobody outside their small circle was to know about the vault as it was a high secret of the order.

Then again, the previously impassable ocean wall was the business of those who minded the ocean, and there *were* people in charge of that aspect of protection, two of whom were in this very room and wore the necessary rings. He looked to one of them, a mere kid.

"Limpet," he said, startling the boy, who had been chewing on a finger beside his friend, Dirt, who had also been chewing on a finger.

"Huh?" the boy said, swallowing at all the eyes looking his way.

Augum found it interesting that they hung on to his every word so much, even when he was merely addressing someone. Was it the power of the dragon they so respected? Or the story he had just told? "Limpet, would you be so kind as to use your ring to contact a Mrs. Seahorse within your order and ask her if she knows anything about ancient Arcaner constructs hidden at the bottom of the ocean?"

"Uh, okay. But the order is secret. You all are not supposed to know about it."

This caused a round of laughter, with Leo chiming in, "Kid, everyone with sea legs knows about the order. Y'all are the nosiest busybodies there are, gettin' in the way of all sorts of trades."

"That's cause your lot trades in nefarious goods—and even slaves," Tammy said, which got some "Oohs" from people.

Leo merely shrugged.

Dirt elbowed Limpet. "Go on, then. Don't matter anyway seeing as we're in the middle of nowhere."

Limpet sighed. "Fine, but I already tried reaching my old mentor and couldn't because of that stupid tower and stuff." Nonetheless, he put the ring to his lips. "Contact Silanna Seahorse. Mrs. Seahorse, this is Limpet. I have a question for you." He paused, scrunching his face in concentration. "Hello? Mrs. Seahorse?" He kept trying but eventually gave up. "I can't reach her either," he told everyone.

"You're too far away from each other," Augum concluded.

"Or it's that tower," Jez said.

"Or even the storm itself," Olaf threw in, earning him nods of agreement from the crowd.

As various low conversations broke out, Jez elbowed Olaf and whispered something in his ear. Olaf then leaned over to Augum to whisper in his ear, "Jez suggests you should search the you-know-what for clues."

Augum whispered back, "Already considered it. Can't take the risk of doing it on a ship for obvious reasons."

Olaf nodded and passed this whisper on to Jez, only to return with a counter. "What reasons?"

Annoyed, Augum smacked his lips. "*Reasons* reasons," was his reply.

Olaf soon returned with, "That's not good enough, monkey. Don't be lazy."

Augum leaned forward to look past him at Jez, placing a hand to the side of his mouth as he whispered, "Because I don't want to lose irreplaceable stuff to a sudden capsize."

For once, she relented, muttering, "I suppose," and took a long sip of her wine.

Carter walked over. "Sir—Commander—I was rather hoping we could get some training in."

"Yeah, *we* want to train too!" Digby shouted so loudly that those sitting nearby winced in displeasure. He raised a tankard and winked at Tammy, who was sipping on a mug of tea. "Want to join in, sweet cheeks?"

She scowled. "Eww."

"You look cute angry. More of that, please."

Augum looked to Carter, who in turn snapped his fingers, shouting, "Digs!"

"Whaaaaat?" Digby sang, glancing at his brother, feigning ignorance.

Carter sliced a hand across his own throat for him to cut it out.

Digby muttered into his tankard, and he and his brother cackled fiendishly, throwing eyes at an increasingly uncomfortable Tammy.

As Carter glared daggers at Digby, who pointedly ignored him, Augum leaned past Olaf once more to speak to Jez. "Hey, Lee mentioned something about finding one of Codus Trazinius's boats down there. Is it possible it was him?"

Jez shrugged. "Sure. But it was just as likely a commission under his banner. How do you think he explored so many lands at once? His charges reported their findings, and he wrote about them." She rubbed two fingers against each other. "Made a heck of a lot of coin flogging that racket. Who knows how much of it was true."

Augum nodded his thanks and leaned back, idly stroking Leera's hair. He returned his attention to the patiently waiting Carter. "Meet me on deck in a quarter of an hour."

"Sir, yes, sir." Carter then went to sit beside Digby, who was resentful of the intrusion as he'd been making jests at Tammy's expense. The tall woman sighed, got up, and walked out of the room cupping her tea with both hands.

Carter started saying something in a hissing tone, but Digby shrugged him off, his eyes on the doorway. He downed his tall tankard, wiped his mouth, used that hand to pat Carter's shoulder condescendingly, and got up to leave the galley. Carter leaned back and shook his head, then began a conversation with Digby's brother, Teague.

With everyone else deep in their own conversations, Augum was the only one aware that Digby had followed Tammy, and so he gently let Leera's head down on the bench and got up, excusing himself from present company. He went out into the passageway and followed where he thought Digby had gone. It wasn't long until he found him standing before Tammy's cabin door—except he was stiff, as if frozen in time, face turned to the side, a fresh red handprint on his cheek.

The door flew open. "And I'll tell you another thing—" Tammy went on, only to notice Augum. "Oh. Hello, Commander."

"I'm not your commander, so you can call me Augum."

"I prefer titles, as it keeps a distance, Dragon Stone."

Augum smiled his understanding and raised a questioning eyebrow whilst throwing a nod at Digby, whose face had gone red from embarrassment after being slapped and paralyzed—and then found in that state by someone he surely considered an enemy.

"You don't survive on a ship full of lonely drunkards by being meek," Tammy explained.

"Shall we conduct a trial?"

"For what? An insult? A few bad words? Slurred speech? I think he learned his lesson. Didn't you, *Digs*? Disgusting pig," she muttered. "Now if you will excuse me, Dragon Stone."

"Of course."

She closed the door, leaving him alone with a still paralyzed and red-faced Digby. Augum walked around so they were eye to eye and folded his arms. "What am I supposed to do with you, huh? You're a poor guardian for Carter, an even worse example, and you have no respect for anyone other than your brother."

Digby's eyes narrowed with loathing.

"That's what I thought," Augum muttered.

The door opened again. "Oh, I forgot. Sorry, Dragon Stone," and she made a reverse *drawing-Digby's-outline* motion with a finger, incanting, "*Paralizo null.*"

Digby animated back to life so abruptly that, in his drunken state, he lost his balance and reached out to brace against Augum, whose reflex was to step aside, allowing Digby to tumble to the floor.

"Pissants, the both of you," Digby hissed, using the wall as an aid in rising back onto his unsteady feet. "Your reckoning is long overdue," he added, scowling at Augum. Then he bared his teeth at Tammy, who looked on with an unimpressed gaze, and stumbled back to the galley, roaring, "Someone feed the Digs a drink!"

Augum and Tammy shared a head-shaking look, and this time it was Augum who excused himself first. His aim was to go back to the galley to keep an eye on Digby, but after Tammy closed her door, he spotted a piece of seaweed slowly rising from the nearby ladder hatch.

"That's weird," he muttered, watching the seaweed poke about like a curious worm. He decided to investigate and approached the ladder. "Who's practicing earth spells down there? Your spell is bleeding out into the hall! You should be more mindful as—" His words caught in his throat upon stepping up to the ladder well and seeing what looked like a whole jungle down in the deck below. "What the ..." The blade of the seaweed, which was attached to a much larger frond, lashed out and coiled around his leg.

As he fell into a bush of writhing seaweed, he made a quick unsheathing motion, shouting, "*Summano arma!*" A lightning longsword appeared in his fist, but by that time, the sword was useless as more seaweed blades had entwined his arm—as they had around his legs and torso. One promptly wound around his face and eyes and another around his throat, with the latter beginning to squeeze. Realizing he had mere heartbeats before the seaweed would prevent him from speaking, he released his sword, allowing it to vanish, and whilst imagining only himself and his clothes teleporting, he envisioned an empty corner of the galley and wheezed, "*Impetus peragro!*" vanishing and reappearing with a *thwomp* in that very corner.

Every head turned in surprise at his sudden appearance. "We're un—" He tried to say, but was overtaken by a coughing fit from having been choked. All the while he was throwing his arms toward the doorway.

Jez was the first to rise to her feet, concerned. "What is it, Augum?"

Beside her, Leera's groggy face appeared from the bench. "What's happening?" she drawled, rubbing puffy eyes with her fists.

"We're under … we're under attack!" he finally sputtered. "Deck below, monster seaweed!"

That announcement got people pouring out at such a frantic pace that the first few, including Digby and his brother Teague, jammed in the doorway.

"Be careful as it's arcane seaweed!" he shouted, rubbing his neck.

"Who's an earthie?" someone from the hall shouted. "Need an earth warlock up front!"

"I am!" Carter shouted back, but the blockade at the doorway prevented him from stepping into the hall.

While some worked together to unclog the entrance, Augum, seeing Jengo nervously shifting his weight foot to foot, told him, "Mahmoute is earth."

"I … I'm not practiced enough in Teleport to risk teleporting down to her," Jengo replied.

Augum nodded. "I'll go. Will I be able to rouse her?"

"Yes. But she will be weak."

"Understood. Get Carter on it in the meantime."

"Yes, Commander."

Augum looked to Leera. She nodded for him to go, and he focused on standing with firm feet in the ward, incanting, "*Impetus peragro!*" He appeared exactly where he'd been hoping and dashed to Mahmoute's bedside, where he gently shook her shoulder.

"Black Eagle Mahmoute," he said. "There's been an attack. We need you." When the woman failed to move, Augum's stomach fell. Her ashen face told him a terrible truth. "Oh …" he whispered.

"I'm not dead," she wheezed.

Were it under any other circumstances, Augum would have laughed. Instead he stepped back. "Black Eagle Mahmoute, we have an urgent situation. Rogue seaweed has infested the lower decks. It almost choked me out. Please, you must hurry."

One of her eyes opened to assess him before the other joined. She raised a wrinkled hand, which he accepted and helped her sit up. "I suppose it is time to return to the world," she said.

Augum aided her in walking, but they didn't need to go far, for the problem infestation had already reached that passageway. The blades were writhing forth toward them. Mahmoute watched it for a moment, grunted, raised a hand, and wordlessly stayed the seaweed's writhing.

"Curious," she said, cocking her head slightly.

Augum kept his elbow extended for her to use as leverage. "What is this?" he asked.

"It appears to be enchanted seaweed. Perhaps an oceanic infestation of some sort ..." She beckoned with her raised hand and one of the vines stretched out to her. She raised a single finger and the blade of seaweed, which had angled at her like a viper, halted a foot from her face, allowing her to snatch it. "*Planta arbora communa*," she incanted. "Seaweed, I am your friend. Show me where you came from." She closed her eyes. "Hmm, most unusual. Most unusual indeed."

"What is it, Black Eagle Mahmoute? What do you see?"

She looked to him. "It came from the sea. It came from *below*."

Something about the way she said it raised the hairs on the back of his neck, but she did not have time to elaborate, for a shriek sounded from above.

"We must help them!" Augum said and bolted without waiting for Mahmoute's reply. He scampered up the nearest ladder—and saw the entire passageway ahead was filled with writhing seaweed.

His mouth went dry as he whispered, "Ye gods ..." With how confined the passage was, he couldn't use his lightning longsword— which would threaten to set the ship alight. In fact, any lightning usage inside a wooden ship was a risk he was not willing to take. As the seaweed writhed toward him, a scroll of all his spells unfurled before his mind—except not a single spell felt like it would do much to the seaweed. In certain situations, such as this one, some elements simply did not fare well against other elements.

He shot back to the ladder, shouting down into the space, "Black Eagle Mahmoute! We need your help up here!"

There was a quick tumbling sound above on the planks, followed by multiple shrieks, with some abruptly going silent as if their mouths had been covered.

"Black Eagle Mah—"

She stumbled into view, already gasping from being out of breath, reminding him of how weak Leera had been after rising from her healing coma. "You must help me up the ladder, Dragon."

"There's no time! You'll have to teleport to the main cabin area!"

Mahmoute swallowed as if the prospect of teleportation worried her, but she nodded.

Not waiting around for her to zip off, Augum bolted away from the coming seaweed to the opposite end of the passageway, where there was another ladder. He scrambled up that ladder—and halted halfway out of the passage hole. The color drained from his face, for the entire passage was filled with seaweed. Amongst that tangled chaos, people, including his friends Olaf and Jengo, Tammy, some crew—even Leera, who was the farthest of the bunch—writhed in the seaweed's iron grip.

Leera had summoned her watery shortsword, but as had happened with him, the seaweed had a strong grip on her arm and fist, and the shortsword wavered about harmlessly. Somehow, they'd all been overwhelmed.

"Teleport to the stern!" Augum roared.

This seemed to snap a bunch of the warlocks out of their panic, for they briefly stopped fighting in order to concentrate before incanting the phrase and popping off with a *thwomp*.

But not Leera, for a vine covered her mouth—and was trying to pry through her lips, though she refused to relent, her head, despite being held by seaweed, shaking violently about.

As he scrambled to get the rest of his body off the ladder, something snagged his foot from below. *No, no, no, no,* he thought, eyes on a flailing Leera, all but ignoring the others still trapped, one of whom was Carter— an earth warlock who himself had been overwhelmed.

Knowing he had to take a risk, he flexed his arm whilst making an unsheathing motion from his hip, incanting, "*Summano arma!*" The lightning longsword reappeared in his fist. He promptly stabbed downward toward his ankle, making a circling motion around his leg. The sword sizzled as it sliced through the seaweed, freeing his leg. He shot off, so frantic that his foot caught on the edge of the ladder entrance, causing him to roll forward like a fool. The tip of the blade sliced through a plank, sending sparks flying and charring the wood.

Augum didn't so much as blink, and after scrambling back to his feet he rushed at the advancing seaweed. Someone began arcanely working on the infestation from the other end of the hall—he thought he'd heard an extra teleport earlier, but he couldn't be sure as he was totally focused on saving Leera.

He slid to a stop before the writhing wall, swinging and slicing within the narrow confines of the passageway, and seaweed began to fly. As careful as he was, the tip of the sword occasionally sliced through a plank, throwing up sparks and creating small flames here and there. Augum in his haste was barely cognizant of the fact that the closest seaweed blades, as if conscious of self-preservation, smacked their flat sides at the flames, smothering them out.

"I'm coming, my love. Keep breathing!" Augum shouted, sword swishing this way and that. She was now in a cocoon of seaweed and her struggles were slowing as the seaweed had completely covered her face. His muscles burned as his strokes took on a desperate vigor. He even started to use his other hand, now and then pointing at incoming seaweed and telekinetically veering it into the path of his slicing sword. A rain of seaweed bits fell to the floor, sword incessantly sizzling.

But there was another problem. The seaweed he'd cut was somehow still alive. It writhed around him and began to attach itself to other bits, until those bits reared up on him like tiny cobras, and he quickly found his feet under attack. Slicing away with a rabid ferocity, Augum noticed only one of Leera's fingers was still free. Instead of panic, a battle-hardened clarity entered his thoughts, and he launched himself into the wall of seaweed, using a long arcing slice to carve a path toward his beloved. He snagged her seaweed-encased leg with an outstretched hand and dragged himself forth, not bothering with his sword anymore as the seaweed had gotten hold of his arm anyhow.

The seaweed closed in on him like miniature hungry serpents. They wrapped around his legs and torso and neck and head and tried getting into his mouth. As he dragged himself up the cocoon around her body, he chomped on a seaweed tentacle and felt it writhe most uncomfortably on his tongue before he spit it out.

Finally his fingers enclosed around her lone finger, which curled up toward him almost lovingly. As more seaweed blades tried to jam themselves into his mouth, he roared, "*Impetus peragro grapa lestato exa exaei!*"

With a *thwomp*, the pair appeared at the bow of the ship, where Leera fell to her knees, gasping for breath, all the while tightly holding onto him. "Came up on me ... so fast ..." she spat between breaths. "Whole wall of it ... suddenly just ... tumbled into us ..."

"I'm going to try to 'port more people out," Augum said.

The ship began to list. The clouds roiled as a fierce wind shrieked through the rigging. Ahead, lightning silently flashed within the darkest cloud he'd ever seen—it looked like a blob of swirling black paint.

"What's happening down there!" the bosun shouted from midship.

Augum looked back to see that people had gathered at the stern. Then he saw something that sent a terrible thrill zipping down his spine—seaweed had started to crawl up the outside of the hull on the port side, the railing closest to the ocean.

"I can handle that," Leera said, using him as leverage to drag herself back to her feet.

"Be careful," he replied.

"You too."

They squeezed hands, shared a fleeting but loving look, then ran off in separate directions, Augum to the nearest hatch and Leera toward the seaweed-entwined railing.

This is bad. This is really, really bad, Augum thought as his feet landed on the floor below with a *thud*. Directly ahead, Rogor was battling a wall of seaweed. He was so strong that he was able to easily rip pieces of seaweed off him, but more would simply latch on, and it was an endless battle—albeit one at an impasse, for neither side was making progress.

"Stay back, lowlander!" Rogor growled.

"You must retreat or you will tire!" Augum replied.

"When I tire, I will retreat. But that will not be for some time, lowlander! Rogor is strong and brave!"

Not wanting to waste another breath arguing with him, Augum, seeing that the path ahead was closed, scampered back up the ladder and sprinted down the pitched deck toward the stern. He ran past people he was glad to see—Alanna and Olaf and Jengo and Limpet and Tammy, all of whom were either supporting each other or standing on a hatchway, using their weight to keep the seaweed from pushing upward. The captain kept glancing between them and his crew—and the vivid black storm cloud ahead.

"Who's left below?" Augum asked.

"Everyone you don't see here," Olaf replied, the hatch thudding below him as something pounded on it.

Jez and Carter and Teague and Digby and Mahmoute and Leo the Leopard and the kid, Dirt, Augum thought, knowing they were either ensnared—or, in the case of Jez and Mahmoute, fighting the infestation. He closed his eyes as he imagined a compartment that wouldn't be filled with seaweed. The only one that came to mind was his own cabin.

"Don't risk it!" Alanna shouted, sensing what he wanted to do.

Augum ignored her and snapped off, "*Impetus peragro!*" He appeared in his cabin—and found himself facing a wall of writhing seaweed that had blown the door open. The blades of seaweed turned—and lunged at him. He thought of the next hopefully safe spot—the galley—and just as the blades lashed around his arms, he snapped off the incantation to Teleport and appeared in the corner of the galley.

Right away he saw Carter holding onto a sobbing Dirt with one arm and the doorway frame with the other, with seaweed tangled around his lower body.

"Commander, it's got me!"

Augum ran to him, grabbed hold of his arm with one hand and the crying kid with the other, and incanted the Group Teleport spell, reappearing on the stern beside Olaf and Jengo.

Even as Carter profusely thanked him, Augum cut him off by asking, "Can you fend it off in any way?" *You're a blasted earth warlock, after all!* he wanted to shout.

"I ... I can try, but I'm either not as strong with the element as I thought or this infestation is way more powerful than it should be."

Augum, who'd been watching Leera fighting off the encroaching vines by blasting them with jets of water, nodded and said, "Do what you can."

"Commander," Jengo interrupted. "Shall I bless thee with boosts?"

"No, save your reservoir. They wouldn't do me any good against this anyhow." Augum then looked to Carter, whom he nodded at. "Bolster him instead, and Mahmoute if you happen to see her."

"You got it."

"Awesome," Carter said, rubbing his hands as Jengo stepped up to him.

Meanwhile Augum closed his eyes and vividly imagined his next spot. "*Impetus peragro!*" he incanted, reappearing in the corner of the galley for the third time. Seaweed was writhing through the doorway.

"Is anyone out there?" Augum shouted. When no reply came, he envisioned standing in the general sleeping quarters of the crew, located near the bottom of the ship and a place he had only ventured into once upon invitation to join a friendly card game. Just as he was about to teleport down, the vines were abruptly yanked backward from the doorway. A moment later, a gasping Mahmoute emerged, taking their place. She was grabbing hold of the wall with one hand for support, while the other was pressed to her mouth as if she were sick. The strangest thing was that her belly was enormous, as if she were with child.

"Are you all right?" Augum asked rather stupidly, hurrying to her.

"I don't have the strength to ... to teleport anymore," she said, cheeks repeatedly and suddenly puffing and collapsing, as if she were holding back vomit. "But I might ... I might be able to ... to finish it off. It is a powerful elemental, one crafted by ... ancient knowledge. You must ... take me down ..."

Augum nodded and placed her arm upon his. Aware she was in grave danger, he wanted to question her about the wisdom of her plan, but she precluded his query by flashing him an annoyed look of determination. He checked in with his stamina reservoir and realized it was low—all that teleporting had added up, something he'd neglected to consider when rejecting Jengo's offer. Knowing there was no time to worry about it and that he would simply have to be very choosy about which spells to cast, he once more envisioned the crew quarters and snapped off the Group Teleport incantation.

They appeared amidst a field of hammocks, by the one he had sat in when playing cards. Nearly the whole room was stuffed with seaweed fronds. These fronds, which had been idling about as if resting, reared up and snaked toward them.

"You'd better go, Arinthian," Mahmoute said.

Augum readied Teleport on his lips, which would suck his reservoir down to a critical level. Yet he hesitated, for she'd never called him by his ancestral name before. He thus stayed to watch what she would do, perhaps lend aid if he could.

She stretched out her arms. Each snagged a seaweed blade, which she telekinetically pulled toward her, but instead of doing something typical of an earth warlock—perhaps make the seaweed wither or vanish altogether—she angled the seaweed into her mouth—and began eating it. It was not an ordinary way of eating, either, but a rabid and fast devouring, which the seaweed blades seemed to want, pushing themselves down her gullet like snakes eager to get at her soul.

Augum wanted to ask her if she was crazy, if this was the only way, but her eyes flicked to him in warning. She devoured foot upon foot of the seaweed, which bypassed him to get at her. Her arm frantically waved at him to get away. He wanted to cast Reveal to see what the tendril geometries looked like. Instead he stood frozen in place, enraptured by this strange ritual.

More and more of the seaweed kept coming in through the door, pulled in like rats by the tail, and he realized there was a method to the madness—she was pulling *all* of the seaweed to herself. One of these seaweed clusters dragged in a cocoon, which jerked Augum from his stupor. He bolted to the cocoon, making an unsheathing motion and incanting, "*Summano arma!*"

The lightning longsword appeared in his fist and he sliced at the seaweed attachments before angling the crackling tip of the blade to pick at the top layer. Once he exposed clothing, he let the sword vanish and ripped the seaweed away with his hands—except it clung on too tightly, forcing him to flex every muscle in his body and incant, "*Virtus vis viray!*"

Muscles bolstered by the 8th degree Strength spell, he tore at the seaweed anew. Strips flew off and reanimated, but instead of slithering to the body or to him, they snaked off toward Mahmoute. He went for the head and quickly exposed a nose with a huge mole on it. He kept ripping away until he revealed a white wig, askew, an ashen face staring with horror-stricken eyes, and a wide-open mouth stuffed to the brim with seaweed.

Augum ceased his efforts to gape at the lifeless face of Teague Bloomington-Southguard, knowing in his soul there was nothing he could do. Digby's elder brother was gone.

The seaweed surrounding his body began to unwind on its own and slithered toward Mahmoute, leaving Teague behind on the floor. Realizing there might be others trapped in this manner, Augum snapped out of his shock and bolted into the passageway, where he saw streams of seaweed coming in from all directions. One of these streams was dragging in a second cocoon, which he ran to and began ripping away with his bare hands, starting with the face, specifically the nose and mouth.

When he once more revealed a mouth stuffed with seaweed, he reached in and tore it out, as if drawing on rope. He must have ripped out several feet before the mouth gasped. He turned the body onto its side and let the man retch out the rest.

"Who is this?" he asked, unable to see the rest of the head on account of the coiled seaweed.

"Who do you think it is, you blasted fool?" snapped the drunken voice of Digby. "You sure took your time, didn't you! Gods be damned, I almost died! Where's my brother?"

Augum's stomach sank. "He's in the room over—"

"Well stop gawking and help me out of this already!"

Augum, who didn't have the heart to tell him that his brother was dead, helped him free a single arm. "You can do the rest. I have to save others," he said and ran off, with Digby roaring, "Come back here and help me, you coward!" which didn't make any sense to Augum, but he didn't have time to worry about him.

He soon found other cocoons and freed them all, which turned out to be crew members. All had survived, for the seaweed had not gone for the nose, only the mouth and the stomach, allowing it to be pulled free. It was a messy process, but Augum worked feverishly, with Leera soon joining him from above—and then Carter. They worked in harmony, efficient with their movements, saying little, each knowing their task.

At one point, Jez careened in from above, shouting, "There you all are! Been fighting a wall of it until it all started moving at once." She joined in the efforts, until every cocoon was freed.

Then they heard a terrible scream of despair emanating from below.

"Digby found his brother," Augum told the others in such a mournful tone they all instinctively knew what he meant. Then Augum blurted, "Mahmoute!" and shot off, the others trailing.

By the time he arrived, Mahmoute was a boulder, with a grotesque abomination of a belly. Even her face was stretched out, yet she ate on, stuffing writhing seaweed into her mouth, her movements tired and slow. Her skin was turning green, as if the seaweed were fusing with her body from within.

Digby kneeled on the floor by his brother. He rocked back and forth, one hand squeezing his brother's lifeless hand, the other scrunching the robe over his heart. "Oh, brother, oh, my sweet, sweet brother ..." he kept repeating. Then he noticed Augum and his face changed. "You killed him!" he roared, spittle shooting forth. "You murdered my brother!"

"Don't be absurd," Jez said, but Digby was inconsolable. He stood and ran at Augum. Jez responded by quickly drawing his outline, incanting, "*Paralizo carcusa cemente*," paralyzing him in place.

Augum, meanwhile, ran to Mahmoute. "How can I help?" he asked.

So stretched was her green flesh that her bulging eyes barely moved toward him. They were red as if she'd been crying, with a profound sadness Augum knew all too well. "Jez!" he shouted without looking away. "Bring Jengo!"

"On it," she replied and hopped off with a *thwomp*.

As Carter kneeled before Teague to whisper a prayer, Leera joined Augum's side.

"What is this?" she whispered, both hands entwining around his arm.

He placed his free hand on top of hers and looked at her, his reply a small shake of the head.

As Mahmoute devoured the last blade of seaweed, there came another *thwomp*, and Jengo and Jez hurried to their side.

"Can you help her?" Augum asked.

Jengo stood staring with a wild look, as if he too had never seen anything like this before. Then he began his usual healing routine, which started with Diagnose. While he worked, Augum called Carter forth to ask, "Do you know anything about this from training in your element? Maybe a school book or an arcanist might have mentioned it. Think hard!"

Carter reluctantly shook his head.

"It is … an old idea …" Mahmoute wheezed. "… for an old spell. Luckily for us … it worked …" She gave the hint of a smile. "You tell Captain Burns … that I wish I had … had more time …"

Jez and Leera slapped a hand over their mouths, with Augum reaching out to pat Mahmoute on the arm. "Let's not be hasty," he said.

"You do not understand. I must now leave …"

"Please let me finish my work," Jengo said.

"No. It is … an ancient elemental … crafted with complex arcanery. I must leave *with* it … or I *become* it. Already I feel it … transforming me …"

Their eyes went to her gargantuan belly, which throbbed menacingly.

"Be good … be brave … and goodbye." As everyone protested at once, she nonetheless closed her eyes, as if envisioning her final resting place. Then, using up the last of her strength, her green face bulged as she raised her chin and proudly roared her final words, "*Impetus peragro!*"

Black Eagle Mahmoute vanished with a *thwomp*, leaving behind a ringing silence.

The five of them stood staring at the spot she had been in only a moment before. No one said a word. Augum imagined the poor woman appearing deep underwater, drowning herself, or perhaps high above the waters, only to fall to an explosive death. He could not fathom the arcanery involved in such an ancient elemental, and he struggled to understand why there had been no other way to dispel it. But he also knew many aspects of ancient arcanery were mysterious and beyond the current understanding of the arcane arts.

With Mahmoute gone, and with Jez constantly drunk, Augum felt a profound sense of responsibility settle upon his shoulders. It was now up to him to ensure their safety. He had to be competent and brave and decisive and unwavering. He had to be strong.

They stood until Olaf ran into the room, shouting, "Tammy's fighting something on the bow!"

They took one look at each other, as if to acknowledge the loss only they had witnessed, before bolting to the bow. No one stopped to unfreeze Digby, for it was safer that he was paralyzed, lest he do something stupid.

Augum, being the fastest amongst them, was the first to skid to a halt upon reaching the bow. Sure enough, there was the gangly Tammy, both arms raised as she battled a vicious column of air that swirled about in multiple vortices working as one. These vortices kept trying to get past her, but she warded them off with artful twirls of the hands, telekinetically nudging and poking and stabbing and hurling them back.

But it was the sight beyond that made the hair on the back of Augum's neck rise. From the dense black cloud ahead, two towers emerged, several leagues apart. In between, four other things were coming straight for them. An iceberg, a tornado of pure fire, a waterspout, and the black cloud itself, which flickered with lightning at an angry pace.

The rest of the elements were about to attack them.

FABRIC FLAPPING IN THE WIND

BRIDGET

Bridget watched the moonlight play about on the ceiling in waves created by the wind-tossed curtains, reminding her of the ocean. She imagined a vast fleet of gargoyle ships being built and provisioned. Empty ships that would return with holds burgeoning with slaves. She imagined reversing time and, instead of helping Grak refill the obelisk, leading an insurrection until the ship sank. Now she had doomed the seven human kingdoms, and they had no idea what was coming …

She had to do something. She had to form a plan.

The gargoyle manor was quiet, the only sounds being the whistle of the wind, the rustle of the trees and grass, and a gentle hum of insects. She looked over to see Sebastian curled up in a ball. Checking that he was snoozing peacefully, she raised the blanket up to his chin. When he did not move, she slipped out from underneath the blanket, placing her feet on the cold stone floor, which she'd washed only that afternoon. There she stood for a moment, listening to the house to make sure none of the gargoyles were up.

Hearing nothing, she padded around the bed in her nightgown, quietly dropped to her knees, reached under the bed, and retrieved the old key hidden there who knew when. Standing, she looked to Sebastian, conscious of the danger, of what awaited all of humanity, of what could happen to them both and especially … to him. She wanted to gently shake him awake to tell him she loved him like her own son. She wanted to claim him as such, even. But her courage failed her.

Turning her back, she walked out of the bedroom and through the short hall and the moonlit kitchen, where she grabbed a cotton blanket she had washed that day, before padding on to the living room. The gargoyles were so confident in their own security that they did not hold watch, and slept high above on a floor only accessible through flight. Grak, when not lifted by a gargoyle, simply jumped on top of a towering scroll shelf, using it as a pivot point to jump onto the mezzanine.

Once in the living room, a gentle scratching and shuffling sound began. A rotund shadow waddled after her into a window-stretched beam of moonlight.

"Hello, Snuffles," she whispered to the armadillo, which watched her like an observing puppy. Allowed to come and go as it pleased when the door was open, which was often, the little creature seemed content with its life, oblivious to the sufferings of the wretches nearby. "You won't tell, will you?"

Snuffles the armadillo's response was to settle in the beam of moonlight, its front paws protruding forth as if waiting for a treat.

"But a treat I have not, little one," she whispered and placed a hand on the oversized bronze door handle. Checking to make sure Snuffles stayed put in the moonbeam, she opened the door, wincing at the slightest creak. Being collared and so high up, Bridget had no hope of escape, so the doors were kept unlocked. She slipped through the space the door afforded and closed it in time to block Snuffles, who had scampered after her as if worried about being left behind.

She winced again upon hearing the *click* of the handle mechanism and pressed her ear against the door to listen. All she heard was the vibrant sound of a sky plateau. The grass, the oak trees, and the insects all sang in nightly harmony that soothed her soul and made her long for her kingdom.

Ahead, a brilliant full moon that looked larger than the sun in the day lit the plateau. The moon whispered at her that this was not the end of her journey but the beginning of a new one. The challenge, of course, was how to start that journey for real.

"In time, Bridget," she whispered to herself. "Be patient. Be loyal, subservient, and humble. And in time ..." She raised a hand, which closed into a fist, and in her mind's eye, she saw herself holding a metaphorical dagger—and using it to impale her gargoyle foes.

Perhaps it will never come to that, she thought, pushing off the door to thrust herself into the moonlight, her feet gliding along the flagstones and cool grass, one hand clutching the key, the blanket tucked under an arm.

Checking that no one was following her, she soon found herself before the pond, with its swaying flowers and gentle frog symphony and overhanging oak. There she placed the neatly folded blanket on the grass, set the key beside it, grabbed the bottom hem of her nightgown, and raised it over her head. Naked and shivering in the wind, she dipped a toe into the water and winced, for it was freezing.

You will persevere, she told herself, for she had experienced many greater sufferings. She continued stepping into the pond, her feet sinking into squishy mud. Although her body screamed from the cold, her mind sought shelter by the roaring warmth of a Castle Arinthian hearth.

Once waist-deep in the water, and with her teeth chattering, she took a series of shuddering breaths to gird her soul and lowered herself into the water. "How in Sithesia do you do this sort of thing, girl?" she asked, wondering how Leera bore the terrible sensation of frigid water. She then thanked the gods for making her an earth warlock.

Finding her footing and allowing her body a few heartbeats to settle into that frigidity, she splayed her hand above the water and incanted, "*Un vun deo.*" A tug pulled her hand down and forward a little. She lowered both hands and began digging through the mud, teeth chattering loudly now. Just as she wanted to give up and try on a less windy day, her hands found something solid. She worked her fingers around its edge and downward, suspecting it was a box.

But she couldn't reach the bottom of it, and so she clenched her teeth and dropped her head below the water, giving her hands access to the bottom. The cut on her forehead stung despite the healing paste Grak had applied. Shoving away the memory of being whipped by the gargoyle king's servant, she propped her feet against the squishy mud and pulled with everything she had. The suction made it a battle, but with some fierce wiggling about, it finally loosened beneath her, and she dragged up a metal box.

The moment her head rose above the water, the wind made her regret stepping into the pond, for it cooled her wet skin to a bone-chilling numbness. Nonetheless encouraged by her find, she weathered the discomfort and washed the mud off the box. Then she placed it onto the grass beside the key, stepped out of the water, and threw the blanket around herself. She jumped in place, rubbing the cotton against her skin, teeth chattering as she repeated, "This sucks, this sucks, this sucks," just as Leera would have.

Except Leera would have used a spell to ward off the cold, she thought. *Not to mention be able to dry herself after*. It was perhaps the first time Bridget wished she were a water warlock.

Body still cold but reaching an equilibrium with the flapping blanket, she dropped to her knees before the box to inspect it. There was a lock built into the front, as she had expected, and the seal between the lid and base seemed tight. She did not recognize the type of metal—one that resisted rust. To complete her investigation, she splayed a hand, incanting, "*Un vun asperio aurum enchantus.*" When the box showed no sign of enchantment, she snuffed Reveal, grabbed the key, and gently worked it into the lock.

Except the key wouldn't quite fit. Grimacing, she raised the box to stand on its back and angled it so the moonlight lit the keyhole. Sure enough, pond detritus had built up within.

"Great," she muttered. Leera would have blasted it with a jet of water to clean it out. What could she do?

Bridget glanced around until she found a fallen branch, which she grabbed and broke into pieces, selecting the sharpest splinter of the lot. Using it like a toothpick, she worked it into the keyhole, methodically prying out the gunk. Then she cupped her hands together, ladled some water with them, and poured it from a height onto the keyhole. She repeated this until no gunk appeared to remain, then tried the key once more.

Click went the mechanism, and Bridget, having experienced so few accomplishments since her capture, expelled a small squeal of delight. She placed the box on its base, grabbed both sides of the lid, and raised it. It wouldn't budge.

"Are you jesting me?" she muttered, shoulders slumping. "No, you will *not* defeat me, you slimy bastard."

She wedged a foot against the base and grabbed the lid with both hands, vowing to try the Strength spell next if this failed. There was a reverse-suction sound and the lid popped open, revealing a wood-lined compartment, the corners of which were cut and fitted with surprising skill. In the center of that compartment was a scroll neatly tied with crimson string—and as a testament to the workmanship of the box, the scroll was powder dry.

Glancing at the manor and seeing no one watching her, she wiped her hands on the blanket to dry them, withdrew the scroll, undid the string, and unfurled it, noting how strong yet supple the parchment was.

"Well slap me fats," she whispered in honor of her beloved Olaf, a smile widening her lips.

It showed this kingdom in relation to others. The problem was that she could not understand any of the hieroglyphs denoting the cities and other notable locations. And at what scale was the map? How many leagues would she have to traverse to reach a border? Days? Tendays? Months? Judging by the tiny size of the landmarks, she suspected the lands depicted were vast.

What she did understand was the *X*, which someone had added at a later date, for it was written in crimson ink—and which had to represent her location. From that *X*, dotted lines ran to multiple distant lands in all directions of the compass, with each kingdom marked by a single visual.

A wolf, also drawn in red ink, represented the kingdom to the south, which Bridget suspected meant wolven. Similar crudely drawn depictions also denoted other kingdoms. The central kingdom with the *X* showed a creature with a pointed tail and wings—surely a gargoyle, with the *X* likely denoting her location. Another one depicted a horned bull standing on its hind legs.

"Perhaps the fabled land of the minotaur," she whispered, feeling like a child discovering other worlds.

Another showed a lizard, also on hind legs, and still another depicted what looked like a lion in the same pose. That one drew particular interest, for she wondered if it was a cousin race of the extinct Dreadnought race of lions.

"Maybe the Dreadnoughts were but one clan of lions," she said, a finger tracing the pictorial. What a strange feeling to hold such a document that would at home be considered nothing but a child's fancy or perhaps a prank. Here, it was revolutionary, turning history on its head.

The dotted red lines that ran in all directions meandered through and around various landmarks of note, ones she could use as guides. The question was, which kingdom would she want to escape to? She knew nothing of minotaurs or lizard kin. She knew wolven were callous, but would these wolven be the same, or worse? And the lion people may well be a completely different race to the Dreadnoughts, or at the very least they could have diverged significantly after eons apart. She would have to be wise with her decision, for what if they chained her anew, even separated her and Sebastian? She resolved to learn more.

The second challenge was *how* to escape with Sebastian, ideally free of the collars. That was something she would have to plan separately.

For now, she committed the map to memory as best she could, returned it to the box, shut it tight, and waded back into the waters, where she suffered the cold anew to rebury it.

After stepping naked out of the water a second time, she froze, for she spotted a gargoyle staring at her from between the trees.

"How long have you been there?" she hissed, snatching the blanket and raising it like a shield, her naked back to the wind.

"Grak hear noise, want to see what Ah-bee-gale do," Grak replied, walking forth to stand ten feet from her, where he watched her with interest.

Bridget kept her front obscured as she worked the blanket around her back to dry herself off. As she did, she watched the disfigured gargoyle with an uneasy tingling in her chest. She realized she had to turn this into an opportunity or all would be lost.

"Y-your k-kind is c-called *g-gerger*," she said, hating her teeth for chattering at the most inopportune time, and she took a moment to force them to calm down. "What does that mean?"

"*Gerger* is word for gorgan cursed with, how you say ...?" He used a hand to indicate between herself and himself.

Bridget, having recently learned that the word gorgan was their word for gargoyle, grimaced as she tried to understand his meaning. "*Gyot?*"

"No, not slave." He kept indicating between them. "Feel sad. Sad for Ah-bee-gale. Sad for other."

At last it dawned on Bridget what he meant. "*Gerger* is the term for a gargoyle cursed with empathy."

"*Empawthee*, yes. Old slave. He know this *empawthee* long time ago." He indicated the manor, telling Bridget he meant a prior slave whose head now likely adorned the manor's walls. He nodded. "*Yoss*, this is right word. Ah-bee-gale people have this ... *empawthee*. *Gerger* cursed with *empawthee*."

Bridget couldn't stop the disdain from infecting her tone. "Empathy is not a curse. It is a blessing. It is a strength. It is the bedrock of friendship and family and community and society." She looked him up and down with a loathing she did not know she could feel, then turned her cheek away in shame. Grak was not the enemy. He was an ally, and she needed to get it together lest she poison the lone well of hope she had. And if what he was saying was true, she needed to make the best of it, even if that meant soiling her dignity.

Bridget dropped to her knees before the disfigured one-eyed gargoyle, with his wings torn off and his body flayed by his own kind. She brought her hands together in supplication and looked up at him. "Grak. My friend. Will you help me and my son? I wish only to return to my homeland, to be free. I wish only for peace between our people. But I know you are preparing for war. I know you are building ships."

He walked up to her, face obscured by shadow.

She kept her own head tilted up at him, eyes pleading along with her words. "I know your people will sail back to my land and conquer us," she continued. "Please. Do not kill us. Help me so that I may help my people. Tell me of the other lands and peoples. Tell me that one is safe for us, so that I may depart to it with my son and —"

Grak's face twisted, and he lashed out with the back of a hand, smashing her face with it. She rolled out of the blanket — and splashed into the pond, where she gasped in shock and pain, her heart shattered.

"Ah-bee-gale must not ask such things," he hissed, glancing back at the dark manor. "Ah-bee-gale want death? Death for son? Death for Grak?" He growled the gargoyle equivalent of "*Huh?*"

Bridget crawled out of the pond and prostrated herself at his feet, where she allowed her nakedness to strip her of the dignity she felt was preventing progress. "Please, you do not understand. The empathy you have is a great strength. A *historic* strength. Use it. Save us. Save my people. Aid us, and you shall know a greatness no gargoyle has ever known …"

Grak towered over her, and she feared he would lash out even more violently upon her exposed back, which would break like tinder under his strength.

Instead he stepped to her side, leaned down, picked up the blanket, and flung it over her. "Ah-bee-gale must not do stupid," he said. "Ah-bee-gale is a *gyot* and Grak is a *gerger*."

A shivering Bridget gathered the blanket around herself and rose into a sitting position, the sting of having paid with her dignity for such a small advance almost beyond bearing. A shadow within her rose and dared her to shove the bastard off the sky island. That shadow took pleasure in imagining Grak trying to use the stubs of his wings as he plummeted, shrieking all the way to a smashing death.

But thinking of Sebastian snoozing peacefully in his bed, only to be rudely awoken by an angry gargoyle master upon learning of a servant's untimely demise, easily corralled such thoughts back into their pen where they belonged.

"Ah-bee-gale must think of son. Ah-bee-gale must be careful."

"Yes," she whispered. "Yes …" Still, she looked up with pleading eyes. "At least tell me of the other lands. The land of the wolf and the lizard and the lion and the bull. Are these lands safe? What are they —"

Grak raised the back of his hand, and Bridget yelped and recoiled, squeezing her eyes shut in preparation for a stinging rebuke.

That rebuke did not come, and when she peeked through the lid of one squinted eye, she saw Grak standing with his head bowed, his lone eye watery.

"Ah-bee-gale want to leave Grak."

"No, not at all. I *don't* want to leave you! You-you-you should come, in fact! Come with us! Come be our guide and protector. Be kind to us, love us ... *save* us ... I beg you with all my heart and soul and—"

Grak threw out his arms and lunged forth with an enraged growl, causing Bridget to throw her hands over her head and hunker in place. Grak hovered over her, snarling his putrid breath, as if contemplating devouring her on the spot.

"I'm sorry," she gibbered. "But you must understand that I don't want to be a slave. I want to be free. I want my *son* to be free ..."

"Grak understand," he replied after a time. "Ah-bee-gale make Grak sad. Ah-bee-gale stay, keep Grak friend. Ah-bee-gale safe here with Grak. Other lands bad. Very bad. Make slave more than gorgan. Make slave ... *gissif*."

"Suffer," Bridget translated, recognizing the word from his sporadic teachings.

"Take son. Eat son. Make Ah-bee-gale arena meat. Ah-bee-gale understand?"

She nodded. "I do. I *do* understand. I don't *want* to leave Grak because Grak is Ah-bee-gale's friend." She patted her chest. "You're my friend, do you understand? We're friends, you and me and Sebastian. We will stay here because it's safe ..." Yet even as she said this, she knew otherwise. She would not stay and would in time craft a plan to leave—and she would do it without Grak, for he was just as dangerous as the other gargoyles ...

For a time, only the wind spoke on their behalf, whispering possibilities. As she sat shivering despite the blanket, Bridget captured one of these possibilities, and her gaze wandered to the pond.

"You know of this secret in the pond," she said, worried that she might be pushing her luck. "Others have tried the journey. Surely someone must have succeeded in reaching one of the other kingdoms."

Grak stood silently nearby, his own gaze upon the distant moonlit horizon. "*Yoss*," he whispered.

That lone word raised Bridget to her feet. "And you helped them," she said daringly, clutching the blanket tight.

Grak snarled, and his hand rose sharply, prompting her to retreat. Then that hand fell and he sighed, gaze returning to the dark horizon. "*Yoss* ..." he admitted.

"There is sanctuary in at least *one* of the other lands …"

"Sanct … ory? Grak not know this word."

"Safety. Freedom."

"Freedom, *yoss*. For some."

"For some?"

"For those who—" He rubbed two broken claws together as he searched for the word. "Who buy freedom. From—" He nodded at the manor.

"Buy freedom from the captain? From Karr Gravak?"

"*Yoss*. Work many, many moons. Whole life. Make good work."

Bridget sighed. No way was she planning on earning her freedom at the cost of her entire life. "So the land of the wolf, for example—are these called wolven?"

"Wol*fan*, *yoss*."

She wondered if he'd misspoken but didn't bother pressing the point.

"They bad. Very bad. No trust. Make slave. Eat slave."

"All right, but how many days would it take to travel by foot to that kingdom, for example?" She made her fingers walk along the air.

"Many *mirsas*."

"What is a *mirsa*?"

"Ten—" He pointed at the sky and moved his hand to the horizon.

"Ten sunsets?"

"Ten sunsets, *yoss*."

"A tenday, then," she whispered to herself. So likely over a month of travel just to get to the land of the wolven.

She tapped her collar. "What about this? How can I take this off?" She had tried disenchanting it using a polished piece of metal as a mirror to watch her fingers work, but just like manacles at home, the enchantments had long sunk to permanence.

He scowled at her, and she knew she was really pushing it, but she needed to know. She sensed she could make a breakthrough if she was bold but careful enough. "Please," she whispered. "I will be loyal and show no signs of my plans. Teach me. Teach me and I will teach you. Find freedom with me. You are a slave as much as I am. *Gerger* is *gyot*. Let us work together. Teach me, Grak. Teach me anything you can. I will be your pupil, you my teacher. And we will be eternal friends. What is the word for friend in gorgan? Hmm?"

Grak stood silently watching the horizon, the wind moving the grass and rustling the branches yet flowing around him as if he were a rock in water.

"Tell me of the other kingdoms at least ..." Something told her there was no word for friend. She bet the closest would be a word like *ally*.

He inhaled deeply and took his time exhaling, his iron gaze never leaving the horizon. "Long is war between the *gengas*," he said, using a gargoyle word Bridget knew to mean kingdoms. "Old war. In time, war make *gengas* equal."

"So you've reached a stalemate."

"Stale ... mat?"

"Stalemate. It means equal positions."

"Stalemate. Equal. *Yoss*. And long is *gyot*."

"You mean the history of human slaves is old?"

"*Yoss*. Old. *Gyot* very old. But in time, *gyot* less and less. You die young. You die sick. Weak. You die many. So price of *gyot* make high in time. Big high. Little *gyot* left here. *Gyot* here stupid. What you see on scroll written when *gyot* still read and make tongue with quill. Few *gyot* make tongue with quill now. Big high price. *Gyot* good *ayga*."

"*Ayga?*"

"It word for—" Grak drew a glyph on his chest, then pointed at Bridget's arm and made a slashing motion, which she took to mean he was referring to her arm rings.

"I think I understand—*ayga* means arcane stamina energy," she said.

"*Yoss. Gyot* make good *ayga* for all gorgan."

"We make good stamina vessels for you gargoyles," Bridget translated.

"*Yoss*." He turned to look at her, and she felt such profound pity in his silence that she involuntarily stepped back, feeling her eyebrows pitch together.

"Now Ah-bee-gale come from far. Come show that big land filled with many *gyot*. Now *gengas*—king *dums* ...?"

"Kingdoms, yes," she said numbly.

"Now kingdoms equal no more. Now all want big *gyot* land. Ah-bee-gale understand?"

Bridget staggered as if struck. "It's not just the gargoyles who will want an abundance of slaves," she gibbered, dropping to her knees, fighting the urge to retch. "It's the other kingdoms too ..."

"*Yoss*," Grak whispered.

"How ... how many of them know what you gargoyles have discovered?"

"*Gengas* know. If not now, soon. They know. They learn."

"Then you're saying all the other *gengas*—these other kingdoms on this continent—they'll try to colonize the new big land—my land—to enslave my people."

"*Yoss. Gyot* is gold. *Gyot* make *genga*—" He flexed both arms, showing his broken claws and making a fearsome warrior expression. "—look big to other *gengas*. Ah-bee-gale understand?"

Bridget rocked back and forth, mouth agape, the shivering worsened by shock. The blanket slipped from her shoulders, but she hardly noticed. Grak went to the blanket and slipped it back up, giving her shoulder a gentle double pat. For a time Bridget sat there, an empty husk devoid of all hope, a puddle of despair.

What was the point of escaping to another beastly kingdom when slaves were inherently precious to *all* the other kingdoms? And what if she only made humans *more* of a target as a result? Yet she couldn't stay here either, steadily getting older until the gargoyles got tired of them and stuck their shriveled heads on a wall …

Her hand closed around the grass. Her numb fingers bit into the dirt until she had a fist of sky earth. A deep rage began to bubble. How she wanted to rip it up and fling it at him and curse him to Hell and then … then what? Run off the edge of the plateau and fall to a screaming death? Was that the extent of her childish plan?

"Get it together, Bridget," she hissed at herself through clenched teeth, letting the clump of grass go. A shadow stepped up to the curtain. For once, she needed its courage and threw open the curtain. She stood, numb to the cold and to her emotions, and gazed upon Grak with a black look, a look he would have feared had he known what was looking at him through her eyes. But it was he who spoke first.

"Many suns and moons ago," he began, "gorgan go over water to your *genga*—your kingdom. But gorgan find *draga* live in your kingdom. *Draga* big. *Draga* strong. *Draga* destroy many gorgan. *Draga* then come, make big war, destroy kingdoms. Kingdoms fear *draga*. Tell many story. Story pass *girku* to *girku*."

"You passed stories from generation to generation of how the dragons destroyed the kingdoms here," Bridget translated, licking her teeth, particularly her canines, with primal satisfaction.

Grak, oblivious to her impudence, merely raised his chin. "But now gorgan go to your kingdom and see only one *draga*. Gorgan come back and no more fear your kingdom because one *draga* nothing. Gorgan now want *gyot*. Want land. Make big kingdom. Make strong gorgan."

Bridget nodded, the reality wilting her bloodlust—but not her resolve. So in that era, there had been many dragons, and now a mere three defended the entire continent of Sithesia—and one of those dragons was in chains. That meant that not only did she have to survive with Sebastian, but she had to somehow prevent all these powerful slave-owning kingdoms from making that journey overseas, as they would no doubt be successful in enslaving the entire continent. After all, what were three dragons against who knew how many such adversaries?

"You will teach me of your people," she said, voice firm with command. "So that together we can save mine. Surely you do not want to see many Ah-bee-gales as slaves, do you? My honorable friend Grak, teach me your tongue, your history, and ..." She grabbed her slave collar and roughly yanked her own neck about. "And in turn, I will teach you about freedom. About our people. About my tongue. About courage."

"Ku ... kurage?"

"Courage. Tenacity. Valor. Strength. Boldness. Bravery."

"Brave. Grak know this word. But brave not in Grak heart. Brave word for *karr*."

"It's not just a word for captains."

"Ah-bee-gale not know gorgan. Not know *karr*. Grak name mean *slap*—" He slapped the air with a hand to show he was being literal, that his very name *meant* being slapped. "Grak is a *gerger kupa*," he spat, voice oozing with disdain for himself.

"You are not a gutterborn." She took a step forth. "You are a survivor."

Grak looked down upon her, his one eye flitting between both of hers as he considered her words. "Ah-bee-gale show Grak Ah-bee-gale people strong. But Ah-bee-gale not know old *hemen*."

"*Hemen*? You mean humans?"

"*Yoss. Hemen* also strong. Long time ago strong in other kingdom."

"Wait, *other* kingdom? You mean outside of the dragon kingdom, or *my* kingdom?"

"Grak not know. Maybe different time. Maybe *hemen* come before *draga, yoss*? Grak not smart in gorgan history."

Bridget swallowed, for the implication was that the gargoyles had perhaps initially found a kingdom like Endraga Ra, where the dragons were wild and ruled the land, and then later found the human kingdom—her continent of Sithesia—from whence they effortlessly took slaves. But it was hard to delve into specifics without understanding the gargoyle tongue, a problem she was determined to resolve in time.

"Gorgans come, take *hemen*," Grak continued. "Other *gengas* come and take *hemen*. Turn *hemen* into *gyot*."

"But when *exactly* did you first turn us into slaves?"

Grak looked to the sky. "Many moons and suns ago. That all Grak know."

Bridget looked to the moon, envisioning a time in history when this could have happened. There were old catastrophes written about in myth. Time before time. In the age of beasts. But also in the age of the Arcaner. In the rise of the power of the dragon. There were some notes in the old scripts and tablets, but most were dismissed as mere mythology. Perhaps they had indeed been telling the truth, yet metaphor and symbolism and the very weight of history itself had hidden that truth.

"You found a way across the oceans," she whispered to herself. "Thus we must close that route—or destroy you ..." The last phrase she mouthed so that Grak could not hear her plans.

A glimmer of hope sparked amidst the moonlight. She cocked her head, realizing the seed had been planted when she had first witnessed the gargoyles harvesting stamina from Ordinaries, something that ought to be impossible. What she had witnessed told her that *all* of humanity possessed an untapped potential to become warlocks. It also implied that there had to be a way to unleash that potential. Perhaps there was a means to do so somewhere in the ancient records, records that may have, like so much knowledge over the eons, been lost to time ...

Bridget craned her neck skyward to look deep into a field of stars. Someone knew. If not the gods, then those charged with keeping knowledge on behalf of humans, knowing they would lose their way over time. Someone like Anna Atticus Stone, who had made it her life's work to bridge the gap between Ley and Sithesia. Or the few remaining Leyan people around her.

Even thinking of them made hope swell within her, a glorious hope ... and a tragic hope, for she knew what it meant to unleash such knowledge. It meant training beyond normal training. Training in the old way. Training with people long thought dead. And it meant arming the populace with a skill set crafted for one thing and one thing only ...

War.

* * *

That night Bridget dreamed of flying above a fleet of twenty-masted ships, aiming to dive and unleash a primal violence that would send them to the bottom. Sebastian rode on her back, shouting, "Yippee! Let's get the fiends and save our kingdom! Yippee!"

But as she flew, she felt something attacking from her right—a giant gargoyle was jabbing her with a spear. That gargoyle morphed into the visage of an angry Anna Atticus Stone, whose long silver braided ponytail was flailing as she jabbed at a fourteen-year-old Bridget with the butt of her staff.

"Get your lazy bones up, Burns!" Mrs. Stone snapped, the jabbing harder now. "It's time to train!"

Bridget bolted awake inside a bright room—to The Brat snickeringly jabbing her with his tail. The moment she locked eyes with him, his gargoyle face scowled, and he whapped her upside the head with the tail, hissing at her in his foul tongue to keep her eyes down.

"What do you want?" she snapped, trying to organize the words he had used, determined to learn the language of the gorgan. But the hard smack had jumbled her thoughts. She rubbed her stinging cheek as she placed a hand on Sebastian, who was awake but pretending to sleep. Upon feeling her touch, he drew the blanket up to his eyes, which he kept averted.

The Brat unfolded his wings, opening them like a parasol, before folding them neatly. He pointed to the window with his tail. "*Giririg, gyot. Tiha yer mah.*"

She almost asked what *tiha* and *mah* meant, but this was not Grak she was dealing with. In the judgment of the gorgan, The Brat was not weakened by empathy—nor was he susceptible to it. Pleading with him would only embolden his foul disposition, and so she held her tongue and nodded.

The Brat swung the tail about, snapping, "*Hohol!*"

"I'm going, I'm going," she said, and slid out of the bed, silently cursing the beast and his prehensile tail. Normally she'd get dressed, but the young gargoyle watched her, so she proceeded to the kitchen. He followed, sneering at her and chuckling to himself, tail idly slapping the floor as he walked. She quickly made herself a simple meal of salted-and-peppered bread and butter and water, with a dried chunk of chicken for meat. She practically shoveled this down her throat, knowing she needed the energy, until the little—at least by gargoyle standards—six-foot beastling lost patience and used his tail to slap the bread from her hand.

"*Hohol, gyot!*" he shouted, a tongue lolling out of his snout as he laughed. He stepped up to her, and she lowered her eyes to avoid getting punished, only to feel his tail slither up her back before suddenly wrapping itself around her throat.

"*Tiha yer mah,*" he repeated, giving her body a shake as he made her look at him.

Prevented from spellcasting, Bridget stood with as much poise as she could, glaring with a cold fury that told him she was not afraid of him. No doubt hoping to see her flail and plead for mercy, he squeezed her throat with his tail so hard that she felt her eye sockets bulge. When she yielded nothing, he let go with a spiteful jerk, once again hissing, "*Tiha yer mah,*" albeit in a slightly disappointed tone.

Stumbling back and rubbing her sore neck, Bridget thought she understood what he'd said, and she whispered, "*Today you're mine ...*" The idea chilled her soul.

Gods have mercy how she wanted to rip the collar off, cast a potent 10th degree Fear into this beastling's brain, and snatch his throat with a reptile claw ...

The Brat lazily flapped his tail toward the bedroom, muttering, "*Hohol, gyot, giri kenga.*"

"Go, slave, and get changed," she mouthed, having learned the word *kenga* on the ship. *I'm going to learn your tongue and use it against you*, she thought, knowing vengeance might never be fulfilled since escape was the plan.

Mercifully, the vicious beast did not follow her to the bedroom, and she went to the trunk and withdrew her day dress.

"Momma?" Sebastian squeaked, blanket lowering to reveal his worried mouth.

"I have to go for the day, Sebby," she said, making a twirling motion with a finger. In turn, he raised the blanket over his head, allowing her to change into her day clothes. "Please be meek in your duties and do as you are told," she said, closing the lid to the trunk, which was his signal to lower the blanket.

"Where are you going?"

"I don't know yet."

"How long will you be gone?"

"I don't know."

"Will you be okay?"

"Yes, I'll be okay."

"Okay."

Having glanced around the room to see that all was well—the hearth was lit, the floor orderly—she swept to him, leaned over, and gave him a warm and tight squeeze. "Promise you'll behave."

"I promise I'll behave. Promise you'll return."

"I promise I'll return. I would never leave you. Ever." She pressed her lips to his forehead and held them there, and felt his hands clasp her forearms. She wanted to tell him that she loved him. Instead she let go, cupped his cheeks, smiled, and playfully mussed his hair. "I'll see you later, kiddo," she said, warming at the memory of Jez doing that very thing to her. Now it was she who felt like a middle-aged woman.

"Okay, Momma. Be safe. Bye ..."

"Bye, Sebby."

The Brat waited for her at the kitchen entrance. He stood before his older brother, who was talking down to him in stern tones, his wings opening and closing slightly with his words, much like a butterfly's — albeit a deadly one. The Brat nodded with a serious face, eyes low. Eyes that quickly realized she was watching. She was careful to stand meekly by the hallway door, gaze on the floor, hands before her in supplication. Her duty today was to learn — and survive. Not to antagonize. Stand up for herself, maybe, but never antagonize.

The older brother finished with a warning growl before turning his back on his younger brother. The Brat waited until his older brother was gone before he snarled at Bridget and hissed, "*Girit, gyot.*"

Come here, slave, Bridget translated as she padded, barefoot as always, to stand before the little brute. He straightened before her, breathing loudly through his nostrils. She braced, expecting a punishment for having witnessed his castigation, but none came. Instead he turned about and walked off, drawling over his shoulder, "*Hehi, gyot.*"

"I'm coming, I'm coming," she muttered under her breath, hurrying to catch up to his long stride.

They met the father outside. The seventeen-foot behemoth was studying an open scroll, Grak standing dutifully behind him, head down as usual. That head rose slightly upon Bridget's emergence from the home, and his face and lone eye revealed no sign that they had spoken the night before.

Thank the gods he is at least good at hiding his secrets, she thought, taking her cue to stand behind The Brat in the same manner as Grak stood behind his master.

The captain ignored his youngest son's arrival as his gargoyle eyes perused the scroll. Upon finishing reading, he furled the scroll up, handed it to Grak, and made a backhanded *off-with-you* motion at him. Grak bowed and took the scroll to the house. Only then did the captain finally turn his attention to the young gargoyle. He gave a sharp series of commands in such a low growl and with such fluid ease that Bridget barely caught a word, but knew it had something to do with that day.

When he finished, the young male hesitated before nodding. That hesitation enraged Captain Gravak, who slapped him so hard that the gargoyle was sent tumbling an incredible ten feet. A stream of what Bridget suspected were gargoyle expletives then tumbled from the captain's snout as he berated his son for disrespect, slovenliness, or hesitation — it was hard for Bridget to ascertain. She stood statue-still, not letting her curious eyes so much as dart in the direction of The Brat or the captain lest she draw attention to herself.

The young male slithered his way back to stand before his imperious father and mumbled something meek.

The captain grunted and sharply took hold of his son's upper arm, snapping, "*Gera fi.*"

Grab it, Bridget reflexively translated in her mind even as The Brat snatched her by the hair and dragged her to stand before him. She winced from the pain but did not cry out. It would not do to show fragility before those who considered empathy a supreme weakness. Still, she most decidedly felt like an *it*. A simple *gyot* doing what was asked of her. And she loathed it beyond measure, so much so that she had to force her fists to unclench.

Patience and fortitude, Bridget, she thought. *Patience and fortitude …*

Luckily The Brat and his father paid her no heed, for upon taking hold of his boy and thus Bridget, the captain touched a rune and growled an incantation, and she felt her body get yanked. After a couple heartbeats of tumbling through the arcane ether, they popped into existence on a roughly cobbled street flanked by rows of homes. But these weren't like gargoyle homes, which had rounded edges and open holes. These were straight-edged and appeared hastily constructed of wood and timber and rope and even fabric, which comprised most of the walls, giving the structures the appearance of a desert tent town.

Bridget glanced around with a slightly open mouth, trying to fathom the meaning of these constructs. Turning in place, she spotted a group of young gargoyles approaching, minded by another winged gargoyle that was only a foot shorter than the captain and with fewer runes on his body.

A teacher and his pupils, Bridget realized.

Every gargoyle, teacher included, bowed upon coming up to the captain. The students kept their eyes low as the teacher paid the captain respect. Bridget noted that The Brat idly picked at a claw, acting like a bored child — until the captain noticed and promptly smacked the back of his head. The young gargoyle snapped to attention, and the captain snarled a few words at the teacher while staring at his son. She suspected the gist of it was that he wanted the teacher to go hard on him.

The teacher nodded along and paid respect with another bow of the head, and the captain said nothing more on the subject. He turned to glare at his son, who was smart enough to keep his head down, until the captain stabbed a rune and shot off once again, leaving his son and Bridget in the care of a gargoyle class.

The teacher exchanged a few words with the recalcitrant student, who grudgingly replied to his queries. Bridget's brow was furrowed throughout as she tried to keep up with their rapid exchanges, but all she gleaned from it was that the young gargoyle was expected to do his duty, whatever that meant in this context.

Then the teacher noticed her and flicked at her to go away. He pointed to a nearby building and said, "*Hohol gor ter yat gyots!*" whilst repeatedly making that dismissive motion.

Bridget looked to the building and saw fellow slaves staring at her from within a large alcove made of loose cloth walls the color of adobe. She approached them, and although they were dressed in the same manner as her, they looked very different. Every single one was at least a full head shorter. All were missing teeth, bent over, malnourished, frizzy-haired, and wild-eyed. They backed away from her as if she were either a pariah or a queen. Their feral eyes kept flitting away, only to reluctantly return. Their grubby fingers, with jagged and broken nails, kept fidgeting with their filthy clothes. As before, they were of all ages, but skewed young, meaning her age or younger. Half were men and half were women.

They muttered in grunts amongst each other, with some serving as questions and others as statements. It took her a moment to realize they weren't grunts at all, but that same monosyllabic language, albeit spoken in a guttural fashion, as if they had spent countless generations trying to imitate the gargoyle tongue unsuccessfully.

Bridget felt such a pang of despair on their behalf that she gave them a small but kind smile. This caused every one of them to jump back as if she had bared her teeth.

"I mean you no harm," she said. They gasped, with some grabbing onto their neighbor. It made her believe this was a lower caste of slaves that was even less accustomed to dignity and decorum, one burdened with a low intelligence cultivated on purpose by the gargoyles. They reeked of sewage and hay so strongly that her eyes watered from the stench and her cheeks prickled from the shame of having such judgmental thoughts.

The largest of these slaves came up to her neck, a stocky older woman with a muscular physique and sagging jowls that reminded her of a Canterran bulldog. She clutched her frizzy hair on either side of her head, hanging onto the clumps as though for comfort. She circled Bridget, sniffing at her and recoiling, only to sniff again, her nostrils flaring. She stank of coil, reminding Bridget of the gargoyle ship and of labor and sweat and agony.

"Yes, I am human just like you are," Bridget said, keeping her tone gentle. She patted her own chest and enunciated the word as she had heard Grak say it. "*Hemen. Hemen,*" she repeated.

Her fluid speech made them all jump back. Some turned to a corner and began growling at the fabric ceiling, which she assumed was a warding prayer, while others twirled fingers skyward, mumbling, "*Ga he me. Gah he me …*"

"I am *hemen* and I originate from a very faraway *genga,*" she said.

The words garnered scandalized whispers, likely on account of her strange accent, fluid speech, and polysyllabic words.

"I am a *gyot* just like you are," she was careful to add as simply as she could. "They captured — I mean, they *took* me in my home king —"

The thick woman whimpered from fright, snatched Bridget's throat with both hands, and began squeezing with a farmer's strength. But the woman was no gargoyle, and Bridget's training kicked in — in one smooth motion, she pushed her head forward and down, then twisted her body away whilst using her hands to hit the woman's wrists, breaking the hold. The woman — and others — shot forth, but Bridget hissed, "*Shyneo!*" fighting the suppressive collar to flare her hand with writhing ivy, which she snapped at any approaching hand.

As if struck by a Fear spell, the lot of them shrieked as one and stampeded against the back fabric wall, knocking it over, which in turn dragged down the surrounding walls. The entire room toppled, ensnaring the screaming slaves, though thankfully the larger carcass of the building remained intact.

Bridget promptly snuffed her hand and stepped away to take shelter in the opposite corner by the doorway — and just in time too, for the towering teacher punched through the alcove entrance. He snatched the thick woman with a single claw, instinctively knowing it was she who had caused the trouble, and throttled her about whilst growl-roaring into her face, "*Gef yer gada, gyot?*"

Since the last three words translated to *you doing, slave?* the first word had to be *what*. Therefore the question had been, *What are you doing, slave?* She was getting closer to being able to cast Tongues on the gargoyle language.

Having shaken the poor woman about like a rag doll, the teacher made a human-like "Bah!" noise and threw her into the fabric wall of a nearby room. She tumbled a few times, gathering the fabric like a snowball, until she was thoroughly entwined in it.

The teacher barked a few words of command, indicating the walls, before leaving, his tail snapping at the ground in warning.

As the slaves dragged themselves to their feet, grumbling amongst each other, Bridget, seeing that none of the others were helping the struggling woman, went to her aid and began uncoiling the fabric. The woman allowed it—until she saw who it was, at which point she bared her teeth like a wild dog. Bridget raised a flat palm, whispering, "It's all right. I mean you no harm," and tugged gently on the rest of the fabric until the woman was able to take over and complete the task.

Interestingly, the other slaves began to work together to erect the fabric walls anew, knowing how the roping worked. A young woman of Bridget's age struggled with one of these sheets, which had torn in the melee. She kept trying to jam the two sides back together with a flummoxed expression, eyes zipping to the others in concern, as if worried she would get blamed for the tear.

And that was exactly what happened when the stocky older woman spotted the younger woman's problem, and she began to curse at her with a string of venomous monosyllables.

"I can help," Bridget said and stepped between the two women. They sprang away, leaving the torn pieces on the ground. Bridget, no longer fearing another attack, beckoned to the unfortunates. "Come and watch," she said with a kind smile, feeling like a teacher trying to teach tiny children something neat. "Look at what is possible." She spread her hands over the tear and incanted, "*Apreyo.*"

It was a struggle to work through the suppressive collar, which significantly slowed the entire casting, yet the two sides of the fabric nonetheless slowly rejoined and sealed with a white light. Upon the flashing of that light, the other slaves shrieked, once again backing away as if having seen a horror.

"No, this is normal," Bridget kept trying to say, but they were lost to their fright, and the teacher soon stormed in there a second time. Before he could point at anyone, Bridget stood to face him.

"I was the one," she said, wanting to spare the others from his torments. He snatched her entire torso with one clawed hand, lifted her, and shook her about whilst growling gargoyle profanities into her face. Her vision bounced along with her body, and after delivering a sufficient rag-dolling, he threw her into one of the newly hoisted fabric walls. She tumbled a few times, her body collecting the fabric.

The teacher hissed a final warning before departing, leaving Bridget tangled in the mess, her head spinning. A shadow rose over her, and her eyes stopped their cartwheeling to see the thick woman, whose grubby fingers extended toward Bridget's neck. Bridget was about to react with a spell—even gibberish would have sufficed—when the woman's fingers closed on the edge of the fabric, and she uncoiled enough of it for Bridget's arm to spring free, at which point the woman promptly retreated.

"Thank you," Bridget said, unwrapping the rest of her body. "How do you say thank you in your tongue? It's different from the gargoyle tongue, isn't it?" But she might as well have been speaking to a herd of cats, for the other slaves huddled together against the far corner, with the stocky woman up front, acting as their leader. They all watched Bridget with simultaneously fearful and curious eyes.

Bridget sighed, got up, hung the fabric back onto its hooks, and went to linger by the alcove entrance, from where she could watch the teacher as he lectured. The tall gargoyle was explaining in seemingly eloquent detail, for he was using complex words Bridget had not heard.

Bridget cocked her head, wondering if this was the moment to try Tongues. She narrowed her eyes, focusing on each word, the pronunciation, the tempo, and gathered everything she had learned about the gargoyle tongue and their culture thus far. Then she idly pressed three fingers into her temple and covered her mouth with her other hand, pretending to cough, before slipping that hand down to her throat and incanting, "*Translateo commona linguino Gorgan*." She added another cough right after so the sounds blended together.

The teacher glanced back in annoyance, and Bridget promptly dropped her head and eyes. He soon continued, and she almost gasped upon being able to understand some of the speech, albeit on a crude level that lacked nuance and depth, as she was limited by her own experience with the language.

"The humans be stacked like this, level after level," the teacher went on, indicating the buildings with his long tail. "But they cunning and attempt hide. Some will go underground, block behind big metal doors. We will answer this upon our return. You must be clever too, my charges, and stop them from going underground like bugs."

The teacher paced to and fro as he spoke, raising his tail or a claw to pontificate the occasional point. Bridget followed every word, filling the missing word gaps as best she could.

"Those of you gaining runes will want learn the art of the *kepa*," and upon using that word, the teacher brought his clawed hands together but kept them apart just so, with the hands offset a certain way that told her the word *kepa* might stand for *pentastone*—but that was a mere guess. "Some these humans know how to use *arcanery*—" Which Bridget heard as the word *ayga*. "—and these are a dangerous kind. They can wound us. Some can summon small beasts. Others big beasts. Even a dragon. But they only have one, and it not big as of old."

The captain's son The Brat scoffed and said, "They only summon fake dragon. It is not real thing."

"Of course it's not the real thing!" the teacher said. "The real thing extinct for many suns and moons! These humans too stupid for such knowledge! But they will be excellent slaves."

The class laughed—or rather, growl-chortled whilst opening and closing their wings and slapping the ground with their tails, as if clapping.

"Now we will practice raids against the humans. This information is fresh, straight from across ocean …" The students leaned forth as the teacher walked on down the street, his voice fading as he described a series of exercises they would be performing. Bridget listened until his voice steadily faded. The last thing she caught was something about it taking the rest of the day.

Eventually they wandered back and the teacher split off to approach the group of slaves. He picked out half to aid in the exercise, telling the remainder—which luckily included Bridget—to stay put for the rest of the day. The chosen half was then herded out and made to take up positions within the timber structures, probably to act as training fodder. By that point, Bridget's Tongues spell had lapsed on account of the suppressive collar, which made long castings immensely difficult. She sighed and took a seat by the entrance, drumming her cheek with her fingers as she watched the gargoyles begin to perform kidnap drills she had seen in person, with the yelps of the slaves mirroring the ones she had heard in Blackhaven.

As the sun rose, her group of bored slaves began to meander out on their own, some heading to a primitive privy, others to a round fountain where they scooped water with their hands which they would noisily slurp. Others hummed to themselves as they wandered in the opposite direction of the drills. For some reason, the teacher ignored this and kept a razor focus on his kidnappers-in-training, who were surely too young to take overseas—or so Bridget hoped.

She studied them for a time, but learning nothing new, she decided to wander as well. The training block was approximately three street blocks long, with the training taking place on the north side and the alcove in the center. Bridget walked all the way to the south end, where she idly glanced over her shoulder to see that everyone else was either bored or preoccupied way down the blocks with drills. Seeing her opportunity, she strolled into another fabric alcove—and promptly dipped underneath the fabric.

To her surprise, the other side was not a city, as she had expected, but a rolling plain of grass. It stretched for leagues and was dotted with the occasional sky tower, what appeared to be farm-type buildings shaped like giant beehives, and rows of farmland with unfamiliar crops and orchards.

"Great, they're farmers to boot," Bridget muttered, shaking her head at how advanced the gargoyle civilization was. Or perhaps the humans were in charge of their farms. If only she had the power to briefly teleport there just to explore …

Although another city rose far in the hazy distance, there was nothing here that interested her, and she dipped back under the fabric and went to the opposite side of the street. This time, she had to needle her way through multiple fabric walls before she found herself staring at a strip of dirt about a city block in width—and on the other side towered a gargoyle city.

"There you are," she whispered, neck craning.

The nearest buildings were dingy, with larvae-like holes in the walls that served as entrances and smaller holes as windows. The buildings themselves rose like giant globular termite columns, and she almost believed that giant insects lived within. But that thought passed when she glimpsed slaves and lower caste gargoyles hustling about beyond the alleys that separated the buildings.

Knowing she had the rest of the day, she thought to take a risk and explore, but before setting out on her own, she spread her hands over a wooden post that held up the fabric walls and incanted, "*Vestigio itemo discovaro.*" Then she raised a hand and made sure to feel the tug that indicated the Object Track enchantment had been successfully placed.

With her way back set, she peeked out from the inner fabric wall to make sure no one was watching or searching for her before setting off. She hurried across the dirt strip and ducked into an alley, from where she took a bit of time to watch the fabric and timber training construct. Upon hearing the continued sound of yelping and the occasional gargoyle roar of triumph after a successful raid, she turned about and walked on down the refuse-filled alley.

There were some things she recognized, like torn slave clothing and worn rope, or pieces of a barrel, a cart, and what looked like shingles torn from a roof. Everything else was unfamiliar, from bent-up pieces of iron to broken columns of stone to what looked like cement molds. And a lot of rags. But one thing she found would be of use—a ripped reed-woven basket, which she hoisted onto her shoulder in order to blend in with the other slaves.

The street she came to was three times as wide as any in Blackhaven and thrice as busy, so busy in fact—and so dense with slaves and gargoyles—that she had to take some time to collect herself whilst watching from the darkness of the alley. The humans were in worse shape than any she had yet seen. Long of tooth and hair, stooped and thin-boned, they walked with a certain waddling gait that showed they carried much on their shoulders, often literally.

Some carried boulders, others baskets overflowing with exotic fruits and vegetables, others stacks of cloth or corn or squash—or at least what *looked* like corn and squash. Others still carried immense stacks of branches or tinder, tied with frayed rope, the stacks so large that they made the humans appear like ants carrying a chunk of bread. One poor old man carried a stack of tied bricks that was so heavy he walked at a snail's pace.

Their gargoyle minders—for those who had one, most did not—towered over them, disinterested and imperial. Even the lowliest gargoyle enjoyed the best-dressed slave making way for them. Here and there cracked the sound of a whip as it came down upon a back, resulting in a yelp of pain, all lost amidst the hubbub of a city brimming with trade.

Of shops there were many, each manned by either a slave or a lower caste gargoyle perched on a log in what Bridget dubbed as the gargoyle squat. Between the many gargoyle and human legs roamed wild dogs and large cats and rotund armadillos and even anteater-like creatures with long snouts that sniffed the ground, searching for sustenance.

Bridget inhaled a deep breath of the feral air, girding her soul. The street smelled pungently of earth and sewage and hay and manure and foreign spices and despair. Then she strode out into the bustle, careful to keep the basket hoisted beside her head, one arm over its lip, the other swinging freely. But she quickly began to catch attention, mostly from fellow slaves, which she suspected was because she was unusually tall compared to them and unusually clean.

She thus dipped into an alley, where she proceeded to muss up her hair and, finding a puddle, muddy up her face and hands. Then she adopted a pronounced stoop, hoisted the basket, and reentered the fray.

It seemed to work, for they paid her much less attention, and she could enjoy the sights and sounds of a city the likes of which had scarcely been imagined in her kingdom or even written about in the most fantastical books. The globular buildings, pockmarked with giant gargoyle holes and perches, loomed like insectoid sentinels, creating great swaths of oblong shade. Gargoyles zipped about from their high entrances like termites leaving stone nests.

One mean-looking gargoyle with a particularly long snout and a bevy of chest runes held the chains of no less than four human slaves, yet as brutish as he looked, his slaves were clean and walked upright. This brute did a double-take upon spotting Bridget, and she got the distinct impression he was mulling adding her to his flock. To make him lose interest, she bent over even more and feigned rubbing her sore back. The ruse worked, for he continued on his way.

The more well-off slaves—who were cleaner, healthier, better dressed, and possessed fewer scars—had the fortune of using pull carts, although they too were often laden with heavy things like ore or marble or stacks of hay so tall they dwarfed the human. Some of these carts were gigantic and it took a team of humans to pull them, with a lower-caste gargoyle whipping their backs to keep pace. The richest of the rich—often festooned with intricate garments or gold or jewelry or various accouterments, sometimes all at once—owned oxen, but there was not a horse in sight for either human or gargoyle.

Another gargoyle, a winged fourteen-footer emblazoned with a slew of complex runes, walked a huge red bear as a pet—or so Bridget assumed, until she realized it might be a guard animal, destined for the arena, or even slaughtered for its hide. It wasn't muzzled, so now and then it would snap its jaws at a slave, only for the gargoyle to lazily yank its chain back.

But since the bear kept snapping at slaves, the gargoyle smacked his gums and dragged the bear over to a scarred slave hawker. After digging in a pouch hanging from his waist, he gave the hawker a handful of golden pebbles, and received in exchange a tiny old man whose limbs shook from a perpetual tremor. The gargoyle grabbed the old man by the neck as a human would a chicken and raised him before the bear.

Although the street barely paid the gruesome sight that followed any attention, Bridget had to turn away and run from the sound. She took shelter in an alley, where she pressed a hand to her chest and buried her head in the crook of her elbow, hiding her tears and sorrow. It took some time for her to convince herself that the old man had lived a full life and this land was fundamentally cruel and she couldn't possibly expect Solian morality in such a beastly place. It was only then that she finally gained enough composure to continue walking.

She continued to take shelter in the occasional alley to observe the strange sights. When walking, she passed all sorts of strange shops, the entrances of which were four times the height of a human. These shops typically had open-window layouts—no glass, with tiered steps that showed off various goods.

Although all had a distinctly foreign look, they sold familiar goods and services, ranging from baking to household items to basket weaving to apothecary. Gargoyle artisans, usually sitting on a perch in the display area beside the entrance, whittled away or hammered works of leather or wood or stone or iron. Gargoyle scribes used giant feathered quills to ink equally giant scrolls or pressed metal nubs into clay tablets. Gemsmiths used delicate claw extenders to pinch gems whilst they set them into exotic jewelry. Haggling was common, with gargoyles often growling at each other over an exotic bird or animal or fish or giant insect or who knew what strange creature, all of which were housed in cramped pens right on the street.

Then there was the slave trade, which was so busy that she witnessed one slave get sold three times back to back. Gargoyles who upsold slaves in this manner dragged the poor wretch to a stall, where the slave would be made more presentable by having another slave brush the person's hair, wash their face and teeth for them while they sat numb, sometimes even change their clothes—only for them to be thrust back onto one of many platforms that dotted the street.

Upon one of these platforms, through a teeming crowd of tall and winged gargoyles, she glimpsed orange fur. She was so curious as to what sort of beast it might be that she halted on the busy street. Whereas the denizens of a normal human street would have walked around her, the wingless gargoyle walking behind her simply stepped on her back, flattening her to the ground as if she were but a piece of trash.

"Ugh ..." she wheezed, her basket rolling away.

Meanwhile, the gargoyle kept walking without so much as a backward glance. No one came to her aid, not even to kick the basket back her way. It bounced around between feet until another gargoyle flattened it under his clawed foot.

Terrified of getting stomped again, Bridget hauled herself back up and scrambled after it, but by the time she retrieved the basket—taking knocks from the apathetic crowd along the way—it was so misshapen that it would require an arcane Repair to get it back to form, a risk she was not willing to take in such a busy place. She nonetheless threw it back onto her shoulder and carried on as if nothing had happened, then tried to find a spot from which to observe what the gargoyles were fighting so loudly over on the platform.

The bidding war was intense, with gargoyles throwing up their arms or flapping their wings or barking a growl at the auctioneer, a winged behemoth of a brute who took no nonsense from the crowd. Bridget kept angling for a better look at what he was selling and finally found a stack of barrels in an alley, which she climbed, gaining a good vantage point.

"Gods," she murmured, for on the platform stood a powerful lion — and not on all fours, but on hind legs, like a human, with his front paws chained. "A Dreadnought ..." she whispered. Except this lion was much larger, perhaps twelve-feet tall, and his halo of a mane was thick and healthy and gave the lion an imperial countenance. Incredibly, the lion had runes emblazoned on his chest similar to those of the gargoyles. Despite knowing his life would be that of a slave, the lion stood with nothing short of intense pride.

Bridget gaped with an open mouth, wondering what the lion's civilization looked like. Myriad questions wanted answering. Was he a cousin of the Dreadnought race that had gone extinct, or a different tribe, or an entirely different race altogether? What language did he speak? Did this lion race outnumber the gargoyles? Was their kingdom larger or smaller? What did his arcanery look like? Did their runes work the same as gargoyle runes? Was the race as callous as the gargoyle race, or were they capable of empathy? Did they too hold human slaves in such numbers as the gargoyles?

Such questions bounced around inside her head until the next-door shopkeeper, a wingless gargoyle with charcoal-stained hands and chipped claws and wearing a huge leather apron, wandered into the alley holding a barrel of water. He splashed this water into the alley and looked up. Their eyes met. Bridget knew she was in trouble and promptly hopped off the barrel. In turn, the gargoyle growled an insult and lashed out with a rather lazy swipe, which for a war-trained Bridget was easy to duck under. This only incensed the beast, and he kicked out at her — another clumsy attempt which she easily hopped over.

She flapped a hand in apology, hoping that would deter the monster, but he kept coming, swatting at her as if trying to squash a pesky fly, all of which she ducked or dodged, even using the basket as a shield, which the gargoyle ripped away. Gulping, Bridget ran off at the first opportunity. The gargoyle did not pursue, but instead yelled into the crowd. Some noticed and took up his call, as if all of gargoyle honor had been impinged.

Onward she ran through the crowd. She dipped under towering legs and under swinging arms, and it was only after ducking under a particularly high-bottomed four-wheeled cart, hauled by a team of what appeared to be giant wildebeests, that she lost her tail.

She walked underneath this cart, head stooped to avoid its bottom, hearing the shopkeeper still raging after her in the distance, until his bleating became one of many in the hubbub of the street. By then the sun had started to cast long shadows, so she decided it was best that she return to the training grounds.

Except when she checked in with the Object Alarm enchantment, she failed to feel the pull of the tug—the blasted suppressive collar must have severed her connection! All thoughts of what she had seen were swept away by the flush of a cold sweat as she dipped out from underneath the cart and hurried back down the street she had walked.

In her haste and without a basket to distract, she had forgotten to keep her back hunched, and thus stuck out amidst a sea of squat slaves. The disguising mud on her face had dried and begun to flake off, and everyone who laid eyes on her seemed to notice her smooth skin and straight and white teeth and general fair complexion.

But she was in too much of a panic to hunker down, desperate to hurry back as quickly as she could as she had spent far too many hours wandering. How long *had* it been, anyway? And how far had she wandered? She'd been relying too much on that arcane connection and thus hadn't bothered to note which shops she'd passed early on, as she'd been too distracted by the crowd.

Gods, what a fool you are, she thought, avoiding eye contact with the gawkers.

A whip-carrying gargoyle female with a single rune in the middle of her chest barked a question at her, but she ignored her and continued onward. Yet even amidst the hustle and bustle of the street, she heard a distinctive uncoiling sound—and the swish of the whip. Instinctively she jumped aside, and the whip snapped at where she'd been standing with a loud *crack*.

"*Gohihol, gyot! Hehi, gyot!*"

I'm not going anywhere with you, Bridget thought as she dipped into the nearest alley—and then raced into its darkness. Footsteps—and more than one pair—followed. Heart thrumming from the terror of getting caught and never seeing Sebastian again and getting sold to someone who would then feed her to his bear, she sprinted into another blind alley and dipped into yet another one—only to find herself staring at a dead end.

Without hesitation, she pressed her back to the stone wall and ran a hand over her body, incanting, "*Armari obscura chameleano.*" But it was a fight to work through the collar, and she had to go over her limbs twice before the spell took—and just in time, for two wingless female gargoyles careened into the alley.

The one with the whip and lone rune blinked at the dead end before barking a question in their tongue. The other, stockier and more muscled, flicked a dismissive hand in a very human-like way whilst saying, "*Goffa fi.*"

Forget it, a frozen Bridget translated, not daring to so much as breathe. And by *it,* the girgoyle meant her as an *it*—a thing not to be bothered with.

The one with the whip mimicked the dismissive motion at the other one, who shrugged, also in a very human-like way, and walked off. But the whip-carrying fiend stayed to survey the alley with suspicious yellow eyes that darted about the stacks of refuse.

Frustrated, the girgoyle lashed out with the whip at a stack of destroyed barrels, making them tumble to the ground with a *crash*. A chunk of wood smacked into Bridget's leg, causing her to grunt in pain. This drew the attention of the beast, who paced forth, sniffing at the air with nostrils that flared like giant vents. That nose caught something, and her eyes widened along with the nostrils. The girgoyle lashed her whip directly across Bridget's body, forcing her to roll aside.

"*Gonto, gyot!*" the girgoyle hollered, lashing at Bridget on the return movement of the whip.

You haven't got me yet! Bridget thought as she cartwheeled over the strike, which snapped at the wall with another *crack*. The girgoyle was surprisingly quick, and with a snap of the arm, she redirected the whip, which coiled around Bridget's leg. She yanked Bridget backward so suddenly that she smashed into the ground on her chest with another grunt of pain.

As the girgoyle advanced on her, Bridget rolled onto her back, pointed with both hands, lashed out telekinetically, and yanked, using the girgoyle's forward momentum to send her flailing into the nearest wall.

Due to the suppressive collar, it was a weak attempt at best, and the girgoyle used her forearm as a shield before her head could smack into the wall. Her nostrils flared along with her rage, and she yanked on the whip, shooting Bridget toward her. Whilst scraping along the ground, Bridget mustered all her focus to shove at the air, roaring, "*Baka!*" and the girgoyle stumbled backward. But the beast promptly recovered and thrust a clawed finger at her lone rune.

Almost whimsically, and in a move that reminded her of Augum, Bridget countered this stabbing by flicking her hand upward, telekinetically nudging the claw up—and directly into one of the beast's eyes, making her howl in pain.

Oops, Bridget thought.

Knowing these weak attempts wouldn't do but not wanting to injure the girgoyle too greatly, she thought to try something more drastic. As the girgoyle winced and tried to blink the pain away, Bridget circled her arm and incanted, "*Voidus vis!*"

A small dark cloud appeared in the area, the 5th degree Darkness spell a pale shadow of its usual strength. Yet it was enough for Bridget to kick off the whip, scramble back to her feet, and sprint away. When the girgoyle pursued, Bridget spun about mid-run, pointed at the beast's foot, and yanked, causing her to trip and tumble, entangling herself in her own whip—a stroke of luck that allowed Bridget to get away.

Before reaching the street, Bridget grabbed hold of the closest piece of refuse she could carry—the broken half of a cartwheel. She hauled this jagged half-moon of spokes onto her shoulders, hunched her back, and hurriedly walked down the street.

The call came once again, but by then she was already a block down, eyes and head low, the cog of half a wheel bent awkwardly beside her head like a broken crown, which also stuck out enough to clear a small path through the crowd.

She kept glancing down alleys, desperate to see open sky—until she finally did. She dipped into the alley and hurried to the end, where she spotted the strip of dirt and, in the distance, the training block of wood and fabric constructs that were meant to look like human dwellings. A wind had sprung up since her departure, and the fabric billowed in long sheets like giant flags.

She dumped the broken wheel and sprinted forth, feet avoiding refuse and thorny weeds and flowers with opalescent petals that glittered in the fading sunlight.

"Please, please, please," she kept saying as she ran, until she was too huffed to say it anymore, hoping she wouldn't get into too much trouble.

She blasted through a sheet of fabric, fought through several more, and found herself standing on the cobblestone street surrounded by gently waving fabric walls. She breathed an immense sigh of relief, for there they all were, the teacher and his pupils, and they were *still* training, with the younger gargoyles now practicing flying to the highest windows, snatching a human slave, and flying long glidepaths to where the teacher stood.

Far down the street, a separate group of older gargoyles with another teacher were seemingly practicing casting elemental onslaughts, in that moment sending a rain of sharp icicles falling upon a field of straw dummies vaguely shaped like humans.

Bridget, having caught her breath by pressing her hands to her knees, straightened, cleared her throat, used the flapping fabric to clean her face and hands as best she could, and meandered along the edge of the street back to the alcove.

There she found the slaves not participating in the exercise huddled like rabbits and asleep, the wind cutting through the alcove like a knife.

Disbelieving her luck, she sat down nearby and watched the exercises. By then, the young gargoyles were so tired that The Brat barely grumbled at her when he passed by on a training run. She interpreted his words as him complaining that he hadn't had a chance to abuse her at all that day, or humiliate her, or something to that effect.

In any case, it was difficult to focus on their clumsy and repetitive attempts at kidnapping, or even much care about what the older ones were doing, when the memory of what she had seen remained as vivid as the afterglow of the sun. The bustling market, the slaves, an upright lion … what a strange world this was. And a much, much larger one than anyone in Sithesia could imagine.

THE ELEMENTS

LEERA

As the wind howled, Leera clung onto *Saltfang's* port railing, eyes glued to water spilling over the starboard railing, the two masts threatening to cross the critical tilt threshold that would capsize the ship. Yet it was the entirety of that moment that painted a picture suitable for the devil's wall.

A storm cloud had descended upon them like a ravenous tiger, plunging the area into darkness lit by a cascade of elements. The air was humid and hot for a change, as a towering tornado of pure fire whirled off the starboard bow with an ear-splitting scream, threatening to burn the ship to cinders. It was only kept at bay by a steady jet of water shooting from Jez, who stood on the bowsprit with her arms raised, a tiny silhouette against a flaming twister. Olaf stood near her, desperately shooting spikes of ice that might as well be cinders thrown at an avalanche.

The heat of the tornado clashed with an icy plume emanating from a gigantic iceberg, which reared up nearby, a building-sized behemoth poised to crush the ship into splinters. But it was being kept at bay by Leo the Leopard, who was blasting it with a steady stream of fire, face lit up maniacally as he seemed to enjoy the thrill of standing so close to death.

At the stern, Tammy battled a waterspout so massive it was is if it had sucked up the ocean itself. The behemoth whirlwind conspired to capsize the ship, the sails of which were tattered rags flapping madly in the wind.

And then there was the black storm cloud surrounding them, which randomly attacked with a bolt of lightning that lit up the entire area —

and smashed into her betrothed, who then channeled it with an outstretched arm into rolling waves. He hung on to the taller of the two masts, his robe torn to ribbons, giving him the appearance of a wraith.

Except for critical crew members, who clung onto the deck like ants in a gale, everyone else was huddled in the doorway to the cabins, surely praying they weren't about to be sent to the bottom of the ocean.

The cacophonic roar of it all was too much for Leera's ears, and it was like she heard nothing but saw everything. The sound was so great it felt like silence, except it vibrated her innards, strumming her organs like a mad lute player.

Amidst the chaos, a choice awaited her. After running about like a madwoman helping everyone take shelter, she had found herself clinging to the port railing after the ship took a sudden tilt. She could aid in the fight against the fiery tornado, the iceberg, or the waterspout, for all three battles hung in equilibrium. But which one would her water spells be most effective against?

Suddenly the waterspout pushed in and *Saltfang* tilted further, and she thought, *This is it, we're done for.* But then Tammy redoubled her efforts, screaming from the strain, her hands raised, and she managed to shove the waterspout back until the ship eased off, and as the water retreated through the spaces between the starboard railing the masts rose a little, avoiding a capsize.

Confirming that the other warlocks were keeping the elemental attacks in check for the moment, Leera looked to the ocean beyond the undefended port railing, fearing an attack from that direction. And that was when she spotted something on the horizon, where lightning flashes lit up the silhouettes of two angry towers that stood out in the darkness like black thorns, their roofs lit up with eerie beacon lights.

Intuitively she knew that these towers were responsible for the mayhem.

Already she had formed a daring plan but had yet to find the courage to pull the crossbow trigger on it. Besides, the ship was making steady progress forward, foot by foot. If only they could get past the range of the attack, perhaps they could survive …

Except the more she observed, the more she realized that was a fool's hope, for there was no way the stamina of her colleagues would last against such a relentless barrage. The ship would have long sunk by the time those cursed towers drifted out of sight.

She also needed to conserve her stamina, for she was the last bulwark of competence left should another elemental attack come, especially from below. As for those sheltering in the cabins, they had little to no experience against such violence and stood little chance against it. Luckily Jengo had arcanely reinvigorated her earlier, and so her body at least felt refreshed—if not profoundly anxious.

As if summoned by her fears, she spotted an approaching bulge amidst the waves. Even as she watched, body tensing with each heartbeat, a gigantic fin began to emerge, carving the water like a knife.

Here we go, Leera thought, readying to fire the crossbow bolt of a daring plan. The shadow that had been salaciously observing all this chaos from behind its curtain sneered that it was useless and the ship would soon sink and all would drown. Yet the part of her that had seen the dragon statue in the black abyss dared to hope.

Become the dragon, the shadow within her pleaded, watching the bulge grow. *Maul it in your other domain, for you are also a queen of the deep ...*

No, not yet, she answered, mollifying its bloodlust for now. *Maybe in time ...*

As she saw the bulge get to within two hundred feet of *Saltfang,* the ship groaned and tilted another precarious degree. There was a *snap* close by, and she looked over in time to witness a trio of barrels break from their lashings, tumble down the deck, and smash against the starboard railing, spilling precious hard tack and biscuit beef and dried fish—all without making a sound, for the attacks overpowered everything with their deafening roar.

And a hundred feet beyond that railing, another monstrous bulge formed—and exploded. The largest serpent she had ever seen, greater even than any told in those harrowing sea tales of old, shot straight into the air. It opened a ship-sized maw filled with tree-length teeth and loosed a deep roar so guttural it was not heard but felt in every bone and organ of Leera's body.

"Mother of the gods," she said, voice muted by the onslaught of sound. In the back of her mind, she heard the echo of a certain sea shanty. *An' it reared up into the sky rumblin' like thunder, ready to fall and smash the ship asunder ...*

For a moment time seemed to still, for the leviathan was so large that it hung there for all to see, dwarfing even the iceberg. Then it slammed back down into the ocean, sending up a monstrous rolling wave.

"Braaaace!" Leera roared as she held on tight, but no one could hear her—though everyone saw it coming anyway, and all held on tight. The ship and the iceberg rose up as the wave passed underneath. *Saltfang* tilted precariously whilst cresting the watery mountain, but managed to roll back the other way once the wave passed, leaving behind a deep trough that lightened Leera's stomach as the ship fell, allowing for a brief reprieve.

After the wave passed, Leera, knowing she had to hurry if she was to have any hope of averting disaster, quickly cast the requisite spells that would keep her alive—Breathe Water and Endure the Deep. Then she hopped up onto the railing and launched herself off the edge of the ship like a frog. Whilst flying through the air, she pointed at her feet and brought her hands together, incanting, "*Kwiko au o dolfa fusio fota talla!*" The 9th degree Speed of the Dolphin fused her feet into a wide flipper by the time she splashed into a lull between waves, which instantly muted the cacophony from above, bolstering her soul with a brief sense of peace she knew only when underwater.

She glimpsed the masts swing into view above, their forms distorted by the shimmering waters. One of them lit up with a flash of lightning, meaning her beloved Augum suffered on behalf of the ship. That lightning diffused itself against waves, and she felt its prickly tickle even this far away.

"*Shyneo,*" she incanted, and her hand lit up with pale light that she brightened to maximum. *Saltfang's* barnacled hull lit up behind her, but her eyes focused forward as she treaded underwater, feeling like a minnow.

A heartbeat later the pointy head of the largest shark she had ever seen emerged from the darkness, with a jaw that could surely swallow the stern of the ship. Even closed, its rows of barrel-sized teeth poked out of its mouth like a phalanx of spears.

Allowing herself to sink, she glanced behind. At the very edge of her light, beyond *Saltfang's* lead keel and beside the bottom-heavy iceberg, the monstrous leviathan swam forth, its serpent body snaking behind it.

Yes, come to the light, Leera thought, waving her brightly lit hand about, which she instinctively knew would attract the predators. Whilst waving, she placed the ring to her lips, incanting, "*Arcanarma,*" arming it, and continued to sink throughout, robe billowing and dragging like a sail.

"Come on, you bastards," she taunted under her breath, wishing she had had the time to strip her robe off earlier. "Come on, come on, come on …" She wondered if she should have turned herself into a dragon for this. Except she had no experience fighting underwater, and didn't want to get chomped in half because of a clumsy maneuver. She didn't even know if the nautical ring power would work in dragon form.

The two monsters rapidly neared, tails whipping fluidly as they raced to be the first to eat her whole. Now it was a question of timing a certain maneuver, for she would not get a second chance.

"Come on, come on, come on …"

Fifty feet. Forty. Thirty …

At twenty feet, their jaws opened wide, and her innards shriveled at the awesome sight of teeth taller than she was, ones that would shortly grind her to fish bits.

Now, now, now! her mind screamed. But she dared wait another few heartbeats, allowing the gap to close to a heart-stopping ten feet, when the mouth suction began, before she kicked out, arms and flipper working with muscle-burning ferocity to shoot her upward. The dull eyes of the behemoths followed the light, blind to each other, until their heads crashed together, unleashing an underwater shockwave so powerful that it sent her tumbling in its wake.

Shoot, shoot, shoot, she thought, urgently working to right herself. By the time she did, the beasts had come to their senses, and the alignment she had been hoping for hadn't materialized.

She couldn't take the shot.

Oh no. Oh no, oh no, oh no, she thought, dolphin tail flapping madly as she swam away from the ship, trying to align a certain position. But the two monsters were now swimming side by side, jaws snapping at her tail, which suddenly felt feeble against their sheer might and speed.

Still, she was fast enough to keep just ahead of the suction of the jaws, a tiny human dolphin trying to stay alive against two predators that would likely never tire.

Left and right and up and down she zipped, dodging and ducking and diving and swooping, all the while searching for that critical alignment. Her muscles burned so fiercely she thought they would tear. Her mind screamed this was impossible and she should just lead them away before teleporting back to the ship.

But that would only stall their inevitable return, and then the rest of her plan would fail when the ship eventually succumbed to the onslaught. No, she needed to pull this off.

Onward she swam, dipping about like a fish caught away from its school, desperately trying maneuver after maneuver in the hopes of attaining alignment.

Yet she began to tire, and the jaws kept snapping closer and closer. At one point the leviathan opened its maw extra wide, creating a huge suction force that pulled her into its maw. Instinctively she reached out, telekinetically snatched a tooth, and pulled herself forth—just as the maw slammed shut a hairsbreadth from her flipper. But instead of swimming straight, Leera grabbed onto its huge scales and used what strength she had left to propel herself up the monster's face—and then used her flipper to kick back and away.

In that moment, as she glided backward, the side of the leviathan's head aligned with the head of the shark at the precise angle she had been searching for.

Gotcha, Leera thought, and slammed her wrists together, roaring, "*Annihilo bato!*"

The ring-empowered surge was enormous, flash-blasting through nearly her entire reservoir of stamina in one go, and two massive jets of water shot forth. The first smashed through the leviathan's bulging eye, and the second through the eye of the shark. Two plumes of crimson innards exploded into the water.

The mammoth bodies of each predator continued in a straight line, tails slowly flapping from the water acting on the fins, until they began to arc downward, gliding into the depths beyond her light, leaving behind a stream of innards … and silence.

Leera tread water in the abyssal darkness, disbelieving she had defeated two monsters in one fell swoop. Had she just performed a Feat of Legend? Would anyone even believe what she had done were she to tell them?

A second crucial choice now awaited. She had enough stamina for one Teleport. She could either return to the ship and watch everyone slowly run out of stamina, or …

No choice, girl, Leera thought. *You must take the risk.*

She envisioned black rock, incanted, "*Impetus peragro!*" and vanished and appeared with a *thwomp* ten feet above the ground, which forced her to land on her flipper—in all the tumult, she had forgotten to nullify her water spells. Since it wasn't the first time she had done that, she bent her knees, tumbled forward to avoid hurting herself, and came to a rest on her back.

After taking a moment to appreciate that she was still alive, albeit back in the land of a steady roar and depleted of stamina, she sat up to nullify her water spells, returning her feet to normal. Then she flopped back to lay there with outstretched arms, catching her breath, muscles screaming from the agony of the battle, vision swallowed by the black rock tower looming above.

A particularly powerful flash of lightning and its subsequent *crack* of thunder jerked her from her stupor, and she shot up. The bright light of an orange flare drew her gaze to the ocean, where she witnessed the fire tornado drill into *Saltfang*. Her first reaction was to whimper and panic and ready herself to overdraw from teleporting to the deck to lend aid — only to realize it was a trick of perspective, for the tornado drifted about on the other side of the ship, kept at bay by the others ... at least for now.

"Get going, girl. They need you back," Leera said and groaningly hauled her tired body up and began half running, half walking around the tower, probing for a way in, eyes on the alert. Augum had told her in detail what the one he and Jez had explored looked like, and this one appeared very similar. With her stamina still critically low, she couldn't even afford to cast Reveal, wanting to save any energy should she encounter a monster of some sort.

The entrance appeared on the other side of the tower, obscuring her view of the ship and the elementals attacking it. But losing sight of everyone was a risk she had to take.

The inside was hollow and dark, yet remembering Augum's description of the first tower, she expected to find stairs on the other side.

"*Shyneo*," she incanted, lighting up her hand with a dim glow just bright enough to see a few feet ahead. Then she ran across the interior — and tripped on something. After getting back to her feet, she swiveled her dimly lit hand low above the floor, revealing a skeleton inside a rusted set of armor. The ribcage was exposed through the rotten breastplate, and all that remained of the sword was the stump of a hilt.

She kept her hand lower as she hurried on, spotting other ancient bodies. One of these had her trundle to a halt, for it was the skeleton of a bull. Except it had an unusually large head and even larger horns, and its bone structure looked like it had been stretched out across the floor, yet the staining on the rock indicated that this was how it had fallen.

"Strange," Leera muttered, thinking a powerful spell must have stretched the bull's skeleton. But then, what was a bull even doing there in the first place? And why was it armored? The flicker of a mythological beast blinked by her mind, but her quest was too urgent to indulge in such things.

Onward she raced, until she found the opposite wall and soon the ruins of a staircase.

"No, no, no," she mumbled, hand rising to see that the stairs began twenty feet up—the rest below lay in a heap of rubble. "I don't have the stamina for this," she said, dropping to her knees, hands splayed over the rubble. She froze. "Then be smart about it, girl," she told herself, mind constructing a theoretical vision of the repair, which would still be cast at 10th degree competence. "Yes, that could work. Believe in your skill." She splayed her hands over the rubble, brow furrowed in concentration.

"*Apreyo*," she incanted, focusing on the highest protrusions and sending pieces forth, working downward from there. Piece by piece, chunks of black stone rose from the floor and fused with the wall.

She quickly felt the horizon of overdraw approach. Still coming off her overdraw sickness, she halted at the foot of the yawning chasm of overdraw. There, she stood upon the precipice, feeling a vicious cold beckoning from the depths. She feared dipping into overdraw so soon after being sick would mean death.

Leera looked up and saw that only half the repair had been completed, meaning the bottom of the staircase was ten feet up.

"Shoot, shoot, shoot," she muttered, pacing back and forth, knowing every heartbeat counted. That pacing ceased. "Then don't waste another—" She interrupted herself to abruptly drop to the ground, crossing her legs beneath her. She snuffed Shine, kept her hands loose in her lap, straightened her back, and closed her eyes to meditate. All she needed was enough to haul herself up, nothing more.

She thought of her beloved Augum. At first her innards screamed from worry, for she saw him getting repeatedly struck by lightning until he fell from the mast, dead.

"That's not the right path," she heard her former mentor, Mrs. Stone, tell her, her old voice an echoey croak in the darkness. "You know what path you need to tread."

"Yes, Mrs. Stone," Leera whispered and refocused her efforts. Bad meditation techniques only hindered the rate of stamina recovery. She switched to thinking about Augum lying beside her on his stomach, feet idly kicking his back as he read a book, a cozy hearth fire crackling before them. And there was Bridget sitting in behind, her legs crossed as she too read a book, and Olaf sat beside her, eyes half asleep as he turned a yellowed page of some old tome. In between them all, cuddling together, sat the husky Sabby and the castle tabby Sir Pawsalot.

Feeling the warmth of the fire, she slowly drew her focus to her toes and then feet and ankles and legs and thighs and chest and arms and hands and fingers and back and neck and head and mind … until peace began to aid in refilling her reservoir.

The moment Leera estimated she had enough stamina for the feat, she jumped up, recast Shine, raised both arms, and channeled her beloved Augum, who had taught her how to do this. After telekinetically latching onto the bottom rung of stairs, she strained her relatively meager—in relation to Augum's—telekinetic muscle and slowly felt her feet rise off the ground.

Up she floated, chest scraping along the rocky wall, stamina rapidly bleeding off again. With the bottom stair a mere foot away, she suddenly hit the wall of overdraw and had to force herself to shut off the tap, which included snuffing Shine. As she plummeted, her hands scrabbled against the rock like a cat, until she managed to snag a small outcrop with her right hand and abruptly halt her fall. Body swinging about in the darkness, she felt the wall with her other hand until it too took hold of the rock, and then one foot found a tiny wedge in the rock, then the other foot.

She rested a little, barely hearing her breath over a windy roar outside that created a *thwooming* echo within the tall structure. Then she worked on figuring out a way up, which she accomplished by letting one hand go and probing about until she found a wedge hold slightly higher. Bit by bit, she climbed in the darkness until her hand at last found the bottom stair, and she hauled herself over it. Luckily the repair held, and she took a precious moment to once more catch her breath, thinking, *Wow are you ever cutting it close of late.*

She then relit her palm with a glow just strong enough to light the staircase ahead. It was an incredibly narrow climb, barely wide enough to fit one person, and each step was awkwardly tall. Seeing that all was well for the next fifty feet, she snuffed her hand to conserve stamina and climbed in the dark, but on all fours to give her the best chance should the stairs collapse.

Every fifty feet or so she relit her hand, scouted the staircase ahead, snuffed her light, and continued on, stamina steadily replenishing. "I've got this," she said, hoping beyond hope that her plan was sound and she wasn't wasting these precious moments on a whim.

In the darkness, she kept envisioning the rippling flames of that fiery tornado, the vivid blue ice of the iceberg as it crackled threateningly, the whirring grind of the waterspout. She tried not to think about the ship sinking to the bottom.

"Hold on, y'all," she said, hearing her friend Alyssa Fairweather, wishing the girl had been able to come. But some Arcaners had needed to remain and hold down the fort back home. The order had to survive.

Later in the ascent, wanting to check her position, Leera spread the fingers of her hand, incanting, "*Shyneo*," —and gasped, for yawning before her was a break in the staircase, which she had inadvertently climbed within two feet of. Had her hand—for she was still climbing on all fours—punched through the air, she might have tumbled forward. She tried not to imagine someone finding her shriveled husk a hundred years later beside the stretched-out skeleton of a bull.

The staircase continued along the wall only five feet away, just close enough to attempt a jump without resorting to using arcanery. It then ascended until it disappeared into an alcove at the roof of the tower.

The light shifted. For a moment she thought someone was nearby, only to realize that it was her palm light that was shifting, subtly waffling about as if caught in an invisible wind.

"What in the …" She gaped at the light that fluctuated like a candle threatening to snuff out. "Never seen *that* before …" But then she remembered Augum and Jez mentioning something about a warping effect, which this had to be. *Stop dawdling and move already*, she thought.

Forcing herself to ignore the weirdness, Leera straightened, backed up, and swung her arms forward a few times to help gather the courage for the attempt. "Gods, you're crazy for trying this," she muttered before running forth with her still-lit hand. Timing the last footstep to push off the edge of the last step, she launched herself into the air. After a heart-stopping moment her hands slapped onto the bottom stair, got a grip, and her legs swung forward from the momentum. She grunted from her chest hitting the stone, hooked her right leg over the stair, and used her core strength to haul herself up, an awkward endeavor while wearing a robe.

"Can't believe that worked," she said, pressing her back against the wall to take a breather, feet dangling off the edge of the thin staircase. For once, she hadn't needed to use her arcanery to complete a feat, which gave extra satisfaction.

Having settled her nerves, she got underway again, this time having the confidence to walk upright. But the higher she rose, the more her Shine casting warped and the stranger she felt, as if something were tearing at her soul.

"Augum warned of this," she said aloud to keep her mind from playing tricks on her.

At long last she reached the alcove, where a fierce wind battered the curving hallway, a pale light beckoning from within. She followed this light until she came to a short staircase that led outside, where she glimpsed a maelstrom of a black sky, as if she were in the center of a necromantic hurricane. She climbed these final stairs and popped her head up above the tower roof, laying eyes on a whirling ball of energy floating above the center of the roof.

"Just as described," she said, voice lost in the din.

Whereas Augum and Jez had had a bad feeling and left the other tower, Leera pressed on toward the energy, barely cognizant that her palm light had been snuffed—not that she needed it anyway. As she approached, her teeth began to vibrate and her bones prickled. It felt like something was trying to hook into her soul or perhaps taint it — an unnerving sensation.

"Can't be good for the health of the soul," she muttered, and raised her left arm to summon her watery shield — only to have it ripped away. "Come on, I need you," she said, and tried again, this time throwing all her concentration into the endeavor. Slowly the shield blinked back into existence, the edges rippling and warping. When she placed the shield before herself, the teeth and bone vibrations ceased and only returned whenever she popped her head above the shield.

"Getting weird here," she said, willing herself to press on, but with each step, the shield got more and more disjointed, until it looked like dough being stretched in all directions. Even hiding behind the shield the teeth-and-bones vibration returned, and she felt like she too was a mass of violent energy. Her thoughts began to scramble, and she saw flashes of light across her vision.

Press on, press on, press on, she thought, but those thoughts twisted into wordplay. *Press on, press off, impress and depress. Egress the temptress ...*

Five feet from the towering ball of energy, Leera raised the wildly fluctuating shield above her, keeping it between her body and the ball of energy, and began to search the ground. *Find and look and search and cry and melt*, her jumbled mind thought. Hunkering, she came right up to the ball of energy, and began to feel as if her own body were being stretched like her shield.

Still she searched, until at last she found it. Embedded in the stone in the center of the roof, directly underneath the ball of energy, was a stone shield depicting the full Arcaner crest. Now acting purely on instinct, Leera pressed her amorphous shield against the crest.

The massive ball of energy instantly vanished, leaving behind a ringing silence within her bones and soul. Although her summoned shield was back to normal, her head throbbed with pain, every bit of her tingled, and her vision was blurry, as if someone had clubbed the side of her skull.

Still, she had the wherewithal to stumble to the edge of the tower, where she saw the ship. Miraculously, the fiery tornado and the waterspout had vanished, and the low-hanging lightning storm had risen to churn high overhead, now only occasionally rumbling with thunder. Although the iceberg remained, she knew the others would unite to defeat it, so she did not have to attempt a dangerous teleport to the other tower to shut that arcane mechanism off.

"So Arcaners were responsible for these too," she mumbled.

A violent nausea built up within, and she keeled over to vomit, her shield vanishing from lack of focus. "Ugh," she moaned, tumbling over to lie on the ground, where she held her knees close to herself. She felt ill in the strangest way, as if she had insulted the Unnameables with a profoundly ancient slight, and now they were punishing her by piercing her body with thousands of tiny needles.

Her mind roiled, thoughts too scrambled to even think about teleporting, let alone attempt it. Meanwhile the queasiness grew stronger, and she retched again and again, until only bile came up. Then she rolled on the ground, body wretchedly uncomfortable and feeling as if it were being attacked from within. Her thoughts once more began to fall apart, and even though she weakly cried out for help, all that came out was, "*Haluup! Alaaap! Aaaaap ...*" It was useless.

Black walls of unconsciousness closed in, and as she faded out, sick to her very soul, a single sound pierced the darkness, one she recognized even through frightening confusion.

TAKING IT ON THE CHIN

AUGUM

With a *thwomp*, Augum appeared on the tower's roof, having followed the pull of his betrothal ring to this spot. He suspected Leera had been responsible for snuffing the tower's light, which in turn vanquished the tornado and waterspout and alleviated the onslaught of the black lightning storm, allowing his lot to work on the iceberg.

"*Shyneo!*" he incanted, flaring his palm with lightning. Sure enough, there was his beloved, lying on the ground near the roof edge. In his haste to reach her, he slipped on the wet stone, then scrambled forth like a squirrel and skidded to a halt beside her, torn robe strips from his mast ordeal whirling about him like a skirt.

"My love?" he said, taking a knee and gently shaking her, but she failed to wake. He placed an ear by her mouth and felt his heart soften upon feeling her breath. Yet she was frightfully pale, and there were two pools of vomit nearby. "You did it, my love. Now it's time to get you help."

He spooled one arm underneath her legs and the other under her neck and lifted her. Then he turned to look toward the ship, lit now only by a half-sized blue iceberg and some palm lights. "*Impetus peragro grapa lestato exa exaei!*" he incanted, reappearing an eyeblink later between the two masts.

"Jengo!" he called out, barely cognizant of Leo the Leopard still lobbing the occasional fireball at the iceberg. *Saltfang*, now free from the threat of the fire tornado and waterspout, sailed on, steadily leaving it behind. "Where's Jengo I need him to—"

"He's below!" Alanna cut in, getting to him first. She took one look at Leera and paled. "Follow me."

Augum hurried after her, ignoring everyone else's questions about Leera. They found Jengo in the infirmary attending to a crew member who had broken his arm after getting blown off the mast. There were five others in there with various minor injuries.

"Found her like this," Augum blurted as Jengo raised his head. "She managed to turn off the swirling ball of energy."

"And I remember what that energy felt like," Jez said, having followed Augum. "It felt dangerous."

Jengo patted the crew member's shoulder and swept to Leera, whom he gestured for Augum to place on a cot. Then he spread a hand over her forehead and incanted, "*Examino potente morbus aurus persona.*"

Augum had never seen the Sierran-born healer's face drain so quickly after casting the 1st degree healing spell Diagnose. The almoner looked up with wide eyes and said, "All of you get out. Now. Faster!" he shouted when people failed to move at a rapid pace, though he grabbed Augum's arm. "You have to stay as you carried her. Just back up."

With a sinking feeling, Augum stepped back a few paces.

"Farther," Jengo said without glancing at him, eyes on Leera's still form.

Augum took another step away and glanced at Jez, who gave him a nod of encouragement before moving to the doorway, where she lingered with a worried-looking Alanna. Everyone else had cleared out.

Olaf abruptly plowed in between the women, shouting, "Aug? What happened?"

Augum raised a hand. "Stay there, Ollie. It's not safe."

Olaf gulped, looked between the women, and gulped again. "I'll be here if you need me though."

Augum returned his attention to Jengo, who had recast the spell and was now slowly moving his hand a finger's width above Leera's body, lips moving as he spoke to himself in an undertone.

"Confused interweavings ... the framework leaving complex tendril evidence ... miniature vascular lacerations ... tiny lacerations to the minor and major organs ... poisoning of the blood ... an emptying of the stomach ... can only be *alchematriosis*—"

"What's that?" Augum blurted.

"An ancient infection."

"Can you cure it?"

Jengo ignored him, his face stony, lips silently moving as he recited complex instructions in preparation to cast his next spell. Then he placed one hand on Leera's head and the other on her stomach, incanting, "*Remedia rexo excella vindiv infecta poisa venoma extracta.*"

Augum recognized the incantation as belonging to the 6th degree Remedy Infection Poison Venom spell. As commander of the Arcaner order, he'd made it a point to be aware of everyone's capabilities, particularly the healer's. But he was also aware of how complex the healing art was and how much Jengo needed to concentrate, and so he stopped himself from asking inane follow-up questions.

"What's happening?" the boyish voice of Limpet asked from behind.

"Hush," Jez snapped in a whisper. "In fact, get out of here. This ain't for your eyes."

"I'll take him up top," Alanna offered.

"I can go myself, thank you very much." Then the boy added a muttered, "Stupid wenches."

"I beg your pardon?" Jez hissed in such lethal tones that Augum heard the rapid footsteps of the boy as he ran off.

"Little brat needs a firm talking to," Jez muttered to Alanna, who only hummed in agreement.

Jengo finished by abruptly raising his hands and recasting Diagnose, head subtly shaking throughout. That head shaking had Augum wringing his hands, and he had to restrain himself from prodding Jengo for more information.

"Pass number two …" Jengo muttered, placing his hands on Leera once more, this time on her neck and upper stomach. "*Remedia rexo excella vindiv infecta poisa venoma extracta.*"

Three passes of this later, with the only sounds being Jengo's mutterings and the ship's steady creaking as it cut through the waves, Jengo plopped down onto the lone chair in the infirmary.

"Water," he said, dabbing at his sweat-dribbled forehead with a sleeve.

Augum raced up to the galley, filled a tankard from one of the tapped barrels, and rushed it to Jengo, who downed the entire tankard in one go.

"I've managed to suck out the alchemical poison," Jengo volunteered. "Now the true healing work begins …"

Augum's mouth opened and closed repeatedly. He was so flummoxed that he could not even stutter out a question, and he was starting to feel strangely queasy and a little bit tingly.

"This is going to be arduous," Jengo said, and he returned to Leera's bedside. "Attempting first round of Remedy Complex Wound," he declared, flashing them all a serious look before refocusing on Leera. He raised his hands above her, and Augum noted how they shook. Then he placed them on her head—one on her forehead and the other pressed to her chin—and slowly and perfunctorily incanted, "*Remedia binda arregando delicato ipulato mortus flaeho rinvara vat finateo.*" Throughout the incantation, his hands delicately and precisely moved along her body.

Augum glanced back at Olaf, and the two friends, well aware of how notoriously difficult the 8th degree healing was to cast, exchanged dark looks.

Jengo's fingers moved with subtle precision as he attempted to heal Leera's innards, repeating the complex incantation over and over and over. How the spell worked was a mystery to Augum, and he almost wanted to cast Reveal to see the tendril geometries, but refrained because he was increasingly queasy and didn't want to push it.

He felt so queasy in fact that he had to sit down on a cot, then lie down lest he puke. He wondered why simply carrying Leera would cause him to feel so sick.

Meanwhile Jengo worked onward despite sweating profusely and looking peakish himself. Augum didn't know if that was on account of the intense spell-casting or from his contact with Leera.

Hours went by, and people came and went at the doorway only to be shooed away by Jez or Alanna. While Jengo worked on through his sickness, Augum's nausea put him to sleep. When he woke up, he found a blanket covering him.

But he wasn't alone. Alanna sat in a chair by the door reading a book, her legs crossed, one foot bouncing. And beside him, Leera slept in a cot that had been pushed in beside his. Somehow, he was holding her hand. He drew that hand, which thankfully was nice and warm, to his lips and gave it a kiss.

Alanna looked up, closed her book, propped a hand on her chin, and smiled. "Famed lovebirds," she whispered.

Augum sat up and pinched his forehead before rubbing his eyes. A slight headache remained from the ordeal, and he was a little tired, but otherwise he felt all right. "What hour is it?"

"Around the tenth hour of the morn. We sailed clear of the towers overnight and have had little trouble since. The storms have mostly abated. Looks like we're through the worst of it."

"Now we know why the ocean was impassable," Augum said, speaking more to himself, hearing the past. "Arcaners of old were trying to protect us, and now their defensive constructs have been penetrated, for the gargoyles have found a way through …"

"Do you think it was a mutual pact? A covenant between gargoyles and humans?"

Augum bit his lower lip. "Those towers, the loop trap below the ocean, all make me doubt these constructs were built in partnership with the winged beasts." He pushed his tongue into his cheek as he tilted his head in thought. "Which brings up a whole host of questions. Why did Arcaners go to such lengths to protect humanity? At what point in history *did* it happen? And why ..." His eyes unfocused as he thought of a third question, which he did not verbalize—why had he never seen any reference to the constructs in any of the Arcaner materials he'd read?

But you did see, didn't you? he thought. *There were hints and mentions sprinkled throughout old texts and history books which you dismissed as mythological allegories ...*

"Those are deep and worthy questions ..." Alanna whispered, and they pondered the matter in the creaking quiet, until she reanimated. "Oh, I hope you don't mind, but I took the liberty of repairing your robe."

Augum raised his robe sleeve before his face, which he remembered had been shredded by the lightning, and found it mostly repaired, with a few unrepairable singe spots remaining.

"Thank you," he said. "Wish I'd brought more robes."

"Heyyyy, lovebuuug," Leera sang in a croaky voice.

Augum slid an arm underneath her and dragged her over to him. Her eyes were closed, but she purred into his chest. "So sleeeepy," she sang, nuzzling up to him.

Alanna stood, clasping her book to her chest. "I'll leave you two be and let Jengo know you're awake," she whispered.

Augum smiled his thanks and Alanna quietly departed. "You did good," he said to his beloved. "No one thought as far ahead as you did. You figured it out and snuffed the tower."

"I guess," Leera mumbled and went on to detail her entire ordeal, her voice tired, her eyes mostly closed as she idly stroked his cheek.

"So the arcanery worked in the same manner as the underwater dragon statue," Augum concluded. "Back up a moment, though. You said it was 'just a couple beasties' underwater, huh? You mean those two massive leviathans, each of which could have easily capsized the ship? Count yourself lucky you jumped into the water before I could hop down to restrain you." He squeezed her. "Don't want to lose my girl ..."

Leera shrugged. "They were a *wee* bit of a challenge, but I managed."

"How are you two feeling?" Jengo asked upon striding in, hands behind his back in a professorial manner.

Augum straightened to greet him.

"Don't get up," Jengo said, taking a seat beside Augum.

"How did you overcome the sickness?" Augum pressed.

"We healers are trained to have a great deal of self-discipline, and that includes working through all manner of sufferings—even if that means casting spells on our own bodies so we may continue."

"You have once again proven your competence, Almoner Okeke," Augum said. He felt terribly guilty for not yet learning how to convey permanent badge honors onto Arcaner shields. The instructions on how to do it were detailed in the book *Codex Arcanera: From Birth to Death, a Life of Honor.* It involved a complex ritual that would take much time to learn, time he had been spending running the order—not to mention helping to rebuild the kingdom and finishing his studies at the academy.

"Yes, you're quite the lifesaver," Leera threw in, smiling warmly at him. "We are forever in your debt."

"You can repay your debt in alms to the poor," Jengo replied, drawing chuckles from the couple.

"They shall be rich through our graces," Augum said.

Jengo spread a hand over Leera's forehead and raised his chin in that teacher-like manner of his. "May I?"

"By all means."

"Examino potente morbus aurus persona. Mmm …" he toned after a time.

"He sounds like Mrs. Stone," Leera whispered to Augum.

"Hold still, please," Jengo said and slowly ran his hand over her entire body before doing the same to Augum. Then he patted Leera's leg. "You'll be fine, but you need more rest. And you, mister—" He threw a pointed look at Augum. "—may return to your duties." Then he stood and began walking out.

"Almoner Okeke," Augum said.

Jengo halted at the doorway and turned his head to look at him.

"Thank you," Augum said, smiling and bowing his head low—and keeping it there.

"Yes, thank you," Leera added, doing the same.

Jengo smiled. "You're welcome," and he strode out.

"He's a miracle maker," Leera mumbled, canoodling closer to Augum by trying to throw a leg over him, but she was so tired that he had to help.

They held each other, speaking softly and with love, until Leera drifted into a deep sleep. Augum then slid out from underneath her, bundled her up in blankets, kissed her forehead, and walked up top to survey the damage.

"We've been on a repair spree all morning," Olaf said upon Augum joining him on deck, where the Arcaner standard bearer was using his warlock arts to mend a sail. "This one's ready!" he hollered, and a crew member swung by to grab the sail. Augum and Olaf then watched the young man haul it back up the mast and expertly reattach it to one of the yardarms.

The day was gray and cloudy and windy, but brilliant sunlight awaited in the east, the direction of their sail. The wind was surprisingly warm, which Augum made a note of to Olaf.

"Cap says we've been on a south-easterly course for a while now," Olaf said, accepting another torn sail from the same crew member. "He says there's better winds down here. How are you feeling, anyway?"

"A little groggy, but all right," Augum replied, and glanced about the deck, noting that all the warlocks were chipping in with the repair work, some of which included repairing wooden parts of the ship. All but one. "Where's Digby?"

"Been a shut-in in his cabin since, you know ..."

Augum nodded. "Put out the word that we'll hold an official memorial ceremony for his brother and for Mahmoute this evening."

"Will do."

Augum walked about the deck, greeting everyone and receiving warm welcomes. Having survived such an onslaught, the crew and passengers felt closer, with the crew realizing how critical a role the warlocks played in keeping everyone alive, and the warlocks realizing how critical a role the crew played in keeping the ship running and on course. Everyone's respect for each other had climbed.

But a certain kid paid him no respect, and when Augum said hello to him and asked him how he was coming along, Limpet, who was fussing with a torn sail beside his young pirate friend, Dirt, merely shrugged and said, "Whatever."

Augum paced over to sit beside the two boys, both of whom shared a look like, *Is he for real?* It was a look Augum knew all too well, having employed it himself many a time when he was their age. He almost told them as much but refrained. Instead he grabbed a damaged sail from a pile, laid it out before his feet, and studied its various tears.

The kids watched him with side eyes, both poking at the sail Limpet was supposedly repairing, obviously trying to make it look like they were busy when they were just killing time and being lazy.

"What are you doing?" Limpet asked.

"Studying the contours of the tearing."

"Why?"

"Allows for a more efficient casting."

"But you've already got a lot of stamina. What do you care?"

"What are you two talking about?" Dirt whispered. "Magic stuff? Bleh."

"I practice this skill for the times I need to repair something during a battle, when every stam counts," Augum replied. "Sometimes a single stam can be the difference between life and death." He spread his hands over the torn canvas, incanting, "*Apreyo*." The tears quickly reformed and sealed with a white light. Augum then rolled the sail up and handed it off to a passing crewman. He nodded over at Limpet's sail. "Let's see it."

Limpet straightened at the challenge. He cleared his throat a few times and hesitantly spread his hands over the sail.

Augum, in the mean, raised a hand and incanted, "*Un vun asperio aurum enchantus*."

"What are you doing?" Limpet snapped.

"Watching your work."

"What, you don't think I can do it? I'm the best warlock here. I'm just young is all."

Augum kept his face placid as he patiently waited for Limpet to begin. It seemed being swept overboard a while back and nearly drowning had failed to humble him.

"He's weird," Dirt whispered, yet the pirate boy had shrunk, as if worried he might draw too much attention to himself, even though he wanted to show solidarity to his friend.

Augum merely raised an eyebrow in wait.

"Fine already," Limpet snapped and, after a bout of concentration, loudly incanted, "*Apreyo!*"

Augum watched his tendril weavings work on the tears, taking mental notes. "Your Repair took three times as long to complete as mine," he said when Limpet dropped his hands. "And you left some tearing here, here and here. See how the seams haven't quite stitched back together?"

"Yeah, so? It's good enough."

"No, it isn't, kid," the walrus-mustachioed bosun, who had been standing nearby watching, chimed in. "I reckon that there sail would tear soon as it caught wind. It's sloppy work, boy, which means I'll have to personally inspect every one of your repairs from now on. Look, kid, if you don't want to do it, best you say so now as I got competent warlocks putting in the effort. We can't have crew wastin' energy haulin' these things up only to have to take 'em down the same day, can we?"

"Gods, I didn't say I was *done* with it," Limpet whined.

Augum wanted to tell him not to lie but refrained, feeling it would be too adversarial and the boy would thenceforth not be willing to listen to anything he said.

The bosun harrumphed and walked off. He soon returned with a smaller sail, but one so tattered it looked like Augum's robe after he'd been getting pummeled by lightning all night. He dumped this sail rather unceremoniously before the boy and flicked at his tilted cap. "Last chance, kid, or I'm bootin' you off the deck as you'll only be in the way."

Limpet threw Augum a pleading look, as if hoping he'd stand up for a fellow warlock, but Augum, who had kept his hand raised and lit with Reveal, only watched the boy, feeling like Mrs. Stone watching a younger version of himself. It was a memory that squeezed his heart with fondness. Yet she was still alive, living in Ley, working to bridge the gap between the planes. Either that or meditating in the orange desert, or maybe fussing about with clay pottery, which was always an amusing thought.

Limpet sighed dramatically but tinkered with the sail this way and that, laying out the strips flat, which told Augum he was capable of learning. He spread his small hands over the sail and incanted, "*Apreyo.*"

Augum watched him work, wondering rather darkly if the boy realized what they might face and that the odds of going home were slim. When Limpet finished, Augum stood and gave his work a smiling nod. He walked off, hearing the bosun say, "Not bad, kid. Not bad at all."

He also heard Dirt say to Limpet, "Something scary about him," which puzzled Augum as he hadn't felt The Callousness of the Predator behind his eyes. He suspected the kids were hearing tales about him.

As Augum next went to the captain to receive an update on the ship's repairs and expected weather events, Carter stepped up to wait his turn to speak.

"Should be smooth sailin' fer the next day or two," the captain said in his dockside twang, eyeing the horizon whilst chewing on the end of his pipe. "But after that, who knows, as we're sailing into uncharted waters. Waters we saltbloods only 'eard about from our grandfathers, who heard it from *their* grandfathers ..."

Augum thanked him for the update and turned to the waiting Carter, who asked to speak with him privately.

"Commander," he whispered after Augum took him aside, "I'd like to report that Digby has locked himself in his cabin and refuses to come out or say much to anyone. He's angry. Very, *very* angry. At, uh ..." Carter scratched the back of his neck.

"At me," Augum said.

"Sir, yes, sir. Blames you for not saving his brother. Thinks you purposely left him to die. In fact, I think he's blaming everything on you, sir. Including me cozying up to the order and stuff."

Augum suddenly felt the urge to visit Leera to make sure she was okay. "Thank you for informing me, Squire," he said, giving Carter a double-pat on the shoulder before leaving him standing on the bridge.

"Training this evening again, sir?"

Augum flashed a thumbs-up over his shoulder as he walked into the main cabin hallway, fearful that Digby might take his anger out on a vulnerable Leera, who was sleeping alone in the infirmary. But he slowed to a halt upon passing Digby's cabin, for he heard quiet sobbing from within.

Augum sighed. Digby was an enemy, someone who loathed him deeply now. Was there any point in trying to communicate? Yet he had communicated with enemies before, even made friends with some. Should he not try now? Except what if it only made things worse? It wasn't like he could put distance between them on a boat.

He battled back and forth like this for a time when the door abruptly opened, with Digby about to step out, probably on his way to the privy or the galley. The thirty-four-year-old froze.

"You," Digby hissed, eyes narrowing, powdered face streaked with tears that ran by his large mole.

Augum stepped back to give himself room to maneuver should Digby act on the violence in his eyes. He gave the slightest nod of acknowledgment but said nothing, standing there with a serene calm that surprised him a little.

Digby stepped out into the narrow hallway, prompting Augum to take another step back. Digby glared at him as he flicked a hand at the door, which slammed shut with a *bang*. "What do you want?" he snapped.

"To pass on my sincere condolences about your brother and to tell you that the captain has allowed us to hold an official memorial ceremony for him and Black Eagle Mahmoute after supper. Both gave their lives battling something we've never seen before. Both will be honored."

Digby's lips curled with malignancy, as if he did not believe a word Augum had said. "You sniveling, whining weasel. You rotten, pretentious chunk of flesh. You *dare* come to me thinking yourself of a higher station? I'm a noble of the royal court. A Bloomington-Southguard, nephew to the lord king. You and your silly little code of honor that you employ whenever it suits you. You high-horse-riding steaming pile of—" He swung a fist at Augum, who had seen the punch forming and thus easily stepped aside. It was then a small effort to telekinetically but gently yank on Digby to get him to stumble forth and face-plant into the wall.

Digby moaned in pain, which sounded more like one of those sniveling whines he had accused Augum of making.

"Violence will not solve the issue between us," Augum said.

Digby hauled himself up and bared crooked yellow teeth as he hissed, "You dare humiliate me? I challenge you to a duel of honor, Augum *Arinthian* Stone," he spat, twisting his tone with mockery.

Augum felt his eyebrows rise slightly. "Thou shalt not duel the lower ranks without serious provocation. The fourth edict of the Sacred Chivalric—"

Digby thrust an accusatory finger into his face. "Ah ha! Even now you hide behind your cheap code of honor, just like a coward would! You *know* I'd wipe the floor with you as your conscience would wilt before the justice I so richly deserve!"

"I have no desire to fight someone who grieves a loss so profoundly," Augum replied, hoping for diplomacy. "The king assigned you a duty to watch over the heir to the throne—"

Digby roared a fake laugh. "The heir! The heir is lost to your sort, to your stupid and useless code. What's that dumb code going to do for the kingdom, huh? Arcaners went extinct for a reason, and you're just wasting people's time with their ashes."

"Your duty is to the young Southguard," Augum repeated, feeling there was no point in countering illogical arguments with logic. "Nephew to the king, your sovereign." Augum transferred his weight to his other foot and sighed. "I did my best for your brother. Perhaps it was not enough, but I tried. We still have half an ocean to cross, and if we are successful in our voyage, we will meet the monsters in their own kingdom. We are but one ship. Think on that. One. Ship. That means we will have to stick together. Work together. Battle together. So carry that grudge if you must, but ask yourself if it serves you to do so. For all our sakes, and especially for yours, I hope you let it off your shoulders."

Digby kept up his glare, but he did not opine.

Augum inclined his head. "I am sorry for your loss," he repeated and turned his back on Digby, fully expecting him to charge again—or throw an arcane cheap shot—but all he heard was his nose-whistling breathing. *Give the man time*, he thought, harnessing the wisdom of his great-grandmother. *He may yet amend his ways.*

He slipped down the ladder and made his way to the infirmary, where he was relieved to find Leera soundly asleep. After tucking her blanket back up to her chin and planting a soft kiss on her forehead, and then her cheek, and then her other cheek because he couldn't help himself—she was, after all, the cutest girl he'd ever seen—he sat on the cot beside hers, drew his legs up, and wrapped his arms around his knees.

From there he watched her sleep, rubbing his scruffy chin on his knees as he worried about the journey ahead. What sort of world would they find? Would they survive that world? Would kids like Dirt and Limpet survive? Would Digby find the courage to see past his own limitations? Was that possible for such people? Would they find Bridget, or was that an impossible task? What if there was more than one race on the other side? What if they landed somewhere completely different and never found the gargoyle lands? What if the gargoyles were already returning with a fleet of ships as large as the one he had laid eyes on? What if ... what if Bridget was already—

"Don't even *think* it," he hissed, angrily jumping back to his feet and wanting to punch his own face. *Don't be so pessimistic*, he chastised himself, pacing back and forth like a restless pigeon. "Besides, her vault door would have gone dark if something like that had happened ..."

Paranoia washing over him, he stopped pacing, flicked at the infirmary door to slam it shut, flared his shield, and incanted, "*Summano vaultus arcanus.*" The vault *whooshed* into existence above an empty cot, and he drew a sigh of relief upon seeing that Bridget's door was lit as brightly as ever. He opened his own to check if she'd left a message, but as usual found nothing.

Disappointed but unsurprised, he swiped at the air, whispering, "*Vaultus null,*" and the vault vanished. Feeling the need to release some energy, he wondered if Jez was up for some daytime training—and almost snorted when she opened the door.

"Want to train, kiddo?"

Augum walked up to her, clamped both hands on her shoulders, and gently shook her back and forth, singing, "You. Read. My. Mind." Then his hands slid off her shoulders as he glanced back hesitantly at Leera.

"She'll be fine, monkey."

Augum stared at the sleeping form of his betrothed and realized he couldn't wreck his nerves worrying about someone attacking her here. And the threat was coming from inside the boat, from an unhinged and grieving man twice his age. How could he neutralize that threat?

Jez, who had crossed her arms whilst watching him, nudged him with an elbow. "What's going on in that gerbil brain of yours?"

Augum slowly turned his head to look at her, an idea dawning on him. A simple, transcendent idea. "Would you by chance be inclined to play master of ceremonies?"

"What? Now?"

"Now."

Jez's eyebrows rose up her forehead. "I don't get it."

Augum flicked his head toward the hallway, silently telling her to follow him, and walked out with her trailing. He made his way up to the main hallway and found the person he was looking for in the galley sulking over half-finished porridge.

Augum allowed his lantern-lit shadow to slide over the man as he stepped before him. "I accept your challenge, Bloomington-Southguard," he said, raising a finger to stall whatever a surprised Digby was going to say. "On the condition that we temper our spells and we are judged by the illustrious—" He indicated at Jez with a graceful hand.

Digby gaped at him. "Er … all right."

Augum nodded. "See you on deck," and left knowing this was the only chance for peace.

"You *do* realize he's a fire warlock, right?" Jez said as they stepped out onto the deck. "And we're on a wooden ship."

That halted Augum in his tracks. "Oh."

"*Oh*, he says," Jez replied, snorting. "Relax, I'll explain to you both how it'll work. We'll do zero-tempers for your lightning and his fire, and that's that."

Augum accepted this solution with a nod and began clearing the deck of sails and people, politely asking them to make room. With Digby still dragging his feet, he asked the captain for permission to duel on his ship.

"I reckon the crew could use some entertainment," the old man said, only to poke Augum in the chest with the pointy end of his pipe. "Just don't send 'er to the bottom, son."

"We will be careful, sir."

"Bosun—furl 'em up then assemble the men midship."

"Aye, aye, Cap," and the bosun hollered a slew of commands that had the crew scrambling to take in the sails. The ship was soon at level keel, with only a light wind ruffling robes and clothes and the various flags of the royal standard and the Solian emblem.

By then, word had spread like wildfire that a duel was going to take place. A visibly nervous Digby stepped onto the deck and was swinging his arms about in a strange attempt to stretch them or something—

Augum had a difficult time telling. Digby then did the same with his legs, and it was only when he started whipping his head about like a bird doing some weird mating call that Augum realized Digby probably hadn't dueled someone in years.

Olaf, who stood alongside watching this bizarre display, shook his head. "Tell me you're going to smear the deck with that powdered face of his, Three Toes."

But Augum wasn't smiling. "He's grieving and needs an outlet. I'm going to provide him with one."

"Uh … you sure that's a good idea there, boss?"

Augum looked over at his best friend. "No."

They had to hide their mouths with their hands to prevent others from seeing their inappropriate smiles. Two people had died, so there was no room for mirth. They should be in mourning.

Then play your part, Augum thought, composing himself.

The crowd gathered, with sailors and warlocks alike grabbing tankards of weak ale and some grub to munch on—salted and honeyed peanuts, figs, cinnamon-spiced dried apple chunks, and buttered chunks of hot bread. When Augum happened to glance at Alanna, she made a show of sighing and shaking her head in disagreement, but he ignored her. He had to follow his intuition on this one, even if it didn't appear to be the sensible thing to do.

Before Augum stepped into the wide ring the crew had formed, located between the two masts, Carter stepped up to Augum. "Sir, Digby hasn't dueled in, well, in a long time."

"I know, Squire."

"Oh. Of course you do. Er … good luck, and I hope you will forgive me for asking this, but take it easy on the poor sap."

"Let's get this show going—gentle sirs, if you please," Jez sang, beckoning for Augum and Digby to step forth.

Augum acknowledged Carter's point with a nod and stepped forth, keeping his limbs loose by flicking out a foot at a time and shaking out his hands. Digby, meanwhile, kept making wild motions with his arms and legs that gave him the appearance of a man trying out his body for the first time.

Leo the Leopard loosed an appreciative whistle as he glanced Digby over. "Look at that rooster calling for the axe," a comment that had some holding their stomachs as they suppressed laughter with their fists.

Even the two kids had a go at him, sniping, "What a weirdo," and "Moves like a donkey," only to be told to hush up by Alanna and Tammy, who stood side by side, arms crossed in identical fashion as if they mutually disapproved of this silly affair.

It is rather silly, Augum thought, swaying from side to side in readiness as he eyed the stubby Digby. *But silly things are necessary for silly men like us.*

"This is a duel of honor," Jez proclaimed. "The rules are as follows. All offensive spells that can cause damage to the ship shall be zero-tempered." She stabbed each of them in the chest with a finger. "That means. No. Damage. *Zero*. Get me?"

The two men nodded, neither removing their gaze from the other.

"No 'porting off, no cheap shots—eye gouges, back-of-the-head swipes, groin kicks, that sort of thing." The kids—and some of the younger crew—snickered at this rule. "Points will be scored on direct hits to the body and visible mind alterations. First to five wins. Nod that you understand."

Augum and Digby nodded, and Jez flicked her hands at them. "Now step back, pay the honors, and try not to kill each other or sink the ship."

Augum and Digby stepped back, bowed, and flared their arm rings— seven fiery bands around Digby's arm, and ten lightning around Augum's. Jez, meanwhile, placed an arm between them. She looked each of them in the eye one last time, flaring her eyes meaningfully at Augum, which he interpreted as *I hope you know what you're doing*, then sliced at the air with that arm, shouting, "Fight!"

As the crew cheered the combatants on, Digby lashed out first, smacking his wrists together and roaring, "*Annihilo!*" sending a pumpkin-sized fireball at Augum, who didn't even have to step aside to let it fly by. It smacked into Dirt, who shrieked like a banshee, only to discover he was uninjured—Digby was sticking to the agreement. Seeing the kid jump about drained the tension from those who had feared the worst, and people visibly relaxed.

"First victim turned into flaming barbecue!" Jez quipped, causing a burble of laughter.

Augum countered by slapping his wrists together, incanting, "*Annihilo!*" and sending a small bolt of lightning at Digby, who didn't summon his shield in time to block the bolt from smacking into his chest with a harmless *sizzle*. Despite it having no effect, Digby lost his balance, no doubt thinking the strike would be harder, and swirled his arms backward to regain his footing. Augum used the opportunity to quickly slap his wrists a second time, sending another bolt into Digby's chest. He fell back on his butt, prompting the kids and crew to laugh.

"That's a quick two-zero for the Arcaner!" Jez called out, flamboyantly dancing around the pair in a whimsical impersonation of some of the more famed masters of ceremonies.

Augum jiggled his wrist, purposely doing it slower than usual, whilst incanting, "*Flustrato.*"

Digby, having received plenty of visual warning, rolled aside in time for the Confusion spell to slap harmlessly into the hull. Whilst still sitting on his butt, he then made a petting-the-air motion, incanting, "*Senna dormo coma torpos!*"

Augum had more than enough time to sidestep the 8th degree spell, and it slapped into a crew member who merely yawned and stretched, easily fighting the spell off, indicating it had been an incompetent casting as they weren't required to temper mind spells.

Jez continued her colorful observations in the background. "The commander easily dodges a Sleep spell—but what our challenger was thinking flinging such a slow-to-cast spell against an experienced dueler like the Arinthian is anyone's guess."

Digby's lips curled, telling Augum his plan wasn't working. Even though he hadn't intended to make a fool of Digby, the poor sap's lack of skill was so apparent that he was naturally making a fool of himself.

Augum thus backed up and beckoned for Digby to stand, sportsmanship the crew rewarded with a cheer.

"Yeah, let 'im 'ave it, landlubber!" a sailor quipped.

"Fair play from the Arcaner," Jez noted, adding, "and we expected nothing less."

Leo cupped his mouth and shouted, "Wipe the butt powder off his face with some of that fancy wrist-slappin', Arcaner!" which caused a round of laughter from the crew.

That one got to Digby, and his face went beet-red as he smashed his wrists together, roaring, "*Annihilo!*" shooting another fireball at Augum, who knew it was a full-strength blast and thus summoned his shield. The fireball slapped into it, and Augum saw its flames lick around the edges.

"Flagrant foul for casting an untempered spell!" Jez shouted. "Do it again and I'll disqualify you."

Realizing that had the fireball hit the ship—or worse, the audience—which could have had deadly repercussions, Augum chose a different tack. Just as a snarling Digby moved to slap his already bruised wrists a second time, Augum yanked on the man's right arm. His hands missed each other and his feet stumbled forth clumsily. Augum then used the advantage zero-tempered spells offered, which was that they could sometimes be cast quicker as they required far less stamina to wield, and slapped his own wrists together, incanting, "*Annihilo bato!*"

Two harmless bolts of lightning smacked into Digby's chest as he stumbled past Augum.

"That's a double!" Jez shouted to the approving roar of the crowd. "Making it four-zip!"

Augum, hoping he still had a chance at mending fences with his adversary, knew he needed to do something only his great-grandmother Anna Atticus Stone would understand, and so he caught Digby's upper arm with a hand as he flailed past, purposely exposing himself to easy retribution. Digby was able to pivot on his other foot, swing about, and clock Augum in the back of the head.

"That's uncalled for!" Jez shouted, hands flapping with disgust. "Point deduction for unsportsmanlike conduct! That's now four to minus one!"

A raging Digby didn't listen to her or the now booing crowd and just kept throwing his fists. That gave Augum the chance to enact his plan — he turned his face *toward* the flailing fist and stood there, letting Digby repeatedly punch him in the face. Flecks of light popped about his vision as his head snapped back again and again. Yet he held onto Digby's other arm, keeping the pair close, as the crowd roared in confusion for him to react.

Jez kept count. "Four-zip! Four-one! Four-two! Four-three! Four-four — it's a tie, unless he snaps out of it!"

A smarting Augum, barely cognizant now, turned his swollen face to a hesitating Digby, giving him the slightest nod. Digby wound all the way back and threw a meaty hook which connected with Augum's cheek. Augum spun in place until he collapsed to his knees, face throbbing, nose bleeding profusely onto his robe.

The deck fell silent as every single jaw hung open. Only the gentle whistle of the wind and the flap of sails could be heard.

"Five-four for Bloomington-Southguard," Jez mumbled, gaping at Augum in disbelief.

Leo scratched his tattooed neck. "Well, *that* was ... different."

A dizzy Augum groaned as he struggled to haul himself to his feet. Multiple people rushed to offer him aid, including Alanna, but he raised a blood-splattered hand to ward them off and managed the task on his own. He turned to his opponent, who stood ashen, jaw hanging as slack as the others.

Augum cleared his throat — only to involuntarily cough out some blood, which dribbled down his chin. After clearing his throat a second time, he smoothed his robe and bowed as tradition demanded. Then he straightened and waited.

Startled, Digby quickly bowed in turn.

Augum accepted this bow with a subtle nod and turned to the crew. "With respect to the gathered, I consider the matter between—" He paused to spit a glob of blood onto the deck like a hoodlum. "—between Lord Digby Bloomington-Southguard and myself squashed."

He wincingly pressed the back of his sleeve against his nose and felt it crackle, meaning it was broken proper. Although it stung something fierce, it was a paltry injury compared to the many he had sustained in the wars.

"I would like to add that Lord Bloomington-Southguard has suffered greatly on account of having lost his brother. Please do not throw salt onto that wound. We have had enough strife and now need to unite for what is to come."

His gaze wandered over the stunned audience. "After supper, we will hold a memorial ceremony for Black Eagle Mahmoute and Lord Teague Blooming-Southguard. I hope you will all attend and honor their memories. Now if you will excuse me," and he hobbled off, for he'd taken such hard knocks that his legs were rather wobbly.

Jengo and Olaf and Jez and Carter and a worried Alanna promptly followed, but he bid all but Jengo to stay on deck with the others and dive right into training, telling them, "Feed the fire while the tinder is lit," something he had thought of in that moment.

As he entered the hallway, Alanna leaned forth to whisper, "M'lord is a wise soul," and she smiled bittersweetly and gave a surprisingly humble bow of her head.

Augum only grunted, perhaps a little sarcastically, and disappeared inside.

"Commander, please stop so that I may heal you already."

"In the infirmary, Almoner Okeke. I wish to sit with my betrothed."

"Thou art a stubborn and—" Jengo indicated the floor. "—a plank-bleeding mule."

"That's the closest you got to a jest in some time."

Jengo snorted a laugh at that, but he followed Augum's hobbling pace as he made his way down to the infirmary, feeling spent and rather old for his age. Once in the infirmary, he allowed Jengo to administer the proper healing.

"But leave the black eye," Augum said. "That's not a request."

Jengo sighed but nodded, and he steadily healed the broken nose, a cracked cheekbone, and several minor cuts. But not the headache, nor the bruise that was forming, nor the blood that remained to be cleaned.

"Shall I fetch someone to—"

"To what, aid in wiping my face?" Augum asked with a wry grin. "Am I a toddler to you?"

"No, Commander, of course not. I forget myself. I just …"

"I know, I know. You care—and care deeply." Augum patted Jengo's tall shoulder. "You're a good soul and a good friend. Perhaps you can see to Digby as a healer and almoner, maybe impart some wisdom as alms?"

Jengo stepped back to glance Augum over. "What the heck's gotten into you? You sound like Mrs. Stone."

"That is one of the greatest compliments one can give this—" Augum swept a hand up and down his bloody robe. "—wretched sap. Now off with ye, lad," he added in a cheap dockside twang, throwing Jengo a light punch to the shoulder. "Go on and mend broken hearts."

Jengo shook his head as he walked off, mumbling something about Augum having lost his mind somewhere across the ocean. Once alone with Leera, Augum shuffled over to a small cask and washbasin. He pointed at the basin, floated it under the tap of the cask, and used his other hand to point at the tap so that it dipped forward, allowing water to rush out. Once half full, he pointed at a shelf with brass guards to prevent slippage in high seas and floated over a cloth from a stack of folded ones. Then he stepped before a polished steel mirror hanging nearby.

"How can I help you, young man?" he said, sensing a certain gaze from the entranceway.

"Why'd you let him win?" Limpet asked quietly, respecting a sleeping Leera. "You could have wiped the floor with that idiot. Even *I* would have."

"That is a difference between us," Augum replied, making the washbasin float before him as he gingerly dipped the cloth into the water and dabbed at his sore face.

Limpet studied him with a cocked head Augum glimpsed through the mirror. "But I want to be like you," he blurted.

Augum kept dabbing, allowing the quiet sound of the water to soothe his tired soul. "And which part of me would that be?"

Limpet wandered into the room and telekinetically flicked at folded blankets sitting on an empty cot, disheveling them slightly, hands dancing about in search of distraction. He plopped down on the cot closest to where Augum was standing and scratched at his red-haired scalp. Then he shrugged. "I don't know."

"But you *do* know," Augum replied, taking his time wiping the spaces between his bloody fingers—how quickly blood traveled when one was not paying attention …

Limpet watched the floating basin revolve slowly in place. "How do you make it float like that and do other stuff?"

Augum dipped the corner of the cloth into the water and used it to wipe a dried blood stain on the heel of his hand. "Practice. Lots of practice."

"You just lost a duel to an inferior."

"Did I?"

Limpet rolled his eyes. "*Obviously.*"

"And what exactly did I lose?"

"Well … I mean … the—" Limpet kept flicking a hand over his shoulder, but he couldn't form a cogent reply, and that hand hung in midair as his face struggled to work out an answer.

As he did so, Augum dunked the entire cloth into the red water, removed it, wrung it out, and wiped his whole face.

"Did I miss anything?" Augum asked, pointing at his own face with the corner of the cloth and angling his jaw this way and that.

Limpet squirmed in his seat, as if he found it incredibly uncomfortable to communicate in this manner. "Er … I don't know."

Augum raised an eyebrow. "You don't?"

"Well, maybe—" Limpet looked away as he subtly tapped the bottom of his chin.

"Ah." Augum wiped the beginnings of a scraggly ocean-born beard, which he hated as it itched and he couldn't wait to shave it off. "How about now? Did I get it all?"

Limpet flicked his gaze at Augum, as if worried that by doing so he might catch the disease of empathy, before mumbling, "You got it all."

"What's that?"

"I said *you got it all!*"

Both of them glanced over at Leera, who rolled in her sleep to face away from them.

Augum pressed his lips together in a thin line at Limpet, who hung his head in shame. Fleetingly, he imagined this very moment happening in the future, but with his own son—or perhaps daughter. He saw Leera hovering in the background, humming away as she fussed with baby clothes, or perhaps read a book, or played with Sir Pawsalot—or their other children. A life blossomed before his mind, watering a fragile seed of hope.

Limpet picked at a scab on his hand. "I want to be a dragon …"

Augum rinsed the cloth in the floating basin. "I told you already, you would die in the trials long before that stage."

"No, I wouldn't."

"Until you understand events such as the one you just witnessed, until you show a little humility and compassion, you will never be allowed to take the first trial. And if I may be so bold as to say, the path you currently tread—the path of arrogance and denial and fear and anger—will only lead to your own destruction."

Limpet shot to his feet and, with balled fists, snarled, "Even *I* could have won such a simple and stupid duel!" He stomped off.

Augum watched him go with a small smile, hoping he'd put a crack in the kid's armor of apathy. "Only time will tell if the lessons sink in …" he whispered, once again hearing Mrs. Stone speaking through him.

Interestingly, hearing that voice and thinking in this manner precluded The Callousness of the Predator from throwing open the curtain and corrupting his thoughts. Somehow, this entire path—a path he could not yet name but intuitively knew existed—was strengthening his ability to keep the predator at bay.

"Interesting," he said, floating the washbasin to a scupper sink—a rusted metal funnel that fed dirty water to the ocean—and had the basin tip itself over the sink until all the bloody water drained away. He rinsed the washbasin out, put it back in its place, and sat with Leera for a time, holding her hand throughout. Then he kissed her forehead, tucked the blanket up to her chin once more, and left the room to change into clothes suitable for the memorial ceremony, knowing he had accomplished his simple quest to allow her to sleep alone in safety—a quest no one else had understood but him.

"Interesting indeed …" he said as he walked, smiling secretly to himself.

SKY MARBLE

BRIDGET

"You cannot come, Sebby," Bridget replied as she scrubbed her soapy nightgown against a washboard, feet on a stepladder.

"But whyyyyyyy?" Sebastian whined, standing opposite the large tub on his own stepladder whilst scraping his nightgown against a separate washboard. A ribbon of brilliant morning sunshine cut across the water. A pleasant breeze cooled them off and played with the row of clothes hanging outside on a nearby line.

"Because you're too young and what the gorgan do is dangerous."

"I don't like it when you leave."

"I don't like it when I leave either."

"Where are you going?"

"I don't know."

"When are you going?"

Bridget flashed the pouty boy a look.

"Well, what *do* you know?" he pressed.

"I know you ought to mind your chores, that much I do know."

"You know more than that," he grumbled, but she let the remark go, and he continued to scrub his gown in silence. He was right, of course, but Bridget did not want to scare him with tales of creatures that would give him nightmares. The boy had a toy of one such creature, the minotaur. She was content to let him keep playing with it as a toy. Why torment him with what he did not need to know?

Bridget heard the telltale swishing of a tail sliding along the floor and the familiar scuffle of claws as they clacked against the planks. The lazy style of noises told her it was Bragga, the nickname Bridget had given the elder daughter of the clan as it sounded so similar to the gorgan's real name, which was a guttural growl. The name also reflected a cruel and preening teenager who was popular amongst her clique. Had she been human, her peers would have called her Bragga the Braggart, as that was what she did whenever Bridget saw her with her teenage friends, who mercifully ignored Bridget on the whole.

Bridget snapped her fingers at Sebastian before turning about on the stepladder to bow her head in preparation for the girgoyle's arrival. Bragga waltzed in with Grak, who held a stubby bottle filled with pink liquid. The teenage girgoyle periodically dipped a brush into it to paint her claws.

"*Gohihol, gyoooooot,*" Bragga drawled, not bothering to look up. "*Yer var hehi vet gat.*"

Attention, slave. You're coming with me, Bridget translated, making progress with their language. If she kept at it, she would have a much easier time with the Tongues spell and would be able to understand nuance and complexity, something she hoped to utilize to her advantage sooner rather than later.

Bridget bowed deeper still, replying, "*Yoss, maso.*"

Bragga looked up. After a pause, she shuffled over, Grak in tow — and lazily slapped Bridget on the cheek. "*Misa, gyot. Maso gu karr.*"

Bridget bowed even deeper, nodding, having already dismissed the lame slap. *Misa* was the feminine form of *master*, meaning it was their word for *mistress*. The word *maso* was therefore used for males like Karr Gravak, the captain.

You must pay closer attention to their subtleties, Bridget thought.

Bragga absently flicked a claw at Grak, who extended the jar to her. She dipped her brush into it and was about to press it to an unfinished claw when she swiped the brush across Bridget's cheek, giggling as she did so. When Bridget flinched only a little, Bragga dipped the brush in again and swiped Bridget's other cheek, taking delight in the play. Despite Bridget not flinching a second time, Bragga did this four more times, until she stepped back and said, "*Mau.*"

Bridget realized the strokes on each cheek emanated from her nose, and visualizing them on her face, she determined she looked like a cat. The girgoyle had inadvertently taught her a new word.

When Grak failed to respond, for he was looking at Bridget with that lone sad eye as he so oft did, Bragga elbowed him in the stomach, causing him to grunt.

"*Mau, mau,*" he agreed, nodding fervently, which told Bridget he was more scared of her than the others. Bridget took note of this and resolved not to annoy the girgoyle further if she could help it.

"*Hehi, mau mau gyot,*" Bragga said with a gorgan chortle and turned about, tail sweeping the floor like a broom.

Bridget stepped off the ladder and dared to steal a quick grab of Sebastian's clammy hand, giving it a reassuring squeeze before following Grak and Bragga.

The rest of the house was empty that morn, the other gorgan family members having departed earlier to attend various daily activities and duties. This made Bridget wonder what Bragga had in mind. She made Grak follow her all the way to the edge of the tiny sky island, where they lingered at her pleasure, Bridget fidgeting and Grak awkwardly holding the vial of pink nail polish as Bragga gingerly took her time painting the last of her claws, her long cow-like tongue sticking out of her snout as she concentrated on getting her nails just right.

The females appear to have their own femininity somewhat like ours, Bridget thought, trying not to stare at the surprisingly familiar display. Gargoyles and girgoyles did not adorn themselves with much, preferring raw power and strength to serve as status symbols, yet there were subtleties that Bridget had yet to comprehend as she still had much to learn about gorgan culture.

Bragga inspected her claws, flipping her hands this way and that. Apparently satisfied, she tossed the brush at Grak, who fumbled it to the ground. When he leaned over to pick it up, she used her tail to push him down, taking childish delight in seeing him roll like an egg.

"*Gerger kupa,*" she said, shaking her head, shocking Bridget with how casually she degraded poor Grak with such beastly language. Then she flicked her hand dismissively, saying, "*Hohol, gerger. Hohol,*" and Grak bowed, flicked his sad eye at Bridget, and silently departed.

Bragga opened her snout in a wide yawn as she extended her wings and arms in a slovenly stretch. After releasing a contented and bored sigh, she idly slapped a pink-clawed hand onto Bridget's shoulder, yanked her forth, flipped her around, and began beating her wings. As she rose, she hooked her legs around Bridget's torso, and the pair took to the air.

Most undignified, Bridget thought half-amusedly, for the position made her hang like a dog. *All I need is a leash*. More uncomfortable was Bragga's strong hold, so strong in fact that Bridget struggled to breathe. Was the girgoyle doing it on purpose or simply didn't notice that she was causing Bridget discomfort? Bridget suspected it was likely the former.

They flew not down, but up into the clear sunlit sky, which surprised Bridget. They rose about two thousand feet before Bragga began a gliding descent. It wasn't long before Bridget realized the destination was another tall platform plateau, which made her nervous as she did not know what to expect.

After a long but steady glide passing several other island plateaus below, during which Bragga barely flapped her wings except to correct her glide path, they touched down on a sky island in the middle of the city, this one four times larger than Captain Gravak's and in the style of a sandy desert that strongly reminded Bridget of Ley. In the center, surrounded by the occasional well-placed and vibrantly pink palm tree, a single-floor white marble palace gleamed in the sun. A path composed of loose white gravel wound toward the entrance of the palace.

Bragga kicked Bridget forth, taking delight in seeing her tumble a few times on the sharp gravel. Bridget had allowed that roll on purpose, not wanting to spring back to her feet too quickly, and even made a show of hauling herself back up. She caught her breath, rubbed her midriff from Bragga's tight hold, and waited for the girgoyle to pass.

Bragga checked to make sure her painted claws hadn't smudged during the flight and, with her tail lazily dragging along the gravel, sashayed forth, idly flicking a claw at Bridget to follow. Bridget did so, but the rocks were so sharp against her bare feet that she hopped onto the pristine sand, hoping no one would mind the footprints she left behind.

Fool, you're an earth warlock, she realized, and with Bragga walking ahead, Bridget turned about, pointed at the sand, and began a continuous smoothing motion. It was a classic earthen trick of Telekinesis that saw the sand smooth over her footsteps, obscuring all trace of her. Sure, sometimes it required more than one motion on account of the suppressive collar, but on the whole the spell was simple enough to succeed.

The pair soon reached wide steps that led up to a golden double-door entranceway flanked by towering pink-leaved palms, and Bridget, satisfied she had gotten away with a minor rebellion, hopped back onto the sharp gravel, wincing as she did so.

Bragga flicked impatiently at Bridget to go up, making a quick fist-pumping motion that Bridget understood as demanding she knock.

Bridget bowed her head. "*Yoss, misa,*" and padded up the steps. Then she knocked on one of the massive golden doors, but she might as well have blown feathers at them for all the noise it made.

"*Taga, gyot!*" Bragga snapped, rolling her eyes in a teenage fashion that would have made Jez scowl with disgust.

Bridget cleared her throat and put the side of her fist to the door. The distant snap of a growl, as if a servant were announcing a house call, responded from within. It was followed by a barking command which used the word *gyot*.

"*Taga, gyot, taga.*"

"Yes, yes, again I will try," Bridget muttered as she raised her fist to repeat the knock—only for a *click* to sound and the door to open inward. She felt her eyes go wide, for standing on the other side was none other than her fellow ship slave Naomi. She was dressed in an identical cotton slave gown as Bridget's and had evidently been allowed to care for herself, for her long curly hair was freshly washed and her brown skin shone in the sun with oil that smelled faintly of citron.

Just as Naomi opened her mouth to say something, someone rudely shoved her aside. Bridget stepped back, ready to bow, only for another slave to emerge—a squat older man with a balding scalp and a roughly trimmed salt-and-pepper beard. She recognized him from the encounter with the royals at the marble pyramid. He had a portly belly and wore the same slave garment, albeit threadbare and worn in parts. He gave Bridget a once-over, which he had to do from below as he was shorter even though he looked twice her age, and promptly bowed—not to her, but to Bragga.

Bragga scoffed and entered without invitation, one of her wings brushing Bridget's face as she passed, making Bridget recoil and flash the girgoyle an involuntary dirty look that she promptly hid.

"Yagiet!" Bragga shouted into the interior, a sprawling white marble hallway lined with two rows of towering marble columns, a long red carpet running in between. The carpet shone a vivid red in contrast to the marble, for it was lit brightly by sunlight shining through long rectangular windows cut into the high ceiling, leaving most of the roof completely open to the sky. Interestingly, the carpet showed no sign of rain, making Bridget wonder if there was glass in the windows that was so clean it was invisible.

Cut into the marble floor sat rectangular pools of crystal-clear water, each long and shallow and strategically positioned to reflect the sky windows, creating a mirror effect. In seemingly random spots, pink broad-leaved palms grew directly from square patches of orange sand, lending the marble palace a sense of eternal desert coziness amidst its glittering and sunny emptiness.

Naomi flared her eyes meaningfully at Bridget, which Bridget took to mean *I can't believe it's you.* Bridget, not wanting to reveal to the male slave that they knew each other, as he was watching her closely, kept a placid countenance and glanced about instead. Doorless rooms branched out from the central corridor, all of which were just as brightly lit by the sun as the central divide, telling Bridget they all had the same rectangular windows open to the sky.

Then she noticed a streak of white floating within the space of a sky window, on what she assumed was spotless glass. She cocked her head, trying to figure out what the streak was, when a small shadow zipped silently through the hallway and a seagull landed not too far away from the white smear, which had to be seagull poop. Its feet seemed to float too, and she realized what she was staring at—an arcane force field, or perhaps arcane glass similar to what was found in the academy's room of masters, though in that case it was structured as an infinite wall.

Gods, Bridget thought, *the gorgan also possess similar ancient knowledge.* She wondered if they had the knowledge to create such constructs, or if this was a holdover from an older era or an extinct race. Brimming with unaskable questions, she realized the others had begun to walk down the hallway and hurried to catch up.

"Yagiet, Yagiet, Yagiet!" Bragga kept calling out, which Bridget figured had to be the name of her friend. "Yag—" Bragga halted and bowed, for a gigantic winged shadow stepped into the hall. The looming figure waited behind a column, as if annoyed he'd had to come out of his room, before stepping forth with a quick growl in the form of a question.

Bridget glimpsed a monstrous gargoyle ripped up with the most amount of scars she had ever seen on a living being. The snout was hideous, as if it belonged to a sea monster, runes covered his torso, and the arms bulged with veiny muscles.

As Bridget bowed along with her fellow slaves, it occurred to her who she was looking at—Naomi's master, Bones, who had lost the bidding war over her to the ship's captain. He was just not wearing his armor. Now here she was in his palace. She felt a blush of regret upon thinking that this could have been her and Sebastian's home. They would have been stronger together with Naomi, with many more places for privacy — not to mention the palace lent a feeling of peace that soothed Bridget's turbulent soul a little.

Bones loosed another short growl, this one not a question but a statement or perhaps a command, and Bragga did not rise from her bow, which meant of course that neither did the three slaves standing behind her, with Bridget in the middle.

The huge gargoyle's claws clicked against the white marble as he walked over. Instead of stopping before Bragga, as would have been customary for the gorgan, he walked right by, until his shadow fell over Bridget, who felt a distinct chill creep down her spine.

He loosed a fluid growling line so low in pitch and so rumbly that Bridget only understood a couple words — *has* and *slave*. How she wished she'd had the prescience to cast Tongues ahead of time! Now, in the solemn silence of the marble palace, it was far too risky to attempt to cast it under her breath.

Bragga hesitated before replying with a string of quick words, one of which was a definite *no*, yet said with utter respect, telling Bridget that Bragga was scared. Bones grunted, spoke again, turned on his heel, and returned to his room. Only when he had vanished out of sight did Bragga rise from her bow, expelling a sigh that sounded like relief. The old slave then rose from his bow, and in turn so did Naomi and Bridget, with the latter two trading secret looks of puzzlement.

Bragga whirled on the old slave, snapping, "*Vir Yagiet, gyot?*"

Where's Yagiet, slave? Bridget translated in her head.

The old man bowed and extended an arm down the corridor. Bragga slapped it aside. It was a light slap for a gargoyle, but hard enough for an old human to yelp in pain. Bragga scoffed at him in disgust as he whimpered quietly, tottering forth at a rapid clip so as not to provoke her further.

Bridget and Naomi allowed Bragga to go on ahead after the old man so that they could walk together in silence, for slaves did not speak idly near their mistresses and masters lest they incur their wrath.

Naomi kept glancing over at Bridget. In contrast with her groomed appearance, her eyes were puffy, indicating she had not been sleeping, and her frame was thin and slightly malnourished. She was already starting to resemble the other slaves.

Upon meeting her gaze, Bridget gave a nod and a slight smile, which was enough for Naomi's face to light up as if it were Endyear. She wondered if the poor girl was making any progress learning either the slave or gargoyle languages, how her frightful master was treating her, and what the family of gorgans that kept her was like in general.

She soon laid eyes on one of those family members, who poked her head out of one of the many rooms lining the long marble hallway and squealed like a human teenager. The girgoyle, who like Bragga only had a handful of runes upon her body, popped out, claws painted a light blue, and the pair did something Bridget had never seen a gargoyle do — dance. At least, that was what it looked like, for each wiggled left to right and back again, tails swishing along the floor like snakes, arms weaving about until they embraced, twirling each other about whilst giggling growlingly. It was like seeing two alligators perform a mating dance, a display so ridiculous that, had it been under any other circumstances, Bridget would have snorted an obnoxious laugh.

Wait until I tell Olaf about this, Bridget thought, allowing herself that comfort.

Yagiet proceeded to talk a league a heartbeat, far too quickly for Bridget to keep up, waxing on about who knew what. The language was more colloquial and perhaps utilized slang. Listening, Bridget picked up on a most human trait, for nearly every statement ended in a high-pitched question. She almost imagined the two females overusing the word *like*. Bridget was so curious about the language and teenage gorgan customs that she was once again tempted to cast Tongues. But due to how silent the hall was and the fact that the old slave kept a vulture-like watch over her, she kept her hands together before her gown, maintaining a placid countenance of serenity and calm that mirrored the palace.

A serenity that shattered when Bragga giddily hopped over, grabbed Bridget by the throat, and threw her toward Yagiet. Bridget tumbled a few times, grunting from the suddenness of the violence and the indignity. Yagiet planted a foot on her back, halting her roll. She then grabbed Bridget by the hair and yanked her to her feet. For some reason, that act punctured the poise, and Bridget found her blood raging.

You vagrant, feral alligator of a dog, you! Bridget screamed internally, allowing the girgoyles to poke and prod her as Bragga discussed various aspects of her new acquisition.

Whilst listening to Bragga brag, Yagiet flicked a blue-painted claw past Bridget's cheek, singing, *"Mau mau, gyot!"* and Bragga stopped bragging in order to join in on a belly-clutching girgoyle laugh.

Bridget had to unclench her fists lest she reveal the extent of her rage, but the two teenagers seemed completely oblivious to her red face and angry eyes, likely because no slave had ever dared usurp their authority—and thinking of Sebastian, Bridget certainly didn't plan on being the first.

Yagiet roughly grabbed Bridget's jaw, forced open her mouth, and yanked her head close to study her teeth as if Bridget were a newly purchased horse. It was particularly humiliating because of the old man, who was so titillated by the display that he made a squeal of delight.

Not wanting to partake in the moment, Bridget's mind ran up to Castle Arinthian, dropped its imaginary drawbridge—which the real castle did not possess—scurried inside, and raised the drawbridge behind her. From within she watched the distant pair of fiendish teenagers continue to poke and prod at her limp body. She turned her back on them and began a cycle of spells, envisioned each going off with perfect precision and potent power, for only in her imagination was the collar absent, her powers unlimited. She used the pair of girgoyles as practice targets, doing some poking and prodding of her own, as well as more lethal combinations that saw the girgoyles blasted into bits, only to promptly reform for the next round of spells.

She finished the 3rd degree before she heard Bragga address her directly and hurried to lower the drawbridge. By then Bragga had to repeat herself, which annoyed the teenager to the point of rearing back with a hand. Bridget returned in time to duck the vicious backhanded slap.

Bragga pointed a claw at Yagiet, singing the gargoyle version of *I told you so!*

Yagiet stepped back and barked at Bragga and her old slave, which Bridget understood to mean she was to showcase her talents.

Shoot, shoot, shoot, Bridget thought, not wanting to show the extent of her powers. She would have to be careful here.

Yagiet indicated between the old slave and Bridget, snapping at Bridget to do something. Bridget stood there staring at the old man, who swallowed and took a cagey step back. Yagiet circled an impatient hand along, once more showing that some gestures were universal and intuitive. Bridget gave her a dumb look, pretending she did not understand.

Bragga, however, wasn't having that and growled menacingly at Bridget, flaring her eyes in that *I know you know what we want* fashion, making Bridget realize she had revealed too much of herself to the teenager. Before she could do anything, Yagiet lost patience and told the old slave to fetch something, but Bridget didn't know the last few words and was left to puzzle over the phrase as the old slave gleefully wrung his hands and hurriedly tottered off.

As he vanished into a distant room, Yagiet went on to complain about Naomi, who went pale upon finding herself the center of attention. Yagiet kept shaking her head as she indicated Naomi from foot to head and even tapped her temple, saying how slow she was on the uptake. Bragga, of course, took this opportunity to further brag about Bridget, claiming who knew what.

The old slave returned before Naomi got a physical prodding from Bragga. He carried with him a pike twice his size and clutched it as awkwardly as a child would a spear. Bridget's heart sank, for she knew what they expected of her. Yet she vowed to take it easy on the cantankerous old fool, who was growing more and more nervous with each step. He bowed before his mistress, then nodded at Naomi and even tried to present the pike to his fellow slave, but Yagiet was having none of it and screamed at him to hold the pike and attack Bridget.

The old man, standing on the carpet and sweating profusely in the direct sunlight, tottered back ten feet and leveled the pike at Bridget. It shook in his hands, but his eyes were narrow with malice. She had no doubt whatsoever that he would run her through if she allowed it.

Yagiet whirled an arm, shouting, "*Gatta, yer hoy gyot! Gatta!*"

The old slave swallowed hard and lamely thrust the pike forth. Bridget took a step back and he fell well short. He nervously glanced at his mistress, who impatiently whirled her claws about for him to press. Throughout, Bragga spoke in low tones whilst indicating Bridget, likely discussing her abilities.

The old man hesitantly shuffled forth and jabbed, and again Bridget stepped back. Bragga smacked her gums in annoyance and made the same clawed *move it along* gesture, but to Bridget.

I don't know what you want me to do here, but fine, Bridget thought, and the next time the old man thrust forth, she grabbed the end of the pike with her hand. For a moment the pair tussled over control of the pike, until the old man revealed a farm strength that nearly cut her hand off when he yanked the pike back.

Having gained confidence, he grinned evilly and made a serious run to stab her heart. Realizing he was getting dangerous, she stepped aside and made an artful yanking motion, incanting, "*Disablo!*" The pike was torn from his hands and sent spinning skyward. Bridget was about to telekinetically snag it when she remembered that she did not want to reveal too much of herself to these fiends, and instead let the pike clatter to the floor.

Yagiet nodded, impressed, but Bragga was incensed, going on about what Bridget was truly capable of—or so Bridget thought based on Bragga's vehement gestures. In short order the old man was forced to pick the pike back up and once more train it on Bridget. This time, Bragga got smart and kicked at the pike so that it swung at Naomi, who yelped and stepped back.

"No!" Bridget blurted, realizing Bragga's clever game. "I'll do it," she added, beckoning the old man to attack her anew. "Come," she said. "Try to hit me again."

To her relief, Bragga allowed him to once again point the pike at her. When he thrust, she yanked on the pike with ardent precision, caught it midair as he fumbled to grab it—she was, after all, much taller than he was—whirled the pike about with a *whoosh*, and trained it on his face.

His beady eyes focused inward upon his nose, and he caught his breath, a bead of sweat dribbling down his wrinkled chin.

Bragga opened both hands in a *You see?* manner, and Yagiet went, "*Eyaaaaaa,*" which was gargoyle teenage for *Ah-ha, I see.*

The shadowy part of Bridget watching from behind the curtain wanted to swing the pike at the girgoyles and poke their stomachs. Instead she dropped it to the marble floor, where it clattered so loudly that both gargoyles scowled in annoyance at her. Realizing her impudence, she blunted their anger with a bow of supplication.

Bragga took the opportunity to continue bragging about Bridget's various other skills, which interestingly led to a rather strange conversation between the pair of teenage gorgan, for their voices quieted and they began pointing to each other's chests and stomachs, asking each other questions and even grunting and intoning, as if trying to keep something secret from the slaves.

Suspecting that they were discussing their training and how they would perform in a battle against warlocks, Bridget listened as carefully as she could. But the girgoyles used complexities in their communication, as if they inherently knew the slaves could understand parts of their language. Only Tongues would stand a chance, yet it was still too silent in the sky palace to cast the spell without raising suspicion, so Bridget remained mute.

As she stood, a shadow reemerged down the hallway, extending between two columns. Naomi saw it too, and Bridget felt her eyes bore into the side of her head. She expected Bones to emerge, but instead she heard a strange crackling noise, as if someone were twisting a bundle of twigs. A second shadow joined the first, and there came a loud screech.

The girgoyles and the old man whirled about.

"Yagiet?" Bragga asked.

Yagiet growled a low reply, and the two girgoyles skittered out of the way. When the slaves began to follow, both girgoyles flicked their hands at them, shooing them off. The girgoyles hid behind one of the columns, from where they peeked out like a pair of schoolchildren hiding from the teacher.

Whilst keeping watch on the old man and the trembling pike he held in his hands, Bridget stepped protectively before Naomi. The shadow lengthened along the carpet, until a boned beast of a gargoyle stepped out from between the columns. It was fifteen feet in height, with decrepit bits of tissue hanging from its naked bones. Its ribbed wings flapped as if remembering the idea of flight, its bleached tail whapping the floor with a *clack*.

"A wraith," Bridget blurted, pushing Naomi away behind her.

There came a growling command from behind the columns, and the wraith lowered its long bone snout and slunk forth like a prowling dog. Behind it, Bones stepped out into the corridor and leaned against one of the columns to observe.

He's a necromantic gargoyle, Bridget realized. *And he wants to see my true capability.* She had to admit it was a clever way to do it, for this time she could not afford half measures. A wraith was dangerous under any circumstances, and would be doubly so while stalking collared prey.

Bridget swallowed as she adjusted her collar, backing away as she tried to form a plan—until the tip of the pike poked her back. She whirled about and yanked at the air, hissing, "*Disablo!*" The old man was all too eager to let the pike twirl toward the high ceiling whilst he ran off to cower behind a column.

"Hide yourself," Bridget ordered, catching the pike, and Naomi took shelter behind another column. It did not surprise Bridget that the girgoyles did not complain, for everyone knew it was Bridget's talents they wished to test.

The fifteen-foot gargoyle wraith began to jog, using its tail for balance, its two arms held wide and claws waiting to rip her to shreds. Bones loomed beyond, a hand gripping his chin in interest. Bridget suspected that any spells she cast would be analyzed and the knowledge used in any future gargoyle invasions of Sithesia—yet what choice did she have?

Centarro, she thought, but that would mean succumbing to the foggy side effects, a dangerous proposition under current circumstances. No, she needed to be in full command of her faculties. As the beast's jog turned into a sprint, Bridget realized the pike would be near useless against such a behemoth, and so she took a few steps forth and hurled it like a javelin. Except she had so rarely practiced that sort of maneuver that the pike turned in midair and hit the beast sideways, bouncing off and rolling along the marble floor before clanking against a column.

Bridget only had heartbeats before the beast would tear her to shreds, and so she fell back on her skills and made a fluid pulling-on-a-bowstring motion with both hands whilst roaring, "*Summano arma flustrato!*" An earthen bow, partly ethereal on account of the blasted slave collar, appeared in her waiting hands, an arrow already nocked. Since she had cast the Bluster of the Dragon simul, that arrow was also primed with the Confusion spell. But would it work against a wraith?

Only one way to find out, Bridget thought as she closed one eye and narrowed the other, clarifying her aim. Beyond, Bones stepped out into the corridor so he could see better, while both girgoyles gasped.

Twang! went the arrow. It flew along the carpet, its shadow trailing perfectly, and stuck the beast directly in its bony forehead. The beast's sprint slowed to a jog and then a trundle as the arrow deposited its Confusion spell into its unprotected undead brain. As the beast halted to a standstill, Bridget tossed her bow aside. It vanished before hitting the floor. She then pointed at the pike, which rolled along the ground and hopped up to her waiting hand, a sequence that elicited more gasps from the girgoyles.

Bridget first walked then jogged and then sprinted up to the giant wraith, and this time when she threw the pike like a javelin, she made sure to let it go at the very last moment so that its tip pierced the skull with maximum impact. There was a distinctive crunching noise as the pike lodged into its oafish brain. Its head snapped back, levering the pike upward. That head kept going, and the entire skeletal frame keeled over and fell back with a great *crash* that echoed up and down the marble hallway, leaving behind a ringing silence.

Bones, who had crossed his muscled arms across his runed chest, nodded to himself before walking off and vanishing behind the columns.

Bridget turned about to see the girgoyles and Naomi and the old man emerge from behind their columns. Whilst the girgoyles gestured at Bridget and murmured in low voices, Naomi stared at her with a proud and amazed smile. The old man, for his part, rocked side to side as he scratched at a callused palm, watching her with suspicion.

Bridget looked to the wraith and saw it crumbling, and the pike clanked to the floor amidst a pile of white and gray dust.

The old man, giving Bridget a wide berth, tottered to the pike, grabbed it, and took up his position behind Bridget and Naomi. Bridget stood in silence with an admiring Naomi, thinking of nothing but the repercussions of the knowledge Bones had gleaned from the ordeal. Judging by the palace and his station, she suspected he was a military commander of some sort and would certainly use what he had learned against her kingdom.

Bragga and Yagiet began strolling along the corridor. Bridget fell in beside Naomi, and the old man followed in the rear, with the pike aimed forward at her back in silent threat. Although Naomi kept trying to catch Bridget's eye, Bridget stole secret glances at the rooms between the fluted marble columns they passed.

Many appeared to be empty, but even those surely held something, for the occasional pink palm stood within, and there loomed shadows hinting at objects. One room held statues of gargoyles with runic inscriptions underneath. Another held marble plinths on top of which appeared to float various weapons of a design Bridget had never seen — perhaps the weapons of conquered enemies. Another room held strange armor that she had also never laid eyes on, another various small human-sized implements such as necklaces and backpacks and quills, all lying either on invisible plinths or floating, which interested Bridget greatly.

One room in particular drew Bridget's attention, for various clay tablets and scrolls floated within—and as with objects in rooms prior, each floated within its own space. How she wished she could spend some time within to study such materials!

Alas, it was not to be, for they soon entered a room with various stalls and an all too familiar black metal obelisk. Bragga, mid-conversation with Yagiet, casually grabbed Bridget's neck and bent her forward into one of these stalls like cattle. She hooked her collar up to the arcane mechanism and, after giving a bow to Yagiet, proceeded to drain Bridget's collar of the stamina that it continually siphoned from her stamina reservoir. Bragga's bow told Bridget the depositing of stamina was likely a gift of thanks for allowing her to come as a guest.

Both girgoyles studied the obelisk looming behind the stalls and traded looks, for it had apparently filled with more blue light than expected. They exchanged words and were so distracted that they didn't notice that Bridget had unhooked the collar of her own volition and gone to stand with Naomi and the old man. Throughout, the old man watched her with particularly narrowed eyes, his hold on the pike tight, as if fearing she would mount a sudden attack.

I would if I had a means to get rid of this blasted collar, Bridget thought, looking to the old man with such a hard stare that he raised his pike at her face. She remained watching him and took small pleasure from unnerving him enough to make him shuffle a step back.

They soon left the room and entered another located near the end of the long hallway. This room had a small oval arena nestled within a larger rectangular room with an open ceiling that allowed in the sunlight. The seating, cut deep into the ground of the sky island, was a classic stepped design carved from marble and large enough for gargoyles to sit comfortably. In the center was a pit with brilliant white sand that fondly reminded Bridget of the Arcaner room in the Academy of Arcane Arts.

She girded herself for another battle. Instead, she and Naomi and the old man were told to stand apart in the upper area of the stepped seating—and luckily in the shade, for the direct sun was getting quite hot. Naomi and Bridget sat together, with the old man sitting behind them, his pike aimed at Bridget's back.

Meanwhile, the pair of teenage girgoyles wandered to the center of the arena, where they proceeded to have a mock fight. It was an odd sight, for they clumsily swiped at each other with their painted claws, mixing in the occasional kick, but they never really connected as the other would flap their wings and jump away. Now and then they tapped one of their few runes and either elemental armor would envelop their bodies or they would throw a weak elemental attack. It became evident to Bridget that neither was very experienced in the art of war or combat.

They trained for some time, tiring each other out, oft appearing to make jests at the other's expense, until the bulky shadow of Bones appeared in the entrance, spilling in and over the stepped seating whilst the grizzled gargoyle himself remained out of view. The two teenagers immediately began fighting in earnest, with Bragga drawing blood after a particularly adept claw strike.

"*Seta, seta,*" boomed the deep voice of Bones, who entered wearing a few human bone adornments, namely the skull necklace. This time Bridget did a double-take, for he was also holding something in his hand she well recognized—a pentastone. The tiny pyramid, made of unknown black stone, reflected the sunlight, throwing quick flicks of light about the large room.

The slaves stood as one and everyone bowed toward the powerful gargoyle, whose wings flapped lazily like a butterfly, giving Bridget the impression he was eager for something.

Bones walked down the seating, skipping entire rows at a time with his long but casual stride, and stepped into the arena to observe the two teenagers. He flicked an impatient hand and they proceeded to go at it once more, awkwardly kicking and swiping and throwing the occasional elemental blast, until he abruptly placed the pentastone before his lips and growled into it. Their elemental armor vanished. Bridget felt the *whoosh* go through her soul and knew she too had been snuffed.

The teenage girgoyles hesitated, unsure as to what to do. Bones barked at them to continue, and they tried shooting elemental blasts at each other, but nothing happened. Bones then used this as an opportunity to go on a complex lecture, which he did in a quiet tone, as if imparting a great battlefield secret. Nonetheless, Bridget's ears perked up, for she suspected he was about to teach something significant.

The lecture went on for about an hour, with him pacing and gesticulating at them and the pentastone. When he pointed at a rune on his body, goosebumps rose on Bridget's skin, for she thought she understood what the large gargoyle was teaching them—how to prevent the snuff.

Bridget sat so far forward in her seat trying to pick up on any tidbit that she alarmed the old man behind her, who poked her back with the pike. She yelped, drawing the attention of all three gargoyles.

All three slaves promptly lowered their heads in submission, and after dispensing a frightful glower, Bones continued his lesson. Bridget watched from afar, following every nuance. Unable to hear the details, for the gargoyles' voices echoed unintelligibly in the all-marble room, she chose another path—a daring one. First, she needed a distraction.

"Cough," she mouthed at Naomi. When Naomi mouthed, *"What?"* Bridget made meaningful eyes and pressed a fist before her mouth, and as subtly and silently as she could, she made the coughing gesture. Naomi nodded and Bridget held up a finger telling her to wait. She kept that finger up until she had gathered her thoughts. By then, enough time had passed that just enough stamina should be available for her to attempt the 3rd degree off-the-books spell Centarro, which would heighten the senses—particularly focus and creativity.

She dropped her finger, and Naomi began coughing. Bridget then incanted under her breath, *"Centeratoraye xao xen,"* and felt the spell trigger. The effect, suppressed by the collar, was weak at best, yet everything still clarified—the brilliant sunlight now streaming in at a slant, threatening to touch her toes; the way the marble gleamed in that sunlight; the freshness of the crisp sky air; and the way Naomi's citron scent subtly clashed with the scent of dried meats and salt and hay coming from the old man.

Naomi yelped in pain, having received a jab from the malicious old man.

"Thank you," Bridget mouthed at her before dropping her head, for they had again garnered the attention of the gargoyles. Only when she heard Bones's voice resume did she perk up to watch. This time, she focused on his gestures, noting their subtleties, how his claws moved this way and that. It coincided with the echoes of his words, and she began to piece together precisely how the rune worked.

Then a miracle happened. While Bridget was still under the influence of Centarro, Bones stepped up to his daughter, Yagiet, who straightened. He raised a claw and held it there ceremonially for a time, before meticulously and slowly drawing something upon Yagiet's chest whilst gutturally incanting, *"Tero kess mero bah ena soff nah."* The gargoyle then pressed the pentastone's base against the flesh, and there was a sizzling noise during which Yagiet screamed in pain. Yet she held firm, allowing the burning to set in, until Bones removed the pentastone, leaving behind the outline of a rune.

With Bridget's focus at an apex, she was able to make out the words, which she engraved into the marble of her memory. Just like the echo of the room, these words bounced around as she solemnly repeated them in her mind. *Tero kess mero bah ena soff nah. Tero kess mero bah ena soff nah. Tero kess mero bah ena soff nah* ...

She also seared into her memory the knowledge that the pentastone had been used to craft the rune upon the body. Pentastones thus had a greater significance than any of them had thought!

She maintained this repetition until the side effects of Centarro began kicking in, and the hallway of her vision and the clarity of her thoughts closed inward with foggy dullness. Due to the collar weakening the original casting, the side effects were also weakened, and so she simply wilted into a dazed but still sitting stupor.

When she came out of that stupor, the sun shone hot across her feet, but something remained. *"Tero kess mero bah ena soff nah,"* she dared to subtly mouth. She had witnessed a powerful moment, and the gargoyles were arrogant enough to consider that moment beyond her learning. Yet that was not too surprising considering the slaves this lot was familiar with could never cast Centarro, or learn the gorgan language with such speed, or have the memory to remember precise pronunciations, a skill learned from countless rote memorizations of complex spell phrases.

The pike abruptly clattered to the floor, and Naomi and Bridget turned to see the old man drowsily fumbling for it. The young women exchanged looks—the old man had dozed off!

The clatter was too much for the big gargoyle, who barked a command at Yagiet, who in turn took to the air and flew over, landing behind the old man to smack him on the back of the head. He yelped and protected his head from further strikes. Then she pointed at the doorway and snapped, *"Hohol, gyots!"*

As the three slaves got up to go, Yagiet snatched the old man's hand and pressed something into it. *"Gergo shorga,"* she growled, a phrase Bridget was unfamiliar with. But she caught a glimpse of the object in the old man's hand—a small marble cube imprinted with a golden rune, and in the middle of that rune was a golden button.

Probably an alarm that alerts the gargoyles of trouble, Bridget thought as she walked after Naomi, who led the way until the old man took charge in the hallway and used the pike to poke at her toward the room beside the arena. The rectangular room, with its open-to-the-sky ceiling, was empty except for three objects—a single palm growing out of a sandy surface, a shallow rectangular pool that perfectly reflected the azure sky, and a huge marble pedestal the size of a coffin, one large enough to fit the largest gargoyle. It was just low enough for Bridget to see golden runic symbols engraved into its top. She surmised it had to be a sarcophagus. Probably someone important in the lineage.

The old man used the pike to herd Naomi and Bridget in front of the coffin, where he allowed them to sit cross-legged on the floor. The old man did the same, taking a seat between them and the entrance at about the distance of the pike, which he held up, enjoying having that small threat over her. He also held the buttoned cube and kept flicking his eyes between it and her, hinting that he wanted her to try something so he could have an excuse to press it.

Bridget thought this was an empty threat, for she suspected that he greatly feared interrupting the gargoyles a second time. She thus came up with a daring plan, which she allowed to gestate with her eyes closed. She even stretched out her legs so that her grubby feet caught the sunlight. Naomi did the same, and the women relaxed, bathing in the sunny silence.

In time, the old man smacked his gums as his eyes began to droop, which Bridget noted through eyes slitted open ever so slightly, for she was watching him like a hawk. He kept adjusting his pose, trying to stay alert, but it was a losing battle—yet not losing enough for Bridget, who thought it was time she helped him along in his quest to catch some shut-eye.

When his eyes were fully closed and he sighed contentedly, telling her he was still awake, she slowly stretched her arms, yawned, and upon lowering those arms, made a long petting motion as subtly as she could, whispering, "*Senna dormo coma torpos.*"

The collar-suppressed 8th degree Sleep spell would have been too weak to impact even a minimally armored mind of a low-degree warlock, but the old man's mind was not only unprotected, but ripe for plunder due to his drowsiness. His tired mind even failed to alert him to words whispered in a silent room, and so he slumped in his sitting position, with the pike angling toward the ground. Bridget caught it with her naked foot and noiselessly lowered it to the floor. The man began snoring, quiet snoozes that would barely make it out of the room.

Naomi grabbed Bridget's arm and violently shook her head, warning her not to try anything, but Bridget had already planned for this. She pressed a hand to her friend's chest and gently pushed her to sit back against the sarcophagus. Then she feigned a petting motion as she mouthed, "Sleep, my friend. Do you understand? Sleep."

Naomi expelled a shuddering breath, swallowed, but surrendered a nod. Bridget gently closed her eyes for her and allowed her to take another deep breath before incanting, "*Senna dormo coma torpos*," and Naomi, being an Ordinary with an unprotected mind, succumbed to the spell, with her head flopping over as she too began to snooze quietly.

Bridget got up and hurried to the doorway, glancing back only once to see that the old man and Naomi were sound asleep. Satisfied, she peeked out of the room. Upon finding the hallway empty and hearing sounds of combat from the arena, she darted down the hallway, checking the other rooms until she at last found the one she was longing for — the room with the floating tablets and scrolls.

They rose to the ceiling, well out of reach, and were lined in neat rows, each piece separated by about a foot. There were rows and rows of such floating scrolls and tablets, all occupying a distinct and perfectly aligned space, creating a library with invisible shelves.

But Bridget's intuition wondered about access to such a room, especially with slaves about. Thus, before stepping inside, she flared her hand and incanted, "*Un vun asperio aurum enchantus.*" Parts of the room lit up with complex tendril geometries, all blue and all centered around the invisible shelving — all but one. A single and thick stripe along the floor that extended from the doorway.

An alarm enchantment, Bridget realized. *And a complex one at that, crafted with foreign hands*. She crouched to examine the workmanship. The band was far too thick to jump across from a standing start. She'd have to make a running jump, a great risk.

But she'd come this far and might as well go all the way. She thus backed up, took a girding breath, sprinted forth, and leaped off near the start of the enchantment. Mid-leap, the physical motion made her lose touch with the fragile Reveal spell, and so she landed on the marble floor not knowing if the back of her foot had caught the alarm.

She listened, heart thrumming against her ribcage, but no new sounds emerged from the hallway, and so she went to work, starting with recasting Reveal. Barely able to hold onto the spell due to the collar, she nonetheless examined the tendril geometries of the shelving system, concluding that all the geometries involved had something to do with the framework of the shelving — meaning they were not alarmed. This was great news, as it meant she should be able to touch the objects without repercussions.

Bridget grabbed the closest tablet, but after finding the hieroglyphs unintelligible, promptly returned it, relieved to see the tablet float back into place.

"There's *got* to be something here I can use," she muttered, ripping tablets off the shelves, but they were all just as indecipherable, and so she switched to snatching scrolls, which were made of fine papyrus and inked in gold. Instinct told her these scrolls were much like human scrolls—one-time castings with a one-time effect. Most were far too complex for her to draw meaning as to their intended use, but some were inked with colorful illustrations, raising her hopes. She saw all sorts—a depiction of a gargoyle with a line drawn down the middle, with one half of the gargoyle grayed out; a gargoyle slapping its wrists; two gargoyles melding together; three cubes in various sizes; a circle within a circle within another circle; and so on, each depiction surrounded with hieroglyphs.

One of these scrolls, a particularly long one with complex and detailed instructions in glyph form, nearly stopped her heart, for it distinctly depicted a chunk of land floating in midair—and upon that land stood a gargoyle castle.

"Ye gods," she mumbled, imagining employing this knowledge to make Castle Arinthian float. She stuck this scroll under an arm and was about to move on when she realized there was now a gaping empty shelf. She looked about and saw that the closest empty shelves were high up.

"Just do it, Bridget," she said, stepping back and raising an arm. She winced as she struggled to flick her suppressed Telekinesis about like a hook on an invisible line. After several flailing attempts, she nudged a scroll that hovered twenty feet above. Another attempt caused it to flip off the shelf and tumble to the floor. She grabbed this and stuck it in the empty space, then looked up to check that it would be difficult to notice that a scroll had been moved on account of the randomly empty shelves on the top layer.

Satisfied, she continued rifling through scrolls, opening and closing them so rapidly that she accidentally tore one. Interestingly, upon flaring her trembling hands above it—she was pushing it in terms of time spent—and attempting a Repair, the golden language of the scroll evaporated into smoke, leaving behind a repaired but empty husk of papyrus.

With nothing to be done about it, she stuck the empty scroll back onto the shelf and continued searching frantically for something of actual value.

Then it happened. One particular scroll, found almost out of reach on a central shelf, showed an illustration of a pentastone being deployed, signified by a bubble of lines shooting outward. Two defending gargoyles stood opposite. One had a rune emblazoned in its chest, the other did not. The lines showed the one without the runes being engulfed by the bubble, while the one with the rune was shielded from it. It went on in great detail about how to cast this rune upon the flesh, including the most important aspect—the gestures, depicted with close ups of a gargoyle hand performing various poses. She knew the pronunciation, and now she had the key.

Bridget held the document like a newborn babe. Combined with the knowledge she had gleaned from studying Bones's use of the pentastone to craft a rune, this was the answer she'd been praying for, and how humanity would be able to protect itself from the vicious snuffing effect. It was a sacred document that she had to protect at all costs. The correct translation, of course, was another matter, but she'd worry about that at a future date.

Yet she couldn't walk out of there with them simply stuffed into her clothing. She had to be smarter than that, more cunning.

After replacing the empty shelf with another scroll from up high, Bridget came up with a daring plan. "Object Invisible," she whispered, realizing the scope of the challenge. The 6th degree spell was notoriously unstable, the bulk of its knowledge lost to time, meaning it was mainly taught for the academy exams and rarely deployed in the field as it fizzled quickly.

That was only half of the problem, the other being that the cursed slave collar would further weaken the spell. Still, it was her one chance at success, so she crouched, placed both scrolls on the floor, and spread her hands over the more important one—the snuffing prevention scroll. After carefully going over each principle that governed the spell no less than three times, even throwing in a quick prayer to the Unnameables, she incanted, "*Obiectum visinabla balan.*"

To her profound relief, the scroll vanished—and remained stable even after she picked it up, indicating a high-quality casting. She gently stuffed it down her front, then repeated the spell with the castle float scroll, using the same level of concentration and thoroughness. Thankfully, this scroll also vanished, and she stuffed it beside the other one.

Then she straightened and adjusted until the shape of the scrolls was barely discernible against the natural folds of the cotton slave garment. Heart thundering that she'd found something truly important and maybe even history-changing, she hurried back to the entrance—and skidded to a halt, for she'd forgotten about the alarm.

She flared her hands and incanted, "*Un vun asperio aurum enchantus,*" and almost fainted upon spotting that the nail of her big toe was hanging over the alarm. As before, she retreated, sprinted forth, and launched herself over the enchantment, once again losing sight of it when the spell failed mid-jump. She landed on the other side so hard that she tumbled, then sprang to her feet ready to spot a gargoyle.

But there was no one in the hallway.

After checking that the scrolls were still invisible—such sudden movements could have easily destabilized the casting—Bridget allowed herself one shuddering breath to calm down before she hurried forth. Already she heard the gargoyle voices, and they seemed to be getting louder—surely they were about to emerge from the arena!

Bridget had to slow her jogging—she didn't want to risk destabilizing the spell by running—to muffle the noise of her feet, and it was an agonizing last few strides to the room with Naomi and the old man. The gargoyles emerged just as she slipped inside. And there was the man, standing and scratching his head as he gaped at a still-snoozing Naomi, pike on the floor.

Bridget thought fast and came up with a story. She smoothed her garment and cleared her throat. The man whirled about and fumbled for the pike, baring his teeth at her, but she feigned casually walking back to her spot, where she sat down to nudge Naomi awake. She startled in time for all three gargoyles to enter the room.

Bridget and Naomi rose to their feet and bowed, while the old man sputtered in monosyllables at Yagiet, telling on Bridget like a brown-nosing schoolkid. When the gargoyles looked to her, she made an awkward gesture downward and said, "Had to go pee." She made another gesture which someone like Leera would have found hilarious, yet the situation was grave, and despite Bridget forcing a sheepish smile, Bones stepped forth to loom over her.

She dared not even breathe, fearing he might sense she was hiding something. Bones seemed to sense this too, for he grabbed her relatively small form with both clawed hands—and ripped her slave dress in half, exposing her nakedness to all.

The old man grinned with evil satisfaction while Naomi looked away, embarrassed on behalf of Bridget. Bones let the torn cloth fall to the floor, and there came the whisper-soft sound of papyrus hitting marble. Bridget stood frozen, heart threatening to punch through her chest. She kept her head down in submission, fearing that making eye contact would give her away. Her only hope was that her Object Invisible castings did not fail then and there, for that would reveal such a grave offense that it might even put Sebastian in mortal peril.

Bones kicked her garment about, checking it. Seeing nothing, he grunted.

But it was Bragga who saved Bridget, for she used the opportunity to brag to Yagiet and Bones that Bridget could do something amazing — she could repair the torn garment. At least, Bridget understood enough from her gesticulations to gather the meaning.

So when Bragga indicated with an impatient hand for Bridget to get on with it, a naked Bridget crouched and, cognizant of the leering old man, incanted, "*Apreyo*," repairing the dress. Then she gathered it up, careful to hold the scrolls within the garment. The gargoyles erupted in almost amenable conversation, praising the humans that they so obviously longed to enslave, with Bones going so far as to tie his lesson in and saying how they would have to work hard as the slaves overseas would be a more difficult challenge to suppress — or so Bridget imagined based on the few Gorgan words she had pieced together.

Meanwhile, she carefully slipped on the dress, feigning salvaging some of her dignity by turning about to hide how she was juggling the scrolls within the garment, a task that made her sweat from nervousness. After making the proper adjustments, she turned around and presented a placid countenance once more, for inside she was on fire.

As the gargoyles closed out their activities and Bragga prepared to fly home with the slave she was so proud to show off, a new hope burned within Bridget. That night, she knew she would place the scrolls into the box hidden within the pond.

Now she could begin crafting a daring escape plan.

THE PROMISED LAND

LEERA

At the bow of a wind-tilted *Saltfang*, a spritely Leera, in the midst of casting a cycle and about to throw a Fear spell at an imaginary opponent, halted. For a distinctly tropical and fruity scent had reached her nose.

"Where is that coming from ..." she muttered, and turned to the ocean, eyes narrowed in search of the source.

"Boat due northeast!" called a crew member stationed on the tallest mast.

The activity on the entire ship stopped all at once as everyone craned their necks. Other warlocks, involved in their own morning cycles, ran forth, forming a crowd.

She squinting whilst adjusting her spectacles to get a better look. It was a warm sunny day, so she used her other hand to shield her eyes. Then she spotted something tiny on the horizon. Amidst calm seas, a lone object bobbed toward them, and there appeared to be the outline of sails ...

"Someone fetch the captain and tell him to bring his spyglass!" Leera shouted over her shoulder.

"Already here, lass," the captain said, pushing through the back of the crowd. "I smell it too," he said before Leera even mentioned it. He stepped up to the bow with the walrus-mustachioed bosun in tow, put one leg up on the bowsprit, placed his long pipe under his arm, and extended the spyglass. He looked through it for a long time before handing it off to Leera.

"Furl 'em by half, and fetch the wolf."

"Furl 'em to the 'alf, boys!" the bosun shouted, then vanished into the crowd as crew scurried along the sails, hurrying to take them down halfway.

Leera, meanwhile, let her spectacles dangle on their leather thong as she squinted into the eyepiece.

"What do you see?" Jez asked, one of many crammed in around her. Everyone was eager to lay eyes on the first contact after months of travel. It had been a long and relatively peaceful voyage since the double tower islands, with only the occasional serpent or storm to deal with. The ship needed repairs and the food stores had dwindled, and so everyone was anxious to find land and replenish their supplies. The sun had bronzed everyone's skin and bleached their hair. Even Leera's tiny arm hairs, usually as black as her hair, had faded to a gentle brown, something that amused Augum.

"Well?" Olaf pressed.

"Looking for it," Leera mumbled, finding nothing but ocean. Then the spyglass sight zipped across an object. She swiveled back and focused the tube by spinning it toward her ever so slightly. There in the center of the field of vision bobbed a boat unlike any she had ever seen before. Wide and oval like a platter, it sat on two parallel wooden hulls and sported a pair of square sails that looked undersized for its strangely oblong shape.

Strangest of all, two fur-clad men stood on its bow, watching them. "Bit hot for coats," she muttered. Except they weren't men at all. "Wolven!" Leera blurted, a word that caused a great stir to rip through crew and passengers alike.

Jez snatched the spyglass from her hands, singing, "Give me that. There's no way we're looking at wolven after so long a voyage and —oh mighty gods there they are …"

The spyglass was passed from person to person, each as disbelieving as the next.

Augum and Leera exchanged wondrous looks.

"This far out?" he said.

"And since when did wolven take to the sea?" she added.

Rogor soon showed up with his usual grumpy expression. He epitomized the idea that wolven did not belong at sea—his fur was matted, he had perpetual dark rings under his puffy eyes, and he had lost a substantial amount of weight. They had all lost some weight at that point, some more than others, but the wolven had suffered most and taken to spending most days in his cabin, studying human books, digesting not only human history but human language.

He snatched the spyglass as if offended that he'd been asked to look through it, and took forever adjusting it before he too froze. He stared the longest of them all, with everyone glancing between him and the distant bobbing speck that was steadily coming closer.

"Wolfan," he blurted.

At first Leera thought she'd misheard him, but then he repeated himself, nodding as he said, "Wolfan ..." The pronunciation was distinctly different too, like combining the words *wool* and *fan*.

Leera flipped both hands open. "Care to explain to us simple lowlanders why you're calling them wol*fan* instead of wol*ven*?"

"A myth come to life," Rogor replied, continually looking through the spyglass, voice distant as if leaping entire eras. "Our people tell stories passed down from elder to cub, generation after generation, for time immemorial."

Leera felt her eyebrows rise up her forehead, impressed by how far his language skills had improved since meeting him. She pictured him languishing in his cabin while using that long snout to sniff up entire pages from human-written books. She had to give him credit—it was more than anyone else had been doing with their time, except for possibly herself and Augum, of course, who'd been dipping into Isobel's training realm on the regular, slowly figuring out small new ways to battle The Callousness of the Predator.

"It is said they seeded our lands with their own before the winds blew them away forever."

"There's more to it than that though, isn't there?" Leera pressed, feeling the wolven would take it as a rude question. Sure enough, he glanced away from the spyglass to raise a snouted lip at her, and she took an involuntary step back from the tall beast who could snap her in half if she wasn't careful. It's not that she enjoyed antagonizing him, it was just that he was so sensitive to the tiniest perception of a slight, a commonality he shared with many of his kind.

"Well *we're* going to call them wolven until proven otherwise," Leera muttered.

Rogor continued to silently hold the spyglass even though others meekly pined for it. "They're turning," he announced, and all eyes went to the horizon. Sure enough, the boat turned about and began to zip away at such a precarious angle that it appeared about to capsize.

"Quite an interesting contraption," Rogor noted as if opining on nothing but the weather.

A flustered Leera kept flipping her hands forward for him to say more, but he only grunted, dumped the spyglass into the captain's hands, and walked off, every single eye trailing him. He did not return to his cabin, but rather went to midship, where he stood between the masts, rubbing his snout as if deep in thought.

"Raise 'em to full and set course after them," the captain said, a command the bosun echoed to the crew. Before long the sails were back up and at full mast and the deck tilted at a steeper angle.

"They're fast little beasties," the captain noted, stuffing his pipe with tobacco, old salt eyes flicking between the work and the horizon. "Trim 'er twelve to port," he casually told the bosun.

"Twelve degrees to port," the bosun told the helmsman, who followed the compass numbers around the lodestone.

"We're going to try to beat them on the diagonal," the captain explained to those assembled.

Seeing that it would be a long sail, people peeled off, returning to their activities, though all kept glancing back to the horizon. A tension — perhaps even excitement — thus settled over the ship, one reflected by the sky, which clouded over as a sharp wind sprang up over the course of the afternoon.

By the time the sun began its final descent behind them in the west, a shimmering line appeared on the horizon in the east. It wasn't long before the man at the very top of the tallest mast shouted, "Laaaand hooooooooo!" and everyone rushed back to the bow, with the captain once more throwing a leg up on the bowsprit, spyglass pressed to his eye, pipe under his arm.

He nodded to himself before passing the spyglass on to his stern-faced bosun, who grunted in the same manner before passing it on to others. When Leera got her turn, she noted that the tiny wolven sailboat was heading right for the land.

Excitement bubbled as people threw out theories. The land had to be teeming with wolven, who worked hand in hand with gargoyles. No, gargoyles were in a different area and these were mere wolf lands. No, they'd just proven the world was round and they'd returned to the western shores of Sithesia. That one drew laughs over how ridiculous the idea sounded, for the prevailing theory was that the world stretched on and on for tens — maybe even hundreds — of thousands of leagues before falling off a steep edge. Another theory suggested that it connected to other planes in a never-ending line of ever-stranger lands, one of which was Ley, another Endraga Ra, another Hell.

Leera reserved her judgment alongside Augum, both of whom kept their opinions to themselves. They stood shoulder to shoulder, with

Augum rubbing his scruffy chin and Leera nibbling at each of her chipped nails, so at least they were evenly unkempt.

She nudged him with her shoulder. "Shall we continue our cycles?"

"Huh? Oh, yeah, sure, I guess."

They resumed their cycles, but were far too distracted for the castings to be effective, and so gave up to watch the horizon alongside the others, which turned into a bit of a theatrical production as people murmured theories with their neighbors. Jez sipped from a goblet of brown wine, the last vestige of the reserves. She, Leo, Olaf, Jengo, Augum and Leera leaned against the starboard railing, watching the landmass clarify in the now crimson and wavering sun.

"They better have invented wine. That's all I care about," Jez said, wincing as she took a sip. "This stuff is horse piss."

"Yet you continue to drink it," Leera remarked, drawing a foul look from her mentor, which Leera pointedly ignored.

"Horse piss is better than nothing," Leo muttered, earning him a stiff nod from Jez.

Jengo shook his head in awe. "A new land of wolven who can fish."

"Which begs the question, where are the gargoyles?" Olaf threw in. He flared eyes at Leera, who leaned over behind Augum's back to whisper in Olaf's ear, "Checked this morning. Still nothing."

"We'd tell you if she left us a note," Augum added in a whisper, leaning close to Olaf so that Leo wouldn't hear. "You know that."

Olaf sighed as he dumped his chin onto his folded arms, which rested on the railing.

Leera reached behind Augum to lightly punch Olaf on the shoulder. "Don't worry. If anyone can survive the gargoyles, it's Bridget."

"Yeah, but how far away are we from her? Where *are* we even?"

No one had an answer to that, and all they could do was continue to theorize and watch. Then a new call from up high.

"Ship to the east! Wait, multiple ships! And … and a port!"

Every single person was now on deck, including the galley crew, who were supposed to be preparing supper. Multiple shapes appeared on the horizon, as if waiting for them.

"Maybe they're anchored," Olaf said.

"Maybe …" Jez whispered, swirling her goblet. "This is it, kiddos. First contact. Do we even know what we're going to say? Are we expecting an attack? An ambush? What's the plan?"

"The plan was we were supposed to see gargoyles," Leera replied. "That plan is out the window. New plan is to—" She raised a finger and circled it about in the air, neck craning until she laid eyes on Rogor and pointed the finger at him. " —have *him* do the talking."

The captain, standing on the stern alongside the helmsman, had the ship tack. *Saltfang* turned across the point of the wind and everyone changed sides to stare out from port. This continued until they could see the ships clearly with the naked eye. The lookout kept calling out new discoveries—a port, buildings, and a city. All of it lit up by the blood-orange sun, and pressing down upon that sun was a bank of sunset-tinted clouds.

"Beautiful in an exotic way," Leera noted, watching the rays of the sun make wide bands across the sky. She particularly enjoyed the way some of those bands lit up the very top of the clouds that had to be fifty thousand feet up, or who knew how high. She imagined soaring through that orangeness, whimsically catching updrafts and downdrafts.

"We should be ready to make a certain *beastly* roar in case they get hostile," Augum said.

Leera nodded. "Agreed, but let's hope it doesn't get to that." If it did, she'd be ready and bring the wrath of the dragon. For all she knew, these so-called wolfan were in cahoots with the gargoyles, and would have to prove otherwise to earn her trust.

She glanced back and saw Rogor mumbling to himself, as if preparing a speech. *Or perhaps the old dog has lost his mind*, she thought, knowing she could never verbalize such a sentiment within his hearing lest he truly lose his temper. She hoped he could keep that temper at bay after meeting his own kind. This begged a certain question, which she posed to Augum.

"How do the, uh, other wolven packs interact with each other if they're enemies? Back at home that is."

Augum shrugged. "If we're talking about how The Dishonored interact with The Honored, they're sort of mortal enemies and mostly fight. But if we're talking about the various packs differentiated by element, they work harmoniously together. I think. Hard to say as they didn't let me catch a glimpse into their society." He drummed his chin with his fingers. "Oh and they sacrifice those among them born into necromancy, so there's that."

"Necromancy ... hadn't thought about that part ..." She wondered what these wolven—*wolfan*—did with those born into the dark art, what their society was like and if it was friendly to humans at all.

The city steadily revealed itself to those lucky enough to take a turn with the spyglass, which included Augum and then Leera.

"It's made of stone," Leera noted, a crowd having gathered around them, as if seeking the shelter of the dragons, the only two who they believed could truly defend them. "Tall blocks of smooth and colorful stone with steeply pitched red clay roofs. There's a market with tiny people—er, wolven or wolfan or whatever. They're wearing clothes!" she remarked, squinting.

"Check one of the ships," Alanna said, tone laced with an eagerness others shared.

Leera swiveled the spyglass to look at the closest series of ships and saw multi-masted vessels that looked like giant floating tortoises, what with all their domed armored hulls and multiple spike-like protrusions. "Whoa, weird," she mumbled.

"More detail, please, or pass it on," Jez said. "Weird don't cut it in this historic moment."

"Fair enough. The ships have an armored carapace, as if they're used to being attacked from the sky."

"Reckon they might like to war with 'em gargoyles," Leo noted.

"The wolfan are lining up on the edge of the domed hull as there's a walkway around the whole thing. The largest of the ships has seven masts, and the spikes appear defensive in nature."

"Maybe as wards against large summoned gargoyles?" Jengo offered, a thought that drew mutters of agreement.

Leera kept the spyglass pressed to her eye, the other one closed. "They've all noticed us and are assembling either a greeting party ... or a raiding party."

That last line prompted the captain to command the bosun, "Weapons at the ready, but on the quiet."

"Arms at the ready, boys, but keep them out of sight!" the bosun called out, and the crew fetched their blades, but kept them hidden on the decks instead of wearing them on their belts as usual. All kicked off their shoes.

Leera kept watch, describing everything she could. "There are catapults in the city. Huge ones, ten times larger than any we've built. There's also ... there's also humans!"

This caused a stir amongst the crew and passengers.

"Are they ... are they slaves?" Limpet squeaked, standing beside his friend Dirt.

"Can't tell. Maybe. They're clothed, though ... I think. Too far away to see and the sun's fading fast. They're lighting torches throughout the city to compensate. It's a pretty civilized place. Houses are built tall and close together and run in rows up a hill. There's a castle!" she blurted, homing in on a structure in the back. "Sort of like our own, but made of orange stone and studded with giant spikes. Bunch of buildings have spikes, actually. Kind of gives the city a bit of a porcupine look if you ask me."

"Rower inbound!" called the top watch.

"Hand it over, young lass," the captain ordered, and Leera had to surrender their lone spyglass. He tucked his pipe under his armpit and used both hands to steady the spyglass, rotating the cylinder with precision as he swiveled it about.

"Sighting was at fifteen degrees to port, Cap," the bosun helpfully muttered.

"Ah, there she is," the old man proclaimed. "Twenty oars per side, low draft, gold plating. An emissary ship, I reckon, full of ambassadors."

Every single one of them, the wolven included, breathed a sigh of relief — these wolfan were willing to talk instead of make immediate war.

"How can you be so sure, sir?" Tammy asked.

"They're dressed all fancy. Eight beasts standin' all formal-like on the bow. Each is wearin' a different color. Reckon they represent the elements."

The warlocks among the group exchanged looks.

"Eight, you said?" Jengo pressed.

Augum and Leera locked eyes, chorusing, "Necromancy." Hearing that word, some among the crew signed skyward, muttered a prayer, and threw salt over their shoulder.

"Can you deal with necromancy?" a young crewman asked Tammy, who looked to Augum and Leera for a reply.

"Of course we can," Leera said without missing a beat. "We handled the Legion and if push comes to shove we will certainly handle whatever this lot throws at us." Her resolve seemed to put the crew at ease, though privately she wasn't as confident as she made herself out to be.

"Furl 'em and prep to drop the iron," the captain ordered.

"Furl 'em and prepare to anchor!" the bosun shouted, and the crew hustled along the yardarms to furl up the sails.

Once the sails were furled, the ship took some time to slow. The crew loosed its lone anchor, which plunged into the water, the chain spinning the deck's windlass until it halted with a great *clang*. From land, they could hear the high-pitched calls of an unfamiliar bird species, a chorus of warbles that sounded strangely poignant, as if the entire species were grieving.

The bosun readjusted his tilted cap against a humid gust. "Anchor secure, Cap."

The captain, watching through the spyglass, grunted. "Prep to receive dignitaries. All whites."

"Crew into whites!" the bosun shouted, and the crew took turns running belowdecks, emerging wearing their whites—a long-sleeved tunic shirt and matching trousers, both edged with blue striping and surprisingly clean. The bosun had them line up in a dignified line. Although they put their shoes back on, they kept their weapons hidden behind nearby crates and barrels.

The closer the emissary ship came, the quieter everyone got, creating a solemn atmosphere. Someone on the foreign ship barked snappy commands, and section by section, the long oars rose into the air, until only a strategic few remained, which were used to orient the ship into final position. By the time it floated alongside and *Saltfang's* crew prepared three boarding planks, the sun kissed the horizon, plunging both ships into a crimson glow enhanced by the glittering ocean.

The eight ambassadors were each thirteen feet in height, one foot higher than the tallest wolven Leera had met in Sithesia. Half were female, as indicated by the presence of ears. All wore loopy jewelry made of precious metals and stones, usually in the form of necklaces or bangles that hung overtop of colored robes embroidered with elemental depictions that were slightly different from Sithesian colors. Green had trees, sky blue had clouds, dark blue had snowflakes, red had flames, indigo had waves, white had soothing swirls, yellow had lightning, with the black robe showing skeletal wolves.

Their bushy tails stuck out from the rear and remained still. Smaller wolfan clothed in drab cloth manned the rest of their ship, most holding an oar rigid-straight.

The eight wolfan muttered amongst each other, their eyes mostly on Rogor, ignoring the humans. Despite the gangplanks, they stayed on their ship. They did this until the fire-robed one raised his whiskered snout and growled out a phrase in greeting.

Rogor stepped up the gangplank and growled a greeting back.

The earth robe responded, and the two sides traded phrases, albeit haltingly and repeating often, as if not fully understanding each other. The few warlocks who could cast Tongues—Jez, Augum and Leera among them—did so quietly. The wolven noticed this and exchanged looks—then remarked on what they saw. Leera couldn't understand the Wolven tongue at all, let alone the Wolfan one, which sounded like a variant, but she couldn't be sure, and so she snuffed the spell. Only Augum, albeit wincingly, seemed to catch some of it, and even then mostly from Rogor.

"Why don't you fill us in on what they be growlin' about over there, highlander," the captain finally said to Rogor.

"They say that I speak in an old dialect and think I am from a lost feral tribe because I am apparently …" Rogor hesitated, grinding his snout as if trying to swallow his pride.

"Apparently what?" the captain pressed.

"… naked and starved and stunted."

Leera tried not to make eye contact with anyone lest she make a face.

"But I am thin on account of the sickening voyage," Rogor went on. "He also asked why I have so many slaves and why you are all dressed so well and where your collars are. I told them you are free, which surprised them, as they believe that slaves can only earn their freedom after doing something extraordinary."

Leera watched as the eight took measure of the humans, here and there pointing one of them out with a claw.

The black robe asked a question. Rogor's reply caused all eight to descend into muttered conversation amongst themselves.

"Please keep translating, highlander," the captain said.

"He wanted to know where we hailed from. I said overseas. Now they are discussing the matter. Their language is more advanced than mine. They speak too quickly and use words I have never heard, longer ones too. To me, it is they who sound like a dialect, albeit one more fluid than our Wolven tongue."

"Ask them about their necromancy," Olaf prodded.

"No, lowlander. That would be rude."

"To you," Olaf muttered. "But maybe not to them."

Leera expected an angry retort from Rogor, but he considered this with a toned "Mmm," then asked a question in Wolven. The black-robed one replied, and everyone looked to Rogor to translate.

"They work in harmony as one," Rogor said rather simply, then followed up with another question. "Their cubs grow up within each element much like our own, but they work together to make war throughout their training."

"War against who?" Leera asked.

Rogor passed on the question in Wolven. The ice robe replied at length, during which Rogor's fuzzy brow rose in surprise.

"What did he say?" the captain pressed, leaning forward as eagerly as everyone else.

"He said they make war against the winged demons, the horned demons, the maned demons, the scaled demons, and a slew of others. He says life is war and asks if we war as well and against who." Rogor raised his snout and replied, but his reply seemed to amuse the ambassadors, who grunted amongst each other, their tails waving about giddily.

"They mock our barbarity," Rogor said in a smaller voice.

Leera wondered if he had caught on to the irony of having his own kind call him a version of a lowlander—a barbarian. Here he was presenting himself as a naked and malnourished wolf who had never warred against these demons, which surely made him appear low in their eyes.

The earth robe chirped something else, and his cohorts nodded along.

Rogor considered their reply for so long that the captain once again prodded him for a translation.

"They also say that we have no true enemies … yet."

This caused the humans to grumble with unease, with the more superstitious amongst the crew going through their usual warding rituals.

The captain snapped his fingers at the unruly line. "Keep 'em sharp."

"Smarten it up, lads!" the bosun snapped, and the line stiffened.

"But it was said with amusement," Rogor added. "So I do not think it was a threat."

The yellow lightning robe asked a follow-up question and Rogor replied before translating. "She wanted to know why you all wear strange colors, and I said you have your own customs around the arcane arts. This confused them. I do not think their slaves are allowed to practice the arts, even the free ones."

The ice wolfen took a turn asking a question, and Rogor once more furrowed his brow in thought.

"What did she ask?" Leera pressed, annoyed that someone kept having to prod him to translate, as if he still didn't fully respect his human shipmates even after all they had gone through together.

"She asked if we can confirm that the winged demons have discovered a new land brimming with slaves. The way she phrased the question tells me it is a rumor amongst their people."

"What are you going to tell them?" Jez asked.

"What do you wish me to tell them?" Rogor countered.

Jez looked to the captain and then Augum and Leera, who in turn looked between their friends. No one seemed to have a reply, until Augum said, "The truth. That they kidnapped our people—a *free* people. Tell them the gargoyles—that is what we call them—found a way overseas and stole some of us, and we are here to reclaim the enslaved."

"Is that wise, lowlander?"

"It is the truth," Leera threw out in defense of her man—and the Arcaner ideal. She looked to the eight ambassadors as she interlaced a hand with Augum's and nodded at them. "Let's see how they respond."

The captain waved his pipe about. "Then ask them if they'd be willing to let us resupply and repair our ship in their port."

Rogor passed this information along in a detailed message. The more he spoke, the more the faces of the ambassadors darkened. They conferred in a group for a while, whispering amongst each other, giving all a turn to speak. After some time they finally dispersed, and the earth robe opened a paw, uttering a long response.

"They invite us to the palace to tell them more, and for some of you to showcase your talents while the remainder repair and resupply the ship. They also say that what I told them about the gargoyles is grave news, but I do not know why they say this."

"Is it a trick?" Digby asked, lingering in the rear of the warlock group, hair and face powdered to perfection today. "Are they wanting to lull us into a false sense of security before enslaving each and every single one of us?"

"I do not know, lowlander, but it seems to me that they have plenty enough slaves. I believe they are curious more than anything. I also do not think they quite believe my story yet."

As the ambassadors stepped away from the planks, all eyes turned to the captain, who considered the matter whilst gumming his pipe. "I reckon you'd have told us not to proceed if you thought it unwise, highlander. Stow the planks, we're going in," he commanded, and the bosun quickly got the crew working on raising anchor and following the emissary ship into port.

Meanwhile, Leera strategized with her friends, all of whom resolved to stay alert in the hours ahead in case of a trap. They also promised to be mindful, respectful, gracious, represent their kingdom and people with honor, and stick close together in case they needed to teleport back to the ship in an emergency.

"Maybe you should sing them a lullaby," Jez told Leo at one point when they had stepped aside with Augum and Leera to strategize additional details, throwing the pirate an elbow and a wink.

Augum and Leera exchanged a knowing look, as Jez and Leo had been spending a suspicious amount of time together of late, usually around the wine goblet.

Leera felt a gentle *whap* on the back of her head.

"Don't you judge me," Jez snapped.

"I didn't say nothin'!"

"The way you share those beady eyes with each other. Been around you two fiends long enough to know *exactly* what's parading about in those monkey minds of yours. Ain't none of your business how this grown woman spends her time." To make her point, she hooked an arm around Leo's bald head, dragged it close to her, and planted a sloppy kiss on his tattooed face.

Leo, for his part, went beet-red, which told Leera they had never even kissed. "So it's not too late to sabotage you two yet!" she blurted.

Jez's face went slack-cold.

"I meant that as a jest," Leera threw in, shrinking a bit, and when Jez's hard eyes followed her, Leera mewed, "Eep," and hid behind Augum, who had to say, "She was jesting, Jez, yeesh," taking a turn defending his woman.

"Yeah, I was jesting," Leera repeated from behind Augum. "You remember what a jest is, right?"

Now it was Leo who elbowed Jez. "Oh, leave the poor dumb lass alone."

Leera ballooned over Augum's shoulder. "Dumb? *Dumb?*"

"Now who can't take a jest," Jez needled, and Leera, catching herself continuing to balloon, deflated whilst slapping a palm over her face. "Ugh, you got me," and the four of them chortled amiably, taking comfort in the levity.

In truth, Leera was happy for Jez to find someone to talk with, maybe even make out with here and there. But she was wary of the pirate, for she did not know him yet. He had a sharp wit, sure, and an adventurous personality, and some skill to boot, but what else was there behind his tattoos and swashbuckling mannerisms? What sort of man was he? Was he even close to being good enough for Jez?

Actually, the more Leera thought about it, the more she soured on the match. In her mind, no one was allowed to steal her beloved mentor's attention away as the bottle diverted it enough as it was.

Their gazes soon returned to the city, which loomed ahead as they followed the dignitary ship into port. Smaller ships took notice of them, some of which were freshly launched, probably just to have a gander at the strangers. Every single one was full of gawking wolfan. A few summoned elemental weapons to see how the humans would react—and although most of the wolfan also had swords and axes and spears and staves, some of their weapons were quite foreign, curving this way and that or possessing spikes or knobs.

One ship was a small oval fishing boat with one grizzled wolfan—and two humans manning the two scraggly sails. These humans, a male and a female, were hunched, sun-bronzed, bare-chested but wearing dirty loincloths and iron collars, wrinkled despite looking relatively young, and callused top to bottom. Their eyes darted about like animals, they were thin, and their remaining teeth were chipped and stained. They sniffed at the air as they approached and started growling at the new arrival.

"If that's what the slaves look like," Leera opined after they had rejoined their friend group, "no wonder they were curious about us."

"My question is, where did they get the humans from?" Jengo asked. "Look at their stooped statures. They almost look like …" He grimaced as he wrung his hands, body swinging in place.

"Inbreds," Olaf said. "You can say it. We were all thinking it."

All manner of boats floated up to them, until the ambassadors summoned their guard detail of wolfan in what looked like purple carapace armor, perhaps made from large beetles or turtles, and had them set arrows alight and shoot warning shots from gigantic bows, which splashed into nearby waters with a *sizzle*. The boats kept their distance after that.

Other ships loomed around them, some monstrous tortoise-like behemoths of wood studded with gigantic steel-tipped spears. They made Leera wonder what sorts of beasts such behemoths had to face — and survive.

"A new world dawns," she whispered, shaking her head at the strangeness before her eyes.

As dusk fell, the city began to glimmer with torchlight. Some of that torchlight had amassed on the dock, where a teeming crowd awaited the new arrivals, indicating word had spread through the city. The crowd was loud, growling and jeering and taunting, with about a third having summoned their elemental weapons — and that included the necromantics among them, who stood with giant black scythes or ball-and-chains or spike-studded truncheons or curved axes or various unfamiliar weapons.

Some of these wolfan were clothed in fancy regalia and flaunted human slaves who were chained or roped by the collar. In a primal display of loyalty, the humans all bared their teeth on behalf of their masters or mistresses.

The emissary ship docked, and a carapace-armored soldier waved the whaler to a spot behind them, whilst other soldiers managed the crowd by linking their beefy arms together, forming a wolfan guard chain.

The pipe-gumming captain approached Leera's group. "I will stay with the ship," he said in a low voice. "Get the boys started on repairs, see if we can barter for supplies without gettin' us all collared." He winked, smiling at his little jest. "Besides our talking wolf friend, choose some among you to meet their procession and act as ambassadors on our kingdom's behalf. You will be my eyes and report back what you see."

They conferred, choosing Augum, Leera, Olaf, and Jengo as the most suitable delegation as they represented the Arcaner ethos, with Jez, Digby, Carter, Alanna, Leo, and Tammy staying behind to guard the ship. Everyone departing quietly set an alarm for the crew so they could teleport back in case something happened.

Once the gangplanks were thrown down and the white-clad crew reassembled in a line, Rogor stepped onto the gangplank, leading their small procession onto land likely untouched by Sithesian civilization in perhaps an eon, if not ever.

The ambassadors awaited their arrival on the other side, now joined by a new pack of wolfan guards, these ones armored to the teeth in thick steel plate painted in cerulean and holding large vermillion-colored shields shaped like beetle husks. They were a disciplined lot who did not so much as glance at the humans or the naked wolven. The throng gathered beyond the ambassadors, on the other hand, taunted Rogor by howling like wolves and beating their chests and spitting his way and wagging their tails at him and shouting obscenities, as if it offended them that he was naked and his slaves walked uncollared.

"Has to be one of the strangest sights I've ever seen," Olaf muttered, glancing back to the ship longingly.

"You don't have to come if you don't want to," Leera said as they waited at the foot of the gangplanks for the ambassadors to give the signal to walk with them. "Everyone will understand," she added, referring to Bridget's absence, for it might affect how he felt being amongst a whole race of slavers.

"No way am I missing this. Have to have *something* interesting to report back to Bridget."

"What, the voyage wasn't interesting enough?" Leera replied.

Olaf snorted. "If harrowing counts as interesting ..."

Leera inhaled deeply and smelled a panoply of scents—fish and tar and iron and earth and stone and various fruits and incenses and myrrhs and oils—creating a pungently novel experience for her. The buildings rose up a surprisingly steep hill, creating a stacked effect, like one of those expensive pop-up card books specialty merchants crafted for the children of rich nobles. The street was cobbled not from stone, but from the end pieces of hardwood that had over time been rounded from heavy use. Far on the horizon, the occasional flash of lightning lit up the outline of a jagged mountain range. To Leera, all of it looked, smelled and felt beautiful in the same sense one would perceive a dangerously exotic jungle.

As the ambassadors began to walk forth in a two-by-two line, with an armored wolfan signaling for Rogor and his troupe to follow, the guards closed ranks behind them, protecting them from the unruly crowd. Meanwhile, another procession formed ahead, two facing lines of horn-blowing wolfan, each wearing a purple tabard with a long train no one dared to step on. When the ambassadors entered their lineup, they blew their horns, which sounded very much like wolfen howls—but louder and higher-pitched. Other wolfan in the city echoed that call, creating a symphony of howls.

"It's like they're warning us what they're capable of," Jengo muttered, eyes darting about like some of the human slaves the wolfan kept on short leashes. Those slaves were of every skin color and tone, raising questions as to their origins.

"Ominous," Olaf added, tugging on Bridget's betrothal ring.

Leera focused in on the tabards as they passed the horn-blowers and spotted intricate gold emblems that distinctly showed a crown above the face of a particularly grizzled wolfan.

"Anyone else feel like we're going to meet royalty?" she asked, wondering if it had been a bad idea leaving Jez behind. What if they were indeed walking straight into a trap? What then? *Then you 'port off just as you discussed*, she thought in an attempt to settle her nerves.

"I would assume that to be the case," Jengo replied, trying to stay in the middle of their group. "We should treat it as an honor and try not to cause offense."

"Speak little, lowlanders," Rogor growled over his shoulder.

"As long as they understand we are free," Augum said to him.

To Leera's dismay, Rogor ignored this remark.

Olaf caught her worry and muttered, "I'll open my yap if need be. Ain't no way we're going to let that furball give the impression we're his personal servants—or worse."

Leera nodded, yet that thought hadn't even occurred to her, and with a fresh anxiety to occupy her mind, she resolved to keep a careful watch over their so-called ally.

They entered a narrow main street in the city running along the bottom of the hill. It was lined with shops that rose into tall and narrow homes that mimicked the tall and narrow people who resided within. The wolfan were less muscular than Sithesian wolven, but they were more discerning in manner and clothing and, in that sense, appeared far more civilized.

The howls from the throng continued sporadically, causing others along the street to hang out of their high windows. The wolfan also had glass and shutters and clay tiles and wooden-wheeled carts, but the designs were different, sometimes drastically so. The shutters were ornate and made with care and oft painted green.

The stonework of the buildings was well placed, cut to form, and sometimes engraved with intricate swirling patterns. Their roofs were studded with strategically placed thorns that were sometimes hidden behind decorations like wooden flowers or trees that almost looked real. Water spouts were made of copper and wells were plentiful. Carts were crafted with care and precision and sometimes looked more beautiful than what was practical for a cart that was, for example, used to transport mere stacks of hay or wood or even manure.

There were no horses or dogs or cats, but there were wolves—and plenty of them. They played on the streets like feral pets that were not only tolerated, but revered. Wolfan petted them and fed them scraps and cubs played with them. Even the cubs were dressed, albeit in simple frocks, always colored too, which Leera suspected denoted their element.

Rogor's head swiveled about in great interest, and Leera got the impression he was absorbing it with some shock, but also creating a mental report for his tribe. She wondered what he would tell them if he ever got back, and if they'd believe him that his own kind had ascended to such civility that he was considered a barbarian. Her curiosity got the better of her judgment and she strode up beside him.

"What are you going to tell your brethren about all this?" she asked.

"That our kind has split off and there is great potential to learn from the other half," Rogor replied, without so much as glancing at her.

"You think you're split equally like that? What if they outnumber you two to one, or ten to one? What if they want to take your lot as slaves?"

At last he looked down on her. "You are a foolish lowlander who does not understand the wolven. I can therefore hardly expect you to fathom the wolfan." He dismissed her with a backhanded flap of his paw.

Lacking the nerve to argue further, Leera drifted back to walk alongside her betrothed, sharing a skeptical look with him. She hardly needed to voice her opinion that she thought Rogor naive for believing these wolfan would be as benevolent as he assumed.

Onward they walked through the city, taking a turn on the road as it wound up the hill. The mob thickened, as did the noise, which continued to draw the more curious sort, who gawked at the humans and the naked wolven as if they were part of a visiting caravan of oddities. Leera saw many humanlike mannerisms—shakes of the head, paw-flips of disbelief to a neighbor, open-snouted gapes. Some clutched their snouts in a manner that made Leera think of a human idly clutching their elbow, others wagged their tails like eager puppies. She even saw a few use charcoal to frantically sketch what they were seeing, which they did so on parchment wrapped around wooden tablets.

"Has to be the strangest parade I've ever been a part of," Leera muttered to Augum, but he was too preoccupied with watching the crowd and the strange buildings to respond, so she repeated the jest to Olaf.

"At least they're not flinging tomatoes at us," Olaf chirped. "Do you think they even have tomatoes? Look at that weird pink palm there. What an oddity."

After he pointed it out, Leera saw other strange plants—what looked like purple aspens and cherry oaks and aquamarine junipers. There was a general tint toward color, as if the wolfan had gone over everything with a bright paintbrush.

As they ascended the winding road up the hill, the homes got wealthier and more ornate—and their roofs more thorny. One particularly gold-ensconced house sported two upright lion statues out front, and the warlocks asked amongst themselves if those were Dreadnoughts. Another had an upright lizard, another still an upright bull, reminding Leera of the dead bull she had seen back at the base of the oceanic tower, which she now recognized as a possible minotaur on account of its unusually large size. Had she only made the connection back then, she could have swiped its horn for the Zygothika ritual.

"Look, that one has a golden collar," Jengo said, pointing out an older woman who wore nicer—and more colorful—clothes embroidered with exotic plants. Although short like all the slaves, she stood straight and possessed all her teeth. What at first glance Leera mistook for a necklace was in fact a thick golden slave collar. She stood apart from the crowd, arms casually at her sides as she stared at the passing retinue as if she were seeing a mirage.

"Anyone else notice that none of the slaves wear spectacles?" Leera noted, pushing her own spectacles back up her nose.

"But some certainly look better cared for than others," Jengo replied.

Better-dressed wolfan and slaves progressively replaced the crowd. More had wolves as pets, which their human slaves oft kept on a golden leash. Leera thought she heard one of the better-dressed slaves speak a word to another, but it was hard to tell with the general mutterings of the crowd.

"We're going to the castle," Augum noted, pointing above a roof, beyond which rose a square minaret with a red clay roof so pitched it looked like a dunce cap, albeit one studded with countless enormous spears.

Leera drew a hand around Augum's waist and squeezed him close to whisper in his ear, "Going to cast Reveal and see if I can make stuff out."

"I'd rather make out with you," he jested.

"Worst timing ever," she quipped back, shoving his shoulder away and muttering, "Boys …"

He grinned as he returned to marveling at the sights.

Leera pretended to descend into a minor coughing fit whilst covering her mouth with one hand and drawing the other up into her crimson sleeve, incanting, "*Un vun asperio aurum enchantus.*" After checking she hadn't drawn undue suspicion, she glanced around—and was surprised to find no enchantments at all on the street. She did, however, spot some blue tendril weavings on the guards' armor. Interestingly, it was too vibrant to have sunk to permanence, meaning they actively engaged in that sort of arcane skill craft.

The more she looked, the more tendrils she spotted. A clay pot enchanted with a simple cantrip that, if she were to guess, promoted growth. A coil of rope was seal-enchanted to a wall without visible use of glue or nails. The wheel crank of a well had a tiny rune underneath, likely enchanted as a trigger for the wheel to turn on its own. The hinges of a door were perhaps enchanted with a basic alarm trigger or one that made the door open and close. Other such simplicities made Leera wonder what sort of wolfan had enchanted them. Perhaps a specialist not unlike a human arcaneologist? Or were all wolfan capable of enchanting objects? She had so many questions …

"Nothing spectacular yet," she told Augum under her breath. "Just minor enchantments on common objects."

Trying not to stare at the soldiers, she kept glancing about, until the roadway straightened to go directly uphill, and they passed massive siege towers fitted with trebuchets built from purple-hued timber. Although the mechanisms weren't enchanted, other enchantments—and these were faded enough to suggest they had sunk to permanence—were ensconced into the structures of the towers.

Such enchantments also stuck to the cobbled roadway, and Leera took delight in studying them as she walked over the tendril web. She surreptitiously reported what she saw to the others. "Tightly enchanted, leading-edge complexities of the first to third order, hues of blue indicating standard spellcraft, sunk to permanence, standard tendril thickness, multiple triggers, all in a stable state but operable. I'd have to crouch to study them further so that's all for now, folks."

After Augum complimented her on a studious report, they passed a massive archway made of huge red blocks, each one inscribed with a runic emblem. These too were enchanted, and interestingly, some of the enchantments were ink-black, indicating necromancy.

"By the way, they utilize all eight elements for protection," Leera added, pretending to scratch her nose to hide her mouth, even though she was pretty sure no one around could understand their tongue.

One of these tendril webs, cast upon a towering trebuchet ensconced atop a spiked building, was so black it might as well have been a void in reality. She wondered what demonic monster it flung, or, more likely — and she subconsciously rubbed her belly — what horrible curse its hurled stones inflicted.

They followed the ambassadors into a courtyard surrounded by a hundred-foot-tall curtain wall, while the rest of the crowd stayed behind the archway. Hundreds of wolfan stood at attention in neat rows within this courtyard, surrounded by archery targets and straw dummies made to look like various beasts, one type of which looked distinctly like a gargoyle.

The procession halted before a pair of massive iron doors studded with spikes. The four Arcaners and lone wolven glanced at each other as the courtyard fell silent. Ahead, no less than twenty horn-blowers raised long horns and blew three deep notes that rattled the pebbles on the wood-cobbled ground.

"Neat," Leera said, enjoying the feeling of her innards ringing to the exotic music of a new continent.

There came two deep *clicks*, followed by the doors rumbling open at a snail's pace to reveal a tall inner hall glittering with so much gold that the four Arcaners gasped.

"By gods, it must be carved out of one solid brick of gold," Olaf said.

Leera, who'd kept her hand splayed, was so distracted by all the luster that she lost focus on Reveal, fizzling it. By then she didn't care as it wasn't like she could inspect any tendril weavings up close — not without the risk of causing offense, a terrible idea in a foreign kingdom of twelve-foot-tall warriors armed to the teeth.

They filed into what Leera at first thought was a gigantic central hall, but it was only the antechamber, for a second inner pair of double doors awaited. These were gold and studded with a pattern of domes. There was probably a name for such a design, but Leera did not know about such things.

A single female horn-blower blasted a deep note, then scaled that note up one octave, then another, then still another, until it was a high-pitched squeal. She halted this note, raised the long horn, and tapped one of the golden doors three times. Three muted taps replied from the other side, followed by a reversing echo of high-to-low pitches of a horn. Another deep *click* sounded, and the doors slowly and silently swung open.

The ambassadors filed in, and Leera got a good look at the eared horn-blower. She was a ten-footer and wore the most colorful silken garment Leera had ever seen, a prismatic, rainbow-hued glittering display of miniature cut jewels. She was so vibrant that any torchlight shining upon her scattered about the antechamber, creating a chromatic display of wonder that made the little girl in Leera want to squeal and hide within that rainbow garment and play peek-a-boo and pretend she was a princess of the elements. It was such a dazzling thing to behold that she tripped over Augum's heel and tumbled to the floor.

"I'm fine!" a red-faced Leera blurted, launching herself back to her feet and smacking the boys' offered hands away. "I'm fine," she huffed, smoothing the crinkles of her robe in an attempt to salvage her dignity.

The inner chamber was vast and filled with eight gigantic braziers hanging on long black chains. Each brazier burned with a different-colored flame that Leera suspected represented the eight elements, for the color scheme matched the wolfans' robes.

These braziers hung twenty feet above a golden floor polished to such a high sheen that it felt like walking on a mirror, giving Leera a mild sensation of vertigo from thinking she was about to fall toward the ceiling.

At the front stood a platform with two thrones, hinting that two rulers ran this kingdom, perhaps a king and queen.

"So very human," Leera whispered as the procession came to a halt.

A wolfan snapped a sharp command and the guard entourage stiffened toward the ambassadors before walking backward until their backs pressed against the golden walls of the great hall. There they stood at attention, holding their spears upright.

Various other small ceremonies then commenced. Heralds trumpeted on their horns, a wolfan sang a musical note, another waved perfumy incense about. Someone drank from a golden chalice, spilling red liquid—perhaps wine—onto the floor in ceremony. Another wolfan, draped in a long white garment, raised his arms skyward and howlingly sang a prayer to a god or gods or The Fates—Leera couldn't say.

At long last, a door on each side of the throned platform opened and out stepped a king and queen wolfan. Each was twelve feet in height, wore a bejeweled royal purple robe, and was obese. They carried their weight forth with great effort, huffing with each step, and both needed help from multiple human slaves to climb to their thrones and sit upon them. These human slaves were by far the most well put together Leera had yet seen, for they had near-perfect teeth, stood erect, were clothed in fine silken garments, and their golden collars were polished to a high shine. Yet even these were smaller humans, standing a foot shorter on average, and all were thin, eyes slightly bloodshot and puffy and encircled by deep purple rings, as if sleep were a precious commodity.

The queen raised a paw adorned with countless bejeweled rings and flicked a finger at the procession, all of whom bowed. Rogor and the four Arcaners took this as their cue to do the same. The bow lasted for too long a time for Leera's comfort, and she almost fell over from the wavering that took hold, until she heard the rustle of cloth as the procession rose. What proceeded was a bevy of reports from the ambassadors, which interestingly was sung in a musical howl-like tone that remained on the same note as the horns, reverberating through the hall—and tempting Leera with drowsiness.

She wanted to groan and snap, "Get it over with, would you!" and did so in her mind. As the ambassadors droned on and on with their reports, the impatient girl within got annoyed, and her attention drifted to those around them, particularly the newly arrived wolfan behind them. There had to be around fifty, each dressed in variations of fine regalia and wildly ostentatious hats—one was composed of the head of what appeared to be a boar, another a pink cow head, another still a gargoyle head. One was even made from an entire peacock, albeit an oversized one. If she had to guess, she suspected these wolfan were the city's nobles.

The chanting report halted, leaving behind an echo. Once that echo died, a dignitary turned about and addressed their group with a question. Rogor bowed his head, stepped forth, and replied. His answer was met with a mix of responses. Some of the nobles gasped, others chortled with distinct skepticism.

"What did he say?" Leera whispered to a Augum, who was squinting, three fingers pressed to his temple and a hand resting idly against his throat, telling her he'd just surreptitiously cast Tongues. Being the only one who had spent a decent amount of time with the wolven, he stood the best chance of understanding their tongue, yet he frowned and shook his head, whispering, "Not quite sure."

Thankfully, Rogor did the translating for them.

"It is as I suspected," Rogor stated over his shoulder. "They do not believe we came from overseas."

This simple statement, or perhaps even the turn of his head to speak to the humans, caused a growling rebuke from the nobility.

The king and queen watched with impassive faces that suggested they had seen and heard it all and were woefully bored with life itself. The king's reply was to extend a single claw—which was studded with tiny jewels—and flick it forth. The minute gesture was enough for one of the ambassadors to raise a follow-up question, leading Rogor to give a long-winded reply. He indicated at the four Arcaners as he made his case, which he did with a surprising level of patience for one with a reputation for impatience. When he finished, the ambassadors and nobles descended into quiet conversation.

Leera cleared her throat loudly at Rogor, who turned to the four Arcaners and in a low voice said, "I have told them of our long voyage and retraced it all the way to the attack upon our lands by the gargoyles. My impression is that they initially thought us an elaborate prank committed by one of their richer nobles, but I think they are starting to believe me."

As the group huddled together to speak in low tones, with Rogor bending forward to allow some semblance of privacy, Olaf's blond eyebrows rose. "They prank each other?" he whispered. "You mean they have a sense of humor?"

An unimpressed Rogor ignored him.

"Did you tell them we're warlocks?" Augum asked.

"I did, but I am not sure the words translated. I am not sure what they think of you."

"Do they think we're your slaves?" Leera pressed.

"I repeated that you are free humans. That you have your own kingdoms and your own arcanery, but again, I do not think they know that word. There are many words in my tongue that are too different from theirs. At least that is my impression. My people would be most interested in this, and I wish more had come to witness this with their own eyes."

"They didn't think any of us would survive the journey though," Augum threw in.

Rogor sighed as he inclined his head, relatively scrawny shoulders drooping.

"Tell them again that we're after our people," Leera added. "Ask them if they are willing to help us."

"Perhaps you have not noticed, lowlander, but they consider humans deeply inferior."

"Then let us display our power," Augum replied. "Let them see that we are to be respected and are not like the humans here."

"I'm curious where they got those humans from," Olaf threw in.

"I can ask, but such a question may cause offense."

"Then for now let us hold off such questions," Augum said.

"Agreed, lowlander. But I will pass on your request for a demonstration."

The procession was soon called to focus again, and another question was asked of Rogor, who gave a detailed response, indicating toward the Arcaners. Then he looked to them. "One of you is permitted to make a demonstration of your powers."

"I'll do it," Leera blurted. "And don't look at me like that," she said when the three other warlocks exchanged uncertain looks. "I won't go crazy. Promise." Being the only female among them, she wanted to show the wolfan that women from overseas were strong too.

Rogor hesitated but inclined his head and stepped aside. She flared her eyes meaningfully at the boys, all of whom took the hint and stepped back. Then she cleared her throat, asked Rogor to translate for her, and cleared her throat again. She ceremoniously raised her right arm and flared ten watery rings. The audience of wolfan gasped upon seeing this display, telling her they had never seen a human use such powers before.

"I've only just begun," she said, a phrase Rogor did not translate, which she thought was prudent, in retrospect. She next raised her left arm, summoned her shield, and slowly turned in place for all to see the full Arcaner crest.

"*Semperis vorto honos*," she boldly declared. "Courage, fortitude, honor."

Rogor echoed these words in the Wolven tongue. All the wolfan leaned forward and squinted as if straining to understand his dialect and meaning and what it was they were seeing. Of particular note — and what drew the most whispers, some in notable alarm — was the depiction upon her shield.

"We are a people from the continent of Sithesia," she continued, with Rogor translating in the background. "A people of seven kingdoms across seven great lands. We wield seven elements — air, earth, healing, lightning, fire, ice, and water —" upon mentioning the last, she made a vicious throwing-toward-the-ground gesture, roaring, "*Grau!*"

The monstrous roar of a crashing wave echoed through the hall, and nearly everyone whirled about, expecting to be inundated by a tsunami. The guards thrust their arms forth, and the king and queen started, their crowns jangling askew on their heads.

Leera allowed the echo of the spell to die before solemnly continuing. "We are a proud people with our own ancient customs and traditions, and our *own* arcanery. She used a finger to draw a five-pointed shape in the air, incanting, "*Summano elementus minimus!*"

A stubby watery elemental appeared before her, its feet slapping against the floor with a watery *squish*. This caused another round of gasps and mutters and canine yips of surprise. Leera would have loved to cast the dragon version of her elemental, but they had explicitly strategized to keep any dragon-related cards close to their chests for now.

She circled her summoned adversary before dipping into a cat-like attack posture whilst slapping her wrists together and roaring, "*Annihilo!*" A jet of water shot forth and obliterated the elemental on the spot, causing more yips, as well as growls of alarm and anger. Rogor continued to speak on her behalf in a calm voice that eased her anxieties and gave her confidence—and kept the wolfan mutterings to a minimum.

"We are a *free* people who can protect ourselves in many ways. Behold, for this is but a taste, and it will harm you not!" When Rogor finished translating, she swept her arms about theatrically, incanting, "*Summano loa storma arregando!*" A dark storm cloud appeared above the nobles and pummeled them with a furious rainstorm of fat drops. They yelped and covered their heads. The cloud rumbled ominously with thunder, and a bolt of harmless lightning snapped at a reedy wolfan female, who yelped—elemental spells such as this oft blended with complementary elements. So as not to cause a panic, Leera let the effect go on only briefly before making a reverse whirling motion whilst incanting, "*Summano null*," and the storm vanished—as did the water that had soaked them all.

After checking themselves over, the throng burst into discussion at this display, nodding to their neighbor, impressed. Some spoke in anger, but even they agreed that this was unexpected.

"We can defend ourselves like you can," Leera declared, making an unsheathing motion from her hip and incanting, "*Summano arma!*" A watery shortsword appeared in her fist, which paired nicely with her large watery shield.

She turned about in place for all to see before shaking out both arms, allowing the summoned sword and shield to vanish. "Please help us find our people. Then we can start to form a relationship on equal terms."

As Rogor translated, she stepped back to join the boys, muttering, "How'd I do?"

"Not too bad, Jones," Augum said with a wry smile. "Not too bad at all."

"I think I covered the main points, but we'll see if the message got through."

The ambassadors conferred quietly with the king and queen, both of whom now sat forward, claws clasped together in their laps. After some time—and a lot of quiet discussion—the ambassadors turned to face Rogor and the Arcaners, with the black-robed one doing the speaking. Rogor nodded along to a series of statements before turning to the Arcaners.

"They declared that they need time to ruminate upon our dilemma. They declare that if what we say is true, we ought to be natural allies against the winged demons, which they call gorgan, their word for gargoyle. The king has temporarily given each of us the title of ambassador and will provide an armed escort so that we may look upon the city with our own eyes. We are to report to them tomorrow at the hour of *tirpat* for a banquet in our honor, at which point they should have come to a conclusion on the matter."

"What time of day is that?" Jengo asked.

Rogor turned to the ambassadors to relay the question and got a quick reply. "When the sun has almost set. The word *tirpat* is the name of a bird that calls at that time of day."

"So humanlike," Leera had to mutter once more with a wondrous shake of her head.

The blue-robed ambassador who represented the air element called forth a tall noble wolfan. The bejeweled noble, dressed in fine and flowing regalia embroidered with the silhouette of a mountainscape, bowed humbly. The wolfan ambassador passed on a set of instructions, and the noble bowed and turned to Rogor to make his introduction.

"This is Kepwa and he will be our minder and guide," Rogor explained. "He will take us to receive our ambassadorial sashes. We must now bow to the royals."

The group turned as one to the royals and bowed, but the king and queen merely watched them with well-practiced boredom, and continued to do so even as they followed Kepwa and departed the hall with an armed escort.

"That went better than expected," Augum muttered to Leera.

"Tell me about it," she replied as they entered a side hall and a high-ceiled room with a long series of golden doors and free-standing cabinets.

Augum rubbed his hands together excitedly. "I'm looking forward to exploring the city," he said.

Leera, wondering if she could snag one of the Zygothika curse reversal ingredients, privately agreed.

WOLFAN MARKETS

AUGUM

As they walked through the courtyard with their escort of ten heavily armed wolfan guards and lone noble minder, Augum adjusted the copper-colored sash that hung diagonally across his chest, enjoying the way the runic inscriptions flowed so neatly down the center.

"What do you think it says?" Jengo asked.

Olaf pressed a finger against the first rune of his own sash and dragged it along as he read aloud. " 'Keep away, soon to be captured and enslaved.' " He snorted at his own jest, one no one else found as funny—except for Leera, who guffawed from beside Augum. Then Olaf's face darkened as his eyes unfocused. He looked to Kepwa, who trailed in the rear, then addressed Rogor. "Can you ask our wolfan minder if it's possible to find a particular human slave in the land of the gorgan?"

Rogor sniffed at the air, as if annoyed to be asked such a petty thing. "Very well, lowlander. I do this because you suffer the absence of your mate. But do not pester me for every little thing. I do not wish to strain the relationship with inanities. Their dialect is also difficult to understand."

"Then aid me in understanding it," Augum said and pressed three fingers into his temple and touched his throat, incanting, "*Translateo commona linguino Wolven.*" He wished he could exchange the *Wolven* part with *Wolfan*, but that would have to be earned through study.

Rogor slowed his walk to speak with the minder, asking in Wolven, "The fat lowlander wishes to know if he can rescue his mate from the gorgan."

The minder's long snout burst with a growling laugh, which ended in a wistful sigh as if he couldn't believe how stupid a question it was.

He replied in Wolfan, but Augum barely understood a mere handful of words. "Only ... death ... free ... gorgan."

Rogor switched to common. "He said that only death can free a slave from the gorgan."

He might as well have stomped on Olaf's heart, for the poor fellow wobbled as if struck and clutched Bridget's betrothal ring, which hung from his neck on a cord.

Augum let the spell lapse and hurried to walk alongside his friend. "Don't worry," he said to Olaf, throwing him a friendly elbow. "They have no idea how tenacious we are. We *will* find her."

Despite his lip quivering, Olaf forced a smile. "Yeah. Right. Of course we will ..."

"And don't forget that Bridget is one smart cookie," Augum added. "If anyone can brain her way out of a predicament, it's the class valedictorian."

"Yeah, I guess she *was* the smartest of the graduating bunch," Olaf said, brightening a little. "Er, no offense, Aug."

"None taken as it's absolutely true." Augum smiled and continued walking alongside in silent support, remembering how Bridget had excelled in all her classes and was the darling of all the arcanists. He was happy she had been chosen as valedictorian, for she embodied everything the academy represented.

They walked through the gates back into the city and were once more quickly beset by curious wolfan, forcing the minder to bark a command at their guard detail, who then formed a loose ring around the group.

They traipsed at a leisurely pace along the cobbled and torchlit street, glancing at this and that and waving at wolfan, but none returned such waves, and even the enslaved humans looked upon them with distrust. The most they received was a tail wag or two, especially from the cubs who perhaps did not know any better. Most often a wolfen would jerk their head away, offering an upturned snout which came across as an insult to Augum.

His eyes pored over the various stalls they passed. One of these caught his attention. "You know what we could use?"

"A route to the gorgan?" Olaf muttered.

"Exactly. A map." He slipped by two of their guards, who were so big, their gazes on the gawkers, that they didn't notice him until he was standing before a stall filled with rows of cubby holes brimming with rolled-up scrolls and stacks of colorful parchments.

Augum pressed three fingers to his temple, cleared his throat whilst placing a hand to it, and incanted, "*Translateo commona linguino Wolven.*

Excuse me," he growled in choppy Wolven to the shopkeeper, a female wolfan who sat upon a tall stool and gaped at him as if he were a ghost. "Do you have a map?" The growls came out strange, and he wasn't sure if he got the word *map* right. For all he knew he was asking for a clump of dirt.

"Get *jabol* back *konta kwa!*" a guard barked, with Augum understanding two of the five words.

"No, let *jabol* explore," Kepwa the minder interrupted, beckoning for the guard to step away from Augum and leave him be.

The towering twelve-footer glared at Augum before returning to his circle of waiting guards.

"What does *jabol* mean?" Augum asked the wolfan shopkeeper, but she continued to gape at him.

Leera broke out of the circle to join Augum's side, squealing, "Oh my gosh this is *so* much fun! Look at all this neat stuff! Did you say you were going to ask for a map?"

"I'm trying," Augum said out of the corner of his mouth, "but I don't think it's sinking in."

Leera waved with both hands, causing the shopkeeper to jump away with a yelp.

At last, Kepwa joined to stand behind them. "The *jabol* wants *deh sot kwap.*"

The shopkeeper glanced between Kepwa, Augum, and Augum's sash before glancing around her parchment-filled shop. She reached into a particular cubicle, the contents of which were too high for Augum to see, and withdrew a rectangular parchment.

"*Jebwa stah*," she said, dangling the parchment way above Augum's head, as if taunting him.

Kepwa reached into a pocket, withdrew a leather pouch, and poured out a pawful of gold, silver and copper pebbles, each engraved with a rune.

As he counted out five copper pebbles, Augum looked to Leera. "Pebbles?"

She shrugged. "Pebbles."

"Pebbles," he replied with a nod. So be it.

Kepwa handed the five copper pebbles over. Upon delivery, the shopkeeper threw the parchment at Augum, who flicked a hand and telekinetically grabbed it before it could slap into his face. The shopkeeper yelped upon seeing him wield arcanery that the wolfan had yet to show they knew and scrambled about as if searching for something to hold onto, but ended up windmilling her hairy arms until she fell back from her chair, causing quite the clatter.

"All right there?" Augum asked over the empty counter.

Upon receiving what he assumed was a growl of embarrassment and anger, Augum politely thanked the shopkeeper and Kepwa in Wolven and he and Leera walked back to the group. Together they gathered around the parchment, which turned out to be a beautifully illustrated map of the entire kingdom, showing a glimpse of three other nearby kingdoms. The only problem was that all the inscriptions were written in Wolfan runic symbols.

"So colorful," Leera cooed.

Augum held up the map before Kepwa and tapped it, asking in Wolven, "Where are we?"

"Your Wolven is abysmal, lowlander," Rogor growled in common when Kepwa glanced to Rogor to help translate, which he did by repeating the phrase, correcting the pronunciation and changing two words out completely. Augum took note to improve his knowledge of the Wolven tongue.

Kepwa nodded his understanding and pointed to a city along the coast. "*Kefa*," he said.

"Is that the name of the city?" Augum growled in Wolven.

"Yes," Kepwa and Rogor chorused in Wolven, a word that seemed to be the same in both languages, as they glanced at each other in mild surprise.

"This is where we are," Augum told Jengo, Olaf and Leera, who leaned in closer around him as he circled the central kingdom, which took up nearly the entire map.

"That has to be the kingdom of the gorgan," Olaf threw in, tapping a depiction of a winged demon in a land north of the wolfan kingdom.

Jengo pointed at a slice of a kingdom squished between others, identified by an upright lion with a large mane. "That's obviously the tip of the lion kingdom," he said.

Leera pressed a finger to a bull-horned demon depiction on the land east of the wolfan kingdom and south of the lion kingdom. "And that's the land of the minotaurs. Because apparently minotaurs exist. Either that or this is all a wild delusion brought on by a powerful curse or something."

The boys blinked at her.

"Er … you all right there, Lee?" Jengo asked.

"Peachy, thanks. Just amusing myself," she added in a mutter.

With the map focused on the wolfan kingdom, Augum was not surprised that only three other kingdoms were hinted at. Suspecting that many more lay about in the lands beyond, he regretted not pressing for a continental map instead.

Like any map, this one showed lakes and rivers and mountains and swamps and plateaus and a wide variety of other features — albeit in a foreign style. The cities were clustered closer together than those in Sithesia and there were more of them, but it was hard to tell for sure as there was no sense of scale. For all Augum knew, the cities were hundreds of leagues apart, their visual depictions exaggerated to look larger and closer together. Nor did all the runic symbols match — some could be monuments or holy sites or who knew what.

Interestingly, the coast ran some ways before it joined the gargoyle lands, the cities of which were also labeled in runic. That meant they could sail directly north into gargoyle country.

Augum pointed to the gargoyle's land as he asked Rogor, "Can you ask Kepwa what the name of this kingdom is?"

Rogor grimaced, probably considering it an inane question but relayed it nonetheless. "Gorga," came the reply.

Augum pointed at the kingdom depicted by the lion. "What about this one?"

"Lona."

Augum moved his finger down to the land of the supposed minotaur. "And this one?"

"Minota."

"And the one we are in?"

"Wolfa."

"At least they're simple," Olaf muttered.

After they were done marveling over it, Augum folded the map and tucked it into a pocket so they could resume their explorative stroll. It was slow going as everything seemed to catch their eye, which prompted Olaf to note in an undertone that, "Our snail pace is making Rogor look a little grumpy."

Augum was about to tell Leera and Jengo that they should pick up their pace as it was far too slow for wolven — and thus surely wolfan — liking, when he spotted a shop stall full of animal skins and horns and bones, among other things. He pinched the shoulder of Leera's robe and gave it a double tug, whispering, "Hey, weren't you in the market for a certain horn?"

Leera, who'd been glancing at a shop full of various sconces and candles and oval oil lamps and unsuccessfully trying to inquire to the aghast shopkeeper how they made their candles, whirled about to exclaim, "Yes, yes, yes!" She hurried into the shop, Augum right behind.

"Did I mention that I might have missed a chance to score a free minotaur horn back in the tower I'd explored on my own?" she said as they glanced about the shop. The place was thin, but twice the height of even the tallest wolfan, and lined with towering shelves and cubbies stuffed with oddities.

"No, you didn't," Augum absently replied, throwing the shopkeeper a nod and a smile.

The shopkeeper was a frumpy old wolfan who was squat for his species. He stood near the top of a movable ladder organizing a cubby of glass jars filled with what suspiciously looked like powdered bones.

"Yeah, still kicking myself for that." Leera waved at the shopkeeper with a silly grin and blurted, "Excuse me, sir, but do you have the horn of an adult minotaur?"

The old wolfan did a double-take upon looking down at her, then gaped as if seeing an apparition.

Augum placed his fists by his head and stuck an index finger out of each hand to imitate horns. "*Minota*," he said.

When the shopkeeper continued to stare, Augum sighed, placed three fingers to his temple, a hand to his throat, and incanted, "*Translateo commona linguino Wolven*." Then in his best growling Wolven, he said, "We're looking for the horn of—" But he got no further, for upon hearing him speak his tongue, the shopkeeper started with a yelp so violently that he fell from the ladder.

Augum's instincts kicked in and he shot both arms out, telekinetically snatching the wolfan in midair. Leera helped, and the pair worked together to lower the squat wolfan to the ground.

Jengo and Olaf and Rogor, who had been perusing things in a shop opposite, glanced over at the commotion, while a few of their guards and their minder, Kepwa, sprinted over as if fearing an attack.

Upon planting his pawed feet on the floor, the shopkeeper began berating Augum and Leera, who edged away from his fiercely gesticulated ravings. Suddenly switching focus to Telekinesis had resulted in Augum losing his grip on the Tongues spell, fizzling it, and so he couldn't understand the wolfan. It took Kepwa explaining in what sounded like an exasperated tone for the shopkeeper to calm down, though his eyes kept darting between Augum and Leera and he kept shaking his wide snout in a disbelieving fashion that Augum was rapidly getting used to.

"No, we're *not* slaves," Augum enunciated, primly smoothing his copper sash.

By then, Rogor had joined them, snapping, "What trouble are you lowlanders getting into now?"

"It was a misunderstanding," Augum replied. "Would you mind kindly telling the shopkeeper that we would like to purchase the horn of an adult minotaur?"

"Why do you need such a thing?"

"It's for a potion of long health," Leera blurted. "Old human recipe," she told the shopkeeper, nodding a little too fervently. "That sort of thing. You know …?"

Augum cringed at the lie but didn't blame her in the least as it was a private matter.

The shopkeeper glanced between her and Augum and Rogor, who seemingly decided it was best to simply translate their query so they could keep the peace and move on. Augum noticed that Kepwa, although he did most of the translating when asked, was studying Rogor with a keen eye, staring at him for prolonged periods whenever the wolven wasn't paying attention to him. He wondered if it was because Kepwa considered Rogor a naked barbarian in relation to their culture or if it was something else entirely.

At last Kepwa managed to successfully translate their wish, and the shopkeeper scratched under his long snout before snuffling a grunt and trotting off to the back of the shop. He soon returned with a huge brown horn.

"*Minotan,*" he said, loudly dumping it onto his counter and growling what they assumed was the cost.

Augum and Leera turned to Kepwa with pleading expressions. Kepwa sighed and grumbled as he once again reached into his pouch. This time, however, he withdrew almost all his gold pebbles, ignoring the silver ones, and handed them over. The shopkeeper in turn passed the horn to Leera, who squealed as she danced from foot to foot, rubbing her shoulder playfully against Augum. The thing was nearly half her size, so it was an awkward dance.

Leera began inquiring about the other two ingredients she needed — the tooth of a giant and the claw of a wyvern—but not only did the shopkeeper scoff at these requests, but Kepwa told Rogor to tell Leera that he did not have the money anyhow for such fantasies.

"Fantasies?" Leera said as they departed the shop, lugging the horn between both arms. "*That's* the word Kepwa used?"

"That's the word the shopkeeper used," Rogor replied. "And our minder expects you to pay him back."

"Tell him there's lots of neat stuff on our ship he can show off to his cubs," Leera said, nodding most fervently at Kepwa while Rogor translated. "But I also have coin," she threw in upon seeing the wolfan's face sour.

Olaf and Jengo, who'd been exploring a shop that sold silk carpets of exotic design, joined Augum and Leera as they walked down the sloping cobbled street.

"Is that a giant ox horn or something?" Olaf asked.

"Minotaur," Leera proudly replied.

Olaf counted on his fingers. "So we have the wolfan, the gorgan, the lonan, and the minotan. How many other races are there on this blasted continent? How big *is* this continent anyway?"

"Very big," Rogor replied. "And there are many races."

"How do you know that?" Jengo pressed.

"Because I asked, lowlander."

Olaf was about to reply when Augum gently elbowed him in the ribs, mouthing, "Another time. Let it go for now." Rogor was already losing patience, and they needed to keep his temper at bay lest it impede their interactions with the wolfan.

Olaf nodded. "You got it."

Wolfan gawkers followed them as they walked. One of these was a family that included no fewer than six cubs, all of whom fought to get a glimpse of the naked wolven and strange free humans who had randomly traipsed into their city as if from a mythical story.

About halfway down the hill, with its winding street, they spotted another entirely new sight—a giant wolfan skeleton carried a huge raw chunk of marble on its shoulder and was minded by a smaller eight-foot wolfan that looked rather young.

Jengo edged away from the sight. "Is that ... is that thing undead?"

Rogor relayed the question to Kepwa, but with additional words. Kepwa in turn replied with a long string of growling phrases. "Their people consider it an honor to be brought back from the dead to serve the living once again," Rogor translated. "The undead are a simpler form of themselves, of course, with no memory of their previous lives. But they are honored nonetheless in the same way you lowlanders honor your ancestors."

"So that's how they integrate necromancy with their culture," Augum noted.

Leera suppressed a smile. "Imagine re-animating eighty-five-year-old Grandpa Cletus so that he could continue slaving away on the farm." She used the tip of the horn to poke Augum in the ribs. "Hey, mister, if this knowledge ever makes it to Sithesia, you do *not* have my permission to reanimate me just so that I can keep doing … whatever it is I was doing prior."

After settling his chortle, Augum, dying of curiosity, touched his throat and temple and recast Tongues before asking Kepwa in Wolven, "What else does your society use necromancy for?"

Kepwa replied with a run-on sentence, and Augum found himself wincing, trying to understand, yet only caught a handful of words before giving up and turning to Rogor for the translation.

"They have many uses," Rogor replied and asked a question of his own. He and Kepwa quickly got into a rather amiable—if that was the way to describe calm growling—conversation on the subject.

Despite paying close attention, Augum failed to keep up and had to wait for Rogor to translate.

"They have many uses for necromancy," Rogor repeated as they slowly trailed the lumbering undead wolfan, whose minder by then had noticed her followers and was constantly gawking back at them out of interest. "Warfare is the biggest use. They use necromantic spells in battle, which includes reanimating the dead and sending them in to aid the vanguard—is that the lowlander word for front line of attack?"

"It is," Augum confirmed. "What else did Kepwa say?" he pressed, not wanting to get sidetracked.

"Besides using necromancy as an honorable afterlife, which is permanent until the undead is slain once again, usually in battle, they also use necromancy to reinvigorate much like healing, but I do not quite understand that portion of the explanation. From what I *do* understand, they use necromancy against prisoners who have done great wrongs, to intimidate those that need intimidating, and to root out spies."

"Spies?" the four Arcaners chorused at once.

"Yes, all kingdoms on this continent use spies, but I do not understand how as his explanation got complex."

A clinking sound interrupted their conversation. Augum turned to find a gnarled old woman sniffing at his feet. She was on all fours and dressed in filthy rags, and a long chain was attached to an iron collar around her neck. That chain was held by a sneering wolfan dressed in pristine silken cloth the color of sunset, which shimmered gently in the torchlight.

The group stopped as the old lady went from sniffing Augum's shoes to Leera's and then Jengo's and Olaf's. When a stray young wolf trotted by to investigate, she bared her teeth at it and growled, and the wolf shot off with a yelp.

"She's probably fifty but looks like Mrs. Stone's age," Leera said. "Look how callused her knees and hands are. My heart hurts for her."

Upon hearing Leera talk, the woman bared black and broken teeth at her and scooted a few steps away before crawling back to sniff at her robe. Leera awkwardly petted her shaggy head, and the woman recoiled once more.

Olaf rubbed the palm of a hand with his thumb. "Um … anyone else have like a thousand questions about human slaves? Because I, for one, am feeling distinctly uncomfortable."

The noble with the chained slave growled something at Rogor, who raised his snout and snarled. The noble swallowed, reined in his slave, and hurried away whilst repeatedly glancing over his shoulder.

"What did he say to you?" Augum asked as they continued on.

Rogor's snarl remained as he replied, "That I am a barbarian and my own slaves appear of a higher caste than me and he feels humiliated on my behalf."

"Have you thought about putting on some clothes?"

"Then I would not represent my highland people. We do not need clothes. Our fur keeps us warm even in the harshest wind. Our fur grows thick and strong, but theirs is weak and brittle. Look to their coats and how they are slathered in oils to mask the thinness of the hairs. They would not survive a day in the highlands."

He spat on the ground toward one of the guards, who had his back turned as he protected their group. But one of the female guards noticed and growled something to her fellow guard. The guard turned around and bared his teeth, and Rogor bared his in reply, until Kepwa snapped off a command and the guard reluctantly resumed his outward watch.

"But their constant disrespect is indeed gnawing on my nerves," Rogor muttered. "They display it in many forms invisible to you lowlanders." He grimaced as he considered the matter.

Leera snorted. "How do you think we humans feel whenever we hear your lot talk about us *lowly* lowlanders?" When the wolven flashed her a fearsome glare, she quickly cleared her throat and waddled away to stand on Augum's other side. She adjusted her hold on the horn and leaned into him, whispering, "This is neat and all, but I miss our castle and our kingdom."

"I miss all that too," Augum replied, wondering how everyone back in Solia was faring. He imagined their friends either attending the academy or training or feasting or running the Arcaner order. He'd long lost track of time, yet his heart felt attached to his homeland even at this great distance.

As they wandered back to the bottom of the city hill, Augum's stomach rumbled. "Anyone else up for some grub?" he asked. Upon hearing a chorus of grunts and snorts of agreement, he suggested they return to the ship's galley.

Kepwa, picking up on the change in mood, growled something to Rogor.

"Our minder suggests we try local fare," Rogor translated.

"Does he have a favorite spot?" Olaf asked.

Rogor asked Kepwa, who replied by gesturing with a flat paw toward the docks where their ship sat moored alongside others. "There is a tavern—I think that is the word. He invites seven of our number to attend, as the number is considered fortuitous among the wolfan. He said something else about entertainment but I am not sure of the wording used."

Leera, Olaf and Jengo looked to Augum with the same silent question.

"I'm fine with that," Augum replied, and they smiled. He was mighty curious as to what a wolfan tavern was like.

Rogor passed on that they would attend and they walked onward, discussing who else to invite from the ship. Soon they spotted their crew mingling on the deck, watching the city and the many wolfan and their slaves that had congregated on the dock to gawk at the strange visitors from overseas. The guards and Kepwa joined the city guard, who kept the mob away from the gangplanks. Everyone on board was relieved to have the four Arcaners and Rogor back, and questioned them about every detail, especially the strange horn Leera had brought back.

"It's just a keepsake," she lied, quickly waddling off to deposit it in her cabin before returning.

Meanwhile, Augum took turns replying to the others and even showed them the map, which drew many oohs and aahs and prompted a whole discussion on the continent and cultures and various races that humans thought belonged to myth.

"This is going to change history," Tammy noted.

"If we get back to tell it," Alanna replied rather darkly.

"On a different topic," Leera sang, throwing open her arms. "Six of our number have been invited to a tavern! Oh, and Rogor of course."

"Any volunteers to attend?" Augum asked. Every single hand went up—except for the captain's, for the man understood his duty was first to the ship. "Right, so we expected that," Augum said with an amiable chortle. "Ollie, you're coming," he said, wanting his best friend as company alongside his woman.

"I can stay back," Jengo offered. "I'm exhausted and have seen enough for today."

"I can stay back too as I'm quite tired," Leera added, though she bit her lip and teetered back and forth as if hoping Augum would reject that idea out of hand. He was about to do just that when Jez blurted, "Great, because Leo and I want a break from this floating privy," and she hooked an arm around the bald pirate's leopard-spot tattooed neck. "Thanks for your sacrifice, monkey," she added, rubbing salt into Leera's wound.

"I too would like to go, please," Alanna said and had the tact to look to Leera and say, "If that is all right with you, that is."

"Er ... of course it is," Leera blurted, albeit with a red face as if being caught out.

"Lovely, thank you." Alanna then cleared her throat gently.

"Oh, you probably want this," Leera said, and removed her copper sash and reluctantly handed it over, with Jengo handing his over to Jez.

"We want to go, we want to go!" Limpet sang, jumping up and down alongside Dirt.

"No chance," Jez snapped, throwing her ambassadorial sash over her head. "You two are *way* too young for taverns, let alone ones on a potentially hostile continent. Go and ... use that fancy ring to try to reach your old mentor or something."

Their faces fell.

"That stopped being possible ages ago," Limpet said, adding in a mutter, "I hate you ..."

"*We* hate you," Dirt corrected, the pair nodding together.

"Well, *I* love you lot," Jez sang back. "Come give momma a kissy-kissy," and she reached out with both arms, which caused the pair to shriek and run away. "Too easy," she said, dusting off her hands.

"I'm coming," Digby declared just as Carter opened his mouth to surely volunteer himself as well. "I need a break from this hovel too," he added and stared at Augum expectantly.

Augum sighed but nodded, feeling it was important to keep the peace amongst the crew. Besides, it would do Digby good to witness a whole other race and their culture.

As they organized themselves, Rogor spoke to the captain, who in turn went below. The old saltblood soon returned carrying a leather pouch, which he handed over to Rogor.

"We ought to at least offer to pay for our meal," Rogor explained upon catching Augum's eye. "Also, I thought it over and I ..." and for the first time that Augum could recall, he witnessed the proud wolven hesitate. "I wish to purchase clothing," Rogor blurted in a most uncharacteristic mumble. "It is best they see me on equal terms for me to be effective in my duties for our two kingdoms."

"Wise decision," Augum said, wanting to be supportive.

"Hey, toss that minder of ours this," Leera said, pressing a coin purse into Augum's hand. "Payment for the you-know-what—" and she flicked her head toward the cabins, referring to the horn.

"I was going to ask you to come," Augum said.

"I know. I was too slow on the uptake." She kissed his cheek, whispered, "Don't have *too* much fun without me," and she winked.

The giddy lot of humans gathered behind Rogor, who led the way to Kepwa at the bottom of the gangplank. Rogor ceremoniously offered his pouch to the minder, who unsurprisingly declined by waving both paws, acting offended that Rogor would even offer.

Augum took the opportunity to offer Leera's pouch on her behalf. This too Kepwa declined, until Rogor explained it was payment for the horn, and Kepwa pocketed it. Rogor then sheepishly explained something else, and Kepwa snorted in the same manner Leera would have. Nonetheless, he gestured for three of his guards to accompany Rogor, and the four departed in a different direction.

"Where the heck is that mangy ball of fur going?" Leo asked, an arm twined around Jez's waist.

Augum couldn't help his lips from thinning upon seeing Leo's hand caress his mentor's waist. He wasn't sure he was ready for such an out-of-the-blue pairing. Even though the rational part of him knew it was none of his business, the emotional part was grossed out—and rather annoyed.

Augum thus didn't respond despite knowing Rogor was going to purchase suitable clothes. Instead he silently led the group of five humans in following Kepwa and his guards to the tavern, located on the docks near the boat.

The building was constructed from dark wood, with large timbers crossing over tarred roof tiles like giant swords. The exterior was decorated with huge orange-colored glass fish floats and pronged rusting fishing spears. A swinging melody floated out from within, with variously pitched howls singing along to the foreign tune.

Kepwa ordered his guards to remain outside as he beckoned the humans to enter after him. They walked through a towering entrance into a smoky establishment with a twenty-foot ceiling. The floor was at the waterline, meaning they had to descend a series of rickety steps to it. The bar area surrounded a central rectangle of water, where wolfan fished with bamboo poles, all puffing on double- and triple-bowled clay pipes, regularly pumping out multi-colored puffs of smoke that stank of seaweed, sweet fruit, and an unfamiliar spicy myrrh.

The rest of the lower establishment was built not out of wood, but out of rock, giving it a cave-like atmosphere. Various holes were cut out of this rock and fitted with rough glass windows and shutters, all of which looked out onto the water from below the docks. Torches sputtered in ornamental cages, tables were wolfan height—way too tall for humans— and instead of chairs there were stools so that the wolfan's tails could wag freely.

Those tails stopped their wagging upon the entrance of the humans. Wolfan crowded the place, but not a single human slave was present. The atmosphere grew tense as the assembled wolfan gaped uncomprehendingly at what they were seeing—a group of humans dressed in relatively fine attire, standing erect as opposed to a typically hunched slave, teeth and hair straight and clean, and their necks absent of a slave collar.

Kepwa raised his snout and growled out a single phrase, albeit adding a dismissive flick of the paw at his human guests. Slowly the patrons returned to their conversations, though mutely so and with many backward glances at the humans making their way down to a table. Except they were so short relative to the tabletop that Kepwa gave an order, and a set of stools—about standard human table height—were brought over.

An eared wolfan female in a flowing and sparkly silver gown wandered over carrying an empty tray. She inclined her head at Kepwa, who said something in Wolfan before turning to Augum and saying something else.

"Let me catch up," Augum blurted and for the umpteenth time went through the motions of casting Tongues, thinking he ought to keep practicing, especially with Rogor absent to translate. "Er, can you repeat what you said?" he said in broken Wolven, using only two words of the Wolfan tongue he had picked up from conversation.

The server yelped as she took an involuntary step back, a paw on her chest. She looked uncertainly to Kepwa, who pressed the lips of his snout together in mild annoyance. "Yes, *gobwat* learning *wolfa* tongue," he told her. "These from far," he added, or so Augum thought he said as he was having a difficult time understanding the phrasing. That was how it went, with Augum wincingly trying to comprehend their language, oft filling in the gaps with assumptions.

"Want what they want?" the server asked.

"Want what they say they want," Kepwa replied. "Ask you."

The server turned to Augum. "Ask what want you want."

Augum blinked. "Is there, er, a menu or something ...?"

Even the server winced upon hearing him chop up her language. "Want what *fish*-fish. Fish want?"

"Fish it is," he replied, hoping his meaning was understood. To make sure, he exaggerated a nod whilst loudly saying, "Fish, yes. *Fish*-fish."

After Kepwa threw in some quickly growled instructions, the server left.

"What was all that growling about?" Jez asked.

"I think I just ordered us fish."

"Very impressive, Commander," Alanna said, smiling so warmly it made Augum uncomfortable. Suddenly he regretted not fighting for Leera to come along.

"Positively *feral* if you ask me," Digby muttered under his breath, a remark all ignored.

Rogor finally joined them, now wearing a plain cream-colored linen garment with a single blue embroidered flower in the middle of the chest. Although the garment did not at all suit his grumpy countenance, it fit in well with the locals.

As he walked over to their table, there came a menacing growl from the bar area, and their heads turned to see one of the wolfan chefs battling with a bamboo rod until he hauled up a juicy pink fish large enough to feed ten humans. The wolfan grabbed it with a paw, slapped it onto a huge butcher's block, set down the rod, grabbed a monstrous cleaver, and in one fluid motion chopped off the head—all whilst puffing on a triple-bowled pipe. After removing the hook, he threw the head into a lidded barrel, then used a long knife to expertly fillet the fish into thick strips of meat.

"All right, now I'm absolutely *famished*," Jez said. "What do they have for drinks? Do they have wine? Can one of you ask them?"

Rogor inquired about the matter to Kepwa, but the minder waved the question aside, which told Augum he'd already sorted the matter out.

Sure enough, the server returned with a tray of eight large ox horns sitting on iron stands. These horns were relatively small for wolven and wolfan, but positively monstrous relative to a human, and it took each of them holding a horn with both hands just to slot it out of its stand.

Kepwa raised his horn ever so slightly as he gave a nod.

"Glad to see some common gestures," Leo said, raising his horn with both hands. "Cheers, mate."

Everyone raised theirs in turn, and they tipped them to their mouths. Augum felt a malty explosion of spices on his tongue that fizzed so much it felt like it burned his throat. Although it was harsh, it tasted surprisingly good. Not wanting to hold such a heavy tankard, he slotted it back into its iron sheath and leaned back against a table leg that rose behind him like a pillar.

Jez and Leo drank the longest, each daring the other to quit first. Jez choked on hers in short order, and Leo let his down with a triumphant grin. "Not too shabby, lass," he said. "Not too shabby at all."

"So do these furballs have any respect for us at all?" Digby asked, glancing around the tavern. "They're eyeing us up like they want to fillet us to the bone like that fish."

In that moment, the chef threw all the fish steaks he'd sliced onto a giant iron griddle, and a plume of smoke threw out a flavorful scent.

When no one replied, Digby smacked his gums at them like a hoodlum, scowled, and raised the horn to his lips. This time he drank greedily, downing more in one go than Leo. "How do you like *that*?" he snapped to them upon finishing more than half his horn, which he kept hold of with one hand despite having to strain to do so.

Augum, realizing it had been a bad idea to bring Digby without Carter, threw Olaf a gentle elbow.

"On it, boss," Olaf mouthed. He sidled up to Digby, threw an arm around his shoulder which was promptly rebuffed, and began a diatribe on the efficiency of servants of the royal court back at home, a topic which soon had Digby's eyes glazing over.

Meanwhile, Jez and Leo got handsy with each other, grinning stupidly and winking and being wholly inappropriate, or so Augum thought despite the glaring hypocrisy.

Kepwa swirled the contents of his horn as he watched them all, with most of his gaze reserved for Rogor, who drank his tankard in oblivious slurping sips that made Kepwa's eye twitch.

"Why do you think he's watching him so much?" Alanna whispered whilst taking a conservative sip, sidling up to Augum and bumping his shoulder.

"Good question," he whispered into his horn, taking a conservative sip of his own. "Maybe he's watching him like a Solian would a Henawa upon their first meeting. The shock of meeting such a strange and foreign culture and whatnot …"

"You get the feeling he's a spy?"

"Absolutely. Wouldn't be doing his job if he wasn't."

Their food arrived on two gigantic silver platters laden with plates. Orange yams with milky butter, a type of soft yellow bread, something that looked like asparagus, and of course juicy orange fish steak, all seasoned with spices, one of which was certainly rosemary, another salt, and another still a red pepper, but the remainder were mysteries.

For cutlery, they were given two-pronged forks the size of small pitchforks and serrated knives the size of shortswords. Everyone, Rogor included, dove into the fare like beasts, with the humans particularly savoring the delectable morsels after such a long voyage.

Olaf sang the highest praise, constantly toning things like, "Mmm, mmm, *mmm*!" and "Oh. My. *Gods*. This is divine. It's like salmon but slightly caramelized. De. Li. Cious!"

Halfway through their bountiful meal, Digby, cheeks bulging with fish steak, took a slurping sip of his horn and loudly said, "Who would have thought talking dogs could make something decent?"

Rogor, who'd been standing beside him, abruptly snatched Digby's throat—and squeezed, popping the food out of his mouth. "Wretched cur, you *dare* insult our hosts in such a way?"

Digby's response was to freeze like a deer, horn still clutched in both hands. Everyone else shouted for Rogor to let Digby go, which he did with a disdainful twist of the paw, and Digby fell backward on his butt, spilling ale all over himself. It was telling how unpopular he was when not one person helped him up.

Kepwa asked what had happened, and when Rogor spat out a growling response, Kepwa snarled at Digby, who by then had hauled himself back to his feet by grabbing Alanna's robe.

"You forget yourself, *sir*, now let go of me," she hissed through clenched teeth. "By insulting our hosts, you have poorly represented our people and ought to return to the ship forthwith."

"You dare," he said at no one in particular, face as crimson as the fish steak sliding down his robe. "You have humiliated me for the last time," and he guzzled what remained of his horn, whirled on his heel, and stumbled off.

"I'll make sure he gets back safe and sound," Jez said with a heavy sigh.

"We both will," Leo blurted, winking at Jez.

They departed while cheekily jabbing at each other physically and verbally, ignoring the patrons who gawked at them as if they were the strangest oddities they'd ever seen.

"That lowlander is disrespectful and has been getting on my nerves for some time," Rogor growled upon meeting Augum's eye. "You would be wise to keep him away from me."

"I understand," Augum replied, wishing he could keep Digby away from everyone.

"Wiser still would be to offer him as a sacrifice of appeasement."

"Now *that* I will not do," Augum replied, drawing a distasteful smack of the gums from Rogor. Feeling more confident with their tongue after doing a lot of careful listening, Augum nonetheless put a hand to his throat and temple and incanted the Tongues spell for Wolfan, then said to Kepwa, "Forgive our friend as he is drunk and mourning the loss of his brother." The words were such a jumble, however, that Kepwa had to look to Rogor to translate what Augum had meant, which Kepwa accepted with a grunting nod.

With the spell still active, Augum thought of a question to ask the minder. "What do your people think of the lands overseas?"

After a thoughtful sip of his horn, Kepwa replied, "Long lands big with dragons. No possible to make sail."

Rogor, able to understand the dialect on a deeper level, clarified. "The wolfan believe that our lands are teeming with dragons and have been infested as such since they last visited eons ago."

Augum traded a meaningful look with Olaf, for there was a time in Arcaner history when their numbers in the dragon rank had been plentiful. He wondered if this sort of knowledge could come in handy should the wolfan ever decide, as the gargoyles had, to make sail and plunder human lands for personal gain ...

They continued finishing their meal, the pace of which had slowed substantially as the portion size was for the stomach of a twelve-foot wolfan. The staff began to clear an area filled with stools, revealing a sandy floor. In no time a pair of drunken wolfan began to wrestle, growling with laughter at each other, until one snorted a laugh of fire — and singed the other's snout. The offended one in turn blew a plume of ice that froze the offender's snout shut. Unable to speak, the latter grunted and moaned and then tackled the first one, and the pair got to roughhousing once more. This drew a drunken crowd, and soon they were trading pebbles, betting with each other.

Another wolfan hopped up on a low stage and began playing, of all instruments, a flute—and a tiny one at that. It was a warbling melody that sounded like a bird call, until it morphed into something rather fun, if not strange in its jumpiness. A wolfan grabbed a huge hide drum from somewhere in back and hopped on stage, and then a third wolfan grabbed a curving stringed instrument as tall as a human and began strumming it. Some wolfan in the now full tavern howled along to a melody they all knew, and the atmosphere shifted to one of a party, albeit an exotic one straight out of a sailor's yarn.

The chatter within the tavern increased, and Augum used it to practice the Tongues spell on the wolfan, picking up the occasional new word after seeing a gesture or mannerism accompany it, or even the tone. The spell greatly facilitated learning in this regard, allowing for relatively rapid improvement—as long as one was paying careful attention.

"Are they that interesting, sir?" Alanna asked with a cheeky smile whilst fiddling with her horn.

"Just doing my duty," Augum absently replied, trying to understand the conversation of a nearby group that kept eyeing them.

Meanwhile the sandy area drew more competitors, some wrestling, others summoning elemental armor and weapons and playfully hacking away at their opponent's armor, obviously not trying to hurt the other.

Jez and Leo had yet to return, which didn't surprise Augum as he suspected they had retired to one of their cabins. Olaf kept sipping his horn and eyeing Alanna's unfinished plate, while Rogor lobbed Kepwa the occasional question about the wolfan, all of which Kepwa responded to with little actual information, which was interesting to Augum—and a little suspicious.

Alanna kept trying to catch Augum's attention, but he became aware of a particularly large wolfan side-eyeing their group. He'd come in recently and was the only one with a human slave, who he kept chained close by. The slave was dressed in hardened leather and was riddled with scars, actually had muscles, and eyed Augum's group—particularly Augum, as if sizing him up for a fight. That wolfan eventually switched to full-on staring, until he paw-punched one of his buddies on the shoulder and the pair sauntered over.

"These your slaves?" the first asked Rogor in Wolfan, flicking a dismissive claw between Augum, Alanna and Olaf. "Why they nice cloth?" His speech was more erudite than Augum could comprehend, but he got the gist of it.

"They are a free people," Rogor replied in Wolven, taking a casual sip of his horn.

"They fight?" The first wolfan tugged on the chain of his slave, who grunted as he taunted Augum with a grin.

"Yes, they can fight," Rogor said.

"I not know accent," the wolfan said, throwing in a couple growled words Augum failed to comprehend.

Rogor set his horn down. "That is because I come from the same land."

"The foreigners," the wolfan's buddy said. "We want a *chagga*. Have show. My slave on yours."

Rogor looked to Kepwa, who said, "*Chagga* is challenge skill. Choose one if want meet challenge." He raised a claw in warning. "His slave arena slave."

"What happens if we do not accept the challenge?" Augum asked in his best imitation of their language.

Hearing him speak caused the two strangers to howl with laughter.

"Then dishonor your people," Kepwa replied. "Show wolfan all humans weak. Wolfan talk."

Augum nodded, understanding the implication that word would spread of their weakness, something he could not risk with a ship in port. "What are the rules of such a duel?" he asked.

"Simple. You kill or be kill."

"What are they saying, Commander?" Alanna pressed, Olaf leaning in to listen.

Augum told them.

"Well, that's a little grim, eh?" Olaf muttered. "Bet you weren't expecting to have a nice time at a tavern in some exotic kingdom only to be asked to lop off a head mid meal, were you, Three Toes?"

"What if I control it?" Augum said under his breath.

"What, you mean, like, make it a slow-motion lopping, or—"

"No, I mean, tire him out or something. Paralyze, that sort of thing. Make it so he loses by default. Show strength through control. Give them a proper taste."

Olaf mouthed, "Ohhh," then punched Augum's chest and winked. "Earn respect the old-fashioned way. You always were the smarter one."

"I accept your challenge," Augum said, not realizing he'd lost focus on the Tongues spell, so his words failed to translate into Wolfan. Instead, he flashed a thumbs-up, yet the gesture still had Kepwa turning to Rogor to confirm it with a wolven growl. Upon hearing this, the slave-owning wolfan flexed all his muscles and howled in delight at the ceiling, and suddenly all the wolfan in the entire tavern did the same—except for Kepwa, who looked on with steel eyes. Meanwhile, the arena slave repeatedly smashed a fist into his muscled chest whilst barking at Augum.

Olaf snorted at Augum. "He thinks this is going to be a physical matchup."

Alanna, on the other hand, was not as enthused. "Forgive me, Commander, but is this wise?"

"I don't know," Augum replied, "but maybe it's time they took us humans more seriously, no?" He particularly wanted to try one idea to see how the wolfan reacted.

"I would never have the daring," Alanna said. "But I understand, and I see why you are a commander." She forced a worried smile.

Everyone made their way to the sandy area, a thirty-foot square surrounded by a crowd of wolfan. By then, word must have spread of the newcomers, for the beasts muttered and gestured at the finely dressed humans. Some tapped their necks, likely noting the absence of slave collars, and others pointed at the starlit horizon through the window, indicating that the humans had come from overseas. The latter was dismissed with visceral gesticulations and elaborate tail wags, giving Augum the impression they were the subject of wild rumors.

The wolfan unchained his slave and pushed him to one side of the makeshift arena, while Augum mentally prepared himself on the sidelines, Olaf and Alanna beside him, Rogor nearby with Kepwa.

"Don't do anything drastic that will scare them into hanging us, good sir," Alanna said.

"Depends what you mean by drastic," Augum replied, removing his ambassadorial sash.

"She means don't rip his guts out and whip them around your head like some crazed barbarian," Olaf threw in, taking Augum's sash and placing it over his own head.

Augum rolled his eyes at them and stepped onto the sandy arena, stretching out his limbs and neck and rolling his shoulders and jumping up and down in place. Having been stuck on a ship for ages, he was ready for some real exertion.

A ten-foot bartender, a female with pierced hoops dangling from her ears and a leather apron, stepped out to stand between them. She made a short speech to the crowd, gesturing to the bar. Augum got the impression she was more interested in selling drinks than the entertainment at hand. Some took bets, others craned their necks to watch over each other's tall shoulders.

Dwarfed by these huge beasts, Augum was only thankful they hadn't attacked his ship right at port. This was his chance to garner respect for his group as free human guests. And it was a chance, if he played it right, to discover more about what the wolfan thought of them.

As the female flicked a dismissive hand at Augum and stepped out of the way, the slave, who been handed a curved blade and a battered tin buckler, shot forth. He screamed a war cry as he ran and swung his blade. Augum countered with a simple backward-yanking motion, pulling the squat warrior's leg forth, sending him tumbling awkwardly to the sandy floor.

Howls of laughter went up, the sort that made Augum believe that the wolfan thought the slave had tripped over his own feet.

To make a point, Augum took the opportunity to formally bow to his opponent and summon ten lightning rings around his arm, causing surprised yips and howls to rip through the wolfan. Some even leaped away, trading uncertain looks with their cohorts, while others scratched at their snouts and furrowed their brows, perplexed by the sight.

Not wanting to let them think it a mere gimmick, Augum resolved to continue making ever-escalating demonstrations. He thus let the warrior get to his feet and swing his blade in lethal arcs before making a second yanking motion, incanting, "*Disablo!*"

The blade twirled out of the warrior's grip. Augum flicked a hand and suspended the hilt in midair—just out of reach of the flailing warrior. As he desperately jumped up and down trying to grab it, the wolfan howled and yelped and grumbled and shook their heads and gaped with open snouts. Some punched their neighbor with a paw, others traded pebbles.

Augum then delighted—or perhaps terrified, it was hard to tell—the crowd by flying that blade about the warrior like a circling bird. The warrior kept flapping his arms at it, trying to smack it down or grab it. Augum guided it along, then abruptly reversed his hand motion, twisted it downward, and snapped his hand forth. The blade turned about, dipped, and smacked the warrior in the face with the flat side, sending him stumbling backward in a daze.

The howls and yips and yelps got so loud that Augum could barely hear himself think, but they also reminded him of the arena crowds during his time as a student in the academy. Part of him enjoyed that roar, for it quickened his blood and sharpened his thinking—and made him think of home.

The warrior kept glancing between the blade and Augum as he tentatively approached. Once near enough, he made one more effort to grab the hilt—and simultaneously kicked sand with his bare foot. It was a tactic he'd obviously used before as his aim could not have been more perfect. Suddenly finding himself blind, a wincing Augum then heard the warrior snatch the blade and the sound of feet rushing forth in the sand. Without missing another heartbeat, Augum shoved at the air, roaring, "*Baka!*" sending the warrior flying into the crowd.

Through blurry eyes, Augum saw that he'd sent him into his own master, which caused another howling round from the wolfan crowd.

A squinting Augum reached out, telekinetically grabbed hold of a horn of ale, and floated it out of its iron sheath and over to his waiting hand. He quickly splashed his face and wiped it with the sleeve of his robe. His eyes stung, but he could at least see properly now.

As the warrior got back to his feet and crept forth, waving his buckler and sword threateningly whilst baring rotten teeth, Augum made an unsheathing motion from his hip, incanting, "*Summano arma grau!*"

A longsword made of crackling lightning appeared in his fist. At the same time, he summoned his crest shield and flared his eyes with lightning. The wolfan responded by acting like wild monkeys as they jumped up and down, tails flailing about so much that Olaf protectively held a cringing Alanna lest she get trampled or thwacked.

Amidst this chaos and Augum's display, the warrior hesitated. Augum swung his blade in a figure-eight pattern and walked forth, flaring his eyes brighter. The warrior retreated — only for his growling master to kick him forward. Forced to engage, the warrior swung, and his blade whistled with lethality. Augum placed his shield before the swing. The moment he felt the distinctive *thwack* of the blade smacking his shield, he withdrew it and sliced with his longsword. The seasoned warrior expertly pivoted and parried, and there came a sizzling noise as Augum's lightning blade cleaved the flimsy buckler in two.

The warrior gasped and sprang back, his buckler falling onto the sand like two halves of a pie. He shook his arm and swung his blade in his own figure-eight pattern before shooting a foot forth — and the blade. Augum, trained to handle such strikes, crossed with a parry and the blades connected with a shower of sparks. But the blade survived, and the opponents sang a steel-and-lightning melody of blade strikes, with neither daring to make a killing blow — the warrior because Augum had a shield that did not allow him to get close, and Augum because he did not want to kill or maim the man.

Augum thought that the warrior's blade arts were in fact better than his. Were it not for the warrior's shorter reach and lack of shield, the slave would have likely bested him.

After sending another shower of sparks into the air, the warrior, frustrated by his lack of progress, once more kicked sand in Augum's face. But Augum was ready, and he closed his eyes against the sand and, whilst letting go of his lightning blade, once again shoved at the air, roaring, "*Baka!*"

His opponent had learned this trick too, and he ducked the invisible shove—and thrust forth. Augum parried by slicing his shield across the blade in time to knock it away. Annoyed, he pointed and stabbed at the air, telekinetically poking and prodding at the warrior, who awkwardly danced about as he tried to regain control of his limbs. During a moment when Augum saw maximum vulnerability, he made a quick yanking motion, incanting, "*Disablo!*" and the warrior's blade was once more sent twirling toward the ceiling.

As the warrior reached for it, Augum kept using his index fingers to telekinetically poke and prod at his limbs. Unused to the power of Telekinesis or how it worked, the now weaponless and shieldless warrior became a marionette on invisible strings that Augum controlled, dipping and dancing and fumbling about, until Augum poked one of his feet into the other and he was sent twirling to the sand in a jumbled mess of twisted limbs.

The tavern flailed as a wild throng, but Rogor and Kepwa watched with tentative unease. Perhaps they thought Augum was showboating, but he had a plan, which he decided to implement when the warrior jumped back onto his stubby feet and unsheathed a tiny hidden dagger from his belt. Sensing the climactic moment had come, Augum stepped back and drew a complex shape in the air, incanting, "*Summano elementus minimus draco!*"

A crackling wagon-sized dragon appeared between him and the warrior.

The place went pin-drop silent. Then, as if struck by a potent Fear spell, the wolfan lost it. The closest howlingly scrambled off so rabidly that some extended their claws and slashed at their neighbors in desperation to get away. Some hunkered behind tables, dipping their head about as if expecting an attack, and others crouched to cower in place, arms covering their heads as they whined like wounded dogs, perhaps praying to be saved or for the gods to protect them or who knew what.

Even Kepwa retreated, paws up and snout open and eyes wide as he gaped at the crackling dragon. That left Olaf still holding Alanna, and Rogor, who stood looking about in confusion.

The warrior-slave, for his part, dropped to his knees, pressed his forehead to the sand, and thrust his arms toward Augum and the dragon, which floated in place, its wings beating with relaxed ease.

Augum felt a rush of power, as if they considered him a god. The shadow behind the curtain of his mind, which he'd been training to suppress, peeked onto the scene and urged him to flex this muscle of godly perception. To rise as a dragon and revel in watching these arrogant wolfan, who considered themselves so superior, soil themselves in their terror.

Yet something like that was already happening, and Augum realized it could be catastrophic. What would casting a dragon mean for his group and the ship? What if he had accidentally transgressed into what the wolfan considered blasphemy? In his attempt to garner his lot wolfan respect, he might have overplayed his hand.

"Draco—sit," Augum thus commanded, and the dragon landed on the arena floor, where it proceeded to tuck in its wings and loaf like a giant cat made of lightning. It sat watching the prostrate warrior with a crackling menace that waited to be called upon with a mere command.

The place once again fell silent as the remaining wolfan edged away, with most having dipped out of the tavern and run off to who knew where. Others crept toward the door, not a single one taking their eyes off either the dragon or Augum. Fearful whispers abounded. Just as Augum prepared to cast Tongues to try to settle them down, one of the wolfan said something. It was like a dam broke and the remainder fled for the exit.

"Wait!" Augum called after them. "We mean you no harm! Shoot, tell them!" he said to Rogor.

Rogor growled after those fleeing but he was ignored.

Only Kepwa and a few other bravely curious wolfan remained. That included the slave-owning wolfan, who was now bowing alongside his slave in the sand, both adjusting to always face Augum.

Augum pressed hands to his throat and temple, cast Tongues, and asked, "What happened?" He flicked a hand for Rogor to aid in translating as he did not trust his skill in their language, and Rogor then asked Kepwa the same question.

"A long time ago, we wolfan almost perished to the dragon," Rogor translated into Solian as Kepwa spoke, allowing for Augum to further bolster his skill with Tongues. "It is said that when our ancestors tried to settle a distant land, they were defeated by dragons, who then followed them home. A great battle unfolded that almost wiped out all the kingdoms at once. Only after striking a pact with the dragons did they return to their land, never to be seen again—as long as none of us ventured there. Since then, a prophecy has foretold the return of the dragon 'upon the hand of a human' if any of us ever dared to venture overseas and step onto their land."

Kepwa scrubbed the air with both paws, voice breaking with fear for the first time. "But you do not understand," Rogor translated on his behalf. "We thought you and your ship had come from an altogether different land. We even thought you were charlatans, or perhaps crazed or confused. None of us believed you were from *Endraga Ra*!"

"Wait, did he just say what I thought he said?" Augum interrupted, exchanging wild looks with Olaf and Alanna. "Endraga Ra?"

"Endraga Ra, yes," Rogor translated. "That is the name of the ancient mythological continent that all thought belonged to a cub's tale. It is not supposed to exist but as an allegory for wrongdoing and arrogance."

Kepwa pressed his paws together as if in prayer as he continued, with Rogor speaking overtop. "Now you have shown us that you are telling the truth. That you are from Endraga Ra and have come to exact vengeance for the breaking of the ancient pact. The prophecy is coming true."

Howls filtered into the tavern from outside.

"What's happening?" Augum asked in broken Wolfan.

Kepwa raised his snout and closed his eyes as he listened. "A call has arisen. They are uniting."

"Uniting for what?" Augum pressed. "For what!"

Kepwa looked away, face falling into shadow. "You know what."

"Annihilation," Augum whispered, looking to Olaf and Alanna, both of whom were pale as ghosts. Overplayed his hand? How about condemned them to a bloody death!

"To the ship," he commanded. "Draco—with me!" and he ran past the slave warrior and his master, both of whom adjusted their bowing positions to face Augum, with the master additionally loosing a yelp as if terrified of sudden execution.

"You must aid us in translating," Augum told Kepwa as he ran by. He stopped at the door to see Kepwa hesitating in place. "Do you understand!" Augum roared at him. "If you want to avert disaster, you will come with me and help translate! There is much you do not understand and much we have to gain if we get this right."

Still the wolfan hesitated, but as the howls spread into the city, Augum could wait no more, and he ran off, Olaf, Alanna and Rogor in tow.

A BEASTLY FEAST

BRIDGET

"No, not like that, like this," Bridget said, scraping the steel at a sharper angle against the flint, until sparks began to fly in earnest against the logs in the stove. The shower of sparks reminded her of a yard full of knights training with swords. "Do you see?"

"Yes, Momma," Sebastian mumbled, taking the flint and steel from her sooty hands and giving it a go. "Like this?"

"Yes, just like that. And you want to strike at the bottom of the tinder pile. Try to get some of the cotton to catch. But you can use anything that's thin and bone-dry. Parchment fiber, dead grass, or wood shavings, which I find are the best. Dry oak is particularly good."

She sat patiently by his side in the kitchen folding linen kitchen cloths she had washed and dried, long slices of morning sunlight lighting up the floor and warming their backs. The manor was silent but for the occasional tweet of a morning bird or the bored croak of a pond frog.

"Did they not teach you this sort of thing in school?"

"I was more of a book reader and wasn't really good with this sort of stuff." He absently pushed on his nose, a habit from having worn spectacles. "Teachers tried to get me to learn all sorts of practical stuff — chandling and hooping and tarring and carpentry and a hundred other things, but I guess I just didn't take to it. My big sister tried to teach me to fish and mend stuff, but then she got all frustrated and said I should just stick to my books. After Momma died Papa got drunk a lot but at least he bought me more books because he said Momma would want me to keep reading. He couldn't read much, being a fisherman and all, but he was real proud that I could."

Bridget felt a tingle of sorrow at the reminder that Sebastian belonged to another family. "Did your sister like reading?"

"She more took after Papa with the family trade, and so she didn't have much of a use for books. But she did like me reading adventure stories to her." He beamed at a sunny window. "She liked that a lot."

Bridget readjusted her pile of neatly folded cloths. "What about your mom?"

"She wasn't much of a reader either but she was awful nice." He smiled at her. "Much like you."

Bridget melted as she pressed a hand to her chest. "Aww, Sebby ..."

"You're my momma now and forever will be."

Bridget had to look away lest she choke up. She cleared her throat and recentered herself by smoothing her garment under her and picking up another cloth to fold. "Did you have a lot of friends at school?"

Sebastian idly played with the flint and steel. "No ..."

"Why's that?"

He shrugged. "I don't know."

"Wait, didn't you once say that you ..." She playfully needled his shoulder with a twisty finger. "... had a crush?"

Sebastian reddened like a summer apple. "Yeah, I guess. She was a bookworm like me with these awful thick spectacles—*much* thicker than mine were—and so she thought she was really, *really* ugly, but *I* thought she was ..."

"She was what?" Bridget pressed, already knowing the answer.

"Well, erm, kind of cute, I guess. But the other girls ..." His face scrunched. "They could be, I don't know, eww, you know?"

"Eww? What do you mean, *eww*?"

"Girls can be gross."

"So can boys."

He shrugged. "I guess."

"You may not think most girls are gross in a few years. In fact, you might think girls are the best thing that ever happened to boys."

Sebastian wilted. "I'll never see a pretty girl again."

"Don't say that."

"What? It's true. The other slaves are beyond gross. Besides, we're never leaving here ..."

Bridget leaned close to whisper, "Yes we are." She smiled, winked, and nodded at the steel. "Keep going."

"Yes, Momma." Sebastian's tongue stuck out from the corner of his mouth as he concentrated on striking the flint. His hands were clumsy though, his strikes uneven. "This is hard. I prefer reading. I miss books."

"I miss books too," Bridget said with a wistful sigh, pressing a folded linen onto her pile. After curling a lock of her hair around an ear, she nodded at his hands. "Longer and slower scrapes at a shallower angle."

"Okay."

The distant croak of the frog returned, reminding Bridget of what lay hidden in the pond—a box, and within that box, a map and now two sacred scrolls. One would allow a castle to fly, and the other, if she could make it work, would brand her flesh with the power to prevent a snuff.

"Look, it lit! It lit, it lit, it lit!"

"Now gently blow on it until it catches. There you go. Careful now."

Sebastian squealed in delight and clapped his hands together clumsily as he looked up at her with that dimpled smile that was so bright it almost made her believe they were living a peaceful country life in their very own kitchen. That smile, which caught the morning sun like the wings of a butterfly, made her imagine Olaf, as her husband, lounging in the living room with one of their other children sitting on his lap as he read a book to her. A gentle breeze would sweep through the house, bringing with it the sound of laughing and playing children.

Bridget closed her eyes and smiled at the fantasy. She imagined leading Sebastian by the hand and the family sitting down together to each read a cozy book. And later, their friends would visit, their own children in tow, and then an abundance of joyful chaos would ensue and they would trade war tales over glasses of white wine …

Bridget felt a tug on her slave dress.

"Momma," Sebastian whispered.

"Mmm?"

"They're here …"

Bridget jolted to find that the matriarch of the family was staring down at her from the kitchen entrance. Absorbed in the vision, Bridget hadn't heard her enter. Grak stood behind the winged girgoyle, his head low even though his mistress could not see him.

Bridget shot to her feet and bowed her head, gently prodding Sebastian to stand beside her and do the same.

The matriarch growled out a phrase, then flicked an impatient claw at Grak, who stepped forth.

"Today is special day," he said in his choppy gargoyle accent. "You prepare feast to …" Grak hesitated as he worked out the wording. "… to give thanks."

Bridget nodded her understanding despite not knowing what that meant. Give thanks to who? Gargoyle gods? Ancestors? Or the household itself?

"You make many dish," Grak went on. "Mistress and me go city to buy food for feast. You will start *potas* and *cotas* and set table for five hands," and he flashed his hand open five times.

Bridget, calculating she had to make enough for twenty-five gargoyles, once more nodded and the matriarch and Grak turned about and left. *Potas* and *cotas* were essentially giant potatoes and carrots large enough to satiate gargoyle hunger. She'd glimpsed farms of these whilst in the grip of the gargoyles as they flew over the land to one place or another.

"A feast? How exciting!"

"Yes, very exciting," Bridget replied tonelessly, trepidation entering her voice — as it always did when dealing with the matriarch, for she was a harsh mistress of a gargoyle, taking no nonsense of any sort, not even from her own children. Bridget had witnessed her smash the back of a hand into her daughter's snout for daring to talk a single growled word back. She ruled the manor with more of an iron fist than the captain, who was too busy with his duties to worry about matters of the household.

"Shall we set the table first, Momma? I'd much rather set the table now and peel potatoes later, if that's okay with you — seeing as we're the only ones here today and all, that is. Ooh, we can pretend it's our home! And there's a big old fire and we own hundreds — no, *thousands* — of really good books and it smells awful nice because we have fancy candles and we have pets — oh my gosh so many pets — "

" — including a dog named Sabby!"

"Yes and a cat and a rooster and a piggy and a duck and a frog and a hamster and even a pony!"

She mussed up his hair, cooing, "And they all love you, Sebby. All of them ..." Suddenly her heart felt as full as it could feel in that time and place, his infectious joy giving her a reprieve from the reality. That gave Bridget an idea, and she added, "Shall we invite our friends to the feast tonight?"

Sebastian gaped at her before clapping his hands whilst jumping up and down, singing, "Yes, yes, yes! All of our friends shall come tonight! And we will have music and dancing, and we can play games!"

Bridget's heart squeezed upon seeing Sebastian so happy, and she had to lean against the table and feel the peace of the sun upon her back to calm herself down. There was so much work to do that they ought not to get *too* carried away ...

She started by putting her stack of folded cloths away, then hung a pot of water over the fire to boil for their morning tea, made from a delectable and tangy orange leaf she did not know at home. But she couldn't resist the sight of a happy Sebastian and so she peeked out to find that he'd already set the hearth fire roaring and was dancing to imaginary music, twirling this way and that as he brought giant gargoyle cutlery to the table.

"Come dance, Momma!"

"Ohhh, alllll riiiight," Bridget sang and twirled into the room, and the pair danced, with Bridget closing her eyes and humming the dreamy tune to the famous ballad "Lover's Lure." Around and around she went, lost in the fantasy of their own beautiful sky home, until she bumped into a perching stool—and heard a great crash of dishes, for Sebastian had placed a stack of perfectly flat porcelain plates upon the stool.

"Oh no, I'm so sorry!" Sebastian cried, hands over his mouth. "Oh no," he whimpered, tears welling. "No, no, no, they're going to beat us to bits ..."

"It's all right. I should have watched where I was going," she said. "And they're not going to beat us because I can repair the damage. Watch," and she crouched over the mess of shards, spread her hands, and incanted, "*Apreyo.*"

Slowly some pieces tumbled back together to reform into plates, but because the spell had to fight through the suppressive collar, it took far longer than usual, so long in fact that Bridget had only gotten through half of the repair when a tall shadow formed in the open entranceway of the home.

Bridget immediately stood at attention and bowed her head, mumbling, "Forgive me, m'lady. It was an accident. I'll have it fixed in no time—" But she didn't get far as the mistress snapped at Grak, who in turn dropped his bundles of supplies and shot forth to smash Bridget's face with the back of his hand, sending her careening across the floor.

"Momma, Momma, Momma!" Sebastian cried out, running to her.

"No!" Bridget hissed at him. "You stand and be quiet! I'm fine! Momma's fine, you hear?"

"I'm sorry. I'm so sorry ..."

"It's fine. It's *fine* ..."

The mistress of the house growled another command, but this time Grak replied, albeit meekly. She snapped a word and Grak nodded. "You must repair, Ah-bee-gale," he said. "You must repair."

"Yes, I was working on it," Bridget said, cheek stinging fiercely, her dignity lying amongst the porcelain pieces on the floor.

"Hurry, Ah-bee-gale. Mistress angry."

"Yes, sorry, right away," and Bridget dropped to her knees before the shards and once more spread her hands, incanting, "*Apreyo.*" The pieces continued to slowly tumble and slide toward each other. "Hurry up, damn you," Bridget hissed at them, but that only broke her fragile collar-suppressed concentration, and the piece halted in place. "*Apreyo!*" she repeated, and the pieces resumed moving, even slower than before. Sensing the mistress was losing patience, Bridget took a shaky breath to calm herself before retraining her focus.

But it was too late, for the mistress barked another command and Grak delivered a stiff kick to her torso, sending her tumbling with a grunt of pain. She hit a wall, where she gasped for breath, for the kick had deflated her lungs.

Sebastian ran to her once more crying apologies and pleading for Grak to stop. Unable to speak on account of her lungs, she let him help her up to a sitting position, where she felt the shadow of Grak slide over her. "Ah-bee-gale repair before we next return," he instructed, adding in a gentle voice full of regret, "Ah-bee-gale must be more careful."

Bridget couldn't stop herself, wheezing, "You ... cowardly ... dog ..."

Grak stood over her, an enigma of a creature.

"I didn't mean that," Bridget blurted, coming to her senses as she scrambled to her feet, keeping Sebastian behind her and using her body as a shield. "I didn't ... I didn't mean that ..." But he had already turned his back on her and left to fetch the supplies he had left at the entrance. The mistress, in the mean, went to a cabinet on the far side of the room where she began to take stock of the remaining fine cutlery and plates and cloths required for that evening's feast.

Bridget and Sebastian silently helped Grak take the sacks of supplies to the kitchen. There Bridget raised a hand in apology, ready to say something to him, but he turned his back on her and departed without another word. It wasn't long until he left with the mistress for a second time to do who knew what.

Bridget sighed, grabbed two battered tin cups, dropped in dried orange leaves from a pouch, and poured in hot water. Then she watched the water steep whilst absently rubbing her aching torso.

"I'm so sorry, Momma," Sebastian squeaked, shuffling forth, hands wringing. "I didn't mean for that to happen ..."

"It's not your fault."

"Did ... did he hurt you?"

"I'm fine. Just a bit sore. You don't know this, but I've been through a lot worse in the war. A *lot* worse."

"Are you finally going to tell me what you did in the war? Being a warlock and all? That nice woman Naomi once whispered to me that you're really famous and many people know you and it made me feel dumb because we were made to take shelter in the cellar during the war and Papa didn't speak to what was happening outside he only said there was evil afoot and not to think too much about it lest it slither in through the cracks …"

"That's for the best. I'm glad your family hid. And maybe one day I'll tell you. But not today." She placed her hands on her hips and flicked her chin at Sebastian. "Why don't you start on the *potas* and *cotas*."

"You *sure* you're all right? You're wincing …"

"I told you that I am! Now you know where the peeler is, right?"

"Yes," he replied in a defeated voice and began shuffling his way there. "Top-left cupboard …"

"Sebby. Sebby—"

He whirled about, eyes on the floor. "What!"

"Sebby—look at me."

"Why?"

"Because I said so."

He briefly looked up at her and she caught a glint of watery eyes. "I don't like them hurting you, Momma …"

"I know, but I'm a tough bird. You understand? Momma's a tough bird. They could knock all my teeth out and I'd still keep my chin high." She went to walk up to him, but he stepped back. She nonetheless took a knee before him and tried to look into his face, but he kept looking away. "It's going to be fine, Sebby," she whispered. "Everything's going to be fine."

"Okay."

"Come here." Bridget opened her arms and wiggled her fingers. "Come give me a hug …"

Reluctantly, he shuffled up to her and allowed her to embrace him.

"Everything's going to be fine," she whispered, stroking his hair and back. "They haven't hurt me. They *can't* hurt me. Do you understand?" She stood him back, hands on his limp shoulders. "I truly have been through much, *much* worse. Like, starving-on-the-edge-of-death worse. Like, captured-behind-bars worse. Like, almost-dying-in-battle-countless-times worse. Do you understand?"

He nodded. "I guess."

She gently clasped his cheeks to force him to look at her, but he looked off to the side. She wiped his tears with her thumbs and kissed his forehead. She let go of him and smiled, but he did not smile back.

"Do you really … do you really believe we'll ever go home?"

"Of course we'll go home. Of *course* we'll go home!" She glanced to the kitchen entrance, making sure it was empty, and leaned closer to murmur, "There's a secret treasure map."

Sebastian's eyes widened. "There is? For real?"

"Yes, for real. It's hidden in a secret chest in the pond and will lead us to the treasure of freedom. As soon as I figure out how to get rid of these collars, you and me are going to embark on a grand adventure, just like in those books you love. We'll pack supplies and set off to trek across new lands and find us a proper ship and undertake a voyage over the ocean—and then find home."

"How will we keep safe?"

She pinched his nose between her knuckles and gave his head a little shake. "With arcanery. I've got a few tricks up my sleeve you don't know about yet. But I'll show you in time, when you're ready. We just have to be meticulous in the planning."

"What does *meticulous* mean?"

"It means we'll have to be very careful and take great care."

"When are we going?"

"Soon, Sebby. Soon. Okay? Look at me. Soon. *Okay?*"

"Okay, Momma. Okay ..."

She patted his cheeks. "Good boy." She kissed his forehead, repeating, "Good boy," and stood, flapping a hand toward the cabinets. "Go on then."

He shuffled to the cabinet, withdrew the peeler, and went to the sack of potatoes.

Bridget watched that shuffle and those droopy shoulders and sighed. The boy was losing faith. She ought to start preparing, which meant crafting a tent and a backpack for each of them, a small one for the boy and a large one for her, roomy enough for the tent, clothes, and spare food. Perhaps this eve's feast would allow her to stash some supplies ...

"Here, this will cheer you up," she said, placing a cup of tea before him. As he took a slurping sip, she took a sip from her own, cupping the tin with both hands and enjoying its aromatic fragrance.

Satisfied he would be busy for a time, she returned to the living area and resumed repairing the plates. With the task complete, she straightened out some of the dinnerware on the table, then went to the kitchen to finish her tea and help Sebastian peel. An hour or so later, Bridget heard Grak and their mistress return.

"Ah-bee-gale!" Grak hollered.

Bridget hurried into the living room area to see Grak holding a gigantic rope sack filled with crates and smaller burlap sacks on his shoulders. He lowered this unwieldy bundle to the floor and indicated for her to help him. The mistress ignored them both as she flew to the second-level mezzanine and vanished into a bedroom.

Meanwhile, Bridget worked to free the sacks and crates from the giant webbed bag, stacking the sacks together and the crates separately. Grak flapped a hand at the sacks and indicated the kitchen, and Bridget hauled one over her shoulders, tottered to the kitchen, and dumped it onto the counter.

Curious, she undid the twine and a bunch of purple eggplant-like vegetables rolled out. Another sack had red onions, another what looked like giant zucchinis, another large water chestnuts, another had orange banana-like fruits, another yellow star-shaped fruits. Wondering when Grak would bring the meat, she poured the contents of each sack into a wooden open-topped kitchen crate and neatly stacked the empty sacks in a cabinet, realizing they would be suitable for making a backpack, as long as she used two layers of fabric. She just needed to craft a needle and steal or make some thread before starting the work in her spare time.

Bridget worked feverishly that morning and afternoon, peeling and slicing and boiling and preparing spices and vegetables and fruits, with Grak working on the arrangements, all the while giving her the silent treatment. Bridget wondered if he was angry with her or if it was something else. She did not ask and kept close to Sebastian throughout, the pair snacking in between moments, sometimes eating a slice of exotic fruit whilst preparing it for serving.

Despite seeing this behavior, Grak didn't seem to mind, probably because he didn't give them a lunch break and knew they would run out of energy if not for the minor offenses.

Sometime in the afternoon the gargoyle children began arriving. By then, the mistress had unpacked the crates, revealing all sorts of golden ornaments, from grand golden candelabras that cleverly slotted together to form a tree-like apparatus, to golden representations of various animals.

The large round table was soon festooned with these gilded items. There were golden plates and platters and double-pronged forks and serrated knives. Side plates and cups and horned tankards set in golden bases were complemented nicely by the flat porcelain plates Bridget had repaired earlier, which were placed underneath the golden plates. There was even a golden statue of a hunched human looking skyward. It stood amidst the golden animals, awaiting final placement.

Outside, wind began to blow and the sky darkened. Bridget, passing a tall window, stole a glance and saw an angry black cloud bank heading in. It had already obscured the sun and would soon loom over the city. The wind pushed the grass about in undulating waves and made the flowers and reeds around the pond dance as if they too would enjoy a feast.

Bridget felt a whap on her back. "*Giri voro, gyot,*" the elder sister snapped, passing by.

"I'm working, I'm working," Bridget muttered under her breath, wiping her sweaty brow with her sleeve. She swept into the kitchen and dove into more organizing and slicing, grinding exotic spices and readying bowls of various flavored salts. Some of the spices would have fetched a premium at a human market, a thought that made her scoff at herself, for what use was it to think about wealth in any capacity when one's very life had been stolen? She was a slave and had no business thinking about anything other than escape. Everything else was a luxury.

Later that afternoon, before the guests arrived, the mistress had Grak line up Bridget and Sebastian in the kitchen for inspection. She used a claw from each hand to flick at Bridget's lanky hair and Sebastian's oily face, snarling something to Grak.

"Ah-bee-gale and boy must wash well," Grak instructed, still refusing to make eye contact with her. "Dress clean. Smell clean. Bow that understand."

"We understand, *misa*," Bridget said, using the gorgan term for mistress.

The mistress's tone changed to one of seriousness as she instructed Grak in a long series of precise growls. He nodded to each line and bowed, only rising after she had left the room, upon which he turned to Bridget, staring at a spot well above her head. "Tonight big guests come. Must behave good. Special ceremony honor of thanks happen. Ah-bee-gale understand?"

"We will do our very best to serve the family," Bridget replied, bowing her head, Sebastian doing the same beside her.

Grak nodded. "Now Ah-bee-gale take son, both wash." He returned to the preparations, which were rapidly nearing completion, the kitchen surfaces now brimming with neatly arranged platters full of sumptuous food.

Bridget, wanting some space and privacy from the hectic day, snagged a large wooden basin and dragged it into the hallway between the kitchen and their room, then carried buckets of hot water to fill it, conscious of the pale blue light emanating from the room with the obelisk. After all this time, the tall obelisk was filled almost to the top, with nearly all of that energy having come from Bridget's collar.

She allowed Sebastian to bathe first while she went to the bedroom. There she prepared fresh clothing she had washed the day before, laying it out neatly on the bed.

"Your turn," Sebastian said, coming into the bedroom wrapped in a towel.

"I won't be long." She went into the hallway, where she stripped down in the dimness and stepped into the bath. The soap was oily but smelled of lemons and sweet flowers and earth. As she dipped her head below the soapy waters, she saw a freshly clothed Sebastian walk by on the way to the kitchen, graciously keeping his face averted to give her privacy.

After scrubbing her long hair underwater, she rose and soaped it up. The kitchen bustled behind her, and she took a moment to enjoy listening to that hubbub, pretending she was in Castle Arinthian listening to the staff clatter away. She did this until the wind whistled through the cracks of the ancient structure, its cold breath raising goosebumps on her skin.

The guests would soon arrive, but the warm bath felt too luxurious, and her bones and soul were weary, and her heart held trepidation about the coming evening. With a house full of surely important guests, she and Sebastian needed to be on top of things—and would have to take care not to perform even the smallest blunder. As she dug her chipped nails into her lathered scalp, she resolved to go over the serving protocols with Sebastian, which Grak had gruffly outlined earlier. The boy had to be on the spot with every service and keep every toe in line. Above all, she would have to figure out a way to instill in him a courage he fundamentally lacked.

Bridget dipped her long hair into the water and took pleasure in rinsing it out, using her fingers like a comb to untangle the long strands. Her hair had once been rich and beautiful, with a vibrant sheen. These days it was dry and limp and riddled with split ends. Yet she had experienced bad hair many times, so why was she suddenly thinking about such a paltry thing? It was only hair. It could regrow and be trimmed and cared for.

"Priorities, Bridget," she whispered to herself as she lathered up an armpit. "Get yourself in order, girl."

She heard the clack of claws upon stone behind her and barely had enough time to cover up with a hand before a growled, "*Hohol, gyot! Hohol!*"

She looked back, a hand over her chest, and saw the older son of the family, his tall wings pressed together behind him. He glanced her over with disgust—and amusement, as indicated by the upturned lip of the snout. He flicked a hand for her to go.

She quickly rinsed off, which only angered him further, for he stepped forth to repeatedly roar, "*Hohol, gyot! Hohol, hohol, hohol!*"

"Yes, yes, yes, I'm going, I'm going," she replied, jumping out of the tub just out of range of a clawed swipe, which would have certainly caused injury. He was brutish and remorseless and would not care one hoof if he wounded her, even mortally.

Recognizing that she had taken too great a risk by basking in that stupid tub, she hurried off, grabbing her towel on the way, and dried off in her bedroom. But the beast entered after her, as if bent on revenge for her slipping his rage. He moved forward and she retreated backward, the towel pressed to her chest. He pulled back an arm and threw it forward, aiming to smash her face, but her training kicked in and she sidestepped the arm, which smashed into the stone wall.

The older son screamed, wiggling out his arm as if to shake off the pain. Bridget, meanwhile, snatched her garment and ran out of there. She dipped into the privy, changed on the spot, and hurried to the kitchen, where she found Sebastian staring at her with eyes as wide as the plums he was preparing.

"It's fine," she said, patting downward at the air as if to settle both of their nerves. "Everything's fine …"

Grak glanced at her, only to return to his task of preparing a large pink fruit with watermelon-like tiger stripes on the outside.

The elder son emerged from the hallway to glare at Bridget. She had set herself on the other side of the central table, but was careful to keep her head down, hands working rapidly to organize a platter full of red berry-like fruit, pretending as if nothing untoward had happened. Using her peripheral vision, she saw the gargoyle take one step toward her, glance at Sebastian and Grak and then the doorway, before moving off into the living room.

Once he was gone, Bridget ceased working on the fruits to white-knuckle the table in an effort to halt the shaking of her hands. The brute had wanted to wound her, grievously, simply because she had taken too long in the bath.

You have to be more careful for the sake of Sebastian, she thought, returning to her labors. *You cannot give them even the smallest excuse to hurt you.*

But the rage within was building, as was the motivation to start the preparations for their escape. The callous shadow, locked in its own collar-suppressed cage, peeked a dark eye out from behind its curtain and asked her if she wanted to indulge in a primordial rage only it could provide.

If only that rage could summon my brethren, she told it, closing the curtain to obscure its violence-coveting gaze.

The house's bustle increased to a frantic pace upon the arrival of the captain, who began barking orders to his family, sending the two youngest to be at Grak's disposal as servants. Grak set The Brat to work alongside Sebastian and the youngest daughter to work alongside Bridget. The daughter lazily cut cubes of a white cheese-like paste and arranged them in neat rows on the plate, taking far longer than it ought to take.

The Brat, meanwhile, cut blood oranges with a long knife, taunting Sebastian with a cruel grin. Bridget side-eyed him as she worked. At some point, he raised that knife toward Sebastian's throat and a keyed-up Bridget lashed out with a yanking motion, roaring, "*Disablo!*" Despite the weakness of the suppressed spell, she sent the knife spinning ceiling-ward. She pointed at it and snapped it into her hand, then stabbed it into a wooden block used for carving.

"No!" she hissed as the iron-handled knife wobbled between them. "No, understand?" Then she said the same in Gorgan. "*Gen! Gen, nadeha? Nadeha, gorgan?*"

The Brat stood stunned. Then he flashed his claws, opened his wings, and roared a vicious curse at Bridget. Sebastian jumped away whilst The Brat advanced around the table despite Grak repeatedly telling him to behave, albeit using the tone of an adult long tired of a kid's intransigence, which failed to halt The Brat's advance.

Bridget used the table as a divider and retreated in the other direction. The Brat's hollering got louder, until a seventeen-foot shadow appeared in the doorway, and he instantly quieted.

Captain Gravak's fierce gaze swept them all before he barked a question that hardly needed interpreting. The Brat began to reply only for his sister to growl and point at him and then at Sebastian and Bridget. The Brat's gray face reddened, telling Bridget his own sister had tattled.

The captain strode to his youngest son, bent down, and hissed something into his long ear. The Brat quickly nodded, and the captain straightened, smacked the boy upside the head, and left. The Brat glared at Bridget, grabbed the knife, and reluctantly shuffled back to his place to resume his work.

Sebastian was about to do the same when Bridget subtly indicated for him to join her at her side.

"Here, wash these," she said, sliding over a crate of green fruit, making a spot for him beside her. When he came over, she wiped a hand on a cloth and petted the back of his head before giving his neck a reassuring and loving squeeze.

"It's all right," she whispered. "Just keep your head down. Okay?"

"Okay," Sebastian stuttered. Yet his hands shook so much he kept dropping the fruit into the water, probably because The Brat kept playing with the knife whilst glaring at him, making not-so-subtle slicing motions with the blade and grinning upon seeing Sebastian cower.

"Just ignore him and keep working," Bridget said, eyeing The Brat to get his attention off Sebastian, but the malicious beastling understood that getting to Sebastian would wound Bridget far more, and so he kept his antics up until the first of the guests arrived, and he and his sister were called out of the kitchen by their mother. Grak also left, and without so much as a glance at Bridget or Sebastian.

"That gargoyle boy scares me," Sebastian said as they heard the distant sounds of gargoyles greeting each other in formal tones.

"I know, Sebby, I know. Just keep away from him."

"Do you think ... do you think we can go soon?" he whispered.

She leaned down, pressed her forehead to his, and whispered, "Yes, but I've got a lot to prepare first. In the mean—" She put a finger to his lips. "—*shhh*, not a word, not even whispered. We are to keep it a secret, so no more talking about it. All right?"

He smiled brightly. "Yes, Momma."

"Good boy." She mussed his hair and used a cloth to clean the rims of platters to make them as presentable as possible, a trick she'd learned from watching servants work back at home.

She wanted to snort derisively at herself. How spoiled she had been being waited on by servants! The luxury she had indulged in—the scented oils, the fine robes and baths and feasts. It was snobbery of the highest order.

A figure appeared at the doorway, and Bridget's heart soared upon seeing her. "Naomi!" she blurted and went forth to sweep her into a twirling hug—only for a familiar squat old man to roughly step between them.

"*Ka, gyot,*" the balding old man said with a sly smile, and made to a grip an invisible pike which he pretended to jab into Bridget's stomach, causing her to take an involuntary step back. "*Ka, gyot,*" he repeated, giving his big belly a double pat as he cackled. For the occasion, he had trimmed his scraggly salt-and-pepper beard and wore a plain but unblemished silken garment.

Naomi, who looked thinner and paler than ever and wore the same garment as before, albeit it was more frayed now, forced a nervous smile, hands writhing together. Yet her eyes remained on the floor even as the old man stepped past them to inspect the fare. As if her spirit had already been broken, she simply refused to look at Bridget, which broke her heart.

Not caring what the man thought, Bridget dared to squeeze Naomi's hand—and took reassurance from Naomi briefly squeezing it back before letting go and sweeping past to aid the old man. Except he was staring at Sebastian and nodding with that same sly smile.

"*Yi re tah di, bo?*" he sang.

"Leave him alone," Bridget snapped, wishing she'd taken the time to speak with the other slaves to understand their crude monosyllabic language instead of mucking about in the city like a fool and almost getting herself captured.

The old man turned to look at Bridget. "*Don war, gyot, ii vi ba pah.*" He shook his head, making a tutting noise with his mouth. "*Oi, pah, pah, gyot. Pah, pah.*"

Something told Bridget the *pah* part had nothing to do with the word father. "Just leave him alone, you weirdo," she reiterated, going to Sebastian and standing between them.

The old man grunted, looked to Naomi, and repeated, "*Pah, pah, gyots. Pah, pah.*"

Naomi shivered at his gaze, her eyes low. She raised a questioning hand at a platter, silently asking for permission to help. He grunted, picked up the largest platter, and flicked his shelf of a chin at her to help. She picked out a large platter as well and followed him to the living room.

Grak stepped in after them and pointed at Sebastian. "*Hehi, Seba.*"

"M-me?"

"*Yoss.*"

Sebastian looked to Bridget, who nodded. "Go ahead. I will be right behind you." She picked out a platter, hoping Grak would let her come along. Mercifully he said nothing as she passed, with the boy awkwardly shuffling in front.

Once out in the living room, she was startled by the sight of gargoyle royalty—no less than ten of the royal family had arrived, along with Bones and some notable others, all of whom mingled in the center of the room. They took notice of Bridget, and word quickly spread until all fell silent as they appraised Bridget and Sebastian with calculating gazes.

Unnerved, Bridget kept her eyes low as she went to place the dish onto the large dining table, squeezing by two hulking gargoyles that loomed like corrupted trees. Their silence unnerved her, and she had a terrible feeling she would again be compared to other slaves like cattle at an auction or perhaps be forced to battle them.

She retreated to stand beside the old man, Naomi, and Sebastian. When the old man bowed, the rest of the slaves did the same, and Grak flicked a hand for them to resume bringing the platters to the table. The conversation reignited and soon the gargoyles were catching up on events and raising tankards like gigantic gray humanoids with wings and snouts.

The slaves moved silently to and fro, delivering plates of fruits and vegetables, until there was hardly any room at the table. Then they were asked to stand in a line off to the side, to be called upon to hold up a platter at a whim. From there, Bridget noted that the various animal statues had been placed in a circle around the room, making her wonder if there would be some sort of game later.

While they stood in line waiting to be called upon, Naomi kept surreptitiously glancing over at Bridget. When the old man got summoned to hold up a platter, she leaned over to whisper, "I can't do this for much longer."

"Yes, you can," Bridget countered out of the side of her mouth.

"You don't understand. They're breaking me. No, already broke me. I know I'm never going home. I know that. And the labor ... it's too hard. I don't get no sleep, and I'm wasting away on their slop."

"You just hang in there. I'm working on something."

"I can't. I can't ..."

The women had to fall silent upon the old man's return.

Here and there a gargoyle would flick at one of them to refill a tankard with their pungent liquor, or bring a cloth and basin of water for claw and snout washing, or hold a platter full of food as high over their heads as they could, all so that nearby gargoyles could idly pick away at it whilst conversing.

The royals had ten of their own human slaves, who stood on the opposite side of the room. All had finely combed and oiled hair and were dressed in fine silken garments, yet their bodies were short and scrawny and their teeth crooked and yellow. They used these slaves for all sorts of additional tasks, from cleaning up spills to cleaning their claws, which the slaves did with bowed heads, buffing each bejeweled claw to perfection. Whenever one of these slaves happened to glance in the direction of Bridget or Sebastian or Naomi or the old man, they would quietly scoff or make a show of raising their noses and turning away.

The younger gargoyles chatted in their own groups but mostly seemed bored, while the adults spoke animatedly, their conversations growing livelier with each drink. Bridget did not dare cast Tongues, lest she get caught out—not that she'd be able to understand the cacophonous burble of conversation anyhow.

The captain stood with his tall wife and the king, while Bones stood with the proud queen and an entourage of dignitaries. These two male patriarchs were the most animated, as if competing for head peacock— who could roar their laughter loudest, make the grandest gesticulations, who had garnered the most accolades. Bridget felt the inevitability of the servant comparison coming, so that by the time it came, she had mentally steeled her mind.

"Ah-bee-gale," Grak said after having been summoned by the captain. He beckoned. "*Hohol*."

Bridget stepped out of her line of servants to attend the captain's side. The male patriarch then proceeded to lift her right arm, showing off what she presumed were her invisible arm rings. He let it fall limp to her side and used a claw to tilt her head this way and that as those present inspected her jawline, her teeth, her nose, her eyes, her neck, her back, her long hair, and so on. She was made to rotate in place so they could comment on her height and posture.

Bones, not wanting to be outdone, went to grab his old manservant and Naomi and dragged them forth by the arms. By then the queen had sauntered over to stand beside the king, and the pair sipped from bejeweled tankards as they watched Bones note the differences between his old man and Naomi, who stood sallow-cheeked and rigid-straight, arms folded across her chest as she was poked and prodded.

Amidst this conversation, which although boastful sounded somewhat amiable, the captain abruptly turned toward a window and swept an arm along the stormy horizon, gurgling something grand. The others all nodded, and for once Bones seemed to agree with the sentiment and raised his tankard in a toast. Everyone with a tankard raised theirs in turn and they toasted to what Bridget suspected was the future domination of her continent.

The slaves were allowed to return to their places, where they stood in nervous anticipation. Even the old man shifted from foot to foot, his beady eyes flicking about at the other slaves as if they were his competition. That piqued Bridget's interest, and she noticed the same nervousness within the royal slave line.

As the outside began to flash with lightning and thunder rolled through the sky palace, and as the slaves refilled the tankards of their beastly masters and mistresses, the party got louder and more animated. The gargoyles picked through the fruits and vegetables and raised complaints, until the captain finally threw up his arms—and clapped three times, making a pronouncement.

Here comes the game, Bridget thought as the senior gargoyles, royals included, gathered around the captain. He in turn led them to the first of the statues posted around the room, a squid-like creature. After a short deliberation, every head shook, and they moved on to the next statue, a lizard standing on its hind legs. That too was a nay, and they moved on to a lion, and on and on until they came to a bull demon—or perhaps a minotaur, it was hard to say. Deliberations about this statue were mixed, with some nods of approval.

The captain set that statue forth to stand apart and they moved on, stopping at the statue of the human. All present nodded and growled their approval. The remaining statues were promptly dismissed, and they returned to deliberating upon the two remaining statues. The old manservant, standing on the other side of Naomi, was sweating profusely as he muttered monosyllabic prayers under his breath.

Naomi and Bridget exchanged tense glances.

"Momma?" Sebastian whispered.

"It's going to be okay," Bridget replied, giving his clammy hand a squeeze.

With the horned upright bull and the human now standing together, the gargoyles turned to the king and queen for a decision. The king raised his snout at the queen, who tapped her own snout with a bejeweled finger. She flicked it at the bull then at the human then at the bull and back again, humming a gorgan tune to herself. Its tempo increased along with the finger pointing, and then it began to slow, until her finger drifted over the bull's head. The gargoyles all hummed the final line together, raising the tone to that of a question. Suddenly the finger shifted to the human, and she swiped its cheek with her claw, proclaiming her choice.

The gargoyles cheered, raising their tankards and glancing to the humans in amusement.

"What's happening?"

"I'm not sure, Sebby. I'm not sure …"

The queen turned to the king and opened her clawed hands in invitation. He bowed to her, turned on his heel, and ambled over to his line of ten humans, every single one of whom stood with bowed head, shoulders quivering. Now it was he who let a clawed finger dance before the slaves, humming the same tune. The guests joined in, creating a humming chorus.

At the apex of the song, the clawed finger swiped the cheek of the scrawniest slave, a girl of no more than sixteen years of age who flinched as the swipe had drawn blood from her cheek. A muscled and wingless gargoyle, a mirror of Grak in disfigurement and holding the same somber expression, gently took hold of her upper arm and led her to stand in the center of the room. In the background, the teenage gargoyles paid each other golden pebbles, having apparently gambled on who the king would choose.

"I'm scared," a shaking Naomi whispered, staring at her feet.

"Everything's going to be fine," Bridget said.

"I'm so scared and I just want all of this to be over already ..."

"Be brave, Naomi. Be brave ..."

"Easy for you to say. You have the heart of a lioness. I'm a kitten who ain't meant for this. My heart's too fragile. Way, *way* too fragile and beaten for this ..."

Grak leaned his torso forth to glare at the women, who promptly fell silent.

Having made his choice, the king opened a hand in invitation to Bones, who took his time dancing his way over to Naomi and the old manservant, drawing amused clucks from the other gargoyles. He raised a claw in ceremony and began flicking it between Naomi's and the old man's heads. The chorus of humming reached a crescendo and Bones's claw slowed. It zipped toward the old man before veering to swipe Naomi's cheek, slicing a thin cut in her flesh and making her jump and yelp.

"It's going to be fine," Bridget said, praying she would be proven right.

Grak took Naomi by the upper arm and led her to the center of the room, where she shook so violently that Bridget feared she would collapse.

Bones raised his tankard to the captain, who looked to his wife. He opened both arms to her. She feigned humility by bowing and drawing her arms to her chest, accepting the gift of choice. She sashayed over in a grotesquely human-like manner and halted before Bridget and Sebastian, tail slowly whipping about like a gigantic snake.

Bridget stared at the black claw that rose above her like a dangling sword, and continued to follow it with her eyes as it swung between her and Sebastian.

"Momma ...?"

"It's all right. It's going to be okay ..." she said in a faraway voice, hypnotized by the swinging claw, its movements mirrored by the tail.

The humming began for a fourth time, with the mistress drawing out the tension until that humming once again reached a crescendo, and the claw began to slow. As it slowed, Bridget's heart rate increased, and she feared her poor heart would jump out of her chest and make a run for it.

It was almost a relief when that claw flicked at Bridget's cheek—except there was no contact. By the time Bridget blinked and then lashed out with her hand in a feeble attempt to snatch the claw, it had already grazed Sebastian's cheek. He whimpered, slapped a hand over the cut, and began to cry, and for the first time, as Bridget grabbed hold of him and drew him to her bosom, she saw her mistress smile. It was not at all like a human smile, but the snouted smile of a triumphant demon. They maintained eye contact, with the mistress grinning until Bridget felt a strong hand come between herself and Sebastian.

"No, you take me," Bridget said to Grak, who loomed over her without looking her in the eye. "Do you understand? You take me," she repeated firmly, fighting his hand, but his strength was far too great and panic took root as she steadily lost the battle of keeping hold of Sebastian. "You take me! Do you understand? *Do you understand!*" The last she roared at the mistress, who had turned her back on them both.

Too frazzled to remember the gargoyle words she knew, Bridget fought with Grak, who kept hold of Sebastian's upper arm, his other hand pressed to Bridget's chest, keeping her at arm's length. The gargoyles chortled at the display, but Bridget's vision barely took them in, for she was focused solely on Sebastian. "It'll be all right," she kept telling him even as she fought Grak, her swings wilder by the heartbeat. "It'll be—let go of him! Let go of my son! Take me, you cowardly son of a—"

Grak shoved her off so violently that she tumbled backward. She promptly jumped back to her feet and charged, hollering at them like only a crazed mother could to take her instead.

The king growled a command, which his Grak-like subject then repeated to the nine remaining royal human slaves, who in turn rushed Bridget as one. She punched the first square in the nose, felling him into a moaning heap. Another she kicked in the stomach, buckling her on the spot. She grabbed the head of a third and smashed it into a fellow servant with a *crunch*, sending both to the ground, knocked out cold. But the remainder swarmed her like bees taking on a hornet. She punched, kicked, scratched and bit, shouting, "Let go of me, you fiends! Let go!"

While she fought, she caught glimpses of the goings-on. The golden statue of the human was lifted — and placed in the center of the table. Like a key inserted into a lock, that was the moment it all clicked. Everything then seemed to happen at once, the moment stretching into forever. The glint of a giant cleaver, previously hidden from all eyes. The fact that the meat had never arrived and the slaves had only prepared fruits and vegetables.

As Bridget fell under the weight of five slaves eager to keep her muzzled, she flexed all her muscles and hissed, *"Virtus vis viray!"* The 8th degree Strength spell coursed through her muscles, amplifying them — but not to the usual power. Yet even as a shadow of its former strength, combined with her rabid tenacity and panic, it was enough for her to throw the lot off her, and she scrambled forth as a hissing, spitting, frothing lioness desperate to save her cub.

A chortling gargoyle royal tried to step between her and her path, but she shoved at the air, roaring, *"Baka!"* sending him stumbling into others, spilling tankards and sending plates crashing to the floor. Onward she moved, each step taking too long. Sebastian stared at the cleaver, but he began turning around to look for her, asking, "Momma?" She springboarded off the royal's chest to sky-punch a lordling in his gargoyle snout. On the way down, she grabbed a third snout and used it as leverage to swing forth. That lordling flipped forward as she kicked out, smashing Grak in the back with both feet, shoving him toward Sebastian.

A moment was all she had, for the others all took notice of a tenacity they had never experienced in a human before. A fleeting moment where she could dip into her vast arsenal of spells. A moment that also stretched, allowing her war-honed mind to unfurl a scroll of possibilities.

The collar had made all forms of Teleport impossible, for she had tested it before. That left violent spells that would likely not have the required impact. But there was Centarro, which she'd tried, yet she doubted she would have enough time for follow-up actions as every single gargoyle in the relatively crowded confines of that home moved toward her, with some summoning their weapons. That left one possible spell that would, if successful, allow for victory.

Except her previous attempts with the spell had failed.

In her heart of hearts, she knew her resolve would allow for a partial casting. The gods would grant her this power this one time, for her son's very life was at stake — and she would save him, her precious boy.

So as she landed, having sent Grak tumbling past Sebastian, and with Sebastian staring at her with wild, watery eyes, Naomi trembling behind him, Bridget raised her front leg and both arms in the praying mantis pose.

"*Xae carna draca arcan doma legenda rava!*" she spat.

For a moment, the room froze into a painting. A moment of forever, during which she felt like she could relax and wander around the room to note all its details. The shelves of scrolls. The table of exotic fruits and vegetables. The spilled drink on the black stone floor. The shrunken and dried-out human heads hanging on the wall. The gathering storm beyond the tall windows.

Yet no bulking happened, and time sped up all at once and a force crashed into her from behind. As she fell, acidic regret set in.

Despite her fervor and iron belief in herself, the slave collar had precluded the spell from triggering.

She had chosen poorly.

She had chosen fatally.

Before slamming into the floor, she was able to glimpse two things — the grinning face of the elder teenage male who had confronted her earlier, and Grak presenting Sebastian toward the cleaver.

It was the floor that took mercy on her, for with her head smashing into it, the ancient stone robbed her of the one thing she could not bear.

Consciousness.

HOWLING CITY

LEERA

"Whaaaat aboooout thiiiiis oooone?" Leera sang, lifting a long-sleeved cream-colored dress and pressing it to her robe front. She leaned left and right showing it off to Tammy, who stood nervously glancing about more at the surroundings than at the dress. "Cute, right?" Leera added, eyebrows bouncing.

"Er, very cute, yeah," Tammy mumbled, side-eyeing a wolfan cub who was in turn side-eyeing her from the shop entrance.

Having grown bored and restless in her cabin while Augum and the others were at the wolfan tavern, Leera had formed an impulsive plan to track down another ingredient for the Zygothika recipe to nullify the curse. The quest had begun with a Group Teleport to an alley she'd spotted on the way back to the ship earlier that evening—except she'd gotten sidetracked after noticing the pretty dresses hanging in this slave clothing shop. Tammy had only agreed to come along if Leera promised to teleport them back at the slightest sign of trouble. After all, they lacked the protection of a minder and the ambassador sashes, which Augum and his lot took to the tavern.

"I mean, I know it's for a rich slave and all," Leera continued as the female wolfan shopkeeper gaped at her with an incredulous expression from behind a high counter, "but the embroidery is just soooo adorable. Look at all these flowers and little animals!"

"I think those are ants."

"They are *so* … not …" Leera flipped the dress around and blinked at the embroidery. "All right, they might be ants. And flies. Or maybe they're bees. Let's say they're bees. Oh, and there's a beetle rolling a dung ball. Lovely. Think anyone would notice? They're quite small."

Tammy shrugged. "I did."

"Hmm. The dung ball might be an issue in high society. Then again, it might be fun explaining it to the pasty-faced hens perpetually preening for advantage at court. Kind of daring to show off one's knees though. Actually, I think I'd feel naked bobbing about in this thing. Bare knees. Bees-knees. Heh, I'm hilarious. Ugh, it's just sooo cuuuuute, but yeah, a little daring for sure."

"It looks like it's for a kid."

"What? No! Not at all! I mean, maybe a little. All right, it might be for a really big kid. Like, a big slave girl. Tall, that is. Wait, an ordinary-sized slave because they're all smaller here. You know what I mean."

Tammy stared down at her from her tall height.

"What?"

"I didn't say anything."

"Tammy wammy bammy momammy. I think I understand. You have a problem with the moral implications. Me wearing slave clothing and all. That's a fair point and-and-and—" Leera pushed up her spectacles. "—and certainly worthy of thoughtful consideration."

Tammy pushed up her own spectacles. "Well, I mean—"

"But it's just soooo cuuuuuute."

"You're melting."

"I'm a cube of ice in a furnace. This is ridiculous. I need to buy it. Hey. Miss Wolfan. Excuuuuse me!" Leera flopped a hand about at the eared wolfan shopkeeper who had been staring at her the entire time. "Is this for sale? I brought money. It's not wolfan money, or wolven money for that matter, but it's our money. You know, from far off." She waved toward the horizon. "A ways out. Overseas and stuff. And it's gold! It's not a pebble, but it's real gold. Look, you can even bite it." She slipped out a Solian crown, gently bit into it, then held it up. "See? Teeth marks. The softness indicates purity. Pu. Ri. Ty. Get me, wolf ears?"

The shopkeeper's snout opened slightly as her ears widened much like a cat's.

"Should I attempt their tongue, you think?" Leera said out of the side of her mouth.

"What if you accidentally insult her?" Tammy whispered. "Or more likely, terrify her?"

"Then we make a run for it with the dress."

"Isn't that against your code?"

"I was jesting. *Obviously* I'd leave the money behind."

"Leera ..."

"Ugh, you're such a priss. You remind me of Bridget. Wish Alyssa was here. She'd be all over this stuff. Fine. *Fine!*" Leera cleared her throat loudly and pushed a hand at the air. "Don't be alarmed. I'm going to try to communicate with you, all right?" she enunciated to the shopkeeper. "Comm. U. Ni. Cate. All right? You ready, wolf ears? Because here we go …" She pressed three fingers to her temple and a hand to her throat, incanting, "*Translateo commona linguino Wolfan.* Hello there, I'd like to purchase this dress, yes?" she said in a growling tongue.

"I don't think forcing a made-up growl is how the spell works," Tammy whispered.

The female wolfan rose from her stool and looked to the cub, who backed out of the shop—and bolted. Her ears were now flat planks, which reminded Leera of Sir Pawsalot before he either bolted—or attacked.

"This dress here," Leera said, continuing her clunky attempt at Wolfan, raising the dress up and down. "I'd like to buy it with my money. My. Mo. Ney. This here coin. See it? Shiny. Shiiiiny."

Tammy winced. "You sound like a feral cat in pain."

"I'm doing my best here."

"You're grinding stones is what you're doing."

"I think I'm doing a great job."

"Then why is she running off as if she's seen a ghost?"

"So … so does that mean we have a deal?" Leera called after the shopkeeper. "She had a nice tail. Bushy." Leera tossed the dress aside and nullified the Tongues spell. "Should have complimented her on it. Maybe that would have made a difference."

"Not sure it would have. For all you know you were telling her how you were raising a family of pet rocks."

"Maybe I should have started simpler. Like a *Hi, how are you?* sort of thing."

"Maybe. Er, it's getting late. We should head back and see if the others are back yet."

"Or I could have offered her the coin. Think I should leave a crown anyway? Just for her trouble? Even as a souvenir? She could tell her grand cubs about how she had two free humans from overseas in her shop and how smart they sounded."

"I'm not sure that would happen. Actually, she's probably running to fetch the authorities. We, uh, we should hop off."

"Yeah, but there's so much more to see!"

"Leera. Please. This is terrifying. Just take us back to the ship."

"Bah, we'll be fine. You can always teleport back yourself."

"I'd really rather not leave you all alone."

"Fine. Then come with me to one more shop. One more." Leera teetered back and forth on her toes at the shop entrance.

"They're starting to howl."

"That's, like, a million leagues away. Probably just a drunken midnight howl. You know, full moon and all. Maybe the silver orb brings it out in them. Bet you the whole city will light up soon."

"Kind of a freakish howl though ..."

"Only because we don't *understand* it. They're essentially wolves, so we're talking pack mentality here. They're probably like, *Oh, hey, there's the moon. Let's all howl at it so we can bring ourselves closer together*. Or maybe it's a worship thing and their god is the moon. In fact, the more I think about it, the more that makes sense, historically and mythically speaking, that is. It's well known that wolves howl at the moon. I mean, that's not just a story, right?"

"Er ..."

"Wow I sound wise."

"See, but ... they're not *just* wolves ..."

Leera waved the matter aside. "They're close enough."

"Actually I think they take offense to—"

"Ooh, there it is! The shop I stole a peek at but didn't get a chance to visit last time! Come on, this is important stuff. Come on, Tammy wammy bammy momammy. Wait, scratch the momammy part. That's just weird."

"Are you drunk or something?"

"What? No! Sober as a clam."

"I don't think clams—"

"Fine, insert whatever fits. I'm not a poet, yeesh. I *did* have a smidge of Nodian coffee though in the galley." She was still buzzing from it, in fact, and it had been more than a smidge.

"At this hour?"

"It's our first night on a new continent. We're making history here. Got a lifetime of sleep ahead. I mean I'm more of a napper myself. You a napper or sleeper? You look like a sleeper to me. Anyway, you coming or high-tailing it out of here? Get it? High-tailing?"

"Yes, quite clever."

"I sure am. Now come on." Leera got behind Tammy and pushed the gangly woman along, but Tammy was reluctant and ended up walking forward with a backward slant as she leaned against Leera's insistent pushing.

"Don't be such a spoilsport."

"Don't be such a bully."

"I'm merely being assertive."

"I'm leaning like a tree, Leera."

"I hate it when you use my name."

"Fine, what do you want me to call you?"

"Never mind all that," Leera said as they entered a shop filled with towering shelves tightly packed with ornaments and curiosities. The shopkeeper, a wheezing gray-haired wolfan with long gray whiskers and a haggard snout, looked up with tired eyes that widened upon the two women's approach. His wheezing tightened, like a bellows struggling for air.

"Excuse me, sir. I'm looking for the tooth—" Leera bared her teeth and tapped at her canine tooth. "—of a giant—" She raised her hand as high as it would go and flattened it, repeating, "A. Gi. Ant. Not a giant ant, but a giant. We're also looking for the claw—" She curled a finger to make her point. "—of a wyvern. Wy. Vern." She muttered aside to Tammy, "Do you know the Wolfan word for wyvern?"

As she had done a lot that evening, Tammy gaped at her with a slightly open mouth.

The old shopkeeper slowly reached under his battered wooden counter, but Leera beat him to it by slapping a golden crown on top, startling him.

"A whole crown!" she sang. "Look how big it is. That's a *lot* of gold. And the teeth marks mean that it's *real* gold. Soft gold. Better than your silly pebbles." She slid the crown forth, smiling toothily and bouncing her eyebrows up and down. "What do you say, ol' wheezy?"

The shopkeeper's eyes flicked to the open entranceway to his shop, from which they could hear the distant echo of more and more howls.

"Bit of a clarion call, isn't it?" Tammy whispered.

"What do you mean by that?"

"It's like a call to battle or something. Ominous, don't you think? Maybe we should get back already—"

"Yeah, yeah, just a few more heartbeats. Those other bozos get to have fun at a tavern. Why can't we?"

"Yeah, but—"

"Wolves howling at the moon, Tammy. Wolves. Howling. At. The. Moon. So what say you, sir?" Leera pointed at the crown and telekinetically nudged it along, which resulted in the shopkeeper yelping, withdrawing a club from under his counter, and taking a clumsy swing at Leera, who not only easily dipped her head back to avoid the swipe, but then yanked at the club, incanting, "*Disablo!*" It twirled into the air. The shopkeeper fumbled for it, but Leera pointed at the club and had it telekinetically zip into her hand.

"Now that was a little rude, don't you think?" Leera said, jamming the club onto a shelf of curiosities behind her. There was a *crash* from the other side of the shelf as something smashed to the floor, followed by the tinkling of ceramic pieces as they tumbled about.

"Er, I can fix that," Leera blurted. "Want to see? We warlocks—" She flicked a finger between herself and Tammy. "—can perform the miracle of Repair. Want to see a miracle? I mean, I think you just did because I don't recall seeing you lot perform Telekinesis even once, but hey."

"Leera, you're scaring the moonlight out of him."

"He's just unsure. Give him time. He's used to unfortunate inbreds who grunt single syllables at him. He's not used to free folk. Free. That's what we are, sir. *Free*. Get me? Tooth of a giant, claw of a wyvern. That's what we need. I know you have them stashed in here somewhere. In fact, can we have a peek around? You wouldn't mind, would you? You know, look—" She pronged two fingers at her eyes then twirled the fingers about. "—around? Look at your goodies? Eh? *Eh?*"

The shopkeeper raised his palms in surrender—then threw up his snout and howled so loudly that Tammy slapped her hands over her ears. Leera, for her part, opened a palm toward the wolfan's throat and closed the hand into a fist, incanting, "*Voidus lingua!*" cutting the wolfan's howl off.

"Don't get to use that one much," Leera muttered, chirpily adding, "Sorry about that, but we're not robbing you or anything. We're being generous here and you're being quite rude, I have to say. First you want to club us—" She thumbed over her shoulder at the club jammed into the shelf. "—and I *will* fix that mess if you just give me the chance—and now you want to call the authorities. Wait, or did you mean to howl at the moon with everyone else? If that was the case then I apologize for, uh, stopping your moon howl or whatever."

The old shopkeeper's snout soundlessly clomped up and down.

"What are you trying to say?"

"I think he's angry, Leera."

"Really? He looks confused more than anything."

"I think we should go."

"Maybe I should attempt another Tongues casting."

"I do not think you growling more random noises at him is going to help much."

"It might."

"Leera ..."

"Ugh, fine." Leera then added under her breath, "Should have taken one of the deck crew."

"What was that?"

"Nothing." Leera gave a long sigh, flapping a raspberry through loose lips, eyes trawling the towering shelves of stuff. "Alll riiight, I guess we can slowly make our way back …"

"Slowly? It's a quick teleport—"

"I know that! I'm just … hold on, look at that." She wiggled a finger at a top shelf. "Is that what I think it is? Is that a wyvern claw?" She looked to the shopkeeper and smiled. "Is that a thingy?" She curled a finger into a *C* shape. "A wyvern claw? Oh, right, you're still muted. Um, would you mind not, uh, screeching like a banshee if I unmute you? We're harmless, promise. I mean, as long as you don't try to club the side of our heads again."

The shopkeeper only stared with the same wild eyes. Outside, the howling slowly strengthened.

"Er … can we be calm while we discuss a suitable arrangement?" Leera thrust a fist forth and opened it, incanting, "*Voidus null.*" Leera pointed at the top shelf, telekinetically snagged the claw, and floated it down to the counter, sliding the coin along beside the scaled claw, which was about the size of a grapefruit. "Go ahead, you can speak now." She indicated her own throat and made her fingers flap up and down. "Make yourself heard, my furry friend."

The old shopkeeper rubbed his throat whilst grinding the teeth of his snout. He looked to the claw on the counter and to the coin. "*Hara,*" he said.

"*Hara?* What's that mean?"

The shopkeeper indicated his own snout, but added a curve to the gesture. Then he flapped both arms and hunched his head forward and down in imitation of a beast that stirred familiarity within Leera.

"A harpy!" she blurted, jumping up and down and clapping excitedly at Tammy. "He's talking about a harpy! This is a harpy claw. Which means they have harpies here. Have you ever seen one? They're gnarled old women creature beast thingies with wings. Kind of look like vultures. Stink like rotten death. Foul tempers. Awful cruel too. Bunch of us ran into some back in the Legion days."

Tammy rolled her eyes.

"Thing is, I guess, uh, I guess a harpy claw isn't what I'm looking for—but at least we're getting somewhere, eh?" Leera wagged a finger over the claw and pushed it aside. "This is a harpy claw. I need a wyvern claw. Wy. Vern." She extended her arms and flapped them, then made a gesture as if extending her face into a snout and waved an arm behind her. "No, I'm not trying to fart," she said. "I'm saying I have a tail like a wyvern. Wy. Vern."

"He doesn't understand," Tammy threw in.

"Give him time."

"Leera."

"Tammy."

"Leera, please. The howls feel super creepy. Let's go back and make sure everything's okay."

"Ugh, but I'm so close! Look at those eyes of his. He's working it out. We're about to make a breakthrough here, I know it."

"You've had too much coffee. We can come back with a translator tomorrow."

Leera, feeling defeated, spread her hands across the wide counter and sighed, fingernails drumming the wood. "What do those howls mean, anyway?" she asked, then threw up her chin and howled, "Awwoooo! Huh? What is that? What sort of weird ritual is happening out there?" She raised her chin even higher, howling, "Awooo—"

Pain exploded across her face and she twirled about before landing on the floor in a grunting heap.

Tammy yelped in alarm like one of the wolfan and pawed at her, screeching if she was all right. Meanwhile, the shopkeeper began loudly howling at the entranceway again.

"Can you hop are you all right can you 'port cause I don't know the group spell?" Tammy frantically asked, grabbing at Leera and trying to get her to stand. But Leera's legs were wobbly, and little bursts of light filled her vision.

"He's got a mean right hook," Leera wheezed, rubbing her face and using the counter as an aid to haul herself back to her feet.

"Enough already," Tammy said. "Let's hop back now and—*guh!*" There was a *thwack* as Tammy abruptly staggered into Leera. The two women looked down and saw a sharp bloody point sticking out from Tammy's chest.

"Gods," Leera whispered and envisioned the deck of the ship, incanting, "*Impetus peragro grapa le—*" only to be cut off when Tammy was yanked backward, revealing that a rope was attached to the bolt. A thirteen-foot wolfan encased in burning armor stood in the doorway, a crossbow-like contraption at his feet, his paws hauling in the rope and dragging a gasping Tammy right along. Another wolfan, this one encased in thick icy armor that billowed plumes of frosty mist, raised his own crossbow-like contraption and aimed it at Leera.

She had enough time for her eyes to widen before there came a *twang* and a second rope-attached bolt shot forth. Crossbow bolts were notoriously difficult to dodge. Luckily, this one was slowed by the rope, giving her just enough time to whirl aside. The bolt zipped above her arm—and smacked into the shopkeeper's chest with a sickly *thwack*.

As Tammy wheezed for breath at the feet of the burning wolfan, hands fumbling at the bloody piece of metal protruding from her chest whilst she stared at it uncomprehendingly, her attacker calmly reloaded his crossbow. Meanwhile the other wolfan tossed aside his crossbow and growled an incantation, summoning a six-foot-long ice blade and matching shield.

Realizing she had to be as quick as possible to get Tammy back to Jengo, Leera's coffee-sharpened mind quickly worked out that a direct hand-to-hand confrontation against such behemoths was out of the question. Ranged spell attacks were the only option—but she also didn't want to cause trouble for the others by killing these uninformed wolfan. She thus wiggled a hand at the iced one, incanting, "*Flustrato!*"

The wolfan took one step forth before his head snapped back, and he halted to gape stupidly at Leera, as if not knowing what to make of what had happened.

Not waiting to see if the Confusion spell had taken root, Leera switched her focus to the other wolfan, who had finished reloading his crossbow and raised it to aim at her. She yanked at it, hissing, "*Disablo!*" and sent it twirling into the air, where it accidentally triggered with a *twang*—and shot a bolt into the first one's unprotected calf. He yowled like a dog and hopped about on one foot.

As the crossbow clattered to the ground, Leera aimed at the fiery wolfan and made a fluid *S*-like motion with a hand whilst incanting, "*Effectus xadius.*" His arms, which were scrambling for the crossbow on the floor, slowed as if he were moving through honey. Leera stuck two hooked fingers out and brought them forth, hissing at the same target, "*Voidus occa!*" That wolfan then began to fumble about with his outstretched paw, telling her the 7th degree Blind spell had worked on his likely unprotected mind—the wolfan appeared susceptible to mind attacks.

As Tammy slumped back to lie on the ground, gasping, Leera ran for her—and shoved the air at the still-hopping ice-armored wolfan, roaring, "*Baka!*" He stumbled off balance and collided with a tall shelf, which in turn fell over and smashed into a second one, and kept going until all the shelves in the shop had crashed to the floor in a cacophonous heap of ornaments and curiosities, adding to the din of the city's undulating howls.

Leera dipped under the wildly swinging and burning arm of the blinded wolfan and slid to a halt before Tammy. She slapped two hands on her and incanted, "*Impetus peragro grapa—*" but was again interrupted, feeling a *whap* on the back of her shoulders that sent her flying over Tammy. She landed on her stomach and rolled over to see the fire-armored wolfan stomping about. One of his booted feet rose above Tammy's head, and Leera telekinetically lashed out, snatched the boot, and halted its stomp.

As she kept the boot at bay—her Telekinesis was strong enough to hold it, but not much else—she realized it was lucky that she'd been interrupted that second time, as teleporting Tammy with a rope attached to the bolt in her chest could have been catastrophic.

Meanwhile, a crowd of wolfan and human slaves began forming behind her. The iced wolfan fought with the pile of curiosities, unable to free himself of the detritus, probably because he was still suffering from Leera's Confusion casting.

Someone in the crowd growled something, and Leera saw torch-backed shadows grow around her. Giving the boot a final strained push, she raised it before abruptly letting go—and shoving at the air, roaring, "*Baka!*" sending the boot and the leg it was attached to spinning. The leg bonked into the other one and the blinded wolfan tripped himself. Leera immediately rolled aside.

As the beast slammed onto the spot she had been laying in, Leera, still rolling but now toward the rope, flexed her right hand, incanting, "*Summano arma!*" A watery shortsword appeared in time to cut the rope connecting the bolt in Tammy's chest to the crossbow.

Leera then let go of the sword, allowing it to vanish, and for the third time slapped her hands on Tammy, incanting, "*Impetus peragro grap—*" and for the third time she was interrupted, this time by a hurled rock from the crowd, which she had to duck lest it split her head open. The wolfan that had thrown it was half the height of the others, a mere teenager, and he yelped right after she looked at him and skittered off into the crowd.

But the other wolfan had started arming themselves, some by summoning their own weapons, others by grabbing whatever was nearby outside—sticks, rakes, pokers, clubs, and more stones, which they threw at Leera, forcing her to summon her shield.

Still on her back and with her shield taking thumps, she realized she needed to scare them off. The 2nd degree elemental spell Slam came to mind, but she dismissed it as being too timid. Needing something more drastic, she used her free hand to draw a complex shape in the air, incanting, "*Summano elementus minimus draco!*"

A horse-sized watery dragon appeared directly above her, wings flapping in place. Incredibly, the crowd shrieked as one and dispersed.

Shocked by how effective the spell had been at frightening them off, she turned her attention to Tammy, who had passed out from the trauma. The blinded wolfan beside her flailed about, arms getting closer and closer to her body. Leera lashed out telekinetically, latched onto Tammy, and dragged her along the ground. This time she double-checked that no one was near her and spotted the wolfen she had shoved into the shelves aiming a bolt at her head, indicating he'd shaken off the Confusion casting. There was a *twang*, and she reflexively whipped her still-summoned shield about. She glimpsed the tip of the bolt coming directly for her eye before the edge of the shield eclipsed it, and the bolt caromed off and *thwacked* into a wall.

Not wanting to leave her dragon behind to cause additional mayhem should they attack it, she made a reverse squiggle, incanting, "*Draco null,*" and the dragon vanished.

As the wolfan reloaded another bolt, she didn't waste another heartbeat and slapped her free hand onto Tammy's shoulder and incanted, "*Impetus peragro grapa lestato exa exaei!*" She heard the *twang* at the same instant as a *thwomp* that propelled herself and Tammy through the arcane ether.

The pair appeared on the deck of the ship between the masts—to a scene of utter chaos. The crew were running about arming themselves whilst hurriedly trying to deploy the sails. The warlocks—those present—were either summoning elemental armor or preparing for an attack. The dock was teeming with a crowd of unruly wolfan, most of whom were doing nothing but taunting, while others were throwing stones, which harmlessly plonked off the hull or slid down a half-furled sail or landed on the deck with a rolling *thud*.

"Jengo, Jengo, Jengo!" Leera shouted.

"Here!" Jengo shouted from above, slamming into the railing that separated the stern from midship. He took one look at Tammy lying before a crouching Leera, vaulted the railing, and rolled upon contact with the deck.

"Bolt to the chest," Leera reported even as he skidded to a halt beside her. "Entry wound is in the rear, exit in the front."

"Got it." Jengo spread his hands over Tammy, incanting, "*Examino potente morbus aurus persona.*"

Leera, heart pounding and innards awash with acidic guilt, watched his face carefully. Her heart almost stopped when his eyes flicked up to her. Just as she thought he was going to say that Tammy wasn't going to make it, he blurted, "We have to get her below. I need to operate right away."

Leera nodded and without hesitation flexed all her muscles, incanting, *"Virtus vis viray!"* With her muscles going taut from the 8th degree Strength spell, she slid an arm under Tammy's legs and another under her shoulders and easily hauled her up. Then she ran after Jengo.

"Please save her," Leera said as they dipped inside the cabins, which muted the outside chaos. "I was only trying to have a little fun and then out of the blue we got surprised and the bastards interrupted my escape attempts *three freaking times* but it wasn't her fault it was mine so you have to save her, all right?"

Jengo didn't break stride. "I'll do what I can."

"What happened here anyway?" she pressed as they stepped up to a ladder.

"Don't know. The wolfan suddenly started howling and before we knew it a crowd had gathered at the dock." He slid down the ladder, turned, and gestured for her to lower Tammy, asking, "Where'd you go?"

"Just went browsing," Leera replied, telekinetically lowering Tammy.

"Browsing what?" Jengo asked, accepting Tammy and holding onto her.

Leera jumped down and took over carrying Tammy. "Doesn't matter," she said as they hurried to the infirmary, where Leera placed Tammy on a cot and Jengo grabbed a bandage roll from a cabinet.

"Where's Aug?" she asked.

Jengo didn't even look up as he began wrapping the bandage around Tammy's torso. "What do you mean? He went to look for you."

Leera felt all the color drain from her face, and she looked to the ship's hull as if seeing the city beyond, imagining Augum scouring tightly packed houses and shops on that city hillside, a shadowy crowd of wolfan gathering behind him …

"Gods," she said and started running off, only to slide to a halt at the doorway to ask, "Is she going to be all right?"

"I don't know … I don't know. Leave me to my work."

Leera nodded. "Good luck," and bolted out of there, the guilt trailing like a kite. But she couldn't worry about Tammy while her beloved was bouncing around in a hostile foreign city looking for her. And every wolfan within earshot of that perpetual howl was going to take a potshot at him.

As she hurried up the first ladder, she realized she could check in with her enchanted betrothal ring once she got up on deck, which would lead her to him. If she was lucky, Augum would do the same and realize she'd already returned.

AN ANCIENT THREAT

AUGUM

Augum ran along the cobbled street, passing wolfan that shot him double-takes, and was about to once again check in with the tracking enchantment of his betrothal ring when what he had been searching for came into view around a bend—a crowd of wolfan and their slaves gathered around a shop. And spilling out from the wide entrance of that shop was a mess of shelves.

"Leera," he blurted, dipping to sneak alongside the buildings at one edge of the street, hoping to get a clear view of her before he struck. What if she'd already been captured or, worse, collared? He'd have to free her without injury and zip back to the ship—ideally before it raised anchor and took to the sea.

His worst fear was finding Leera's ring—but without her. The thought alone gave him a cold sweat, and he increased his pace to a jog, dipping past huge carved patio chairs and tables and around torches and standing shop signs.

Wolfan had spilled out from their homes and a nearby tavern to gawk at the street chaos. Upon spotting Augum, some joined in the howls that already echoed from every direction. Even as he skulked toward the gathering, he witnessed a wolfan standing upon a tiny third-story balcony raise her snout to the cloud-obscured moon and howl.

The crowd turned about as one, and one of the human slaves pointed directly at Augum, shouting a word of alarm. Augum went to the center of the street, where he walked forth with confidence while a range of ideas patrolled past his battle-hardened mind. The fastest solution quickly won out—a scare tactic he'd already seen work.

As the mob summoned weapons and armor, showcasing the entire gamut of elements, including necromancy as represented by a wolfan encased in night-black bone armor and holding a giant summoned bone axe, Augum used a finger to draw a complex shape in the air, incanting, "*Summano elementus minimus draco!*"

A lightning dragon sizzled to life before him, its wings flapping to keep it stationary in the air. The mob, standing a hundred feet off, froze.

To accentuate the effect, Augum made a lashing-the-ground motion, animalistically roaring, "*Grau!*" A *crack* of thunder sounded, rattling the windows and ripping down the street. Those who'd come to their balconies yelped and scooted back inside. Gawkers jumped into alleys. And the mob dispersed as if struck by lightning.

Augum ran forth into the shop, only to find it empty —and a slew of wolfan watching to see what he'd do from a ways down the street.

"Shoot, where are you, girl?" he whispered and raised his left hand, focusing on the betrothal ring. Feeling the pull, he looked toward the distant sea sparkling in the moonlight. Among that sparkling were the dark silhouettes of ships at dock.

"She's gone back," he blurted and did a reverse squiggle at the dragon, incanting, "*Draco null.*" It vanished, and he refocused to envision standing on *Saltfang's* deck whilst incanting, "*Impetus pe—*"

There came a *twang* from the nearest alley. Battle instincts already heightened, Augum twirled aside —and felt something zip through the loose fabric of his robe. He spotted the culprit in the alley, a beast of a wolfan hidden in darkness, frantically reloading a giant crossbow-like contraption.

Augum slapped his wrists together, roaring, "*Annihilo!*" and sent a bolt of tempered lightning into his face. The wolfan screamed and threw the crossbow-like weapon into the air in panic, surely thinking his face had been blown off.

Augum didn't stick around to see how he coped with still being alive —he'd tempered the bolt to a strong zap but nothing more —and he once again envisioned the deck of the ship, incanting, "*Impetus peragro!*"

With a *thwomp*, he appeared on *Saltfang's* deck —and took an arm to the face. Staggering back, he squinted through watery eyes at the perpetrator —only to be enveloped in a sudden hug.

"Oh my gosh I was *just* about to 'port off to look for you!" Leera squealed, showering his face with kisses. "And sorry about that I didn't see you coming and you're such a knight you went out to look for me but you managed to check the ring didn't you you silly goose and so you came back here—"

"What happened?" he asked, gently prying her off so he could look around. The mob at the dock had grown to several hundred wolfan, with more pouring in from the city hill by the heartbeat.

"I, uh, I went shopping and the hairballs started howling and next thing we know Tammy got hit and after a scuffle I brought her back here. Jengo's doing his thing with her below."

"She going to be all right?"

"She better be or I'll slit my own throat out of guilt."

"Don't make those sorts of jests."

"Where have you two fools been?" the voice of Jez floated down to them.

Augum looked up to see her standing at the railing that separated the high stern from midship, encased in a thin film of watery armor.

"Around, but we're back now," Augum replied. "What's the situation?"

"Whole city is about to come down on top of us. Cap raised anchor and sails are unfurled, but she won't budge."

"They lampooned us somehow," Leera said. "I'll dive and check."

"I'll join you," Jez said, and the two women ran to the side of the ship, where they prepped their usual spells in readiness to dive into the water.

Trusting that they'd keep each other safe, Augum ran to each of his fellow warlocks, checking to make sure they were safe and prepared for what was to come.

"Stay on bow watch and eyeball those other trawlers," Augum commanded to Olaf. "And keep your armor and shield up in case they take potshots from other decks."

"You got it."

"Stay close to your cousin," he told Carter, grabbing his shoulder. "Watch each other's backs. Where is he, anyway?"

"Uh, I'm embarrassed to say that Digby is passed out in his cabin, drunk."

"Then pair up with Olaf at the bow. Elemental armor, tempered attacks unless directly threatened. Need to save our stamina. Pass that command off to Ollie."

"Sir, yes, sir," and Carter ran off.

"Kid—kid!"

"It's *Limpet*."

"Limpet, right. I want you and your friend below watching for hull breaches in case the wolfan get cute."

"You don't want us on deck? We can be—"

"No, we need eyes below. Go, go, go."

"Fine, I guess," and Limpet schlepped off with his friend to the cabins.

"This is the most terrifying situation I've ever been in," Alanna said when he found her pressing two fists to her mouth as she stared wild-eyed at the ever-growing mob on the docks.

"You're a warlock," Augum replied. "You've trained for this."

"I wasn't trained to go up against an entire army. You know what the training says to do against such odds?"

Augum nodded. "I do."

"But we can't exactly run, can we? Ship's stuck. And even if those of you who can cast Group Teleport teamed up to whisk us all out, where would we go? Can't roam about in a whole kingdom brimming with wolfan. They'd hunt us down in no time and then—"

"I know, I know, we're working on it."

"Then work on it!" she snapped, tears flowing down her cheeks. "I don't want to die here or get chained up as a slave. You understand me, Augum Arinthian Stone? Do something. *Do something!*"

She's losing it, he thought. Not all too surprising considering she was used to a posh life at court where the greatest drama was who had worn the worst outfit at whatever ball was the flavor of that tenday. He figured the best thing for her would be to keep her mind occupied.

"I want you to go below and check on Tammy. See if Jengo needs anything. And hey—you hang in there. We'll figure this out," he said and next flagged down the tattooed fire warlock that had caught Jez's eye. "Leo—"

"I already know what to do, son," the bald man said, eyes on the dock mob, one leg up on the railing, a fiery shield on one arm, the other idly twirling a curved flaming blade. "We faced worse odds when the navy came slicing up our lot back in the pirate wars. I survived the onslaught then. I'll survive it now. And don't you worry. I can play with others. You just show them who's the top dog around here, if you get me drift."

Augum wanted to clap him on the shoulder but refrained, not wanting to come across as condescending to an elder, especially a 15th degree. "Good," he said instead and moved on to check in with the crew and captain.

"They must have chained us from below," the captain said as he stood by the helmsman at the stern. "She's at full sail and we're sitting ducks."

"Army inbound!" a sailor shouted from the masts. "Thousands of 'em!"

All eyes swept to the city. Streaming in from the hillside was an entire army of armored wolfan, shining with all eight elements.

"Unnameables save our souls …" the captain whispered. "We're dead unless you lot make believers of us all." He looked Augum dead in the eye and gummed his pipe, which had long gone out. "Is it real? What you lot can do?"

Augum steeled his jaw. "You'll find out soon enough. Don't let the crew attack unless the wolfan start boarding."

The captain gave the slightest nod. He was silent, but his eyes said, *I hope you know what you're doing, son.*

I do too, Augum thought, walking to the railing and looking to the water in search of Jez and Leera, and saw the wavy glow of their palm lights below the water. When he looked up, he spotted a whole armada bearing down on them, some ships monstrous in size. Even *if* the women unhooked the ship, there was almost no hope of slipping by those behemoths unscathed.

He looked to the city and the countless thousands of wolfan who would soon overwhelm the ship like ants invading a discarded apple. There was only one hope, Augum realized. One precious, tiny hope.

Knowing he had to make it count, he searched for Rogor and found him standing apart at the midship railing, staring at the incoming army as if in a trance. Augum then vaulted over the railing that separated the wheel deck and midship, bending his knees as he landed on the deck below, and ran up to him.

"I have a plan," he said.

Rogor continued to stare at the approaching army.

"I'll need your help to pull it off," Augum continued, not wanting to ask the wolven to snap out of it.

"I always knew I would die in battle. I did not know it would be against impossible odds."

"If we do this right, there will be no battle."

"You are a fool."

"And you need to help me translate."

"What can you possibly say to stop an entire army that fears a repetition of myth?"

"You leave that to me and just aid me in correcting the occasional word as my Wolfan is still terrible."

Rogor looked down at Augum, searching his eyes. "You waste precious moments. Today we die, lowlander. It is best that you take time to prepare your soul."

"Not if I can help it," Augum replied and turned upon hearing the call of his name. Jez and Leera were climbing aboard, having been hauled up by a rope ladder the crew had thrown down to them.

"No fewer than twenty chains attached to the hull," Jez reported, dripping water as she and Leera walked up to him. "Not going anywhere anytime soon."

"Would take an hour to detach," Leera threw in, shaking her head. "Like it or not, we're stuck here."

"Hope you got a plan, kiddo, or we're wolf toast."

"I do," Augum replied, closing in and placing a hand on each of their shoulders. "I'm going to cast *the spell*. When I'm done, I need you—" He tapped Leera's shoulder. "—to silence me, whisk me below, and confine me to a cabin."

"And I'll stay on deck to guard," Jez said.

"Exactly. If I do my job, all you'll need to do is watch a mob slowly disperse."

A pale Alanna reemerged from below. "Tammy's going to be fine," she reported.

Leera pressed both hands to her chest. "Thank The Fates. And holy gods am I going to have to make one heck of an apology to that girl."

"That's nice and all, except a gigantic army of foreign hairballs is about to grind us into mincemeat," Jez said, nodding past Augum. "So whatever you got planned you better hop to it, kiddo."

Augum glanced over his shoulder and felt his knees weaken. He'd made some speeches in his life, but he'd never tried such an important one whilst speaking a tongue he barely fathomed.

"May the Unnameables help us ..." Alanna whispered, backing away.

Augum felt a gentle punch to his chest. "Hey—monkey."

"What?"

"History's watching." Jez smiled. "And I believe in you."

"Me too," Leera blurted. "And I love you." She kissed him on the cheek, then on the lips, and they embraced. "Let me know if you need me," she whispered.

Alanna, who'd been watching them, looked away the moment he noticed her. "Just hang back for now," he said, soothingly rubbing Leera's back. He lingered with her for a sweet moment, then gave her a final squeeze before letting go and rejoining Rogor.

"This was a foolish quest," Rogor said, all the fight drained from his voice. "I never should have left my people."

"Perhaps." Augum watched the massive crowd steadily thicken, hearing the echo of Jez's words. *History's watching ...*

"Some of your people are trapped as slaves in the land of the gargoyle," Augum said to Rogor. "And you're their only hope. Now help *me* help *you* get to them. Ready yourself."

As the horde of armored wolfan approached the dock, Augum focused on the intricacies of the ancient Spirit of the Dragon simul. He took a single meditative breath, then raised one leg and both arms in the praying mantis pose, incanting, "*Xae carna draca arcan doma legenda rava!*"

His vision rose as his body bulked into a behemoth. He felt wings sprout from his back that when extended would stretch two barns in width wingtip to wingtip. As those folded wings pushed against the sails, long black claws emerged from his hands and feet. His muscles expanded and tightened, while his reservoir of stamina amplified along with the potency of any future castings. An invisible wave of natural arcane Fear splashed ahead onto the dock.

The response was immediate. Those closest on the docks tucked tail and bolted as if stung. Behind them, the army halted on the spot, with many breaking ranks and running off. From the city beyond rose a tide of frightened yelps and howls. Not since mythical times had the wolfan seen a dragon in their midst. As far as they knew, their prophecy was coming to life. He even heard some of the ship's crew whimper in terror behind him.

Augum didn't want to let panic take over, but he also needed more than what his current faculties could deliver. And so he rose on his hind legs, careful not to expand his wings lest they think he was about to take flight, and took a moment to focus on the subtleties of existence—his massive pounding dragon heart as it beat against his scaled chest; the way the ship tilted ever so slightly in the water beneath his girth; the exotic smell of this new yet old land—the salt of the ocean, the oily tar of the docks, the fishy smell, the strange spices and fruits and flowers.

Then he narrowed his eyes and incanted under his breath, "*Centeratoraye xao xen.*" The dragon-amplified effect of the ancient 3rd degree Leyan-taught spell known only as Centarro was immediate. His thoughts clarified and expanded as if placed before a prism. The horizon of possibilities seemed endless. He felt the pulse of existence itself with each beat of his dragon heart. Focus became a weapon.

Profoundly conscious of every subtlety, Augum pressed three clawed fingers to his temple and a hand to his throat, incanting, "*Translateo commona linguino Wolfan.*" The spell blasted through his mind, and combined with the focus-enhancing effects of Centarro, he felt like he could draw upon every guttural word he'd heard the wolfan express since his arrival. The missing words he would fill with those he knew in Wolven and those Rogor would supply.

He looked down at Rogor, who had taken a step to the side, gazing up at Augum with a quiet terror Augum knew all too well. Yet Augum needed him calm and focused, and so he intimated peace by consciously ceasing the powerful arcane Fear aura natural to all dragons. Then he gave a slight nod, whispering in Wolfan, "Are you ready, Rogor of the wolven clans?"

Rogor's snout flinched as if he had not expected such perfect eloquence. "I am ready," he said in Wolfan.

Augum marveled at how effortlessly knowledge he'd only picked up in passing surfaced in his mind. He could now combine his knowledge of Wolven and Wolfan, the difference in the distant dialects clarifying, for they were the roots of the same tree.

Augum touched his throat once more, incanting, "*Amplifico*," and felt his throat strengthen with the 5th degree Amplify spell. He raised his dragon snout to the city before him and boomed in Wolfan, "Greetings!" In his Centarric state, he took an interest in observing the invisible wave of the word hit its listeners and the varied reactions it provoked. Some yelped, some howled, some ran, some gawked, some took immediate shelter only to peek out from their hiding spots.

"We come from overseas," Augum said in Wolfan, his mightily amplified words slamming into the city, leaving behind echoes that he knew should die before he continued. So he spoke slowly, every word timed for maximum echoed effect. "And we come in peace. I know of your history. Of the myths of old. Of the dragons of a bygone era."

Augum looked to Rogor, who in turn said, "The word for bygone is *heira*."

"Forgive me, the word I meant to say is *bygone*," Augum corrected, using the newly supplied word. "But we have not come to fulfill an ancient prophecy. We have come to begin a new dawn. A new era. One … of cooperation."

He looked to Rogor, silently asking if he had used the correct growl for the word *cooperation*. Somehow, Rogor knew his intimation, and he inclined his head in acknowledgment of the unspoken question.

Augum lowered himself to a seated position so that his dragon legs hung over the side of the ship. He relaxed his wings and placed his scaled arms on his knees, evoking a sense of peace over the city. And he could see the subtleties of relaxation expand in a wave before him. He sighed pleasantly as he sat like this, taking his time between speaking, conscious of his will controlling so many beings.

"The gargoyles—whom you call the gorgan—have broken the ancient covenant separating our two continents. They have stolen our people—and the people of the wolven, ancient cousins of yours whose tongue I partly speak, a tongue you will know as a dialect."

He looked to Rogor, who said, "*Raera* is the correct word."

"A tongue you will know as a *dialect*," Augum repeated, correcting the word supplied by Rogor. "Forgive me, for I am still learning both dialects," he said, adding a genuine chuckle which further eased the tension that was as visible to his Centarric mind as an arcane tendril after a Reveal casting.

"The gorgan have no doubt turned our kidnapped people into slaves, and we believe they plan to return to our lands to continue to plunder them for riches and slaves." Now the crux of the matter, which Augum prepared for by allowing a silence to ring between the nations. "This would ignite a war that would make true the prophecy you fear … the return of hordes of dragons."

He let that thought simmer, which translated into a low murmur that rolled through the city. A Centarric Augum waited until that murmur subsided before continuing. "That brings us to the question at hand. We—" He pressed the tips of his claws to his scaled chest. "—come in peace, asking for your aid in rescuing those of our kindred the gorgan have kidnapped. Will you aid us?" He raised his chin to roar, "Will you aid us and become our allies so that together we may create a new dawn, a new era? Will you aid us!"

He let his words roll across the city and dissipate, sensing the tide of fear and anger turning into curiosity. He also sensed that he hadn't quite won them over yet. As well, a fog began to settle over his mind, for his careful phrasing and its intricate timing had come at the cost of time itself. Centarro would soon expire and with it any hope of further communication. Thus, one last push was required.

Thinking back on his history of public speaking, an idea occurred to him, a profoundly simple one too. One that could be spoken in a language all creatures understood—fear.

He rose back to his feet and opened his arms in invitation. "We await your verdict," he boomed. "Do you wish to have peace with us, or do you wish …" He extended his mighty wings, pushing past *Saltfang's* yardarms, and rattled them—and continued to rattle them while he sent forth an amplified and invisible aura of Fear that splashed forth into the city, creating a wolfan wave of terror. "… *war!*" he finished, and stopped the rattle of the wings and the Fear aura with the death of the echo of the word *war*.

He then ceremoniously folded his wings and lowered his extended arms. "We hope you … you choose peace and …" The words started to fail his beleaguered mind. Centarro was fading, its side effects kicking in hard.

"Cooperation," Rogor whispered in Wolfan.

"Cooperation," Augum said. "We hope you choose a new … a new dawn …"

He turned his back on them, the words tumbling into incomprehension. He placed a clawed hand to his throat, muttering, "*Amplifico null.*" But he was cognizant enough to know that his every gesture was being perceived and judged and would echo through history. And so he sat down again, his back exposed to the wolfan in a show of humility and patience.

With sand trickling in the hourglass of time, he knew he only had moments before he would have to force reversion lest the foggy side effects kick in while he was in dragon form, and then anything could happen. *Please …* he thought. *Step forth.*

Behind him, he heard much deliberation. Then a voice spoke up with sacred words he had been longing to hear.

"We wish to aid you in your quest," Kepwa said, his words causing a murmur to flare outward. "We wish to cooperate."

Augum nodded. He stood, barely cognizant now, barely able to see past the fog. But the ceremony of it was critical. He turned, made a show of nodding, bowed, and whispered, "*Xae carna null.*" Rapidly, he shrank back down into human form.

The callous predator threw open the curtain and stepped into his foggy mind, but it could not utter so much as a sentence, for the Centarric confusion muddled his thoughts, turning them into rags, so much so that no one even bothered casting Mute on him. Instead, a ridiculously pretty girl with freckled cheeks and oval spectacles and shoulder-length raven hair took him by the arm and led him to the cabins.

"You did it my love," she kept whispering, squeezing his numb arm. "You did it …"

RAINS OF RAGE

BRIDGET

Like a pond leaf floating to the surface, Bridget became aware of darkness and the whistling of the wind and the creaking of shutters. She became aware of the rough cloth of bedding beneath her face and the tight grip of rope around her wrists and ankles — and especially of cloth tied tightly around her head and mouth, so tightly her head felt like a watermelon about to explode.

Her muddled mind searched for clarity, perusing the pieces of what had happened. She and Sebastian had prepared food. That much she remembered. The bread crumbs of that memory led to seeing him have a bath before she took her turn. She remembered the peace of soaping herself up, the peace of the warm water. Then she remembered one of those beastly creatures wanting to hurt her, but she escaped to the kitchen. Then the guests arrived and along with them Naomi and that old man slave. The gorgan feast began, and then a certain game …

Goosebumps rose on her flesh as scattered details of that game reemerged. Of the king and queen and Bones and the captain and his cursed wife swiping fearful pink cheeks, leaving behind thin streaks of blood. She remembered the look of terror in the eyes of Naomi and Sebastian. The last of those details was the glint of a cleaver. The meal had consisted only of fruits and vegetables for the explicit reason that a chosen beast would provide the meat. But the gargoyles had not chosen to fetch a lion or a minotaur or any other such beast. They had chosen from their own human slave stock.

The horror was so potent that Bridget felt her mind reel directly into frothing insanity. She began to shake uncontrollably, battling the tight bonds of cloth and rope and reality. Seizing with incomprehension, she flopped about like a fish until she accidentally rolled off the bed and slammed onto the cold floor.

The wind whistled on, rattling the window, the sounds naked and lonely. "Sebby!" she screamed, but all that came through the cloth over her mouth was a muffled moan. "Sebby! Sebby ..."

Only the wind answered, shrieking its lonely song, taunting her.

She wiggled like a worm to and fro, adding in a roll until she bumped into the edge of the bed. She scraped her head against its edge, finally managing to slide the face binding up over her eyes. The remaining bindings around her wrists and ankles were so tight they cut off circulation, causing a tingling numbness in her limbs. She'd need something sharp. She needed a plan.

The kitchen, she thought and rolled in that direction, the sounds of her rolling lost in the continued shriek of wind. Now and then, a flash of distant lightning lit up the windows in the otherwise near-total darkness. Despite using the afterglow of the flashes, the pale blue light spilling into the hallway from the obelisk, and what she could feel with her bound hands to guide herself along, she still repeatedly bumped her head into corners and walls.

In time, another flash lit up the kitchen, and she wormed her way to the cabinets with the cutlery. Awkwardly bending her knees and pushing her back against a cabinet, she slid her way to a standing position. Then she turned and, with the few fingers available to her, fumbled about inside a cubby. Her fingers danced over spoons and two-pronged forks until they came across a knife.

Too dull, she thought, feeling its edge, the equivalent of a butter knife. Her fingers continued dancing along the iron cutlery until she felt a prick. She followed the point down and felt dull serrations. *This ought to do it*, she thought and wiggled the metal about until her fingers closed over the handle. She then angled the knife and sawed at the rope, but her fingers in relation to that angle had too weak a hold for the serrations to damage the rope.

Bridget halted, thinking, *Cast Strength, you fool!* But would it work through a gag, not to mention with the added challenge of the slave collar? There was only one way to find out ...

She tensed every muscle in her body, muffled words incanting into the rag, "*Virtus vis viray.*" She felt a tightness enter her muscles, but it was so minimal that the spell would likely have been considered a failure during an academy exam. She nonetheless angled the knife and tried again with the serrations. The cutting still felt useless, but she kept sawing away until she felt a sudden loosening of the rope. Heart thrumming from impending success, she continued until more fingers were freed, allowing for a stronger grip. Soon she managed to wiggle a hand from the rope, then the other.

Quickly she worked to saw through her ankle rope, then slid the knife under her gag and cut it off. Free of the bonds, she nullified the Strength spell, felt her way back to the bedroom, and stood there in the wind-whistling darkness, breathing heavily, fearful of what she might see.

She raised a trembling hand and flared her fingers, incanting, "*Shyneo.*" A weak green light pulsed to life ... revealing an empty bed. All that remained of Sebastian were his nightclothes, laid out neatly as she had done in the hours prior to the guests arriving, and his toy minotaur carving.

He could be sleeping elsewhere! she realized and hurried out of the room, holding her palm low, the light just dim enough to see by. She found the living room empty, the food long cleared. Only a single golden statue of a human slave stood on the table. Everything was clean, spotless even, as if wiped by someone who wanted to leave no trace of a crime.

She searched the area, but all that remained was the top floor, and she knew he would not be there. Instead, she drifted back into the kitchen like a ghost. There her eyes fell upon a sleeve hanging out from a basket in the far corner of the kitchen. Upon that sleeve was a dark blotchy stain.

Her breath shivered as she took hold of the counter to steady herself, for her knees had turned to jelly. The light from her palm, pulsing to the panicked rhythm of her heart, flared out as she lost focus. She stood in total darkness, barely hearing the wind over the blood rushing through her ears.

A flash of lightning lit up the kitchen, and her eyes, still fixed upon the sleeve, saw it in the afterglow. The sleeve engraved itself into her vision, and it was all she saw, all she thought about.

It's not real, her mind whispered to her. *None of this is real. It is but a nightmare that you will wake from, safe in your bed at home. All of this is an illusion ...*

Like broken glass scattering across a stone floor, such thoughts soon fell apart, for she was still alive. And time inexorably trundled forth, a never-ending battering ram of suffering. She could not stand there forever. Eventually, she needed to know the truth.

Step by shaky step, whilst holding whatever she could grab for support, she moved through the dark kitchen until she felt herself standing over the basket. Another flash of lightning revealed a bundle of clothes, each splotched with dark stains. She could even smell the faint tang of iron from the blood, the whiff rousing a shadow from behind the curtain of her mind. She let it come forth and move that curtain aside.

I need you, she told it. *Lend me your strength, callous one …*

With a shuddering breath, she fell to her knees before the basket and raised a quivering palm. "*Shyneo*," she whispered, and once again her palm lit up with pale green ivy that pulsed frantically in time to the beat of her broken heart. With each pulse, more and more details emerged. There were three distinct garments. One had belonged to the royal human slave, another to Naomi, and the third …

She slapped both hands over her mouth, fighting to keep the scream inside so violently that she fell back. Shrieking internally, she fled into the castle of her mind, careened through the doors, ran up the dark steps, and fumbled her way to a window. From there, hollering and crying and shrieking and punching whatever was in reach, bloodying her imaginary knuckles, she watched her real self flail about on the kitchen floor like a speared fish on a beach.

Back in the kitchen, the tears rolled over her fingers as the muffled screaming continued, a screaming that subsided into shoulder-heaving sobs. Yet the hands remained firmly clasped over her mouth, strengthened by a callous shadow that in some twisted way enjoyed wanting to snuff the breath from her lungs.

If only it were that simple.

Time passed as it was wont to do, but it did not ease the pain. Instead, it magnified it. The pain morphed into a rage she had also never experienced before. It was a rage that grew deep roots into the caverns of her mind, darkening the corners and making the shadows that much more vivid.

A potency surged and, with it, a clarity.

Behind the window of the castle, Bridget raised her chin, face cold as ice, knuckles bloody. She turned about and took one methodic step after another, striding through the open gate and reentering the gargoyle kitchen. There her eyes trawled the darkness. A flash of lightning lit up the walls, revealing a set of implements. One of these was a sharpened iron poker designed to skewer meat over a fire.

She went to it and took the implement into her hand. It was heavy and long enough to act like a half spear, but it would do.

She left the kitchen, feet padding on the cold stone, the menace thick in her veins. Led by the shadow within, she stepped into the center of the room and looked up at the high mezzanine, lit by the slightest glint of moonlight peeking out from behind the storm clouds. The gargoyles had felt safe leaving her bound up, thinking she could not reach the second floor due to the height involved, but they had underestimated the resolve of a wronged mother.

Bridget glanced about until her eyes fell on a towering scroll shelf about ten feet away from the mezzanine. Remembering that Grak used it as a jump-off point, she paced up to the stone shelf and flexed all her muscles, hissing, "*Virtus vis viray.*" Her muscles went taut with a diluted version of the Strength spell. She placed her hands on the side of the shelf and pushed, but had to instantly stop when the shelf squeaked against the stone floor.

Undeterred, Bridget padded into the kitchen, grabbed a large stoneware flask of oil for cooking, walked back to the scroll shelf, and poured the oil along the floor all the way to the mezzanine, adding an extra amount against the shelf's base. Then she set the flask aside and once again pushed on the side of the shelf. This time it slid with ease. She avoided the oil by splaying her feet on either side of the oily slick, until the scroll shelf stood underneath the mezzanine. Then she climbed it, carefully straightened on its top, rose onto her tippytoes, and closed her fingers over the stone mezzanine floor.

Since the gargoyles flew up to the mezzanine, they did not need a railing, so it was relatively easy, especially with a partial Strength casting, to drag herself over the edge. For the first time she found herself on the forbidden second floor. By then the moonlight had vanished, once more plunging her into total darkness. As she rested from the effort and listened for any sounds indicating she had been detected, she felt her muscles weaken back to normality—the suppressive collar had snuffed the Strength spell.

She did not rest for long, and with the wind shrieking a death song, she stood patiently waiting for another flash. When it came, she identified the rooms. The farthest and largest would belong to the captain and his wife. Next would be those of the elder son and the elder daughter. Then the younger son and younger daughter. A thinner door likely led to a gargoyle privy, and last was the smallest door, which she skulked toward like a prowler. She felt her knuckles whiten as they gripped the iron poker. In her mind's eye, those knuckles were bloody.

Unlike the others, this door was plain and lacked a handle. Before opening it, however, she once again flexed every muscle in her body, incanting under her breath, "*Virtus vis viray.*" The words felt ceremonial, as if she was about to conduct an ancient ritual.

With her muscles tightened, yet their potency hampered by the collar, she placed her free hand against the door and gently pushed. It swung with a squeak that easily disappeared in the whistle of the wind.

The inside was a plain room with a moderately high ceiling. There was one stubby dresser, a blanket box, and a bed situated under a crude window. Beyond, a flash of lightning lit up a pink-leafed tree canopy that swayed violently about in the wind.

Bridget stepped inside, quietly closed the door, and moved to the side of the bed. While she waited for another flash to light up the darkness, she became conscious of how calm her breathing was, how capable she was to execute her plan. A cold reality revealed itself to her.

There was no bottom to her violence. She was capable of the greatest cruelties. Of inflicting the most potent harm.

The flash came, revealing the sleeping form of Grak. Carefully she raised the poker, gripped it with both hands to allow for maximum thrust, and pressed it to his throat.

Grak squeaked.

"*Shyneo*," she growled, injecting menace into her voice. Her hand lit up with ivy, revealing the poker—and Grak's terrified face. His lone eye was wide, his snout open in shock. She saw the stubs of his torn-off wings and the various scars inflicted on him over his lifetime. Above all, she saw the cowardice, written as plain on his mangled face as a headline on parchment.

"Ah-bee-gale ...?" he wheezed, for the poker was hard against his throat.

"That's only my middle name," she hissed. "My real name is Bridget Burns, and I am a dragon. A *draga*."

"I not understand ..."

She had been planning on asking him something else, but she could not ignore the question that burned brightly in her beacon-fire mind. "Where is my son?" she hissed.

"Ah-bee-gale ... please ..."

"Where is my son, Grak?"

"He ... he gone."

"Gone where?"

"Ah-bee-gale, please, I n-n-n-ot want this. I not want Seb hap-p-p-pen."

Her voice was as iron as the poker. "Where is my son, Grak?"

"Ah-bee-gale ... Ah-bee-gale I sorry, but Seb ... they eat Seb. They eat him. He gone. He gone, Ah-bee-gale ..."

A tide of potent grief shook her resolve and threatened to overwhelm her. Before it could triumph, Bridget pressed the poker in harder, and Grak squealed in pain. She let him struggle under the weight of the sharp tip, not caring that it had drawn blood. She leaned in, unafraid of his broken claws, hissing, "The collar. Remove it."

"I ... I c-c-can't ..."

"But you know how." His lack of reply told her she was right. "Tell me or I will impale your brain with this poker."

"Ah-bee-gale ... p-p-please, I get in big trouble ..."

Bridget pressed the poker in and he surrendered a pathetic squeak. "Tell me or die, coward. Last chance, Grak. Last. Chance."

"All right, all right, all right, Grak tell. Please, Ah-bee-gale, Grak tell ..." He swallowed, body trembling. "There is device ... it in master and mistress bedroom. Must close it around collar."

"Is there a runic unlocking phrase?"

Grak hesitated. "Yes ..."

"What is it?"

"I not know."

"Yes you do. You've heard it spoken many times before when they bought new slaves. Tell it to me. Now."

"All right, all right. Please, Ah-bee-gale, it hurt much ..."

"Say it."

"It is *tikitat bah nat faz mah yat.*"

"Again."

He repeated himself.

"Again."

He said it a third time, allowing her to commit it to memory and confirm the pronunciation.

"P-p-please, Ah-bee-gale, I not want Seb die ..."

"Yet you allowed it and you serve them still. How many have you killed in that way?"

"Ah-bee-gale, please ..."

She sensed his hands moving. Before they reached her, she thrust the poker through his throat. He gurgled around the iron, body convulsing. She had stabbed him with such force that she felt the tip jam well into the bedframe. His hands, which had been going for her, scrambled to his throat. She stepped back and in the dim light of her palm watched him rabidly scramble at the poker like a fly pinned to a board.

"Goodbye, coward Grak," she whispered as his fumbling steadily weakened, until he went still altogether, never to move again.

Part of her wanted to deliver the Final Valediction, but the callous vengeance thrumming through her veins dismissed the idea. These particular beasts here, who had murdered her friend and her son, did not deserve such grace. The only thing they deserved was her cold vengeance, and one by one, she would extract it.

She padded out of the room, skipping the rooms of their brood, and stepped up to the towering door to the master bedroom. She raised a hand to it, only to pause. Instead of touching the handle, she flared her dimly lit hand, whispering, "*Un vun asperio aurum enchantus.*" The handle flared with a blue tendril web. It was alarmed.

She leaned in to study it. The tendrils were rather crude, simple even, and she tracked down the lead tendrils and their endings before switching to the 10th degree Disenchant. "*Exotus mia enchantus due dai ideum exat,*" she whispered and pinched the core tendril. She tugged it just so, carefully untangling it, and the entire apparatus fell apart, the trap dissolving.

With her palm still dimly lit, she gently pulled the handle downward. With a *click* the door swung inward, revealing a spacious room with a high ceiling and golden furniture that glittered in her pale light. A giant gilded bed, a massive wardrobe, numerous dressers, the blanket box at the foot of the bed, and a huge gilded mirror on a stand stood like silent witnesses to a coming crime.

A bolt of lightning flashed outside quadruple windows, and a deep rumble shivered through the ancient manor. She used it as cover to move up to the bed where the two enormous gargoyles slept side by side. There she loomed over her captors, feeling nothing. Part of her wanted to strike then and there, but that would only throw her life away, for striking one would cause the other to react. And as little as she valued that life, vengeance kept her wanting to continue it.

Bridget stepped back and looked about. Where was this contraption? What did it look like? Her eyes went to the blanket box. She padded up to it, gently opened the lid to peek inside with her lit palm, and found only blankets. She next went to the towering wardrobe and opened the first of four doors, which were so heavy she had to use both hands. The first compartment had various pieces of clothing hanging on sticks. The second door had gorgan jewelry, the third long garments. The fourth was filled with long and colorful pieces of what appeared to be ceremonial cloth, each hanging on a horizontal spindle.

Disappointed, she glanced back at the sleeping forms, thanking the gods for the loud wind and thunder, which obscured her quiet noises. She spread the fingers of a hand and concentrated on tracking down the intent of concealment, then whispered, "*Un vun deo.*"

It was difficult to get the spell to light, for the suppressive collar made it feel like she was trying to focus through a pane of glass that dispersed the energies, and although she felt a few tugs, the spell soon failed. She refocused with a deep breath and tried again, and this time numerous invisible tendrils tugged at her from all directions.

All were relatively weak — all but one, which led directly to the fourth compartment, the door of which was still open. Carefully she followed its subtle trail until she was crouching before the chunky bottom of the wardrobe, where her dim palm light revealed a line in the base — the outline of a secret trapdoor. The wardrobe was built with a base thick enough to hide a human underneath, so who knew what was in there.

Bridget searched the edge of the trapdoor without touching it and found a hidden latch at the very back. She snuffed Unconceal and spread the fingers of her lit palm, whispering, "*Un vun asperio aurum enchantus.*" The entire door lit up with dense tendril geometries — and they were *black*, meaning this trap was enchanted with a necromantic curse.

Her thoughts drifted to Leera and how she suffered from a curse inflicted upon her in the Canterran war. What sort of gorgan malignance lay in wait for her here? Resolving not to find out, she studied the foreign intricacies of the trap then switched focus to Disenchant, whispering, "*Exotus mia enchantus duo dai ideum exat.*" Gently she tugged at the black noodle tendril she had identified as the most susceptible to collapse, unspooling it like a loose thread that would undo a sweater.

The tendril caught in a knot, and a portion of that tendril web flashed — until the flash met the knotted area, where it died. Bridget held her breath. She'd likely broken the trap, except instead of vanishing, it sat there as a failed disenchantment. That meant she could either try lifting the trapdoor or find another tendril to unspool.

She chose the latter, and whilst holding her breath, tracked down a less promising but potentially crucial secondary tendril. This time she pinched the relatively fat tendril with delicate fingers and ever so gently tugged it, making sure to weave the tendril in such a way that it did not create a knot. The unwinding felt like it took forever, but at long last that portion of the tendril web dissolved, causing the other portions to fall apart and vanish.

Finally she allowed herself to take a breath. She checked over her shoulder and froze, for the mistress was moving about. Bridget snuffed her palm and listened. The shuffling of cloth continued as the mistress either tried to get more comfortable or was getting ready to rise, perhaps to visit the privy.

Realizing she couldn't chance the latter and not knowing how good gargoyle night vision was, Bridget slipped into the wardrobe and closed the door after herself. She heard a tired groan from the other side and the sound of claws clicking against the floor—the mistress had woken and was shuffling by.

Knowing she had to move fast, Bridget waited until the sound of her mistress faded out of the room. Then she straddled the trapdoor with her feet, grabbed hold of the latch, and gently lifted it, wincing at the slightest noise. The door turned out to be nothing but a panel, which she lifted and propped against the back wall of the wardrobe. She then slipped her hand up into her long sleeve to conceal the light and murmured, "*Shyneo.*"

An empty secret compartment revealed itself, one that ran the length of the wardrobe. She lowered her foot and was about to touch the floor when she realized the gargoyles could have laid another trap down there, and so she once again spread the fingers of a hand and cast Reveal. Mercifully, no trap appeared.

Unless the spell failed to light through the collar, she reminded herself. She thus refocused—and tried again. To her horror, another black tendril web appeared, this one along the entire floor of the wardrobe. Who knew what would have happened had she so much as grazed it with her foot.

She propped her knees painfully against the hard edge of the opening and once again went through the Disenchant process, which began with a detailed observation of the intricacies of the tendril web. She was about to grab the most susceptible tendril when she heard the telltale sound of foot claws clacking against the floor and froze—losing her concentration on the Disenchant spell. The sound continued until it halted, and Bridget's heart slammed against her chest as she expected the door of the wardrobe to be flung open.

Instead there came a creak as the mistress got back into bed, and Bridget allowed herself to breathe again. She waited for a time before recasting Disenchant, grabbed the susceptible tendril, and ever so slowly dragged it toward her, moving it this way and that to avoid creating a knot. At a critical point, a portion of the tendril web vanished, and the remaining tendril webs collapsed back into the arcane ether.

After taking a moment to calm her nerves, Bridget stepped down into the compartment, where she gently settled onto her knees to have a look about. At the nearest end, neatly aligned within a series of specially built cubby holes, were a series of scrolls, each tied with a golden ribbon. And stacked at the foot of these scrolls were gigantic gold bars that gleamed in her dim ivy light.

As the wind whistled outside the wardrobe, muted by its thick wood, Bridget telekinetically snatched a scroll and floated it forth. She undid the golden ribbon and unfurled the parchment, revealing a dense miasma of runes in list form, with what looked like runic numeric symbols. It told her that these documents were financial in nature and thus useless to her.

She dumped the scroll and tried lifting one of the gold bars, which was as long as her arm. It did not budge, meaning it would be way too heavy to carry. She thus turned her attention to the far end of the wardrobe, where there sat a large object covered in crimson cloth. She crawled to it, checked that there was no alarm, and slid the cloth off, finding herself staring at a charcoal-black lidded box.

Carefully, Bridget removed the lid, set it aside, and peeked into the box. Inside was a chunky clamp mechanism made of gleaming steel and stamped with runic engravings.

"There you are," she whispered.

She reached in, but the mechanism was too heavy to lift, forcing her to flex all her muscles and incant, "*Virtus vis viray.*" With her thin muscles amplified, she was able to lift the clamp out of the box, barely avoiding scraping the ceiling of the wardrobe compartment. Not wanting to hold its massive weight, she laid it down on its edge and whispered, "*Virtus null,*" snuffing the Strength spell.

Then she studied the runic engravings, but they were gibberish to her. Instead, she once again spread the fingers of her lit hand and whispered, "*Un vun asperio aurum enchantus.*" The clamp lit up with dense tendril geometries, all of which were slightly faded, indicating the contraption was old. She wondered how many slaves it had collared and how many it had freed.

She studied the tendrils in great detail until she thought she had identified the rune she needed to press along with the incantation. Then she lay down on her back, slipped her head through the opening, and closed the clamp around the collar. After taking a calming breath, she pressed a thumb to the previously identified runic engraving and whispered, "*Tikitat bah nat faz mah yat.*"

There was a *click*—and a release of pressure around her neck. Like a dam bursting, a deluge of stamina flooded into her reservoir, and a sense of profound relief washed over her body and soul.

Something else also barged into her soul, however—a cold callousness she welcomed at its full strength, as now her captors would truly feel her wrath …

She swiveled her head as if she could see through the wood of the wardrobe, seeing the sleeping forms, albeit through lizard eyes. Oh, how she would savor what was about to happen …

After sliding out from under the clamp and gently placing the slave collar on the floor of the wardrobe, she looked at the wall of the wardrobe with lizard eyes, imagining seeing her soon-to-be-victims sleeping peacefully beyond. The potential power of raw nature coursed through her veins, expressing a nearly overwhelming urge to be set free.

Soon I let you completely loose, she thought at the callousness prowling her mind, licking its chops in anticipation.

After taking a nostril-flaring breath, Bridget crawled to the trapdoor and stood up into the wardrobe. Just as she stepped up into the main compartment, she accidentally knocked the trapdoor, which clunked into the wooden wall of the wardrobe.

There came a distinct squeak of the bed, followed by the mistress saying, "*Gozda kah?*" which Bridget assumed was Gorgan for *Who's there?*

Vengeance is who, Bridget thought, mind coalescing around the most powerful spell in her arsenal. A spell so old it had long transformed into a child's tale … until the trio had brought it back to life.

As there came a flurry of noises from the bedroom, Bridget raised a leg and both arms, pushing aside the hanging strips of ceremonial cloth as she did so. With her mind organized and focused, she loudly incanted, "*Xae carna draca arcan doma legenda rava!*"

Her body began to bulk. The wood of the wardrobe cracked and splintered before exploding off her expanding form. The mistress, who had jumped out of bed alongside the captain—shrieked a sound filled with gorgan fear. Bridget's vision rose above the detritus of the wardrobe as her wings grew and scratched along the wall. Yet her gaze was solely on the captain and the mistress, both of whom were frantically touching runes on their bodies and shouting for their brood to wake.

Bridget's head thumped against the ceiling and her knees pushed against the side of the bed and the blanket box as her body continued to grow. She raised her arms and pressed her clawed hands against the high ceiling until it cracked and abruptly ruptured, making her feel like a newborn dragon bursting through its egg. Rain poured into the now-open structure, with flashes of lightning illuminating the wet interior. The other gargoyles had awakened and were shouting and preparing to attack.

The captain and the mistress encased themselves in earth and lightning armor respectively and summoned elemental weapons—a great curved blade for the master, and a scythe-like polearm for the mistress. Both readied to attack her.

"*Gohihol, gorgan,* for now it is you who will watch!" Bridget roared, and as the captain shot forth to swing his blade, she flicked a claw, sending him shooting back into the wall, where he slammed with a visceral *crunch*. The mistress swung her own blade at Bridget's hand, but Bridget easily raised it out of range and smacked her with the back of her other hand, sending her flying and crunching into the wall in the same manner. Bridget squiggled the captain's outline, incanting, *"Paralizo carcusa cemente!"* He froze on the spot, totally paralyzed. As their brood screechingly piled into the room with their own summoned weapons, Bridget repeated the Paralyze spell against the mistress.

As if she were nothing but a pesky fly, the brood screeched and waved their blades and shields about in an attempt to scare her off. While they did so, Bridget saw Sebastian swatting at a fly buzzing about in the sun, saying, "Look how *big* it is, Momma! It's so funny-looking, isn't it?"

And she had replied, "Don't touch it. Who knows what it will do to you. Best to leave it alone."

"Okay," he had said, and she remembered him watching it fly about the room before vanishing through the open window. He had been a simple boy entertained by simple things. And now he was gone ...

"Are you watching?" she hissed to the paralyzed captain and mistress. *"Gohihol! Teva!"* Bridget roared, using the Gorgan words for *attention* and *watch*. Then she whipped an arm back and lashed forth, snatching the four gargoyle progeny with her clawed hand, before stuffing them into her maw.

The gargoyle shrieks were abruptly replaced by the grinding sound of flesh being gnawed. Throughout that chewing, Bridget carefully watched the captain and his wife and how their eyes quivered. She took her time savoring the taste of raw vengeance.

Having chewed and swallowed them, Bridget spat out their bloody night clothes, which landed on the captain and his wife and hung off them in strips. She then let the sound of the wind and the rain fill the void, letting the two appreciate what they had just witnessed.

The pair stood motionless, their eyes frantically shooting about, trying to look anywhere but up at the mighty dragon before them.

"Yes, I come from stories told long ago," Bridget rumbled. "And now ..."

She raised a claw, hung it above the captain, and began to hum from memory a certain tune she'd heard earlier that evening. And as she hummed, recalling her son humming innocently between idle moments, she moved the claw to the mistress and back to the captain, and back to the mistress, and on like that, until the melody reached its climactic peak and the claw slowed to a halt above the captain.

Bridget sliced his cheek open. The blood mixed with the rain and dripped onto the clothing of his brood, and as she made a fist above his head, Bridget noted how the captain's eyes were as wide as saucers. She kept the scaled fist there, letting the mistress appreciate the guillotine that both of them had unwittingly crafted, before slamming the fist down onto the captain's head, crumpling him like parchment.

The mistress could only stare up at Bridget with glazed horror as the claw moved to her cheek. Paralyzed, she could not even wince when Bridget cut her too. For a moment the pair stood, Bridget's head in the sky, looking down upon her former captor, the mistress's husband and brood's clothing lying in torn pieces at her feet. The mistress's cheek bled down her chest, her lightning armor crackling uselessly.

"And so it ends," Bridget said, the fight rapidly draining from her soul. Like the rain, grief was seeping in, and she could not hold the dam back. Soon it would break and the sorrow would crash through like a tidal wave. Flashes of a smiling and playful Sebastian already tormented her vision.

Amidst these flashes, she saw herself raise a fist—and smash it into the mistress's chest, ramming her into the wall with a satisfying and insect-like *crunch*. As the armor's light blinked out, Bridget ground that fist left and right, pulping the mistress into the ancient stone until she was nothing but a bloody remnant of the powerful gargoyle she had been.

Bridget then slumped back to sit amidst the debris, whispering, "Now you are dead. It is finished. *I* ... am finished ..."

She sat there as the rain ran down in rivulets upon her scales, at last allowing the sorrow to breach the walls of her castle. She had never wept as a dragon, but she wept then, shoulders and wings quivering as her body convulsed with deep, heaving sobs.

She cried for her dead friend Naomi, for the wretched slaves, for the disappointment she had felt with Grak, for those like her who had been kidnapped and dispersed in this terrible kingdom and those who would be kidnapped if she failed to stop the gargoyles.

Mostly, she cried for Sebastian, for his gentleness and kindness and innocence, for his broad smile and the scent of his hair. For the clumsy way he flopped his hands about as he spoke and how he loved to grab her arms when making a particularly thrilling point. She thought of these things and countless others, until the ancient simul sucked up every vestige of her stamina and she reverted.

Like icy mist, the callousness seeped into her soul, supplanting all feeling. She stood amidst the piles of debris and puddles of blood and mangled bone and surveyed them with cool detachment. There was nothing here for her. All that remained was a series of tasks to continue the brutal art of survival.

Not thinking of the family she had slain in vengeance or of the friend and son she had lost, she plodded onward, dumping one foot before the other, soul numb from having experienced so much. She jumped from the mezzanine onto the scroll shelf and surveyed the room. Rainwater had already begun to dribble down from the cracked ceiling, mixing with the oil slick that trailed behind the scroll shelf like the path of a giant slug.

Feeling the need for destruction but unable to satisfy it on account of being cut off from her arcanery, Bridget pressed her feet against the edges of the scroll shelf and swung her body back and forth until the scroll shelf toppled. As it fell, she jumped off and landed on the table, cracking it in two—and sending the golden statue of the human tumbling along the floor. She jumped off the table in time for the scroll shelf to crash into it, destroying both into splinters.

Bridget rolled to a halt before the wall of human heads. Sebastian was not there, nor was Naomi.

She was conscious of the loss but could not feel it. Conscious of the human inside her who hurt. For now, The Callousness of the Predator protected her from these frailties and worked in harmony with her as she opened the main doors and walked out into the cold waters of the pond, where she dredged up the box with numb fingers.

By the time she carried it to the kitchen, the callousness had begun to wear off, and she fell to the floor as a flood of emotions washed over her like a tidal wave.

Racked with a second round of grief, she flopped about on that floor, a soggy and muddy mess of a being. The feeling that she had been left behind was so acute that her eyes found a dull blade and she considered committing a terrible and final act ...

She stared at the blade, seeing its form more clearly during flashes of lightning but barely hearing the thunder. Then a window blew open from a particularly strong gust, bringing with it rain and wind and blustery cold.

For a time she waffled on whether to live or die. The feeling of loss itself was, in its own way, a thing of wretched beauty, reminding her that life itself was fleeting and oh so fragile. She wouldn't be here long anyway, in this realm, in this kingdom, in this time, in existence itself. And maybe she had more vengeance to extract ...

It was the wind that reminded her to move. She had to leave before the first blush of dawn as other gargoyles, passing by the structure during flight, would see the damage. She could not risk being here in daylight, and so she hauled her reluctant bundle of flesh and bones off the floor. As the storm slammed a shutter against the outside wall, she went to prepare food and supplies, angrily stuffing them into a thick burlap sack which she would use as a makeshift backpack.

After pummeling the outside of the backpack with open hands, she punched a cabinet—and then wailed on it with both fists whilst roaring a blood-curdling scream of the most exquisite pain. She kept this shrieking lament up until the cabinet lay in pieces and she ran out of energy. Then, her knuckles as bloody as in her mind's eye, she crumpled in a heap by the backpack, convulsing with ever more dry sobs, until even those petered out to simple gasps.

Sometime later, the wretch of what had been Bridget hauled herself to her feet. She picked up the backpack and trundled to the bedroom, where she numbly withdrew some clothes—including her original robe—from the blanket box. Then she stood listening to the wind. A flash of lightning lit up rivulets of rain as they washed down the window in small waves. Another flash lit up the bed, and upon that bed sat the small hand-carved figure of a minotaur.

Bridget raised a hand, beckoned, and the minotaur floated forth until she grabbed it. She held it gently, remembering Sebastian playing with it. A finger caressed its snout in the same manner she had idly rubbed Sebastian's neck when he had been ill at ease. Her touch had soothed his anxieties, as his presence had soothed hers.

Now he was gone, and she was alone, and this place was haunted with memories of him.

Clutching the toy in her hand, she went to the doorway and turned to face the room.

"Goodbye, my beloved son," she whispered into the darkness. A final flash of lightning etched the room forever into her mind. Its simple bed, crudely hewn trunk, and shelf of dusty scrolls. Its stone floor and tall windows and open hearth. The room of a slave.

Bridget walked through the empty house, conscious of the destruction and death on the floor above. Just another tally to add to the many surely experienced by this house of horror.

She came up to the two front doors, numbly opened one, and walked out into the wind and rain. As her feet splashed into puddles on the way to the edge of the sky island, she heard something waddling after her. Upon stopping, the waddling stopped too. She turned her head and saw the little armadillo, Snuffles, looking up at her, as if wondering where she was going. They stared at each other, the wind whipping Bridget's soggy hair about her face, until she answered the silent question.

"Far away from here, my friend," she whispered. "Goodbye, little one."

Onward she walked, and this time Snuffles did not follow. She looked back to see the little creature watching her, perhaps saying goodbye in its own way. She walked past pink trees and past the pond, until she stood on the very edge of the sky plateau. There she turned to look at the ancient house once again. Having painted its fearsome countenance onto the canvas of her mind, she turned about and put her mind to the trek ahead, which would begin with a Teleport incantation.

A long road awaited. Where it led, she did not know, but she had an invasion to stop. And that meant reaching out to her friends through the Arcaner vault ... at least in time. First, she needed to grieve. When the time came to reach out, the question was whether her friends would undertake the voyage overseas ... or if they were already on their way?

As the low moon peeked out from behind a storm cloud, Bridget looked down at the toy minotaur clutched in her hand. The rain made it shiny, the drops mirroring the tears that ran invisibly down her cheeks.

She would live for Sebastian.

IN THE DARKNESS, LIGHT

LEERA

In a dark ship cabin a humming Leera folded up her robe and quietly placed it on top of her trunk. With Augum already snoozing in the bunk, she couldn't wait to hop in beside him so the pair could snuggle. Spooning together was her favorite way of falling asleep. The only thing missing was a sleeping Sir Pawsalot curled up around her head.

"Oh, don't you forget now," she whispered, having promised Olaf that she'd check the vault for a message from Bridget. She thus summoned her shield, lighting up the cabin with its cool watery light, and whispered, "*Summano vaultus arcanus.*"

The vault appeared with a quiet *whoosh*, its ghostly light adding to hers.

Except there was something off about its light. When Leera noticed it, she froze. For a time, she could only gape whilst trying to fathom what it meant.

"Aug," she finally hissed. When he failed to rouse, she nudged him. "Aug!"

"Muh …?"

"Look."

"At what?"

"Just get over here."

He groaned as he sat up, rubbing his eyes. The light soon caught his attention, and he stepped off the bunk to join her. Together they gaped at the sight of the floating triple-doored vault.

"Oh no," Leera whispered. "Oh no …"

For Bridget's door had dimmed by half.

PERSONAL THOUGHTS FROM THE AUTHOR

Dun, dun, duuuuuun …

I know, crazy, right? I hadn't planned any of that. It just happened. And now Bridget will have to face it.

The big question is, what will happen next? And did you enjoy the adventure in whole?

Hope you're excited about the next book in the *Arcane Legacy* saga, because I've already started loosely plotting it out. The writing begins January 1st 2026 (title to be announced late 2026).

Having always wanted to write a sea voyage, I loved writing *Storms of the Ancients*. There's something cozy about experiencing a stormy life at sea. The creaking of the ship as it rolls about in the waves. A hot meal in a smoky galley. Lightning flickering through wave-splashed windows. The wind and the rain and the sway of iron lanterns …

I thought it'd be fun to let the reader finally experience a dive into the abyss with Leera, Augum learning to tame lightning on a new level, and Bridget desperately trying to survive without losing what remained of her dignity.

What's always interesting to me is that regardless of whatever plan I have for the trio, they go their own way, write their own tale. I know I've said this before, but I'm more of a scribe in that sense, writing the story they dictate to me, moment by moment, even in the editing phase.

I don't know where things are going to go from here for our illustrious trio, but I'm strapped in for the ride and look forward to every bit of it. All I know is I can make the best plans, but the trio are, well, rather spirited and independent people.

Some of you have been reading since the trio were fourteen-year-old fledgling warlocks stepping into the then-abandoned Castle Arinthian for the very first time in *Arcane (The Arinthian Line, book 1)*, when they had jumped at shadows and scared each other for fun. Some of you joined during the *Chronicles of Anna Atticus Stone* series, getting to know Anna first before delving into Augum, Bridget and Leera's saga.

I've been a full-time author now for over ten years, having spent most of those years with the trio and, of course, Anna Atticus Stone and the rest of the cast. For these experiences I am supremely grateful to you, dear reader, for continuing to support my work. Without you, I don't know what I'd be doing with my life right now.

On another topic, one that's been making headlines this year, we live in a time where the machine is making inroads into human creativity. My statement on the matter is that I am proud to say that the writing of this work, the editing, the cover, the audiobooks, and even the formatting are all 100% human labor. And it will continue to be that way.

Speaking of which, some people see the emdash (—) and think it means that a work is generated. To set the record straight, the engines *stole* the idea of the emdash from authors after being trained on millions of books. Authors used the emdash first. I *love* the emdash. The emdash will only be relinquished from my cold, dead hands.

Regardless of how you slice it, we live in tumultuous (interesting?) times. I've now gotten to that age where mortality has begun knocking on the doors of those I know. That includes some of my readers, who I have gotten to know over the years.

Here and then, I think about those souls and reflect on the time we got to spend together, no matter how short. Perhaps writing these stories and having my characters face mortality is one way of me trying to come to terms with it.

Thank you all again for your amazing support and for sharing *your* time with me.

And if you're curious, check out the new glossary section at the back of the book, which details spells, simuls, robe colors, and general lore.

All my best to you and those you love,

—**Sever**

P.S. A gentle reminder that honest reviews play a vital part in readers discovering new books. Please consider leaving one on Amazon for *Storms of the Ancients*, or any of my works you have read (bonus points for leaving one on Goodreads too).

P.P.S. To receive email notice of my new releases, as well as news relevant to my work, subscribe to my newsletter at **severbronny.com/contact**. I don't email often, so you don't have to worry about mailbox clutter.

November 2025

ADVANCE READER TEAM

Want a chance to read my next book before its retail release? Consider joining my Advance Reader Team at severbronny.com/team (spots are limited, as is the application window).

EMAIL THE AUTHOR

Want to tell me what you thought of the book, ask a question, report an error, or just say hello? Email me at sever@severbronny.com

FOLLOW ME ON AMAZON

Hit the "Follow" button on my author profile ensuring you will get an email from Amazon whenever I release a new book or put up a pre-order.

CONNECT VIA SOCIAL MEDIA

Home: severbronny.com
Facebook: facebook.com/authorseverbronny
Reddit: reddit.com/r/severbronny
Instagram: @severbronny
Fan-run Discord: Link can be found at severbronny.com/discussion
X: @severbronny
Bluesky: @severbronny

Visit severbronny.com for world lore, a glossary of spells, simuls, general terms, an author FAQ, and much more. And via severbronny.com/discussion you can visit the fan-run Discord to chat with fellow readers, duel in the arena, chat about lore and world theories, even role-play within the world.

ALSO BY SEVER BRONNY:

THE ARINTHIAN LINE

Pursued by a murderous tyrant, fourteen-year-old warlocks Augum, Bridget and Leera train under the legendary Anna Atticus Stone — while exploring the secrets of an ancient abandoned castle. The saga that began it all.

Arcane
Riven
Valor
Clash
Legend

FURY OF A RISING DRAGON

When a kingdom threatens invasion, sixteen-year-olds Augum, Bridget and Leera attempt to resurrect an ancient and forbidden order of warlock-knights, hoping to summon dragons to their aid.

Burden's Edge
Honor's Price
Mercy's Trial
Champion's Wrath

CHRONICLES OF ANNA ATTICUS STONE

Young warlock prodigy Anna Atticus Stone is tormented by her
vile sister as she tries to get into the mysterious Academy of
Arcane Arts. But her sister has other plans.

Prodigy of Thunder
The Arcane Artist
Flames of Stone

 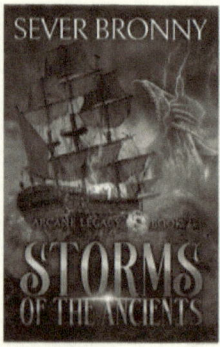

ARCANE LEGACY

Augum, Bridget and Leera face an overwhelming demonic menace
from an unknown land. But who is predator and who is prey?

Whispers of Wrath
Storms of the Ancients
Future titles to be announced

All available from Amazon

Arcane (The Arinthian Line, book 1) blurb:

Nominated for the Epic Fantasy Fanatics Readers Choice Award

Orphan and former farm slave Augum dreams of becoming a warlock. But that would take courage and aptitude, both of which he lacks. Doesn't help that his mentor is a cranky recluse who sends him on strange errands.

When a vicious tyrant ravages the kingdom in a quest for seven mythic artifacts, Augum discovers his mentor possesses one. They flee to a mysterious castle with other aspiring warlocks, including two quirky girls. Adventure ensues as the aspirants explore the castle's secrets and learn spellcraft.

But not everything is as it seems, and when a sudden betrayal plunges the group into a terrifying ordeal, survival will hinge on Augum's daring, his aptitude in the arcane arts . . . and on friendships forged in fire.

An enduring bestseller, Arcane is the beginning of an epic coming-of-age fantasy saga beloved by fans the world over.

**Audiobooks narrated by Grammy and
Hugo winner Stefan Rudnicki
Suitable for ages 10 to retiree**

THE SACRED CHIVALRIC CODE OF THE ARCANER

Thou shall never refuse a challenge from an equal.

Thou shall never turn thy back on a foe.

Thou shall always show thy stripes before thine enemy.

Thou shall not duel the lower ranks without serious provocation.

Thou shall be gallant and fair to those unable to learn the craft.

Thou shall never take the life of a weaponless Ordinary.

Thou shall always accept a bent knee.

Thou shall give succor to widows and orphans and beggars.

Thou shall refuse pecuniary reward for doing thy duty.

Thou shall fight for the welfare of all.

Thou shall guard the honor of the arcane craft.

Thou shall seek knowledge that contributes to the craft.

Thou shall preserve and honor the Hallowed Trust.

Thou shall never break thy word.

Thou shall serve thy lord and king and kingdom with valor and courage and an open heart.

But thou shall also root out corruption in all its forms, and the sanctity of the truth shall vanquish any title.

Thou shall swear fealty to this code of honor, for it is the war ye are locked in from this moment on.

SPELL GLOSSARY

- **Note:** Spells which have not yet been published in detail will not have their trigger phrases listed. Triggers with blank underlines indicate scenario-specific input needed by caster.
- (OTB): Off-the-books
- Highlighted rows are elemental spells
- For brevity, most extensions and off-the-books elemental spells are omitted from this glossary. See fan-run Discord for a more complete list: severbronny.com/discussion

DEG	NAME	TRIGGER
1st	Telekinesis	(non-verbal)
	Repair	*Apreyo*
	Unconceal	*Un vun deo*
	Shine	*Shyneo*
2nd	Shield	(non-verbal)
	Push	*Baka*
	Disarm	*Disablo*
	Slam	*Grau*
3rd	Mind Armor	(non-verbal)
	Object Alarm	*Concutio del alarmo*
	Object Track	*Vestigio itemo discovaro*
	The First Offensive	*Annihilo*
(OTB)	Centarro	*Centeratoraye xao xen*
4th	Fear	*Dreadus terrablus*
	Deafness	*Voidus aurus*
	Confusion	*Flustrato*
	Summon Minor Elemental	*Summano elementus minimus*
5th	Amplify	*Amplifico*
	Darkness	*Voidus vis*
	Paralyze	*Paralizo carcusa cemente*
	Summon Weapon	*Summano arma*
6th	Mute	*Voidus lingua*
	Object Invisible	*Obiectum visinabla balan*
	Seal	*Obdura del boundera sen*
	Elemental Armor	*Armari elementus totalus*
7th	Slow	*Effectus xadius*
	Blind	*Voidus occa*

	Minor Illusion	*Illusea _____*
	Summon Minor Wall	*Summano valla minimus girata barricada*
8th	**Sleep**	*Senna dormo coma torpos*
	Chameleon	*Armari obscura chameleano*
	Strength	*Virtus vis viray*
	The Second Offensive	*Annihilo bato*
9th	**Teleport**	*Impetus peragro*
	Shrink	*Smolla boda infintessima axtenay su*
	Frenzy	*Enta frenza harka natar*
	Craft Trap	*Infusio gato captum* + other spell incantation
10th	**Area Alarm**	*Concutio del arregando alarmo*
	Sphere of Protection	*Sfaera au praentergo buboa*
	Disenchant	*Exotus mia enchantus duo dai ideum exat*
	Summon Minor Event	*Summano _____*
11th	**Reveal**	*Un vun asperio aurum enchantus*
	Greater Repair	*Apreyo enchantus delicato obiectum roa*
	Arcane Drain	*Arcan rosso*
	Enchant Weapon	
12th	**Decoy**	*Impostra persona _____*
	Compel Truth	*Kompella o minad veta honesta*
	Tongues	*Translateo commona linguino ___*
	Summon Major Wall	*Summano valla marjorus girata barricada*
13th	**Create Simple Object**	*Obiectum minfassa _____*
	Complex Enchantment	
	Memory Wipe	*Erassa memora au o minad*
	The Third Offensive	*Annihilo ito*
14th	**Paralyze Group**	*Paralizo carcusa cemente____*
	Bewitch	*Hoodvinka _____*
	Major Illusion	
	Summon Major Elemental	*Summano elementus marjorus*
15th	**Invisibility**	*Arcan persona visinabla balan*
	Sanctuary	
	Metamorphosis	*Persona morpha mat agateo kipat*

	Summon Midling Event	
16th	**Convey Degree**	*(Ritual)*
	Memorial Ceremony	*(Ritual in song)*
	Modify Memory	
	Summon Army	
17th	**Portal**	*Portus ea ire itum*
	Teleport Group	*Impetus peragro grapa lestato exa exaei*
	Immunity	
	Incarnate	
18th	**Area Conceal**	
	Area Spell Void	
	Create Scroll	*Infusio skrul _____*
	The Fourth Offensive	*Annihilo dio*
19th	**Doppelganger**	
	Combat Portal	*Portus da / ata ei portus da*
	Possession	
	Summon Champion	*Summano elementus kampiona*
	Elemental	
20th	**Arcastrate**	
	Slow Time	*Muerto tempus ideus deo didaeiee*
	Indestructible Object	
	Summon Major Event	

20th degree mastery and beyond:

Yet to be published (some spells already explored, others hinted at). See fan-run Discord server for theories and observations: severbronny.com/discussion

ARCANER SIMULS

Birth of the Dragon
Summano elementus minimus draco
Spells involved: Summon Minor Elemental
Degree: 5th
Effect: Summons a small dragon in place of a standard elemental. Dragon has slightly greater ferocity and strength.

Roar of the Dragon
Summano arma grau
Spells involved: Slam + Summon Weapon
Degree: 6th
Effect: Primes summoned weapon with X hits of Slam, where X is warlock's degree

Awe of the Dragon
Summano arma dreadus terrablus
Spells involved: Fear + Summon Weapon
Degree: 6th
Effect: Primes summoned weapon with X hits of Fear, where X is warlock's degree

Bluster of the Dragon
Summano arma flustrato
Spells involved: Confusion + Summon Weapon
Degree: 6th
Effect: Primes summoned weapon with X hits of Confusion, where X is warlock's degree

Mirror of the Dragon
Mimicus
Spells involved: Shield + Reflect
Degree: 7th